THE EAGLE AND THE DOVE

BOOKS BY
RUTH FREEMAN SOLOMON

The Candlesticks and the Cross
The Eagle and the Dove

THE EAGLE

AND

THE DOVE

Ruth Freeman Solomon

G. P. Putnam's Sons, New York

*Library of Congress Catalog
Card Number: 73-97081*

Second Impression
PRINTED IN THE UNITED STATES OF AMERICA

DEDICATED TO
Joseph,
Leonard, George, Daniel,
Joshua, and Jared

Foreword

This is a work of fiction.

I have taken liberties with dates. To mention three:

The expulsion of the Jews from Moscow took place on the first day of Passover, 1891.

The Odessa Pogrom is a composite pogrom based upon the massacres which took place in Russia and the Ukraine between the years 1891 and 1897.

Tzarevich Nicholas became Tzar Nicholas II in 1894, inheriting the throne on November 1.

Part I

1

DAVID VON GLASMAN sat in his magnificent library brooding over Piotr Stolypin. Even sitting alone behind his desk, David radiated a formidable power and intelligence. Tall, slim, always dignified, and a trifle aloof, his austere features were lit by magnificent dark eyes. He dressed elegantly even for a man of wealth, and in continental fashion. David possessed one of the sharpest minds in Europe, sharp enough to make him the friend and adviser of the Empress Marie Fedorovna. Luckily for the Empress, only Jews recognized him for a Jew.

The library was the heart of the great white manor house built almost two centuries before on the banks of the Dnieper outside the city of Kiev by David's ancestor, the renowned architect Aaron von Glasman. This was the room in which David lived. Here he received the distinguished guests who came flocking to visit. Here he saw to business; for while he had inherited enormous wealth, he had increased it many times over through his astuteness and contacts throughout the world, contacts that reached from London to New York, from France to Manchuria. A delight to the eye, the room also soothed the spirit, exquisitely suited as it was to reflection and conversation. In summer, awnings shrouded the windows, which looked out on wide terraces of greenery, lawns, and flower beds. In winter, the windows were heavily shuttered, brightened by brilliant foliage brought in from the greenhouses and displayed in celadon bowls and extravagant brass containers.

Color was everywhere. Heavy Persian rugs covered the parquet floors, their warm reds and blues echoing in the sofas and chairs, all glowing softly under the suspended light of a brass chandelier. One huge wall, twenty feet or more in height, held hundreds of books bound in forest-green leather embossed in gold. Gold studded with pearls and rubies formed the base of the Chinese lion dog guarding the stone fireplace, and the tooled leather top of the room's most magnificent treasure, Aaron's walnut desk, was edged with gold. The white jade chess set, the big globe, the profusion of paintings by the masters, testified to the breadth of David's interests, and the T-shaped table behind one of the sofas, ready to receive a samovar or a tray of drinks and food, signaled his hospitality.

But for all the sumptuous elegance of the house, with its gleaming crystal of high-fired Chinese ceramics, Dutch and Italian masterpieces, wall tapestries, and Fabergé eggs of lapis lazuli cradled in gold, the real treasure was the land. Twenty-two miles long and eleven miles wide at its widest point, it contained a great pristine forest, a wild and lonely place in winter with its hard-packed snow and howling wolves. This great tract of land, burgeoning with prosperity, sloped down to the river—almost as if the Dnieper itself belonged to the Von Glasmans.

When Aaron von Glasman had designed a new and splendid St. Petersburg for Tzar Peter the Great at the dawn of the eighteenth century, he had been rewarded with this rich domain along the Dnieper. Peter had made only one condition. There was a gypsy settlement on the land, a colorful community of swarthy-featured people living in brightly colored wagons. They were ruled by a queen, a dark romantic woman—storyteller, upholder of tradition, possessor of mysterious powers—who had borne Peter a daughter. Not until Aaron von Glasman gave his oath: "I, and those after me, shall be responsible for the gypsy queen and her people," did the Emperor award Aaron with clear title to the land and promise freedom, rights, and royal protection for the Von Glasman family in perpetuity.

Aaron built his house and founded his dynasty, but he himself brought the serpent into his earthly paradise. He plucked the forbidden apple. He was the first of the Von Glasman men to lie by the side of a gypsy queen.

In the intervening century and a half, the gypsies had made only one change in their style of life: They left their painted wagons and moved into sturdy houses. The women remained partial to garish colors and to cooking in pots hung from iron hooks high over wood fires. In this land of wheatfields, no gypsy concerned himself with agriculture; their business was horses, timber, and—when the queen proclaimed a day lucky—bold stealing. And they remained faithful to the Von Glasmans.

The current of loyalty that ran between the gypsies and the family was strong and unyielding, and thus in David's time the family included, besides his wife Ruth and their two daughters, his first cousin the gypsy queen Rifka and her daughter Tamara.

Being almost of an age, the three girls had grown up together, and Ronya, the apple of David's eye, only a year younger than Tamara but two years younger than her sister Katya, was the gypsy girl's inseparable companion.

In the great houses and in the Jewish streets in Kiev, whenever the company was at a loss for a topic of conversation, there was always the gypsy Rifka. Surprisingly, most of the stories about her were true. As for her daughter Tamara, the impression she gave was nakedly, uncomplicatedly, sensual.

Ruth von Glasman eyed the intimacy between Ronya and Tamara with a certain alarm. "David," she would often protest, "you are deceiving yourself if you think Tamara can live in two worlds. One moment she is a gypsy girl with a dagger in her belt, and the next she is being brought up to sit at our table. And Ronya belongs here at home. Why is she growing up in the camp? There's no need for her to ride and shoot like a Tartar."

But David was not in the least influenced by Ruth; if anything, he increased her alarm by bringing in a Hungarian carnival performer, putting a whip in Ronya's hand, and saying: "Teach her how to use it, so that if she meets the devil, she can cut him in two."

Heaven, for David, was his house in Kiev, to which he retreated at cherished intervals in his crowded public life to play the role of father and, secondarily, that of husband to his serene and patient wife.

Now near evening on a bright late summer day in 1880, David was sitting quietly at Aaron's desk, the last rays of sun streaming in over his shoulder onto a sheet of paper lying before him. A straight line had been drawn down the middle of the sheet. On the left side was the heading "Pro"; on the right "Con."

David had a decision to make. Actually, over the years it had very nearly made itself, but before the house guests and the family gathered, he wanted to review the history of the entire relationship between his nineteen-year-old daughter Katya and Piotr Stolypin. To David von Glasman, caution was as natural as breathing. David knew that Piotr had come to Kiev with his father to ask for Katya's hand in marriage. She, in turn, had spurned the dashing young officers, the admiring university students, the sons of the local landowners who paid her court and showed a distinct preference for Piotr, whose family had vast holdings along the Volga and in the Kharkov region. What David did not know was that Piotr stirred no storm of passion in the heart of his elder daughter. In a curious way this was his strongest appeal for her. She felt safe with him, having first met him when he was a prim little boy of nine and she a pretty five-year-old; she thought he would make a good husband. In time perhaps, she would even fall in love.

The methods by which David evaluated Piotr were those he would

13

use to buy a horse or hire an agent to track down a valuable document. He ran his eyes down the two lists once again.

His concentration was broken by the sound of the library door opening and a rustling of garments.

"Am I intruding?"

He raised his head. "No, not at all."

Ruth shut the door behind her and came over to him. She looked cool and summery in green silk that matched her green eyes and set off her fair Viennese coloring.

David, who made a point of noticing clothes, reached out and touched her sleeve, murmuring approvingly, "Most attractive. New?"

"Yes, dear," she replied absently.

David returned to his arguments, unaware of the intense concern on her face. It was rare for Ruth to reveal her feelings so openly. Marriage with David had added self-command to her well-bred manners and reserve, and she was used to keeping her own counsel. Today, however, she sat down at his elbow and asked to look at his summary. "Let's compare our assessments of Piotr Stolypin."

David had been surprised to discover that Ruth was not at all taken with Piotr and thought his father Nikolai sharp and tricky, intensely Russian. The single occasion on which she had met Yevgenia Stolypin, Piotr's mother—a stiff and awkward woman, totally subservient to her family—she had felt sorry for her but without any desire to pursue the friendship. David rather liked Piotr's plump, unworldly mother, who lived on her husband's land, controlled by his strong will. He was thinking of her now: white-faced, a little stupid—always on her knees, as it were. Poor woman. At the moment, however, he was more in sympathy with Yevgenia Stolypin than with Ruth. Reminding her that facts alone were of interest to him, he asked, "Why do you oppose this match? What objections can there be to a young man richly endowed with intelligence, energy, ambition, and good looks—not dramatic good looks, I grant, but moral earnestness is far more important. Piotr will never allow vodka or passion to ruin his life."

Instead of pouring out her heart, Ruth concurred dryly. "Yes, dear, intellect and solidness are written all over him."

David looked at her sharply, and she saw in his dark eyes the same piercing quality that she distrusted in Piotr's blue ones. But David she loved.

"I'm sorry," she said, softening. "My only concern is Katya's happiness. I simply don't think Piotr can give her the things she needs."

David smiled patiently. "Do you think I intend to send your precious Katya to the Stolypin manor house? No, my dear, Katya will live in a palace. She'll have a title and a bigger allowance than she can spend. Nikolai Stolypin even insists upon settling an income of twelve thousand rubles a year on her, and though it's unnecessary, it would be a lie to pretend that I'm not pleased." David paused. "True, Nikolai is somewhat coarse but, still, he's ambitious for his son. Piotr is interested in politics and eager to make a career for himself in government. I shall arrange for him to enter the Ministry of the Interior. After that—" He made an eloquent gesture.

Ruth looked at him disappointedly. "Aren't your plans a little premature?"

David hesitated, then said, "No, I don't think so."

They were both glad when the door opened and the Stolypins walked in with Katya.

Piotr did not take after either of his parents. Tall like his father, he looked aristocratic in evening clothes. His sandy hair was cut short and always brushed carefully back from his high forehead. He was respectful, his manners were good, and his voice was pleasant, but Ruth noticed that he wore white gloves almost constantly and that, when he smiled, he smiled briefly. She could not help feeling that there was some reason for the gloves and something behind his smile, which never seemed to embrace anyone with the slightest degree of affection.

Ready for the party to which Piotr was escorting her, Katya looked enchanting in a billowing white dress that left her slim arms bare. A single blue jewel flashed in her brown hair. She had something of her mother's dignity and breeding and a delicate grace all her own, but tonight these were eclipsed by the happiness that suffused her creamy skin with a soft glow.

"We've come to say good-night," she announced.

David rose and lifted her hand to his lips. "Enjoy the party."

Ruth smiled at her. "When you get home, if my light is still on—" Moved by Katya's sudden look, she corrected herself hastily. "No, it will be too late. I'll see you tomorrow. Remember, we have an appointment to go shopping. Lisette's new fabrics have arrived from Paris."

Katya was formal with Nikolai Stolypin and Piotr stiff with the Von Glasmans. However, both fathers smiled pleasantly, and as she passed through the door on her way out Katya turned and waved.

Nikolai Stolypin lit a cigarette and lowered his thick square body onto the sofa. "Just look at them," he said, immensely pleased with the situation: Obviously, everything was progressing just as he hoped. He felt safe enough to suggest that perhaps he should give thought to concluding his stay.

"You must be anxious to get back to Yevgenia," Ruth said without hesitation.

"Well, yes. But that has nothing to do with Piotr," he said jovially.

"Life is exciting for a young man in love and about to take a wife. Let him stay on and enjoy it."

Ruth felt a moment of irritation as she glanced at David. It was not uncommon for him to keep things from her. "Has Piotr already spoken to you?" she asked with astonishment.

A laugh came from Nikolai. "He will, he will."

"I agree wholeheartedly," said David. "Piotr must stay on. A drink before dinner, Stolypin?"

Nikolai shrugged. "Anything."

David gave him a vodka, poured whiskey for himself and a sherry for Ruth. "Where's Ronya?" he asked, resuming his seat.

"Rifka has taken the girls to a new restaurant. Tamara was not invited to the party," Ruth explained to Nikolai, "hence the treat in town."

David smiled at Nikolai. "Those two are devoted to each other."

Over the years he had courted David von Glasman, Nikolai Stolypin had hidden his feelings about the gypsies and guarded his tongue for fear of losing David's friendship. Nikolai relished his new closeness with David and now, with a surge of confidence, he hitched himself forward on the sofa and said, "It strikes me that Tamara takes advantage of her position. It's selfish, particularly now, when Ronya will be invited to functions honoring Katya and Piotr."

David glanced at him sharply but made no reply.

"Is that how Piotr feels?" Ruth asked casually.

Nikolai nodded and took it upon himself to speak for his son. "Tamara makes Piotr uncomfortable. He has never found the gypsies appealing."

"How interesting!" Ruth said, carefully avoiding David's eyes.

David's displeasure deepened. Presently, dinner was announced, and he was the first to his feet.

Simply getting through the meal with Stolypin was an effort for Ruth, but for politeness' sake she made herself accompany the men to the library and pour the coffee before making her excuses. An hour later Nikolai made his way heavily to bed.

David waited up for Ronya.

She peeped around the library door shortly after Nikolai's departure and, seeing her father alone, ran across to kiss him good-night. He took her face in his hands, brightening at the sight of her luxuriant copper-colored hair and big dark eyes that always looked so infinitely deep. Her face still kept its look of innocence, but beneath was the divine promise of eagerness and dauntless passion.

"Did you enjoy your evening?"

"Not especially," she said with a rueful grin, fingering the long fringed sash that tied her paisley dress, setting off her slim figure to advantage. "Tamara didn't smile all evening—not even once. She says if Katya had wanted it, that dreadful creature Ludmilla would have been compelled to include her in the invitation."

"I see," David said wryly. "And what do you think?"

Normally Ronya's full lips seemed to smile even in repose, but now they turned down in contempt for Piotr. "I think—poor Katya, it must be awful to let oneself be influenced by an arrogant snob."

David shot her a look. "That's hardly justified."

When Ronya remained silent, David's expression suddenly changed, and he inquired lightly, "Would it be presumptuous of me to ask what you will do if the man you choose considers gypsies beneath his notice?"

Ronya planted her small, fine-boned body firmly before him. "Why do you imply Katya chose Piotr, when she had no choice?" she demanded, her voice strong with feeling. "Gospodin Stolypin has made no secret of the fact that he chose you, and you threw them together summer after summer. Why? That's like throwing Katya away."

It was difficult for David not to be angry, but impossible for him to be angry with Ronya. The slamming of the front door would have been a welcome distraction, had it not been the sound of Katya's feet running up the stairway at the incredibly early hour of ten o'clock. David and Ronya instinctively made for the library door. Following Katya, formidably austere for a young man, was Piotr. He gave them a stiff bow and continued on his way upstairs. Ronya's heart began to beat fast, and she raced up the stairs past him. David's face showed puzzlement and concern, and he reached Katya's room hard on Stolypin's heels.

Katya was in the bathroom. "Give me five minutes," she said, her voice muffled.

Ronya stood irresolutely just outside the bathroom door. "May I come in?"

"Ronya, darling, give me my robe," Katya said, stretching out a hand.

David touched Ronya's arm. "You know Katya," he said softly, "it's useless to press her."

Ronya gave her father a semblance of a smile and let him lead her to her sister's room, where they both sat down on her gaily patterned sofa.

Shut away from the rest of the house, Katya's room was ordered, uncluttered, and quiet, as befitted her personality. It held Katya's treasures, her books, and little things she held dear—the family photographs on the mantelpiece, a little child's chair, her favorite doll, her grandmother's gold hairpin box. The curtains were drawn and only the soft night-light was on, making the room cozy and shadowy. It smelled of the lingering scent of Katya's perfume and flowers.

Ten minutes passed before Katya reappeared. She had unpinned her hair and removed her dress. Her face was strained but composed, and David by now had mastered his alarm, assuming nothing more serious than a lovers' quarrel.

"How much longer do you intend to keep us in suspense?" Ronya said abruptly. "What happened?"

"Nothing really." Katya's voice was grave. "I got only what I deserved."

"Honestly, Katya—"

"Unless you have a good reason you ought not to have left the party," David said.

Instead of replying, Katya forced her mind back to the events of the evening. Even now it was not easy for her to tell them what happened. . . .

When Piotr asked her to leave the dance floor and walk in the garden, Katya felt certain that his purpose was to declare himself. She found herself thinking, *There are good reasons for marrying Piotr, but do I really want to marry him? Perhaps he will be content with an unannounced engagement for a time—at least until we find out whether we can be happy together.*

They wandered out into the mildness of a summer garden fragrant with roses. Trees moved gently in the breeze, and the stars were very bright. They stopped presently and Katya rested her back lightly against a tree. Piotr's lips were tightly compressed, and the silence between them was sharp.

Katya wondered: *Does he regret coming outside? Or is he more bashful than I realized?* She gave a little sigh.

Piotr seemed to force himself to speak. "I do love you, Katya." She knew he was deliberately weighing what he had to say. She took a half step toward him and said, "Piotr, would you kiss me? You never have, and I want to know—"

"No," Piotr said forcefully, "I don't propose to do that. Hear me out, please. . . ."

In confusion Katya turned away from David and Ronya. "I'm sorry," she said.

It seemed very odd to Ronya that Katya should find it so difficult to speak. "Would you like a glass of tea?"

She shook her head.

"Perhaps a sherry," David suggested.

"Oh no, Father. I ought to have come right out with it." She went on doggedly, "Piotr said he wants two things. He wants to be Prime Minister of Russia one day, and he wants a title, and he wants these more than he wants me. He said so very bluntly. He said: 'In Russia it is sheer stupidity to marry a Jewess!' "

In the shocked silence that followed, her head drooped and she was again with Piotr. She recalled the rush of tears that came as she ran down a path in the garden. It was edged with spotted geraniums, she remembered.

Piotr hurried after her. "Wait, Katya." He caught up with her and put a hand under her elbow. At the sight of her tears, gentleness showed in his face for the first time. "Do you think badly of me?"

"Decide for yourself," she answered.

"Let me take you home."

She let him lead her to her mother's carriage waiting in the cobble-stoned entrance. The coachman looked at them with some surprise, as if to say: "Why on earth would anyone leave a party scarcely begun?"

On the way home Katya began to regain her composure, so that when Piotr said, "I suppose you'll never forgive me," she was mistress of herself again.

She put away her handkerchief and even managed a smile. "Don't worry, Piotr. I shan't die of a broken heart and I shan't remain an old maid. If I can, I'll even help you get to the top."

All at once, Katya was aware of her father's voice. She raised her head. Then Ronya, her black eyes bright with anger, her chin up: "Father asked whether you have told us everything there is to tell?"

Katya thought, *Heavens, he's going to make a fuss.* She was right. Whatever Jesus may have said to the ancient Jews about loving their enemies, David von Glasman shared no such attitude. His was a hard-headed philosophy utterly contrary to the resigned acceptance of injury and insult. "Please, Father," she pleaded, "I don't want vengeance, I don't want you to punish Piotr. We didn't part enemies."

David surveyed his daughter gravely. Her generous attitude toward young Stolypin tired his patience—more, it offended him. But David von Glasman was by birth and by choice a gentleman: Whatever he thought privately he would keep to himself (perhaps sharing it only with Ruth and Rifka); he would make his plans secretly without placing the burden on Katya. Instead of losing his temper, he got up from the sofa. "I wish that I could at least say that Piotr's attitude is either unexpected or surprising, but I cannot. I had great confidence in him, rightfully crediting him with considerable intelligence, which only proves to me that stupidity can be found in unlikely places and that the most blatant form of stupidity is prejudice."

David kissed both girls good-night. But already he had set himself two new goals: first, to elevate Katya to the foremost rank in high society and, second, to thwart Piotr Stolypin.

Katya felt deeply relieved, while Ronya marveled at their father's easy acceptance of Piotr's cruel rejection. But her first thought was to protect her sister from the inevitable gossip.

"Father, we should have ready some sort of explanation."

"There'll be no gossip. We will say that Madame Stolypin is quite ill and Piotr has been called home. By the time we return from St. Petersburg—"

"St. Petersburg!" Ronya cried out excitedly. "Me, too?"

Katya was equally surprised.

"You, too, I promise. But don't breathe a word of this to your mother," he warned.

Ronya stayed with Katya. Far above Piotr in importance loomed St. Petersburg; she almost forgave him. In a rush of excitement she ran over to Katya, put her arms around her, and kissed her. "Please promise me something," her sister said.

"Anything," said Ronya.

"Don't tell Tamara about St. Petersburg. Somehow she'll spoil it."

Ronya drew up sharply. "That's mean."

"No, it isn't, it's the truth. Anyway, you promised."

Ronya turned away. The fun had gone as quickly as it had come.

Ruth's sitting room was a supremely beautiful room formally furnished with the best of Louis XV. That evening asters blazed in the vases and tea waited, as David opened the door, shrugging his shoulders into a velvet smoking jacket. Ruth looked up, a trace of a frown on her forehead. "I'd very nearly given you up. What has kept you, David?"

Without answering, he pulled the bell cord.

At this late hour, he expected one of the maidservants, but Evdokia Ziniatovski, the housekeeper, only three months in the Von Glasmans' employ and anxious to please, answered the ring. As she crossed the threshold, David said in a clear voice, "Gospodin Stolypin's wife is ill. He will be leaving, and his son with him, first thing in the morning. Go see if they need help with their packing."

The woman turned to the lady of the house. "Do you think I should take a girl as well?"

"Yes, take two maids with you," Ruth replied, struggling to mask her surprise. "You may start now." She could hardly wait for Evdokia to depart.

A thousand thoughts raced through her mind and a sudden feeling of panic.

"David, please tell me what has happened. I feel frightened."

His voice slow and dispassionate, David began to relate the events of the evening.

Ruth listened in silence, but as she understood his true feelings, her fingers gripped her teacup, and slowly her sea-green eyes turned deep emerald.

Down the hall in one of the guest bedrooms, Piotr Stolypin was seeing David von Glasman as his father saw him and weighing the moment to break into the torrent of abuse.

"Fool—damn fool—big fool!" Nikolai shouted, his stock of insults exhausted. He whirled away from Piotr, his body rigid with fury. "You've dug your own grave! You're through!" He slumped down in his chair, his big red face in his hands, nearly weeping.

"Listen, Father," Piotr said without emotion, "I have analyzed my position carefully. There is going to be less and less tolerance and equality shown the Jews. The people coming into power despise and hate them. They're dedicated to destroying them. If I wish to achieve my aims I must not indulge in sentimentality and romanticism. Passion, if practiced, becomes a habit, a habit I can't afford. I want to rely solely upon myself."

Nikolai's rage broke into a fresh blaze. "Upon yourself?" he roared, jumping up. "No help from the outside? That's about the stupidest—" He stopped and gesticulated speechlessly at Piotr. "Stupid! You're stupid! What about David von Glasman? What about his influence? Can't you see him with the Empress? Can't you hear him? I can. After he's told his story, the Empress will be as offended as if Katya were her own daughter. And mark you this—"

Piotr looked at his father with distaste. His mouth hardened. "David von Glasman is, I regret to say, a Jew."

Nikolai groaned. "A Jew! You know what the Jew did when I first hinted at an alliance? He laughed. He pointed out that we Stolypins are not of the nobility or even of the aristocracy, and that closes the door as far as marriage between the two families is concerned.

"Well, I was smart. I behaved as though it would kill me if he refused me. You know why I did it. For you."

Piotr gave his father a sardonic smile. "Come now, Father, you did it for his land. Land makes your heart beat like a drum. Well this land, gypsies included, is to be left to Ronya, not Katya. You picked the wrong sister."

Stolypin snorted.

"Father, this once, let me tell you. I was the one following Von Glasman around with a notebook and pencil in hand as he inspected his lands and holdings. I can remember incident after incident. Ronya is to have this house and the land. Her branch of the family stays here. Katya is to establish a second branch of the family, a Russified, titled branch, in St. Petersburg. All their lives the girls have been brought up with this understanding."

Nikolai felt himself grow sick inside. "Damn it, Piotr—are you out of your mind? Once married to Katya—" Exhausted with emotion, he sighed heavily. "What's the difference? Ever since those damn maids pulled out your valises and emptied your bureau drawers . . ." He turned a gray face away from his son, poured himself an immense drink, and downed it. He glared at Piotr. "Let's get out of here."

Piotr Stolypin nodded. Picking up two of the suitcases, he led his father down the hall past Ruth's sitting room, where the lights were still burning.

"David," Ruth was saying, "I understand exactly how you feel, but are you being honest with me about Katya's feelings?"

David pinched out his cigar. "Yes, principally Katya has suffered a shock. Ronya is greatly relieved."

"I'm glad," Ruth said with intense relief. "I'll add—good riddance."

"And I shed no tears. This farm boy will learn soon enough the price of prejudice."

"Please don't talk like that, David. There's no need for revenge. The important thing is that Katya is not committed to a young man whose aim is power and who lacks moral strength."

David sat for a time without talking. His eyes narrowed. He was looking into his own soul.

Prime Minister: that was the one thing he had wanted all his life. This was a secret no one knew, not even Ruth. There was little satisfaction in the knowledge that all St. Petersburg granted—however grudgingly—that in England or France, where the attitude toward Jews was more liberal, David von Glasman might have become Prime Minister. Russia was not England or France.

David shrugged. His hand reached out and touched Ruth's. "Let's go to bed. For the present there is nothing left to say."

2

Two weeks later, fate lent a hand. David received an urgent summons from his Empress. Now the way was easy. He wrote to his trusted secretary, Ladislaus, calling him to St. Petersburg.

The evening before David left Kiev, Rifka and Tamara were invited to dinner. Ruth made the invitation, but it was at David's suggestion. Tamara was, as usual, already at the manor house. She simply stayed on.

Rifka came into the library at about six o'clock, unannounced, to find Ruth, her innate elegance enhanced by a simple gray-green dress, rearranging some late roses. Ruth looked up as the door opened.

A knee-length skirt of bright patchwork gathered and caught at the waist with a red silk rope. Rings on her tapering hands. Long flowing black hair held together with a diamond clasp. Black eyes made blacker by bold painting. Rifka had always possessed an exotic beauty all her own, and the attention she lavished on herself had kept her a handsome woman. If with the passing of the years, fiery dignity had come to dominate the sensuality in her face and bearing, there was still a hint remaining of the Rifka who had caused more than one duel.

Ruth took it all in and smiled. "Very striking, Rifka. I'd swear you're not a day over thirty."

Rifka laughed aloud. "I'd tear your hair out if you'd said fifty-nine."

Heavens, fifty-nine! Ruth thought. *And David, too. I always think of him as young.*

Rifka came across the room and buried her face in the flowers.

"Why the lantern?"

"Old Auntie reminded me there'd be no moon," Rifka said, putting it down. "Where's David?"

"Dressing," Ruth said.

Rifka watched her deftly place the last rose in the bowl, then: "You know what the peasants are talking about?"

Ruth made no reply.

"About Piotr. They say the master swore an oath that if ever he set foot on this land he'd be flogged."

"What utter rubbish! I suppose the maids got that started. They dreaded him. Nothing they did pleased him. They were overjoyed to be told to pack his clothes."

"Strangely enough," Rifka said, "I shared David's early opinion of him. I thought he'd make Katya a useful husband."

"Why strangely?"

"Because ordinarily I don't like cold men, and I distrust the landed gentry."

"I'm sure David thought he'd do well in the government. It never hurts to have a son-in-law in powerful places."

Rifka smiled. "Don't worry. David is in control of himself. The angrier he gets, the cooler he is. Now that he's decided to change his strategy, there'll be no stopping him. I wouldn't be surprised if he had leanings toward a duke for Katya." Very much at home, Rifka sauntered across to the bell cord and rang for a servant just as the housekeeper came into the room. Evdokia bobbed a small curtsy to Ruth and said, "You have orders for me, my mistress?"

Ruth let her eyes go to Rifka. "I suppose we ought to wait, but I'm sure David will not think badly of us if we drink an *apéritif*. We can keep him company with another."

Bottles, decanters, and glasses had already been made ready on a small lamp-lit table by the window. Evdokia poured sherry for Ruth and skillfully prepared vodka, Cossack style, for Rifka—a glassful, well sprinkled with coarse black pepper. Rifka tossed it down, accepted a large red tomato, and sank her fine white teeth into it. It cooled her mouth. She smacked her lips. "Why won't you ever try it, Ruth? Once you're used to it, you'll never want anything else."

Ruth laughed. "Perish the thought. You know my aversion to Cossack ways."

Ronya and Tamara flung open the door, hand in hand and bursting with laughter at some shared joke, and the room seemed to come alive. Ronya planted herself on a stool next to her mother and launched into a sea of talk, eyes sparkling as she related the adventures of the afternoon. Ruth looked from her to Tamara, who, in spite of her flaming blouse beneath a purple vest and burgeoning orange skirt, had sat down with unaccustomed demureness. The subtle resemblance in the two firm-boned faces was uncanny, yet one great difference overcame all else: Ronya was an exquisite bud still closed, while Tamara's voluptuous mouth and lissom, full-blown body spoke of a sensuality bordering on the animal.

A few minutes later Katya came in with David. Rifka's lips tightened as she saw her muslin blouse and beige skirt and recognized this informality as a deliberate, though covert, slight: To Katya, gypsies were not worth a grand dinner dress. Katya nodded and smiled at Rifka, but the nod barely stirred the high-piled dark hair and the smile did not warm the cool brown eyes. For years they had been locked in a silent struggle, the result of the lifelong antagonism between Katya and Tamara, a tension they, like Ruth, made an enormous effort to keep hidden from David.

He went over to the fire, with one hand took the gold tumbler Rifka was offering him, and with the other beckoned Ronya over. He surveyed the women; he enjoyed seeing them all together, and he was in a particularly good mood tonight. Lifting the tumbler he toasted his "harem."

24

It was almost nine o'clock when they returned to the library from dinner. After coffee and brandy, David deliberately ground out the stub of his cigar. When it was completely extinguished, he looked around the room, aware that all eyes were on him. "I have made up my mind about certain matters," he said. "I have a statement or two to make."

He waited until they were all settled, then went on. "After I have concluded my business with the Empress, I shall devote myself to finding a suitable setting for Katya. That should not be too difficult— mansions and titles are always available."

"At a price," Rifka interjected.

"Precisely," David nodded.

Avoiding her mother's eyes, Ronya rose and stood by her father. She brushed some ash from his sleeve as she said, "Have you told Mother about my going with you and Katya to St. Petersburg?"

There was a frozen silence. Ruth and Rifka stared at David in consternation. They had not guessed his schemes included Ronya. Then Tamara exploded.

"Going to St. Petersburg? If Ronya is going, so am I!"

No one spoke. They were all feeling Ruth's hurt. As usual, David had made his plans alone.

Tamara was gripped with the fear that Ruth's anger would be turned against her, a fear compounded by the realization that David looked upon her as an unexpected complication. Past victories told her that whatever chance she might have rested with Ronya.

"I'll just die if you go without me," she said, more softly.

"Please, Tamara," Ronya said apologetically, "don't make it hard for me. I won't be away very long, and I'll write every day."

"Well, thank you!" Tamara snapped scornfully. "In that case, you stay home and I'll write the letters."

"Katya's my sister," said Ronya comfortably, "and besides, I've never been to St. Petersburg."

"Well, neither have I. I've never been anywhere except in gypsy wagons."

"But you *are* a gypsy," Katya put in.

Ruth set down her demitasse in displeasure. "That's enough," she said with finality. "There is no need for you to go to St. Petersburg, Ronya, and that solves your difficulty with Tamara."

Ronya looked at her mother in dismay. "But Father—" she began, spinning around to David.

"Not so fast," he said firmly. "Ronya is not the bone of contention. She certainly is going. We are speaking of Tamara. As a possible solution," he turned to Rifka, "will you consider taking Tamara with you?"

"I knew you'd suggest that. Do you want me to dig my own grave by revealing I have a grown daughter? No, David, unless I go to St. Petersburg alone, I might as well stay home."

Tamara opened her mouth to protest, but there had been an implacable note in her mother's voice. She stood up, gazing uncertainly at the rigid faces, and then flounced out of the room. Ronya threw an anguished glance at her father and mother and ran after her.

Adjusting the tulle over her shoulders, Ruth said, "Katya, I'm sure you have no enthusiasm for the turn this conversation has taken. You may go."

Her parents watched her pass coolly from the room. She beguiled no one: Katya was pleased with her victory over Tamara.

When she had gone, David turned to Ruth. "What's the matter with you? You look ready to tear Rifka and me to pieces."

"I'd like to. I am appalled."

"At me," Rifka smiled.

"Yes, at you," Ruth answered. "I—"

David cut her short. "I never expected you'd want to leave Ronya alone in Kiev. Furthermore—"

"Wait, David," Rifka said, rising. "I'm leaving." She picked up her lantern and went quickly to the door. "I'll see you and Paul in a few days. Good luck."

She was hardly out of the room when David said, "Would you do me the kindness of sparing me an unpleasant argument?"

Ruth could feel her husband's chilliness; nevertheless, she said to him beseechingly, "I am not going to St. Petersburg, and I beg of you —don't take Ronya."

David neither spoke nor moved. She tried again.

"It is not merely that high society is corrupt and wanton. She is so completely virginal—a little girl living in a world of romantic dreams, waiting for a man far better than men really are, who will slay dragons to reach her."

"Odd," David remarked, "that you confuse chastity with innocence. Even odder is the fact that you do not understand your own daughter. Ronya is no romantic child. She is a creature of immense contradictions with the hard-sure courage to stand up to the Almighty, if need be."

"David, stop! You blaspheme!"

"And you, my dear, are bluffing."

"No, David, I am not. I cannot bear St. Petersburg—but that is of minor importance. I refuse to lend support to this business of using Katya, of mating Ronya, so you can have the grandsons you think are your due."

26

"Think what you wish," David said coldly. "Ronya will accompany her sister to St. Petersburg."

Ruth flinched. In the profound silence that followed, she left the room.

The seconds slipped away. David's throat was dry. He rose slowly and poured himself a brandy, and in a few slow strides returned to his chair and sat down again. A great lassitude came over him, and he closed his eyes and let his mind drift.

He recalled a warm, sleepy afternoon, some months after Ronya's eleventh birthday. He had come upon the girls quite by accident on a path leading from the camp to the manor house. Ronya was huddled on the ground behind a bush while Katya and Tamara kept watch. It was Ronya who told him loudly to go away.

"What has happened?" he asked.

Again Ronya. "I can't tell you."

Tamara and Katya remained motionless, watching. Suddenly Katya stepped forward and took his arm. "Come, Father," she said, "let's go home. Ronya will be along later."

It was on the tip of his tongue to demand an explanation, but Ronya lifted her head and cried out, "Can't you see, Father, that I want you to go?"

An hour or so later, Ruth joined him in the library. Quite shaken, she said, "David, Ronya's menstrual flow has started." She took a deep breath. "Good God in heaven, how sad that childhood is to be so small a portion of her life."

David remembered asking Ruth whether it disturbed her to find only relative equality in nature and that Ronya had surged ahead of Katya. "Yes, I am disturbed," Ruth had answered gravely. "It would have been better after Katya. After Tamara, too."

David had decided there was no point in pursuing the discussion. Pouring two brandies from the crystal and silver decanter, he said, "Let us drink to Ronya."

Ruth lifted her glass. "To both our girls." Her brandy finished, her face softened. "Shall I send Ronya to you?"

"Please. Give me a few minutes."

At the sound of Ronya's step, David closed the wall safe, pocketed what he had removed from it, and re-hung a magnificent painting of a city silhouetted in the glowing light of sunshine and mist.

For some moments he remained silent, watching Ronya standing in the doorway—comparing hers with a remembered face, the same sparkling black eyes, the same reddish-brown hair. Strange! Though the room was warm, David felt suddenly cold. Determinedly he pushed back the memory that had taken hold of him.

"Come here, my love," he said.

She came to him and let herself be clasped against his chest, but only for an instant. Now, years later, David remembered the moment clearly.

"I know I'll never convince Mother, but I hope you accept my word for it. I *did* see the one whom I shall marry, so you don't have to worry about me and boys."

David smiled. "I know you can be trusted. Whether or not that strange boy you once saw for a few minutes in Odessa may eventually become your husband is of small consequence at the moment. Just remember—" he said, regarding her intently, "should a boy dare approach you, cut him down with your whip."

Ronya said nothing.

David drew from his pocket two brilliant blue-white diamonds. "Gold loops are for little girls," he said softly. "These earrings are now yours. They were my mother's, and she was thirteen years old when her father locked them in her ears."

"But Katya is thirteen years old."

"I have saved these for you, Ronya. Katya will have duplicates— soon, I expect."

"That is not the same, Father. And, if I were Katya, I would resent it."

David recalled the silence that fell between them. His head felt heavy, and he dozed. When he awoke, his mind traveled farther into the past, and another, fearful memory was rekindled.

The land was unchanged, the house practically unchanged, even the peasants in their sheepskin coats were unchanged. He saw the estate when there was mist in the air, when the rain came in a steady downpour, when the summer roses were in bloom. Gypsy men played mouth organs or whittled sticks, telling tales over a bottle of vodka. He saw their garishly dressed women, listening, watching. He saw two children, himself and Rifka, walking along rutted roads, solemnly swearing loyalty to each other. And then he saw the boulder. . . .

They ascend the boulder slowly and on tiptoe. (David could no longer remember why they sneaked along. Most likely it was a game Rifka invented that required cunning and silence.) Suddenly they hear a soft moan and, looking down into the tall grass, they see his sister Sophia, nearly naked, beneath the weight of Azov the gypsy. They watch as Azov raises himself and caresses Sophia, gently rubbing his hand over her breasts. They hear Sophia, urging him on, and see her fingers clench into his bare shoulder, her face contort, and again, the gentle moan. Sophia opens her eyes, she smiles and whispers into Azov's ear, and he, unmoving, nods, then laughs aloud.

The past faded, David finished his brandy at a gulp. With slow, heavy steps he went up to his bedroom, realizing that the time had come: Ruth, his wife, had to know. He went quietly toward the bed. "Are you awake?" he asked.

"Yes, dear. Turn up the lamp if you wish."

When David returned the room was well-lighted and Ruth was sitting up, resting her head against her pillow.

He got into bed beside her. "I don't want to sleep," he said, and then, his voice tight, he told her he had something to tell her: "A black secret. An unforgettable horror."

Ruth, her hand extended to take his, drew it back in foreboding.

Relentlessly, he went on: "I have a sister. Her name is Sophia. She calls herself Sophia Azov, and she and our Ronya are—at least in looks—identical twins, one generation apart."

"No!" Ruth cried.

"Yes." David nodded his head slowly. "She is twelve years older than I. She was the absolute center of my life and deeply attached to me. When I wanted something, it was to her I went; when I was hurt, she comforted me. After our mother died, our father was lost in shock, and it was Sophia who took upon herself the task of looking after me. If I was afraid of the dark I crept into her bed. She made up enchanting stories, and sang the songs I loved, and taught me not to be afraid to visit our mother's grave. I came to feel that Sophia was part of me, that she belonged to me. It was very wonderful while it lasted."

Abruptly David stopped talking.

"What happened?" Ruth said at last.

"I don't know where to begin."

"Begin anywhere, but tell it all." For over twenty years David had let her believe that he was an only child!

Eyes half closed, voice barely above a whisper, David resumed his strange tale. "She fell in love with Azov, the brother of Rifka's mother. When the consummation of that love became apparent, people said that the tragedy was inevitable—a motherless young beauty allowed to run wild around the gypsy campfires. People said other things, heartless, cold-blooded things." David paused, and then his voice grew strong. "Sophia's dishonor brought my father out of his somnambulism. First he silenced the gossip. He used a strong hand, he knew how. Then he took Sophia out of Russia. He left Azov's punishment to the gypsy queen.

"Rifka and I were then about eight years old, and it was decreed by her mother, the queen, that she and I should bear witness to the castration. It was horrible—one can never imagine how horrible. But the truth is"—David paused—"I was glad, because I hated Azov with a passionate hatred.

"He died by bits in a cage. He failed to observe the taboo. He dared to debauch a daughter of the Von Glasman house."

"Oh, my God!"

David looked for no words of comfort. "You are never to breathe a word of this to Ronya or to Katya," he said after a long silence. "Give me your promise."

Ruth was so surprised, she seemed for a moment not to have heard.

"Well?" David demanded.

"In heaven's name, why?" Then, seeing his severe face, she said, "Certainly, of course, David. I promise."

He hesitated a moment and added, "I have obtained the same pledge from Rifka. Tamara will remain ignorant of Sophia."

Ruth mused upon David's double standard. It was all right for his father's brother to sire Rifka, but not for a gypsy to awaken desire in his sister. But she gave no hint of what she was thinking. Instead, seizing the opportunity, she said, "You have remained in touch with Sophia, haven't you?"

David nodded. "I spent years finding her. If it hadn't been for Ladislaus, I might never have succeeded."

"Do you see her?"

"Every few years. We meet in Paris, and we write to each other through an intermediary."

"Did she ever marry?"

"No. When Father brought her and her son to New York, he established them in a luxurious house and explained that she was widowed, and a widow she has remained."

"And Ladislaus?"

"Ladislaus is in my employ. Eventually, he will serve Ronya."

Ruth looked at David a long moment. "Why is Ladislaus never allowed to see you here in this house?"

"Mainly because he chooses to present himself as himself only on rare occasions, which, frankly, pleases me. After the girls are married, well—" David turned down the lamp, put his arms around Ruth, and no more was said that night. Past dawn, Ruth slept and dreamed.

The next morning, all alone in the house except for the servants, Ruth found it impossible to get Sophia out of her mind. Principally, she thought about her dream, in which Ronya and Sophia were entangled, like butterflies caught in the same net. She sought some meaning to the dream, but the thoughts that came to her, though vague, seemed too fanciful and absurd, and she tried to put an end to them by concentrating upon David's less disturbing disclosures. Gradually her gloom lifted. At the noonday meal, David kept silent, his eyes fixed on Ronya as though she were changed from yesterday. If

Ronya perceived this, she made no sign. Soon afterward, David withdrew to his room for a nap, and Katya returned to Kiev and her dressmaker, whose seamstresses were putting the finishing touches to several costumes created, cut, and basted by a Paris designer. The gypsies were making wine, and Ronya and Tamara ran off to stamp grapes brought straight from the Crimea.

Ruth thought about taking a rest; instead she ordered her carriage. It was a perfect early autumn day. The sky was clear blue, the air hung windless and, though the gardens were still ablaze with chrysanthemums, dahlias, and even some late-blooming roses, the lawns were browning and the leaves on the trees turning yellow. Ruth's feeling of urgency lessened, and instead of driving straight to the Levinsky house, she told the coachman to make a detour. He took the horses past the solid, whitewashed peasant houses, past the barns and the corrals, and down to the river, so that Ruth reached the Jewish quarter later than she intended.

Simon Levinsky, chief rabbi of Kiev, was her dearest friend—for many years her only friend—and it was with him that she shared confidences. But before her visit with the rabbi, Ruth first enjoyed tea and honey cakes and gossiped a little with Lena, his wife, bringing a breath of the outside world into her life that was bounded by strict Jewish tradition.

The rabbi turned to his son. "The day is almost over, Joseph. Go back to the Torah. A lifetime passes before one masters the five books of Moses."

Joseph replied with a nod. "Please tell Ronya," he said to Ruth, "that once the High Holy Days are over, I shall keep my promise and teach her Hebrew."

"I know how much Ronya relies upon your friendship, Joseph," Ruth said softly; she suspected that this slim, solemn youth loved her daughter Ronya. "But I am afraid teaching her Hebrew may be impossible—at least for a time. David is taking both girls to St. Petersburg quite soon. It may turn out to be a prolonged stay."

The young man's face fell.

"I'd like to hear why," the rabbi said in dismay.

Ruth remained silent. She would say no more in Joseph's presence. Simon Levinsky sighed heavily and gestured to the door. "You may leave, Joseph."

For a few moments they remained in absolute silence. Finally the rabbi asked Ruth what was worrying her.

"So many things," she answered. "It seems that David and I have one disagreement after another about the girls, and my wishes are simply dismissed. David makes all the decisions. He has such a talent for acting with stunning certainty."

31

He sighed.

Ruth fixed her great emerald-colored eyes on her friend. Bitterness flooded her face and her voice. " 'The Lord God planted a garden in Eden, in the east, and placed there a man whom He had formed.' David will place Ronya, whom he has tried to form, in his garden of Eden to till it, to tend it, to bear its heirs. Through Ronya, David becomes immortal.

"The Lord David commanded Katya, saying, 'Of each generation one is given to Christianity. Of every responsibility you are free save one. Let not the wild beasts of the earth, the birds of the sky, take you from Her, flesh of your flesh, bone of your bone—the One, called Ronya. Hence, if need be, leave your husband and cling to Her. Serve the house of Von Glasman.' "

Left weak by her outburst, her lips trembling a little, she pressed her handkerchief to her mouth.

The rabbi gazed compassionately at this woman who was ordinarily so restrained and seemingly uncomplicated. "David von Glasman is not the Lord God," he said at last.

Already a little remorseful, Ruth said, "Forgive my outburst, Simon. And, in all fairness to David, I must say I am exaggerating."

"Come, Ruth, you can't fool me. What is David up to? I know how arrogant he can be. And what about young Stolypin? Rumor has it that David considers him a fairly acceptable catch."

"No longer." Ruth put away the handkerchief.

The rabbi sat watching her, puzzled.

"Frankly, I'm not overanxious about Katya. She flirted—in a perfectly respectable way, of course—with all the attractive young men around here, and she finds David's promise of a great title very agreeable. It seems to me she's put Piotr completely out of her mind, so the dent he made in her heart must indeed have been slight. It's Ronya who troubles me. She is not yet eighteen and has never looked at a man romantically."

"So what are you worried about?"

"I'm against exposing Ronya to St. Petersburg. There's danger in it. But as I've said, it's useless to oppose David, especially as Ronya is determined to go."

"In that case," the rabbi said mildly, "let us hope for the best."

And half humorously he added; "It's unlikely that David will hand over the most beautiful girl in the Ukraine to a stranger; of that we can be certain."

Ruth gave him an engaging smile. "You are a comfort to me, Simon." She hesitated, then: "I wonder whether you know anything about a woman who once lived hereabouts. Her name is Sophia."

Caught completely by surprise, the rabbi fell silent, remembering the exquisite creature with black eyes and chestnut hair gleaming like copper in the sun, with skin so white and delicate.

"I see you knew her."

"Knew her? Certainly I knew her."

"And the stories?"

He stared at Ruth, troubled, trying to fathom the purpose behind her questions. Finally he said, "The scandal spread rapidly over the entire *gubernia*. Among the Jews, it was concluded that sooner or later it was bound to happen. But oddly enough, not even the women blamed Sophia. It was Erich von Glasman who was condemned, particularly for making Sophia's shame public. Shortly before they left, Erich came to see us, bringing David. My father, then rabbi, could not understand why Erich insisted upon exile. 'Let them marry,' he begged. That infuriated Von Glasman. 'I should have pressed a whip into my daughter's hand and taught her to fight,' he replied, and told my father that he would be away from Russia for months, maybe years, and asked him to see to David's education. In all other matters, the gypsy queen was to take complete charge. He said, 'I want David and Rifka raised as brother and sister.' "

"It's crazy," Ruth remarked. "How long did Erich von Glasman stay away?"

"He never came back. I think he never intended to."

"Poor little David," she said, and got up. "It's time for me to go."

"I'll walk you to your carriage."

"Simon, may I ask you one more question?"

The rabbi smiled. "I daresay I can handle it."

"David claims Sophia and Ronya are alike. Do you agree?"

"They have the same face. Character is hard to judge; so much lies beneath the surface. The important point is, Ronya has a mother. And a father, in the best sense of the word."

"And," Ruth added, "a whip in her hand."

Ruth rode home, sunk in thought.

At supper all was pleasant, with Katya and Ronya carrying on a lively conversation. But later, when they were alone, Ruth turned to David. "Will you take me to America? I want to meet Sophia."

"Perhaps, after Ronya is settled."

Ruth moved close to David and kissed him, and she made the kiss last until he put his arms around her and pressed his body to hers.

3

As was their habit, her Majesty the Empress and David met behind closed doors, with no others present. He was led into one of the smaller sitting rooms in her private apartment, where she sat waiting amid a welter of ornate French furniture, brocades, imperial Easter eggs, gold sprays of lily of the valley, jeweled peacocks, miniature imperial coaches, jade jars, and music boxes in rose diamonds.

The Empress prodded. David responded with a plan designed to bloom into rubles for the royal coffer; finance was his métier. But knowing that David von Glasman, her Disraeli, her Rothschild, had private channels of information, the Empress sought every bit of news he could give of every subject, not only political and financial; and for her, David, despite all his reserve, was not above lightening his conversation with gossip—he always had the best and latest version of the newest international scandals.

The Empress was enjoying herself. "David, my friend," she said at length, "you are always such a pleasure to us. Allow us to reward you in some fashion."

This was the opportunity David was waiting for. He gave a brief and straightforward account of Katya's abortive romance.

The Empress understood dignity, she understood damaged pride, and the picture of beautiful, rich, bereft Katya stirred her imagination. After a moment's deliberation she said, "We know of at least fifteen eligible suitors. A few, however, are widowers." She gave David a fleeting but shrewd glance and went on decisively, "Bring your daughter to St. Petersburg where she can be seen at the opera, at the ballet, at the foreign embassies. We shall give a ball."

David envisioned the scene: bare-shouldered court ladies, dukes in glittering uniforms, bemedaled drawing-room warriors, races, receptions, dances, dinners. Yes, David smilingly allowed, his Katya was about to enter the established order's most jealously guarded preserve.

Wordlessly he bowed low.

Personal matters concluded, they played the game they had been playing for years. David gave his Empress a sculptured icon; rosettes of precious stones decorated the saint's dress.

With feigned surprise the Empress scolded him for his extravagance.

David's answer was nothing but the truth. "Your Majesty does me honor."

Characteristically, the visit ended on a serious note. David urged the Empress to reconcile the Tzar to the direction in which the world was moving.

"We cannot agree," she answered evenly. "We in Russia do not search for modern views of government."

David said no more. His interest was in harmony. As he prepared to take his leave, he was rewarded for his restraint. The Empress rose to her feet and gazing up at him, said, "Our word: No title will ever be bestowed upon Piotr Stolypin."

The evening was mild and the distance short—just a few blocks once one turned off the elegant wide main street.

The solidly respectable old house was in darkness, or so it seemed from the street; but David was watched for, and Ladislaus opened the door as he approached.

Ladislaus' tall, gaunt form and veiled, melancholy, tea-colored eyes were never seen in the Kiev house. A man without name or country, he served David secretly and with passionate devotion. After all, he owed his life to David von Glasman. The story was an old one, but since David and Ladislaus were both closemouthed, it had never gone further. By birth Ladislaus was a Pole; when he was only nineteen his father was accused of high treason and shot himself before trial; the son was court-martialed in the father's place. David took up his cause and made himself Ladislaus' champion, and thanks to David's notable defense in court and uncounted bribes, he was acquitted. But Ladislaus was made to forfeit his broad acres and his ancient name. He forgot nothing, neither the injury done him nor his debt to David. He was David's right hand in executing business; his eyes and ears when he traveled, often in disguise; his brain when summing up a man or using a tool.

"Ladislaus," David laughed as he shrugged himself out of his coat, "you're taller and thinner than ever. A string bean."

But Ladislaus was used to comments about his appearance. "Countless disguises spare me my own image," he said, pressing David's hand.

"Is Paul here?"

"In the study," Ladislaus answered, as he led the way across the hall.

"How is he?"

"Suave, articulate, and better-looking than ever."

David's face lit up. Rarely demonstrative or even affectionate, particularly with men, he entertained a real tenderness for Paul, his favorite among Rifka's sons. Yet he did not go straight to the study. Instead, as was his custom, he first went up the stairs to the room Rifka used as her dressing room when she stayed in the house.

Ladislaus entered the study to find Paul standing near a tall window screened with heavy damask drapery. Books lined the walls of the comfortable, rather staid room.

35

"Do you suppose he has brought her yet another present?" Paul asked, seeing Ladislaus was alone.

"Yes," he replied, "she'll find it locked in the safe when she comes."

"Ruth von Glasman is an amazing woman. She accepts all David's devotion and generosity to my mother without resentment."

"Ruth is a lady," Ladislaus said evenly. "If she has feelings in this matter, she believes in keeping them to herself."

"Yes, I suppose so," Paul said faintly, moving idly over to the ceiling-high tiled stove.

Ladislaus watched him admire a table nearby topped with lapis lazuli. "A priceless treasure, isn't it?"

"What was this place like when David bought it for my mother?"

"Awful. The exterior was run-down and neglected, the plaster was peeling away from the brick, and the inside was crowded with fussy little ornaments—antimacassars, bits of lace, cut glass. We threw everything out. David would not keep a single thing."

Paul looked around the sparkling clean room, now so in keeping with David's impeccable taste—magnificent woods, great wing chairs, shelves filled with books. Marvelous! Who but David would put so much into a house so rarely used?

The door opened then. Paul went to David quickly, and they clasped hands for a long moment.

Ladislaus smiled sympathetically. He could see that Paul wanted to throw himself into David's arms.

David took note of the firm mouth, the strong chin. "You look well, Paul."

"I've put on weight."

"It becomes you."

"And how are you, David?"

"Am I ever sick?"

Ladislaus drifted over to the stove and watched them with an absorbed air. What if Paul had not rushed into too early a marriage . . . No, he told himself, polish does not change quartz into a diamond. David loves him like a son, but he knows that Paul is not good enough for Katya.

Ladislaus knew almost all there was to know about Paul. He liked him but was wary of him. In his childhood, when it became clear to him that he was born a bastard, Paul began to show a mean streak. By the time he was twelve he was a problem, and by fourteen he was in serious trouble.

There was the matter of his murdering his mother's lover. David was in Paris at the time, but when Rifka's summons came, he laid aside all personal and financial interests and hurried back to Kiev.

36

Resolutely, he set about finding a solution. David paid a bribe. A key witness lost his memory. David collected a debt. A police officer destroyed a record. Still, weeks passed in costly litigation before the court set Paul free.

Immediately, he was sent off to an excellent school in England, equipped with a new identity—David's well-born protégé. Paul took on the manners of a gentleman. Every year, David went to see him, and his pride and confidence in him grew.

Paul's absence from Russia lasted nine years. Then David brought him home, introduced him to St. Petersburg, and obtained for him a position of some influence in the Tzar's secret police. Paul was enormously intelligent and strikingly handsome, and women fell in love with him, but no one stirred his interest deeply until he met an engineer's daughter, an attractive girl with a quiet face and a passive disposition. Impetuously, Paul proposed marriage to her, and she overcame her timidity surprisingly fast and accepted him. On their wedding night she prayed aloud to the Holy Virgin to protect her against his lust. At first Paul stroked and kissed and courted her; but after they had had two daughters and she still delivered herself to loud prayer, he left her alone.

Ladislaus did not know the details of Paul's married life, but he suspected that all was not well. Paul appeared to have every reason to be a happy man; he seemed happy: but Ladislaus had a long memory.

"Come and sit down, Ladislaus."

A buxom serving maid had brought in tea and lemons and a bowl of salted nuts, and the three men talked companionably before settling down to business.

"Tell me about Mother and Tamara. How's Fedor?"

"All well. Rifka is waiting for the latest styles from Paris."

"Mother decked out in Paris elegance!" Paul half smiled. "That conjures up an enticing picture."

"Be appropriately surprised when she arrives. She thinks you will not guess that she is coming. I keep telling her that behind your handsome face is a keen brain, but she likes to fancy herself enigmatic."

Paul's smile widened. "Well, you're quite right about us both."

The twinkle in David's eyes disappeared suddenly. "It is as well that you are astute and discreet. You have not yet been tempted to tell your wife about us, about your mother and me?"

Paul shook his head. "No. I know I cannot tell her and, in any case, Helena lives in a world too far removed from ours. I could no more tell her about Rifka the gypsy queen and Von Glasman the Jew than I could put my trust in my captain. Their minds are closed, rigid, numbed." There was a pause, in which Paul included Ladislaus by a glance. "You must not think I'm unhappy. We get along, and in many ways she is very understanding. She has her own interests. She never intrudes into my professional life and never complains, even though I am often away for long periods of time."

How curious, Ladislaus thought, that none of them seemed to feel at all discomfited by Paul's confidences.

"A satisfactory arrangement is often more valuable to a man than a more passionate relationship," David remarked.

Ladislaus pictured a girl without glow, and he felt sorry for Paul. Instead he said, "Well, David, I have found the perfect house. It's within easy walking distance of the palace and has enough bedrooms and sitting-room suites and modern bathrooms. It is expensively furnished in very good taste and has a splendid ballroom, so it's thoroughly adequate for entertaining. There's a balcony that overlooks the square, which gives you a private viewing place for parades. I have spoken to the owner, Gospodin Kaluzhny. He was very friendly—explained that he was needed at home in Georgia and is willing to rent the house for four months, provided you are prepared to keep on his house servants and his coachman, whom he praised highly. So I made him your offer. He was delighted—in fact he said that you have such a reputation for generosity and honesty that there is no need to sign legal papers."

"Well done," David said. "Now I want a carriage and a matching pair. Find a butler, one who knows how to keep the servants in line. Stock the cellar."

Ladislaus nodded.

"I daresay Gospodin Kaluzhny's silver and linens and so on are excellent. Nevertheless, check them. Have a look at the wall hangings and the paintings. If they are of a religious nature, store them and find appropriate replacements."

Ladislaus' expression betrayed nothing, but he thought: *Strange man. You are prepared to give your daughter to Christianity, but the Virgin and saints and Mary Magdalene dressed in red must go.*

David turned to Paul and, thinking himself dismissed, Ladislaus made a move toward the door.

"No, don't go yet," David said, without turning his head. "Listen to what Paul has to say."

Ladislaus sat down again.

Then Paul made his report. "I've made a list of the matrimonial prospects, especially the titled ones. Frankly, there aren't many I'd recommend."

David raised an eyebrow.

"You ruled out widowers, with or without children . . ." Paul said uncomfortably.

38

"I think you have something else on your mind," David said. "Say what you don't want to say."

"To what purpose, David?" he said ruefully. "You have already read my mind."

David addressed himself to Ladislaus. "Paul grants us that Katya's situation is impressive, still he does not shut his eyes to the fact that very few among those truly desirable will want to marry the daughter of a Jew. What do you say, Ladislaus?"

Ladislaus crushed out his cigarette carefully. "Somewhere in Russia there is a man who is not afraid. You'll find him, or he'll find you."

"Yes. I think so, too," David said thoughtfully. He turned back to Paul. "You have the information I asked you for?"

Paul reached for his briefcase.

"No, don't show me. Tell me."

"Duke Demetrius Kosta," Paul began, leaning back in his chair. "They say his ancestors were rulers as far back as the twelfth century. That may be true. He doesn't lack connections—of any kind, unfortunately."

David's eyebrows rose questioningly.

Paul screwed up his mouth in disgust. "From time to time, the Duke employs the services of a male prostitute. Sometimes he takes a peasant boy. So far, the homosexual episodes in his life have been well hidden."

Unmoved, David said, "What about your other assignment?"

"I think he'll make his bid. He's bound to."

"Money?"

"He's desperate. He has been waiting for his aunt to die. She just has and left a pittance, for all her miserliness."

David was not entirely surprised, nor was he disheartened. "Destroy all the written notes and evidence. When I come back I shall go into the matter of choosing a suitable son-in-law. When I have the name for you, I want every detail of his life, not an assortment of bits and pieces."

"Yes, David, I understand."

It was Ladislaus who brought up the most delicate subject of all. "David, have you thought about the biggest problem? It's likely that, no matter who he is, he'll make a condition: that Katya be converted to Christianity."

There was an expectant silence, as both men's eyes riveted to David. All he said was, "I have it in mind."

The door to high society opened with a royal invitation to view the mounted guard of honor on parade one warm, still, fall day. This dazzling ceremony was very much part of the glamor surrounding the royal family, and it was no accident that David and his daughters viewed the parade from locations very near the Empress. This honor was noticed and noted. Also marked, and later imitated, was the splendid costume worn by Katya. The style was severely plain, high-necked, long-sleeved, but it was made of a most unusual fabric, fine beige tweed embroidered with a tiny apricot-colored figure. A scarf of thin apricot silk was folded delicately around her neck. She wore no jewels, and the small hat that framed her face was inconspicuous—a deliberate choice. This combination of richness and simplicity was exactly right for the time, the place, and the event. Katya was by no means unaware of the stir she made and held herself with superb assurance.

Ronya did not go unwatched. Her dress was clear apple-green and so fine a wool that the skirt swirled around her as she turned from side to side, eager not to miss a thing. Her hat swung from her hand, and when a glance reached her she glanced back and smiled. Everything was new and exciting, and Ronya was alive to every trifle.

She was the first to notice the tallish man with close-clipped fair hair who stood a few paces behind the Empress. He had stared at Katya quite persistently when the Von Glasmans had arrived and picked their way through the crowd of spectators to their places, and since then every time Ronya had risked a covert look he had been immobile, silent, and transfixed, apparently aware of nothing but her. Ronya wondered who he was. He looked about thirty. Even from this distance she could see that his eyes were blue, like the Tzar's, and that he was a Muscovite, for he was wearing the gold braid and crimson sash that denoted Moscow's nobility.

All at once, there was a volley of rifle fire; yet Ronya noticed that even then he had not changed position and that, even after the hussars rode out, his gaze remained intently on her sister.

The hussars were followed by the colorful dragoons, and they in turn by the Cossacks in their dress uniform—long red coats trimmed with purple, sabers clanging against shining black boots. But everybody in the square in front of the Winter Palace—the grand dukes and duchesses, the famous of the aristocracy on the viewing platform, and the droshky drivers, the ragged children, the beggars, the women in dingy black shawls, craning around the soldiers guarding the square—waited for the Imperial Guard, the elite of the Cavalry. At last, to a roar of applause, they rode out, 105 strong, dazzling in scarlet tunics laced with gold and gold helmets. They were led by a young giant, who wore no helmet and whose hair shone brighter than the sun.

40

Ronya was conscious of nothing but the beautiful face of the young captain of the guard. It seemed to fill her senses, blocking out the square, the horsemen, the murmuring spectators, the shrill words of command.

"There he is!" she said in wonder. "There he is, Father. The man I have been waiting for all my life."

"Sh! Keep your voice down," Katya whispered, looking straight ahead.

Ronya was trembling. "Father, answer me!"

She had his full attention now. "You can't be serious."

"But I am!"

An incident in time. A man on a horse. A girl at a parade. Everything changed forever.

"We'll talk at home," David said briefly.

With a sigh Ronya turned her eyes back to the golden horseman.

The parade moved on. Captain Boris Pirov rode forward, stopped in front of her Imperial Highness the Empress Marie, and snapped to attention. He executed his salute and held the salute until he had passed the reviewing stand.

Most of the Empress' guests did not catch the fragment of a smile that swiftly faded, but David von Glasman saw. For a brief second his mind was shaken with disappointment: Shame, Marie Fedorovna; then it returned to Ronya.

The band played "God Save the Tzar." The Empress turned to go, her ladies following. As David and the girls started across the Nevsky Prospekt, they were stopped by a young man in gold braid and crimson sash, who bowed respectfully and said, "Your pardon, Gospodin von Glasman. Allow me to introduce myself: the Count Alexis Brusilov. Do me the honor of accepting my carriage."

Ronya's eyes danced. She stole a look at Katya.

"I must warn you"—David produced his most charming smile—"it will be a short drive. That pink marble palace across the way is ours."

Ronya put her hand on David's arm. "Please, Father, let yourself be persuaded," she said, her whole face lit up with mischief. "We have been standing for so long, and my feet hurt."

Alexis beamed down at her.

"Then, if you allow me," David said, "my daughters. Katya. The imp is Ronya."

Alexis bowed slightly and gave his arm to Katya.

They crossed the street in Alexis' magnificent carriage pulled by four gray geldings and driven by a huge red-bearded Moscow coachman. In minutes they were at the front door.

"I cannot say that our cook has no equal," David said, with a nicely measured blend of dignity and warmth, as though not conscious of the absurdity of getting into a carriage to travel a few yards, "but do join us for luncheon."

"Sir," Alexis answered, "my pleasure. Thank you."

Alexis' ardent tone amused Ronya. She glanced at Katya, trying not to laugh, and then at Alexis to see if she was observed. But he was too preoccupied with Katya to notice anything.

The meal, substantial and lavish, was served with great parade by a pompous butler, who had been less than anxious to serve "the Jew," whom he had never seen before he entered his service; but at the arrival of an invitation bearing the imperial crest the butler lost his misgivings. With the appearance of Count Alexis Brusilov, the butler strolled about, heavily important. Though she seemed magnificently aloof, Katya was on a golden cloud; to Alexis she was a dazzling dream.

It was David who did most of the talking, and he talked well, with immense charm. Ronya stayed determinedly quiet, refusing to be engaging, although she did ask one question, casually.

"Count, can you tell me the name of the captain of the Imperial Guard?"

"Ah, you noticed him, did you?" Alexis said. "I'm not surprised. Boris Pirov. Haven't you heard about him yet? People talk about nothing else. He's an Odessa Tartar and national champion—the finest horseman Russia has ever produced. They say that previous champions were nothing to him. The stories about him are endless—you'll hear a lot about him from the ladies when you have been in St. Petersburg a few days more."

David changed the subject.

It was ten past two when they left the table.

"Sir, I'm wondering," Alexis said, "if you would allow me to walk in the garden with Katya."

Katya sent a mute appeal to her father, who nodded his permission but cautioned, "For ten minutes only."

Ronya followed Katya to her room and watched her in the long, gold-framed mirror as she smoothed her hair and chose a cloak; but she could not tell what her sister was thinking, what she was feeling. For once she did not pester Katya with questions, but as Katya started out of the room she said, "You two look wonderful together."

Katya turned her head slowly and looked Ronya in the face. In a voice that said more than words, she replied, "Thank you, Ronya."

Alexis was waiting for her at the foot of the stairs. She took his arm and led him silently through the passageway and into the garden. They strolled along the graveled paths between almost leafless trees,

42

not speaking. When they came to a spot that was half hidden by trees and shrubs, they stopped. Alexis looked about to assure himself that no gardener was in sight. Katya walked on until she came to a stone bench. There she sat down and studied Alexis, submitting herself to his close scrutiny. Alexis' lips parted. "I've had no experience of love, but I think I have fallen in love with you, Katya von Glasman."

"When you are certain, speak to my father," Katya answered gravely. "He'll listen."

"Katya! Are you telling me that you regard me favorably?"

"I am."

"Extraordinary!" Alexis held out his hand and drew her to her feet.

"We must go back," she said.

"Surely we haven't used up our ten minutes already."

"Don't you believe in moderation?" Katya laughed, starting toward the house.

Alexis shrugged and caught up with her. "May I see you this evening?"

"I'll ask Father to include you in our plans."

They parted at the gate.

Dressing for the Presentation Ball was no small undertaking. It required the services of a hairdresser whose talent was greatly praised by the ladies of St. Petersburg. It kept maids running—a petticoat wanted pressing, a tuck required a skilled seamstress, Katya's right slipper needed stretching.

Ronya was dressed first. She ran downstairs to David who, with every attribute of a gentleman, looked remarkably grand in white tie and tails. Ronya pirouetted gracefully. "How do I look?"

David put his arms around her and kissed her. "Ravishing."

"I disagree," Ronya said, with passionate conviction. "I've no bosom showing and barely any instep."

David smiled. "It happens that we are on a mission for Katya."

"What about Boris Pirov? Is he to have his first look at me totally covered in yellow, high-waisted, and sashed? I look like a buttercup."

"More like a refreshing lemon drop," David teased.

"Please, Father, let me change into something fetching. Everything depends upon Boris Pirov falling in love with me."

David smiled at her. Small and slight, her hair piled in curls just above the nape of her neck, her eyes brilliant with feeling, she looked enchanting. "Trust me, my love. I know how you should dress."

Never had she questioned her father's judgment; it was difficult to do so now. Still she felt robbed of an opportunity. She considered a moment. "Will you be charming to Boris Pirov?"

43

"Probably." (Only later, much later, did Ronya learn that upon David's request the name of Boris Pirov had been removed from the list of guests, and by that time she had also learned more disturbing truths about her father.)

Taking his "probably" for a pledge, Ronya flung her arms around her father's neck and kissed him. Then she wriggled out of his embrace. "I'm going up to Katya."

"Stay a moment, Ronya. I want to talk to you."

He waited until she took a chair, then began at once. "I have seen you exhaust a wild mare into submission and felt no fear on your behalf, but now I am afraid. The people you will meet tonight will look charming and behave charmingly. For tonight, they will suppress prejudice and suspicion and accept us as the Empress Marie wishes us to be accepted. Don't be taken in. Pretense—all of it."

Ronya frowned. "In that case, Father, is it not a mistake for us to be here?"

"Where else could Katya have captured the attention of Count Alexis Brusilov?" David said wryly. "But it is getting late. Under no circumstances are you to go exploring or accept an invitation beyond the public rooms." David sat down alongside Ronya. "Court ladies, though they smell of French perfume, are frequently no better behaved than some of our peasant girls who smell of sweat. Do you understand?"

Ronya nodded. *How extraordinary,* she thought. *Fragrance the symbol of rank.* Still, she did not like the subject and was relieved when Katya came in.

Her gown, yards and yards of the softest, palest pink beaded over with tiny white brilliants, was cut low, and she wore diamonds in her black hair.

"Katya, you look gorgeous! Absolutely divine!"

Katya turned an ardent gaze on David. "And how do I look to you, Father?"

"Like a countess—naturally." His voice was warm and friendly, but it was not the voice he used to Ronya. *Damn! Damn!* Katya thought to herself. *But I should be used to it by now.*

Still trying, she said, "Father, have you any last-minute instructions for me?"

"Speak French. You too, my love," he added, to Ronya.

They entered the Winter Palace, as directed, by a side door. There they were met by the Empress' private secretary and escorted into a small drawing room hung with portraits of Tzar Peter the Great and the Empress Catherine. The pictures were prime examples of mediocrity, but the room was filled with roses and, despite the stiff portraits, exuded an aura of intimacy. There they were left alone for a moment. Katya and Ronya stood on either side of David, still and silent, until the major-domo announced them. Proudly they accompanied him into a gigantic gallery flooded with light. The room was of white marble with gilded ceiling: its walls were covered with Van Dykes, Rembrandts, Rubenses, Renaissance watercolors, and fine Belgian tapestries.

Under an immense gold and crystal chandelier stood the Empress, a dazzling, dark-eyed beauty whose numerous diamonds were so bright the eye could hardly bear their glare. Around her were her ladies in billowing gowns and her Cossack guards in scarlet uniforms and eagle-crested helmets. The grand master of ceremonies tapped his gold-handled wooden staff, and as Katya and Ronya sank into a curtsy a hush fell over the group.

The Empress Marie extended her hand. "We are delighted to receive you, old friend."

"My daughters share my happiness, your Imperial Highness," David replied and, following the proper etiquette, presented Katya and then Ronya.

The Empress' guests—every one of consequence was there (except for the Tzarevich Nicholas and his German wife Alexandra)—kept close watch as Count Alexis Brusilov, elegant in gold braid and jeweled medals, presented Katya with a glass of champagne and escorted her from the receiving line. Later everyone remarked on how he was brimming with pleasure and pride and hardly left her side the entire evening and that the Jewess behaved as if capturing the oldest title and one of the richest men in tzardom was nothing at all. The Empress' reception, a lavish, joyous affair, lasted until midnight. Ronya envied the women their fashionable décolletage, noted the careful pairing off, danced, and looked for Boris Pirov.

At one a sumptuous supper was served in an adjacent room. Katya and Alexis withdrew to a table for two. Ronya sat near David and the Empress, stuffing herself with sturgeon and stuffed eggs and staring fruitlessly through the double glass door. Rather than weep with disappointment, she refilled her plate and then danced again with the young officers, all in brilliant uniforms and flushed with drink. She danced to the imperial band, to balalaikas, to gypsy violins. She danced quadrilles, mazurkas, and waltzes with spirit and grace, her eyes constantly looking around the room. She responded to the compliments showered on her with indifference. But this very indifference was appealing; more eyes were turned in her direction than in Katya's.

45

"Ronya could have her pick among them," the Empress said to David with a smile. "To tell the truth, old friend, I'd like her near me, in the city her ancestor built upon the marshes."

David understood what the Empress meant, and his heart sank. It was impolitic to refuse a royal command, even though it was disguised as a hint; but taking advantage of his privileged status, he answered respectfully, "The fact is, your Majesty, Ronya has already become interested in a young man."

"Oh? Something serious?"

"Just a childish infatuation."

The Empress looked closer at David.

"I am taking her home, your Majesty."

The Presentation Ball was a sparkling success. When Alexis finally handed the girls over to David, it was after five in the morning.

It was an unseasonably mild dawn. Through open windows the river's gentle breeze brought in salt air from the Gulf of Finland. Katya was sitting at her dressing table in a trailing blue silk robe brushing out her hair. Ronya had been wandering restlessly about the room, unable to bring herself to undress. Katya gave her a sharp glance.

"Well, if you ask me," she said, "it was rude of Boris Pirov. Everyone knows no gala is complete without him. Now, of a sudden, he does not come near the palace. Perhaps—" Katya broke off and put down the hairbrush, then picked it up again and went on resolutely, "perhaps he thinks that because we're Jews—"

"Don't, Katya," Ronya interrupted passionately, "don't talk like that."

"Why not? He's a Tartar."

Ronya stood irresolute for a moment and then swung around and went out onto the balcony. She gripped the iron railing until it hurt her hands and remembered what Alexis had replied when she asked why he hadn't come.

"Little Ronya with the copper hair," he said, "listen to me. When women look at Boris Pirov, something happens to them. Their hearts hammer, they can hardly breathe. Or so I hear."

"What else do you hear?"

"Isn't that enough?"

"Not if there's more."

"People like to gossip, Ronya. Don't rely on what people say. Trust your heart."

Ronya looked down at the road, remembering the beautiful boy with the hazel eyes and golden curls she had met long ago at the dacha in Odessa. The memory eased her sadness, and gradually her

46

imagination began to stir. Soon she was luxuriating in the fantasies building in her mind about herself and Boris.

Her daydreams were disrupted when Katya came out carrying coffee and whipped cream tarts. It took a great deal to spoil Ronya's appetite. Seating themselves on a pastel-blue wrought-iron seat with the tray between them, they ate in companionable silence.

It was Ronya who first heard the distant sound of horses' hoofs on the cobblestones. Her heart leaped, and she rushed to the railing.

Not the Imperial Guard, but a fierce Cossack Cavalry unit from the Ukraine, the men who kept watch over St. Petersburg, rode into the morning scene.

Katya longed to say, this is idiotic, Ronya, but she could not bring herself to speak. She watched Ronya stand at the railing until the Cossacks could no longer be heard, then came over. "Go to sleep, Ronya. We'll talk about the ball tomorrow."

"It is tomorrow."

Dejectedly, Ronya started for her own room. She removed all her clothes and took a bath. The bath made her feel better, and she shook off her disappointment and sat down to write to Tamara, as she did every day.

> Dearest Tamara,
> I've been awake around the clock, and I'm not tired.
> Last night was wonderful. It was warm, and there was a full moon, and the air here smells of the sea and reminds me of Odessa. But the city itself makes me think of Venice and Paris.

Ronya remembered then that Tamara had never seen Italy or France or any of the countries she had been to with her father, and now Tamara was not in St. Petersburg. That seemed very wrong. Ronya brooded upon it and decided to talk to Paul about Tamara. She returned to the letter.

> I could write and write—the glistening jewels, the elaborate hair styles, the low low necklines (almost embarrassing). There was a lot of drinking—lots and lots of champagne—and dancing, and toward the end, intoxicated singing. Oh, but I wish you could have seen the Empress in her trailing skirt and jeweled hair! She is beautiful! A curious thing, though. She reminds me a little of me (she's small), and a lot of you (she has the same throaty voice). I know that sounds silly, but it's true.
> The men here all seem so desperately determined to flirt. One really made a nuisance of himself. Finally, I just laughed at him.
> About Katya. Compared to her, all the women looked wilted or common—except the Empress. Whichever way I turned, it seemed

to me that people were staring at Katya. Father was so proud of the admiration she received.

So you want more about Alexis. Well, as I told you, he's rather nice-looking. Fairly tall, in fact, but somehow he looks only medium sized. His skin is clear—no mustache. He has exquisite fingernails. His expression is sensible, dignified, and good. He rarely drinks vodka—he sips champagne. I've noticed that he is a delicate eater.

Don't think I'm being coy—or saving best for last. B.P. did not appear. Since he is in the habit of attending all Court functions, Katya concluded that the Von Glasmans from Kiev do not interest him. I don't know why, but I don't share her view. Now that the evening is over, in a way I think perhaps it is just as well that he didn't come. I wasn't the only one with eyes glued to the door. Besides, I looked ridiculous. Father tried to turn me into a child. Honestly! It amused the Empress, who saw through his device and thought it droll.

I haven't seen your mother, but Paul drops in every day. He strolls in hatless and sweeps me off my feet. He dances around the room with me and I tease him: "You're a married man." He laughs —"What of it? We have fun." With Katya he is most proper, the implication being that she's grown up and I'm not. Oh, well—why bother to prove otherwise? I've Boris Pirov to worry about.

Share this letter with Mother, and please tell her that Katya wants to write about Alexis and about the ball herself. Kiss Mother, and don't let her get lonesome. Remind her that once she gets to the camp she enjoys herself.

Good-bye. Don't forget to write.

Love and Kisses,
Ronya

P.S. I miss you.

Love,
R.v.G.

4

It was the morning after the Presentation Ball, and David von Glasman, dressed with severe propriety in a black frock coat which struck a somber note against the green curtains and brown leather and red bookbindings of his study, sat in a deep cushioned chair reading a report. Upon this report he would make his decision. As he read, his expression softened. He liked the fact that Count Alexis Brusilov was more interested in rare books, in the Dutch and Italian masters, in translucent enamels, in polite diplomacy, than in women. His title was older and far nobler than that of the Romanovs, which pleased David's ambition. His wealth was of small importance, but just the same, it was nice to know that there was one suitor whom no one could charge with fortune-hunting. Besides, Katya needed something to strengthen her self-confidence. Alexis was an orphan with no brothers or sisters, and this was a double blessing; no need for Katya to be watchful, a very comfortable situation for a countess born to Judaism.

The report went on, but David stopped reading. His plans were formed. He leaned back, closed his eyes, and listened to the bells ringing from the church steeples as he waited for Alexis to arrive.

Alexis was on time, seconds before eleven. David liked that (he had dinned promptness into Katya and Ronya). He rose and greeted him with a firm handshake. "Good morning, Gospodin von Glasman," Alexis responded with a straightforward smile. "Fine weather."

"Yes, another day of sun," David answered genially. "The girls keep asking, 'Where's the fog?' " David indicated chairs by the window.

Alexis sat down and looked collectedly about the well-kept study and out into the grounds. If he felt any sense of strain, he did not show it. The butler entered with tea, and while he waited upon them nothing of importance was said. But as soon as the tea cart was wheeled from the room, David came to the point. "Ordinarily I do not believe in pressing matters. However, I feel the time for our departure is near. Shall we have a candid talk?"

"Sir," said Alexis, "since I saw your daughter, my life is not my own. I love Katya, and I want to marry her. It is my earnest hope that you find me eligible."

"I do."

As if he wished to reassure himself, Alexis said, "You do."

"I do." David smiled.

"Thank you, sir." Then Alexis grasped the implication. "That means you have investigated me rather thoroughly."

David neither confirmed nor denied this. He credited Alexis with the knowledge that he had private channels of information.

"What shall I add, sir? That I am a dilettante, that there is nothing lurid in my life, that I shall love Katya and place her on a pedestal high above all other women."

"You talk like a young man in love. But you know perfectly well that Katya's Jewishness will be a constant source of worry to you. Married to her, your life will be entirely different from the one you know. You will be obliged to care for Ronya and protect her interests, and it will be said of your heir, the next Count Brusilov, 'He has Von

49

Glasman blood.' Are you prepared to accept these responsibilities—burdens, if you will? Do I have your word that when accounting for your deeds to God, you will say, 'Katya von Glasman was my life. Her happiness, her welfare, held first priority in my feelings and actions. I did not yield to the pressure of prejudice'?"

Alexis did not hesitate an instant. "You have my word, I swear it."

David regarded the young man, a flicker of mild amusement in his eyes. "But the truth must be faced. There'll be no heir to your title if you make a morganatic marriage."

Alexis flushed slightly; he would have liked to deny it. But then he thought: David von Glasman is not the sort of man who has to be coddled. "To be received as my wife," he said, "Katya must accept Christian baptism."

David inclined his head. "I am glad we understand each other. Now," he said in a warmer tone, "I had better tell you some of our family secrets."

Alexis sensed the change in the atmosphere and relaxed his formal manner.

"The first Von Glasman to capture the attention of a Russian was my gifted ancestor, the architect Aaron von Glasman. When Peter the Great asked Aaron to come and build him a city, Aaron refused to leave Germany; but later, he and the Tzar came to an agreement: For his part in creating St. Petersburg, Aaron was to have something very important of his own—thousands of acres of rich black earth and thick stands of timber along the shores of the Dnieper on the outskirts of Kiev. However, there was one obstacle. Peter's gypsy mistress, the Queen Natalia, lived with her people on the land. The gypsy camp had been there for centuries, and Peter was especially well disposed toward Natalia, for she bore him a daughter and trained his war horses. The Tzar Peter and the Jew Aaron gave each other a hard and binding promise. Along with clear title to the land, the Tzar awarded Aaron von Glasman royal protection in perpetuity, and Aaron made the Von Glasmans forever responsible for honoring the queen and protecting the gypsy camp. The Romanovs have kept Peter's word, and Aaron's descendants have stayed unswervingly loyal to his pledge."

Alexis had not taken his eyes off David as he talked. "I have no wish to overburden you with stories and confidences—"

"But I'm fascinated," Alexis said eagerly. "The history Katya gave me was sketchy, and when I pleaded for details she told me that you, sir, and Ronya are the storytellers in the family."

"Did Katya tell you about our present queen, our cousin Rifka, and about Tamara?"

"Very little."

David smiled. "There's nothing strange about that. As Ronya's brother-in-law, you'll be very much involved with them."

"Yes," Alexis answered, "I want to be."

David paused for reflection and decided that this was not the time to talk about Rifka's four sons.

But, to David's surprise, Alexis remarked, "It doesn't seem right to jump from Natalia to Rifka. Are there no diaries or letters?"

"Yes, records, letters, Aaron's diary." David hesitated. It had always been Ronya who had wanted to know where the secrets lay buried. He wondered what Alexis would make of some of them.

"Aaron wrote in veiled terms, but it is certain that he succumbed— not without a struggle—to Natalia's daughter, another Tamara. Tamara's child was a girl. She was received as royal by the gypsies." Then, without pause or change of tone: "Since then, many of the Von Glasman men have fathered gypsy children."

Alexis could scarcely conceal his amazement. David thought it best to make his point quickly. "The children of the family play around the campfires, and the gypsy children come up to the manor house. The gypsy queen is ruler, magician, judge, and executioner. She is honored by the family, and when she gives birth, the Von Glasman wife names her child. The children of both sides learn early the loyalty expected of them by tradition. They do not forget it."

Alexis did not feel that David expected any comment. He supposed almost every family had a two-hundred-year-old skeleton in its closet, but not many had such exotic present-day connections.

"But that's enough for now," David said. "We will have many opportunities to talk about the old stories. The girls will be down in a short time, and before they arrive I must tell you about my eldest aunt, the one for whom Katya is named."

Alexis' mind was full of questions about Tamara, and he wondered about Ruth—why had she been left in Kiev? He felt a strong curiosity about Paul, whom he had met. He sensed more there than met the eye. "Very well, sir."

"She was allowed to marry outside her faith," David said shortly. "Her grandson, my cousin, is now Bishop of Moscow."

Good God, Alexis thought, not my bishop! Despite his pledge to David, Alexis was still a Russian, and a Muscovite at that.

David guessed at what must have been going through Alexis' mind. He waited a few moments, until the color had returned to Alexis' face.

"I am sorry," said the young man. "It's not that I'm distressed, sir— only stunned."

"I told you it won't be easy."

"You aren't angry, are you, sir?"

"No, you've done well. Very well, considering."

His face brighter, Alexis glanced shrewdly at David. "Will our cousin the bishop administer Christianity to Katya?"

"Yes. Do not expect her to be piously orthodox."

Alexis did not blunder twice. "As to that, sir, I shall leave it to Katya. Whatever she wishes."

"Our situation is a bit ticklish, you can understand," said David. "Discretion—no, caution—is needed. You are not among those the Empress suggested for Katya, so she will be less than delighted that Katya has captured a title suitable for a king's daughter." David paused, then went on, "Nor can I give Katya a dazzling wedding in Kiev, where the Von Glasmans have lived as Jews for generations."

"As for that, sir," Alexis said immediately, "Katya and I can be married in Moscow, as quietly as you wish."

"Good," David said. "I'll make the arrangements. Well, Alexis, you must come to Kiev with us and meet Katya's mother. I am looking forward to showing you the estate."

The door opened, and Ronya stepped in. "Are you through talking?" She came toward them smiling. "Is it all settled?"

All through dinner that night, Ronya thought with pleasure about Katya and Alexis.

"Are you tired, my love?"

Ronya shook her head.

"Why so silent?"

"I can hardly wait for Katya to come home, and for us to be alone. I want to hear all about Alexis' castle." Suddenly Ronya said, "Father, why did you tell Alexis to bring Katya home early?"

"Come along to the study, Ronya. We'll sit by the fire."

"I planned to go upstairs and write to Mother and Tamara, and I've a book to finish. I left off just where the heroine is having the most exciting adventure with two fascinating men who love her desperately."

"Please, Ronya," David said. He went to the door and held it open.

She followed him into the study, staring suspiciously at his back with great shining eyes, but she said nothing, and seated herself in her favorite chair.

David stood with his back to the fire. "Katya's engagement came sooner than I expected. So we are returning to Kiev now. I have canceled all our engagements and notified your mother that Alexis accompanies us."

"No! I won't go!" Ronya sprang up. "You said that after Katya you'd devote yourself to me. You said he has a reputation for honor, despite his faltering morals and his excesses. You said I could do worse. You led me to believe that all my hopes and dreams are possible. Why are you behaving traitorously to me?"

David patted her shoulder. "Ronya, Ronya, why are you so impetuous? Consider what your marriage means to me."

"Consider what my marriage means to me," Ronya retorted with spirit. "That's more to the point."

"A complete biography of Boris Pirov is being assembled," David said wearily. "Even the air he breathes is being studied. It takes time."

"Father," she said quickly, "you know perfectly well you're temporizing."

"Yes, you're right." He sighed. "Very well, my love. We'll talk about Boris Pirov. You had better sit down."

He led her to the sofa, and they sat down side by side.

"I'm sorry, child," he said in a low voice, looking away from her into the fire, "I wanted to spare you."

Ronya looked up at him with such misery in her eyes that his heart ached. "Is he secretly married, Father? Is he committed to someone?"

"No."

"Oh—thank heaven!" Ronya exclaimed swiftly. Then she said, "Tell me."

"I've met Boris' father only twice, but I have a very low opinion of him, Ronya. Colonel Itil Pirov is a known opportunist and liar."

"You can't hold Boris responsible for his father or blame him for his father's lack of character."

"But can we brush aside the tragic fact that his mother is a pagan Tartar woman?"

Ronya looked down at the rug. "I don't care."

"Let me tell you about the Tartar woman, then tell me afterward whether you care. Boris' mother belongs to a fierce Tartar clan, and when she's on a rampage, the Jews in Odessa are afraid to close their eyes at night and sleep. Even in daytime they strain their eyes in the direction of the caves, on the lookout for her blond braids. She's done dreadful things, Ronya. I won't go into details, but I think you should keep in mind that if you marry her son, she'll be grandmother to your children."

"She'll be a stranger to my children," Ronya said stubbornly.

"That is naïve, my child."

"I'm not making light of Boris' ancestry," Ronya said, "but you're making too much of it. And the thing I don't understand, Father, is how it is right for Katya to marry a Muscovite—notorious Jew haters —and wrong for me to marry a Tartar?"

"There is no comparison between Count Alexis Brusilov, a gentle man, and that ruffian Boris Pirov," David said firmly.

53

"And there's no comparison between the ladylike Katya von Glasman and me!"

David now was convinced his original tactic was wisest: Take her home, and then search for a man attractive and compelling enough to dim her image of Boris Pirov. Since no country and no stratum of society was inaccessible to David von Glasman, he had little doubt such a man could be found. "We're going home, Ronya. Trust your father."

Ronya knew her father's mind well. She guessed what he was thinking, and while it came to her as no shock, still she found it maddening that he could confuse love with obstinacy and not know the difference between them.

"Father."

He turned toward her.

"Bring us together. Let's see what sort of person he is."

"So that if Boris Pirov gives you reason, you'll think twice about marrying him?"

Ronya's black eyes were shining. "It's no use, Father. Boris is my destiny. I feel it. I'll marry Boris, take the rough and stormy, and overcome it."

His face frozen, David said, "I have to ask the Empress for his release from the Imperial Guard. As you know, they are forbidden to resign or marry without the consent of the Tzar. But now is not the time for that."

"Because of Katya and Alexis?"

"That's right."

"When?"

"When I'm certain I will not be refused."

Ronya's voice trembled with emotion. "How long must I wait? Until you arrange matters so that there is something the crown wants, like another country that belongs to its own people, like another monopoly—so that each time a man drinks a glass of vodka or buys medicine from an apothecary, he pays exorbitantly to the Romanovs?"

"Exactly. And when I am in full possession of Marie's gratitude once more, I shall say, 'Please, your Majesty, may I have Captain Boris Pirov?' For him, I shall pay exorbitantly—*ad infinitum*," he added bitterly.

David's distress caused Ronya's eyes to fill with tears. "Are you angry with me, Father?"

"No, love! Never! For all his vaunted manhood, that Tartar will never come between you and me!"

The intensity with which he spoke confused her. Suddenly Ronya found herself wishing for Ruth, never ruffled, always calm. But she wanted more from David. "Please, Father," she pleaded, "invite Boris to Kiev. There'll be dozens of parties for Katya and Alexis, and they'd make such a nice beginning to our courtship."

"No, Ronya, that I won't do," he said, shaking his head vehemently. "I won't provide Boris Pirov with an opportunity for gratuitous sampling. He gets quite enough among the ladies at Court."

Ronya blushed. David was conscious of sudden shame. His eyes dropped to his long lean hands. "I'm sorry, Ronya."

"That's all right, Father," she said quietly. "I know women go mad over him—it worries me to death. What's to prevent his falling in love with one of them, unless he learns of me?"

David was haunted by another quiet voice, another vivid face crowned with copper-colored hair. He steadied his hands and stood up. "It is still my fervent hope that you'll get over Boris Pirov. However, if six months from now you have not recovered from your insanity, and if further investigation reveals nothing disgracefully lurid, I will deliver Boris Pirov to you on your wedding day. There will be no previous meeting between you."

Ronya capitulated. "All right, Father."

5

Naked, Boris Pirov lit a fresh cigarette and poured himself another glass of vodka. It was three o'clock in the morning. "Come back to bed," the woman called. He ignored her. She raised herself on one elbow. "Boris? Come back to bed."

He went out on the balcony and looked down on the deserted street below. He tried to think but, feeling ridiculous, stalked back into the bedroom, crushed out his cigarette angrily, and started to dress.

The woman put on a lace robe and climbed out of bed. "What's happened? Boris? Is there something wrong?" .

He thought: *Something ridiculous, impossible, damn insulting, that's what's happened.* He pulled on his boots and with repugnance glanced at the woman. "Good-bye, madam." He bowed mockingly. "My regards to your husband."

Boris did not return to the barracks. He walked in the gray predawn until he came to a droshky stand. The driver was asleep, propped against the seat. Boris took the reins and, when he pulled up at the house, told the driver not to wait, adding a generous tip.

The night hostess looked at him without interest. "What kind of girl do you want?"

"No girl."

The woman, dressed formally in black satin in keeping with the vulgar opulence of the establishment, glanced at him speculatively and made a second try. "We've a new Chinese, very pretty, very clean. Shall I wake her?"

"I want a clean room, a clean tub, a clean glass, and an unopened bottle of vodka. Nothing else."

"Shall I order breakfast for the captain?"

Boris nodded. "About nine. Send it up with a porter."

He took the key from her hand, waved her away, and walked up the stairs. The room was the usual sort, heavily decorated yet impersonal. He stretched out on top of the bed.

Boris glanced at his watch. Another hour had gone by. Over and over, the memory of his monarch's words: "The most beautiful girl in the Ukraine, perhaps even in all Russia. An enchanting, charming girl with dark dark eyes under beautifully arched brows." The girl! All the time the Empress had emphasized the girl—not the lavish world in which she lived, not the astonishingly important father. Finally, the Empress had concluded the one-sided conversation with a backhanded solicitude. "A reminder, my dear Boris. We cannot stay forever young and in the honor guard, can we?"

Boris lit another cigarette and took a deep breath.

Curious, how the memory of the little girl with the raspberries came back to him. He couldn't remember how old he was, but it was a long time ago in Odessa.

His mother had stormed up to him in a thundering rage: "Flying high, those damn Jews in their castle on the hill, flying very high indeed." Then her voice had gone flat. "I let the Jew hire ten of my men."

Boris remembered jumping on his pony and riding out to the spectacular house overlooking the sea. It was made of native stone, built to withstand the ravages of time, fire, and warfare. Sure enough, his mother's Tartars were there. He strolled over the tiers of terraces that spread out over the entire landscape, marveling at the view. He was walking down a path through the woods, when he came upon a little girl eating raspberries. She glanced up at him with a smile. "Are you my fairy-tale prince?"

He grinned.

"I live in Kiev," she said, "but summers we come here. Father says hiring Tartars is buying insurance."

The boy looked at her and said nothing.

56

"Do you like raspberries?"

"Sometimes."

"Would you like some now?"

"No."

"I have plenty." She offered them to him again.

This time he took some, and she rewarded him with a smile so warm that he had to look away.

"You forgot to say, 'Thank you.' "

The boy said, "Let's start all over again," and put out his hand. She tipped raspberries into it. "Thank you." He grinned. "How's that?"

"I love you."

The boy felt happy. He wanted to say, "I'm glad," but instead stood very still. Then he said, "You're an unusual little girl," and walked away.

When he asked his mother that night about the people in the house by the sea, she replied, "Von Glasman is the name. People call him the German, but he's a Jew all right."

"Got any children?" he asked casually.

"Two little daughters. And a gypsy brat—probably his."

It was amazing how exactly he remembered it all. A grin spread across his face. What a twist of fate!

The warm feeling that suddenly came over him made him wary. Forcing his mind to the matter at hand, he tried to reach a decision. "If I do, I get a ravishing young beauty with a fortune, my own stables, a reserve commission of major, and Count Alexis Brusilov for a brother-in-law. If I don't, I get Cavalry duty in Siberia with the Cossacks. What a choice!"

He made up his mind. "All right, I'll see Von Glasman. It ought to be interesting."

He extinguished his cigarette and turned over. Just as he was drifting off to sleep, he wondered: *Is Von Glasman still buying insurance?* The thought infuriated him.

They met in Rifka's house. Neither man pretended special warmth or even friendliness; still, both paid strict attention to the niceties of good manners. The housekeeper brought tea, which Boris refused, and vodka, which he accepted. Face to face, they eyed each other appraisingly. David had the advantage; there was nothing about Boris Pirov he did not know. He was prepared for the majestic size, the golden coloring, the magnificent bone structure and Tartar cheekbones, but he was quite unprepared for the engaging grin, for the man's authoritative power. And Boris, on his own part, had failed to reckon with David's confidence; here was the public David von Glasman, the aloof diplomat, the cool professional.

57

Avoiding all pleasantry, David began. He spoke directly and honestly. "I know it's not the pleasantest thing in the world for a good officer to be summarily relieved of all duty."

With a mocking smile, Boris leaned back in his chair. "I'm glad you know. That helps a lot."

David shrugged and drank his tea. "I had to do it."

"What do you mean you 'had to'? And why me?"

"That in its proper time."

Boris reminded himself that he had come prepared to dislike David von Glasman. "Tell me more about Ronya."

How to begin? "There is no way to describe Ronya," he said at last. How could he describe laughter—more than he'd ever known? Or honesty? Or flawless taste? Or the tigress ready to leap? So he said, "There is a girl who demands Boris Pirov and swears she will take no other. What can I do? Lose her?"

Boris sensed that David had never intended to make this confidence. Generously, he responded with silence.

David went on again. "You will have to be married by a rabbi in the Jewish faith."

Boris' mouth turned up in a grin. "My people and yours aren't exactly close friends. A rabbi would have to be mad to perform a marriage ceremony between a Tartar and a Jewess."

"Leave that to me." Then, carefully, David added, "A certain surgical procedure has to take place first. Circumcision by a *mohel* according to rite and regulation."

Boris' face suddenly changed. His eyes burned like fire. His voice sounded like the crack of Ronya's whip. "Forget it!"

David von Glasman was startled at the words that fell from his lips. "It is forgotten." He was conscious of a grudging respect.

For a long moment a dead silence. Then David reached into his inside pocket and took out an envelope. "A letter of credit. Your tailor, your bootmaker. You'll be needing to return hospitality. Give a farewell party."

Boris' eyes hardened.

"Well?"

"A warning to you, sir: Don't put me through tests. I don't like it."

David stared at Boris coldly. "All you have to do is say, 'Good-bye,' and walk away."

"Oh yes," Boris sneered, "just walk away." He brooded on this and added honestly, "I'm caught, and you know it." His eyes flickered toward the envelope, and he held out his hand.

David handed it to him.

Boris lit a cigarette and sat thinking hard for a moment or two. "It may interest you to know, sir, that when the Empress explained my duty to me, she said nothing about staying married. She also suggested that I maintain full ties with the Cavalry—in case. . . ."

David smiled condescendingly. "The idea of an annulment does not entirely displease me."

"In that case, sir, I'll make an effort to keep the marriage permanent. When do you want me in Kiev?"

"Exactly six weeks from today."

"I'll be there."

Presumably the meeting was over, but Boris sat on. At last he spoke, and David thought he caught a note of shyness in his voice. "Sir, I have my severance pay. The Empress was generous. Do you know Ronya's ring size?"

With a hint of a smile, David reached into his pocket and brought out a ring box, from which he took a circle of string. "Ronya sent you this."

Boris surveyed the circle carefully. "This can't be right."

"Ronya is deceptively slender. Though her hands are elegant and beautifully shaped, they are strong, useful hands."

"Christ! Every time I conjure up a picture of her, I have to revise it." Boris rose and drew himself to his full height. "With your permission, sir."

David allowed him to get as far as the door. "Wait! Come back at about five. Go directly to the stables. Ronya has sent you a present."

"Don't tell me she has sent me a horse."

"From Odessa."

"Not a Tartar stallion!"

"Pure white."

Boris' profane exclamation startled David von Glasman. He wondered: Could it be that Ronya's instinct was right?

6

Colonel Itil Pirov kept a private flat as well as his quarters at the Cavalry post. He went there to entertain. Every morning a scrubwoman appeared, cleaned up, and left immediately. Another maid, less disheveled and decently uniformed, came later; she brought a few flowers, arranged cold snacks on a platter, served the meal, and departed. The flat was convenient. No one actually saw Colonel Pirov getting cozy with the wives of his brother officers.

When Boris came into his father's sitting room—dark brown leather and a scattering of newspapers and riding whips—the French champagne (bought on credit) was chilled and waiting. Colonel Pirov, still erect and soldierly at fifty-seven though some gray had crept into his dark hair, was comfortably arranged with his feet up on a small table. He raised his hand in a sketchy salute.

"Hello, son," he said amiably. "I'm prepared for a celebration."

Boris took the proffered glass. "Suppose I decided to tell Von Glasman to go to hell."

His father smiled tolerantly. "For some reason, I didn't think you would choose Siberia. Besides, you're too smart to throw a fortune wrapped in a delectable little package down the drain."

Boris could not deny this—he only wished he could—yet beneath the wounded pride he felt himself drawn to Ronya, and for some reasons beside her beauty or his curiosity. But he kept this to himself. "You're right," he said. "Stupidity is not one of my shortcomings." He moved away and sat down.

Taking the champagne with him, Pirov moved closer to Boris. Balancing the bottle on the windowsill, he asked, "How did the Empress persuade you?"

"Unscrupulously. She murmured flattery in my ears. I melted. She quenched my thirst. By the time I caught on to her scheme, I was facing a walk—either south or east—the direction up to me."

Itil slapped his knee with pleasure. "What a woman! Five feet two and she led the Tzar by the nose. And how he loved it, God rest his soul."

Boris reached for the bottle.

"How did it go with Von Glasman?"

"Just as you expected."

Itil chuckled. "How about that? Ten to one I make general."

"It figures," Boris said mockingly.

His father ignored the insult. This time he refilled the glasses himself. *"A votre santé."*

"Let's eat."

"Lunch is at two o'clock. Let's pop another cork."

By the time they had finished the second bottle, Itil had become expansive. Suddenly he gave a whistle. "Christ, I'd forgotten all about your mother."

"I haven't. She won't like it."

"She won't quarrel with money."

Boris looked out of the window as Itil fiddled with his empty glass.

"You mean you care?" Itil said in amazement. "You know she's insane."

"Only a trifle."

"But on several subjects," Itil insisted.

Turning his gaze full on his father, Boris said, "She was all I had." Itil was not offended.

After lunch the table was cleared and they were comfortably sipping cups of coffee—black, strong, with chicory—when Boris asked if his father would mind a personal question.

"Anything."

"Why did you and my mother marry?"

The older man let his breath out slowly. "Who can answer for your mother? I had just returned from guard duty in Siberia and was sent to Odessa to put down a minor Tartar uprising. One night she came into my tent with a priest. In the morning she was gone. Five days later she appeared again, leading two horses, and made me follow her to a cave up in the hills. After a time, I got accustomed to her comings and goings and to the peculiar places she chose for lovemaking. When my transfer orders came, she just said 'Good-bye.' I said, 'Don't you want to come with me?' She said, 'Leave Odessa? Have you got any more crazy notions?' I knew her well enough by then to read the warning, so I asked, 'What would you consider crazy?' 'Divorce,' she said, and burst out laughing.

"At first, I managed to see her every few months, but then I was ordered to the Crimean front only a few days before Sevastopol fell, September 9, 1855—you were born on that day. Your mother held me personally responsible for the fall of Sevastopol. She cursed me in language a drunken sergeant wouldn't use and between curses screamed military doctrine at me: Russia had all the advantages—we had a single command—our army was bigger—we knew the terrain . . . you must have heard her when she gets excited about military matters. She cursed the Tzar and said she and her Tartars would have been able to hold on to an impregnable fortress. Then came her ultimatum: 'I live here in Odessa. The boy belongs to me. You belong to the Army. Travel. Remember—no divorce.' I insisted on visiting you occasionally, and she agreed grudgingly. 'All right,' she said. 'Don't come too often.' "

Itil lit two cigarettes and passed one to Boris. There was a grin of genuine amusement on his face. "You ready for the rest?"

Boris nodded. He was not smiling.

"We never quarreled, just drifted. The years passed, and one day you appeared, a cadet at the academy. Then suddenly you were almost nineteen and competing for the national championship. Do you remember when she rode in with her Tartars? St. Petersburg never saw anything like it." Itil shook an admiring head. "You know the rest—most of it. You won, and the Tartars went wild—they tore up the town. When I opened my eyes next day I thought I was dreaming. There she was, naked . . ."

"Look . . ." Boris was on his feet. The laughter died out of his father's face.

Boris reached for more champagne. The last bottle was empty.

"I've an appointment to keep. I must go to the jeweler's."

Itil got to his feet. "Thank you for coming by."

Boris hesitated, then took out David's letter of credit and a roll of bills.

Boris tossed the roll onto the table. "Pay your bills and try to stay out of debt. I won't be here to follow you around the gambling clubs winning back what you lose."

His eyes on the rubles, Itil said with some pride, "And more."

Boris handed over the paper money. "This is my severance pay. Buy Ronya a wedding present."

"Well, now. She has everything."

Boris just looked at him and Itil dropped his eyes. "All right. I'll go with you."

The next stop was at a fashionable jeweler's. "I want a gold wedding band," Boris said to the man behind the counter.

"Choose from our samples, Captain," said the clerk, laying a tray of rings before him. "We'll make one to size."

Boris made his selection, a wide heavy circle of bright yellow gold, completely plain.

"What engraving, sir?"

"Leave it unadorned. It's for a strong, useful hand," Boris answered. As he spoke, his eyes focused on a heart-shaped pin. In its center was a slightly blue diamond, surrounded by smaller stones of varying sizes.

Boris picked it up and asked its price.

"A king's ransom, Captain."

"Translate that into rubles."

The clerk named the figure.

Itil whistled in disbelief.

"Hold it for me," Boris said. "I'll be back tomorrow."

When Boris had left, Itil browsed around the shop until he found a gold clasp plump with colored stones.

The jeweler shuddered. There had been transactions between them before.

Itil grinned. "Don't be alarmed. I have money."

"Where?"

Itil rubbed his breast pocket.

"Show me."

Itil put Boris' severance pay on the counter.

Miraculously the distrust disappeared from the jeweler's eyes.

When the package was ready, Itil Pirov took it to the post office and sent it to Odessa. Crazy or not, she was still his wife.

Boris swung himself into the saddle and rode hard, and at five fifteen he was at his destination. He slid off his mount, threw the reins over a post, and held out his hand to the man leaning against the stable door. "Sorry I'm late. I was detained." As he spoke, his eyes took in this man in gypsy dress. Tangerine-brown complexion, coarse black hair, slanting eyes, and the arms and shoulders of a blacksmith. Boris knew enough about men to know that he was a good fighter, that he knew how to pitch a tent, hunt and fish, and tame a horse. A useful man.

He took Boris' hand only because it was forced on him. "Fedor is the name." He led Boris inside the stable. He stopped some distance from the stallion.

"Christ!" Boris said. "In all my life I've never seen one more beautiful."

"He's a devil. Don't be too eager to put a saddle on him. The priest and I finally got him roped. That was enough for both of us."

Boris picked up a bit of straw. Chewing thoughtfully, he said, "The priest?" When Fedor did not answer, he asked, "Where's the priest now?"

"Went back to Kiev with David. I'm charged to stay here with you."

Boris grinned. "I apologize for the trouble I'm giving you. Tell me about the priest."

"Nothing to tell. Ivan Tromokov was born on the land. He was smart, so David let him study. Then he sent him to the seminary in Moscow. The bishop made him his protégé. Now he is our priest."

Boris wondered why a not overclean gypsy with one pierced ear and a knife stuck in his belt called the master of the manor by his first name. He decided not to ask. Instead, he said, "Usually, priests escape the role of nursemaid to a wild stallion."

"You've got a lot to learn. Our priest is the best goddamn rider in Russia next to you. And he's not a man I'd pick a fight with."

"I'm impressed."

Resolutely, Boris turned from Fedor and, like a lover approaching his beloved, he began caressing the stallion with words. The nearer he came, the softer his tone. His eyes fixed on the animal, Boris circled him slowly, like a dancer, giving him the opportunity to make his own judgment. Seeing that the stallion approved of him, Boris gradually moved in closer, smiling, comforting, praising: "Lord, you're splendid."

The horse did not stir; he stood scrutinizing Boris. Boris fell silent and stood absolutely still, waiting for the stallion to do whatever he wished, when he was ready. At last, neck outstretched, the horse cocked his head. Still moving with care, Boris took off the rope. The stallion moved forward, his big eyes serene. Boris started to stroke his nose and, as he stroked, he talked, taking the stallion into his thoughts, into his heart. He laid his lips close to the horse's ear. "Ah, beautiful—I'll be back. Tomorrow, we'll run for exercise." Much as he hated to leave the stallion, Boris had to spend the night at cards.

The stallion understood. Head tossing up and down, he neighed.

Boris was not looking forward to riding all the way back to the barracks, but when Fedor offered him supper, he thanked him and declined. "I want a hot tub and clean clothes."

"You don't need to go far," Fedor said. "Almost everything of yours is upstairs in the front bedroom, even your guns."

Boris was damned annoyed with David von Glasman. By what right did he instruct strange hands to explore another's possessions?

As if he knew what Boris was thinking, Fedor said: "It was Ronya's idea. She understands about a man and his horse. I wish she could have seen you and that wild beast. I could hardly believe it myself."

Boris thought, *Again, Ronya!*

"Let's go up to the house," he said, his good humor restored.

About an hour later Boris came down. He opened a door: an empty sitting room. He tried another and found himself in a dining room where a cold supper was laid out: vodka, lemons, caviar, smoked salmon, cold boiled potatoes, black bread spread thick with butter, breasts of chicken peppered lightly, sour cream, cheeses, baked apples sprinkled generously with cinnamon. The samovar was humming.

Boris wondered if someone proposed he and Fedor eat that mountain of food. He shrugged, poured himself a tall vodka, and stood at the curtained window looking out at a sudden downpour of unexpected rain. His body idle, his mind was running over a puzzle. How did Ronya von Glasman manage to get hold of a sacred white stallion? And how in hell did her two friends—a gypsy in corduroy and a peasant priest—get the horse out of Odessa and to St. Petersburg?

At the sound of steps Boris turned around slowly. Coming into the room with Fedor was a man he knew to be a highly placed member of the secret police, whom he knew as Paul Zotov.

Paul offered his hand and said courteously, "Hello, Pirov. I'm glad to see you here."

64

Remembering how remarkably often he had run into this Zotov in recent months, Boris took the powerful but immaculately groomed hand in his and said dryly, "I'm flattered."

"I see you're beginning to fit the pieces together."

Boris stared into the sensual, strong face. "I'm not sure. I'm no expert in sizing up methods and motives riddled with intrigue."

"With a jewel like Ronya, we had to be sure." There was something passionately proprietary in Paul's voice. Suddenly a gleam of Tartar fierceness sprang into his eyes. He came close to Paul. "The jewel had better be whole."

Fedor's hand moved toward the ever-ready dagger, his strong teeth bared in a ferocious snarl.

Boris refused to let the gypsy with the massive shoulders push him into a false move. He waited with Tartar stillness, deciding the blow he would use to fell the gypsy, and concentrated on Paul, whom he recognized instinctively as the more dangerous opponent.

But Paul had not taken offense. He openly admired the way Boris handled himself. It was a pleasure to meet someone who looked as though he could subdue Fedor with one hand. Paul made a slight gesture, barely moving his head, and Fedor put away the knife. He pulled out a cigarette and started smoking.

"Even in a girl without her captivating appeal and physical grace, Ronya's complete virtue would be astounding," Paul said firmly. "As for Fedor, he worships Ronya. Value him. No girl ever had a better watchdog."

Boris turned to Fedor, ashamed. "I was wrong. I ask your pardon. And I ask Ronya's pardon."

Fedor passed a finger over the big piece of gold dangling from his ear. "Forget it," he said tightly.

Boris grinned. "You're a sullen bastard."

Fedor reddened, anger flared anew in his eyes, and all at once the atmosphere was stone-heavy again.

"Now what?" Boris said.

Paul was shaking his head, which told Boris better than words that his intended jocularity was no joke.

"Oh, hell. I'm sorry."

Instead of answering, Paul poured drinks. Fedor tossed his down as if a glass of vodka followed by a mug of beer was nothing at all. He had a second and then said, "Well, are we going to eat?"

Fedor downed the supper heartily, but Paul and Boris ate with indifference and were relieved when Fedor drew himself away from the table. "All right if I go back to the barn," he said, looking searchingly at Boris, "and woo the stallion?"

Boris' eyes rested on Fedor. "I don't advise it."

Very slowly, Fedor turned and walked out.

"God almighty!" Paul's voice was filled with incredulity. "A horse Fedor can't handle!"

Boris laughed.

"Let's go into the study," Paul said. "It'll be easier to talk."

The lamps were lit, the curtains pulled, and a fire burned in the stove against the wet chill of the March night. Boris sat smoking quietly, remembering that all through supper Paul had been cheerful and disarming and had acted as host. With the brandy, he asked, "Is this your house?"

"I was about to say something about that." Paul drank some more of his brandy. Then he asked, "What do you know about the Von Glasmans and their gypsies?"

Not even glancing at him, Boris said, "Not much."

"Tell me what you do know."

"Well, I hear the gypsy queens and the family have much to do with each other."

"Boris, it was David's intention not to tell you anything—just to let things emerge—but Ronya protested, and her mother supported her. Ruth said, 'Things are hard enough for him. He has a bride he's not interested in yet.'"

Flashing his grin, Boris cut in, "I wouldn't go that far."

"David decided that I should explain things to you and prepare you for Kiev."

Boris thought, *Why you?* He said it aloud.

"Because the present gypsy queen, Rifka, whose house this is, is my mother."

Paul could see the interest in Boris' face. He sprang his second surprise. "Fedor also is her son. We're half brothers."

Boris' eyes widened. It was inconceivable that these two men could be related.

Paul's cool gray eyes took it all in. "Our mother has two other sons and a daughter. We're all bastards, related to each other only through her."

Boris grinned wickedly. "If that's bait, Paul, I'm not biting."

Paul frowned.

"Relax, Paul. I haven't any quarrel with bastards. Let's have another brandy."

Paul lifted the brandy decanter and poured.

"But then where are the other two brothers—in Kiev?"

"That needs explaining. First," Paul said thoughtfully, "you must understand that Rifka, my mother, is as much an aristocrat as David, and almost as rich. She lives in great splendor, and she travels more in

66

the manner of a reigning monarch than of a gypsy queen. David loves and respects her. Now, as for my brothers, David took into consideration each boy's father. Fedor was easy. He's the eldest, fathered by a gypsy duke—gypsy life is his style.

"Sergey and Alexander were different, and David dealt differently with them. He supervised their education himself, and as he found each boy ready, the boy vanished from Kiev. Sergey lives quietly in Geneva; he handles important documents and large sums of money. Alexander mingles with all sets—receptions in London, opera in Paris, dinners at private clubs in Berlin—providing they stand for financial and political power; Alexander's reports are intensely shrewd."

Boris nodded and thought, *What about you?* Though Paul's mind followed the thought, he did not, at present, feel like being completely honest about himself.

"Well, that brings us to Tamara—a bawdy baggage, who will no doubt gyrate her golden derriere in your direction."

Boris passed the tip of his tongue over his lips. *Jesus,* he wondered, *am I being told, "Enjoy it, it comes with Ronya's dowry," or "Keep off"?*

"Tamara is much younger than all of us. One day she'll be queen. She is the inseparable companion of David's Ronya."

"David's?"

"Yes," Paul said slowly. "I always think of her as David's little girl."

Boris' mouth tightened. "She's about to be my wife. That makes her mine now. Well," he said, putting the matter aside, "tell me about Ronya and Tamara."

"David has never worried about the friendship between the girls, but I think Ruth does. I've always suspected that she doesn't like it when Ronya runs off with Tamara. Of course, David knows that Ronya is as safe at the camp as in his own house, and in any case, she has her whip—"

"Whip?" Boris jerked his hand up. He thought he must have misheard.

"Oh, yes," Paul said, offhand, "she's very good. She can flick out a candle flame. David hired a Hungarian carnival performer to teach her when she was a child." Paul smiled at Boris, who looked strange. "As I said, Tamara and Ronya are like sisters. Even if David wanted to wean Ronya from Tamara, I'm not altogether sure that he could do it. Close as Ronya and David are, she has a will to match his, and Tamara she would fight to keep.

"Well," he said abruptly, "I don't suppose there's anything else, except to warn you that my wife knows nothing about my past, or my real identity. She must never know."

"Your wife?"

"Yes," Paul said, "I have a wife and two daughters. I trapped myself into a marriage when I was very young—for none of the usual reasons. With a mother as vivid as mine, I was attracted by reticence. I revered a female who would scarcely smile at a man without benefit of clergy." Meeting his level gaze, he answered Boris' unspoken question. "Now we live our own lives. Mine, as you know, is lusty. Helena lives hers timidly—she's fanatically religious."

Touched that Paul had given him his trust, Boris followed with a confidence of his own. "Because of my mother, I was always on guard against tall, broad-shouldered women with loud laughter." Rather overwhelmed at himself, Boris went on, "I was about ready to refuse the Empress and take the consequences, when she said, 'You must not mind that Ronya is small. The Tzar was your height, and much heavier—a great bear of a man—and he took my littleness with delight. Our life together was filled with joy.' " He rose and Paul accompanied him outside.

As they were driving along in Paul's hired carriage, Boris laid a hand on his arm. "One question. How did Ronya get hold of the white stallion?"

Paul chuckled. "She outsmarted your mother."

"Yes? How?" Boris said, shaking his head in disbelief.

"By coercing me, David, Ladislaus—he's David's secretary—Fedor, and the good priest Ivan Tromokov into committing a felony."

For the rest of his life, Boris would be able to hear Paul describe how he himself stole the envelope and the paper with the imperial seal. How Ronya composed the letter purporting to come from Dowager Empress Marie requesting from the Tartar woman, as one dignitary to another, a favor for Russia. Boris, the golden eagle, was in need of an Olympian stallion—pure white, of superb intelligence, of great stamina, strength, and courage—in order to bring the world equestrian championship home to the land of the two-headed eagle. How the Tartar woman was commanded to deliver the stallion to the railroad station in St. Petersburg, where two trusted deputies would take charge. How the Tartar woman was further commanded to accept, as a token of gratitude, an immense bundle of gold (supplied by David). How David entrusted the letter and the gold pieces to Ladislaus who, passing as a royal courier, made the delivery.

Boris began to laugh. He laughed long and loud. He was still laughing when he and Paul walked arm in arm into the casino, where they embarked on a night of gambling. Paul did well enough. Boris broke the bank before they called it quits.

Fedor woke from a deep sleep with a big thirst. On his way to the cold box, he saw that the door to Boris' room was ajar. He looked in: Empty. Fedor drank his two tankards of beer and went back to bed. At about six he passed the room again; it annoyed him that Boris had not bothered to return. He told the housekeeper that breakfast would have to wait—he was going out to the stallion. He had been dreaming all night of being able to gloat over the priest: "I made loving sounds to him just like Boris, and he purred like a kitten." What he saw when he got to the barn was Boris asleep beside the stallion, his arm around the animal's sleek, powerful neck, both their heads resting on neatly folded blankets. Slipping from Boris' pockets were paper rubles by the thousand.

Late afternoon brought Paul back to the house. He carried a folded newspaper, which he handed to Boris. "You're front page news."

Boris opened the paper. The headline boldly proclaimed: WEDDING BELLS FOR BORIS PIROV, RUSSIA'S CHAMPION RIDER.

The first paragraph spoke of the recent visit of two sisters from the Ukraine, both beautiful, both heiresses. The elder sister had captured the heart of Count Alexis Brusilov, descendant of Kalita, Prince of Moscow. The article fully traced in historical detail the glory of the princes of Moscow, seat of the Orthodox Church.

Next followed what amounted to an essay on Boris. It retold legends of the Tartars, Boris' ancestors, when they were the masters of Russia. Inserted in italics (the reader was left to draw his own inference): *"Boris Godunov, later Tzar Boris, owed his position largely to a fortunate marriage. Boris proved his worth until, gradually, the unfortunate and unaccepted looked upon him as upon God."*

This was followed by stories of Boris' colorful bachelorhood—he was described as everything from a huge, golden ruffian to a forceful officer and an authority on cavalry warfare.

Long before Boris reached the last paragraph, he learned that the promise made but two days ago was already fulfilled: He was a major.

Boris came to the last word and marveled. Not once were the Von Glasman girls identified by name.

He was about to comment when Paul said, "I have your mail."

Among the invitations, mainly from court ladies, was a summons from the Empress. Ostensibly, the royal guard was commanded to attend an official palace ceremony, the purpose of which was not clear. Actually, when the time came, the Empress received Boris alone. He was led into one of the smaller sitting rooms in her private apartment where, amid ornate French furniture, brocades, imperial Easter eggs, sprays of gold lily of the valley, jeweled peacocks, miniature imperial coaches, jade jars, and music boxes in rose diamonds, she sat waiting.

She gazed upon him with unconcealed admiration and said: "On this occasion we speak as friends. Be seated."

Boris put his lips to the Empress' hand and took a straight chair that enabled him to face her fully. And, indeed, the Empress kept her eyes on him as she spoke, using the personal "I" rather than the imperial "We."

"I have reviewed my long association with David von Glasman. I have asked myself many times: 'Did I help my friend by granting his daughter her wish, or did I fail him?' If I have failed him, then you, Boris Pirov, will have failed your Empress.

"However, so convinced am I that you shall not fail me, I shall not even entertain such an eventuality. For this reason I make you a present."

The ring the Empress put on Boris' finger was not extravagant, not a jewel from the recently established House of Fabergé. It was the imperial crown and the initials B.P. appliquéd into a stone of jet-black onyx, held secure in a solid band of gold.

A lady in waiting brought in a decanter of wine, and they drank together. The Empress said, "May the ring bring you delight."

Boris was a man who liked to give as well as receive. He sent the Empress his gold ornamented racing trophy with the name Boris Pirov written in tiny stones.

In the next six weeks Boris taught the stallion to stand still for hours with or without reins. He made him behave like a gentleman on city streets and took him miles out of the city and showed him how to hunt. They jumped fences and high bushes and went swimming. He taught the stallion all the intricacies of the show ring. And he trained him for battle. For six weeks Boris stayed away from cards, he did not go near a woman, and he rarely poured himself a vodka until sundown.

On his last night in St. Petersburg, Boris asked himself by what witchcraft Ronya had divined the way to bring him peace. He left for Kiev happy, until he remembered David von Glasman, a rival to beware of. And the blond Tartar woman, his mother.

7

David von Glasman still had one last problem, and it was an awkward one. He turned the question over in his mind as the carriage jolted along. How could he persuade Russia's greatest Talmudic scholar and the chief rabbi of Kiev to marry a Jewess to a Tartar? It seemed to David that Simon Levinsky could not refuse him—reason, friendship, personal indebtedness—every consideration should urge him to agree. Yet in his heart David had doubts: The rabbi was capable of a firm and irrevocable No.

David shrugged. "A nuisance but no disaster. For a price, I can call in a liberal thinker from Germany."

The carriage stopped outside a little box of a house made of old red brick next to the synagogue. Lena showed him into the parlor, a small low-ceilinged room made stuffy by the heat of the porcelain stove. David sat down on an uncomfortable horsehair sofa and waited for her to tell the rabbi of his arrival. When he entered the bare little chamber the rabbi called his study, only friendship and gentle sincerity showed in Simon's bearded face. The rabbi stood up to shake hands and give him the traditional skullcap, and he returned to his desk only after David was seated.

"Good evening, David. To what do I owe this honor?"

David smiled slightly. "Beyond a doubt, you know why I have come. It's all over Kiev."

Ashamed for the Court Jew, the rabbi had to use great restraint to speak calmly. "It is all over the whole Ukraine that you give your Ronya to a heathen, to the enemy."

"My dear Simon," he said, "if that were so, I would not be here."

The rabbi contemplated him. "So, why are you here? Maybe to tell me that my Joseph does not dream in vain?"

How stupid of the boy to imagine my Ronya could content herself with him, David thought. Aloud, he said, "I am sorry about Joseph."

The rabbi had his thoughts too: *Ronya von Glasman is the last Jewess in Russia I'd pick for a* rebbitzen. "Don't be sorry," he said. "I told my Joseph, 'Dreaming is splendid—still, untroubled sleep is better.' "

It was apparent that getting down to business in a businesslike fashion was out of the question. Decision could be hours away. Amused, David reflected, *When I need help from the Empress, I ask for it. Here there is no escaping the manysidedness of Jewish logic. In the mind of this small, graceful man are stored the sayings in the Talmud, a thousand years of Jewish witticism, tales of the foolishness, the incongruities, the pathos, the gaiety of our people. Patience!* "One wise saying calls for another," he said pleasantly. "It is also stated: 'To do justice and give judgment, the wise judge has both the will and the courage to cut through the underbrush of deceit and legal technicalities.' "

Simon nodded and thought for a while. "David," he said, "I am a tolerant man, but what possible excuse is there for me to be lenient in this matter? Not since the Roman Titus sacked the Temple and led our people in chains through Rome has anyone so sorely oppressed the Jews and mocked at their sorrow as the Odessa Tartars."

David did not disagree. "Please see my side of it. I have two daughters and no sons. In time the children of one daughter will forget me. From Ronya—"

The rabbi interrupted. "You are pleased—honored—that Katya is a countess."

"True. However, as I was saying, from Ronya must come my heir and my immortality. My land must not fall into strange hands."

"Then in heaven's name, give Ronya in marriage to a Jew. With her beauty and your wealth, you have the whole world to choose from."

"That's right but no answer, because Ronya will not be dissuaded. It's like a sickness."

The rabbi dropped his attempt at politeness. "What did you expect? Did you teach your daughter to observe the Sabbath? Did you forbid her to eat *trafe?* Did you instruct her in modest piety? French and German you taught her, not Yiddish and Hebrew. Generations of ease and luxury have corrupted your Jewish values, David."

Bless Friday evening candles and all will be well, David thought mockingly. *What rubbish!* Deliberately, he said, "I can manage Boris Pirov."

Simon Levinsky raised his pale eyes. "And if you find that you can't, what then?"

"Suppose I refuse to answer that question."

"That's up to you. But remember, David, my friend, it is infinitely better to be loved than to be feared."

This, too, David let pass and elected to come to the point. "Simon, I want you to marry Boris Pirov to my Ronya. A handsome stock of precedence says that you may, for among our people, as among all people, mixed marriages have existed for thousands of years. King Solomon, the wisest of men, took a Pharaoh's daughter for a wife."

Simon pondered for some minutes. "This cannot be settled at one meeting. I have to think about it."

"How long?"

"Come back tomorrow."

"Regrettably, that is impossible. I must have your answer tonight. You think. I'll wait."

With a sigh, the rabbi consulted his watch. "Lena is in the kitchen. She likes to sit and watch Joseph study. Ask her to give you a glass of tea and come back in half an hour."

At the door, David turned. "Remember, Simon. The rabbis of old who compiled the Talmud were robust people endowed with practical good sense."

"Without doubt."

As he turned to leave again, Simon called, "Don't expect a *mazel tov* from Lena. Among the Jews, Ronya von Glasman is not exactly a heroine."

The door banged shut—David's only reply.

When he was alone, Simon Levinsky let his thoughts wander. He found himself remembering a woman whose son had been sent to Vienna to study medicine on Von Glasman money, a girl who was able to make a good marriage because of a Von Glasman dowry, a community whose study hall was a Von Glasman gift, poor families who got through bad winters on the money David gave to their rabbi, villages that narrowly escaped a pogrom because of David's intervention with the Cossack chiefs.

The rabbi tapped his nose, then patted it absently. A new expression came to his face.

"I owe David a debt," he said aloud. "My father was indebted to his father. Joseph will be indebted to Ronya. I can't believe that when God let Aaron von Glasman give up everything and come to Russia, He did it without real reason." He meditated for a while, head bent.

"If I do not bless this marriage, someone else will. I feel it is my duty, for only if I bless her marriage can I demand of Ronya a pledge, that whatever her husband remains in his heart, her children shall be Jews. That is the Law—the children belong to the mother."

The rabbi raised his head: "O Lord of the Universe, help me. If I am wrong, stop me. Send a sign."

When David returned at the appointed time, the rabbi was ready. "Your premonition was right. The answer God sent is the answer you expected. I am instructed to place the man of Ronya's choice as close as possible to her people."

The lines in David's face relaxed. "Splendid." He hastened on. "Ruth is in a great hurry to send the invitations. We introduce our count and countess at Ronya's reception and celebrate their homecoming."

Katya and Alexis had made their vows in the Church of the Twelve Apostles to the tolling of the Tzar Kolokol bell. They were joined in marriage at dawn, when the melodic chime of bells sounded from inside the Kremlin and streams of people came to worship in the white stone cathedrals in Krasnaya Square. Neither David nor Ruth had witnessed the marriage, but they had shared in the wedding breakfast. The servants came to kneel before their new mistress—the face of Alexis' faithful old nurse was streaked with tears. David recalled how erect and proud Alexis had looked at this moment, Katya's laughter like music, Ruth happy in their happiness, Ronya, her chin trembling,

73

her dark eyes bright with anticipation of that day when the glory would be hers.

David started to rise, but Simon held up a restraining finger. "Not so fast, my friend. You know the rules. First of all, Boris Pirov must carry out the requirements of our religion. Then he must be instructed in Judaism."

"It has been done. It was done in St. Petersburg."

This was a wholly unexpected answer. Their entire argument was based on the assumption that Boris was a Gentile. If he had been converted already— The rabbi stared hard at his guest, puzzled. "In the presence of a *minyan*—ten men—he was circumcised by a proper *mohel* according to ritual?"

"Yes."

"You were present?"

David's eyes did not flicker. "Yes."

Simon Levinsky could not say why, but he knew that David von Glasman was lying. "I see," he said.

It was late. David started to get up again, but he was waved back into his chair. "More?"

The rabbi slowly began to speak. "Listen to me, David. Two hours before your first guest arrives, I shall come to your house, alone. Send a carriage in time. Without further inquiry, and in the presence of her immediate family—no gypsies, no priest, no Jew-hating landowners, no peasants, no Cossacks—I shall perform the marriage ceremony between Ronya von Glasman and Boris Pirov. With all my heart, I'll give Ronya my blessing. Him, I'll wish no harm. Then I shall leave. How you celebrate afterward, what prophecy Rifka foresees when she conducts the ceremonial of reading from the molten lead, is none of my business. Agreed?"

"Agreed," David replied, with no intention of keeping his word. "I had planned it a little differently; however, it is agreed. Thank you," he said, removed his skullcap, and left without words.

Later, the rabbi discovered on the wooden stand in the hall a heavy envelope containing money for a new roof to the *shul* and for the orphaned, the old, the infirm, and a sheet of paper bearing the instruction: "To be distributed on my Ronya's wedding day."

8

On a clear warm April morning in the year 1881, with Fedor in the lead, Boris approached the estate. He guided the stallion up a steep rise from the Dnieper and looked down in wonderment on Ronya's heritage. It was strange: He felt at once that all he ever wanted lay here at his feet.

Directly ahead, though some distance away, was a flowering green meadow where stood a stone church. Simple and severe, it followed no rule of architecture but was constructed by Aaron, its creator, with sureness and fulfilled its purpose—not even to worship did the peasants have to leave the land. Fringing the meadow on the far side were peasant cottages, and on its right was laid out a compound of barns, carriage house, blacksmith shop, corrals, and exercise rings, with its own group of houses for the families of grooms, drivers, trainers, coachmen, and stable hands. These houses, like the peasants' cottages, were constructed of local clay, plaster trimmed, and fenced, each with its own backyard. In the far distance, open fields sloped down to the River Dnieper. They were edged by forest, the remnants of which dotted the land between the groups of buildings and formed a pine grove massed between the meadow and the fields.

From where Boris sat on his stallion, though he strained his eyes to where Fedor was pointing, he could not see the great white house or the surrounding gardens, since the orchards blocked his view. Nor could he see the guest cottage, where Katya and Alexis, tired from their long European wedding trip, were resting undisturbed. But in the opposite direction, where the true forest began, he caught a glimpse beyond the stout peasant houses of the sturdy gypsy houses, of the tents pitched around the gypsy encampment, of painted wagons with their tongues resting on wooden blocks.

Fedor had the sense to know that these moments belonged to Boris. He rode off to his two wives and many children and left Boris to find his way alone.

Boris had intended to explore the stables by himself—this was why he had ridden in hours before he was expected—but now he found he wanted to be united with Ronya in marriage before claiming David's princely gift. He took the stallion down the hill and trotted quietly toward the stables. A little way short of the nearest buildings he sighted a groom—a rough fellow—leaning against a tree, sucking a straw and regarding him with intense and obvious curiosity. When Boris was satisfied the groom knew his business, he turned the stallion over to him and left the stables.

He passed a hulking peasant already drunk on vodka; he heard a dog howling in the distance. All else was hushed and still. The first green shoots were pushing through the bare earth, from which the last snow had only just melted. At length he reached the house, majestic beyond expectation: The pillared sweep of the classical façade was punctuated by long graceful windows, and a curved double stairway led up to the massive door.

No one answered his knock; but he knew he was early and figured, rightly, that everyone was busy with last minute preparations. He tried the door. It opened. Boris lingered in the hall. Spectacular! He stood under a crystal chandelier, delighting in the vastness and great height, his eyes drawn up the grand horseshoe staircase to the gallery above. On the walls he recognized an El Greco, a Rubens, and Belgian tapestries which he knew to be companion pieces to those in the Winter Palace in St. Petersburg. At ease, Boris lit a cigarette and called out, "Anyone at home?"

There was no answer. He drew on his cigarette and shrugged: Obviously the whole house was at sixes and sevens and there was no point in waiting in the hall. His luggage had arrived some days ago and must be in whichever of the upstairs rooms he had been allotted. He began to climb the stairs—the front door slammed. He paused and glanced over his shoulder. There was his mother. Boris saw her through the smoke of his cigarette—tall and narrow-hipped, breeches and high boots, blond hair plaited Tartar fashion in many braids.

For a moment he was silent, feeling her ageless strength, and then with sudden longing he cried out, "Mother!"

The sound of his voice floated up to Ronya, where she lay on a chaise longue confined in her room in accordance with custom. She threw a chiffon wrapper over her nakedness and darted barefoot to the stairway. Halfway down the stairs she stopped, transfixed.

"Mother, I'm glad you've come. I'm glad you've come alone."

The Tartar woman laughed a screaming laugh, her head thrown back. Fear caught at Ronya's heart.

"No need to be glad," the woman said.

"Stay," Boris pleaded. "Give me your blessing."

"You're throwing yourself away."

"No, Mother, I'm fulfilling myself."

The Tartar woman's eyes were flat and wicked, her voice rose high and harsh: "Marry the Jewess, and I give you my curse. Limbs rotting, may you die alone."

Still as stone, Boris stared at his mother.

"Choose!"

Gazing down on the two blond heads bathed in the sunlight pouring in through the tall windows, Ronya spoke, "Yes, Boris Pirov, choose!"

Startled, they both looked up at her as she stood erect in the strong light, her frail garment barely concealing the vibrancy of her young body. She stared Boris full in the face unembarrassed, and he knew then that he loved her, that he would always love her.

76

The ice around the Tartar woman's heart melted. She had come for her son and stumbled on a young goddess. Looking up into Ronya's face, she boomed out, her voice filling the vaulted hall, "Come to the Tartars and be my daughter, lovely one."

Ronya's knees began to shake. Without a word, she turned and ran and locked herself in her room.

Boris' eyes went back to his mother. She saw his hard cold look and knew she had met defeat for the first time. "The golden ones never escape," she screamed. And she was gone.

Boris was still staring at the door which had slammed behind her when a buxom, rose-cheeked young woman bounced into the hall. "You!" she exclaimed.

"You must be Lydia," said Boris, remembering the name of the girl who was Ronya's servant, friend, and confidante. Seeing her surprise, he added, "Fedor mentioned you."

Lydia beamed. "You look totally bewildered."

Boris came down to her. "I am," he said. "Where is everyone?"

"Well, we thought Katya and Alexis should be away from the excitement, so we put them in a cottage normally used by guests. They're still there. Ronya usually sleeps late, but today she was up for an early breakfast. She must be back in bed by now fast asleep. The master and mistress ought to be home with Colonel Pirov any minute." She paused for breath, then rattled on. "I'm under orders from Ronya, my mistress, to take good care of you."

She leaned close. "The new housekeeper has no luck with the servants. Lazy wenches—still churning butter. And on top of that, she lent Rifka some of the household help for the entire morning." Lydia confided, as if this explained everything, "She's Polish."

Boris grinned. "That's unfortunate," he said understandingly and won Lydia's heart forever. Like the Cossacks, Lydia had no use for Roman Catholics.

"Hungry?"

Boris was hungry.

Lydia took him into a small, sunny alcove and sat him at a round table covered with a creamy lace cloth and a delightful flower arrangement. She gave him a hot towel for his hands, fed him stuffed goose and very hot tea, and talked conspiratorially about the wedding presents and reverently about the priest, Ivan Tromokov; and all the while she talked she surveyed him appraisingly. Boris did not mind. He was used to being stared at.

He was listening to a breathless description of the wedding cake, when the door opened and there stood Ruth.

Boris jumped to his feet. "I bet a million rubles," he grinned, "you're Ronya."

Ruth laughed with pleasure. "I'm afraid not." She gave him her hand. "Hello, Boris Pirov, and welcome. May you be happy here."

Leaning forward, he looked into her eyes. "Thank you, Ruth, my mother." On impulse, he kissed her full on the mouth.

Ruth, who had never been so treated by a virtual stranger, was caught short; but she understood perfectly the depth and the honesty of his gesture, even as she knew instinctively that her own association with him would always be close and loving. Stepping back, she noted carefully the sculptured profile, the firm-set jaw, the smile that revealed perfect teeth, the hazel eyes set wide apart and slightly Asiatic —they had a way of looking at a woman that made her feel desirable.

"You make an ideal son, Boris," she said, squeezing his hand gently. "Now, come along. Let me take you to your room"—Ruth glanced over at Lydia, who could barely control her eagerness—"because Lydia can hardly wait to run from here to Ronya."

They went up the stairs and Ruth led him along the hall. "This room is yours," she said, opening a door. "Ronya felt that sometimes you would want privacy."

Boris looked around. It was a good room, a man's room, with a fine marble fireplace, a sturdy bed, a treasure of a chest under a magnificent relic of a mirror. On one wall was a Goya, against another was a splendid desk, and between two massive leather chairs was a low table bearing vodka, brandy, and an array of liqueurs. The room faced the morning sun and was filled with light. Boris crossed to the window and looked out on well-kept lawns sprinkled with flower beds.

"Do you like it?" Ruth said, watching him.

"Very much." His eyes were on a vase of flowers on the desk. "Where's Ronya's room?"

"Directly across the hall."

Boris' glance flickered to the door. "You will have to be ready a little early, Boris," Ruth went on. "Rabbi Levinsky wants to see you and Ronya before the ceremony, separately. He has something private to say to each of you."

Boris glanced at her.

Ruth sat down in a deep chair by the window. "I don't think anything complex is involved." She considered him earnestly and continued, "Boris dear, it is very important to me that you allow Simon Levinsky to like you. He is my best friend."

Boris suddenly realized that Ruth's life with David was no long honeymoon, and it raised her in his estimation. "I'll do my best to make a good impression," he said, taking the other chair. "I have never in my whole life as much as said 'hello' to a rabbi before."

Ruth smiled faintly. The first rabbi to whom she had ever spoken was Simon's father. It was Simon who secretly instructed her in Judaism after David had married her in a civil ceremony in Vienna. "He'll take that into consideration, I'm sure."

"Ruth, my mother," Boris said slowly, "there's something I would like to know."

"Anything."

"I don't understand why Ronya's father dislikes me. It's even less clear why, disliking me as he does, he's doing all he is doing—the stables, all the ready money I need to buy horses from the Tartars, unlimited accounts with horse dealers. And the wedding. He could give in to Ronya without—" Boris shrugged, as if there was just too much to say. "It never entered my head that the wedding would be a brilliant social event—flowers from the Crimea, fireworks, guests from all over, presents from the four corners of the earth."

"I assure you, dear, there are never simple answers where David is concerned." She took a moment to decide how to answer Boris and continued resolutely, picking her words with care: "You must understand that David is experiencing a sense of loss. He is bound to feel, well, a little envious of you and your happiness; only David is very practiced at evading anything he finds unbecoming, particularly where he himself is involved, and will invent all kinds of elaborate tricks to fool people."

Boris certainly was no stranger to rivalry; he understood, too, that there was more to the situation than he had bargained for, but Ruth's words seemed to be leading him down a dark street. He shut his mind to it. To hell with David von Glasman!

Ruth saw that she had lost him and wondered if he thought her outrageously disloyal or if he was intuitive enough to understand women—that for a daughter, a loving wife becomes a passionate mother, crying out, "Leave her to life."

For a moment Ruth was lost in contemplation. Then Boris said, "I have so many different images of Ronya, I can't sort them out."

"Ronya is not altogether easy to describe," Ruth replied. "Her eyes. I'm perpetually conscious of her eyes—so intensely aflame and at the same time filled with a deep tenderness, sadness."

Boris found himself remembering an incident out of his boyhood, an initiation involving a skinny young girl with big sorrowful eyes. Later when he said, "She had Jewish eyes," the Tartar woman was content.

Ruth stood. "Will you be ready at about two thirty?"

There was a rap on the door and, before either of them could speak, Tamara whisked into the room and closed the door behind her.

"Tamara," Ruth exclaimed, "what in the world are you doing here?"

Tamara leaned against the door. She was at her most flamboyant in a gypsyish dress unbuttoned halfway down the front.

Ignoring Ruth—she had not bargained on finding her there—she pressed her admiring glance upon Boris. "I just thought I'd drop by and keep the groom from getting lonesome."

Boris took in every detail—the long shining black hair, the smooth copper skin and sensual mouth, the luxurious body and long dancer's legs.

Devilishly taunting him, Tamara came close. "Now I understand why Ronya would think of no one else."

Boris felt acutely uncomfortable. He knew Tamara at once for what she was: She spelled trouble—but at the same time her snapping brown eyes and scarlet mouth charged the room with desire. He realized he desired her and hated himself for it.

Ruth, fighting back tears of anger and shame, thrust herself between them. "Go at once, Tamara," she said icily, "your conduct is most inappropriate."

Boris held open the door. "You've been told to leave."

Tamara swept out, giving him a full smile as she brushed by. Boris closed the door behind her. "Thank you, Boris," said Ruth. "Well, that's Tamara. I don't know how much you've been told—"

Before Boris could answer, she went on, "Her mother has spoiled her from birth. She is willful, destructive, childishly grasping. Whatever Ronya has, she wants, and she'll go to any lengths to get it. She never takes no for an answer." Then, as if embarrassed by the outburst, she excused herself, leaving him to his disquieted thoughts.

Boris immersed himself instead in a soothing bath, after which he vigorously scrubbed his hair until it shone like gold. As he was about to pour himself a vodka, he heard a voice very much like Ruth's call his name from the hall. "Boris? I'm Katya." Another voice added, "I'm Alexis." Then, "May we come in?"

Boris flung his silk dressing gown about him and drew Katya and Alexis delightedly into the room. He lifted Katya off her feet and kissed her and embraced Alexis warmly.

"We have only a moment to wish you happiness," Katya explained. "The rabbi has already talked to Ronya."

"Stay a minute," Boris protested. "Have a drink."

"We can't," Alexis said. "David has asked us to go down and receive Paul. He'll be arriving any minute." He clasped Boris' hand again. "Luck and happiness, Boris. Come, Katya, we'll be late."

Neither the hot tub nor Katya's and Alexis' visit entirely took Boris' mind off Tamara. Intrigued, he let his thoughts wander: The family, accustomed to relationships between the Von Glasman men and the gypsy queens, should not take it amiss were he to fool around with Tamara. Actually Boris knew better. He sensed Tamara was danger. Therefore—"Damn!" he said to himself. "I'm thinking like an idiot."

"It's time, son," said Itil. "The rabbi wants you in the library."

David was waiting below to make the introductions to the rabbi. But first he apologized for not having welcomed Boris in person. "I started up the stairs at least three times, and each time I was called away to handle an emergency. The peasants are drunk, the gypsies are drunk, and two of our coachmen have been arrested—one accused of stealing a horse."

Boris laughed. "May I speak bluntly?"

David nodded.

"You run a lousy stable."

David pondered a moment. "Of course," he smiled, "that is why Boris Pirov is here."

Boris felt a flicker of fondness for Von Glasman. But the rabbi broke in. "Leave us, David."

Taking Boris' arm, David steered him to a chair. "Why?"

"You must do as I say."

David shrugged and obeyed.

The rabbi turned to find himself being observed by a wholly composed young giant with an engaging smile. "As you know," he said pleasantly, "I went to see Ronya. What you don't know is that she ignored my interrogation and opened an unexpected attack on me. 'Understand this,' she said, 'I shall never forsake my people or forget that I am a Jewess. Now leave Boris alone. He's had enough.' "

The rabbi saw the proud, pleased look on Boris' face. He smiled in full friendliness and said simply, "Boris Pirov, is it agreed—do I have your word that the children will be raised as Jews?"

"Yes," Boris said, "it is agreed."

"Your father is outside the door. Go with him into the drawing room. Stand under the canopy. I'll meet you there."

Boris thought a moment. "Will you say, 'Who gives this man?' "

"Yes. In our religion the parents of the bride and the parents of the groom give the girl and the man to each other. In your case—"

Boris stopped him. "Look, rabbi, nobody gives me. I give myself to Ronya von Glasman."

Their eyes met and held for a long moment. "Boris Pirov," the rabbi said, "I like the way you talk."

The congregation gathered in the drawing room to witness the marriage of Ronya and Boris was a study in contrasts. The corpulent

Lydia, strong as granite, her broad face illuminated with pleasure that her little mistress was about to commit herself to a man. A priest of the Orthodox Church, a big, square, heavy man who towered over the others, a simple man of the people who trusted in God and his horse and who saw grandeur in the Russian peasant, a priest whose public joy was vodka and whose private sorrow was the inhumanity of man. Rifka, the gypsy queen named for a Jewess, a woman of worldliness and power. Paul, her son, who had everything in abundance except integrity. Tamara, her daughter, inevitably doomed. Katya and Alexis, count and countess, joyous with each other. And off to one side, next to Itil Pirov, a tall thin man wearing a black beard that hid his face and thick spectacles that hid his eyes. Everything else about him was white, for his caftan covered him from chin to toe.

The object of everyone's eyes, Boris stood under the wedding canopy made of white roses and sprays of lily of the valley. Now they could all understand Ronya's determination to have him and no other man. In consequence of her choice, the peasants and gypsies born on the ancestral estate she would inherit would have for master a Tartar prince, a celebrity, the favorite of an Empress. The landed gentry would be no less enthusiastic: None among them had ever worn the white breeches, the white boots, the embroidered tunic, the seven rows of gold braid designating the Imperial Guard.

Boris stared across the white velvet carpet to the double doors. It seemed a lifetime before they opened. He could not believe his eyes when he saw her, glowing in the extravagant splendor of tiers and tiers of white, in long Venetian lace, with twin strands of matched pearls. Conscious of his eyes resting on her, Ronya left her parents and ran to him. She looked up at him with great shining eyes, and Boris saw tears on her lashes. To everyone's everlasting surprise, he lifted her long veil lightly and kissed the tip of her nose. Then he dropped the veil and turned to the rabbi. Artlessly, Ronya slipped her hand in his.

"The time has come," Simon Levinsky began, his duty now a pleasure.

"Ronya von Glasman, you chose this man. Before God, do you swear to love him, to attend him, to share your views with him, to make him happy?"

Triumphantly Ronya raised her voice, "Yes."

The rabbi called on Boris. "Boris Pirov, do you swear to love and to honor Ronya von Glasman, and for her to forsake all others?"

"I do." Turning to Ronya, he promised, "Until death do us part."

When he put the ring on her finger, Ronya had to hold back tears.

The rabbi pronounced them man and wife.

A big grin lit up Boris' face. He lifted Ronya's veil and her lips welcomed his. Then with a deafening bang he smashed the ceremonial cup, and to the tinkling of the crystal chandelier the congregation called out: *"Mazel tov."*

Hand in hand, they walked the length of the room; the double doors swung open before them, and they passed through into the central hall. Ronya pulled Boris into a cloak closet. She lifted her beautiful face. "Kiss me."

Boris took her into his arms. "Little dove," he said, "let's get the hell out of here."

Ronya's soft fingers touched his face. "We can't, my love. The peasant children are waiting to sing to us—Father Tromokov has been rehearsing them for weeks—and the reception starts at five."

Boris knew there was no escape.

The vast hall was waxed and glistening, and even at this distance the bustle from the kitchen could be heard. He capitulated to the toasts, the gifts, the guests, the supper. He drew her closer, and the kiss that started tenderly ended with her trembling and dazed, so that he had to support her.

"Are you all right?"

"I'm not sure."

Boris held her tight. "I'm glad, Ronya. Glad that you found me."

Still looking into his eyes, Ronya said, "I love you."

In spite of the radiant happiness of the newlyweds, happiness they made no effort to conceal, Tamara had eyes only for Boris. She interrupted when he stood among a group of men, continually put her hands on him, followed him wherever he went, and sat next to him at the improvised bar, her legs crossed, tilting vodka and licking her lips.

Totally disregarding Ronya, she forced herself upon him, claiming a dance. He had done his share of drinking; it hardly mattered to him who his partner was or what he thought of her. His feet sprang from the ground, he soared in erotic leaps. In perfect harmony, Tamara vulgarly pressed against his body, as they danced to a beat as wild as the soil that nurtured them. It was a spectacular show, dazzling everyone who saw it. They left singing Boris' praise and condemning Tamara. Still, though the local gentry prided themselves on their broadmindedness, they never had expected such a sight—not under David von Glasman's roof.

David himself suffered. Though he did not interfere, remaining cool and calm, the sight of the conquering Tartar brought back a terrible past—it did not matter that he loved Ronya, he hated Boris more.

Ruth, concealing her own distress, stepped across the white carpet on which a brief few hours ago Ronya had walked between her and David to the wedding canopy and touched Boris' shoulder.

"Darling, will you dance with your mother-in-law?"

"Yes, lovely lady," Boris exclaimed with a broad grin. Swiftly his arm was around her, and Tamara was left standing alone.

"You're a splendid dancer, Boris." *Too splendid,* she thought.

Boris understood her. He gazed down at her in admiration and sincere affection. "I love Ronya and hate tramps. You're not to worry."

"I must say," Ruth replied, "it doesn't take you young people long to know you're in love."

"Tell me, does Ronya still love raspberries?"

"Why, yes." Ruth gazed up at him. "How strange that you should ask."

Boris pressed her hand and swept her faster into the waltz. She followed him effortlessly until the music stopped.

They were still hand in hand when Tamara rushed over and clutched at Boris' sleeve. "Will you dance with me again, later?" She felt a firm touch on her arm and turned. It was Paul. He put his hand under her elbow. "Dine with me, Tamara."

Boris and Ruth started to move slowly toward the buffet tables where Ronya was talking to Katya and Alexis, her back resolutely turned to the room. Their progress was slow, for at every step they had to stop and accept congratulations and handshakes. All at once they were intercepted by the bearded gentleman in white, who bowed from the waist and said, "Do me the honor, Madam von Glasman, of drinking a glass of champagne with me."

Privately Boris considered this conspicuous guest a queer bird, but in a way he was glad that it was he who had taken Ruth away; all evening Boris had felt pangs of jealousy as the handsomest and most distinguished men showered attention and flattery on the Von Glasman women.

As the distance between them and Boris lengthened, Ruth said softly, "Really, Ladislaus!"

He offered his arm and she took it. "Don't you think me ingenious?"

"What are you?" she laughed. "A Chassid in white instead of black, or a desert Arab in a caftan?"

Ladislaus removed his glasses. "I'm worried, Ruth."

"In that case, Ladislaus, what shall I do?"

"Take David away. How you manage doesn't matter. He's a taut string. He'll snap."

"Even my resourcefulness is unequal to that," Ruth said, her tone hushed and sad.

The buffet tables had been crowded, but when the music again began, everyone drifted to the ballroom. The older guests settled

84

themselves to watch the dancers; footmen entered with lavish trays of desserts and champagne. Alexis offered Katya his arm, but Boris and Ronya stayed where they were, Ronya unhappily poking at the food on her plate with a fork.

"You don't want that."

Her eyes downcast, Ronya put the plate down slowly.

Boris put a finger under her chin and tilted her face up. "If you as much as gain an ounce," he said only half in jest, "I'll—"

"And if you ever dance like that again with anyone but me, I'll make you regret it."

Boris increased the pressure to her chin. "I don't take kindly to threats."

Ronya said nothing.

Boris saw her lips quivering and looked into her eyes, sensing something of her feelings. Softening, he lifted his finger from her chin and touched her mouth caressingly. "We'll be quicker settling this in bed. Let's go, dove."

"We can't," said Ronya. "We're obliged to stay until Rifka reads the molten lead."

Boris lifted a glass from the tray of a passing waiter and, from the way he tossed down the drink, it was evident what he thought of that ritual.

As soon as Ruth had taken Boris away from Tamara, David went over to Rifka, magnificent in purple and diamonds. "Tell your daughter she is attracting too much attention upon herself and shame upon all of us."

"David, don't be stuffy," Rifka replied, catching Itil Pirov's eyes.

Masking his anger with a smile, he said, "Come with me."

He led her to the library and closed the door. "Rifka," he said, sternly, "I think we had better have a talk."

Rifka seated herself on the sofa. "About what? Or should I have said, about whom?"

David sat down beside her. "About my Ronya. I can see which way the wind is blowing, and I don't like it. I am telling you to put a stop to Tamara's lascivious games."

A cruel smile played around Rifka's lips. "I won't, David, because Tamara's behavior fits my design."

David asked scornfully, "To what lengths, dear cousin, to achieve your aims?"

Without taking her eyes off him, Rifka replied, "To your lengths, David. I want Boris for the same reasons you want him. Stud! Can't you just see the gorgeous golden babies?"

"Good God, Rifka! You're a fool to risk—"

"I have not finished," Rifka interrupted. "After Boris has done his duty by Ronya, he can service Tamara. After that—the devil take him, for all I care."

Furiously, David warned, "Don't hurt my baby—or my good name."

There was a look of victory on Rifka's face. "Tamara and I have our duty, David. We are queens."

David thought of the lifetime he had loved and trusted her. Served her. He rose, walked slowly to the door, and when he spoke his voice was low, contained: "Your scheme is far from foolproof, Rifka. I own the blond Tartar."

When Rifka approached Ronya, she found her in a circle by the side of Boris. They were all laughing as they watched Ivan Tromokov balance a glass filled with vodka on his forehead.

"That's good, really good—for a priest. But, among us Tartars, we gallop a wild stallion as we anchor a trifle like that."

The priest gulped, upsetting the glass. "That I want to see."

"How about a wager?" Boris said, a trace of a grin at the corners of his mouth. "Say a thousand rubles?"

Rifka laid a hand on Ronya's arm. "It's time for the molten metal." She led her away and showed her where to stand.

Boris turned away from those around him and watched her, composed and still, her head proudly poised, directly under the dramatic glow of a crystal chandelier. He longed for the moment when they would be able to retire. He saw himself closing their door tightly, holding her in his arms, tasting her crimson lips, and slowly and gently leading her—

Tamara abruptly cut off the vision. "Let's get a breath of air," she whispered, pulling him toward the door.

"Christ, let go!"

"Must you behave like a slut?" Again it was Paul. "Come stand with me."

Tamara shrugged off the insult. "There'll be other times," she said, smiling smugly at Boris as she moved away with Paul.

David saw the exchange between Boris and Tamara, and he judged. But instead of blaming Tamara alone, he believed Boris, too, was willing. The thought that his son-in-law could commit adultery on his wedding night made him shake. It took all his control not to betray his feelings, so that when Rifka called for him, as father of the bride, he kissed Ronya and placed himself at her side without so much as a cursory glance at Rifka.

The guests crowded around and the servants and musicians craned over their shoulders. Rifka called for silence in a room already silent. "David von Glasman," she said, "ask the question."

David's face froze into a ruthless mask. "I have no question to ask."

No one was prepared for this; they could hardly believe it. No one trusted himself to look at his neighbor. In the intense stillness that followed, Boris sensed that something had gone wrong. He looked about him. Rifka was staring, unable to speak. He looked across at Ruth and had the impression that she nodded encouragement at David. Katya's eyes, filled with tears, were on David. Paul, livid, glared savagely at Tamara, and she looked thoroughly terrified. Slowly, Boris' gaze went to Father Tromokov. The priest looked grave, but Boris had no idea what he was thinking.

Boris riveted his eyes anxiously on Ronya, and he knew from the way she held her head and from the intense glance she directed at him that her uncertainty was over and her mind made up. She was ready to take command. She beckoned him to her side, so that she stood between him and her father, and then, as if nothing had happened, she began: "Queen Rifka, my cousin, I, Ronya, ask the question. Have you made use of the metal?"

"I have foreknowledge," Rifka said, regaining her dignity.

For a brief instant, the fifty-nine-year-old queen and the nineteen-year-old girl measured each other. "You have my permission," Ronya said. "Speak."

"The molten lead proclaims two lives in two lands for Ronya von Glasman Pirov. She will live by her own law and mourn at her own wall."

For several moments Rifka remained silent, watching Boris.

Ronya spoke again. "Queen Rifka, my cousin, is there more?"

"There is." Eyes still fixed on Boris, she addressed him: "Know that Ronya who brought you here will recover from each tribulation. True daughter of her people, she will bestow many gifts, upon herself the greatest of all—life."

Boris had had enough of Rifka and her gypsy rubbish. In some strange way, despite her opulent costume and glittering jewels, she reminded him of his mother—crafty women, who scorned laws and had no use for men, for whom sex was merely a diversion, an elemental appetite; women with an overpowering mission.

When she had finished speaking, Rifka turned away from the circle, then paused for an instant in front of Paul.

"Will I see you tomorrow?"

"No," Paul said, without explanation.

Rifka concealed her hurt and summoned Tamara with a glance. "Come with me."

A few minutes after they had left, Itil Pirov went out after them. Paul saw. He remembered.

As the guests began to take their leave Ronya slipped away. She undressed hastily and sank herself in a scented bath. She wanted to remain there, let the warm water enfold her and quiet the tension deep within her, but she was afraid to do so, even though Katya had assured her that Alexis would keep an eye on Boris and make sure that he stayed downstairs until she had had time to put the finishing touches to her bridal toilette and slide between the silken softness of her sheets.

Time was slipping away. *Funny,* Boris thought, *a girl all my own at last and I'm expected to stand at the door, shaking hands, mouthing platitudes to idiots who haven't the sense to go home.* Boris groaned inwardly and signaled to the butler. "Vodka," he said curtly. "Serve it in a big glass."

At long last, the final good-bye: Boris wanted to cheer. He felt a touch on his shoulder. It was David. "I'll meet you in the library."

Boris decided to ignore the summons to a midnight tête-à-tête with his father-in-law, but as he reached the stairs he wondered if it might not be a good idea to look into the library. Maybe Ruth was there, and Katya and Alexis. Maybe the family wanted one last drink together. He found the room deserted. He strode up and down a few times; a minute later he left.

David was waiting at the foot of the stairway. Though his voice was pitched low, his manner was hostile. "Until you arrived, there was no blight upon my relationship with my cousin Rifka. I did not expect this complication, and I resent it."

It seemed pointless to discuss the gypsy woman or her daughter. Keeping his feelings under control, Boris said good-humoredly, "Come now, must we argue, sir? This is my wedding night."

David's dark eyes shone with anger. "Soaking up vodka like a common peasant soldier! You were in no pressing hurry to go to your bride."

Boris thought: *Hell, if you want to make a scene, you'll get no help from me.* Nevertheless, he did not dismiss the implication lightly. "You'll never see me drunk, sir."

David knew perfectly well that Boris had a hideaway in the bachelor officers' quarters at the local Cavalry barracks and had sent much of his personal gear there, including his store of wines and liquor.

"At the moment I have something more important than vodka to discuss."

"Tomorrow."

"Now," David said authoritatively.

Boris shrugged, seemingly imperturbable.

"I want it clearly understood that while you reside in my house you'll conduct yourself with gentlemanly decorum."

88

Anger flashed in Boris' eyes, but he said, "I'll remember that."

David flushed. His mouth worked in indignation. "Chivalrous bearing toward a woman, any woman, be she actress, whore, or empress, distinguishes the gentleman from the savage."

A sneering began to creep over Boris' face. "Interesting. Anything else?"

"Yes."

"Make it brief!"

Boris' coolness infuriated David. Never in his adult life had he known such agitation. He desperately needed to believe that the man Ronya had chosen would fail her—unlike her father who would remain constant forever. He was shaking with rage. "I had no trouble bringing you to Kiev. It was comparatively easy. It will be even easier to get rid of you."

Ronya his weapon, Boris said, "I'll keep that in mind."

Lost in his own turmoil, David, who customarily saw everything, did not see the Tartar savagery explode in Boris' face. He heard his footsteps taking the stairs two at a time.

Spent, David moaned, *I—I alone—arranged this marriage. Rifka spoke the truth, I need him for stud. But—oh God! I did not know how much it would hurt.*

Bursting into his room, Boris snatched up a bottle and gulped a long drink. Part of his mind urged him to stay where he was and not go to Ronya still half mad with rage; yet he knew instinctively that if he spent his rankling wrath on vodka he would be playing into David's hands. But why? Why had David done this to him? All he could fathom was that more was involved than David had divulged. He threw off his clothes, snatched a robe and, still consumed with thoughts of David, stalked across the dark hall to Ronya.

Boris found her, face uplifted, unafraid, willing to give herself in complete surrender. The eyes that met his were shining with love. Esteem for her, hate for the father, fought in him. He did not yield. He felt that if he did, it would be the end of him. Without a word, he caught the soft female material curving gently around her glorious nakedness and ripped it off with one strong sweep. Yielding to the primitive need to best a rival, he dropped his dressing gown on the floor and threw himself on her in swift attack. Ronya fought, but it was like striking a stone wall. Boris paid no heed. With insolent disregard for her virginity, he took her without restraint. It was quickly done. His victory over David von Glasman won, Boris rolled over on his side and drifted off to exhausted sleep.

Stricken by the senseless act, Ronya's head spun, her thoughts awhirl. How to account for it? The vodka? No—this was by design. Why? She knew he loved her. All her wondering settled nothing. Ronya tried to lie still but was unable to do so. There *must* be some reason! She reached over and stirred him awake.

Boris raised his head instantly.

She asked one word: "Why?"

Boris gave her a long searching look. Bathed in soft light, she was beautiful. Her rich copper-brown hair spread adorning the pillow, her uncovered breasts were the most perfect he had ever seen, her lips were made for love. Boris seized her roughly and dragged her over to him.

"Tell your father to stay out of my way."

So that was it! "And what if he doesn't?" she asked, her exquisite brows imperious, her voice a shade too composed.

"You get more of the same," Boris said, his mouth cruel.

Ronya gave him a rebellious stare. "I hate you."

Boris laughed suddenly. "Like hell you do."

Ronya jerked herself free. Without another word, she got to her feet and stalked off to the bathroom. She came back very proper in plain white cotton with white lace ruffles, looking young and bewitchingly precious and smelling faintly of some elusive perfume. She stretched out on her back and instantly fell fast asleep. Boris touched his lips lightly to her eyes, her lips, her throat.

A soft murmur escaped her.

Boris raised an arm and put out the light. His hands reached out and drew her to him. Holding her, his big powerful frame relaxed, and he slept.

Just a few miles away, in the dark of a gypsy wagon, Itil Pirov had a sweating, panting Tamara. He brought no pleasure to her pain.

She gave no nectar.

9

At about five Boris woke with a start, drenched in perspiration. He had been dreaming of Odessa—he could smell the sea and recognize the rocks he used to climb, and he heard the screams of the sea gulls just as he had thousands of times before. He could not remember much of the dream—only that there was a quarrel and he lost Ronya.

"Daughters sometimes do," she said, when she told him she was going back to her father. Then he was dead; he killed himself.

Boris' eyes moved to Ronya's head, cushioned against his shoulder. He whispered her name softly and swore an oath. "So help me. No one is going to take you from me, little dove. Not ever."

He could feel a hot tightness, the swell of desire, but he let her sleep. He bathed and shaved, and when he came out of his room he was dressed in high boots and rough work clothes. Half an hour later, having helped himself to breakfast, he was fetching oats for the stallion.

Next he took a good look around, and what he saw disgusted him. First and foremost, the place was deserted—at this hour! True, the horses did not seem neglected or mistreated, but neither did they look overloved. Boris went to work. In a stable he was no gentleman Cavalry officer, no clever trick rider, but a professional, son of a people who lived with horses from birth.

At about seven thirty Fedor appeared, accompanied by a burly groom and a short, bowlegged fellow with massive shoulders and enormous hands called Sad Eyes because of his drooping eyelids.

Eyes ablaze, Boris exploded. "You lazy sons of bitches!"

Fedor was a man of one mood—surliness. He grunted sullenly and went to work.

Sad Eyes smiled; smiling did not fit his face. "There's one thing I got to know, sir—did you really drink the priest under the table last night?"

"Of course."

Sad Eyes gave him a long, considered appraisal. Then, "Would you care to shake hands, sir?"

Boris gave him his hand.

Near noon they heard a rollicking cheer and went out into the big cobbled yard. Boris stared in amazement. The priest was there, surrounded by the stable hands and numerous peasants. Some of the men were quite old, some just boys with cropped heads, some had come up from the fields wearing thick shabby boots and rope belts to their coarse blouses. They were celebrating the fact that now they had for their own the national hero. He was young and strong—a golden eagle, who stirred their imagination with his dash and his Tartar toughness. They had brought food and kegs of beer, and in high spirits and full of talk Boris and those who lived on the land lunched in equality. An hour later the peasants marched off singing. The priest stayed.

Boris heaved himself to his feet and, ordering his men back to work, clapped the priest on the back and said, "Come with us."

The men turned to find Tamara standing in the stable doorway, hip jutted out. She sent Boris a glance of weighty invitation.

Later the men described to their women how she looked in exact detail—toned bronze set off by a wide ruffled skirt and a blouse that left her shoulders bare.

Boris turned slowly to Fedor. "Tell your sister to get the hell out of here."

"You tell her."

Boris swung one blow, and down went Fedor. Then he thrust out a hand and pulled him to his feet. "Next time you disobey an order," he said steelily, "you can get off the land."

Boris swung around to Sad Eyes. "I want no women hanging around the stables. Spread the word."

"Yes, sir."

Tamara stood laughing, mocking Boris with her eyes, as he turned his back and strode rapidly away.

Father Tromokov caught up with him. "Boris, you should apologize to Fedor. Tamara will be his queen. He may not give her an order."

"You know I won't do that."

"I know," the priest said in a resigned tone, "but that's unfortunate. You've made yourself an enemy."

"Am I advised to be on my guard?"

"Yes."

Boris eyed Ivan Tromokov strangely. "I thought you two were comrades."

The priest laughed pleasantly. "I humor him."

When Boris came in, Ruth and Katya had already retired to their rooms to rest before dinner. David and Alexis had been away since early afternoon visiting a farm a few miles from the Von Glasman property. The bank that held the mortgage was foreclosing on the absentee landlord, and David was bidding for it. Lydia, on the watch for Boris, met him at the door to tell him the news.

"Your father and Paul have gone; they've left you notes. Colonel Pirov took the ten fifteen for Odessa. Ruth, my mistress, was beginning to worry when you didn't appear for the noonday meal, but Ronya guessed you were in the stables."

As she waddled up the stairs beside him, Lydia betrayed a confidence. "This morning Tamara came wandering in, just as she always does. Ronya and Katya were up in the attic with the maids packing away the wedding gifts. Leave it to Tamara! She found them—and you should have seen Ronya pull off her shoe. She yelled, 'Get out of here, you Judas. I won't miss with the second one.' The maids haven't stopped talking about it yet."

"Lydia, you're a jewel. Thanks for the briefing."

The girl chuckled.

He walked up to Ronya's door and tried the knob. It was locked. He moved slowly away.

As he soaked in his hot tub, Boris thought about the locked door. When the water got cold, he pulled the plug, returned to his room, and stretched out on the bed. He thought about the outrageous thing he had done to Ronya. He thought about it a long time. When it began to get dark, he got up and opened the closet. Most of his suits and uniforms were gone—Ronya must have had them moved into her own room. Boris raised an eyebrow, dressed, and went downstairs.

There was music coming from the drawing room and, in a moment, Ronya's voice, "In here, darling."

She met him at the door. Boris stood looking at her, not knowing whether to bend down and kiss her or not. He decided against it, but she lifted her face, and he drew her into his arms, grinning inwardly. Ronya slipped her hand into his and led him into the room.

It was Katya who was playing, with Alexis sitting beside her on the piano stool. Ruth and David were finishing a game of checkers. Alexis poured a drink, brought it over to Boris, and leaned against the piano watching him—warm with Ruth and Katya but chilly with David, who stayed very much out of Boris' way and made himself pleasant to Ronya. He was urging her to take a more active role in the management of the estate. She said, "Yes, Father," at the right moments, but it was apparent that her thoughts belonged to Boris and, after a while, he went over and put an arm around her shoulder. They were all glad when dinner was announced.

They were drinking the last of the wine when Rifka and Tamara came in unannounced. For a change, both were dressed with wonderful simplicity. Rifka looked stately; Tamara looked less like a gypsy and more like a nice friendly girl who happened to be beautiful.

Rifka sipped her brandy reflectively, her eyes dwelling on Boris. Then she broke the silence. "I've never spoken to you of this before, David, but now I shall."

David sighed heavily. "You use my name, but you direct your remarks elsewhere. To whom are you speaking?"

She turned and eyed him. "I was about to say I really can't spare Fedor. I'm increasing his responsibilities at the camp, and he just won't have time. Can you replace him in the stables?"

David stroked his chin thoughtfully. *Hm-m-m,* he thought, *I wonder what this is all about.* But he had learned his lesson; direct tactics—hurling threats or insulting him with money—were useless with Boris. David's strength lay in the mistakes he'd force Boris to make and, if Tamara was part of them, he was past caring.

"It's for you to say, Boris," he said airily. "In the stables you rule undisputed—except," he smiled his most charming smile, "allow me claim to my carriage."

Alexis saw that David's performance fooled Ruth and the girls, but not Rifka. Boris he was not sure about, because the glance Boris sent David did not quite harmonize with the words he spoke.

"Thank you, sir." He leveled his eyes on Rifka. "I don't feel entitled to a foreman until the stables start making money. I'll do Fedor's job."

Rifka merely smiled. She turned to Ruth. "When is your first free date? I must plan the party Tamara is giving for Ronya and Boris. I want a Saturday."

"As far as I can remember, there's not a free Saturday until mid-June," said Ruth.

"Fine. There's nothing better for a party than the hot sun by the river followed by a summer evening."

On the way out of the dining room, Tamara linked her arm with Ronya's. "What about tomorrow? We could ride, or take a picnic lunch into the woods, or go into town, if you wanted."

"I'll let you know."

At the front door, Tamara hung back, but Rifka said with unusual sternness, "Come home with me. At once."

At half past nine, Alexis yawned. Katya said, "I'm tired, too."

Ronya looked at Boris lovingly from under her arched eyebrows and whispered, "Give me a few moments."

Softer still, he murmured, "First tell me that you don't hate me, dove."

She drew back and looked away.

Fifteen minutes later, torn between amusement and irritation, he was staring at her locked door. He had underestimated her.

He got out his pocket knife. A twist of the blade, and the door swung open. With a smile of triumph, he stepped into the room only to be pulled up short.

"Jesus!" he roared in surprise.

There was Ronya naked—tantalizingly, thrillingly, mouthwateringly naked—a whip in her hand.

With no thought to the open door, Boris started to strip, keeping his eyes on Ronya, who stood firmly braced, buttocks tight, belly sucked in, mouth inviting. His eyes teased her, and mocked her, and admired her, but she stayed still and ready without any change of expression.

He was unbuttoning his shirt when he heard the sharp indrawn breath.

David was staring into the room. The man was pale with shock, his face twisted in terrible suffering.

The laughter died out of Boris' eyes. Swearing under his breath, he kicked shut the door.

He pulled off the last of his clothes and, as naked as she, moved toward her. Ronya raised her arm and slashed with the whip, and Boris laughed as he felt the leather bite into his flesh.

"Don't you dare use me as pawn in your fight with my father!" Ronya flung at him, as the whip flickered out at him again and raised a weal on his shoulder.

Boris met her angry glare with laughter, still advancing on her, and as she lifted her arm again he caught her wrist. "Drop it, dove."

Ronya obeyed. She felt herself being lifted in his arms and carried into the bed. He played with her, caressed her, kissed her, until her responses became fiercely passionate.

In the long minutes that followed, Ronya learned what lovemaking meant, and in the glory of her wild surrender, Boris learned what love meant.

They rested in silence until Ronya sighed contentedly, "Imagine!"

Boris had been thinking the same thing and asking himself how one little girl could bring a man so much happiness.

"Boris?"

"What, dove?" he replied without opening his eyes.

"Will you ever love another woman?"

Raising his head, he looked down into Ronya's luminous eyes. "Never!"

"Will you be faithful to me?"

Again he answered without hesitation, "No, Ronya."

The half smile faded from her lips and the light from her eyes, and Boris was looking down into the deepest, darkest sadness he had ever seen.

"Why not?" It was a plea.

"I'm not altogether sure, Ronya," he said softly. "Maybe it's because I'm a man, and to stay a man I must behave like one. Maybe, because I was born a Tartar, now and again I'll go back to being one. Maybe because I'm afraid of getting too dependent on you."

Suddenly, Ronya's hands clenched into tight little fists. She lifted her head in defiance. "I've given a lot of thought to love, Boris. You can't make me believe that you can take away what belongs to me and still leave me whole. And you can't fool me—I'll know, and I'll remember, and I'll pay you back."

His eyes narrowed, and his fingers clenched themselves so hard into her shoulders that the color drained from her flesh. "If *ever* you so much as look at another man, I'll kill him," he said, his voice cold and dangerous. Suddenly he pushed her back against the pillow.

She watched him step over to his clothes and take something out of a pocket. As he settled his head against the pillow again he tossed the heart-shaped pin into her lap. "This caught my fancy in St. Petersburg."

Ronya picked up the pin and cradled it in the palm of her hand. Settled on one elbow, Boris watched her face. "It's beautiful."

"Like you, dove."

Clasping her pin, Ronya stretched herself against him, her hair falling in disarray over his chest. "Hold me," she murmured, "hold me tight."

His arms gathered her to him, and they slept.

Ruth smiled. "Look at me, David." He turned. "Leave Ronya to her husband just as you've left Katya to hers, and devote yourself to me."

"How can you—?" David cried. "Have you no shame?"

"David."

"No, let me finish."

Ruth got up from her dressing table. "I don't want to be told again. I don't want to know how Ronya stood, or how he laughed, or how they made love afterward. I want you to give up your obsession with Ronya and look at me."

"You astound me." David's face was blank, his voice cold.

Ruth sighed despairingly and picked up her hairbrush. "*You* taught Ronya to turn quickly to her whip and, as a matter of fact," she swung around and pointed her brush at him, "you took extraordinary pride in her virtuosity, so that wherever you went you recounted stories about her, exaggerated accounts of her physical tussles with lads who had something on their minds other than reciting verses. But now that Ronya has turned her whip excitingly on her lover, you are embarrassed."

Nothing she said made an impression on him; his mind closed her out. There came an end to the sound of her voice, and he put his thoughts into words. "I am curious to know. Please explain to me why she would take her whip to him unless he tried to force her to do something repugnant to her."

Ruth burst into laughter.

David stiffened, waited for her to finish.

"Oh, David—where is your good sense? Were Boris' demands—well—what you imagine, would she greet him stark naked?"

David's eyes wavered; presently, he started to undress. At the bathroom door he looked back at her a moment, and Ruth was startled by the depth of suffering in his face and found herself wondering, *Is he ill?*

Later, when the room was in darkness and in complete silence except for their breathing, she put out her hand and touched him. "David." She waited for him to answer and, when he did not do so, she said quietly. "Boris is a proud man. Give him and Ronya a house of their own—in the pine grove, near the stream, there's the most perfect site."

"Ruth, understand this: Here, in this house, Ronya will remain, and my grandsons, and their grandsons after them."

"All right, dear, but we could go." Even in the dark, Ruth could sense his glare. Hastily she added, "And return—I meant—" Suddenly she had an inspiration. "Oh, David, do take me to America on a holiday. I want to meet Sophia."

"Go to sleep, Ruth. This is no time to plan trips."

"Then you must kiss me good-night, *mon cher,*" she said softly.

His cold lips touched her cheek.

But as Ruth slept, David stared up into the darkness and mused upon something that remained stubbornly elusive—a picture, a memory? Whatever it was, it could not liberate itself from his subconscious.

So for yet another night David found no peace. Just before daybreak, he made up his mind and was able to shut Boris out of his mind for a few hours. Immediately after breakfast, he locked himself in the library and composed a coded message to be delivered in St. Petersburg:

Dear Paul,

Please convey my regards to Madam Titiana, for whom I have an assignment. I want a twenty-four-hour-a-day surveillance on Boris.

Not a whisper of this to Rifka. Say nothing to Ladislaus. Keep attention away from yourself.

Yours,
David

That afternoon, when the family saw Alexis and Katya off on the Moscow train, everything looked normal. The people standing on the platform staring at the Von Glasman sisters with their husbands and their parents said to each other, "What a handsome family. You can't help liking people like that, even if they are Jews and Jew lovers."

The whistle blew. Boris lifted Katya onto the train and stayed with her and Alexis until it started to gather speed. Then he jumped and ran back to Ronya.

Even David smiled when she said, "I was afraid Katya persuaded you to leave me and elope with her."

10

The weeks passed. David and Boris maintained an uneasy truce but remained adversaries. Ruth and Ronya pretended not to notice, but they knew the reckoning was just a matter of time.

At first, everything arranged itself to suit Ronya. Rifka ordered Tamara to keep away from Boris and stop pestering him. She did not think that anything was likely to happen until he got bored and restless. "But your day will come," she promised with assurance. "Meanwhile, enjoy yourself, experiment—I've shown you how to take care." Curiously enough, neither Rifka nor Tamara considered this unnatural or immoral, nor did their attitude toward Ronya change in the slightest. They loved her.

Boris reveled in his new life. The stables presented a fine challenge. Before he could acquire more horses, he needed more space. The new building began: barns, storage sheds, corrals. Boris did all the designing and planning and much of the carpentry. He explored the forest and the family land, feeling that he and the stallion should be able to find their way blindfolded in Ronya's domain. Besides, the forest and the river stood for freedom and adventure, and he needed to make them his. His leisure he spent with Ronya. They rode together, she in stylish riding habits, the tips of her dainty boots peeping out beneath her skirts. They paid calls, Ronya in dashing wide-brimmed hats and the rustle of silk. At night, her hair came down, and they made robust love.

Twenty-three days after they were married, three things happened. Ronya missed her period; it rained; and Boris returned to the big house early, thinking that a little poker or three-handed pinochle at the barracks and a few drinks were just the thing for a drizzly Saturday afternoon.

Though she had been expecting it for days, her misery showed in her face when he told her where he was going. He took her into his arms. "Dove, I've got to return to a man's world."

"Why?" she said mulishly.

"You know why. I've undertaken to breed and train mounts for the Cavalry, so I need spirited horses, and I can't wait much longer before going to Odessa to get them. What's more, I need good men, not grubby muzhiks, and I don't want too many Cossacks around."

Ronya fixed her eyes on him. "I suppose you'll drink a lot and play cards all night."

"Sure," Boris said with a grin, "and dance a lot, and sing a lot—

there's nothing like a Cavalry post on a Saturday night for fun. And if I leave now," he said teasingly, "I'll get there in time to gallop around the ring picking up handkerchiefs full of rubles with my lips."

Anger rising, Ronya wiggled out of his embrace. "Will there be girls?"

"I certainly hope so."

"Will you amuse yourself with them?"

"Look here, Ronya—"

"Will you?" she repeated, adamant.

Because her voice was harsh, Boris almost said, "Maybe," but just then her eyes filled with tears, and she looked little and fragile and vulnerable. He sat down and pulled her into his lap. "I won't amuse myself with women, dove. And—"

Ronya threw her arms around his neck, all at once gay. "Oh, Boris, I love you!"

"Wait, dove, I haven't finished." He went on, very seriously: "I'll never lie to you."

Eyes full of mischief, she said, "And I'll never lie to you, but I might fib a little sometimes." She gave him a last hug and got up quickly. "If you decide to sleep at the barracks, I won't be angry. I'll catch up on my reading for consolation."

The three men assigned to watch Boris considered themselves lucky: well paid, well fed, well housed, they had nothing to do. The girl was a different story. She disliked Kiev and wanted to leave. In all fairness to David, big-bosomed, long-legged Annette with the thick mass of blond hair was Paul's idea. He wanted to get rid of her, and he figured he owed Boris a bit of grief—not that Paul liked Fedor, but blood being thicker than water a little retaliation seemed in order.

Naturally, when she gave the girl her order, Madam Titiana made no mention of Paul's involvement in the affair. She simply suggested that Annette might combine a profitable job with a little vacation in the south at just the right time of year. St. Petersburg was still gloomy with the tail end of winter. It was a tribute to the fascination Paul exercised over his women that Annette was reluctant to take the hint. As all the girls in her house and every soul in the St. Petersburg underworld knew, behind Madam Titiana's little twinkling gypsy eyes lay ruthlessness, and behind the genial welcome for which her house was famous lay infinite power and contacts; it was not at all wise to ignore Madam Titiana's suggestions. A somewhat more pressing mention of Kiev was enough. Annette collected her belongings and asked, "How do I meet Pirov?"

"Hang around the Officers' Club," said Titiana. "Sooner or later, he'll show."

A few minutes on the road, and Boris thought he was being followed. Ten minutes later he knew for sure. He merely grinned and rode on.

The men gave Boris a rousing welcome. Seizing him by the arm, the colonel said, "Pirov, let me order you a drink."

They joined a group of young officers, who were doing a lot of drinking and laughing. After a time, Boris moved his head to indicate a civilian at the far end of the room. "Who's the short fellow in the city clothes, with the sharp eyes?"

The colonel shrugged. "Damned if I know. He's got a pass."

"From whom?"

"Provided by the Admiralty."

"Proper identification?"

"Yes, of course."

Boris surveyed his tail and, guessing it was his father-in-law's doing, almost burst out laughing.

The colonel put down his glass. "Another?"

"No, thanks."

"You want to go upstairs?"

"Yes, sir. I'd like to unpack."

The tall colonel, with the thick graying hair, said, "You're all set, Pirov. I've assigned you an orderly and one of our best rooms—a fireplace, bathroom, and a terrace overlooking the parade ground. We want you to like it here."

"Thank you, sir."

"Sorry I can't dine with you tonight, Pirov, but come to my house next week."

"May I bring my wife?"

The colonel smiled. "I order you to bring your wife. Say Wednesday at eight?"

It was after nine when Boris came down to dinner. By the time the music had started, he was leaning back in his chair drinking black coffee. Annette brought herself to his notice by stopping at his table and saying, "If I had a bottle of champagne, I'd drink it here with you."

"Be my guest."

A few moments later, one of the servants came with the bottle.

Boris smoked a cigarette and watched her drink. Then he said, "Where's your pal?"

The girl looked up from her glass. "I'm everyone's pal."

They danced. The dance concluded, he bought her a drink. They each smoked a cigarette and danced again, and he bought her another drink. From time to time, Boris' eyes rested briefly on the civilian, and it seemed to him that the girl's eyes were on the stranger too. Nearly an hour passed in dancing and drinking, and then the girl said, "Want to go to bed?"

"Can't. I promised my wife I wouldn't."

Her eyes widened—he could see her thinking, *Good God, some excuse* —and she said, "Three wasted weeks in Kiev. I'm so sick and tired of this damn place."

Boris gave her an innocent grin. "What do you mean?"

"Forget it." Annette was very busy lighting her own cigarette. "I talk too much."

"Stay here." He beckoned to the waiter. "Don't let the lady get thirsty." He went into the cardroom and played for an hour or so. When he came back for Annette, he bought a bottle and took her upstairs.

"Sit down," he said. "I'll pour."

That was not what she expected. "Oh, come on. Don't let's waste any more time. I'm sleepy."

"Talk."

Annette looked up at him, bewildered. "What do you expect me to say?"

Boris saw the distrust in her eyes, the tenseness in her body. He put a cigarette between her lips and lit it, took her by the hand, and made her sit down with him on the bed. He put a finger under her chin and turned her face up. "You don't like Kiev, but you can't go back to wherever you came from until you fulfill your assignment, which is to compromise me—right?"

The girl made a choking sound. He dropped his hand. "Relax. I'm going to help you, because your orders fit right into my plan."

Frowning, Annette bent and crushed out her cigarette. When it was thoroughly extinguished she said, "I see." Her mouth twisted into a crooked smile and she started carefully unhooking her dress.

Boris took her hands and put them in her lap. "I want you to concoct a filthy tale. Tell your employer that I shared you in a drunken spree with—"

"Two other girls?"

Boris started to laugh. "That's enough."

Annette had associated with many men, but Boris was outside her experience. There was something about him that she liked. "Don't worry," she said. "I know what to say."

Boris pulled out his wallet and tossed all his money on the coverlet. He lit a cigarette for himself and got off the bed. "Good-bye. Good luck to you." He uncorked the bottle and stepped out of the door, closing it quietly behind him.

No one saw him leave the post. No one heard him enter the house. When Ronya, disturbed in her sleep, opened her eyes slightly, she was in his arms. "Did you win?" she asked sleepily.

"I broke even—I think." Then he put his mouth against hers.

Boris spent the rest of the night thinking about David's shabby tactics. Clearly, the man hated him and wanted to get rid of him. The why of it no longer made much difference. His instincts urged him to force a showdown, and he began to concentrate on ways and means—and consequences. Trained from infancy to be master of a horse, a woman, a situation, Boris dwelled on his enemy's personality. He knew that when the ultimatum came—"Ronya, choose!"—it had to come from David, not from him. He decided that his best weapon was to provide David's agents with plenty to report. Having made his decision, Boris lit a cigarette slowly and pondered the ease with which he contemplated sliding back into the corrupt world of transgression and abandonment. He found himself thinking about Ruth and realized that what little hesitation he felt centered on her. To say nothing of his yearning for Ronya, his deep, all-pervading love, he knew the hold he had on her—the exciting sweetness he alone brought her.

Boris prepared. Whereas in St. Petersburg his escapades just occurred, in Kiev they were done with deliberation or staged. Boris took good care of Ronya. They were of one flesh.

Time passed, and Boris saw that David made no move. His attitude seemed to imply, Do as you please and be damned. Boris' eyes narrowed in thought: *I haven't goaded him enough.* He found himself a town house, shamefully overpriced, with nothing to recommend it except a fantastic view, and paid for it by overdrawing his account by thousands. He furnished it on credit, stocked it with the best of everything, and held open house. His easy and liberal hospitality soon gathered a disreputable circle there, and though Boris himself did not show up often—he found professional tarts tiresome—with each visit tall tales of his debaucheries were carried back to David. Had Boris known why David dawdled, he could have spared himself and Ronya much grief.

David was not satisfied with merely presenting Ronya with a list of Boris' philanderings. What was the use? He could not rid his mind of that evening four months ago when his eyes fastened on Ronya's loveliness as she swung her whip across the body of her lover, evoking in him the response her eyes desired. No, it was too late for a minor skirmish. David sought and found, so he thought, the one thing Ronya could not forgive, could not live with. But he waited—Ruth still looked on Boris lovingly, and Ronya must be undisturbed for three months so as to make sure she would retain his grandson in her belly.

The showdown came at about the time David intended, but somehow not in the way he had intended. It was in a fit of anger that he revealed his secret.

It began with Tamara. One day she arrived uninvited at six in the afternoon, her hair pinned in a chignon atop her head, her lips as red as wine, her skin golden amber. She sat out the conversation and, when they went in to dinner, moved in with them, darting bold, persistent glances at Boris and more often than not, finding his gaze lingering on her.

Dinner was finished when she spoke up. "Boris, is it true that the Tartars give their wives priority, but a Tartar without a sweetheart to love is as unthinkable as a Tartar woman without her braids?"

Boris grinned. "I'll let you know when it's your turn."

Tamara threw back her head and laughed, wild, beautiful, full of life.

Ruth and David knew that Tamara had men and that she gloried in her new freedom, but bringing that freedom into their house was beyond endurance. As Ruth rose in protest, anxiously Ronya said, "Please, Mother, Tamara is only teasing."

But David was on his feet, pale and inflexible. "Boris, a word with you." His voice was very low, but the women stiffened at the sound.

A gleam of excitement came into Boris' eyes, and he got up with relief. At last, he thought, with gratitude for Tamara. He lifted Ruth's hand to his lips as he passed her and followed in David's wake.

In the library the men eyed each other coldly.

"Pull up a chair, Boris."

"I'll stand."

"In that case, I'll keep to the essentials."

Boris waited.

David dropped into an armchair; he did not like Boris looking down at him while he stood. "Am I to assume silence means acquiescence?"

Boris' brows contracted. "Assume what you wish."

David nodded. "In that case," he said slowly, "I must ask you a question. Will you satisfy my curiosity and tell me why you do the things you do? I should very much like to know."

"I've been trying to live up—or rather, down—to your opinion of me, sir."

David leaned forward, his keen eyes peering intently at Boris. Vehemently he hurled his accusation. "Whom were you living down to when you rode against the Jews in a pogrom? Your mother?"

Boris flinched as though struck. "You son of a bitch!" he spat, his voice hoarse and rough with pain. For a minute he stood where he was, rigid, immobile, forcing down the black rage that possessed him, dragging his eyes away from the narrowed, hating, black eyes before him, willing his body to move. Stiffly he opened the door and reeled as though drunk down the central hall, colliding with Ronya and Tamara in the dining-room doorway. Ruth was just behind them. He lifted Ronya off her feet and swung her away from Tamara. "Get the hell out of here. Go home," he bellowed harshly.

"Oh my God," Ruth gasped. She shoved Tamara aside and ran to David.

Ghastly white, Ronya sagged against Boris. "Did you lift a hand against my father?" she cried despairingly.

He wet his dry lips. "No, dove, no."

Without a backward glance at Tamara, who was left to make her bewildered and disconsolate way home, Boris mounted the stairs with Ronya in his arms, carried her into her room in the dark, put her gently down on her chaise, and turned up one lamp. Moving quickly, he found brandy and glasses in a cabinet Ronya kept stocked to please him and thrust half a glassful into her hand.

"Please, Boris, what happened between you and Father?"

He looked closely into her face. Her color was coming back. "He's all right. No need to worry about him."

"What about you, my darling?"

Boris lowered himself into his special big armchair, took a cigarette from a white jade box and a match from his pocket. "Here, take a puff."

"You first."

He drew on the cigarette deeply, blew a smoke ring, and absently ground it out.

Ronya stared into the hazel eyes flecked with green and gold and waited. Boris finished the brandy. "Get undressed, Ronya."

She pushed her glass away and started to unpin her hair.

He was already in bed when she came to him, her body unconcealed in a flimsy kimono over a transparent nightgown. It perturbed him somewhat that her pregnancy did not show. Pondering his own perversity that now for the first and only time he wanted her pregnant, he propped up the pillows for her.

"Come, Boris. Please."

Boris turned toward her. "Tomorrow your father will tell you I rode in a pogrom. He'll make it sound bad. I want to tell you about it myself—"

Ronya's eyes grew big and her hands flew to her ears. In a voice that tore at him, she cried, "No, I'm carrying our child—I don't want to hear."

104

Boris took her hands in his. "You've got to," he said softly.

She closed her fingers tightly over his and held on.

"My mother loathed my birthday because it fell on the day the French dragoons and the Turks whipped the Russian hussars and Cossacks," he began with self-loathing. "Instead of a celebration and presents like other children, I was forced into some senseless daring adventure. On each anniversary of the fall of Sevastopol, my mother acted like a lunatic. Sometimes a brawl with the Cossacks melted her fury. Sometimes she called some of her men together and they rode against the Jews—looting, sometimes burning. If the Jews' shrieks were loud enough, she rarely harmed anyone, but if the Jewish streets were deserted, she did the shrieking herself. 'Discourtesy! Impudence! Folly! No one to greet me.' She saw no inconsistency in the fact that at the same time other Tartars, also hers, were patrolling and guarding the dachas of rich Jews from all over the Ukraine.

"By the time I was fourteen, I was already near my present height. I was skilled with dagger and sword, expert with a gun, and even better with my fists. I could find my way in any direction without a compass, and my mastery of horsemanship was total. With the audacity and ingenuity my mother taught me, I was winning competitions against circus riders and ferocious Cossacks."

Ronya felt a growing compassion; her fingers relaxed their hold. Looking into her upturned face, he sighed, "Ronya, Ronya.

"Today I realize my mother must have liked the girl and thought her just plain lucky to get me. Anyway, she picked her, arranged for no more than a bit of modest looting—no arson, no beatings, no destruction. Her plan went like clockwork. Two armed Tartars burst into the girl's home and dragged her family into the street. It was a cold, damp night. I can still hear their pleas. My mother ignored them and concentrated on me. 'All yours,' she said, and shoved me inside." Boris stopped, but then went resolutely on.

"The girl was a surprise—a pale little thing with delicate features and long smooth braids. Her eyes were remarkable. For the first time, I saw *Judenschmerz*. I wanted to run, but there was my mother outside, leaning against the door smoking a cigarette.

"The girl backed away from me. I felt sorry for her and was looking about for a way to make her understand that she need not be afraid, but before I could speak a word she screamed, 'If you want me you'll have to take me dead.'

"I lowered my voice to a whisper. 'I don't want you, but unless we fool the Tartar woman, she'll give you to someone else. Will you trust me and do as I say?'

"She stared at me in terror.

105

"I said, 'Start screaming, and make it loud, while I rough you up a little.'

"Her eyes were fixed on me in horror as I ripped her blouse and skirt and mussed her hair. She struggled and screamed as much as I wanted—I don't suppose she believed me. Then I retreated to a corner across the room. 'Now, stay quiet,' I said.

"I'd never had a girl. It was she who whispered from her side of the room, 'I think you've had enough time.'

"I made her lie on the floor, and I bent down and made her scratch my face. I said, 'Start whimpering, and when I open the door make noises like a wounded animal.'

"She lifted her eyes to me and whispered, 'What's your name?'

"I told her.

"She said, 'Thank you, Boris Pirov.' She was smiling a little.

"My mother judged me a man: I had ravished a Jewish maiden. The next day she entered me in military school and left me there, and after graduation I was accepted as a cadet at the Cavalry Academy. In St. Petersburg I learned a lot about women."

Boris' voice stopped abruptly.

"Darling," Ronya said at last, "I remind you of that girl?"

Boris' gaze lingered on her beauty. "A little," he agreed slowly.

She smiled as her fingers reached his lips in a soft caress. "I'm glad. Now," she said, "we must decide: Do you want to leave?"

Boris drew her to him and embraced her hungrily. "No, dove, I want a fresh start, I want us to stay a family."

With these words, Boris smashed David's hold on Ronya.

Across the corridor, a heated exchange was taking place.

Ruth was clutching the arms of her chair. "I don't believe it. Boris could no more participate in plunder and rape than you could."

"In a narrow Jewish street lined with dingy houses and small shops dozens of weeping men and women witnessed the wretched crime."

"But David, you admitted that later the girl swore Boris never touched her, that he was kind to her."

David shrugged. "No one stood in the open doorway watching, but it is difficult to imagine an innocent girl managing to fake a rape with such consummate skill."

"The Odessa Jews must be mistaken. The girl spoke the truth. I know Boris."

"Then you declare yourself Boris' ally?" he asked icily.

"David." Ruth took a deep breath. "Your evidence against Boris is worthless. Don't degrade yourself by burdening Ronya with it."

David's voice lost none of its firmness. "No matter what happened or did not happen, tomorrow I shall present Ronya with *all* the data I have against Boris. She'll leave with us. If, however, she remains stubborn, she'll come later. She's bound to. It's inevitable. Her infatuation will spend itself."

"Speak of the pogrom," Ruth said, rising, "and you'll go without me. I'll stay with the children."

David stared at her, genuinely shocked.

"Please, David. I beg you to do as I ask."

David took Ruth's arm and steered her toward their bedroom. "I won't mention the pogrom," he said finally.

Summoned, Ronya went to him. David was standing. "Shut the door, love."

Ronya took a chair, as David seated himself at his desk. Picking up a bundle of letters, he said, "A complete history. Do you want the details?"

"You think I don't know?"

"Does it not disturb you?"

"Somewhat."

He was unprepared for her apparent tranquillity. "Do you want to say anything before I go on?"

"Father, I don't want Boris tame—only faithful. An occasional spree of vodka and cards—"

"Faithful! Why does a man with a home buy a house unless he needs it for his mistress?"

Ronya felt a sinking sensation.

"Ronya!"

She collected herself quickly. "You caught me by surprise, Father. Where is the house?"

"I have no address for the moment, only a notification from the bank that Boris has seriously overdrawn his account and that the deed he left as security is worthless because he paid more than twice what the house is worth."

Though Ronya did not dismiss entirely the possibility of a woman, she thought it unlikely. But she did not shrug off the house. What did it mean? Then an idea struck her. Perhaps Boris, more affected by David's insults than he admitted, had acquired the house for her.

"Father," she said, "you must promise me to take no notice. The house is clearly Boris' affair. Let him carry out his plans without interference from you and without being answerable to you."

"My child, you talk nonsense. However, it does not matter. I am taking you and your mother out of Russia for a time. Once your marriage is annulled and Boris is legally and physically removed from our lives, we shall be notified in Vienna and we'll return immediately. I want my grandson born here in this house."

Ronya heard her father's words and suddenly felt a welling anger.

"What a hateful thing, Father, to scheme against Boris. What has he done wrong? His first reaction to an attractive woman is interest—what man's isn't? He likes vodka—what Russian doesn't? He maintains his ties with the Odessa Tartars—why not?"

David sighed. "I do not understand you, Ronya. My sources have gathered shocking evidence. Boris Pirov is the most easily seduced man in the province."

"I dispute your evidence, Father."

"My child, I am not unmindful of your loyalty, but I will not permit you to squander your life on an irresponsible libertine."

"Why are you determined to destroy Boris with trumped-up charges? Where is your justice? If you want evidence, go back to the boy who never had a sister, never had a sweetheart—only a mother with a swagger to her walk, who was often cruel to him, who forced him into hair-raising stunts. Still, she was his mother, and he relied on her."

Moved in spite of himself, David said, "I gave Boris Pirov the chance to leave behind the world of ruffians, loose women, and vulgarity. I credited him with the decency to be grateful."

Ronya thought, *Monstrous, Father, monstrous.* "Yes," she said, hardening, "let's talk about what you did for Boris, who came into this household fancying himself a son. You made him a stranger, an outsider, a Gentile on probation. Did you once invite him to dinner, just the two of you? Did you ever ask his advice, even his opinion? Did you ever let him do something nice for you, just so you could say thank you? No! Whenever he came into a room, mother's face lit up with a smile of welcome. Yours tightened. Always, you were 'just leaving.' He suppressed his hurt, and it wasn't until you pushed him too far that he took to cards and a bit of hard drinking."

David dabbed his forehead lightly with his handkerchief. "I have built my whole life around you, Ronya, my child."

A great resurgence of love for him took hold of her. Her big eyes brimming with tears, she said beseechingly, "Reach out your hand to Boris and call him 'Son.' I don't want to give you up, Father."

"Too late, love. For your sake, to protect you, I cannot. The enchantment will pass, I swear it."

Ronya left him. She went quickly. Changing into street clothes, she walked rapidly down to the stables. As she suspected, Boris was on the lookout for her. He smiled, but his eyes were serious. "Come inside."

"I was about to ask you to drive me into town."

"Harness Lady," he called out to Sad Eyes.

His grasp on her wrist gentle, Boris lifted her into the open carriage. The reins jingled as he shook up the mare. "Where to?"

"The bank."

"Did you reach a settlement?" he asked quietly.

Ronya nodded.

"They're leaving?"

She nodded again. "Vienna."

"I gather that your father regards me—" As he searched for the right word, she lifted her face and stared into his eyes. "He *never* mentioned the pogrom."

Boris returned her stare unbelievingly for a moment. "Your father is easy to hate, but hard to dislike."

When Ronya entered, Von Kaufman, Kiev's foremost banking official, almost ran the length of the room to greet her. He took her hand and raised it to his lips.

"I am very angry with you," she said, pulling back her hand.

He looked stricken. "Ronya, my dear, what have I done to incur your displeasure—?" He cast a swift look around him and hurried her out of earshot of his employees. Ronya made no explanation until the doors to his office were closed, but then her reticence disappeared, and the astounded man listened aghast.

"Believe me, Ronya, I had no wish to invite your anger. Letters of that sort go out as a matter of routine. However, I shall transfer the money from your account into Boris' at once." He still looked worried. "Am I forgiven?"

Ronya shook her head. "No, not until you promise you'll talk about my husband to me and to no one else—ever. Do you understand?"

The banker pondered: *And what if Von Glasman inquires?*

Ronya divined his thought. "Well, which is it to be? David von Glasman or Ronya Pirov?"

The banker's frown deepened. "It's a difficult choice."

They looked at each other.

"All right," Von Kaufman said softly. "I'll tell my old friend that you've made certain matters confidential between us."

"Thank you. And the address of the house?"

They made their way home in silence. Absently holding the reins, Boris lit cigarette after cigarette, disturbed that Ronya meant to keep her business at the bank her own secret. Not that he particularly wanted to know, but her silence was so uncharacteristic, almost ominous—

Indeed it was. Ronya knew the house stood between her and Boris, and she was desperate to know whether he meant to go there to get away from her. Suddenly she recalled how her father judged the purchase, and she hated the house. But she did not speak of it. She would wait until she saw in his eyes that the house did not matter to him. He had forgotten it.

As if he could feel her unhappiness, Boris obeyed his intuitive impulse. "Love," he said, "there's an inn nearby. It's right on the beach. Let's not go home."

Ronya looked up and smiled mischievously. "But I have no change of clothing."

"Who needs clothes to make love?"

Moving closer to each other, they met in laughter.

For the next few days, Boris and David avoided each other. Boris spent the whole day at the stables and took Ronya out to dine. David placed himself at Ruth's disposal, and she kept him busy mingling with old friends, none of whom guessed that anything was wrong. Even the house servants accepted as fact the announcement that master and mistress were to pay a prolonged visit to her people in Vienna. David's lawyer assumed some sort of power struggle, but his banker believed that David wanted Ronya to learn her way around the tough and competitive world of big business, deliberately given that impression by David, who murmured such banalities as "Experience the best teacher . . . in my lifetime . . . if she needs help, I'll still be around . . ."

Rifka and Tamara were invited to dinner by Ruth, on their last evening in Kiev, and Boris, who had no intention of appearing, was persuaded to go into dinner only after a very confidential talk with his mother-in-law. Wandering about the house tense and restless, he came upon her and, to make certain they were left alone, took her up to an unoccupied attic room. There, amid old trunks and forgotten furniture, he ungently seized her hands.

"Ruth, my mother," he said, "listen. I don't want you to go, it isn't right. I'll take Ronya, and we'll start a home of our own. Believe me, *Ruth my mother,* I'll take care of her, good care of her."

"Will you go back on active duty?" Ruth asked quietly.

"No, that's no life for Ronya."

"What will you do? I suppose you have given it some thought."

"I've spent long hours thinking."

Ruth guessed the significance of his reluctance to elaborate. "Will you live by your wits?" she asked. "Turn professional and use your reputation to draw the crowds?"

He met her searching look. "Yes, horses and cards. In two years, maybe less, I'll have my own stables again."

Ruth was wise enough not to show her disapproval. "Boris dear, do you want to leave this house and this land?"

There was directness, truth, and pain in his "No!"

"Come here, my son."

He dropped to the floor and laid his head in her lap. Twisting a golden curl around her finger, she said, "Hear me out. I want to go, really I do. Once away from here, little by little and with the help of God, I'll teach David to live without Ronya. Oddly enough, when David has mastered this, we can come home to you and Ronya and to our grandchild. That's why we must go."

Boris regarded her worshipfully. "If you were my real mother," he said, "I would be different."

"I hope not. I love you the way you are."

Boris felt a tear spill down his cheek: In all his memory, he could not remember a tear before.

"And now, will you do something for me?"

"Anything."

"Please come down to dinner this evening."

At close range, Rifka looked much older than she had a few months ago. Dressed in solid, heavy black—even her cloth-covered buttons were black—she wore a black shawl over her shoulder, no makeup, and not a single jewel. Tamara, by contrast, came dressed in riches. As soon as she saw the flash of her skirt, Ronya said, "I never saw so much gold embroidery. You look like the sultan's favorite concubine." But Tamara didn't laugh, her eyes burned into Boris'. He was unmoved, thinking about David and wondering why he delayed coming down. He went to a window and watched the moon disappear behind a cloud. Ronya joined him there and just as she said, "Shall I go see?" she heard her father come in. Boris remained at the window.

After kissing Ronya, the first thing David did was to go to Rifka. He gave her a grave appraising look and said, "You've lost weight. Are you ill?"

"No, consumed." Rising, she gave David a measured look and added, "With curiosity and with wretchedness." She hesitated a fraction of a minute, then said, "Your decision is cowardly. It's madness and, by narrowing our family circle, you leave me with no age peers—with no friends either."

Boris was interested to know what David's reply would be. He shifted his position and turned his head in their direction, at the same time seeing that Ronya watched with attention to every word and that Ruth sat, her face absolutely tragic, watching, never taking her eyes off David.

David automatically nodded his head in greeting and then took no further interest in Boris. He returned to Rifka. "That's one point of view."

It was a direct rejection, but Rifka refused to believe that the relationship between them had widened beyond repair. David was still the one she most loved, the one she most respected and enjoyed, and the person to whom she felt closest. She turned to Ruth. Ruth nodded her understanding. A minute passed in which they stayed in absolute silence, and then David spoke. "The premise basic to your logic is that I still care about you. I do not. You grow old, Rifka, my cousin. I cannot help you and you cannot help me."

It took a moment for her to understand. Then she turned a greenish gray, her knees gave way and, sagging, she fell to the floor.

Nothing changed in David's face.

Boris picked her up in his arms and stepped to the sofa. There, cold to his touch, he put her down. Rifka lay back exhausted, her eyes closed. Boris turned and looked at Tamara. "Bring a brandy."

"I'll get it." Ronya hurried over and held the glass while Rifka sipped from it. "Let me rest a little."

Boris stepped back.

Rifka gazed up at David, her wide dark eyes were stunned. He gave her a cold, disdainful look and turned to Ruth. "I will eat in my room. Tea and toast, and perhaps a baked apple."

Her throat too dry to answer, Ruth walked a few steps and automatically, before realizing it, pulled the velvet cord that buzzed a maid.

David left without speaking again.

Still sipping brandy, Rifka allowed herself to be helped to her feet. She walked with Boris into the dining room. Within a few minutes dinner was served. It was a magnificent meal. But with no murmur of conversation and only the soft clatter of sterling and crystal, it was soon over. After coffee, with no censure in her voice for David, Ruth said firmly, "Tamara, your mother is weary. Take her home. You, Ronya, go to your father."

Ronya went, walking slowly, hearing her father's voice saying the things he said to Rifka and hoping he wouldn't attack Boris again. Ronya could see she was expected. Finally David said very sadly, "Ronya, my child, when you have reached the limit of your endurance—"

Ronya shook her head. "Don't, Father. Don't keep on saying the same thing, because we both know I won't leave Boris nor will he let me go." Then Ronya said, "Say good-bye to me now, Father. I'll not come down tomorrow."

David opened his arms.

11

In later years Boris was to realize that when Ronya was hurt and sad, she made a conscious effort to refocus her mind on the business of living. When her parents had gone and she came out of her room, she looked drawn but there was a no-nonsense air about her, as if to say, "David, my father, entrusted this land and its people to me and I will be worthy of his trust." She began to make changes immediately. Handing Lydia a big bunch of keys, she put her in charge of all the household servants.

By dinner time, eight hours after her parents' train had pulled out of the railroad station, the servants were finished with scrubbing and polishing and struggling with heavy furniture. The house was full of color, and the smells from the kitchen made Boris' mouth water when he came in on his way from the stables. He found Ronya, in a strikingly deep neckline, seated at her dressing table pinning a jewel in her hair.

He kissed her and pulled off his boots.

"You're late."

He pulled off his socks. "Are we entertaining?"

"Each other and Father Tromokov."

Boris wiggled his toes.

"I thought you'd be in sooner. I wanted to tell you about a plan I have before I told Father Tromokov."

"I was very busy, Ronya."

Ronya rose and, turning her back to him, said, "Unhook me, please."

Boris grinned and obliged, and his hands slid from the last hook to stroke her back, his eyes appreciatively running over her smooth whiteness.

Ronya moved away and carefully laid down the dress. "Come, I'll talk to you while you shave and bathe—I'll even scrub your back."

By the time the priest had entered the house and drunk a little vodka, Ronya's powers of persuasion had triumphed; while not exactly enthusiastic about her idea of a school for the peasant children, Boris had at least agreed to the experiment.

Ivan Tromokov was sprawled in the largest chair in the library. The summer air drifted gently in through the open windows, the vodka was spreading a pleasant warmth through his body, and here to crown it all came Ronya, glowing in a dress the color of a rose.

"Well!" he exclaimed, getting gallantly to his feet, "you light up the room, Ronya!"

Ronya laughed and whirled about, her skirts flying. "You see," she said, glancing up at Boris, "Tamara isn't the only one with dancing feet."

"It's not her dancing feet," Boris teased, "it's her swaying hips."

During the hour they were at the table, Ronya and the priest talked about the school. Boris listened without speaking, though at times his face mirrored his thoughts.

Disappointed by his lack of enthusiasm, Ronya said, "Still unconvinced?"

"In a way. Teach a peasant to read and write and he'll want a better life."

The priest chuckled. "Can't give you an argument on that."

"No, no," Boris said uncomfortably, "you don't understand what I mean."

"Now, Boris, I know you're not mouthing the idiocies put out by the reactionaries. Speak your mind."

"How about the work force? What happens to the economy, especially in the Ukraine, if the peasants leave the fields?"

"Machines will do the work. Russia will move on to a more sophisticated economy, more urban than rural."

"Factories! Like Moscow."

"Boris," Ronya broke in, "some day Russia and progress must meet head on."

Boris pushed away his dessert plate. "Dove, I'll run the stables, you run the estate. When you need a strong right arm, I'll be here. Only explain this: If education for the masses is desirable, how is it that David von Glasman, obviously a generous man and a strong believer in learning, never established a school?"

The priest and Ronya exchanged glances. There was a smile in her eyes as she said, "My eagle still knows nothing about being a Jew." Then, turning serious, she spoke directly to Boris. "Von Glasman the Jew was obliged to tread lightly. He dared not risk projects frowned upon by his neighbors. The Jew's daughter, merely by marrying the national hero and adding Pirov to her name, may dare more."

"Do you mind if I amplify a bit?" the priest asked.

"I'd like to hear," Boris said, offering the priest a cigarette.

As the match flared, Lydia came in with a fresh pot of coffee, and it was not until she had gone back to the kitchen that the priest went on. "David did a lot for us peasants, but he had to soften his good deeds with good judgment. Not too much, too fast, too openly. He had to protect himself. The landowners are a tight group, jealous and mean, and they take alarm easily. They grow fat on excessive rents and killing work hours. In this rich wheat country, the peasant slaves for mere

114

existence, he's virtually a chattel. Mark my words, Boris, riots and violence and revolution will be the answer."

Boris thought, *Nonsense,* but shrugged eloquently.

Yet before they left the table, it had been settled—a teacher and classes three days a week for the first year, using the church as a schoolhouse.

Ronya rose, meaning to leave the men together, but Boris paused as he opened the door for her. "Come into the library with us, dove. We'll drink a toast to Ruth and David."

As they sipped their brandy, the conversation passed to the gypsies, and Boris brought up a subject close to his heart. From the beginning he had passionately resented their routine destruction of the forest in the interest of sheer selfishness. But it wasn't Rifka's greed he found so surprising, it was David's indifference. Until now, however, Boris hesitated to put his feelings into words. David's departure put an end to his hesitancy. "At the rate she's cutting, in another generation there'll be no forest," he said to Ronya.

She looked at him in dismay. If his prediction were true her children's children would never know that strange, wonderful wilderness of green smells, leafed shade, splashing streams, deep blackness, and wild animals. The priest, too, chafed at the wanton way in which the gypsies cut timber. "Let Boris put an end to it as quickly as possible, Ronya."

"Shall I talk to Rifka?" he asked.

"No, darling," said Ronya. "The responsibility is mine." Then she excused herself. Begging the priest to stay and talk to Boris, she went upstairs. She made herself ready for bed, then sat down to write to Katya.

> Dearest Katya,
>
> What a day! Boris drove them to the station. Mother insisted. "For appearances' sake," she said.
>
> As I look back at the last few months, I am at a complete loss to understand Father. It seems that from the moment Boris actually became mine, Father set himself up as a Messiah whose sole purpose in life was to save me from the man I love. Over and over, he harped upon Boris' alleged weaknesses—women, cards, vodka— only he made it sound like rapist, cheat, drunkard.
>
> Boris is still downstairs with Father Tromokov. Well, at last he has his school. Let's make him a present of a regular schoolhouse next year.
>
> In regard to your questions: Of course Tamara is in and out of the house and flirts with Boris. The bigger I get, the better she's going to look. I don't understand why she doesn't get herself a man of her own.
>
> Katya, I miss you so, and now you'll be in Vienna for the holidays instead of coming here.

Darling, I hear Boris.

Good-night, dear Katya. Kiss Alexis for me, and Paul, too, when you see him.

Much love,
Ronya

Boris came through the door, whistling. "I thought I'd find you asleep, considering the day you've had."

Ronya loosened her hair and let it tumble to her waist. "I'm not tired."

Boris studied her a moment. In repose her face seemed sad. "Do you miss him already?"

Ronya sensed his fear and did not answer immediately. She went to him, and when he took her in his arms she said, her voice low and gentle, "Not him, darling—them. In all my daydreams, I imagined you for me, and for Katya I picked someone more like Father. I used to think we'd all live here in this house, loving each other, and the house would ring with the laughter of family and friends and children. Many, many children."

"I know," Boris said quietly. Then softly, "Do you know why I love you?"

"Why?"

"Because you smell so good."

Ronya's dark eyes went even darker.

Boris carried her into bed, kissing her as he went. Much later, holding her against his heart, he whispered, "There's nobody on earth like you, Ronya. Nobody."

In the morning, Ronya's head was still resting on his shoulder. He gazed at her delicate loveliness, put off getting up, and soon fell asleep again. When next he opened his eyes, Ronya was bending over him, with searching, exploring fingers. The sounds of their lovemaking filled the room.

"I feel so happy," she said at last.

"I should sleep in my own room."

"It's still all right."

"Did the doctor say so?"

Ronya said mischievously, "The doctor said that I am a young lady of extraordinary physical strength, who requires being made love to at least twice a day."

Boris grinned, kissed the tip of her nose, and glanced at the clock. It was a little after eleven. He leaped to his feet.

At breakfast Ronya was strangely quiet. Boris wondered whether

116

David, forgotten during their lovemaking, had surfaced between them again. He shook his head. *Forget David,* he told himself. He picked up his glass and finished his tea.

"Boris, are you as good as you were when you first won the national championship?"

Only momentarily was he taken by surprise. "I'm better."

"In what way?"

"I'm heavier, I'm stronger. I have the kind of confidence that comes with winning five years in a row."

"That's good."

Boris hadn't the faintest suspicion of what she had in mind.

"How long does it take to get ready for international competition?"

Of course—the stallion! He threw back his head in a roar of laughter. "Well, now, that depends. If I were still in the Cavalry, training would be easy. I'd swear off women, spend my seven or eight hours in bed sleeping, and my days—"

"Stop teasing. You have five months less nineteen days to get ready."

It was tempting, no denying it. His whole life so far had prepared him for this one event—winning the world championship and adding to the folklore of the Tartars. He could see it all: the excitement of Paris, the uniforms, the posters, the color, the pageantry, the parade with the horses at a canter through slush and snow, the brass bands, the unbelievable feats of bravery, the fierce competition, the stallion at full gallop, the crowds, the cheers. And, the victory his, the homecoming.

Boris could feel Ronya's fathomless eyes on him, guessing his vivid imaginings, sensing his innermost desires. He lifted his eyes to her. "But what about you, dove?"

"You'll be back in time. And bring back the title, my eagle."

Boris swept her upstairs to their bedroom. She lost count of the number of his one-arm push-ups with her sitting on his back, inhaling and exhaling with her on his stomach, the leg lifts with her on his knees. When it was over, he was not even breathing hard. He took a cold bath and donned work clothes. He had not meant to take her along, but Ronya was already in pants and riding boots. Boris ran seven miles his first day of training; while Ronya, her glistening braids falling to her waist Cossack fashion—one over her bosom, one over her back—jogged along on a gentle mare.

The perfection of the day held all through the evening. They ate from trays in the library, and then Boris went upstairs and she curled up with a book. It was quite late when she crept into bed without making a sound, but even in his deep sleep Boris felt her and opened his arms.

He rose at dawn and set off for the stables. A ringing neigh shrilled out from one of the stalls. Boris headed for his recently acquired wild mare. Her nostrils flared, her eyes whitened, she reared and plunged forward, trying to escape her stall. Boris wanted to include in his performance some ferocious stunts spectacularly Russian, and for long minutes he studied the mare but finally decided against her—she was tough and beautiful with her sleek brown coat but, wild as the wind, it would take too long to train her. Boris walked slowly through the stables, appraising every horse in the stalls; until finally, besides the stallion, he picked three horses to take to France, all splendid, powerful, jet black, all carrying their size with easy grace. Reared for battle, instructed in the art of competition, these horses were trained to follow all commands and fear nothing, especially loud frightening noises.

With Tartar patience and expertise, Boris set about the important business of making the stallions understand that from now on it was all work—teamwork—no fighting, no lashing out with their forelegs, no thundering around each other, tails flying. The horses sensed Boris' inner excitement and they worked hard, each horse doing his best for him. At about eleven he led the horses down to the river and swam with them, and they returned to the stables, refreshed and jaunty, to find young spectators assembled there. Word of Boris' morning activities had percolated through the stables and out into the village. While the horses were fed and rested, the boys and girls squatted on the ground and waited.

By late afternoon the practice ring was jammed with women who had left their houses and with men who had abandoned the fields to watch the master leap from horse to horse. When the black horses began to tire, Boris sent them back to the stable and mounted his white stallion. The happy cheering crowd loved this horse madly because he needed neither a tight rein nor the flick of a whip to follow commands. As Boris, riding bareback, gently stroked him, the stallion pranced around playful as a puppy. Then Boris whispered into his ear and, nose uplifted, the stallion shot forward in wild abandon.

Ronya arrived just in time to see Tamara push her way through the crowd and run alongside the horse. As she gathered herself to jump, Boris reached down and lifted her over the stallion's shoulders. Standing body to body, they flew around the ring. Turning to face the stallion's tail, Boris caught sight of Ronya less than fifty paces away. In the minutes it took to slow down the stallion, lower Tamara to the ground, dismount, and disentangle himself from the audience that swarmed around him, Ronya disappeared.

He ran down the path that led to the house, but she was nowhere to be seen. She watched him from behind a tree and, when he was out of sight, picked up her skirts and ran the other way toward the camp. By the time she reached Rifka's door, waiting for Tamara, she had a grip on herself.

"Listen," she said, stalking into Rifka's elegant living room as Tamara arrived. "Keep away from my husband."

Tamara glanced up at her through long lashes. "I love him."

Love! Ronya wheeled on her savagely. "No, you don't, you just need a man."

Tamara sat carelessly on the edge of a table and swung her long, shapely legs, laughing. "Ronya, you're still naïve. It's not just any man I need—or even a special man—it's your golden eagle. When you chose, you chose for both of us."

Ronya gasped. Then she launched into a torrent of invective.

Springing up, Tamara put her arms around her. "Stop, Ronya, stop, it's bad for the baby."

Just then Rifka came in and took in the situation at a glance. "A Cossack isn't a Cossack without a horse," she said, "and love is like death. You can't argue with it. Make peace and stay friends. You'll both face your fate."

"Well?" Tamara smiled, still cradling Ronya in her arms.

Ronya struggled with herself. "The mouth of a wolf you have, never satisfied," but she touched Tamara's hand for a brief moment, and when Rifka said, "Stay for supper," she accepted, mollified.

All evening Boris waited for her, first angry, then remorseful. At about nine, a vague alarm took hold of him and he stormed into Lydia's bedroom. "Where is she?"

In spite of her better judgment, Lydia felt sorry for him. Her broad shrewd face creased sympathetically. "Try Rifka's house."

His eyes narrowed to slits. "Why the devil would she go there?"

With absolute simplicity Lydia said, "Ronya and Tamara love each other. They always have. They always will."

Boris found them gay and laughing. Gripping her wrist hard, he pulled Ronya to her feet. "I'm glad you're enjoying yourself."

Her eyes bright, she said defiantly, "I'm pleased you're glad. I'm enjoying myself *very* much."

His grip tightened. "Come on."

With the reins of his horse looped over his arm, Boris led Ronya home in silence. The stables were no place for him to train. Besides, he needed an indoor ring as well. He decided to get up with the sun and move the horses to the Cavalry post. Carefully he stamped out his cigarette. And there was Tamara: It would be senseless to get mixed up with her. Once conquered, she'd grow stale, become a millstone around his neck. He must train hard.

Everything was going well. All day Boris worked, increasing his stamina and skill. His nights, unless he was too tired or too hungry, he spent at home. Eating lightly, he turned in early and slept a dreamless sleep. His path and Tamara's seldom crossed. Ronya was content: There remained only four weeks before the competition and about seven or eight weeks before her confinement.

On the nineteenth of November, the day before Boris' departure, it started to snow lightly late in the afternoon, and Boris rode in after dinner, his gray gelding patched with white. A groom came to take the horse, and Boris swung himself out of the saddle and headed for the house. He was glad to be home.

He found Ronya in the library, drinking coffee in a warm circle of lamplight. She put down her cup and said, "I've been praying for snow, so now, with no time left to work the horses, it snows."

"It doesn't matter, dove. No horse of mine will be beaten by weather." He took her hands and kissed her. "Has Sergey written?"

"Today. The post came shortly after eleven." She handed him the letter.

Hôtel des Invalides
Paris

Dear Ronya and Boris,

For the last five days I have been quietly lodged at this obscure hotel, whose one claim to fame is that Napoleon once lived here.

Colonel Georges Bernard, the son-in-law of enormously rich Alsatian Jews, who has recently returned from service with the African Light Cavalry, has offered to stable your horses and house your men in his villa, which is barely an hour's ride from St. Lazare Station. You'll only need three men, and Fedor is made to order for the job. If you want four more horses in sympathy with the brutes you've already trained, Colonel Bernard will supply them.

Boris, you will be living at 99 Rue de Varenne, which has a bedroom suite and two additional bedrooms. I have chosen it because the drawing room is admirably suited for entertaining. It is a luxurious room with a particularly fine gilded ceiling. The house comes staffed.

The weather: The outdoor events will take place in snow possibly, in slush certainly; snow followed by rain is typical of Paris in the winter. It might be well to count on sharp frost and fierce winds. Fog is also a possibility. Four years ago, two riders were lost for days.

Too bad, Boris, you are to see Paris in the bluish gray of winter, its chestnut trees leafless. Paris should be seen, for the first time, in late spring or early summer when its streets are packed with people, its rooftops glowing in the sun, its gardens, profusions of green dotted with tulips, peonies, and begonias.

120

I earnestly hope that everything is to your liking. I would prefer to remain in Paris and welcome you, but unfortunately I am compelled to return to Geneva to attend to a business matter.

Bonne chance. Au revoir.

Yours,
Sergey

Boris concluded that Sergey's specialty was spending Von Glasman money. One thing for certain: He was not staying by himself in a house with a gilded ceiling.

"It happens, Boris darling, that you're not staying by yourself. The suite is to be occupied by the lady who has rented the house, and you will be sharing a bathroom with her daughter, who will be using the larger of the two bedrooms."

"Ruth! Katya!" he exclaimed.

"Surprised?"

"Overjoyed."

Boris was in bed before Ronya completed her toilette. She looked out of the window as she closed the curtains. "It's snowing harder." She put out the light and slid into his arms.

"The train leaves midafternoon, but we shall have to leave early enough to get the horses loaded."

Ronya nodded in acknowledgment and decided it was the right time to tell Boris about the doctor, who in all probability was already on his way from Vienna. How like her father to give her a resident obstetrician as a present.

Boris said nothing for several minutes. "How old is the doctor?"

"Mother's letter did not say, but he must be quite old—he is a *Herr Professor.*"

Boris imagined him. Fleshy, not much hair, a kindly face, no particular coloring, good hands. "Tell him to take good care of my dove."

Early the next morning Boris rose. After swallowing a glass of tea, he went to the camp, where he found Fedor drinking warm beer. The room was untidy, and two women, one stoutish and one rather striking, were sitting at a table, gossiping and eating kasha. Of all the children, only one was there, a small bright-eyed boy.

The woman turned surprised eyes on Boris. Fedor's expression did not change.

Boris grinned. "You've heard about Paris?"

Fedor nodded.

"I can use you."

Fedor's eyes showed interest.

Boris' grin widened. "You might enjoy it. We leave today."

Fedor stood up and spilled the beer into the sink. "I'll be ready."

Boris returned to his bedroom and his sleeping wife. "Wake up, dove."

Her face buried in the pillow, Ronya murmured sleepily.

He took her into his arms, as she rubbed her eyes and half sat up. "Promise me—"

"Ssh, dove," Boris placed a finger over her lips. "It doesn't need to be said."

Ronya's heart warmed, and she wound her arms around his neck.

Boris kissed her over and over. "I love you, Ronya. I'll be lonely without you."

He walked out of the room quickly.

12

Ronya, my own,

I love you, I love you, and if it were not for Mother and Katya, I think I might turn around and come home.

I've not put the horses through their paces so far—I'm letting them get used to the damp chill of Paris. At present, I'm leaving a lot to Fedor and Sad Eyes and devoting myself to some lovely ladies—one quite ancient.

I've seen Notre Dame and Sacré Coeur and the Louvre and Versailles, strolled along the grand boulevards, and drunk innumerable *apéritifs*.

I must present myself at the embassy before Monday. I am told our ambassador is arranging an elaborate reception for us.

Dove, this is the longest letter I have ever written.

Do you miss me? If you don't, do, and if you do, miss me more. I love you, Ronya. Take good care of yourself.

Yours always,
Boris

P.S. Nearly forgot. I like Georges Bernard. He smells of horses, and saddle leather and, because he's passionate for escargot, slightly of garlic.

Love,
B

Dearest Ronya,

Would you believe it? Boris was thinking of going home. Only a thin wall separates our rooms, and last night I heard him call out your name.

Sight-seeing with Boris is fun. Everywhere we go, people stare at him.

Paris is all aflutter over the coming event. Boris is the heavy favorite, and the enthusiasm for him is not confined to any one class, partly because Russians are extremely popular in Paris.

The invitations to dinners, dances, private theatricals, and so on are too many to enumerate, and too tedious to describe, but Boris has decided that we shall attend only official functions, and only if they're mandatory.

Monday, Boris starts working out with eight horses. He plans to spend a lot of time observing the competition. Some riders—the Italian, the Englishman, an Arabic-speaking tribesman, a Turk, and a North American Indian from Canada with the pleasing name "Little Eagle Eye"—are already here. Of course, the Frenchman.

Ronya, you have no idea how nervous Father is about you. He's so afraid that something might go wrong. I can't tell you what a relief it is to him (and us) that the foremost specialist in Vienna will deliver the baby.

Mother sends her love. She'll write soon.

> Your loving sister,
> Katya

Two days later a package came from Boris, and among the stunning array of silks and satins and velvets there was a present for Lydia, a huge Chinese fan of peacock feathers.

A cold wind came through the iced tree branches. The contestants, all well mounted, rode into the empty outdoor arena. Each man swung a leg across his horse, slid down, shook hands all around. Then the judges entered the arena, among them a big, loose-limbed man, formerly a colonel in the French Foreign Legion. He cupped his hands to his mouth and called: "Gentlemen."

The men clustered around.

"This world competition is divided into various parts. The first two days will be filled with usual routine events: jumps, races, trick riding, stunts. The mock battles are scheduled for the third day. The committee has spent considerable time setting up rules. The fool who breaks one may not live long enough to be disqualified. Temper bravery with wisdom. This is a competition—not a battle for survival.

"On the fourth day you're off on a speed and endurance contest over an obstacle course. You will be required to endure darkness, bad weather, difficult terrain. You are all experienced horsemen and com-

123

petition riders. It's up to you whether you fear God or the devil, but the man who rides in with a bloodstained whip in his hand will be disqualified. The horse must not be mistreated, and you will be judged, apart from speed, by the way man and horse withstand the elements.

"Gentlemen, because this is the coldest, wettest, most dismal season on record, you'll ride in pairs and score as a team. You'll choose your partners now. You have exactly seven minutes in which to do so. Good luck and godspeed."

Neither Boris nor Little Eagle Eye bothered to scan the entire company. Boris had already noticed the man with the hard weathered face, who had the look of a scout and made no sound when he walked. The Indian, for his part, estimated that the blond giant could easily outride, outjump, outrun, and outmaneuver all of them.

A few words in French was all that was required between them.

In the jumping event Boris scored high. He scored high in all the traditional competition events, as did the others. But in the trick riding he pulled far ahead with a Tartar stunt, one the Cossacks learned from the Tartars. It was a trick he did at home for the amusement of the peasant children. Laying out a ring of twenty white handkerchiefs, in each of which was tied a five franc note, he galloped around the ring picking up each handkerchief with his teeth. Then, still at top speed, he slid under his horse's belly, emerged on the other side, and rode from the ring standing on his head.

The roar that went up was frightening. People swarmed onto the field, and it took the gendarmes a good twenty minutes to restore order.

In the sham battle Boris and his stallion were at their best. Amid the confusion of Turk charging Arab and the imperious Frenchman demonstrating his toughness, Boris unseated rider after rider with dispassionate proficiency.

At dawn of the fourth day the contestants rode out at a gallop. Boris made his way up a side street where he reined in. "Come," he said to Little Eagle Eye, "there's no need for us to hurry. How about a bowl of hot onion soup and a beefsteak?"

The Indian's face creased in a sudden smile.

All that night and the next day they rode over the zigzag obstacle course, narrow and rocky twisted paths which passed through tunnels, around the frozen edge of the Seine, over icy suspension bridges, through brush and bramble. Toward evening, still looking fit, the golden eagle and Little Eagle Eye thundered into the finish—a cheering crowd wild with excitement cleared a path for them, the winners by several hours and many points.

On the last day of the competition, Boris' stunt was of such suicidal daring that the crowd held its breath. Ruth, who had watched every one of his exhibitions glowing with pride, did not have the courage to look. But a strong excitement showed on many women's faces—Boris Pirov and his stallions had an overwhelming effect on the spectators.

As four huge stallions raced wildly into the ring, Boris, riding two other horses—a foot on each—started after them, constantly building speed, and then at the height of their stampede cut in front of them and brought them to a dead stop.

Handing his horses to the grooms, he reemerged on the white stallion, who under Boris' sure hand danced, jumped, and whirled in time to the music.

Boris easily won the world championship—and his place among the immortals.

He was showered with invitations to the dinners and balls of the season; Paris, the courtesan, showered its affection on him, its adored new hero, and he basked in the glory. *How can Ronya think it wrong?* he asked himself. *Hadn't his ambassador ordered him to cooperate?* Paris detained him, and he delayed his *adieu.*

In Russia, every newspaper in the land carried the story: THE GOLDEN TARTAR WINS . . .

In Odessa, the Tartars went crazy.

In the big cities, even as far as Vladivostok, there was jubilation, particularly among cavalrymen.

In the villages and small towns where the Jews lived, however, there were few who knew or cared about horse shows or daring riders, and Boris Pirov was as far removed from them as the gladiators of ancient Rome. The ghetto Jews were hardworking and pious; their thoughts flew to God.

But in Kiev for days normal activities were suspended in an orgy of celebration, and among these Jews there were many who took pride in the thought that something of him belonged to them now.

Ronya waited quietly for the adulation and madness to subside. One day, she shut herself up in the library and calculated the gross expense of her husband's triumph. Subtracting the prize money and allowing a token figure for value of the prestige brought to the Pirov Stables, she arrived at a net cost, a sum she sent by messenger to Rabbi Levinsky.

The letter she received in return read:

Ronya, I rejoice. My heart murmurs thanks and I send you my blessing. You have climbed three steps of the golden ladder of charity because you gave cheerfully, proportionately, and unsolicitedly. But though to give and remain unknown is commendable, let our people know you remain ours.

When your child is born send for me.
My Lena and my Joseph send you greetings.

Your *rebbe* Simon Levinsky

P.S. Ronya, I almost forgot. Soon our new cantor arrives. People will travel any distance to hear him sing, so far and wide has his fame spread. Come to *shul* some Sabbath eve. Bring your husband.

13

Doctor Erick Stiller possessed more than average height and good looks and a brilliant mind and, until he lost the wife he adored, life had been exceptionally good to him. It was his sadness and restlessness, not the great fee offered by David von Glasman, that caused him to accept a maternity case in Kiev. His mistake was that he expected the delivery to be difficult and the situation relaxing. Nothing in his experience had prepared him for Ronya and certainly not for Boris.

Ronya, her lips tightly shut, did as she was told without fuss and in less than three hours from the onset of labor delivered a perfectly formed, healthy male child of good size. Almost immediately thereafter she found the strength to start exercising in bed, and on the third day he found her standing, her weight evenly distributed on both bare feet, stretching and bending. The man in him watched her graceful movements with approval, but the doctor, trained in a culture that pampered the rich and highborn, said: "Don't rush things, my dear. Overdoing it is the main cause of female troubles."

"I suppose you're right, but confinement is such a bore," Ronya said as Doctor Stiller reached out to help her back to bed—trying not to notice the hair becomingly held in place by a bow that matched the clinging nightdress, bare at the shoulders. Just then Boris opened Ronya's door.

Stiller, absorbed in Ronya, hardly noticed they were no longer alone. Ronya, however, was immediately aware of Boris' presence and said hastily, "Please put me down."

The doctor smiled. "That is my intention. You're going back to bed and you're to stay there. That's an order."

"And you, Doctor, have exactly one hour in which to pack your belongings and get out of this house. That, too, is an order."

126

The doctor turned, baffled, and he saw at once that Boris was vulnerable as any man in love with a breathtakingly beautiful woman and that jealousy could easily funnel into violence. Well bred, Doctor Stiller had no desire to fight; his patient, young and strong, had no need of him. He turned to her and said, "I wonder if you can suggest a good inn, or is there a train I can catch?"

The fierce glow in Ronya's eyes made him recognize, all at once, that these two people were very much alike. Somewhat to his own amusement—and to assuage his masculine pride—he found himself feeling slightly sorry for Boris, because he saw Ronya was sure of herself, whereas Boris was somewhat uncertain.

Keeping her eyes on Boris and her voice low, Ronya said, "I am sorry to say, Doctor, that my husband's rudeness does not surprise me, since I know him to be more at home with ruffians than with gentlemen."

Outwardly, Boris appeared calmer, but the wise doctor was not deceived. "Good-bye, Madam Pirov," he said, offering her his hand, "you are a marvelous patient."

Ronya took the proffered hand. "Please tell my father that you are the very nicest present he could have sent me."

That was the last straw. "It might be smarter," Boris said, "to let go my wife's hand and start moving."

Ronya waited until Doctor Stiller had let himself out of the room, then picked up a small vase filled with hothouse roses. Her aim was good, but Boris sensed it coming and ducked. "I'll be back," he said over his shoulder.

Boris made sure that the specialist from Vienna would remember his ride to the railroad station, but if he expected Doctor Stiller to shout to him to rein in, he was denied that satisfaction. As the doctor held on grimly, he was smiling and thinking with enjoyment: How often does a physician get the world's champion equestrian for a driver?

I should have guessed it, Boris said to himself angrily. *Damn David von Glasman—he sent a real man to steal Ronya.*

They got to the station with minutes to spare. Boris swung down Stiller's baggage, nodded briefly, and turned to go. But the doctor stopped him with a hand on his arm. "Grant me a moment."

Boris nodded warily.

"I know you think poorly of circumcision and of *mohels,* and your wife seems to be terrified at the thought, but in fact they do their job well, often better than surgeons. Even so, afterward, when Igor is back in his cradle, look at the dressing—sometimes they bandage too tightly."

Boris stiffly thanked the doctor for his advice and drove home wondering how he and Ronya would make up their quarrel, since he could not make love to her. Thinking of her made him eager for her, and he drove home at the same breakneck speed he had driven to the station.

He had been prepared to be indulgent with Ronya for her slight indiscretion, but when he found her waiting for him still simmering with anger, he thought, *All right, we'll have it out.* He went to the cabinet, took out a bottle of vodka, and poured a stiff drink. "The next son of a bitch who lays a hand on you won't get off so easily. I'll break his arm. And for the next one I'll break both arms, and I'll kill if I have to, until you learn that I won't stand for any damn foolishness from you."

"You don't intimidate me," Ronya said, infuriated, "and I bitterly regret that I have allowed you to isolate me from the community. From now on I shall go to the theater, and the ballet, and the opera, and concerts. I am going to entertain and be entertained, and visit Katya, both in St. Petersburg and in Moscow, and reopen our dacha in Odessa. If you don't like it—too bad."

Boris stared at her over the rim of his glass. *What if sometime she stops loving me?* he asked himself in torment. He admitted to himself he felt most secure when Ronya needed him physically; other women still tempted him, but his need for Ronya was so overwhelming it frightened him. He could not be a whole man without her. Still, he disliked her declaration of independence. He swallowed the last of the vodka. "Ronya, I advise you to keep your social calendar to my liking."

Suddenly tired, Ronya gave up the fight: "Oh—go eat your supper."

Boris saw the shadow of fatigue in her eyes. "I don't like eating alone," he said. "I'll send up a tray and eat here with you."

He stayed with her the rest of the night, holding and caressing her.

In the nursery, a fat peasant woman watched over Igor and when he cried, she took him to her warm breast. "Drink more," she said, rocking him, and Igor sucked contentedly.

The stables were quiet. Too quiet. Every horse for sale had been sold and delivered. Boris was bored. To a degree, the weather was responsible, for until the frost broke he could not look for new horses; but also he had taken it into his head to be faithful—at least, to give it a try for a time. The more he thought about Ronya's generosity—gracefully accepting his loitering in Paris, where he was feted and admired so that he returned home with barely a minute to spare before their son was born—the sharper grew his wish to put an end to their one area of violent conflict.

Besides, in the last week, with the Viennese doctor constantly in his thoughts, Boris had begun to wonder: What if Ronya, in spite of her Jewish concept of marriage, were suddenly to decide what's sauce for the goose is sauce for the gander? Among his own people, with all the strong tradition of family, a woman rarely defied her husband but still managed to have her fun. She learned to ride a horse, drink vodka, and fight like a man; and even if she loved her own man best, if he wasn't at home or if he was sleeping in the barn with another woman, she found someone to take his place. The mere thought of another man near Ronya filled him with rage.

Still, he was careful not to make any promises—not even to himself.

Instead, he used some of his prize money to give most of his men a holiday and searched for jobs to keep himself busy. He repaired, he shared Fedor's routine duties and, to the annoyance of his comrades, he stayed away from the barracks, from the gambling casino, from temptation. And he deceived himself about himself, until the seventh day following Igor's birth. Partly it was because Boris craved a woman's body—abstinence came hard; partly, it was due to anxiety and fear for his son, whose coming circumcision he regarded with deep-rooted horror. Mostly, it was due to Ronya. Nervous, afraid for her son, her impatience with Boris was a cover-up. Not until too late, however, did he understand that.

Boris glanced at his watch—only a quarter of eleven and nothing to do. He sat down and wrote a brief note to Ruth. At eleven, he went upstairs, but halted at Ronya's door when he heard Tamara speaking.

"Ah, yes," she was saying, "it is true. When she is to be confined, a Chinese wife finds a concubine to take her place with her husband. The wife calls the girl 'little sister' and is very good to her."

Boris predicted Ronya's response. "Little sister, my foot—big whore. I'd cut her heart out before I'd—"

"Ronya von Glasman, it's a sin to force a man to go to prostitutes."

"The name is Pirov—if you please."

Boris shook his head and turned away, smiling. He had every intention of settling down until Tamara left but, without ever consciously deciding to do so, he drifted out to the stables and saddled a horse.

At the barracks, where he was greeted like a long-lost brother and congratulated on all sides, he drank a little, missed lunch, and won a couple of hands at cards. As usual, there were a few girls hanging about. Two of them he already knew. He sized up the third: She seemed placid and graceless—compared to the perfection and fire of Ronya's body.

His unacknowledged design unaccomplished, Boris left the barracks as the short winter day was fading and headed for home.

In Ronya's room a huge fire was burning in the grate. Tamara, a picture of domesticity, lay on the sofa.

He kissed Ronya tenderly and grinned at Tamara as she held up her mouth and begged, "Me too."

Ronya was not smiling; she barely acknowledged Boris' presence. Her face pale and strained, her hair scraped back in a tight knot, she sat in her bed rocking Igor, who was wearing nothing but a diaper.

"The room is stifling hot, dove."

Ronya glanced up and gathered the baby closer. She looked worried and nervous.

"Want tea?" Tamara asked, uncrossing her legs. Her eyes were mocking him; she knew what he wanted.

Suddenly angry with Ronya, Boris turned on Tamara. "Get the hell out of here."

Tamara laughed.

"Please go," Ronya said quietly.

Tamara made it her business to brush past Boris on her way out.

Christ, what a whore! Boris thought. Then he caught Ronya's eyes staring up at him, but before he could speak she said accusingly, "The wet nurse is gone, and I let myself go dry because I wanted to be pretty for you."

"That's no catastrophe," Boris said easily. "There must be a hundred available wet nurses in Kiev." He pulled over a chair and swung his booted feet up on the bed.

"Boris! The clean bedspread!"

Boris jerked himself to his feet. "For Christ's sake, Ronya, when have you ever cared about the bedspread? What the devil is wrong with you?"

Ronya's eyes went back to Igor. "Poor little darling," she said, face and voice totally absorbed in the sleeping child, "he hates diluted cow's milk. Babies are so vulnerable."

"Ronya."

She did not answer.

Christ, she doesn't give a damn, he thought. Hot anger and jealousy flared up in him. Making a supreme effort, he said conciliatingly, "Have you sent for a new wet nurse?"

"Of course."

He regarded her a moment without speaking, then left the room to eat a belated lunch in the kitchen. In half an hour, he was back.

Igor lay snuggled against her bare breast, and she was gazing at him lovingly, a faint smile on her lips.

"Dove," Boris put out his hand and touched her hair, "give him to one of the maids. Let me hold you."

"No," she said, eyes fixed on Igor.

"All right, Ronya!" He stormed out of the room. He would cool his lust for Ronya with a night on the town. On the stairway he pushed past Lydia, who was escorting Igor's new wet nurse.

When Boris came striding into the stable, he saw by the light of a lantern hanging on a nail that he did not have to ride into town after all. Skirts and petticoats well up, legs, arms, and neck bare, Tamara was ready for him.

His mouth curling with scorn, he threw off his sheepskin jacket and unbuckled his belt, and even as he plunged, his brain said, *What in hell are you getting yourself into this mess for?*

With consummation, which came almost instantly, such a storm of disgust rose in him that he rolled over and lay face down in the straw, nauseated.

Lydia's small, smart eyes had fastened on Boris as he shouldered his way past her and down the stairs. She walked hastily into Ronya's room, pushing the wet nurse before her, took Igor from Ronya, and gave him to the woman. "Olga, this is your mistress," she announced abruptly, crossing to the nursery door and flinging it open. "Through here is the nursery. Go."

She shut the door after the nurse and made for the bed, where she sat herself down and compelled Ronya to meet her eyes. "I just met him on the stairs. Tamara took his horse and, as sure as God, that she-wolf is up to some devilment."

Ronya knew the twin devils were there—opportunity and hunger. She knew of his hunger. She had seen it in his face, felt it in his hands, heard it in his voice. She sat staring, fighting back panic; then, as she recognized—suddenly she had not the slightest doubt—what had been tormenting her all day, panic left her and cold hatred took hold. "I shall kill her," she swore.

Lydia waited attentively for her orders.

"How can I get to the stable?"

"There's my cart and the old mare."

"All right. I'll meet you at the back door. Hurry. He must be nearly there."

Lydia dragged from the closet a long warm cloak and then ran to do as she was told. Ronya, on her feet and ready, pulled Boris' revolver from its holster and checked it. It was loaded.

Clinging to the balustrade, she made her way down the stairs, thankful that she met none of the servants on the way. She did not have long to wait. Lydia appeared out of the darkness with the horse and cart, helped Ronya up, and handed over the reins.

Lydia watched her drive with eyes full of pity.

"Poor little mistress. Sweet Jesus," she prayed, permitting herself a silent curse, "a pox on that gypsy slut."

In a clump of pines some distance away from the main barn where Boris housed his saddle horses, Ronya pulled up and climbed down from the cart. "Lydia, stand guard behind that tree. No matter what, see to it that no one comes near."

She crept forward toward the stable door, keeping close to the trees to the left of the path. Had she gone to the right instead, she would have seen Tamara's lookout stationed by the carriage house door.

It seemed to Tamara a long time since Boris had rolled away from her body. He was still lying motionless, his face buried in the straw. Hoisting herself up on one elbow, she said in a light but coaxing voice, "That didn't count, Boris, you were too quick, and that's unworthy of a golden stallion.

"Come on, Boris, just one kiss. Please."

He shut out the sound of her voice, just as he heard a light rustling of straw. "S-s-sh," he whispered, and raised his head. In the dim yellow light just inside the door, he saw Ronya taking careful aim, and he knew by the slight movement of her head that she knew he had seen her and that she meant to maim or kill Tamara and spare him.

Before Ronya could fire, Boris smashed his hand into Tamara's face, knocking her to the floor.

For an eternity all was still. Then Tamara groaned and spat out two teeth, and Ronya turned and ran.

Tamara wiped her nose with her skirt, leaned forward, and spat again, and reaching out with both hands clutched Boris' tunic. "That's not what I wanted from you, but if that's what you want from me, you can have it. Just hold me, and tell me that you love me."

Boris groaned. Disengaging himself, he got to his feet and dragged up his trousers. "Listen Tamara." His voice was cold and cruel. "The little fondness I had for you has turned to loathing. Leave me be."

"I don't mean like you love Ronya," she implored him. "I don't ask for that."

He took a long look at her and then, like Ronya, turned and ran. Once outside, he was violently sick. Still retching, his eyes fixed on the ground, he suddenly focused on a pair of boots and looked up. Fedor was standing before him holding a pail of water.

"You goddamn son of a bitch, I told you to keep your sister away from the stables."

Fedor did not answer.

"I suppose that's for me."

The man nodded.

"Well, pour it over my head."

Silently Fedor did as he was told, then stood rubbing his jaw with the palm of his hand. Boris could tell he was trying to come to a decision, and he waited. Fedor shoved his hand into a pocket and brought out the pistol. "Here," he said, offering it to Boris, "Ronya dropped it."

Boris pocketed the weapon. "If you ever tell Tamara that Ronya saw us," he said, "I'll break you in half—so help me."

Fedor thought for a moment, his dark eyes studying Boris. "Maybe you will, and maybe you won't. I'll talk it over with Rifka, my queen."

Depressed and deeply ashamed, Boris made his way back to his own room, where he found on the windowsill a white orchid in a flower pot and a message from Ronya:

> Boris:
> What happened will not blow over by the time the wisteria is in bloom on the terrace. The best thing now is to think of Igor; a boy needs his father. Hence, the white orchid. I have been nursing it for months in the greenhouse. It's from your son. I had planned to give it to you tomorrow.
> I've had enough of bed and shall dine downstairs this evening. If you care to join me, please do. Eight thirty.
>
> Ronya

Boris folded the note back into its envelope and locked it away. After a scorching hot bath, he girded himself for the difficult evening ahead by putting on a handsome suit newly arrived from his St. Petersburg tailor, and he called a maid. "Get rid of those clothes," he told her, pointing to the pile on the floor. "Burn them—they're contaminated." Seeing her startled expression, he added, "Don't worry, it's not catching."

He met Ronya at the door of her bedroom. He saw that she had dressed equally carefully, and her braided hair was put up and held in place with jeweled hairpins.

At the table neither of them ate much, but Ronya, with an air of normality, talked continuously about the *briss*. When the main course was cleared, Boris took matters into his own hands. He dismissed the servants, saying that he would ring for dessert when they were ready, and when Ronya made yet another remark about the *briss,* he said, "Goddamn it, Ronya, stop! Stop being polite. I left you in search of a whore, and I found one. That's all there is. It didn't mean a thing."

"Oh, Boris!" Switching from the pure Russian they were speaking to melodious Ukrainian, she said, "I'm trying so hard."

"Dove—" Boris began, but stopped short as he heard the door open and the rustle of satin behind him. He gave her a quick, inquiring look.

133

Ronya rose, nodded formally to Rifka, who was standing just inside the door, and led them both into the library where no one could overhear them.

If Rifka counted on finding them upset, she was disappointed. Boris offered her a drink and took one himself. Ronya broke the silence, speaking quietly and evenly. "Rifka, my cousin, my husband has told me what happened late this afternoon."

Rifka started to speak, but Ronya silenced her. "Hear me out."

Rifka sighed and shrugged, as Boris' eyes narrowed slightly.

Ronya ran her tongue over her lips. "I asked you here simply to tell you that Tamara is not welcome in this house, except on those occasions when duty demands that I receive her."

A smile played around Rifka's mouth. "Ronya, child, don't take it so hard. This has happened before, it will happen again. It is understood that Von Glasman women are linked to the gypsy queens through their men."

In spite of her anger, her grief and pain and need for vengeance, Ronya hung tightly to her dignity. "Order Tamara to stay away from me, please."

As Boris sat motionless, concentrating on the women, Rifka played her first card. "Listen, child. You can have David, your father, back."

Boris made no move; he sat still as a jade Buddha. From the look on Ronya's face, Rifka could see she had said the wrong thing, but she felt impelled to go on. "I have to tell him."

"Why?" Ronya cried out. "Why do you have to hurt him and Mother?"

"Because I choose to," Rifka said, rising.

Boris spoke for the first time. "I'll see you to the door."

Rifka picked up her sable wrap. "You're to be congratulated, Boris, fathering a future queen."

"Oh? You're sure about that?"

"Oh, yes, very sure. We gypsy queens know when to conceive."

Staring down at her, Boris mocked, "Is that why you had Fedor?"

For a moment, Rifka froze, feeling the pounding of her heart, and then she said savagely, "You unadorned, unadulterated bastard."

"That's right," he said mildly. Then, sharp and sudden: "Tell Tamara to get rid of it."

Rifka threw back her head and laughed. "Fool! Why do you think I tolerated Tamara's pursuit of you these many months? I need your seed."

He shook his head. "It's useless, Rifka. I'll deny it." Then, softly, "Apart from Ronya, everyone in the province knows that your daughter is a tramp."

"Yes? And what are you?"

Boris nodded. "You've got a point." He opened the door, escorted her outside, and helped her into her buggy.

When he got upstairs, he was surprised to find Ronya's door open. She turned on him as he came into the room. "Why are you here?"

"Well, for one thing, dove, I'm here to trade," he said softly, moving toward her slowly and warily. "I go to bed with you and hold you in my arms, and I wear that skullcap tomorrow as proudly as it's ever been worn. Send me away . . ."

Trembling as though from a chill, Ronya rubbed her bare arms. Encouraged by her silence, he got her into bed. "I love you, dove," he said as he put out the light. He undressed in the darkness and took her in his arms. "I know it's a hell of a lot to ask, Ronya, but forget what happened today, and I'll promise you anything."

"Never!"

Boris waited a little and then started to stroke her. "Go to sleep, dove."

She opened her mouth to say "I can't," and found to her surprise that she was sighing, "I'm very tired."

Boris waited until she was asleep, then bent over her, staring at her in the dark. Holding her, looking at her led to long, long caresses, cautious at first. Ronya's beautiful face remained serene, but he began to suspect that she was aware of his embrace, divined his passion, and that her longing for him was as great as his for her. Bringing his mouth down hard on hers, he sought proof, and she savored his kisses in her sleep and returned them. Convinced of the extent of her love, Boris grew calmer. He slept the rest of the long, dark night, and when he wakened he still held Ronya clasped tight to his naked flesh.

Among the Jews, a male child is circumcised on the eighth day of his life, at which ceremony he receives his name formally. He can be circumcised by his father or an elder of the congregation, but usually it is a *mohel*, a professional. A fee is paid, presents are given the child, mostly ornaments of gold or silver. The Von Glasmans, for centuries freethinkers, did not carry the child to the synagogue, there to be circumcised to the left of the Ark. Bathed in perfumed oil, he was put upon a wooden table covered with exquisitely hand-loomed white linen and in the presence of family and friends (the unpurified mother remaining in her confinement bed) and in memory of Elijah the Prophet, who was the angel or messenger of the covenant, the *mohel* performed the act, symbolically cutting off the sins of the flesh. All was done in strict accordance with Jewish ritual. The Von Glasmans named their girl children on the eighth day, too, and they celebrated as joyously and gave as generously for daughters as they did for sons. The giving was not entirely from the goodness of their hearts, or from brooding upon the grief of the Jew throughout the ages, or to assure for themselves a good entry in the Heavenly Book of Accounts; it was to release themselves from guilt, an atoning, for the Talmud says: "Write not 'the poor man' but 'thy brother,' to show that both are equal."

Now with her parents away, and to reward Ronya for her generosity and to honor her son, Rabbi Simon Levinsky brought with him a *minyan* of ten adult Jewish males including Kiev's gifted cantor—the quorum necessary for holding public worship.

Boris himself lifted Igor onto a silk cushion and gave him a gauze teat containing a lump of sugar dipped in brandy, and he held him while the cantor sang sweet lullabies about pearls and sandalwood, about birds and angels and grandmothers. Igor was easily tranquillized into deep, coma-like sleep.

The rabbi prayed: "Praised be Thou, O Lord our God, King of the Universe, who hast sanctified us with Thy commandments and enjoined us to celebrate the rite of circumcision."

With the first drop of blood, the rabbi intoned and the congregation swayed to the rhythm of his singsong delivery.

" 'And God said to Abraham: You therefore shall keep My covenant, and your seed after you, throughout their generation. Every male among you shall be circumcised. You shall be circumcised in the flesh of your foreskin, that it may be a sign of the covenant between Me and you.' "

During the bandaging Igor cried, but Boris calmed him with more brandy, and then it was over.

The men congratulated Boris: *"Mazel tov. Mazel tov."*

The rabbi said, "A man who brings his son to be circumcised is to be compared with a high priest bringing an offering of grain and a libation to the temple altar. From this they say that a man must prepare a joyous feast on the day on which he is privileged to circumcise his son."

Boris grinned. "Fair enough. A feast in accordance with religious law awaits you."

The men toasted mother and child in ritual wine and each other in whiskey.

"Gentlemen," Boris said, "if you will allow me a few moments with my Ronya, I shall rejoin you in the dining room. Rabbi Levinsky will show you the way."

As soon as the dining-room door was shut behind them, a babble broke out, the gossip inevitable when Jews get together.

"Did you hear?" said one elder. " 'My Ronya,' he calls her. I shed tears that David is robbed of a daughter."

Another agreed.

A third man spoke up immediately. "So—why not 'my Ronya'? If you will think a moment, you will realize that David himself created his fate. Whenever did Von Glasman cleave to his creator?"

"Permit me," said the sage of the congregation. "I believe with our learned rabbi: Boris fulfilled the duty of procreation, and today he made the rising of his flesh the servant of God."

A supporter exclaimed ardently, "He has proved deserving! May he and Ronya keep this union firmly on the pillars of purity and sanctity and build a proper Jewish home."

Several chimed in. "Amen, amen. With *nachas* in their Jewish children."

But one purist remained unswayed. "Where was the godfather? Who authorized Boris Pirov to hold his own son? By what right did he do this? I fervently believe that we performed the deed out of kindness. The mountain came to Mohammed. Next time, let the stranger come to the synagogue."

Three letters left Kiev in the same mail pouch.

Rifka presented facts, but beneath there was less than truth, and beneath the veneer of understanding less than magnanimity.

Ronya wrote the truth. She knew more about it.

Boris wrote:

> Ruth, my Mother,
>   I wish I could spare you, but I can't. I wish I could say "I'll never disappoint you again." However, all I can tell you for certain is that I love Ronya, and that I cherish her above life.
>   I have the temerity to ask your forgiveness. More—I need your love.
>
> Yours,
Boris

Ruth went to a small case and from it took a gold watch. She dashed off a note:

> Boris, my very dear,
>   This was my father's. Now it is yours.
>   My faith in you remains unblemished, my love for you undiminished.
>
> I kiss you,
Mother

137

14

Ronya remembered, as did Boris, that the flat of his hand had saved Tamara from her bullet. Only Tamara, swept back and forth between consciousness and oblivion, did not remember, did not know. She knew only that Boris had rolled off and away, leaving her unsatisfied and, then, with a savagery born as she believed out of shame and loathing, he hit her.

Now, nine months later, immense pains ripped at her, sweat poured, her heavy belly heaved like waves on a stormy sea. When she could, she screamed. "Ronya! Boris! I need you!"

"Don't wait for them, Tamara," Rifka pleaded, "don't wait, you'll die." Finally, in despair, she had to tell: "They refuse to come. Boris says he'll see you in the grave first, and Ronya has locked herself in her room and hung her mirrors with black."

At midnight of the second day, a baby came. She was a monster, a freak, with an enormous misshapen head, a pathetic little body, six fingers on her right hand and four toes on her left foot.

With dark, ugly oaths, Rifka pressed her thumbs against its neck and choked the feeble life out of the poor little thing. She wrapped it in a cotton blanket and flung it aside, muttering savagely, "For you, miserable dead thing, I sacrificed my child and betrayed David. I needed a girl related by blood to Ronya's heir and, God forgive me, I wanted a granddaughter all white and gold."

With great effort she turned back to Tamara and, cupping her hands at the outlet, waited for the afterbirth. Instead she saw a head coming down the passage. One violent contraction of the uterus, and the baby was precipitated right out and into her hands. An endless moment, and he gave a lusty cry. His skin was white, his eyebrows and eyelashes gold, even his still wet hair was light in color.

In violence conceived, in violence born, the child was tenderly bathed in warm oil, his masculine perfection clothed in the softest, whitest cloth, and he was put in a cradle. A few feet away his mother, raw, fevered, and in pain, lay hemorrhaging. Exhausted, Rifka waited for morning.

Fedor came in at about seven and found them all asleep. He went to the crib and studied the child. "A Blond One!" Gently he woke Rifka, who went immediately to Tamara. She stared down at her daughter for a long time. Finally she turned to Fedor and said in a hushed voice, "She rests as though dead from her humiliation, but she will live."

"Will she remain beautiful?" Fedor asked, trembling.

Rifka nodded. "And barren." She commanded him to pick up the bundle lying on the floor and beckoned him out of the room. Outside, she gave him his instructions.

Fedor rose from his stool as Boris entered the carriage house.

"I got your message."

Fedor nodded impersonally. Kicking at the burlap sack, he said, "That's yours."

"What is it?" Boris asked cautiously.

"Open it."

Boris thought, *Hell, why not?* He threw open the sack and recoiled in horror. The umbilical cord, all blood, remained untied; the repellent head, the piteous torso covered with a white, flaky, cheeselike matter.

For an endless moment he stood frozen, and then came awareness of Fedor. Rage boiled in him, and with an incoherent curse he struck out—one shattering blow. Fedor went down.

Boris snatched up an ax that lay propped against the wall and turned on his heel without a backward glance. He took a short cut through the meadow to the priest's house, his set face ignoring the peasant children who called out to him. As Father Tromokov opened the door in answer to his peremptory knock, he said, "Get to the carriage house. Don't waste time," and was gone before the priest could speak.

Boris strode swiftly through the gardens to the house, in long, rapid strides that kept pace with his anger. Smashing the ax through the lock to Ronya's door, he knocked out the panels in pent-up fury and burst into the room. He ripped aside the curtains, flung open the windows to let in the morning's bright sunlight, and tore down the mirror's black coverings. Then he turned on Ronya, lying in bed, and said in a terrifying voice: "Get up. Done is done. After breakfast, we'll talk. Tonight we resume our marriage."

"You need fresh air and exercise," he said after she had eaten. "Let's walk."

They drove down to the river where, backs against a big boulder, Boris told her everything, with as little detail as possible. They both remained quiet for a long time as Ronya concentrated on the autumn landscape. Finally, staring at the grass before her, she asked, "Do you think Fedor's badly hurt?"

"I'm pretty sure I cracked his jaw. He may even have a concussion. He landed hard."

Boris could see her lips trembling. "Look at me, dove."

She raised her eyes.

He straightened his shoulders. "I'm glad it's dead." Her eyes widened. "I am too," she said, with desperate truth.

Then, softly she added, "But you have a son."

His wide mouth tightened into a hard glance, and his lips showed white against his wind-tanned skin. "Sure," he said sharply, "his name is Igor. You ought to know that."

Ronya felt a sharp stab of pity. "Boris—listen. About eight this morning there was a hard knock on my door and a white paper was slipped beneath it. It was a note from Rifka announcing the birth of twins and saying, without explanation, 'The boy lives.' " Ronya glanced at Boris anxiously. "She says the gypsies are already calling him the Blond One."

Boris lit a cigarette and let the match flare between his fingers. "I've heard enough. Let's go, Ronya."

She took a slow, deep breath and went on. " 'Tamara's flame will fire men to passion, but to no avail,' Rifka said. 'Tamara sacrificed all to the Tartar invader.' "

Ronya did not know how she found herself so suddenly in his arms. She felt his lips hard against hers, and then he held her at arm's length. "I wasn't the first with Tamara, and no man will ever be the only one. She's a whore."

Ronya seemed dazed.

"So help me, dove," Boris said vehemently, "I wasn't the first. You're the only virgin I've ever had. You are the only woman I ever took by force. And you are my only love, now and forever."

Boris held her tightly, and when he released her he saw that her shining eyes were moist. He carried her back to the carriage.

"Boris, one more thing," she said, as they drove off. "When Fedor recovers, he'll have to find a new home with some other tribe. I won't have him here. I'll make him pay."

Hope rose in Boris. If Ronya was prepared to get rid of Fedor—maybe, now—"Dove, get rid of them all. Please."

She shook her head, and could feel his disappointment. "Darling, I want you to understand about Rifka. She has been moving Tamara and me toward this all our lives. To her you are of no consequence as a person, you are only the instrument by which she has linked her gypsies in kinship with my heirs. To induce a girl child, every day Rifka made Tamara drink a concoction of herbs mixed with ground worms, the feces of flies, and fresh honey. In a way, Rifka's hopes are now dashed—at least postponed for another generation. That's why she sent you that pitiful dead thing."

"Dove," Boris said bitterly, "a man has a better chance against a Siberian wolf-bitch than a woman like Tamara. Lust and frenzy burn in her like boiling water in a caldron. Shelter her, and she'll spill it all out again."

Ronya shook her head. "I am responsible for the gypsy camp, and since Tamara was born to be queen, I am responsible for her too."

There was nothing left to say.

It was a long blissful night, and Ronya was to remember his gentleness for the rest of her life. In the morning she said, "We were in Eden."

Far back in time, when another Tamara was princess of the tribe, Aaron von Glasman, a civilized man, a scholar, in the winter of his life, heard strange music and yielded to the wonderful, the terrible, the forbidden. Natalie, the queen, waited eight days after Tamara's child was born and then dispatched a messenger to Aaron. "The blood of the Romany is mixed with the blood of the Jew. We shall light candles, for not to light them is the sin. The honor of choosing a name comes to the mistress of the estate. Take heed, Aaron. Bring Naomi."

Now, in Ronya's time, came this message from Rifka: "Tamara lies in a darkened room, bleeding and in pain. The candles will not be lighted, for to light them is the sin. But the eighth day is upon us. The Blond One must be named. Take heed, Ronya. Bring Boris."

Ronya waited until noon, and when Boris did not return to the house she realized he would be eating with the men, for he had his usual stable work to do and had to make ready for a Cavalry delivery. She had no alternative but to send for him. He came running into the house, alarmed. "Ronya? What's wrong?"

"There's nothing wrong," she said and came to the point quickly.

Boris said nothing until she had finished, but it was clear he was angry. "Ronya, you're a lunatic to hold with that hypocritical rubbish. Refuse."

"I can't."

"I'm against your going there."

"I must."

He shrugged. "Personally I don't care what name you give the bastard as long as it's not mine." He turned to the door and Ronya, ashamed to walk among the gypsies alone, screamed, "You have a cold heart, Tartar."

She went to the nursery and picked up Igor. "Come, sweetheart, come meet your brother."

She went to the camp on foot. In one arm she carried Igor, in the other five hundred gold pieces in a purple velvet bag.

They all came out, all but Tamara. Rifka took Igor, which made Ronya feel even more alone. Then a daughter of Fedor's came out carrying Tamara's child and put him in Ronya's arms. Ronya stared down at him; he made her think of Boris, and she wanted him.

Rifka spoke first. "Blessed with gifts—a sovereign spirit, a noble heart."

Ronya spoke. "Until time has passed, and your father sees what I see, and after you have waited and waited and he has called you 'son,' I name thee 'The Blond One.' "

It was dark when Ronya walked home with a sleeping Igor. There was no one to see her, and she let the tears fall.

Boris was gone for ten days, twice the normal time for a Cavalry delivery. He presented himself to Ronya, freshly shaved and bathed, early on the eleventh day. It was a beautiful morning. He sank down into the bed and pulled her to his nakedness, pressing his lips on hers. She flung her arms around his neck with answering passion. Skillfully and slowly he made love to her, until he heard her small cry of contentment. When he tucked the light blanket around her and went quietly away, she was blissfully asleep.

Ronya stayed in all day and rose only to do the cooking herself. She arranged the flowers and set the table, using spode and crystal and sterling and her mother's Meissen candelabra, and leaving time enough to make herself lovely.

Boris remembered other times like this, when she had turned their evening meal into an occasion, and nearly always it had been an artful ruse—she wanted something of him.

At the dinner table, it seemed Ronya intended nothing more than the obvious—a triumphant meal served with French wines and agreeable chatter of no consequence—but before she joined him in the library she changed into a negligee of a clear, true red, as bright as a red raspberry. Boris' eyes lit up at this new transformation. He pulled her down to sit with him on the sofa and, as she stretched luxuriously against the sofa arm, he drew off her slippers, took her feet into his big hands, and with the easy touch of a man sure of his strength, began to rub them.

She wanted to close her eyes and slip into the delicious languor induced by Boris' fingers, but the only way to deal with a problem is to deal with it. "Boris, please hear me out, and don't answer until you've had a brandy and time to think."

He nodded.

"No. Promise with words."

Boris grinned. "Only if you promise not to exhaust me with verbosity."

Ronya searched his face as she talked. "Yesterday, Rifka sent for me, and I went. Strangely enough, I wasn't really surprised when I found Tamara waiting. In truth, darling, I was glad to see her looking beautiful and on her feet.

" 'Ronya,' she said, 'I'm not going to beat about the bush. The Blond One is of no use to me, and he'll be better off with you than here. If you want Boris' bastard, you can have him.' "

She looked full in his face. "I want him, Boris. I want your second son very much. He belongs here with us."

The soothing fingers closed convulsively over her foot, so that she cried out in pain. In a voice pitched low but piercingly savage, he said so vehemently that Ronya, accustomed to his Tartar furies, recoiled, "Two things you will never get of me. I'll never be a Jew. I'll never call the bastard of a gypsy slut 'son.' Understood?"

"Boris, that's a terrible—"

"Let me finish! Two animals coupled in a barn, and a goddamn sperm found its way inside. You want that dirt in this house? I'm revolted."

Ronya lit a cigarette to give herself time to regain her self-control. "You have no contract with God, therefore the future is not yours to divine. As for that runaway sperm, it was yours. That makes you his father and him your son. Just like Igor. Exactly."

"Ronya, enough! Or so help me I'll—"

"You'll what?"

Boris wanted to get up, but he allowed himself to be held down by her feet.

Gradually they both relaxed. Boris began to feel guilty, for hurting her, for his unnecessary remark about the Jews. And in spite of himself he loved her for wanting the bastard. "Ronya," he said at last, "have a drink with me, please."

She accepted with reluctance, and in a moment the brandy was poured and he was back beside her. "Ronya, you know how I feel about you, don't you?"

"Yes," she said softly. "If a time were to come when events forced you to choose, you would choose me again."

He raised his glass. "Dove, that's for certain. But—knowing what you know—would you choose me again?"

Had Ronya smiled he would have been satisfied, but when seconds went by and she was gravely silent, as if she needed to think and decide, he cried out sharply, "For Christ's sake, answer!"

"Oh, yes I'd choose you," she said quickly, "only I'd do it differently."

"How?"

Again she considered her answer; then she said in measured tones,

"I would manage an introduction without my father. And I'd ask, 'Will you be faithful?' Before I agreed to be your wife."

She snuggled against his shoulder. "Darling, do you know the story of Hadassah? She was called Esther."

"No."

"The details are a bit complicated, and complicated details bore you, so I shall summarize."

"An excellent idea."

"Be serious."

"All right, dove."

"Very long ago, Mordecai, a rich Jew, rose to power and influence in the court of Ahasuerus, whose kingdom extended from India to Ethiopia. When the king commanded all the fair young virgins to be gathered into the house of women, Mordecai gave his niece and ward into the custody of the king's chamberlain, the keeper of women. The king began to love Esther above all other women. Soon he loved her so much that he made her his queen, and Esther the Jewess wore the royal crown on her head.

"But the Jews had an enemy in great favor with the king, and his name was Hamen. Hamen told the king that the Jews were dangerous traitors, and he obtained the king's signature to an act ordering the destruction of all Jews, young and old.

"Esther prepared a great feast to which she invited the king's ministers, Hamen included. Full of wine, the king looked upon his wife Esther, the most desirable woman in the kingdom, and said, 'Whatever thy petition, Queen Esther, it shall be granted thee, and whatever thy request, even to half the kingdom, it shall be performed.'

"And Esther answered, 'Give me the lives of my people.' She pointed to the wicked Hamen and called him 'Enemy.'

"The king rose in wrath and said, 'Hang him!' And he gave the Jews the right of self-defense, and thus Esther reconciled the king to the Jews."

Ronya looked up to find Boris staring at the clock. At times, his Tartarness seemed impregnable.

"Well?"

Boris grinned. "Beyond question, Esther was a heroine."

"The story was told more to acquaint you with Ahasuerus, the king."

Boris' grin faded. "I got the point, dove."

When they went up to bed, Boris went into his own room. Ronya was relieved to see him go. She ran to her writing table, and after several false starts wrote to Katya and Alexis, ardently urging them to adopt the Blond One.

In his room, Boris, too, was seated at his desk.

144

Ruth, my Mother,

I know you find it gratifying that under Ronya's tutelage I am acquiring an education beyond the gymnasium and the Cavalry Academy. I have just finished a series of biographies, and now I am reading a history on Eastern civilization and Tolstoy's works. Ronya, Ivan Tromokov, and I all have different opinions about Tolstoy, and we have some hot arguments.

All this reading, brought about by Ronya, is aimed at keeping me at home evenings. Between us, Ronya overvalues the power of the written page. Lately I find that I have a special need to stay close to home, and that when I am my "other self" I feel turned against myself.

Ruth, my Mother, I know you keep the contents of our letters a secret, as I do. I want you to hear the whole truth. Away from Ronya I am assailed with frightening doubts. Still, I can take domesticity only so long, then it begins to get to me and I feel fenced in, trapped.

I am not able to end this letter without telling you that Ronya is obsessed by what happened. She can't undo, and she won't let go. Now she wants the boy—as if Igor isn't handful enough for her. I calculate the only way I can shut the bastard out is to give Ronya another child. I hope it will be a girl this time, and no matter what her name to me she will be Ruth, for you whom I love.

Please keep writing to me. I read and re-read your letters, and to you I can talk of everything. Like Ronya, you have a way of making your point with a fable, only quite often Ronya makes hers painfully direct. You, my Mother, are a more gentle interpreter of my feelings.

Your Boris

Ronya's letter reached Katya at her husband's palace on the Moskva River. When the Tartars burned Moscow in 1237, the original house that stood on the site was saved, for it stood at the water's edge. Now it remained a monument in the beautiful modern city of short summers and long, hard, ice-solid winters.

The letter was a shock to Katya. Though she felt herself rich in fertility, she was convinced she would never give Alexis an heir, for she experienced no strength, no glory in his mild sexuality. Yet her marriage was very important to her. She thought of Alexis, always, with love. She felt comfort in his kisses, peace in his arms.

Ronya's letter made her aware of passion; it was like the ringing of the city's five thousand bells. It made her feel undone and unequal, because Ronya had Igor, born from the fire of married love.

Without a thought of sharing Ronya's request with Alexis, she took it upon herself to answer.

Ronya, I must say you are not overburdened with good sense or good taste. How dare you suggest that Alexis give his lofty, honorable name to Tamara's bastard? If it is a blond one you want, I'm certain Boris will oblige you, and if you are so anxious that I have a son and Alexis an heir, I'll take Igor—happily, gratefully, forever and ever in debt to you. You see—my love for you outweighs my low opinion of Boris.

I must mention Mother. Do you know that Boris is her chief confidant? Imagine—a woman of her breeding sympathetic to his excesses. What has happened to her?

There is no sense in going on, but this I must say: Father is failing. Go to him, bring a little excitement back into his life. If you decide on Vienna, I'll go with you. My heart goes out to Father in his loneliness for you, but if you remain obstinate I'll see you in Kiev in three weeks as planned.

I do love you, my little sister.

Your Katya

Ronya read the letter, and tore it to pieces.

15

In Vienna, David lived in incomparable luxury; and despite Ronya's refusal to turn from Boris, he nourished the conviction that in time—next year, the year after—Ronya, lost without him, would ask him to come home. He would make his return to Kiev dependent on certain stipulations, for by then Boris' powerful hold on her would have considerably diminished; by then conceivably he might have been carried from some arena, feet first. It was perfectly possible. From the very beginning of his self-imposed exile, David had deluded himself in other ways. From all reports Ronya was taking successfully to business:

"Ronya manages the estate better than did your overseer, whom she has discharged for taking more than a fair share from the tenant peasants. The new agreements she has made with the grain and wheat wholesalers are advantageous to her as a grower. Mindful of the future, she has quarreled with Rifka because the gypsies were cutting too much timber and has put a stop to that. And since some of the finest of pelts—the best sable, mink, fox, and ermine—come from our thick forests around the Dnieper, she has persuaded your son-in-law to trade in furs as well as horses. Enclosed are financial statements. You will find them impressive."

146

No girl involves herself so deeply unless she is seeking to fill her empty hours, David concluded after much thought. What contented girl would bother with the few extra rubles pocketed by the overseer?

When, on the birth of Igor, it was reported to him that the child was all Von Glasman, he felt a rush of masculine pride: For all of Boris' strength and sexual vitality, his—through Ronya—were the determining factors of heredity.

This was followed less than two weeks later by three letters almost impossible to believe—the shocking news that Boris could mate in the straw like a stable boy with a peasant wench and then go raving mad and give Tamara a savage beating.

"That perverted monster!" he cried.

Ruth tried to reason with him. "David, you are determined to put all the blame on Boris. What about Tamara's part in this, and Ronya's?"

"My daughter was perfectly justified in reacting as she did, considering the circumstances."

Ruth sighed. "Rifka did her job well. I believe that *she* and *we* are more to blame than Boris and Tamara."

"We?" David said, shocked.

"Yes, my dear, we helped fashion Tamara. I always thought she would break Ronya's heart one day. From the day our little Ronya was born, Rifka had just one goal—to feed Tamara from Ronya's plate. I begged you to protect Ronya from the gypsies. You would never listen. And what explanation did you give? You told me not to concern myself with matters I did not understand. You said, 'You are not a Russian, Ruth.' You made me feel less than Rifka, but I loved you too much to argue. I was afraid that if I forced a choice, you might get rid of me and not the gypsies."

"Nonsense!"

Ruth touched David's arm. "Listen to me, dear. Now that this dreadful thing has happened, Boris needs a friend." Her voice filled with pleading. "If you call him son now, Tamara will never matter again. Boris will throw away everything truly alien to his real self—his Tartar life, his women."

David's eyes blazed. "Do you think that after this my Ronya will want him?"

"Yes," she said quietly.

"And I," David said, "think exactly the opposite."

Fiercely he held on to his belief that Ronya would beg him to come home, and Ruth was astonished at the energy with which he planned their triumphant return to Kiev. Ruth refused to entertain false hope; still, she was comforted to see him less tormented.

It happened on a Friday afternoon some nine months later.

Waiting in her sitting room for her hairdresser—they were to dine at one of the foreign embassies and then go on to the opera—Ruth learned that David was shut up in his study with Ladislaus. She was pleased; Ladislaus, a great favorite of hers, always came to talk with her after he and David had finished their business. But when David walked into the room alone a few minutes later, she realized from one glance at his set face that Tamara's child had been born. Prepared though she had been, she felt the sob rise in her throat and choked it down. She dismissed her maid, and she and David regarded each other in silence. He seemed surprisingly composed. Handing her the letter, he sat down and waited without speaking while she read it.

Brutally unrefined in her language, Rifka described the birth in all its horrible detail and castigated both Boris and Ronya for their harsh treatment of Tamara. She accused Ronya of injustice and heartlessness in shielding Boris and banishing Fedor from his ancestral home and hinted that Fedor might not survive Boris' blow. "I am alarmed that he still has severe headaches and blurred vision."

Ruth laid the letter down, her heart heavy with foreboding. "David, we must go home."

He looked distastefully at Rifka's letter. "Why do you think Ladislaus is here? I am counting on just that. Fedor will be fully compensated, and once Boris removes himself from Kiev, I'll provide for him too. He'll leave with more to his name than a few caves and some barren hills in Odessa. As for Ronya, she will love again. Only yesterday I ran into Doctor Erick Stiller on the Goethegasse. There is no mistaking his interest in Ronya. He called out—"

"David," she broke in disapprovingly, "how can you think of such a thing at a time like this?"

Torn from his pleasant speculations, he admitted to himself that they were indeed premature; still, it had entered his mind at their first meeting that the doctor was just the sort of husband he wanted for Ronya. He leaned back in his chair, closed his eyes, and started to compose the letter he would write to her.

"David—" Ruth began. He did not stir. She sighed and slowly went over to him. "David, listen."

His eyes opened.

"You haven't given a thought to Tamara's pain, have you?"

"No. Nor—beyond a generous gift—to her brat, damn him."

Ruth's voice seemed to be coming from a distance, interrupting his thoughts of Ronya; David made himself listen.

"I am thinking that you understand finance and politics, but you don't understand people."

148

"Nonsense. A man who doesn't understand people is no more financier or politician than you are."

"In that case, hear me out and prove me wrong. Answer truthfully, David. In the too many times you have left me alone, exposed to tall, blue-eyed, light-haired men, did you ever consider I might be unfaithful to you?"

There was no need to think. "Never."

Her gaze remained steadily on him. "Do you suppose Katya might one day accept an anonymous seed to provide her with a child of her own to love and prevent the end of a glorious name?"

David's voice rose. "Never!"

"Why, my love? Why couldn't I? Why can't Katya?"

"Because you are what you are," he answered sharply. "What's your point?"

"That is my point: Basically, people do not change. Sometimes they develop, but habits are hard to break and to imbue new values is indeed difficult. Is it possible that you persuaded yourself that merely by being transferred from St. Petersburg to Kiev, Boris would all at once become a paragon of virtue?"

David said irritably, "Am I being told that you regard what happened in Kiev as no scandal, no insult, no injury? Just a naughty habit, a bit of spice to give zest to everyday existence?"

"The thing that happened has been happening for generations between the Von Glasman men and gypsy women. I am sorry Tamara put herself in Boris' path, I am sorry Boris accepted the invitation, I am sorry that Ronya took so terrible a blow, but she took it without complaint to us or to Katya, and her love for Boris stays bright. Why don't we take our cue from her? The fact is, in Russia, adultery and illegitimacy are in fashion."

"Ronya is not a Von Glasman wife. She *is* a Von Glasman," David said brutally.

"Like Sophia?"

Without answering, David got to his feet. Halfway to the door, he stopped, hesitated. "What did you mean by that?"

I wonder . . . Ruth thought. *If I'm right, and I open his eyes, perhaps . . . I'll chance it,* she decided.

"David," she said gently, "I implore you to think about it. Is it possible that Boris reminds you of Azov?"

Ruth could see him visibly struggle to control his trembling. Then, he turned away.

Left alone, Ruth chided herself. "It was a mistake, I did wrong." She shut her eyes, but the look on David's face stayed with her.

In his study, David sat for a while staring into space, his mind blank; then he pulled himself together and set about writing to Ronya.

Ronya, dearest child,
No word from you; studied, biting censure from Rifka. Do not let it worry you. Boris and Tamara are suited to one another. As for Fedor, I am making plans for him, plans that, if it be your wish, can include Rifka and all her tribe. I have sent Ladislaus to Hungary to buy land. Hungary answers my need because it is a country with a large enough gypsy population to sweeten Fedor's life.

Ronya, my love, your mother and I are willing to come home, and as soon as we get there I shall start to arrange the annulment of your marriage.

Or, if you prefer, I am willing to take you and my grandson out of Russia—Vienna, London, Berlin, New York, Rome, Paris—anywhere. I can serve Mother Russia in all parts of the world.

I await your answer. And know, sweet child, that for you everything is possible.

Thank God our separation is over. It has been a long time—fifteen months, two weeks, and five days.
Your devoted and ever-loving father,
David

David checked the mail every day. Nothing from Ronya. He waited. "Shall I go to Kiev and hurry Ronya up?" he asked Ruth.

"Don't, David, please don't."

"Perhaps the letter was lost in transit. I shall write another."

"No, David, I beg of you, don't."

"I cannot permit Ronya to think that I am impotent to help her."

"She knows, dear, you have a giant's strength. Wait."

Finally, it came.

Dear Father,
I have tried to write parts of this letter a hundred times—maybe I needed your letter to give me the impetus to do so. Still I have waited before picking up my pen, afraid I would say hurtful things I would regret. Yet there is one thing I feel impelled to say: Your letter is immoral, even if it is well meaning.

Father, I shall never forgive Tamara as long as I live, yet already I am finding it hard to hate her. Tamara is part of me, just as Rifka is part of you, and just as the Blond One is now part of Igor. It was you who taught me to be part of the whole farcical tradition—the gypsy queens, the Tartar woman's curse—and if you had entrusted me with less, if you had left open the door of choice, I could agree with Boris that we should get rid of Tamara, get rid of them all.

But I'm being unfair. It's not your fault, any more than your involvement was your father's fault. Like you, I remember that so far the crown has never broken Tzar Peter's promise to Aaron von Glasman, and like you, I don't want to be the first Von Glasman to break Aaron's promise to his Emperor.

Now I want to tell you about Boris' second son. He is the most beautiful child I have ever seen and deserves better than a gypsy camp, but Boris' rejection of him is as deliberate and unfair as your blundering rejection of Boris. And that brings us to the chief point of this letter.

I am not leaving Boris. I love him and astonishingly enough, he loves me even more than I love him. I am not sure that I am capable of loving as consummately as he loves. I know that in a few weeks or months he'll do something he shouldn't again, but I also know that one day he will be all I want him to be.

And there are other considerations: I want more children, and there is Igor to think of.

Father, you worry me, partly because you want of me what I cannot give. I cannot be satisfied being your whole life. There are many kinds of love, and I need the kind of love I have for Boris, which has nothing to do with you. Besides, what of Mother and Katya? How do you think they feel stripped of their rightful share?

Your abuse of Boris startles me. I've been poring over the old family journals and diaries and thinking about their wretched revelations.

"Tempted by a dalliance with the young beauty already an accomplished harlot."

"By the side of my serene Naomi, I am aware of the mystery of wide Asiatic eyes that are clear blue. I long for them."

So they go, Father. On and on.

"Today, I put fantasy in action. God help me!"

And this: "It is a girl child. The choosing of a name came to my Naomi. Given the imp, she hugged it to her, and said, 'Abra was the favorite of Solomon. I name thee Abra.' (I'd have named her Ara for the goddess of destruction!)"

How, Father, is Boris worse than Aaron von Glasman?

How am I better than Naomi?

Father, you have no idea how much Boris misses Mother. You have no idea how much I want Igor to know his grandparents. Come home. Boris is not the sort of man who holds grudges.

I do love you, Father, and I do miss you. Kiss Mother for us.

Your daughter,
Ronya

David sat for a time with his head bowed. Then he roused himself and went to his room.

He found Ruth waiting for him. Her dark hair parted in the middle, she looked in her blue lace negligee the image of a young girl. She crossed the room and kissed him affectionately. "Well," she asked sitting down, "what's Ronya's answer?"

151

David stared up at Ronya's portrait above his bed. "For the present, it is as you said," he answered sadly.

A wave of pity flowed over her.

For a while neither spoke, and then he said, "I'll give Ronya her head a bit longer."

"David dear," she said gently, "traditionally daughters have left their fathers to become wives, and that is as it should be."

"Why is it," he said, lowering himself into an armchair, "that women take pleasure in voicing platitudes? I do not reproach Ronya for choosing a husband, nor do I wish to put myself in his place.

"The differences and antagonisms between me and the Tartar are in direct proportion to his exploitation of Ronya. I merely wish to put an end to his cruelty and duplicity. It is absurd to assume otherwise. However, nothing can be effected except with Ronya's cooperation, and this requires further patience. I am by no means through with Boris Pirov."

Ruth's eyes and ears picked up the difference in him. He was making the same motions, the same sounds, but now there was no strength in his voice, simply a thin, unconvincing repetition of the dead words. He sounded like an old man.

Her heart went out to him. "David dear, sorrow passes, anger passes."

"It makes little difference to me now."

Ruth wanted to cry out, "What about me, David? Shall I never get you back?" She checked herself. Poor, tortured man, what could he say? "Please, David," she said at last, "may I see Ronya's letter?"

He carried it over to her. "Forgive me, Ruth, I don't mean half I say." He rang the bell. To the servant who answered his ring he said, "My carriage, please."

On his return from his attorney, at whose offices he made a series of provisions and signed several legal documents, he found a letter from Katya.

Katya, angry with Boris and even more furious with Tamara, blamed Ronya for not getting rid of the gypsies once and for all, and begged David to bring Ruth back to Kiev and banish the whole tribe. The last sentence of the letter stuck in his mind:

"As Alexis says, 'No one seems to realize how young Ronya is.' "

He went to his journal and wrote: "Without a dream a man dies."

The next day, David overslept and woke feeling unwell. "I'm getting a cold," he thought. He remained under his feather bed taking hot tea and a little clear soup. Ruth suggested she call in their doctor.

"For what ails me, a doctor has no cure," he said.

This acceptance of defeat frightened her, but since he had no fever and no sign of physical ailment, she decided to wait. David dozed and between naps seemed sunk in gloom. Toward evening, she said, "I'd feel much easier if you let me send for Ladislaus."

David answered, "Not yet."

Within twenty-four hours, except for a mild sluggishness, he appeared relatively well.

In an effort to distract him, Ruth pretended an interest in a lecture at the university and, David, apathetic, yielded to her wish. Uninterested in the lecturer's theme of moral intolerance, he sat inattentive until he was shaken into awareness by a quotation from the Englishman Locke: "The power parents have over children arises from duty —to take care of an offspring during the state of childhood. But when the child comes to the estate that made the father a free man, the son is a free man, too."

After he and Ruth got home, David went into his study and began to read—Descartes, Spinoza, Locke.

"Locke," he read, "maintained that all man's knowledge originates from sense perception. The human mind, at birth, is a blank—a white paper—upon which absolutely nothing is inscribed. Not until the newborn child begins to have experiences to perceive the external world with its senses is anything registered."

Suddenly tired, he closed his eyes. His mind drifted. He sat back, raised his feet onto a black leather ottoman, and let it drift. His mind went blank—a white paper upon which absolutely nothing was inscribed. Then it came back to him—Ronya in her wondrous nudity— the whip—the man, gloriously ready. At long last David von Glasman knew. He wanted to be Boris, just as—in the deeply buried, nearly forgotten long ago—he had wanted to take Azov's place with Sophia. Poor little fellow, lonely and alone, caught in a desperate fight for a sister whom he needed for survival, the tortured memory of Sophia and her lover in fierce mating stirring in the man the primitive passion of father for daughter.

David lost consciousness.

When he came to, self-deception no longer possible, David made a stern evaluation of himself. All his conspicuous accomplishments, all his high motives, all his personal ambitions for Alexis, for his grandson, obscured by Shame—the mocking god.

At dinner, Ruth saw that his remoteness had taken on a new dimension. Truly alarmed, she made herself calm, for David expected calmness from her at the most terrifying times. Speaking quietly, she said, "David, I want to go home. I must."

David looked up, but his eyes remained blank, unfocused. "Home?"

"Yes, home. Kiev, where my children were born, where my grandson is, where we shared a life."

There was a long silence. "Go if you want to. For me, because I have made a fool of myself, one place is exactly the same as any other, so I shall remain here, thereby rendering unto Boris the things that are Boris'."

He did not allow her to reply. He walked silently out of the room and went to his bedroom, from which he never voluntarily emerged again.

Each day the doctor called, but David spurned his suggestions. He refused all solids. During the day, unless he dozed against his pillows, he stared at Ronya's portrait. At night, he read and often wrote.

Days passed. The doctor confided in Ruth, "He is willing his own death, but he is a strong man in perfect health; it will take time."

In January of 1893, some days after Igor's birthday, Ruth gave David an ultimatum. "Come with me to the Mediterranean and regain your strength, or I send for Boris."

In appreciation of her strategy, David rewarded her with a feeble smile. "You have managed my capitulation."

In June, Ruth contrived to get him to Baden-Baden; there, too, he continued his pattern of starvation and inertness. By midwinter they were back in Vienna. Skeleton thin, David reestablished himself in his room.

Ruth cried. "Oh God, why must it be? Please," she pleaded, "let me send for the children."

"I do not want them."

She dropped down on his bed. "I have a letter from Katya. She and Alexis are in Kiev. They don't understand why you don't want to see them." She saw he listened spiritlessly and almost wished his former tormented look back—it was better than nothingness. She wanted to weep. "I have a wonderful surprise for you. Ronya wants Katya and Alexis to bring Igor here for a visit with us. Boris agrees."

"That's very handsome of Boris."

She forced a happy smile. "Then it's all settled. I'll tell them to come at once."

He reached across the bed and took her hand. "No."

"David, for my sake. Please."

"I made a fool of myself," David said, more melancholy than ever.

"David, why do you keep saying that?"

David did not answer her, nor did he know he still held her hand. He was staring at Ronya's portrait, absorbed. "It is said that every man has his own insanity. Ronya is mine."

154

Ruth raised her own eyes to her daughter's portrait. Seeking an answer, she appraised the face—part sensual, part innocent, pronounced cheekbones, high-arched brows, a wide mouth with a tentative smile on full, slightly parted lips. Black eyes, intent and seeking, and a little sad. The artist had captured something of her glow—the warm skin, the swell of her breasts. She thought, *Poor baby, the center of a twisted tangle, none of it your making.* Ruth looked away. She disengaged her hand and put out the lights. A cold winter moon shone through the windows, and by its thin light she sat and watched David doze, his mouth a little open.

One morning, suddenly speaking strongly, David said to her, "Summon Ladislaus. When he arrives, I want to see him alone."

The summons had to go through Sergey in Geneva.

By evening of the seventh day, Ladislaus was at David's bedside. A wave of pity swept over him. Clasping the cadaverous form—his savior, his mentor—he kissed him Russian style. "God Almighty," he said, "your long silence was baffling. Where's Ronya? Where's Katya? Why aren't they here?"

David smiled his old smile. "Calm yourself."

Ladislaus took out his handkerchief and wiped his eyes.

"Pull up a chair."

"I'm worried, David. What will happen to Ruth, to all of us, if anything happens to you?"

"Shed no tears," David answered. "Death is sleep, sleep as long as the Jewish exile, sleep until the coming of the Messiah."

"David, why?"

"Because I caused my own defeat."

Ladislaus wished he could be sure he understood what David meant. He thought a little and then said diffidently, "Ruth tells me the doctor believes you are bewitched, that you yourself have cast the spell."

"We have a saying, 'Whatever one desires most, one dreams about.' I dream only of death."

"I don't understand you. With all you have to live for—"

"My death is not the death of Moses. Don't act as if it were," David said, with something of his former asperity.

Ladislaus glanced at the man in the bed. Blinking back tears, he said, "I never thought it would end like this. I don't know what to say."

Nodding, David said, "We have another saying. 'The deeper the sorrow, the less tongue it has.' " And he added with his old twinkle, "We Jews are full of sayings."

Ladislaus smiled and waited.

155

After a few minutes, David began speaking again, his voice devoid of emotion. "I want to be buried in Kiev on my own land alongside my forebears. Leave the plots next to mine empty. To my right is Ruth's resting place. The one on my left is for a woman who calls herself Sophia Azov. She lives in New York City, she is my sister. When she dies, bring her home. There will be no legal tangles there. Paul has my will and a letter I have written to Ronya. Both are explicit. Both will be delivered to her after my death. You, of course, will remain on salary for the rest of your life. A bit extra is on deposit in Geneva; upon request, Sergey will turn it over to you. As for this house and its furnishings, take your instructions from Ruth. Ronya's portrait I bequeath to Boris. Tell him she will grow into it. The artist saw in the girl the woman to be. He had a strong certainty about Ronya. He was right."

Bewildered, Ladislaus managed to say, "David, I think you should rest before you tell me more."

The next day, David sent for Ladislaus early. The night had not refreshed him. His skin had a gray tinge and, though he spoke steadily, his voice was weak. Without wasting time, he told Ladislaus to keep Ronya informed on world intrigue. "But don't burden her. I'm sure Ruth will want to go to Sophia." David's voice trailed away. Ladislaus could hear his labored breathing in the quiet room and he silently willed strength into his mentor. "When she travels, travel with her. Keep in close touch. I feel Ronya will need you."

"I shall serve her," Ladislaus promised.

The effort of speaking seemed to have exhausted him. Ladislaus took his hand.

"Go, Ladislaus, my friend," he said in a whisper.

"Please, David, let me stay."

"I am tired."

David relapsed into apathy.

The next day, he did not speak, hardly opening his eyes, neither eating nor drinking. The day after, he thought little Ronya had fallen off her sled, which upset him so much he spoke harshly to Ruth, telling her to take better care of the child. The doctor sedated him. After a long sleep, he roused himself long enough to tell Ruth that he loved her, and that at times her eyes were the color of the sea and at other times much darker with specks of emerald green in them. Then he died.

Ruth's tears were endless, so long had she held them back. Ladislaus sat beside her motionless. Eventually the doctor came and gave her an injection of morphia and Ladislaus carried her into her own room. He sat with her all through the night. When she stirred, his long, strong fingers stroked her hair.

156

16

He was gone just three years, one month, and sixteen days, and now he was home. David's family wanted no strangers around the black marble coffin in the family cemetery deep in the pine grove. Time enough later, after the burial, for the landowners, the rich Jews and obscure Jews, the military, the politicians, the writers and artists whom he had supported in life, the peasants and the gypsies to pay their respects.

In Vienna, Ruth tore the clothing opposite her heart with her nails and washed David with her own hands. When he was enveloped in a white sheet, she lit the candles and stood watch, forbidding herself even a glass of water.

From the moment Boris, Father Tromokov, and two of Rifka's trusted men carried the heavy casket from the train and into the house, everything was arranged in accordance with Ruth's wishes. The coffin was placed, foot toward the door, on a low catafalque covered with Oriental rugs. A *talith* with fringes was draped over it, and lighted candles were placed at the head. The family—Rifka, Tamara, and Paul included—waited with David for the funeral escort sent by the Jewish congregation headed by Rabbi Simon Levinsky, who had left his son Joseph, now an ordained rabbi, in the synagogue with a quorum of ten men reciting the Kaddish for the dead.

Thirty paces from the grave, the pallbearers halted the coffin seven times, indicative of the seven portals of hell.

Ruth began the burial service: "Praised be Thou, O Lord our God, King of the Universe, who created you in justice, who maintained you in justice, who caused you to die in justice."

When the coffin was laid in the grave, the rabbi recited: "May his repose be in paradise, and may his soul be bound up in the bond of eternal life, and may his repose be peace."

The few mourners stood in two rows, through which Ruth passed first, followed by Ronya and Katya holding hands. Before David's wife and daughters left the burial ground, they plucked some grass and threw it behind them, saying, "He remembereth that we are dust."

The grave was filled.

The ladies of the congregation supplied the first meal, the meal of condolence, for on the first day of mourning the mourner is not permitted to prepare his own food. After the meal the Jews left; except for Simon Levinsky, they did not return. Most of the people who called were Ukrainians, though some came from as far as Moscow, St. Petersburg, and the Crimea, and their presence attested to David's importance and to the high esteem in which he was held. For seven days Ruth kept the candles burning for David's departed soul.

Ronya stayed in her own room much of the time, making her first survey of the papers that Paul had given her—David's will, letters, and a political appraisal of the future of Russia and his concern regarding the situation of the Jews under a Tzar distinguished for his stupidity and a Tzarina who fervently believed that Judaism must be suppressed and that the only virtues were German.

At the moment, she was principally interested in the letters, of which there were two.

> Ronya, dearest child,
> I say it in my will, but first I say it here to you alone. I have made Boris rich—comparatively rich; money has a way of magnifying a man's faults and virtues.
> You ask, how does Boris deserve the riches I bestow upon him? It is my final fling at victory, my revenge. You will not leave him; I make it easy for him to leave you.
> Don't think for a moment, Ronya my own, that I allow myself to believe this will happen. I have known Boris long enough to know that, though he spends lavishly, money does not matter to him. Well, the kind of money I leave him doesn't matter to me.
> For you, my darling, life must never become empty. You plan a life with Boris. Whatever happens, don't *ever* leave your children, so that more children are but a matter of time. As long as there are children, there is no boredom. Children are the sun and the earth. They are the music.
> There are no words to express how much you mean to me. I think you know.
> God bless you, Ronya.
>
> > Your loving father,
> > David von Glasman

Ronya laid the letter down and tore open a second envelope, this one sealed in wax and labeled: "Postscript—read last."

> Dearest Ronya,
> I have come upon something about which I cannot be specific. Frankly, it would not be proper.
> I cannot go to my Maker without confessing to you, Ronya my child, that my hostile feelings toward Boris have drawn their source from elsewhere.
> I wish to make an apology, and therefore bequeath to Boris my most precious possession, your portrait.
> Still, the Talmud, which allows polygamy, makes adultery a cap-

ital crime. In our faith, all who go down to hell shall come up again except these three:

"He who commits adultery."

"He who shames another in public."

"He who gives another a bad name."

So, my daughter, though I have sinned against Boris, when you meet me in a place called Gan Eden, it shall be without Boris the adulterer.

Your father,
David von Glasman

David's letters set many emotions stirring; together they puzzled Ronya and infuriated her. She let the papers drop on the desk.

Father, why did you not keep silent? Why do you talk to me from the grave? Why do you confuse me? I don't want to be reminded that I let you go because I was beginning not to like you. You shaped me. You taught me to think, to reject false premises, to be determined, to face facts. But you taught me intrigue, too—and deviousness.

Ronya sighed, knowing that she had better concentrate on making herself beautiful for the coming ordeal. Boris had to be told about her father's last vengeful wile.

She chose a pale yellow ruffled shirtwaist and a wrap-around skirt of a deeper yellow. Piling her hair high on her head, she tied it with a violet ribbon and put the finishing touches with diamond earrings and her cherished heart-shaped pin. It was the first time since David's death that she had given a single thought to her looks. Then she sat down to wait for Boris, who she knew would soon be coming in from the stables to dress for dinner.

As soon as he entered the room, he took in her careful appearance and air of suppressed excitement. The smile that started deep in his eyes never reached his lips. "What's happened, dove?"

"I have something to tell you," Ronya replied.

Boris had a strong inkling she was going to tell him that she was pregnant. His arms went around her, and he kissed her warmly. He put his lips to her ear. "I know, little dove."

"I don't think you do," she said, leaning heavily against him.

Something in her tone made Boris stiffen. "Well," he said, pulling off his boots and sinking into his armchair. "What have you got to say?"

"Something quite unpleasant. My father has left you quite a lot of money."

A sharp frown appeared between his brows. "For what reason?"

She produced the first of David's letters. "Here. Read."

Boris read intently, while she watched closely, and before he had finished the last sentence she said, "Well, what do you think?"

He shrugged. "Set to music this makes one hell of a sad ballad."

Ronya was amazed. "You take the affront so calmly! I expected a full-scale Tartar rage."

Boris looked at her thoughtfully. "I am thinking that much of this is my fault. I did earn David's disrespect."

Ronya was grateful; Boris knew it and smiled. "I'm in a position to be generous. An enchanting female, only slightly pregnant, is in love with me."

"Are you going to take the money?"

"Sure," he replied with a grin.

Now the sharp frown appeared between Ronya's brows. "That's out of character, Boris."

"Yes."

Ronya thought, *This is not possible.* "What will you do with it?"

His grin broadened. "You'll think of something, Ronya."

Ronya's face began to glow.

"Let's go to bed."

"This," she said, reaching into her pocket, "is in the nature of a postscript."

Boris read the second letter and raised an eyebrow. But his curiosity was not as intense as hers. All he cared about was Ronya's portrait; he had been meaning to ask Ruth for it. "I appreciate the portrait more than I can say," he said seriously.

"What was my father thinking? What was he feeling? Shall we ask Mother?"

His response was immediate and emphatic. "No, she's had troubles enough the last few years. Let's go to bed."

Ronya sighed with relief that everything had gone so smoothly. "I want a cigarette, and you have some explaining to do."

"No cigarette," he said, with an air of finality.

"How long have you known?"

"Since Lydia told me that we've run out of dill pickles," he said teasingly.

That night Boris did not sleep. He lay awake thinking about the happiness Ronya found in Igor and even in the bastard. He felt a rising anxiety about the months ahead. He knew for certain—he had a sixth sense about it—that Ronya was carrying a boy. Her face wreathed in smiles, tired and happy, she'd look at him and call him David, for her father. "Goddamn," Boris thought. "One son has purpose. Who in hell needs two? Or more." Feeling bleak, he clasped Ronya in his arms. "Ronya, don't get absorbed in the baby. Think of me."

160

From the moment she came home, Ruth devoted herself to Igor and he brought her much joy and a few sharp surprises. Right off, he told her, "I am going on four, and my brother is almost three. We play together, and he loves me the best in all the world."

Swift in making judgments, Igor was exceptionally articulate for his age. The adults tried to protect him from the knowledge of death, but he delighted in relating his experiences with dead birds, dead bugs, and one dead kitten to the despair of his beloved Aunt Katya and Rifka. He began to harbor a dreadful fear. It never occurred to him that death could embrace Ronya or Boris, both of whom he considered Titans, everlasting and all powerful; his fear centered on Ruth, who let him light the candles and play with her jewels and, when it was time for a nap, took him and the Blond One into her own bed, where she told them fascinating stories and sang them wonderful songs.

As his fear sharpened, his demands on Ruth for attention increased, and even Katya reprimanded him one day for pestering his grandmother.

Motioning Katya to keep quiet, Ruth asked, "What is the trouble, sweetheart?"

"Are you old?"

"Why do you ask, Igor? Does it matter?"

"Yes, Ruth, my grandmother. Old people die."

She took him by the hand and drew him close. "I promise to stay young."

Igor freed himself with a quick motion and said in his clear little voice, "I wish you were three going on four, then you could be my girl-friend as well as my grandmother."

Katya first noticed how frequently Ruth visited Rifka. She found Ronya in the kitchen one afternoon two weeks after the funeral flavoring the beef and rice filling for the stuffed cabbage and kneading her yeast dough for a second rising.

"Mother home?" she asked, sinking into Boris' rocking chair.

"She's at the camp."

"Isn't Mother spending an awful lot of time at the camp?" Katya asked, eying Ronya closely.

"Yes."

"Why do you suppose she's doing that?"

"She likes being with Rifka, and she takes Igor to play with the Blond One—like you, she feels I shouldn't impose him on Boris." Ronya shot Katya a quick look. "But she's beginning to love him very much."

"He is an adorable, lovable child."

Ronya was delighted. "Oh, Katya darling, I am so glad you finally see him as he is. You ought to have him."

Katya sighed. "You never give up, do you?"

"And you never give in."

"For the last time," Katya said angrily, "Tamara's bastard cannot carry my husband's title. Besides," she added, to soften her remark, "Rifka won't give him up."

"Yes, she will. To give her grandson your husband's title, she'd throw in her right arm."

"I cannot, I will not forget how and where he was begotten," Katya replied righteously. Her tone changed. "I don't understand you. Why don't you loathe Tamara?"

"I do," Ronya answered, swallowing to keep too much feeling from her voice. "I loathe her, detest her, want to cut her to ribbons with my whip—and I still love her."

Ronya turned back to her dough. "This is the second time I've asked. It's the last. I'll never bother you again."

While Katya and Ronya were arguing in the kitchen, Boris and Alexis were smoking companionably in the library. Two weeks now, and David's will remained unread. A suspicion had begun to dawn in their minds that, for some reason known only to themselves, the women had no appetite for its contents.

"Do you think I ought to leave Katya here, and come back when they're ready?"

"No, we ought to get it over with. Let's talk to Ruth."

Rather reluctantly they got to their feet; the library was pleasant and quiet, and neither was anxious to distress Ruth. But when they went to her upstairs sitting room, they found a new maid lackadaisically rubbing wax polish on the antique furniture.

Assuming she belonged to his mother-in-law, Boris asked, "Where can we find your mistress?"

It was Lydia's niece, Tanya. She was no proper servant but was being allowed to help in the house because her husband and brother were both serving prison sentences. Actually, Lydia did not trust her— she was sly and would have been light-fingered if her aunt had not kept a sharp eye on her. Lydia always made her leave at night and sleep at her grandfather's, the peasant cottage closest to the camp.

"Oh, sir," the girl answered pertly, "there's a love affair between her and the pots and pans. She'd live in the spice cabinet if she could."

Boris' nostrils flared, and the girl realized her mistake. She started to apologize, but Boris cut her off sharply. "Don't you ever speak of your mistress in that fashion again or you'll be looking for another job —Lydia or no Lydia."

"Insolent girl," Alexis remarked once they were out in the hall.

"It's not surprising that Ronya is resented in the kitchen," Boris said. "The servants have nowhere to go for a glass of tea and a bit of gossip."

Alexis chuckled. "Put a samovar in the ballroom for the servants, but don't, I beg you, take Ronya out of the kitchen. The flavors she produces are sheer heaven."

Boris made no reply; but as they descended the stairs, he said decisively, "The kitchen is the only ugly room in this magnificent house. It has no light, no air. We'll abandon it—give it back to the wenches. I'll build Ronya a new kitchen, one with every modern convenience and lots of space—and a herb garden just outside the door. It will face south and catch the sun; a room for people and for visiting—just right for Ronya."

Alexis chuckled. "Very amusing. We set out to find Ruth, and the house winds up with another room. Incidentally, where are we going?"

"To Rifka's house. Sometimes I wonder—did Ruth come to be with us or her?"

"You know, it's really quite strange. Katya told me that there was a time when David couldn't drag Ruth to the camp."

"Rifka is looking haggard," Boris said thoughtfully. "I wonder if she's ill. But I keep forgetting she's not that young. A damned shame that a beautiful woman can't keep back time."

"Some nights," Alexis said quietly, "I fantasize Katya's hair pure pewter, I see a little shawl over her shoulders. I like the picture. I look forward to the small delights of old age."

Boris sighed. "Old age!" Then his beguiling grin came. "I guess it's all right for old people."

They were almost at Rifka's house when Tamara came in sight, dawdling along the path with a great bunch of wild flowers in her arms. She brightened as soon as she saw them. "Hello," she said, "you must be on your way to Mother's. I'm sent packing when she and Ruth start reminiscing, but today I caught something really unusual," she said eagerly. "There's a letter from America. Someone in New York doesn't want to be interred in Kiev."

Boris took her in with one sweeping glance: lips blood-red, eye sockets smeared with green, a vitality radiating excitement. *Damn her,* he thought. He kept his silence.

Alexis disliked and resented Tamara intensely; her uninhibited sexuality offended him. Generally he pointedly ignored her, but now he said reprovingly, "Obviously Ruth and Rifka share something they prefer to keep private. Why chatter about a fragment of conversational pickings?"

"Pardon me," Tamara said heatedly. "Sorry my chatter doesn't amuse you." But she joined them.

It was a very silent trio that stepped into Rifka's parlor, where they found the two women seated in straight chairs by a tea cart and Igor and the Blond One playing quietly in a corner with stuffed animals.

Boris dropped into an armchair. "We missed you, Mother, so we've come to escort you home—are we interrupting?"

"No," Ruth said gravely. "You've caught us almost at the end of our conversation."

Rifka offered Alexis a cup of tea. "No, thanks," he said with careful politeness, "I think I'll talk to the children."

"Play game?" the Blond One said hopefully.

Rifka was assailed by curiosity. Alexis and Boris were not the kind of men who dropped in for a social call; clearly they had come for some purpose. And it was obvious that Tamara could hardly contain her desire to be alone with Boris.

"Here," Tamara said, "let me give you a vodka."

Boris looked at her. "Not if you pour."

The suddenness of Tamara's throaty laugh came as a surprise. In mischievous remembrance, she explained, "I doctored a drink, and he was out cold for hours."

Boris' eyes narrowed menacingly, but persistently Tamara went on. "He needed the rest."

Boris controlled his anger for Ruth's sake. Rising, she said, "I'll get my handbag and my wrap. I put them in the hall, I think. Come along, Igor."

The Blond One dashed to Ruth and tagged at her skirt. "I go, I go."

"Not now, angel. Igor and I will come for you tomorrow."

The Blond One went back to his corner and began fondling a little gray elephant.

Not once were Boris' eyes drawn to his bastard son.

If only he were mine! Alexis thought. He kissed the boy tenderly and prepared to follow Ruth.

Halfway out of the door, she came to a halt. "Do walk on a little," she said, "I'll be only a minute. Take Igor with you."

"What's wrong?" Rifka said.

"It's a private matter," Ruth said with a sidelong glance at Tamara. "Would you mind leaving us?"

"Out!" Rifka commanded. "Her imperviousness to her son sickens me."

Ruth found herself looking down at her hands. She did not like to talk about Tamara.

"Well?" Rifka's tone was abrupt.

Ruth looked up. "The letter. Will you destroy it?"

"That might be best."

"Must the girls know?" Ruth said shyly. "Would there be any point in telling them?"

"None," Rifka said with feeling. "Let them continue to think that David was an only child and I the only companion of his youth. If they find out about Sophia later, then they find out."

"Thank you, Rifka. I'll see you tomorrow."

The sun was setting as they headed in the direction of home, Igor running ahead playing some private game of his own. Whereas Alexis took uneven steps to match Ruth's pace, Boris, despite his size, walked along as if her legs belonged to him. *How beautifully he moves,* Ruth thought. After a while, she said, "There is a reason for your coming for me, isn't there?"

"Yes," Boris said.

"Nothing serious, I hope."

"I have to go back to St. Petersburg," Alexis said, "but I also have to be in Kiev for the reading of David's will. I have been wondering if you have decided on a date."

Ruth sighed. "I've put off thinking about it. It is so utterly marvelous to be with all my children and with Rifka after the loneliness of Vienna."

"I can come back."

Ruth felt the cool breeze and shivered, and Boris placed his arm gently around her shoulder. Close to Boris, she felt warmer. They walked on in silence until they came to the front door. Here, with the last of the sun's rays going from the horizon, Ruth said, "David's will has not been read because I play a game, called 'Pretend.' It would not surprise me a bit if both girls are playing the same game. So much of David's life was spent away from home, it is easy to bask in the belief that he will return."

Alexis admired Ruth and had a deep affection for her. "If that's helpful for a while, there is no harm."

But Boris loved Ruth. He loved her for herself and for loving him. Looking directly into her eyes, he said, "David is on a journey from which there is no return. To deny it is to remain forever enslaved."

Ruth considered carefully. "I shall ask Ronya to make the arrangements. David entrusted his will to her. He did not want me to have it." Very quietly, she added, "Poor David, he saw value only in Ronya. I minded more for her than for Katya and me. What a burden for one little girl! Still, he prepared her for it. He put an old head on her young shoulders."

Alexis frowned.

165

Boris made a mental note to prepare Ronya for a difficult situation while there was still time.

They could have all been spared discomfort had they known that Ronya, deeply sensitive on this point, far from usurping her mother's position as head of the family, had sent the sealed will to Rabbi Simon Levinsky, asking him to keep it until he heard from Ruth.

"Although addressed to me, the will is really for you. I am certain my father meant it so," she wrote tactfully.

17

On the evening appointed for the reading of David von Glasman's will, the gentle fragrance of apple blossom permeated the library. The rabbi, a bearded intellectual, intense and fragile, sat down at a desk near the window, allowing the others to group themselves around him in a small irregular circle. Boris followed him into the room, leading Ruth and Ronya. Recognizing this as a formal occasion, he had put on his regimental dress uniform; across his chest glittered an array of medals. It was the kind of clothing he liked. It was impressive; it suited his size.

Of the women, only David's widow wore black, but it was opulent, not funereal: velvet embroidered with the sheerest silver threads, set off by a double rope of pink pearls. In contrast, Ronya had chosen to dress simply, remembering the clothes David had liked her to wear. As Boris handed her into a chair and took his place between her and Ruth, the emerald on her finger glowed softly, echoing the pale apple green of her long-sleeved muslin dress.

Paul, who had purposely found police business in Kiev to coincide with the reading of the will, chose a chair near Ronya.

Alexis and the priest sat on a sofa on either side of Katya, Alexis' somber evening dress and the priest's black gown a splendid foil to her sumptuous sky-blue satin, with which she wore David's wedding gift, huge Oriental sapphires surrounded by diamonds—Katya enjoyed looking every inch the countess and besides, this was a night for paying tribute to her father's love of magnificence. Next to her the priest, Ivan Tromokov, though he wore the robes and cross of his church, looked even more the rough soldier-horseman than usual.

At Ronya's invitation Lydia was there too, but sensitive of her position, she pulled a chair as close to the door as possible and sat respectfully on the edge of the seat.

Rifka came in with Tamara and her two granddaughters and saw at a glance that they had been isolated. The others had formed a close circle around the rabbi, and the gypsies were forced to find chairs and sit behind them. She noted this as yet another injury, and it rankled.

But no matter, she said to herself angrily, *David will have deeded the camp to me, in which case Tamara can do as she pleases and Ronya may as well be prepared to like it.*

She made one of the girls fetch her a big armchair upholstered in crimson velvet, in which she enthroned herself regally, conscious of the picture she made—burgundy-red satin and jewels that nearly outshone those of the Von Glasmans against the crimson of the chair. Boris gave her a sidelong look. He could appreciate that in her younger days she had driven men mad; she still retained the remnants of a striking and unconventional beauty.

His eyes avoided Tamara, but he could not help seeing the emphatically painted eyes and mouth, the dress of brilliantly ornamented orange, green, blue, and gold—the skirt cut to display a trim ankle—the belt of many-colored stones fastened with a huge gold buckle. The gaudy skirts and petticoats, the colored stones, the gold were worn for a purpose: The evil spirits who live in black holes and swarm the earth in the dark night do not dare venture among colors as light and bright as the summer sun. The two young girls, Fedor's daughters, wore simple blouses and dirndl skirts and strings of beads, but as brightly colored as Tamara's silks. They had escaped banishment with Fedor because the tribe needed one or the other to produce a queen to follow Tamara.

There was silence until everyone was settled.

Then the rabbi broke the seal and pulled the will from its envelope. Written in David's meticulous script, though duly witnessed and made legal, it was not a formal document.

It began:

> I have provided for my beloved wife Ruth von Glasman, for relatives, friends, and employees separate from my main estate. In this, my last testament, I am mainly concerned with my daughters, namely Katya von Glasman Brusilov and Ronya von Glasman Pirov.

I instruct Ronya to give the Tintoretto, a Rembrandt, and an El Greco from my collection to my esteemed son-in-law, Count Alexis Brusilov. All other objects of art are to remain in the house in Kiev and pass through Ronya to her heirs.

To Boris Pirov I leave Ronya's portrait, unconditionally. When this will has been read, Ronya must notify Sergey in Geneva, and he will remit to Boris Pirov a certain sum of money, which Boris Pirov may have in any currency he chooses. Thus I make the world open to Boris Pirov. He may take his leave of Kiev at any time without forfeiting the abundant life.

The rabbi could not go on. He heard identical gasps from Ruth and Katya. There was no sound from Count Brusilov, the priest, or Paul. The rabbi did not care about the gypsies, but he could not help catch the ephemeral smile on Tamara's lips. He did not want to look at the Pirovs. He imagined he could see the fury in his eyes, the agony in hers. He was mistaken.

Boris felt forced to speak. "It is pointless," he said quietly, "for you all to speculate on my feelings and Ronya's. This is no thundering surprise to either of us—or to Paul. David gave Ronya and Paul advance notice, and Ronya took me into her confidence." Boris had not meant to say more than this, but he found himself continuing, his gaze on Rifka, his voice taking on a hardness. "Rest easy. Nothing—nobody— can take Ronya from me. Only death can take me from her."

Rifka thought: *Wait, Blond Tartar. Some day—*

Tamara was not dismayed: She had no wish to take Boris away from Ronya.

Katya waited hopefully. Perhaps David, who had manipulated an Empress, had found a way to get rid of the gypsies.

The rabbi looked around. Such craziness! If David had wanted a nice Jewish lad for a son-in-law, he would have been a different kind of father. He heaved a sigh and went back to the will.

Father Ivan Tromokov will take the needs of his people to Ronya; she will do her duty. She will also honor Hebrew charity. I know she will open her purse wide; I caution her to open it quietly: Jewish prosperity excites animosity.

Remember, today in Vienna there is furous anti-Semitic agitation. The ritual murder theme arises again and again. Here at the Universität zu Wien, a brilliant young thinker named Freud believes that anti-Semitism is based on the idea—the Jewish idea—of the "Chosen People." He says: "If God holds Israel near, other nations feel themselves kept at a distance."

I leave this reminder to you. Change in Russia is bound to come. If it comes from the crown in the form of increased liberty and the betterment of the lot of the masses, well and good. If, however, either extreme—reactionary or revolutionary—takes complete control, be prepared to run. Have ready portable wealth. Continue to acquire gems—flawless diamonds, large emeralds.

Now to the heart of this document.

I put everything into Ronya's hands, with one provision. My daughter Katya, who is wedded to Count Alexis Brusilov, is provided with resources far beyond anyone's wants. However, should she ever, for whatever reason, be reduced in circumstance, I command Ronya to provide her sister with her full share. Katya is to live in the plenty I regard essential for her.

David's total rejection of Tamara was final; nowhere was she mentioned. And because Rifka had allowed Tamara to plunge into illicit passion and promiscuity, her dream for an independent little kingdom lay shattered. The land remained Von Glasman land, Ronya's to guard.

No one said anything.

Deeply attuned to moods, the rabbi searched faces. The priest wore a pleasant expression. Ivan Tromokov understood what David had done and was impressed. He was also peased that Rifka had lost out. He detested her rigged magic and sorcery, and he could never forget the morning Boris sent him to the carriage house—to find that pathetic little monstrosity stuffed into a burlap sack.

Behind Ruth's control was heartache. *Oh, David, David! How could you?*

Boris' face was still, but not a reined-in stillness like Paul's. David had concentrated all his forces against him and lost. Emerging the victor can be a remarkable experience.

They all had the distinct feeling that Rifka was near the breaking point. Frighteningly pale, she was breathing harshly and trying to hold her hands still.

Tamara suspected her mother's bitterness. However, it happened that David's will suited her, because it restored Ronya to her. Accepting the estate, Ronya had to accept all its responsibilities. There was real comfort in that.

Alexis, enthralled, was watching everyone intently.

Lydia quietly stepped into the hall. When she returned, it was with a loaded cart.

Eventually, all eyes except Rifka's were fixed on Ronya. Not one of them saw clearly what she was feeling. Paul came the closest because he knew how well David had prepared her to take his place, but even so he could not be sure. Maybe what David expected was much more than a girl could provide.

Rabbi Levinsky broke the silence. "Speak the truth, little Ronya—

David's little princess. Do you feel your father treated you badly? Did he put too much in your charge?"

Katya came over to Ronya, embraced her, kissed her. "We think our father's arrangement excellent, don't we, Ronya?"

"Yes, Katya."

"And we're not being politely filial," Katya added. "We mean it."

"Well, well," Alexis said, and assumed the responsibility of the host. He gave Ruth and the girls dry sherry, Boris and the priest vodka. Rifka found herself with a brandy snifter in her hand. "Thank you, Alexis. I need a drink badly. I'm cold."

As soon as they all held their drinks, Alexis proposed a toast: "To David von Glasman—our genius. He ties us all to Ronya, thereby making sure that not one of us escapes him entirely. So be it."

Meanwhile, Ruth had decided to speak out on David's unkind and ungenerous bequest to Boris. "Dear Boris," she said, turning to him, "I wish it were in my power to take back David's insult. At least know that I disapprove, and that I express my regret."

"No need, Mother, not the slightest need."

Father Tromokov chuckled. "Boris, I'll relieve you of your money any time."

Ruth immediately endorsed the priest. "He'll put it to good use, Boris."

Boris laughed. "Sorry, Ronya has already claimed it."

A slow smile came to Ruth's face. Deeply relieved that the problem had resolved itself, she relaxed and let the rabbi claim her attention.

"There's something directly connected with David's generosity," Simon Levinsky began, "something distinctly pleasant, that I'd like to tell you all about."

Boris knew that the rabbi, in common with most Jews, loved to talk. Ordinarily, he would have evaded the ordeal, but this particular evening he felt a strong responsibility to the memory of David von Glasman, which astounded him not a little. He lit a cigarette and said politely, "Please do."

Before Simon could speak, Paul pushed his chair back and asked to be excused. "I've been up since five, and I have an early morning appointment with our new man in Kiev, a fellow by the name of Krasmikov. Come, girls," he said to his nieces. "I'll take you home."

Ronya put down her teacup. "Aren't you sleeping here?"

"No, I'm meeting Krasmikov at the camp. There's something we want to discuss with my mother."

He strode out of the room with the girls as they all turned to Rabbi Levinsky.

Simon Levinsky leaned forward across David's desk, and everyone recognized that he was about to give himself up to the pure pleasure of speech. In no hurry, Simon started with his son Joseph.

"It pains me that Joseph refuses to see Ronya's marriage in a proper light. He is young, and the young are in love with conviction, but he will mature, his eyes will open, and he'll see that there are two men in a man. One impels him to virtue, the other to sin. Both are natural. Opposed as I was at the start to the marriage of Ronya and Boris, I have come to know that God placed Boris in Ronya's sight, God, and no one else. God has a habit of making the right people fall in love. Why a Jewess and a Tartar? I do not know. When the reason comes, it will be a satisfying one, for God's purpose will be fulfilled. This I must believe, since I was God's instrument. I have dwelled upon this theme, because my Joseph will need Ronya in much the same way I needed her father." The rabbi looked across the room at Ronya directly. "I ask her to give him her support, because soon the congregation will elect Joseph their chief rabbi. I look forward to the day eagerly."

Had the rabbi made this announcement in an ordinary Jewish household, there would have been a buzz of excited comment. Here, only Ruth, Ronya, and the priest cared. The rabbi took his disappointment calmly, and since no one else asked the question, he asked it himself: "What is to become of the old rabbi? After all, he isn't so old. What will he do? He still belongs to God."

Without waiting, he answered himself, and thus finished his story.

"I shall wait twelve months, until the dedication of the tombstone. I will honor my departed friend David with memorial prayers, and on the following day my Lena and I shall leave for the land of Israel, where our hearts will feed on honey. For this I have yearned all my life.

"In Jerusalem I shall repair to the synagogue, there to hear the Chassidim discussing the Torah. With no worldly duties remaining to me, I shall sing and seek the truth, so that my mind will be filled with wisdom.

"All this David von Glasman has made possible. Thanks to him, Lena and I will never want."

"That's wonderful, Simon," said Ruth.

It seemed to Boris the evening would never end. Torah, Jerusalem, God on throne loving, hating, arranging miracles and marriage. Christ! Still, he made the effort. "I am happy for you," he said, shaking Simon's hand, and then he refilled everyone's glasses, pouring extra long ones for himself and the priest, and proposed a toast. They drank a *L'chaim* to Lena and Simon, after which Boris stationed himself next to Ruth, hoping that she would put an end to the staggering amount of talk.

Ronya could see that Alexis, who thoroughly enjoyed the continuing drama of the Von Glasman-Pirov household, was willing to listen all night, whereas Boris was very nearly out of humor. She rose. "Mother, may Boris and I go, now? I'm exhausted."

Tamara suddenly giggled. Coming after an evening's solemnity, the giggle was infectious and they all laughed. Even Boris permitted himself a grin.

"Sit down, Ronya," Rifka commanded. "I had no idea you were such a feeble fibber."

"All right, so I'm not exhausted, but I shall still say good-night. Will you come, darling?"

"Of course, dove." Just then Rifka said, "I, too, have an important announcement to make."

Ronya sat down.

"I'll not detain you, Rabbi," Rifka said. "If you wish to make your *adieux*, I will wait."

Simon Levinsky was glad to go. He gave a formal bow to the gypsies, shook hands with Katya and Alexis and the priest, and with his usual affection, reminded Ruth to come see him. Holding Ronya's hands in his, swaying a little, he scrutinized her face. "David's death is a grievous blow to the Jews of Kiev. Now you take his place. Thank God, you possess the qualities required for your unique role."

Boris escorted the rabbi to a Pirov carriage.

Deeply unhappy, miserable about David's death, disappointed in his will, Rifka was gripped by violent resentment. She awaited Boris' return quite prepared to pay Ronya back for all Tamara's suffering and public humiliation. Fifteen minutes passed before he reappeared.

Rifka was far too clever to create an atmosphere of belligerence by open recriminations. "You may all rest assured that though I address my remarks mainly to Ronya I am talking to all of you, for not one of us is a mere bystander."

Rifka waited, then went on.

"Now Ronya is mistress here, and master, too. This is the first time in the history of the estate that a woman rules—a very young woman. The chances are that neither she nor any of you will ever know the reason for the totality of her rule. What am I leading up to? This: Normally, Tamara would have waited until my death to become queen, but just as David abdicated in his lifetime, so shall I. With Ronya mistress, Tamara must be queen. This is fitting.

"I must wait until we have observed my cousin's first *jahrzeit*. At David's headstone, Tamara will kneel at the feet of her queen and swear the oath of allegiance to the gypsy nation. Eight days later, before some of the greatest names in Mother Russia, Ronya will hand Tamara the rod of queenly office, place the crown upon her head, and raise Queen Tamara to her feet. They will exchange the kiss of everlasting loyalty to each other."

Rifka included Boris in a meaningful glance. "Ronya and Tamara are a team—to work, to play, to share. Especially to share—and with matching energy."

A smile of unclouded delight formed on Tamara's lips, and impulsively she clasped Rifka's hand. "Oh, Mother, how wonderful! Thank you." Only then did she realize that there was no responding delight in the others.

"The light on or off?" Boris asked.

"On," Ronya replied. "I want to look at you."

He waited until she lay in his arms and then said, "My father's regiments are on maneuvers just this side of Odessa. I want to join them for a week—two at the most."

This was unexpected. "When?"

"Tomorrow."

"Why?" she said bitterly, and added with even more bitterness, "Have you had all the domesticity you can handle at one stretch? Or is it Tamara you're running from?"

Boris' eyes gleamed, his grip on Ronya tightened. "Don't you *ever* say that again."

Ronya lifted her face to his. "Is that your answer, Boris?"

Silently, he studied her face. The deep sadness in her eyes tormented him. Stroking, caressing, his marvelous fingers began to move. Ronya lowered her head onto the pillow and let herself go loose against his strong body. He began to kiss her, and she tried to pull away, but he held her all the closer. "All right, Ronya, I grant I sprung it on you without warning, but I should think by now you'd know that every year I join the Cavalry for at least part of the war exercises."

"Is it possible that you've forgotten Katya and Alexis will still be here tomorrow?"

Boris looked at her in astonishment. "Christ! Is that all? All right, I'll catch up with my regiment a day later."

Now Ronya leaned closer, and her hand began stroking.

"I love you," she said, softly, slowly.

Strength flowed back, and with it passion. He gathered her to him, and she clung to his body, rubbing her cheek against his. Their mouths met. Later, after the giving and taking, she cushioned her head against his shoulder.

Boris' big hands moved over her still-slim nakedness. "Ronya, oh Ronya."

He fell asleep holding her, and she lay in his arms torturing herself with visions of women who moved with the Cavalry, husky peasant wenches with stolid faces, skinny girls from the factories, all searching for an easier life, corrupt beauties—many of them well-born flowers of the degenerate aristocracy, shameless in their lust for hard-sinewed men.

Ronya drifted into sleep hating women. She dreamed of Boris on his white stallion being pursued by scores of women. She caught up with the women and saw that they all were pale reflections of Tamara and of herself.

18

Krasmikov had known Paul for years but was a stranger to his personal life. He had made Boris' acquaintance less than two weeks ago and knew only he was married to a vibrant, shining-eyed Jewess, said to be one of the richest women in Russia, and that he had a blond bastard by a beautiful gypsy girl, whose grandfather was the Jewess' great-uncle. From the moment Krasmikov set foot in Kiev, he had wanted to meet Tamara.

He conceived a plan that would bring him in contact with the gypsies. It was not devoid of merit; the coincidence was that he sent it to Paul of all people. Paul thought it made to order. He knew that Krasmikov was nothing but a minor scoundrel, reactionary and bigoted like all the secret police, trying hard to push himself into the limelight. Dishonest and unscrupulous, he was at least not vicious, and Paul had a shrewd suspicion (based on a thorough study of Krasmikov's dossier and supplemented by private investigations of his own) that once introduced to Tamara, Krasmikov would be easy to influence. If he took his views from Tamara, he would be less of a threat to Ronya than most of the secret police, and since Paul could not put a sympathetic liberal in charge in Kiev, Krasmikov was the next best thing. Paul sent the plan to Rifka and told Krasmikov that he would come to Kiev and talk about it.

Krasmikov was nervous; it was the first time he had been nervous about meeting a woman. And he was full of confusion. He had expected brawling gypsy youngsters rolling in the dirt, bare-legged women washing clothes in the stream, a jumble of livestock, tents, wagons, equipment. Instead, he came upon an attractive scene, color-ful and romantic, and impressively prosperous.

Paul smiled. "What did you anticipate?"

"Not this."

Rifka received them.

Krasmikov sensed immediately that Paul's relationship with the gypsy woman was intense, that he somehow belonged in her house. This to Krasmikov implied that Zotov had had his way with the daughter, too, and his desire to see Tamara mounted.

Amused, Rifka waited patiently for Krasmikov to take in the room. She could understand his reaction. The elegance of her possessions had the same effect upon visitors with far more sophistication than this bumpkin police officer. Finally, she nodded him to a chair. Paul re-mained standing.

Her manner almost abrupt, Rifka said, "I find myself no longer in-terested. I shall therefore allow you to speak to my daughter. If you can persuade her to do business on your terms, she has my permission to proceed."

Krasmikov barely had time to jump to his feet before Rifka left the room.

In a few minutes the door swung open again, and Tamara pushed through with a tray bearing a bottle of scotch, one of vodka, and three glasses.

Tamara saw a brawny six-footer with narrow eyes, dark gray in color and slightly slanting. The impression he gave was one of coarse sensuality. He was no Boris Pirov, no Paul Zotov.

Unprepared for the impact of her bold appraisal, Krasmikov stared back at the warm copper tones of her skin, the long-legged stance, the high full breasts under the transparent blouse. Vulnerable as a school-boy, he felt the thrust of desire and was betrayed by the flush on his face.

Tamara smiled, and Krasmikov felt a more intense and compli-cated sensation far beyond his understanding.

"Tamara," Paul said, "may I present Andrei Krasmikov?"

Tamara put down the tray and held out a languid hand. Her amusement deepened as Krasmikov stammered a barely coherent greeting.

"He's here to put a proposition before you. He thinks your gypsies may be able to steal for him"—Paul smiled a little—"when required. And on the theory that people reveal all sorts of secrets to fortune-tell-ers, he wants to use your prettiest girls and plant them here and there where they will be most useful."

Tamara waited to see if Paul had something to say about payment;

satisfied he meant to leave this to her, she said, "What do you drink, Krasmikov? Paul takes scotch."

Now it was clear that they were lovers, and Krasmikov immediately felt a racking envy. "Vodka," he said, and his hand shook as he took the glass.

"Nothing for me," Paul said and briskly left the room.

Tamara lifted her glass and wet her lips, and said as she put it down, "Come on. Follow me."

Krasmikov halted just inside the bedroom door and stood in stunned silence. What if they were discovered? And then, looking around the extravagantly opulent room, he began to feel uneasy. It was not the sort of room a strange man sneaked into—things were moving far too fast. He had expected everything—getting the gypsies to consider the plan, persuading Tamara to sleep with him—to be more difficult. Nothing was as he had imagined.

The corners of Tamara's mouth curled in mischief. "Shut the door, drink your vodka, and relax. We won't be disturbed."

Krasmikov pulled himself together. If this was how she wanted it, why should he complain? He downed the vodka, and thus fortified, he lifted her down to the bed, started to rip off her blouse, his hands reaching for her breasts.

Tamara moved sharply. "I don't need assistance to undress."

Krasmikov inhaled deeply; he was having trouble breathing. He threw off his own clothes. When presently he turned back to Tamara, she was naked.

Feverishly, he let his eyes travel over her.

Tamara looked up at him, laughing. "Am I beautiful?"

"God, yes!" Krasmikov sputtered.

Still laughing, she reached for him. He lowered himself onto her, and his hands slid under her back. He started kissing her, his tongue searching.

Tamara favored him with the most uniquely violent sex he ever had. And he—strong as an ox, and no inexperienced flounderer—gave her nearly all she asked of a man. Tamara's need included everything.

Afterward, Krasmikov wanted to say something tender. But he was interrupted by Tamara. "Well, let's get down to brass tacks. My people spy and steal for you. What does the secret police guarantee me? Gold alone isn't enough. I want protection for—"

With a gesture of protest, he said, "Tamara, I want you to love me. I don't want—" He tried to take her in his arms.

Tamara drew back, cold and distant.

"I adore you," he said, alarmed.

"It's nice to be appreciated," Tamara said mockingly. She seemed bored.

Krasmikov thought, *Impossible.* Searching her face earnestly, he said, "I'll marry you."

"I need a bath." Tamara rose to her feet.

Krasmikov thought, *I don't understand it.* It was almost embarrassing to recall all the things she had made him do to her; stranger still, he had liked doing them. *No,* he decided, *I can't lose her. Eventually, she'll begin to love me. I must find a way to see her again.* "I don't suppose I can take you out to dinner?"

"Why not?" Tamara answered without looking at him. "Come back for me at about eight."

It was a glorious day, bright sunshine and gentle breeze. The flowering shrubs were in early bloom, some still in bud, and the air smelled strongly of honeysuckle.

The only disagreeable note had been struck by Boris' telegram:

CAVALRY MOVING UP TO THE ROMANIAN BORDER. AM RIDING WITH THEM.

YOURS, B.

Wandering through the orchard in search of the boys, Ronya determined not to let the telegram spoil the morning. She spied the children sprawled in the big swing, deep in conversation and a bowl of raisins, their faces alive in the sunshine. Though nine months younger, the Blond One was as tall as Igor and every bit as strong. She smiled to herself, wondering if the new one would be beautiful like dark Igor, or beautiful like the Blond One, or just beautiful like her golden one.

It was not long before Igor spotted her and called, "Come get in the swing."

She sat down next to him.

"Ronya, my mother," he said earnestly, "can the Blond One sleep with me tonight?"

With no Boris home to complain that she spoiled Igor and let him come between them, she said, "Of course, darling."

"I want the Blond One to live with us all the time."

"His mother wants him, too. We'll just have to be satisfied with having him as often as we can."

The Blond One looked at her as if to say, you know better. "She doesn't want me," he said.

Carrying a handful of raisins to his mouth, Igor flushed deeply. "She beats him hard with a broom. Last winter she chopped up his sled for firewood and stole his mittens."

"Nonsense. Don't tell fibs and make derogatory remarks about people."

Igor chewed his raisins. "What's derogatory?"

"Not nice. Disrespectful."

Igor's question and Ronya's answer meant to the Blond One that their word game had started. Now, he supposed, it was his turn. "What's a bastard?" he asked.

Her hands clenched, she paled.

The children noticed nothing. Igor assumed it was his turn to answer. "You are, and you have to accept it—that's what Father Tromokov said."

Ronya thought, *Damn you to hell, Tamara.*

Igor could not be quiet long. "Am I a bastard, Mamma?"

She could hardly bear to meet his eyes. "No, dear. And, it isn't right to think of the Blond One as a bastard. Just remember that he's your brother, and that we all love him very much."

"Especially God," Igor said. "He loves bastards better than regular people. That's why regular people like the peasant kids are jealous."

Ronya did not want to pursue the question, but she was curious. "How do you know, Igor?"

"Father Tromokov told us. He said, 'God loves the bastards the best, he made so many of them.' "

At noon, Ronya greeted Gospodin von Kaufman, her banker. She was dressed in a ribbed silk dress of dark purple, which made her look taller and thinner. Her piled-up mass of hair added to the illusion of height.

The elderly banker stared at her in admiration as she crossed the room to her father's desk. He always marveled at the wonderful combination: beauty, overcharged with exulting femininity and astounding business acumen. It delighted him.

He did not rush into business talk, because he had something else on his mind.

"Tell me, Ronya," he said, drawing a chair up to the desk, "will you open the Odessa house this season?"

"I don't know. That depends upon Boris. However, the caretaker and his family are always there, and the Tartars are still retained as protectors, so the house is always ready. Mother might take Igor and meet Katya and Alexis there, but not before mid-August."

"Forgive my presumption. My wife is having a difficult time, and the doctor recommends a complete rest in the sea air. I thought—"

"Of course," Ronya replied at once. "When do you want the house?"

"The sooner the better. Say for two weeks?"

"Stay the month, or longer. The servants complain they never have enough to do."

That settled, Von Kaufman thought, *Well, to business.* But he was remembering that he almost said to Ronya, "My wife *gives me* a difficult time." He thought of his wife then, old and dried out at sixty, constant ailments, always dressed in murky shades. Bah! The proper Kievan banker almost made a face and wondered what Ronya would think if he did.

Meanwhile, Ronya was trying to figure out the true reason for the rash of increased mortgage foreclosures on acreage owned by the nobility. The number of estates and stock-breeding farms available in the Kiev Guberniya alone was staggering, and the prices almost embarrassingly low.

Von Kaufman had some of the answers.

"Don't worry about the owners, Ronya. They don't live on the land. Some don't even live in Russia. The principal parcel you want belongs to the scion of an old family who lives in Biarritz up to his aristocratic ears in debt. Unless you buy—he wants all cash—I shall have to force him out. He hasn't paid even an occasional interest on the loan in the last three years. The owners of the other parcels are also practically bankrupt. What with incessant peasant unrest, high interest rates on mortgages, and low productivity per acre, they're losing their shirts. You can pick up all three estates for a song."

Ronya's mouth, sensuously full with Boris, was determined with her banker. "I want the wheat fields. I can make them pay. I don't want the run-down manor houses. Can you get rid of them?"

"Yes, that can be arranged later."

"All right. Close the deals. And don't drive too hard a bargain. Pay a fair price."

Von Kaufman chuckled. "Ronya, you're so much like your father."

Ronya took it as a compliment. "Thank you. That's nice to hear." She reached into a desk drawer and took out a letter. "Our purchasing agent in Geneva recommends an American reaper. It's manufactured by a concern," she glanced at the letter, "called International Harvester Company. I have instructed him to buy three reapers for a start."

Von Kaufman shifted in his chair. "Why reapers? You've got a big labor force."

"I want labor-saving devices, just as I want schools. Father Tromokov and I are working on a plan whereby our peasants will work the land on a percentage basis. I'm not being entirely unselfish. With machinery our peasants will produce more, and our harvest will increase threefold. With the incentive of a better life, the land will hold its people and I will not lose what you call my 'labor force,' as other landowners are losing theirs."

179

The banker weighed Ronya's ideas and found them extravagant. "A church, a school, a holiday at every opportunity. Ridiculous! What if you make a few peasants happy? The lot of the rest is still hopeless. Don't throw away good money on reapers, Ronya."

Ronya gave him an impish smile. "It's not my money I'm throwing away. It's Boris'."

"I had no idea," he said seriously, "that Boris could afford to import agricultural machinery from America."

Keeping her face still and the laughter out of her eyes, she said, "Recently Boris came into an inheritance."

Von Kaufman was deeply surprised that Boris Pirov was buying reapers with his inheritance. Horses, yes. High living and womanizing, maybe. But he knew better than to let slip any but good words about Boris. He got to his feet. "Ronya, a schnapps before lunch, if you permit."

"Please do. Help yourself."

The banker poured himself a glass of cognac from the decanter, and he sipped it slowly, thoughtfully.

That evening, Ronya left the boys to her mother. She made herself comfortable in a robe and braids and settled herself in a deep chair in the library with a book. A peaceful, pleasant hour passed before Ruth came in.

"Are they asleep?"

"Heavens, no," Ruth laughed. "They're on a perpetual talkfest and refuse to settle down." She sank into a chair. "You know, darling, I'm anxious about the Blond One. By keeping him here while Boris is gone, don't you make it worse for him when he has to go back to Tamara? And I won't be surprised if Igor is upset, too. There'll be grief, Ronya."

"A situation Boris has created, not I," Ronya flared up, black eyes blazing. "The Blond One ought never go back there again—for his sake and mine."

"I can understand how his being here has certain advantages," Ruth said, "but it is a complicated problem. I do believe—"

"If you talked to Boris—if you asked it of him—" Ronya saw the expression that passed over Ruth's face and stopped speaking. She knew her mother would never help her get the Blond One.

"This snuggling down with you will end when Boris returns. Igor will blame him."

Ronya put away her book. "Mother, can you remember me at four?"

"I can, and a devilishly precocious four you were." Ruth laughed, but the face Ronya turned to her mother was concerned, as she told her of her conversation with the children about bastards.

"They're bright," was all that Ruth said.

"Mother, do you mind if I smoke?"

"You know I do. I've always minded."

"You've been plotting with Boris."

"Yes, darling," Ruth smiled. "We discuss your bad habits."

"His, too?" Ronya asked pointedly, with no smile.

"His, too." Ruth strolled over to close the window, straightening a white jade chessman on the way back to her chair. "When do you think he will be back?"

Ronya told her about the telegram.

"Boris is a born soldier. It's natural enough that he does not want to separate himself from the Cavalry entirely. Besides, he loves the outdoor life and the companionship of men."

Ruth had meant to comfort her, but this evening Ronya was impervious to comforting words. "Yes he does, and he loves the indoor life and the companionship of women."

"Patience, child, and tolerance."

Ronya felt neither patient nor tolerant. She reached into a bowl of apples and bit into a big red one.

"Mother, how is it that you have never told me what you think about Tamara and the Blond One? Everyone else has."

"Everyone?"

"Yes."

There was such grief in Ronya's voice and she looked so slight and porcelain-fragile that Ruth wanted to take her into the softness of a mother's embrace; but she did not deceive herself that Ronya was really fragile. "*Milaska, milaska,*" she said, "we shall not talk of it."

Ronya's chin went up. "Why not?"

"Because Boris speaks the truth. Tamara is nothing."

"How can you say that?" Ronya asked accusingly.

Ruth smiled fondly. "It is fortunate, Ronya, that you are small, lovely, and desirable, for you are indeed a formidable woman."

"What does that mean?" Ronya asked, a note of indignation in her voice.

"It means, dear, that you are more capable, more efficient, more assured, that you have more sense and more stamina, than most women."

"Mother, I never heard a compliment sound more like a complaint."

Ruth looked at her daughter and assessed her mood. The time had come; it was necessary to speak. As she formulated her thoughts, Ronya shot out, "Why do you let Rifka monopolize you?"

"Light a cigarette if you want to, Ronya. It's a long story."

Ronya was invaded by a sense of foreboding.

"Your father and I met on a glorious Sunday in spring," Ruth began. "Hans, my eldest brother, brought David home. They were both at the university in Vienna. I remember thinking that he was the most beautiful, the most brilliant, the most cultivated man I should ever see. I was barely seventeen.

"A year later, only a few weeks before we were to be married, my father learned that David was a Jew. Poor David, it never occurred to him that his friend Hans thought otherwise. As for Hans, David was rich, accepted in the highest society—what could he be but one of us?

"Meanwhile, unknown to me—and in all honesty completely unimportant to David—my father and my brothers had borrowed huge sums of money from him. My grandparents, who had gone through at least two fortunes, were also in debt to him.

"My family did not turn up its aristocratic nose at the Jew. They toasted us in champagne, briskly wished us well, and suggested that we marry in Russia—from where it was unlikely much news would travel. Their friends would lose track of me.

"It was David, not I, who insisted on legalizing my status before making the journey to Russia.

"I was not proud of my family and was very proud of my husband, and I found it very easy to do the one thing he asked of me—become a Jewess."

Ruth stopped. "I'm getting a little ahead of myself. Your father had told me about Rifka early in our courtship, so I was prepared for her, but she was completely unprepared for me. Your father never realized that all the years he was away, Rifka had fancied herself the future mistress of the Von Glasman estate. It never failed to surprise me that she dared believe my David would marry her and accept her four bastard sons.

"I think that for years Rifka secretly hated me. I know I hated her, and I was constantly vying with her for first place in your father's life. The first years were miserable. But when he was away—and he was away so much of the time—I was almost totally dependent upon Rifka, and I must say she took good care of me."

Ruth looked into her daughter's intent face and took her hands. For an instant she held them tightly; then, relaxing her grip, she went on, putting her thoughts into neat, orderly sentences.

"David was frequently caustic and austere. Of course, he could be warm, attentive, amusing, and persuasive. He was never unfaithful— and he was never as thoroughly and completely committed to me as Boris is to you. Also, whatever the cause, David was rarely able to be uninhibited and completely comfortable in the act of physical love."

Ruth let that sink in before adding: "I believe this reticence was the main reason your father took every opportunity to travel on state business." She came to her main point. "I am telling you everything because I want you to know that Boris, with his faults, is a better husband than David was, with his virtues. I was never as happy or as fulfilled as you are, Ronya. Be thankful."

Ronya was embarrassed and acutely uncomfortable; but though she blushed slightly, she met Ruth's eyes and said generously, "I know you spoke for my good. Thank you, Mother."

Ruth said admiringly, "That's kind of you, my child, and largely true. I shall explain how I feel about Rifka now and tell you what we plan to do—I want my children's blessing on our venture."

"Your venture?" Ronya sat up with a start. "What do you mean? Has she been trying to involve you in some plan of hers? Oh, Mother, why do you let her monopolize you?"

"Darling, it doesn't matter why. I have come to love Rifka and enjoy her company. Our past differences no longer matter—we've outlived them. Now, we can help each other." She looked at her daughter thoughtfully. "Can you understand that?"

"Yes. You both spent so many years loving the same man. Now you share your memories of him."

Ruth's eyes, deep green as the sea, suddenly filled with tears, and she turned away, groping for her handkerchief. When she had wiped away all trace of tears, she turned back to Ronya. "All of you, Boris in particular, have made it perfectly clear that I belong here, and here—except for a brief journey now and then—I stay. All of you have taken for granted that I'll be content. I don't reproach you for that, but when you and Katya are my age, you'll know that it isn't old at all, and that the zest for life and living does not dull and soften. I am not ready to settle into the passive role of widowed grandmother."

What was passing through her mind showed on Ronya's expressive face. Ruth thought, *Heavens, I hadn't thought of that!* She shook her head. "No, darling, not a man. I will never remarry."

Ronya was not altogether reassured; she had a feeling that Ruth was leading up to something utterly unacceptable. She sat in frowning silence. "In that case, I see no real reason for you not sharing yourself with us, and allowing us to share our lives with you."

"I am not divorcing myself from my family, just separating myself for a time." Ruth sounded determined. "Rifka and I have decided to roam the world. First of all, we plan to leave for New York after Tamara's coronation, to see all of the New World. From there, we'll decide where to go next. Ladislaus will be with us much of the time. He promised your father."

"Mother, it should sound wonderful, but it doesn't. I feel it in my bones that the whole situation— Why didn't you tell us this before Katya and Alexis left?"

"I wanted you to get used to it first. I am depending on you for support."

Privately, Ronya thought, *At least, we have months to find a way of dissuading her.*

Privately, Ruth thought about Rifka. In her mind's eye, she saw how tired she appeared, her once exquisite hands now blue-veined, and she mentally chided Ronya for forgetting how much of her childhood had been brightened by Rifka.

"What are you thinking, Mother?"

"That a precious part of my life perished with your father. There is nothing I can do about that. I want to fill the part that is left to me with new experiences. What are you thinking?"

"That I don't want to be around when you tell Boris."

19

A few days later, Ronya opened her eyes at about ten in the morning with a yearning for sweets and ordered for breakfast layer cake filled with raspberry jam and covered with chocolate and a pot of strong coffee. Whenever she was pregnant she longed for sweets and sours, and it was her good fortune that she never became fat.

Ordinarily, Lydia was in her element watching Ronya eat, but now she stood subdued, eyes downcast.

Ronya took only two mouthfuls of cake and was finished with it. She put down her fork, savored the good, hot coffee, and waited for what seemed a long time for Lydia to speak. At last, she said, "You might as well tell me."

"I'm upset," said Lydia.

"So I see."

"I never approved of that sticky-fingered lout. First he corrupted her brother. Now he's going to leave her."

"I expect you're talking about Tanya's husband."

Lydia nodded.

"Has he been released from prison?"

"Not yet, thank heaven."

184

Ronya raised her eyebrows.

"A letter came. Tanya can't read. Maybe I didn't make it out good."

"Who wrote it for him?"

Lydia shrugged.

"Tell Tanya to come in."

As Ronya suspected, the maid was just outside the door.

Ronya did not like Tanya, but seeing the red nose and lids swollen from crying, she felt sorry for the girl.

Tanya gave her the letter and waited nervously.

"Sit down, Tanya. You too, Lydia. It has no salutation. It simply starts." With considerable difficulty, stopping to figure out the clumsily written words, Ronya read the letter aloud.

a pal of mines carrying out this letter—you'll know its from me for sure by my X. I aint coming back to live with your grandfather —from the beginning me and the old man dont get along—he's satisfied with warm beer and cold potatoes—not me. Im going to america—the streets are paved in pure gold—I hear a fella dont need to know reading and writing neither to make his fortune but if he is meaning to make money fast he better get himself a sizable stake—theres where you come in with that aunt of yours in the big house—if you aint going to help me I aint taking you to america. dont write me here—they read the letters—my friend rentovsky will bring me the answer—he'll come see you pretty soon—I'll be out in december—maybe you'll see me and maybe you wont—depends on the information I get from the general—that's what we call him— yours truly X

Ronya lifted her head.

Lydia sniffed angrily.

Tanya seemed to be waiting, holding her breath. Then the tears came. "Begging your pardon, Mistress Ronya," she cried, holding out trembling fingers for her letter.

"You've got until December," Ronya said. "Give America lots of thought."

"Yes, ma'am."

"I want to be told the moment that man Rentovsky arrives."

Tanya walked down the hall thinking, *Like hell you'll be told.*

"A fine thing," Lydia began.

"I hate to say this to you, Lydia, but I don't want Tanya's husband here. If she decides to go with him, I'll help."

Lydia sighed. "Ha, little mistress, when dealing with a thief, it isn't that easy. There's trouble ahead."

A couple of hours later, Boris' telegram came, and Ronya ran down to the family dining room to share the news with Ruth and the boys. "He's on his way!"

Ruth gave her a glad smile, but Igor said, "He'll spoil all our fun."

Ruth looked out of the window. Mortified, Ronya said tartly, "Make sure, young man, you never say that again—do you hear?"

Igor peered up at her in a temper. It was amazing how much like a Tartar he could look, in spite of his Von Glasman looks. "You can't make me."

"I think I can," she said, none too gently.

"If you spank me," Igor threatened, "I won't eat my kasha."

"Don't."

"I'll wet my bed," he added desperately.

"I wouldn't do that, Igor," the Blond One interjected. "If you do, he won't take us hunting."

No one noticed the old peasant standing in the doorway until he said, bowing low, "A thousand pardons. I was told to wait, but I heard voices, and they led me here."

They all looked up with a start to see the old man in baggy pants and peasant blouse still bowing deeply. Ronya went over to the bent figure, and just as she reached him, he straightened and nearly bumped into her. "Pardon, young mistress," he gasped, "pardon." Poor old man, his agitation was unmistakable.

Ronya said kindly, "Vadim, you could use a glass of tea. Come and sit down."

"I can't stay long enough for tea," Vadim stammered, almost incoherent. "The beast is drunk. God alone knows what he'll do."

Ronya did not have to question him. Vadim's son-in-law Nikolai was notorious for drunkenness and wife-beating. "How did you come here—with a cart?"

"A mule harnessed to a cart—not fitting for you, Mistress."

"I'll pick up my whip. I'll only be a few moments."

The peasant crossed himself, muttering, "Jesus save her," and backed out.

Ruth recovered from her surprise and looked at Ronya aghast. "You'll be too late. Send Father Tromokov."

But Ronya had already run from the room.

The peasants made way for Ronya as she entered the cottage. The first of the four rooms, a small parlor, was empty. In the next room she found Nikolai sprawled across a dirty, unmade bed. The room looked as though it had been turned upside down, the furniture and clothes thrown all about. It was like an oven and reeked foully. There was no sign of Alevitina, his wife. The kitchen was clean. On the mantel over the cooking fire was a pottery jar filled with straw flowers. The big table of stout wood planks, flanked by long wooden benches, was laid with three bowls. The clock and the iron pots and pans hung in place on the walls. The door to the tiny room where the old man slept was bolted.

Ronya knocked. "Alevitina, it is I, Ronya."

There was no response.

Ronya went outside to where the people stood, and there among them she saw Viktor, one of Boris' harness makers. "Get an ax," she told him, "we shall have to break the door down."

"I have one of my hammers," he said, rolling up his sleeves.

Excitedly, the crowd moved closer to the front door as Vadim and Viktor went with Ronya. Viktor's strong right arm swung down, and the door flew open.

Alevitina sat sagging in a rocker in the corner, talking to herself. Both of her eyes were blackened, her lower lip was badly cut, and her whole neck scratched. Even when she saw Ronya, she did not move.

Ronya told Vadim to bring a basin of water and a clean cloth and to start heating water for coffee. She told Viktor to get Nikolai on his feet. "Sober him up enough to stand. Get help. And tell them, outside, they are about to see what I do to a coward who hits a woman."

Ronya sat down on the bed opposite Alevitina and started to bathe her face and neck.

When it dawned on the peasant woman what Ronya intended, she burst out, "You'll break my heart if you hurt him."

"She's crazy, Mistress Ronya," her father shouted from the kitchen. "Don't listen to her."

Alevitina began to wring her hands and cry. Between sobs, she wailed, "What if he deserts me?"

"Save your breath," Ronya said. "The last time he hit you, I warned him—"

Vadim reappeared. "Whip him, Mistress Ronya. He's a dirty louse, a mean pig. Even a dog treats a bitch better."

It took over an hour, but by the time Nikolai was on his feet, leaning heavily against a tree, Alevitina was washed and dressed in a stiffly starched blouse and full skirt, with a red silk shawl on her head. Women with children in their arms were jostling each other for a better view. Old grandmothers brought out chairs. A few big boys climbed trees; little boys were lifted onto shoulders. Father Tromokov, accompanied by Sad Eyes, a few trainers, and several grooms, was there to watch. Even some gypsies wandered over and spread out on the grass.

Ronya hefted the whip in her hand. Viktor took a closer grip on Ni-

187

kolai. The lash whistled down on Nikolai's shoulders. He jerked upright and screamed an incoherent oath. The lash came down again and again, and no matter how much he squirmed and how far he tried to run, Ronya's whip found him.

Tears were running from his eyes, sweat was dripping from his forehead and blood from his back, when he begged for mercy and swore he would never beat his wife again.

The wife cried, "Enough, enough."

The old father laughed, "Jesus! Look at the pig squirm."

The women shook with laughter. What a champion they had in Ronya!

The gypsies shouted.

Ronya raised her arm. There was still Alevitina's bruised mouth to avenge. She cut across his face just once, and blood ran from his mouth and fell on her whip.

Alevitina ran to him. "Poor baby. Let me get you in the house."

Ronya arrived at Rifka's house exactly at the hour appointed. Rifka was out, and there was an awkward initial ten minutes with Tamara. But eventually Ronya melted under Tamara's cheerful friendliness and, though she said nothing, Tamara soon became aware of it and felt happier. With no intention of flattering, she said, "You're more beautiful than ever, Ronya."

"I wish there were some way to house a lodger without swelling around the middle," Ronya said whimsically.

Tamara sank back into her chair. "Don't you like being pregnant?"

"I want children, but I hate being pregnant."

Though nothing showed in her face, Tamara was thinking about her own sterility, and her heart thudded.

"Did your mother get the package the apothecary sent to us by mistake?" Ronya asked.

"Yes. It was a tonic—beef, iron, and wine."

"To stimulate the appetite?"

"Yes." Tamara read the surprise in Ronya's eyes, and said, "Damned if it makes sense. She's taught me eight different formulas for curing a lagging appetite. Why would she buy anything as mundane as that combination?"

"Maybe for the iron." Curious, and slightly vexed, Ronya asked, "Incidentally, where is your mother?"

"I don't know. Keeping us waiting is very uncharacteristic of her. I can't help thinking—"

"That she goes to a doctor," Ronya interposed.

The sound of the front door shutting ended the conversation. Rifka walked heavily into the room and sank all too gratefully into a chair.

"Are you losing weight?" Ronya asked quickly. "You look thinner."

With a shrug of her shoulders, Rifka answered evasively, "I have no makeup on."

Tamara gaped at her mother.

With eyes in the back of her head, Rifka said, "You needn't stare at me like that, Tamara." Concentrating her attention on Ronya, she said, "Boris will have another son. There is comfort knowing that David, your father, will have a namesake."

Ronya looked pleased. "You're sure?"

"Positive. You are destined to bear sons."

"How many?"

"I shall have to look in the crystal to answer that. The moon is on the rise. When it is full, I shall look carefully and see. Now, you both know that by abdicating I am doing something no other Romany queen has ever done. I am breaking with tradition. However, I find myself less concerned with tradition than that Tamara's coronation will be accomplished with all the pomp and ceremony due her."

Coming to Ronya's defense, Tamara said, "Ronya knows what she must do."

Rifka raised a brow. "Indeed? My cousin is gone. Were I gone, too, Boris and Katya would think of a hundred different ways of arguing you into leaving the ceremonies to the gypsies."

"No, they wouldn't," Ronya said hotly. "Katya is just as aware of duty as I am, and Boris does not allow himself to interfere in beliefs other people hold sacred. I think you owe me an apology."

Tormented by nausea and a general feeling of debility, Rifka was easily roused to irritation. Her temper was very close to the surface. The least little criticism, imagined or real, Rifka saw as a threat or ridicule. She hated ridicule worse than death.

"Nothing of the sort," she said shortly. Her voice shaking with rage, she repeated a joke Boris had once made about the elaborate gypsy coronation: "More Romanov than Romany," he had commented with a laugh. Katya had laughed too. Rifka had never forgiven either of them for this incident.

"He was making a joke," Tamara protested, "and you took him seriously."

"No." Rifka was emphatic. "It was definitely meant to be what it was. Ridicule."

"Banter, yes. Ridicule, no."

Well! Tamara leagued with them against her. "You are a fool, Tamara."

Tamara rose and went with quick steps to the door.

189

Ronya saw that Rifka was shaking and realized that she was a sick woman—anger made her look years older. Rifka was abdicating because she no longer had the strength to rule.

"Let us assume that you are right and Boris was poking fun at our ways," Ronya said gently, "that doesn't change anything. I have been taught all of my life what I must do, and I shall do it."

"How admirable!" Rifka said sarcastically. She pulled herself up out of the chair and called, "Tamara, we're waiting."

Tamara reappeared from the direction of the kitchen. "Mother, the reason you tire so easily is you don't eat enough. I've ordered some food. Rest awhile. Ronya is in no hurry to go home."

The food made a difference. Rifka's ill-humor vanished, and some of her vigor returned. "Several days ago," she said, "Ruth told me that mid-May of 'eighty-seven is definitely out of the question as a coronation date."

Ronya nodded. "Rabbi Levinsky insists we separate the placing of father's headstone from—" She searched for a kind way of quoting the rabbi.

"Did he say 'gypsy rubbish'?"

"He said 'pagan.'"

If Rifka was seething, Ronya could not detect it from her manner.

"We've had a letter from Katya. The Grand Duchess Elizabeth has asked Katya to make herself available for the entire month of May. Also it is thought that the Empress Marie will join Nicholas and Alexandra in St. Petersburg and then go to Moscow by carriage. Most likely, she'll command Boris to lead her escort."

"The possibility of the Empress Marie leaving the gaiety of the Riviera is doubtful," Rifka remarked. "The dislike between her and Alexandra is too strong. That leaves Boris free to play a major role in Tamara's coronation. As for Katya—neither she nor Alexis have an official part in the ceremonies. Katya's interest in the gypsies is small."

Angrily miserable, Tamara made no effort to hide her feelings. "I refuse absolutely. I'd rather not be queen in advance of my time than be crowned without Katya, and I am not willing to take a chance that Boris won't be there."

Ronya said quietly, "Ruth my mother has promised that she won't leave us until the new baby is at least six months old."

Rifka was pleased to see the girls taking a united stand. It raised her hopes for the future. As she was about to capitulate, her cat, sleek and agile, jumped in her lap. Rifka gave the cat an amused look and said, eying the girls, "Very well. Name a substitute date."

Tamara shot a glance at Ronya.

"You choose," Ronya said.

With a delighted smile, Tamara said, "July 2—one year from today."

Still left in the air was the question of Tamara's half brothers. Rifka, naturally, wanted all four of her sons present at the ceremony. For Sergey the visit to Kiev presented no difficulty. The banker had no wife to ask, "When, where, why, and for how long?"

Paul and Alexander, on the other hand, had to be very careful. Just as nobody in St. Petersburg knew about Paul's connection with gypsies, so no one in Paris had the faintest glimmer of suspicion that Alexander was the son of a gypsy queen. Quite the contrary, known as Monsieur le Graf Alexander Bok, he and his French family were received in the finest houses.

"Will Alexander's disappearance invite comment from his wife?" Ronya asked.

"I have no fears on that score," Rifka replied. "He has lived all these years without betraying himself, so he must have ways of getting about without her knowledge."

"There's no risk with Paul. His job presents him with excuses to come to Kiev."

"Besides," Tamara laughed, "he has Helena duped into thinking that national security depends on his strong back and silent tongue."

"Nonsense," said Rifka, "she is neither duped nor dazzled. The unvarnished truth is, she doesn't give a damn, as long as she can collect rare icons and holy hermits and go on pilgrimages. Fedor, I want him here."

"No," Ronya said bluntly.

"Where is your sense of justice, Ronya? Fedor loved you and hovered over you more years than I like to count. In the forest, when you and Tamara were put in his charge, he barely spared his sister a glance. Always his attention was on little Ronya."

Ronya swallowed painfully. All Rifka said was true. She called up his black deed, his disloyalty to Boris, and she made herself say, "Rifka, my cousin, I have told you before. Fedor may never again show his face on my land."

"Be generous. Give him another chance."

"David, my father, was generous. Fedor has everything he wants."

It cost Rifka something to beg but, for her son, she made the effort. "We were tremendously upset that day. What Fedor did, I told him to do, and I wasn't thinking clearly. Blame me."

"I do," Ronya said sadly. "But that does not alter my decision at all. Fedor made public our shame."

Rifka's eyes narrowed, but she only nodded her head.

When Tamara saw talk of Fedor was over—the bad time ended—

she became animated. She looked at Ronya hopefully. "Stay for supper. Please."

With memories of other times and other suppers, Ronya agreed.

"I'll send for Ruth," Rifka said, pleasantly surprised. "I think I'll lie down for an hour."

Tamara flipped her cigarette, man-style, into the fireplace. "It's a shame you haven't seen my wagon," she said to Ronya. "Come. Let me show it to you now."

Again, Ronya's face closed in sudden sadness, and she glanced at Tamara from under long, dark lashes.

At once Tamara sensed the nature of her fear and quickly reassured her. "Never," she said.

Without speaking, they went outdoors and down a long stretch of the road until, well away from the encampment, they came to a ridge. About two hundred yards beyond its crest stood the wagon.

Ronya propped herself against the doorway and waited while Tamara closed the curtains and lit a lamp. As soon as the whole interior was filled with subdued light, she called out delightedly, "Ready." Ronya had not known what to expect—certainly not a *mezuzah* on the door. That was characteristic of Tamara—combining her tie to the Von Glasmans with her fondness for magic. Ronya gasped as she took in the Oriental carpeting, the dark-red damask curtains, the magnificent collection of pillows piled high on the luxurious low couchlike bed, the huge Venetian mirror. All she could see in the small kitchen were silver champagne buckets.

There was no mistaking the hopefulness with which Tamara awaited her reaction. Losing patience, she cried, "Isn't it divine?"

Her eyes crinkled in smile, Ronya said, "Splendiferous!"

"Do you see a likeness?"

"Oh, my God!" Ronya exclaimed, in paroxysms of laughter. "Cleopatra's barge. I haven't thought of our game in years."

"Ronya, let's kiss and make up," Tamara begged, looking at her with adoring eyes.

Ronya's laughter turned to a sigh. Looking unhappy, she sat down on the bed.

Tamara curled up on the floor at her feet.

"I should not have forgotten myself," Ronya started guardedly. "If I led you to believe I could forgive you, I'm sorry. But I would like to talk for a bit. I've heard rumors—quite a few. Are they true?"

Tamara looked amused. "I can't say I don't know what you mean."

"You're to be queen. You ought to be more . . . decorous."

Tamara chuckled. "The only thing a gypsy minds is sleeping alone."

192

"Tamara, have you ever thought of a disease? Suppose . . ."

Tamara laughed mischievously. "Never. I pick my men from among the most fastidious husbands in Kiev. With strangers, I take meticulous precautions."

"I'm being serious."

"From your advantageous position, you complicate love by insisting it be accompanied by legality, morality, fidelity, normality. I guess that makes you a splendid wife.

"I separate love and pleasure, and I don't invest sex with too much importance. It's just an animal function like eating or going to the bathroom. That makes me a splendid whore."

Tamara could not help peeking up at Ronya to see how she was taking it. It seemed incredible. Ronya was interested—was watching her with bright eyes.

Sunk in the depths of the divan that passed for a bed, Ronya shook her head in disbelief but said pleasantly, "Go on."

Because she remembered vividly how often Ronya had silenced her and run from her, Tamara asked, "How far do I go? I don't want to offend you."

"As long as you don't get the wild idea that we're close again, or that you are free to call uninvited once Boris returns, you may go as far as you like, because I want to understand you. I really do."

Tamara spoke a little breathlessly. This might be her chance to regain Ronya, the Ronya she had lost. "You feel I'm dishonored because a healthy male awakens a response in me. How can I convince you all women are like that? We're all alley cats."

"Me, too? Katya? My mother?"

"Well—maybe not your mother. You think I'm immoral and disloyal, because I am content to love your husband. You can't understand that above him—above everyone—I love you."

"I've heard enough."

"Damn your bourgeois morality! It's bloodless."

"I'm thinking," Ronya said with a half smile on her lips, "of supper."

Tamara laughed her throaty laugh. "Ronya—you're crazy."

20

All morning Ronya tried to suppress her excitement.

"Why don't you pile your hair on top of your head?" Ruth said. "It promises to be a hot day."

Ronya glanced at her image in the mirror. "I suppose I should," but left it falling in braids down her back.

"It's a pity to spend the day indoors," Ruth said gently. "It may be a long wait. Go for a walk."

Ronya rose to her feet obediently. "Boris ought to be back any minute."

"He'll find you, dear."

As soon as Ronya was out on the lawn, she saw the children playing together near a red-barked myrtle tree. She slowed her pace and let them catch up with her. Igor ran ahead, but the Blond One tucked his hand in hers and walked beside her.

"The best hunting," he said, "is after the first frost."

Igor ran back. "He promised me a rifle," he said rapidly. "Will I get it?"

"Your father keeps his word," Ronya said quietly.

Igor shot her a Boris look. "We need two rifles."

Ronya glared at him. "Don't you *always* get two of everything?"

Igor smiled and caught the Blond One's other hand. "See—I told you."

With the children at her heels, Ronya left the camellia garden, just past its June prime, and went into the fuchsia garden, a spectacular display of blues, purples, and white. Finally, they reached one of her favorite spots, a dell bordered with hydrangea shrubs.

The boys disappeared to climb trees. Ronya stretched out on the grass. She rolled her skirts up above her knees and gave her bare legs to the sun. She fell asleep.

When the boys reappeared, Igor remembered he had something to tell the Blond One. "She has a new baby staying in her stomach. It has to get big before it can climb out."

The Blond One considered it a waste of thought to wonder about a new baby and preferred to concentrate on the rifles.

Igor had decided on the very same thing. "If we wait at the stables," he whispered, "we'll get to see them sooner."

Nearly a half hour went by. Boris found her lying in the grass with her skirts billowing far higher than her knees. He knelt beside her and pulled them down, and stayed there watching the gleam of her hair in the sun. Then he took her face between his hands and pressed his mouth on hers. Ronya awoke with a start. She saw him looking down at her, tan and fit, hard as nails, his sun-bleached hair long and tousled. Her eyes lit up, and she held out her arms, clasping him to her with all her strength.

"You've been gone a long time."

194

She felt the quickening, felt his muscles tighten. "An eternity, dove."

"How much did you miss me?" she murmured.

He took her into the comforting warmth of his arms and, holding her against him, kissed her eyes, her nose, her mouth.

She saw the glow in his eyes. His yearning reached her. "Let's go home," she urged softly.

Boris caught her hand and rose from his knees.

The next morning, Boris was up at dawn—not that he had meant to get up early. He had heard the thrush call and the light step of a Tartar boot meant to be heard.

Quietly getting out of bed, he pulled on a pair of trousers and stepped soundlessly out onto the balcony. The Tartar was waiting below. Seeing Boris' tense expression, the Tartar's own eyes softened and he smiled. No words. Boris understood. His mother was well. Boris let his breath out slowly.

The Tartar said, "Our stomachs are empty."

"Where are the others?"

"Riding in."

"How many?"

"Two."

"Leave the way you came. I'll meet you downstairs."

Neither Boris' voice nor the Tartar's hoarse whispers disturbed Ronya.

Boris pulled on a pair of boots and a lightweight sweater Ruth had knit for him and went with quick, light steps to the back of the house in time to see a pure white pony being led out of a trailer by a big dark man named Spartak.

"Brace yourself," Spartak said, grinning at Boris. "Snow Girl is here as a birthday present from your mother to Igor."

Jerking off his hat, his companion (Boris searched his memory for the man's name . . . Piotr, that was it) ran a hand over his bald head and said, gazing at the pony admiringly, "Ain't she a beauty?"

Boris had already gone over to the pony and was running his eyes and hands over her. "She sure as hell is."

"The trip was slow," said Grigori, the Tartar who had ridden in first. "She comes from the north, and she's only happy when she's cool. We had our orders to keep her happy."

Boris was not listening. The gift struck him as distinctly odd. Why would the Tartar woman claim Jewish Igor for a grandson? What did the gift imply? Boris, who knew horseflesh better than anyone, with the exception of his mother, who had bought and sold ponies for years, had never seen the likes of Snow Girl.

In spite of his preoccupation, he remembered the men were hungry. He told them to secure the horses and put the pony back in her trailer, and then took them into the kitchen for an impromptu picnic which would tide them over until there was some sign of movement in the house and a real breakfast could be made.

There was a remarkable store of food in Ronya's cold box and on her shelves; and in her deep cellar, several feet down into the ground, were crocks of dill pickles and sweet cucumbers and tangy sour tomatoes, barrels of herrings in wine and spices, and powerful beverages of alcohol poured over dried cherries or plums. Although the Tartars loved these fiery liquids, they chose to start the day with ice-cold buttermilk. But even before they ate, they led their horses to water and treated Snow Girl to a carrot and a cube of sugar.

At six o'clock, Lydia came downstairs. She stood in the doorway a moment, looking at the three Mongolian-featured Asian Tartars eating corn bread and beans, and managed not to appear startled.

Boris pulled himself out of his chair. "Lydia," he said, "these men are my people: Piotr, Spartak and Grigori. Gentlemen, our housekeeper, Lydia. Lydia will take good care of you. I ask to be excused for a few moments."

Relaxed and at home in the kitchen, the Tartars were enjoying themselves. "Sure," said Piotr carefully, "take your time."

Boris went at once to Ronya. He sat down on the bed and planted a kiss on her mouth. "Wake up, dove."

Ronya murmured.

Boris shook her, and she struggled out of sleep. "Has something bad happened?"

"No."

"You frightened me."

"Sorry, dove."

Puzzled and curious, Ronya still looked fearful.

Conscious that the Tartars expected him to return to the kitchen and do his duty as host—no Tartar spent time with his wife when he had male visitors to entertain—Boris spoke rapidly: "Please get up and dress. My mother has sent Igor a pony with some of her men, and I want you to breakfast with us."

Still half asleep, and alarmed that Boris' mother had come into their lives again, Ronya put out a beseeching hand. "Sit down, Boris."

"I haven't time." He turned and started for the door.

"Please," she cried out.

He came swiftly back, torn by the note in her voice.

"Why in God's name does your mother suddenly take notice of Igor's existence? He was born in January. Why a birthday present in July?"

196

"Well," Boris said jokingly, trying to soothe her, "if I were to face my mother with your questions, she'd toss her braids and say, 'I'm his grandmother. I've got my rights.' "

Impulsively, Ronya pulled him toward her. "I took her son," she said in a low trembling voice. "Is the gift a repentance for cursing you? Or is it an evil impulse?"

Boris heard the Tartar curse again. *Marry the Jewess, and limbs rotting, may you die alone.* Gently, he freed his arm. "Neither, Ronya." He kissed her. "I must go."

Boris walked the Tartars through the gardens and along the stream in the pine grove. They skirted the whitewashed peasant cottages. The men were attentive to his comments, but silent. Peasants and grain were not subjects that interested them; they were waiting for the stables. As they emerged from the peasant compound, Piotr, the spokesman, asked, "Do we pass the gypsy camp?"

"No."

Piotr's mouth turned down in disappointment. "A pity. We don't have to go back today, or even tomorrow. Your mother granted us a holiday."

"I'll fix you up later in town," Boris said with a grin. "All right?"

"All right," agreed Piotr. But catching a glimpse of the camp, he suggested, "Why go looking for something when it's to be had just a few hundred yards around the bend?"

Suddenly Boris seemed to become very distant; the Tartars knew better than to press the point.

The stables had grown. Now they spread over acres and acres, and they reflected the plenty of Ronya's patrimony. Tree-shaded pastures and open corrals took up much of the area. In addition there was a race and training track and a wide arena encircled by wooden bleachers. Boris and his stallion were performers, and they enjoyed perfecting their acrobatic feats in front of an audience; besides, the small arena was a good way of conditioning riders and horses to noise and visual distractions. For bad weather, there was an indoor schooling ring.

Flowering vines curled around the buildings, which opened onto big yards and driveways lined with trees. The renovations included superb stalls for all the horses, but the stallion's stall was the handsomest of all. Above all, the entire layout shone; Boris employed a sizable troop of stable boys, kept constantly at work caring for the horses and the land.

An hour later, after a very thorough tour of each of the buildings, which the three Tartars scrutinized with minute attention, they left Boris to do some necessary chores.

He cut back to the largest of the barns to find Sad Eyes. "What do you think of Snow Girl?"

"I reckon we got dogs bigger."

"Would you say she's a mild little lady?"

Sad Eyes nodded.

"Give me an hour, then put her through her paces. I want to know how she reacts to commands. Then get the vet over here. Tell him that if she has so much as a single flea on her, I want him to fish it out. Afterward, put her in isolation. If Igor shows up, don't let him see her. If he asks questions, distract him. Let one of the men give him some drill with the rifle."

"Yes, sir," said Sad Eyes, and he watched Boris out of sight before squatting down against a tree stump to think about the white pony. When it came to Igor, Boris was careful.

Boris and his guests walked a half mile down a lane and came to rich grassland still wet with the morning dew, where his slender-legged racehorses were pastured.

"That," said Piotr, "is the prettiest sight I ever did see."

Boris grinned at him.

Grigori and Spartak nudged each other. Piotr finally turned his eyes from the horses to Boris. "We've heard a lot about your stables, and everything we heard was nothing but the truth."

Boris laughed. "Well, I'm lucky I can afford to pour every kopek I make back into the stables."

"That's great," Piotr said admiringly, "really great. A man couldn't ask for anything more."

"My wife is expecting us. Shall we go?"

"Mind if we wash up?"

"There'll be rooms prepared for you at the house."

The three Tartars were used to water that came from a pump.

"We didn't look for hospitality at the big house, Boris. We could go down to the stream and spread out our bedrolls. We brought fresh clothes."

They reminded him of his mother, who liked to bathe in streams or plunge into the sea. With a smile, he said, "Fifty yards north of the big barn, take a left turn. Keep close to the fence. You'll come to some cabins. You'll find everything you need there."

"Thanks, Boris," Piotr said. "That suits us better."

"Whenever you're ready, come to the house."

While Boris soaked himself in the newly installed white marble tub, over six feet long and more than three feet wide, Ronya asked him to tell her about Snow Girl.

"She's a yearling. Full grown, she'll still be tiny. She looks perfect. Seems gentle and sweet-natured. We'll see if she's trained to take orders."

198

"Is it possible that she was drugged?"

"I don't think so."

Absently, Ronya began twirling a wisp of hair. "Do you suppose that a grandchild is an Achilles' heel?"

"Beats me. Throw me a towel."

She brought him a giant-sized towel. He took it with one hand and seized her with the other, ignoring her protests and gathering her close.

Ronya tilted her head. She forgot the mussed dress. "How much do you love me?"

He answered with a grin, "I'd sure like to show you," but could see that this did not reassure her. "What's wrong?"

Ronya stirred in his arms, and he felt her quiver. He let go the towel and took her face in his hands. "Don't be uneasy."

She smiled a bit forlornly. "It's not the pony. Partly, it's being pregnant—I guess." She would have continued but sensed he was thinking about his guests again. "I think I'll go change my dress."

Boris did not withdraw his hands. "Listen, dove. I promised the men a night on the town."

Ronya went rigid. *Barely home, and already—* She could not even bear to complete the thought. "Let me go."

Except for the greater pressure of his fingers, Boris took no notice. His voice, when it came, was pleasant. "I'll take them to the club for a few drinks and dinner, and then I'll turn them over to an acquaintance of mine. I'll be home by eleven, at the latest. We'll compare ideas for your new kitchen. I've made a drawing of the fireplace. It's huge, big enough to roast an ox."

The change in Ronya was instantaneous.

Boris smiled at her. "All right?"

"Very all right."

"Can you stand more?"

"I'm not sure."

"The pup I brought home for Igor has fallen in love with the stallion. It's no use bringing her into the house; she won't stay."

Ronya laughed with relief.

His lips touched her nose. Releasing her gently, he said, "Get out of that dress, Ronya, I don't like it."

"What's wrong with it?"

"Wear something more—ah—"

"Spectacular?"

"Less! That one reveals too much bosom."

Dressed like the three visitors in the Tartar clothes—white boots, white pants, embroidered blouse—Boris made the introductions.

All three were dark-complexioned with broad, high cheekbones, short noses, and very slanted eyes. The two younger men were dazzled by Ronya, but Piotr's eyes went to Ruth. All in all, it was a very pleasant meal. Ruth had a way of making people feel at ease. Ronya kept them laughing. Igor, until Boris sent him out, had all sorts of fascinating tidbits to contribute. Lydia and the serving maids pressed food on them. Around three in the afternoon, they rode off to Kiev on their Mongolian ponies, led by Boris on the stallion.

That evening, Piotr spoke to Boris from the warmth of vodka. "So help me, Boris, when I saw Ruth, your mother-in-law, I thought she's a prize I'd sure like to have around my campfire."

Boris came in at eleven sharp. Before going to his own room, he looked in on Igor. Gazing down at his sleeping son, at the chiseled nose, the high cheekbones, he pondered on his intense love for the boy. True, it was overshadowed by his love for Ronya, but this Boris understood. What brought him moments of perplexity was his irrational jealousy.

Some half hour later, he entered Ronya's room. She was in bed, sitting beneath a soft light, reading, and Boris could not remember ever seeing her more beautiful. Her gleaming hair falling in disarray, she looked no older than when he married her. His eyes traveled to the rounded near-perfection of her breasts, and Ronya saw with pride that Boris could discern little change beneath the sheer lace.

Boris got into bed and stretched out his long legs.

"Ronya—" he began. He looked at her. The color of his eyes deepened, and Ronya knew that he was going to say something she did not want to hear. Dreading it, she pushed herself up higher on the pillow, her brows knitted in concentration.

Presently, he took both her hands in his and said, his voice deep, "I don't want to share you."

"The new baby?" she whispered.

She saw the fierceness creep into his eyes and remembered his reaction to Igor when he was born; and that brought back, as though it were yesterday, the time she found him with Tamara. Suddenly, her dark eyes were fiercer than his. "My father," she said coldly, "did not want me to be a wife. You make the same mistake when you deny me the right to enjoy my babies."

Boris gripped her hands so tightly that she cried out. He let go, but his rage was terrible. "That's a hateful thing to say."

Ronya laid her slim, pain-filled hands on the blanket. "That," she said, glaring at him, "was a stupid thing to do."

With a sudden stab of shame, he drew her to him. Holding her close against his chest, his lips brushing her ear, he slid down between the silk sheets whispering, "You're mine."

Her anger forgotten, Ronya pressed her body against his.

Boris leaned over her, and she raised herself a little. Trembling under his touch, she flung her arms around his neck and her lips moved against his.

Afterward, leaning on an elbow, he scrutinized her intently.

"What's the matter, darling?"

"We're a couple of fools making love like that."

"Don't be silly."

"Ronya, I'm serious."

"You don't have to be frightened, darling. I won't lose the baby."

Ronya snuggled her firm buttocks into Boris' abdomen. He felt the delicious warmth of her body and fell asleep at once.

Much to the children's relief, the perfect weather lasted until the next day. When the veterinarian came to look at Snow Girl, Ronya had gone to the stables specially to hear what he had to say. He pronounced the pony beautifully mannered and trained and in perfect health. Getting a pony such as Snow Girl was an event to be celebrated, and Ronya immediately invited all the children of the neighboring landowners for a hayride next day, promising a picnic by the river and a riding display by Boris.

Punctually at eleven o'clock there arrived ten little girls dressed in ruffles and lace and eight little boys dressed like admirals in imitation of the Tzar, escorted by six nursemaids in black with white ribboned caps. Six carriages rolled up the drive in turn to unload their passengers and be dispatched to the stables, where coachmen and horses were offered the famous Pirov hospitality by Boris' men. Igor and the Blond One could barely contain their excitement.

Regiments of servants staggered out of the house carrying large hampers of food, jugs of sweet cider, and gallons of lemonade, which they loaded into a cart drawn up behind Ronya's.

When Ruth came out to join Ronya, she stopped short at the sight of the piles of provisions in the cart. "You are taking enough to feed the entire Russian army," she said, climbing into the buggy.

"Yes, I suppose so, but there'll be peasant children and gypsy children tagging along in their own wagons. There always are."

Leaving the rest of the procession to organize itself, Ronya drove to the path that led to the church. Pulling up, she handed the reins over to her mother and jumped down. "I'll only be a minute."

Ruth settled back to wait and let her eyes follow Ronya, who was peering in at the doorway of the church.

"Father Tromokov?"

"Why don't you come in?" the priest bellowed from the cool interior.

"Because I can't," answered Ronya. "I'm bare-armed and have no kerchief on my head."

Father Tromokov came striding out.

"I suppose," Ronya began, "you've heard about the pony."

He nodded. "I sure have."

"Were you surprised?"

"Happily so." He gave Ronya a long look from under his bushy eyebrows. "Something special must be brewing."

"Boris doesn't think so."

"Let's walk over to the buggy. I've something to tell you."

Ruth reached down to clasp his hand, as he cleared his throat. "Rifka hasn't sought me out in years. She came to see me so early this morning the sun was barely up, with a white-nosed black pony. Very politely she asked me to tell Boris that the pony was for the Blond One. I agreed, of course."

Ronya bit back an astonished exclamation, and Ruth gave a knowing smile. Father Tromokov went on, pleased at the little sensation he had caused. "She said, 'Isn't it amazing how quickly everyone on the land knows everything? There are no secrets.' When I took the pony to the stables at about ten, I met Boris leading a magnificent pony—all black. It seemed to me that one black pony was enough for one blond boy, so I turned around straightaway and gave Rifka back her pony."

"Did Boris see you?" Ronya asked.

"Indeed, he did. He had time to stop me, but he didn't. He just looked rather sheepish and walked on."

A radiant smile spread over Ronya's face.

"Are you coming to Igor's party?"

"I'll be there," Father Tromokov said, helping her into the buggy.

As they moved off, Ruth said, "Now, aren't you glad you didn't speak to Boris about a second pony?"

It was exactly the right weather for a hayride—not a cloud in the sky, the birds singing in the trees. Boris, sporting a stunning paisley scarf around his neck, led the way, followed by Father Tromokov and Sad Eyes. Behind them came Ronya's buggy. Then followed a procession of peasant carts filled with hay and the gleeful shouts of children. At the end of the line, though no one had invited her, Tamara rode in a wagon decorated with squares and cubes in bright colors. From her wagon emanated the rhythmic beat of guitars and a fiddle. There was no sound at all coming from Boris' wagon, where Igor and the Blond One sat in silent awe, each holding onto his pony as if he would never let go.

They passed green pastures where cows munched contentedly and mares grazed. They passed herds of sheep. They passed the wheat fields, where the songs of the peasants came floating to them across the wheat, songs sung in rounds, one group calling joyfully to others.

When they came to the grassy banks of the Dnieper, the wagons were brought to a halt. Boris jumped down, strode over to the buggy and lifted Ruth down, and then Ronya. He put a minute kiss on the tip of Ronya's nose and started unloading, helped by the priest and Sad Eyes.

"Where do you want it, Ronya?"

Ronya paused, looked around, turned to Ruth. "Where do you think, Mother?"

Ruth laughed.

"Over there," Ronya pointed, "by the boulder. It's got a nice flat top."

The picnic was a glorious triumph. The cold meats and salads, the hard-boiled eggs, the cheeses and fruits, were devoured. The little cakes were consumed by the dozen.

Tamara had the good sense to stick close to Ruth, and the smiles she directed at Ronya seemed to say, "See how good I am. Trust me again." But as the day progressed, and Boris avoided her, and Ronya was barely polite, and no one invited her to dance, her smile died.

The children were content to run and wade in the river and gape at the ponies, and skip the games for prizes, because they were longing for the last part of the day. What was a hayride, or even a picnic, compared to a horse show? It was easy to collect them into the wagons for the return journey.

Ronya was still a considerable distance from the stables when her ears caught the boisterous shouts of happy children. "They got here unusually fast," she said to Ruth, "or we were awfully slow."

Annoyed because Ronya had insisted on staying behind to clean up, Ruth said, "Some day you'll remember you have servants to do the work."

"Boris agrees with you," retorted Ronya, "but I remind him that in the stables he's as I am in the house. We both feel no one can do the work as well as we can."

"That's hardly the same. Boris makes the stables his job. He should be able to outthink and outspeed his hands. They respect him for it. Your zeal is a little silly."

Somewhat taken aback by the scolding, and wondering what crime it was to pick up after Igor's party, Ronya turned away and concentrated on getting the buggy to the big open space in front of the stables, since the shouts were not coming from the direction of the arena.

In one group stood the nursemaids come to collect their charges. Most of them were young, and they smiled or fluttered their eyelashes in kittenish glances at the lean, rugged riders and trainers who worked for Boris. The visiting coachmen took measure of the well-kept buildings that housed the horses and equipment; they knew that what they were seeing was the best in the country. Boris' stable boys—wide smiles spread across their Slavic faces—leaned against doors, rails, and trees. Their pride in the Pirov stables was immense. Some of the gypsy and peasant families were about—with their children, throngs of them, laughing and shouting.

Igor was sitting, easy and erect, on Snow Girl, eyes glued on his father. The Blond One was on Blackie, ramrod straight, the glint of wonder in his eyes; he, too, was watching his father.

The ponies had the place of honor. Surrounding them were the children and grandchildren of the neighboring landowners having the most marvelous time of their young lives, for Boris Pirov, the world's champion horseman, was putting on a daring show for them, and he was as magnificent as on the day Ronya first saw him in St. Petersburg.

Standing upright on a spirited black horse, with the white stallion waiting quietly behind him, Boris made a slight bow in the direction of Ruth and Ronya. He waited until Ronya had driven past him and edged her way into a good viewing place, then gave the command. The black horse broke into a gallop. The waiting stallion sprang forward to its side and matched its pace stride for stride. After one circuit of the big yard, Boris leaped onto the stallion's bare back and, without slackening its speed, slid under its belly, emerged on the other side, and stood facing the stallion's tail.

He completed another circuit before bringing the two horses to a standstill and signaling a groom forward to take charge of the black horse. The children clapped and shouted, and the gypsies gave piercing whistles. Even the nursemaids had taken their eyes off the men.

Next, Boris took the opportunity to teach Igor a lesson. He wanted the boy to understand what he meant by: "If you have one morsel of food, feed the horse; you go hungry. If you have one drink of water, give it to the horse; you go thirsty. You'll be trusting your life to his courage and loyalty and stamina."

Boris took off his paisley scarf and tied it over his eyes. He and the stallion did some old tricks. Then Boris turned his head slowly in Ronya's direction and, guiding the stallion with his knees alone, he came up to the buggy at a gallop. The mare began to snort, but Ronya calmed her. Still blindfolded, Boris jumped from the stallion, remounted, and rode away.

For a finale, Boris rode with one foot on the white stallion's back and one foot on the black's.

204

No applause, no cheers came from Igor or the Blond One. They were awestruck. It was as though both boys somehow knew that the day would come when Boris' strength and daring would haunt them.

"How long is it now," Ruth said to Ronya, "since Boris introduced me to his skill and prowess? Five years? My heart still pounds, I turn cold."

Proudly Ronya answered, "A golden god on a winged steed."

21

By mid-July, Boris and Ronya were so absorbed in building the new kitchen that Boris spent more time toiling in the house than running the stables.

Jack of all trades, Boris was artisan and laborer, cabinetmaker, bricklayer, structural engineer, and plumber. Ronya was inspector and surveyor. Igor was subforeman and errand boy. Ruth, who had never understood Ronya's passion for cooking and baking, was grateful for her daughter's happiness. *Oh David,* she thought, *you should have lived to see it.*

By the end of November, everything was finished, just as Boris planned. Snug and cozy against the cold, the kitchen gave Ronya an open view of the grounds, high and low storage cabinets, copper pots filled with winter greenery, display shelves for the ancient blue china, a long table topped at one end with unpolished black marble on which to roll pastry dough and at the other with a thick chopping block. Boris had his huge rocking chair, Igor a wooden rocking horse. Even Ruth had one of the servants carry down her favorite chair. "I promised Igor I'd read aloud to him and, as long as you're both here, it's hard to keep him upstairs."

Boris, absorbed in the newspaper, raised his head and grinned at her. "Don't worry, Mother. As soon as the novelty wears off, we'll reinhabit the house."

It started to snow on the second Sunday in December, and it snowed continuously for five days and nights. No one, not even Kiev's centenarian, could remember when there was so much snow. The sun was low and gave off little light and almost no heat. And so it was cold—colder than the northern coast of Russia—and, except for the blinding whiteness of the great snowdrifts, dark. The snow froze, and the new snow fell on the frozen snow. Even the Dnieper was almost completely frozen over. On the sixth day, it stopped snowing.

Ronya, who under the circumstances felt no qualms about doing so, conscripted her peasants for shoveling, and even though they were land workers and well off, for her they willingly turned themselves into domestic serfs. When their fingers turned blue and their toes stiffened in the sub-zero cold, they came into the snug kitchen where there were always men drinking hot tea and casting sidelong glances at the fat-thighed housemaids. However, there was no nonsense in Mistress Ronya's house—Lydia made certain of that.

Boris was completely disgusted with himself. Sheer jealousy had made him veto Ronya's suggestion that Dr. Erick Stiller be asked to deliver the coming baby. "I should have let him come," he admitted to Ruth.

"I'm sure there is no reason to worry, dear. Ronya is young and strong, and I'm certain the local doctor is competent."

Boris' eyes narrowed. "We need a smooth road for a dog sled."

"Rifka is a superb midwife."

Boris downed a glass of vodka. "No," he said tersely.

In his sleep, Boris heard the sound of the door opening. He disengaged himself from Ronya and lifted himself to look at the time. Barely five in the morning. Thinking that it was Igor who had come into their room, he could scarcely believe his eyes when he saw who it was. The very first words Boris addressed to his bastard son were: "What in the hell are you doing here?"

The Blond One was wearing fur boots and a red fox parka over his little nightshirt, and his bare head was damp from the heavy mist. He stood by Boris' side of the bed and trembled. Before Boris could question him, Ronya suddenly sat up. Her eyes full of sleep, she leaned over Boris and reached for the child.

Boris lifted the Blond One onto the bed and pulled off his wet boots. "Talk," he said.

The Blond One crawled over Boris and put his arms around Ronya's neck, tears running down his cheeks. "Rifka, my grandmother, fell down and got dead."

"Where's your mother?" Boris demanded, bristling.

The Blond One snuggled closer to Ronya and made no reply.

Boris and Ronya exchanged a significant glance.

Boris quickly started to get dressed, and Ronya, looking at his naked torso, said, "Dress warm."

206

Ronya pulled her nightdress down over her belly under the covers, and helped the Blond One off with his parka. He crept into the warm space his father had left, buried his blond head in Ronya's bosom, and burst into heartbreaking sobs. Ronya held him closely, and from time to time she cried too.

After a time his sobs lessened and, under Ronya's gentle questioning, told how he had found Rifka sprawled on the bathroom floor in a pool of blood. He remembered that out in the woods one day Boris had told Igor, "Never panic." He said, "I forced myself not to run out in the snow in my bare feet."

"You're a smart boy and a brave one, and you were right to come here."

"Will I live with you now?" the Blond One asked.

"We'll see, darling. I hope so."

The smell of fresh blood assailed his nostrils. Done with self-centeredness and vanity, Rifka lay face down between the tub and the sink. Kneeling, Boris saw that death, which must have been instantaneous, was probably due to a massive hemorrhage. Without touching the body, he rose to his feet. He glanced down at the woman who had lavished such consummate attention upon herself in life; then, astounded at the wave of repugnance that swept over him, he left quickly. He swung open the front door, letting the cold December air pour into his lungs, and set out with determination for the wagon.

Boris realized that Tamara was probably not alone. To make sure, he plunged through the snow to the fringe of the forest and there discovered the sleds. Judging by the loads, the hunting must have been good, but the dogs looked tired and hungry. Two sleds secured together: Tamara had two callers. Even though Boris had no illusions about her, he felt sickened at the thought. He separated the sleds and drove the long narrow lead sled, pulled by eight dogs, up to the wagon. Moving out of sight, he pelted the dogs with icy snowballs, hitting them on the neck, back, and in the eyes. A hunter himself, he knew how to enrage dogs. Blinded and stung by the snow, hungry and tired, the dogs howled frantically. They turned savagely on each other, entangled in the traces and jerking the loaded sled dangerously.

The men inside the wagon came racing out, still pulling up their bearskin hunting breeches. Boris knew them both. The big-boned, pockmarked man was a jobber dealing in fine skins. He had a wife and thirteen children. The other man, still in the full vigor of youth, was a trapper and hunter. His sister was said to be the highest-priced tart in town.

The men kicked and cursed until they had got the dogs calmed down and drove off to retrieve the other sled.

Boris entered the wagon. Tamara lay outstretched, naked, her jet-black hair hanging loose over the side of the bed. Boris took in the slack, slightly open mouth, the lithe body, the long, beautiful legs. His eyes turned to the litter of empty bottles, broken glass, and cigarette butts, and back to Tamara. He cried out with revulsion:

"You rotten slut."

As he spun around, Tamara sat up and staggered to her feet. She caught up with him at the door, still half asleep, clasped her arms around his thighs, clung to him, begged, "Don't leave me, I love you."

Boris felt nothing but disgust. "You bitch. You pig."

Befuddled with sleep, she slipped to the floor, mumbling, "I love you, I love you."

He caught hold of her wrists, pulled her to her feet, and shook her. "Your mother is dead."

She did not hear. Consumed by her passion for Boris, she forgot that she was disheveled, that a bare hour ago, weary and satiated, she had slipped as though drugged into the vacuity of sleep. She knew only that Boris was backing out of her reach, her desire was being denied her. "Come to bed. I'll make you happier than you've ever been, I promise."

Boris slapped her across the face and ran out of the wagon.

"Wait—wait," she cried. The freezing air bit at her naked body. Boris was gone. She closed the door and flung herself down on the bed, weeping hopelessly. She pressed her tear-swollen face into the pillows, sighing brokenly between sobs, torturing herself: "If only Boris had let me know he was ready to come to me at last, if only he hadn't found me with them."

After a while she clutched at the idea that if he came once, he'd come again. Hastily she wiped away her tears and splashed water over her face. As she dressed, she made herself concentrate: What had Boris said about Rifka? Something strange. Suddenly, combing the snarls out of her hair, she remembered. Rifka, dead! "Oh, my God!" she cried. Heart pounding, she snatched up her sable wrap and started to run.

Back at Rifka's house, Boris got towels and a sheet and, going into the bathroom, he turned on the taps full force. He returned and removed Rifka's bloodstained nightdress, washed her clean, smoothed her hair, wrapped her gently in the white sheet, and then lifted her off the floor and carried her back to her own bed. He sat down on a straight chair in the silent room and waited for Tamara.

He felt her eyes burning on him as she entered, but he could not look at her. Tamara dropped to her knees beside him and pressed her face against his legs, her eyes full of tears. "Please give me another

208

chance, Boris. The others are nothing. Love me, and you'll never catch me with anyone again."

Boris pushed her away and stood up. "Don't you see your mother?"

As though speaking to herself, she said, "It makes no difference to her now." She got up. "Put your arms around me, Boris."

"Damn you, Tamara, you're an animal."

Tamara fell moaning across Rifka's body. "Mother, Mother. I'm alone."

Boris left the bedroom. In seconds the front door slammed shut.

Tamara cried a long time. Then she found the vodka bottle.

Outside, the camp was awake, alive with the sounds and smells of a new day—children, bundled to the teeth, playing in the snow, dogs barking, mules kicking up the white powdered dust.

Boris came to Old Auntie's house and had barely set foot on the porch, when the wizened old woman came and opened the door, as always, smoking her clay pipe. She settled him at one end of the wooden kitchen table and filled two glasses of hot tea and two heaping bowls of kasha and meat from a pot on the stove, before sitting down at the other end of the table. "You're going to tell me she's dead," she said.

Boris nodded.

"Don't mention the name of the dead one," she warned, "lest her ghost hear and haunt you."

"I'll be careful," he said seriously.

Old Auntie rolled and lit a cigarette and handed it to him. He took a puff and asked, "Where are Fedor's daughters?"

"Sleeping on straw, dancing for coins on the roads of Spain, preparing themselves in our ways and our skills."

He looked surprised, and the old woman eyed him from her chair. "Did they not tell you," she asked, "that Tamara was trained in the same fashion?"

Boris made no reply.

Old Auntie chuckled. "When Ronya accompanied her father to the great cities, Tamara, our new queen, was sent to dwell among my kind, dressed in the poorest of clothes. She begged in the streets, she kept her fingers nimble for stealing, she hawked trifles at fairs—she learned all the tricks of the cunning."

He finished his cigarette and picked up his parka. "Come," he said, "I'll take you to Rifka."

To his relief, she said, "Go home to Ronya. I can manage all right."

"Thanks, Old Auntie."

The bath Boris took was scalding hot. It washed him clean, but it did not wash away the image of the once proud and graceful Rifka motionless and stained red. He felt a ripple of horror at the profound finality of death. His mind slid to Tamara and her moral collapse. Boris sighed heavily and sought to free his mind of death and filth by evoking Ronya's image. His state of mind was such that had Ronya asked it of him, he would have sworn fidelity; and having given his promise, he would have kept it.

They met in the library.

"What happened?" she said, apprehensively. "What took you so long?"

Boris turned from the winter landscape of bare trees and frozen snow. Her hair, even in the dim sunlight, was a shining, copperish, autumn-leaf brown. He took her in his arms and breathed in her perfume.

"How do you know that Rifka is dead?" he said, when he had led her gently to the sofa and sat down beside her.

Without thinking, Ronya answered, "The Blond One told us," and in a flash realized the stupidity of taking the word of a frightened three-year-old as fact.

Boris nodded. "I did the same thing. Felt no doubt at all—just rushed off, prepared to find a corpse." He smiled wryly. "He was not mistaken."

Ronya remained silent, and watched Boris hold a match to a cigarette and inhale quietly. She saw his face change; he was getting ready to say something about the Blond One.

"You think the boy has penetrated my protective guard. You're wrong, Ronya. As soon as the situation permits, I want him out of the house. Meanwhile, I want to see him as infrequently as possible. Clear?"

"Crystal clear." It was said without rancor; this was not the time to start a quarrel. "It's getting late. We must go to Mother. I'm afraid she already suspects something."

As he so often did, Boris sat completely still, staring at Ronya's lovely face. Now, as always, it gave him pleasure, but his mind was on Tamara. He made his decision: to tell Ronya everything.

Ronya heard him out, thinking how strange it was that the Tamara she once loved had turned into the Tamara who misused her perfect body and dedicated herself to moral corrosion. The why of it mystified her. She tried desperately to understand. Her good sense assured her that Boris was not to blame for Tamara's numerous and varied assignations. She paled as an answer came in mind: From early girlhood, she herself had been Tamara's conscience.

Suddenly Boris was handing her a glass of brandy. "Here, drink this."

Her color returned, and with it came the realization of what lay before them. She heard David's voice in her mind: "Here on this land, we heed tradition. We weep with our peasants and mourn with our gypsies."

"Boris," she said, "we are going to have to prepare for an influx of nomad gypsies. I don't know how, but the word has gone out. They are on their way right now from all over Russia, and from Poland, Romania, and Hungary. They'll be riding into the camp soon. In summer, it's easy—they set down their wagons and tents in the meadows and clearings, but in winter. . . ."

Boris thought the possibility of a gypsy invasion in the worst of winter extremely remote, so he let Ronya go on without tackling the problems of housing and unlimited hospitality.

"We, not the sorrowing tribe, must feed the visitors. We shall have to make arrangements for a constant supply of food, day and night. Fortunately only cold food is allowed, but we must provide peasant girls to keep the samovars bubbling and the coffee pots filled. After six days the gypsies will light their fires and feast. It will be all over in six weeks, when Rifka's tent will be burned."

Boris, who shared his Tartar people's contempt for gypsies, thinking them a greasy, dirty, thieving, shiftless lot, concealed his feelings. By now he was worried. *What if they do come?* he thought. The horses did not bother him—he had plenty of feed and shelter—but the nightmare of a flood of people and their demands excited his revulsion. As did the danger of a winter fire.

Ronya guessed at his thoughts and found his hand. Her touch was sufficient to quiet his resentment. Up at five, she looked positively glowing. Her vitality, like everything about her—the way she ate, the way she slept—pleasured him. He felt the strong stir of desire, and this too communicated itself to her. A blush flitted across her face. "We must go to Mother," she said.

After they had broken the news to Ruth and left her sorrowing but calm after the first grief-stricken shock, Ronya went to her room—ostensibly to rest, for that afternoon she and Ruth were to go to Tamara. Boris had protested, but both women knew what they must do.

But instead of resting, she rang for Lydia. While she waited, she twisted bright ribbons into her braids, which she then wound peasant-fashion around her head, and fastened her heart-shaped diamond pin to her dress. Jewels and gay colors were proper gypsy mourning.

Lydia looked tired and strained when she came in. Ronya made her sit down, and she sank gratefully into a chair. "It's nice to rest my feet."

"I'm not surprised," Ronya said. "I don't want you exhausted. Hire more help."

"More easily said than done, my mistress. The days of good servants are over. The young people flock to Moscow to work in the factories."

This was a timeworn complaint. Ronya gave her an affectionate glance, which turned into a worried frown. It was not usual for Lydia to look so harassed.

"Why haven't I seen Tanya lately?" she asked suddenly.

Lydia's face darkened. "She is preparing to go to America. No one can stop her."

Ronya had been having visions of two convicts descending upon them and was only too thankful for Tanya's decision. "I have a present for her. I hope it helps open the door to a good life."

Lydia thanked Ronya and pulled a kerchief from her pocket and dabbed her eyes.

Ronya smiled at her fondly and started giving orders for feeding the gypsies—especially the children. Lydia did not like gypsies, she never would. "A handsome kopek that'll cost," she grumbled, generations and generations of peasant frugality in her soul.

"We can afford it. We've practically doubled our grain-growing acreage these past few years."

Lydia brightened with pride. Getting to her feet, she said, "For dinner, we have chicken breasts in champagne and wax beans."

Tamara looked flamboyant, expensive, and more tired than sad. She greeted them nervously and gave Ruth a cheek to kiss. Ronya was profoundly grateful that Tamara led them into the darkened bedroom without offering to kiss her.

Rifka looked asleep, peaceful and serene. Ruth lowered her head, kissed Rifka lightly, and broke down in tears. She turned her tear-stained face toward the girls and said, "Please, let me say good-bye to my friend."

Tamara and Ronya withdrew and walked down the hall where they sat in gloom drinking tea. Tamara was first to speak.

"Boris told you everything, didn't he?" she said fiercely.

"Yes," Ronya answered. Her voice was husky.

"Ronya, I have no idea of how much he saw. Please tell me. Don't be delicate."

"He saw them pulling on their breeches as they rushed out to the dog sled. He saw the manner in which you had been used. How could you let them?" Ronya said wretchedly.

Her firm chin held high, her white teeth glistening, Tamara scoffed, "You know the old saying: 'The appetite grows with eating.' "

Ronya understood that her bravado only masked her shame, and said nothing.

Tamara waited for Ronya to vilify her, turn from her in loathing. When she did not, her whole attitude changed. "Look at me, Ronya," she pleaded. "Aren't I worthwhile?"

Ronya looked at her and replied in an impersonal voice, "Very."

"Then why aren't you and Boris nice to me? If only you were, I'd never need a drink, I'd never make men fight over me to prove my desirability to Boris, and—and—it wouldn't take two men to appease my starvation." She burst into sobs.

Ronya remained unmoved.

"Stay with me tonight, Ronya."

"No."

It was another slap in the face. Tamara uttered an ugly laugh. "Boris told you about me, that sanctimonious debaucher. Well, why was he sniffing around here at dawn?"

"I think," Ronya said quietly, "that you should respect your mother's corpse and my mother's sorrow."

Tamara thrust her head forward. "You're right to be jealous," she screamed. "Boris will never give me up. He can't. I'm in his blood."

"You're a liar." Ronya's voice had a cold, murderous ring to it.

Tamara cringed. She lifted the cold tea to her lips with a shaking hand.

Ronya rose. "You are going to provide a decent home for the Blond One," she said in a strong even voice, "and you're going to behave yourself. There'll be no more wagon, no more whoring, no more drunkenness. The next man with whom you establish an arrangement—make it a bit more permanent and a lot less public. From now on, you'll leave the stink of whoredom to the whores. They get paid for it."

Tamara had already decided on a less dissolute life, principally because the men who came to her bed were mere shapes, who left her feeling foul and slimy, but Ronya had opened the door on another matter: the Blond One. True, early each morning he had made his way to the big house, and each evening someone brought him back; but still Rifka had provided his official home. Tamara knew she had to unlock her heart and make room for him. That decision turned another key, opened another door. She hated Rifka's house, hated it with a bitter loathing from the day her baby girl lay stuffed in a sack, killed by its own grandmother.

"I want to get out of this house. I want one exclusively mine, one with no echo of agony or death."

Ronya felt the same about Rifka's house and for the same reason. "I think that's smart. Come spring, you may cut timber, all you want."

It disturbed Ronya that Tamara made no inquiry about the Blond One. Finally, she mentioned him.

"Why—I took it for granted he's with you." It did not occur to her to ask how the Blond One came to be with Ronya. "Can you keep him for a time?"

"Yes, but not indefinitely."

Ruth entered looking calm and grave. "I think we must go," she said.

They left Tamara seated before the samovar.

Boris opened his eyes to find Ronya smiling down at him. "I trust you had a good nap."

He lifted his hand and touched her face. He felt a prickling of uneasiness. She looked different. He caught her to him.

"Hurry, darling," she said, returning his kiss, "dinner is at eight."

Boris swung his powerful legs out of bed. When he had shaved, he rubbed his palm over his smooth, wind-tanned face and gave himself a thoughtful glance in the mirror. He wished Ronya free of the child in her womb and wished fervently that he would be able to stay faithful to her until she was ready for him. He was not sure he would, and it disturbed him.

It was eleven o'clock when Ronya, lying between the cool, fresh sheets watching the clock, concluded that her pains were no false alarm. She was in the start of labor. She thought of Doctor Stiller in Vienna, how easily he had performed his part at Igor's birth, how safe and confident he had made her feel. She sat up, put on slippers and a warm robe over her long white nightdress, and dragging a blanket, went downstairs to the library, where Boris and the priest were playing cards. She made herself comfortable on the couch.

The priest looked over at her and chuckled. "Boris was born under a lucky star. He wins every hand."

Boris flashed her a grin from his cards. "Did you get lonesome?"

"Well, not exactly."

She was thinking about how much she disliked the local obstetrician; she did not care if he got to her in time or not. Father Tromokov's sister-in-law Marya was an excellent midwife, and her house was only a stone's throw from the church.

At the same time, she was annoyed because Boris seemed to have nothing on his mind but the card game and the priest's genial company. It was his fault that Erick Stiller was not here: He had refused to send Stiller an apology and ask him to come to Kiev again. To punish him a little, she said, "Do you suppose delivering a woman is much different from delivering a mare or a bitch?"

214

"I don't know about midwifery to a woman. Why do you ask, dove?"

"Because," Ronya said sweetly, "you are about to find out."

Boris flung down his cards and jumped to his feet. "Christ! When?"

Her dark eyes dancing mischievously, Ronya replied, "In a few minutes."

"Stop play-acting, Ronya," he said anxiously. "Tell the truth."

Ronya's eyes flew wide open, she choked back a scream, and the teasing grin vanished. When the hard pain subsided, she said, "That was a bad one, really bad. Get Marya, please. Hurry."

Boris overcame his momentary paralysis. He sent the priest for the doctor; he himself raced to the kitchen shouting for men to run for Marya and help the priest with the sleigh.

Father Ivan Tromokov broke into a run. Once out of the door, he saw the weather had changed. The darkness was at its deepest, the wind on the rise, and even Siberia could not match Kiev for coldness.

Hastily, Boris came back to Ronya.

"Hold me," she said.

He gathered her into his arms and, looking down at her wide soft mouth and the sublime curve of her chin, carried her back to bed. He sat down on the edge and stroked her hair. "Do you want your mother?"

"No. Let her sleep."

Ronya suffered each terrible pain with eyes and lips tightly closed, but the pain showed. One minute she grew stiff, the next she relaxed. "Oh, Christ!" Boris cried.

Ronya opened her eyes, breathing hard, and seized his hand.

Then Boris stretched out on the bed and laid his body next to hers. "I love you, Ronya. More than life, I love you."

"I know, my darling," Ronya gasped, drenched in perspiration.

David was born an hour before dawn. Like a gypsy, he came in the storm.

When Ronya had slept an hour, she heard the wail of the wind and opened her eyes. She had a moment of terror, but then she saw Boris resting in his wing chair, feet up on a small table, thinking exhaustedly about the hell a woman goes through to give a man a son. She murmured his name, and the next instant she was in his arms.

"Ronya . . ." he said. "My Ronya."

"You're trembling, darling."

Rubbing his cheek against hers, he said softly, "We have a second son, little dove."

"I know. I remember. Does he look like you?"

Boris grinned suddenly. "Damned if I know."

"I want to see him."

Boris released her and pulled the bell cord but remained by her bedside.

They showed her David. Ruth carried him in and laid him in her arms. Ronya leaned over and kissed the baby's forehead. Her heart pounded.

"Well, dove? Does he look like me?"

"He's so big." Ronya's voice was husky rather than proud.

22

After Ruth and Ronya departed that afternoon, Tamara sat staring at the samovar in long and lonely sadness. Nearly an hour passed before she was roused by a commotion outside her door. Three strange gypsies, bundled in eiderdown jackets over layers of wool, had come into the camp. Huddled around them were barking dogs and a noisy crowd of her own people, who were shrieking in disappointment that only these three, out of the many traveling bands, had arrived to pay homage to their dead queen. They cursed and hurled insults at the absent cowards who feared to challenge the ice, the freezing cold, and the swirling wind in their high-wheeled wagons.

Tamara sent her young men away to erect the death tent in a clearing in the forest and fill it with the fragrance of incense, under the supervision of Kako, who had been top man in the camp since Fedor's banishment. The men worked in silence, ignoring the brutal cold. They draped the interior with white velvet and laid a floor of boards, covering them with brocade. Tall candelabra flanked the silk-swathed platform on which the coffin was to rest.

The girls were set to braid sharp-colored wool into bows, to fashion silk kerchiefs into flowers, to tear the skirts of their bright dresses into strips. During the six days of Rifka's lying in state, the bronze coffin would be shrouded with these offerings. The older women collected bracelets, earrings, and gold pieces. At the end of the six days and nights, Rifka's casket would be lowered into its grave to the music of a gypsy orchestra. A hundred different fires would be lit, and everywhere there would be the smell of burning wood and roasting pig. After the feast, Tamara and her people would gather around the open grave and pelt it with the gold and then, wailing and screeching, they would take handfuls of dirt and fill the grave. Every sixth day for six weeks the feast would be repeated, and then Tamara would put a match to the death tent and declare the mourning over, for by then Rifka would have arrived in the Nation of the Dead.

Meanwhile, Tamara was preparing her mother for the grave. She dressed her in her most exquisite belongings, in embroidered silks and satins, and decked her with her priceless jewels. She painted her face carefully and with artistry. She scattered around her a fortune in gold.

By night, all was ready.

In pitch-darkness and with a freezing wind on the rise, Rifka, reverently covered with jewels and gold and bright, bright colors, was carried in torchlight procession to the death tent. It was freezing in the tent. In the presence of the important members of the tribe—all men and each a head of a household—Tamara, also adorned with gold, gave the dead queen her oath of commitment and loyalty. The men joined hands, and their voices rose high in an ardent oath of loyalty to Tamara. This was but the token ceremony, made even shorter by the weather. The honor guard took their posts and were left to the hardships of their watch.

Rifka's house was tightly secured against the raw, icy gale. Tamara lay on her back and stared at the ceiling. "Why go on thinking about it?" she asked herself over and over, but her mind kept bringing back Boris' face—the fierce nostrils, the naked contempt, the way he whirled and ran from her. That was as far as her mind got.

Fatigued to the point of exhaustion, Tamara decided: To hell with staring at the ceiling. She slid out of bed and in the dark went to the kitchen, where she turned up a lamp, brewed poppyheads, and then drank the tea. She rinsed the glass and, in the minutes it took her to feel drowsy, she inspected the shine on the brass candlesticks. Like Ronya, she had a born passion for a meticulously clean house. When she returned to her bedroom, she carefully straightened the sheets and arranged the pillows.

A few minutes after she returned to bed, she lost consciousness. She heard neither the thundering roar of the storm nor the knocks of the two men who had come to ask permission to get help and bring the coffin back into the shelter of the house.

It soon became clear to Kako and Yokka that something was wrong.

"Better find out," said Kako.

Stamping their feet in their bearskin boots, they tested the doors and windows. It took Kako only a few minutes to force open a window and crawl through. He let Yokka in at the back door. Exchanging nervous glances, they began to search the house.

217

They stood apprehensively on the threshold of Tamara's bedroom, hardly daring to wake their new queen. But it was obvious that her sleep was not normal. It was too complete; and it frightened them.

Kako cocked his big head at Tamara and then, seeing no response, said grimly, "I've got to do it." He struggled out of his boots and coat, sat down on the bed, and holding her at a respectful distance, started to shake her. That did no good. Nerving himself, he picked her up in his arms, carried her into the bathroom, and put her in the tub.

"I beg your pardon, Tamara, my queen," he said, as he arranged her flannel nightdress with impersonal hands. Then he turned on the cold water faucet and let the tub fill, splashing the water in her face.

In the meantime, Yokka was in the kitchen making strong hot coffee. At the sound of running water, he frowned in perplexity and followed the sound into the bathroom, where he stood in the doorway and regarded the whole procedure with thoughtful gravity.

"She stirs," Kako said without looking up. "Bring blankets and the hot drink."

It took over an hour to arouse Tamara, and another ten minutes for meaning to penetrate her mind.

"Tamara, my queen," said Kako, "no tent on earth was ever constructed to withstand such foul weather. Ripped and crushed by the wind, it has fallen."

Tamara listened. "The wind does not sound especially strong."

Kako scratched his head. Yokka concentrated with open mouth.

"It has died down," said Kako.

"True," said Yokka.

"Nevertheless," said Kako, "there is no more tent."

Tamara put an end to the discussion. "Bring Rifka, my mother, home."

The two men slowly put on their boots, their fur coats, and their mittens, and picked up their caps. "Tamara, my queen," Kako said hesitantly, "I have something to say. Once this house becomes the death house, it is condemned. It must burn."

"Yes," Tamara answered. "After the burial, I shall set fire to it."

Tamara put on a fresh nightgown and a robe and went into Rifka's room. She sat down and waited there in the darkness.

In physical appearance, Tanya's husband and his mentor Rentovsky, better known among his friends as the General, were enough alike to be taken for brothers. Both were of medium height, with short, thick, hairy arms and legs and disproportionately long torsos. Both had broad peasant faces, Rentovsky's characterized by calculating brutality, and Oleg's by coarseness.

By a lucky coincidence, they arrived in Kiev when Tanya's grandfather was visiting a relative in a village some distance away.

Tanya did not matter to Oleg. He and Rentovsky had already agreed to make her common property. Their return was for one reason and one reason only—money.

A couple of hours before the blinding, tearing wind reached its peak, Oleg and Rentovsky skirted the edge of the camp on foot without attracting attention but under a circumstance that caught their notice. A long line of gypsies was on the march. Women in jackets and kerchiefs and felt boots, men with faces hidden by ear flaps pressed close together in family groups and pushed forward over the snow with howls and sobs and bursts of wailing. They followed the eight coppery, ferocious-looking men carrying a coffin. At the head of the procession was Tamara in a long, hooded sable cape.

Watching in the shelter of the trees, Oleg murmured to himself, "Christ, Rifka's dead."

"Come on," Rentovsky said roughly. "I'm cold to my guts."

"A hundred steps and we're there."

Rentovsky pulled a cigarette butt from behind his ear and lit it. "Look here, she'll have the money, won't she?"

Oleg fixed his eyes on the cottage. "Sure."

Tanya was watching for them at the window. As soon as her eyes made out the glow of the cigarette, she snatched up a black shawl and ran out to meet them. Heart pounding, eyes for Oleg alone, she raised her lips to be kissed.

Unmoving, Oleg said, "We're hungry."

"Come," said Tanya, and turned about quickly.

The kitchen was warm and lit by two oil lamps. The brass samovar was boiling. Tanya poured thick soup from a pitcher into a pot, set it on the stove, and started cutting black Cossack bread. Without looking at her, Oleg went into the pantry and came back with a jug of vodka.

Rentovsky sat drinking, eyes fixed on Tanya. "Not bad."

As they sat down to potato soup, cold roast veal, and turnip salad, Oleg asked, "Where's the old man?"

"He went to stay with his sister until after the New Year."

"That makes things good for you," he told Rentovsky. "You've got a whole mattress to yourself."

Rentovsky pressed thin lips into a grimace that passed for a smile. "I've got something besides sleep on my mind."

Oleg poked Tanya. "You hear?"

Her cheeks flaming, Tanya recalled the times Oleg had rented her out. She tried to close her mind against the brute sitting opposite her, a greasy kerchief around his neck and a week's growth of whiskers on his face.

Rentovsky, gay with drink, guffawed. "You won't be disappointed when I get around to it, but right now I'm more interested in money."

Instinctively, Tanya turned her eyes to the image of her saint in its niche on the wall, until Oleg said, "Why don't you answer?"

Tanya made a mistake. She said, "I've got something to tell you. But don't get mad, let me finish."

Oleg raised his hand. "What the devil!"

Rentovsky caught his sleeve. "Relax. She knows you for a hothead. Let's hear what she has to say."

Meeting Rentovsky's eyes, Tanya took a deep breath. "I could only touch my Aunt Lydia for two third-class ship tickets, new clothes, bedding, and a set of pewter ware. I found Grandfather's savings—I found it yesterday—three hundred rubles, but"—Tanya was quite conscious of her husband's fury but kept her eyes on Rentovsky—"I'm going to tell you where to find more gold and more jewels than you've ever dreamed of." She turned to Oleg. "Rifka's coffin. Have you forgotten how the gypsies bury their queens?"

Oleg froze in the act of lighting a cigarette. "Jesus!"

Rentovsky looked at Tanya with new interest. "How many men guard the coffin?"

"Two. And there are two of you—with me to help."

Rentovsky gave another of his loud laughs. "Well," he said, "you're a marvel."

A little dazed by the new situation, Oleg pulled Tanya down on his lap and gave her hot lips a moist kiss. It made him proud that the General liked his wife.

"All right," exclaimed the General, "playtime's over."

Tanya sat up on Oleg's lap and pulled her skirts down. She looked as though she had more to say. Rentovsky nodded his head, giving consent.

"The gypsies drink a lot at wakes. If I bring them vodka, they won't refuse it."

Rentovsky snapped his fingers. "Good idea. You keep them busy, and we'll put them out of action with the butt of my revolver."

"That might not work," Oleg objected. "Those bastards are tough."

"So I fire a couple of bullets. Who's to hear?"

Tanya sprang to her feet, her face flushed with excitement now that it was settled.

"Damn my soul," Rentovsky exclaimed enthusiastically and seized the vodka jug. He drank, passed the jug to Oleg, and patted the pistol in his belt.

Oleg rose. "We'll need rope and runners." He shrugged himself into his overcoat, got an oil lantern, and went out to the barn.

Their luck held. They reached Rifka's coffin less than fifteen minutes after it had been abandoned. Instead of having to overcome the gypsies, their only struggle was to get it securely tied onto runners and themselves hitched to it. They were unconcerned with tracks as they dragged it over the snow; a new snow was falling.

They pulled the coffin into the house and shut the door. Upon prying it open, Oleg let out a gasp. Then he threw back his head and roared with breathless laughter. Rentovsky was too exhilarated over the brightness and the sparkle to make a sound. And besides, there was the woman to appreciate—it was she who had the brains, that was clear to the General. Tanya was in paradise. Never had she seen such a look of pleasure on her husband's face. And as for Rentovsky—

As soon as Rifka was robbed of her jewels and her coffin of its gold, Rentovsky was anxious to get away.

Tanya turned her worried eyes to Rentovsky. "First, we must hide her where my grandfather won't find her."

"That's right," Oleg agreed hastily. "I'd sooner face the devil than Boris Pirov."

"The hell with him," Rentovsky said. "I spit in his face."

Oleg shook his head.

Tanya said, "We won't get far."

"Why not? We've got a good head start."

The thought of Boris gave Oleg courage to defy the General. "I can't say I enjoy digging, but we hide that coffin or we're caught before we start."

For some seconds, Rentovsky debated. Then he spat on the floor. "Lift your end."

Tanya lit the hanging kerosene lamp and led the way, as the two men carried the great coffin down to the dirt cellar.

An hour after putting Rifka in her shallow grave, they harnessed the old man's horse to his wagon, which they had loaded with blankets, tarpaulins, food, oats, and Tanya's belongings, including a goose-down feather bed. Avoiding the main roads, they traveled cross country through rough terrain, making for Poland. At times, they waded almost knee deep in snow, pushing the wagon and pulling the horse. Tanya nearly collapsed, but the men pushed ahead relentlessly, threatening to leave her behind.

They came to Warsaw and found a fence who agreed to buy their jewels. Which is when their luck ran out—

When Ronya awoke the second time, it was evening. In all, she had slept over eighteen hours, natural sleep that healed her exhausted body. In answer to her ring, Lydia came bustling in with a tray, her cheeks flushed, her eyes bright, and full of news: Paul was on a train stuck in the snow two hours from Kiev, and Boris had set out after him with a troika.

"And the baby?" asked Ronya.

"What no one can believe is his size. He looks and sucks like a three-month-old child. The doctor is completely befuddled. 'How,' he asks, 'did he grow so big in someone so small?' "

"Lydia," Ronya said anxiously, "am I torn?"

Lydia patted her head. "No, little one. When I saw that you were having a hard time, I went downstairs to Father Tromokov. Together we prayed. God understood."

"Thank you, Lydia. Take this tray out of the way."

Lydia put the tray on the floor and watched with lively interest as Ronya pulled down the covers, pulled up her nightgown, and examined herself very carefully for stretch marks. There were none. Ronya smiled quietly at Lydia, who exclaimed triumphantly, "Just like a young virgin."

Ronya barely had time to cover herself before Ruth came in, followed by Tamara, who glared at Lydia. "You told her!" she accused the girl.

"Told me what? What's happened?" Ronya asked.

Tamara sent her an incredulous glance. "Don't tell me you haven't heard! Rifka, my mother, has been stolen—kidnapped!"

"What?" cried Ronya in astonishment.

Tamara settled herself on the bed. Without a glance at Ruth, she said, "Are you equal to a long story?"

Ronya nodded.

Luxuriating in Ronya's undivided attention, Tamara gave a long description of her drugged sleep and the guards' efforts to wake her, rising to a dramatic climax at Kako and Yokka's discovery of the theft.

"I still felt drugged and struggled to clear my mind. I got to my feet slowly and stared at them. I saw they were in a cold sweat, and thought they had lost possession of their faculties. So I said, 'Rubbish. It's the storm. It plays a game with you. With daylight, we'll find the coffin safe.'

"Kako broke down then, and Yokka was on the verge of hysteria, wailing wild-eyed about a stolen soul. He cried, 'Tamara, my queen, do you realize the consequences?'

"Kako ran out and came back with Old Auntie. First she tossed down a couple of drinks, then peered up into my face, and at last she

222

said, 'What can you expect? She broke the law. For that, her soul, lost forever, will bark and howl in pain like a hyena. And when it can, it will invade the body of a woman and serve the devil—unless, within the hour, a male child is born.'

"Well," concluded Tamara, "that's the whole story."

Knitting furiously, Ruth said, without raising her eyes, "It surely is."

Ronya was lost in thought. "What time did you see Old Auntie?"

"Really, Ronya," Ruth interposed, "what difference? Everyone knows Old Auntie has been crazy for years."

"What time?" Ronya repeated.

"Around dawn," said Tamara.

"What else did she say?"

"She said, 'There are truths beyond truth.' "

Ronya knew she ought to think the gypsy beliefs were rubbish, but she could not dismiss them so easily. So, for the moment, she said nothing.

At length, Tamara remarked, "Aren't you going to say anything?"

"I want to think about it. What happened today?"

"Not much. I wanted to talk things over with you and Boris, but controlled my impulse to rush right over here."

"Well, naturally," said Ruth, "I would not allow Boris or you to be disturbed after your long ordeal. Wisely, Tamara returned to the camp and led a search. Boris went there at about two. I went along. He circled the area and decided it was a waste of time and so we came home."

"Hasn't anyone called in the police?" Ronya asked in surprise.

Tamara shook her head. "We decided to wait for Paul."

"That's a good idea," Ronya agreed. "Meanwhile, talk to your people. Tell them not to lose hope."

"I have. I told them that David's birth gives my mother's soul time. We have nothing to fear."

"That's a cheerful thought," Ruth said sarcastically.

Tamara looked at her sharply, and decided to read the molten lead in advance of its proper time.

Ronya shivered.

Rembering Ruth's instructions—"Your job will be to protect your mistress as much as possible from Tamara"—Lydia announced to Tamara that her sleigh and driver had arrived.

"What driver?" Tamara asked in surprise. "Who sent for him?"

"I did," Ruth said frankly. "I think we've all put enough strain on Ronya."

Tamara turned to Ronya. "I would like to see David again—please."

"Have you seen the Blond One?"

"No," Tamara said, eyes blazing, "and I don't want to."

They all stared at Ronya.

"Fetch David," she said to Lydia.

"But he's sleeping like an angel in his cradle."

Ronya ignored her, and Lydia went out to get the child.

After Tamara had held David for a few minutes, Ronya said, "Give him to me now, and please go. I'll see you again tomorrow."

Tamara gave Ronya a quick kiss full on the mouth. "Thanks, Ronya. Until tomorrow."

The stars came out, and the crescent of the moon rose—a beautiful night after the storm. Boris came into Ronya's room deep in conversation with Paul, whom he had driven to the house in the troika. They broke off for a minute to congratulate her, then drew up chairs to the bed and plunged back into the discussion.

"Yes, Boris, you're right. The mystery started before the crime. But who—and how?"

"The thieves think they hold a fortune in jewels," Boris said thoughtfully.

Paul stared at him. "They don't?"

Boris shook his head.

"Mother told us that she has the real ones," Ronya put in. "Rifka had copies made of her jewelry, and it's the fakes that she's wearing. But even Tamara doesn't know that yet."

"Good God," said Paul blankly. "And Tamara? What has she told the people?"

"Tamara has suspended all official mourning until such time as we again possess your mother's remains," Boris answered.

Paul's mouth set in a bitter line. Rifka's death had shaken him badly.

Boris fetched drinks for them both, and deftly turned the conversation to other topics. None of them mentioned the theft again until Paul rose to leave, when he said, "I'll ride into town in the morning and see that Leo Mischuk is assigned to the case. He's first-rate."

The next day, the hunt for Rifka began in earnest.

A detachment of police and deputized woodsmen descended upon the estate, under the orders of Lieutenant Leo Mischuk, a rising police officer whose cool professionalism and zeal for justice distinguished him from the majority of Russian law enforcers.

When Mischuk presented himself at the house, it was his first meeting with Boris. Mischuk, a bachelor, lived his career ten hours a day, six days a week. Naturally, Boris was not unknown to him; even if Boris were not a national hero, the husband of Ronya von Glasman could not live unnoticed in Kiev.

Boris himself opened the door to Mischuk, and as they shook hands, he gathered an encouraging impression of a bigger than average frame kept trim by moderation and exercise, medium height, coarse, close-cropped hair, and keenly intelligent deep-set blue-gray eyes, with the slight Asiatic tilt characteristic of most Russians not of the peasant class. Boris and Mischuk were both in their early thirties, but Mischuk looked older.

Mischuk had already conferred with Paul, who had told him that the stolen jewels were false, and he proposed to leave the hunt for Rifka to Boris, while he himself interrogated known fences and called in his informers. That settled, Boris took him over to the camp, where Tamara was waiting for them with Paul, who was present in the capacity of police officer and friend of the Pirovs.

They found Tamara gracefully arranged in a chair near the fireplace, her feet raised on a footstool.

Paul made the introductions. Mischuk bowed and smiled faintly at Tamara without saying anything. She returned his smile with an appraising look.

He sat quietly observing her, while Boris described briefly the division of responsibility. She was as he had imagined her—yet he had not expected her to be quite so beautiful. At the same time, he realized that he did not like her much, without knowing why.

Paul was talking. "Your mother," he said to Tamara, careful to keep a formal note in his voice, "was buried in cleverly reproduced duplicates of her jewelry. She protected her real jewels by leaving them with Ruth von Glasman. I gather that's in keeping with her character and explains Old Auntie's remark, 'She broke the law.'"

At first Tamara was panic-stricken. To cheat the spirits for a handful of precious stones! Desperately she longed to share her fears with her brother, to remind him of the mysterious tales they had both been taught; but the need to preserve the secret of his identity kept her silent.

Without asking, Boris made drinks for all.

Mischuk shrewdly guessed there was something going on from which he was excluded. Interesting. He continued to sit quietly, studying his strong, well-shaped hands: There would be time enough to find out what it was.

The drink helped Tamara to regain her self-control. "In your line of work, you've seen most things," she said to Paul. "What's your opinion?"

Mischuk turned to him, too. "Please. I'd be most interested in your ideas."

Leaning back in his chair, his legs extended in front of him, Paul said: "Point one: Those who robbed your mother were well acquainted with the estate. Perhaps her abductors originally planned only a robbery. Her sudden death may have changed the nature of their crime, and they may have counted on the storm to provide them with perfect cover.

"Point two: The jewelry will be taken out of Russia. Because of the gold pieces in the coffin, the thieves can go far.

"Point three: I'm convinced, beyond doubt, that the thieves were waiting in or near the camp, possibly in one of the empty wagons."

Mischuk nodded in agreement. "Set your mind at rest, madam," he said politely. "We shall find them once they try to sell the false stones."

Boris leaned forward. "Do you know Krasmikov?"

His face impassive, Mischuk replied, "I know him."

"Would the Kiev secret police have names unknown to you or data not available to you?"

Trying not to sound too critical, Mischuk replied, "Unfortunately, yes."

Boris raised an eyebrow at Paul, who said in a measured, official tone, "Krasmikov will make his files available to you."

Mischuk was not surprised. He looked from Paul to Boris, and smiled for the first time. "Thank you."

Boris got to his feet, a signal for Paul and Mischuk to stand up also. For once, Tamara made no attempt to detain Boris. She said nothing but, "Please tell Ronya I'll visit her sometime tomorrow," and saw the men to the door. Only Paul took her hand when they said good-bye.

Boris knew it was a useless, futile job; but still, in spite of the new snow, he and his men diligently looked everywhere. They combed the woods on snowshoes, searched cottages, wagons, barns, hedges, even caves—any likely hiding place. When the police hunted through the church, there was an instant outcry from the peasants. After talking it over among themselves, they decided upon sending a delegation to Ronya to make a complaint. However, Father Tromokov had no difficulty in quashing the idea. Silencing the resentment with his customary pungency, he led a vigorous deputation in an invasion of the stables, where they spent hours whirling about in the hay lofts, tossing straw and poking about in corners. Boris' hands swore vengeance for the havoc the priest created.

Among the gypsies hot blood was roused by the questions Boris asked. How could he imagine that any of them, brought up in strict

226

observance of gypsy lore, could be implicated in the theft? They decided to speak to Tamara about it. The fact that Boris was Ronya's husband gave him no right to deliver such an insult.

The neighbors were annoyed, partly out of fear. Who wanted police poking around and spying—but what could one do?

From dawn until dark this turmoil went on for three days, and then Boris called off the search.

The Von Glasman gypsies were not a truly matriarchal clan. They gave their allegiance to a queen rather than a duke, but the individual family units were dominated by the males. Each man had his wives and a cluster of children. Quite possibly, even probably, not all the children were his, but that did not matter. When one man takes on two or more robust young women, particularly in a society where promiscuity is not frowned upon, possessiveness and jealousy are comparatively rare.

This cultural trait may have accounted to some extent for Tamara's behavior; as a matter of fact, her people understood her wagon far better than they understood virginity beyond the age of twelve. So when the gypsies assembled to hear her speak, they were not interested in her personal life. They wanted to know whether she had the ability to rule. Was her loyalty indisputable? Would she guard and protect them? Would she advance their fortunes—for through the generations, the Von Glasmans had restricted them more and more. Now it pleased Ronya to protect the forest from the gypsy axes. As for horses, at first they were gratified that the great Boris Pirov had acquired the stables—it provided reflected glory—but they soon discovered that the golden Tartar was no gullible amateur to be flattered and duped. Nor would he accept all the horses they brought in. If anything, he rejected more than he bought of the herds they captured. His preference was for Tartar horses and Mongolian ponies.

Tamara came to the meeting prepared. She made a planned entrance, walking into the room proudly. Beautiful! The men began to smile. She stepped into the center of the circle. "We are a free people beholden to no one," she began without hesitation. Their smiles broadened, and Tamara knew the men were with her.

The heads of at least seventy families were crowded together in Tamara's living room, with Old Auntie watching impassively from a chair. Tamara surveyed her men with flattering glances. It was a clever tactic; gypsy men admired female cunning.

Looking affectionately into their eyes, she thanked them for their magnificent behavior in the crisis.

All around her, heads nodded affirmatively.

Next she hastened over to Old Auntie. Holding the back of her chair and bending over the old woman, she declared, "I have read the molten lead, and the signs are good. Therefore we shall not be reckless with drink, for being drunk we grow angry and foolish."

She paused, and Old Auntie took this as an invitation to speak. "Blind to all else, a soul is on a journey. Be heedful and obey the queen."

The men were now hers.

With a quick change of mood, Tamara walked among them, giving orders. She put them to work and kept them working hard. Even the children were assigned chores.

She reinstated old customs. She encouraged her people to leave the comfort of their warm houses during the day and live outdoors; the horse dealers had a preference for wagons, while the coppersmiths showed a distinct partiality for tents. Large fires were built, and the snow smelled of burning wood. Pigs were rubbed with garlic and roasted, and there was a communal feast every night. Tamara put a temporary ban on hard drinking and enforced discipline; even the yapping dogs were made to behave.

When there was nothing left in the encampment that was battered or broken, when all the harnesses were repaired and the wheel axles greased, Tamara ordered that every dwelling and every barn should be repainted in bright yellow, clear green, pure white, and rust red— strong colors, strong enough to chase away evil spirits if any were about.

The gypsies waited for Rifka's return, unafraid. They knew that in Tamara they had a queen who would watch over them.

23

It was five days after David's birth. Boris was watching Ronya exercise strength back into her muscles. A surge of pride took hold of him; childbearing left her breathtaking loveliness unmarred. Strange that of the many women he had had in his life, he remained enraptured only with his wife. His whole being revolved around her.

She was lying on the bed panting, her eyes closed. He sat down beside her. "That's enough, dove."

Ronya opened her eyes. "What time did you and Paul come home last night?"

"Late," he replied. Half rising, he kissed her full on the mouth. "I've got to go. If the train pulls in on time, I'll have Katya and Alexis here by noon."

As soon as the door was shut, Ronya pulled the lacy nightdress over her head and rose to stare at her naked body in the full-length mirror. She twisted and turned until she had examined every inch. She understood about time and change, yet the strong voice of her heart whispered, "Guard your good looks." She nodded at her reflection in the mirror.

On his way out, passing the Chinese Chippendale console in the hall, Boris noticed a plain white envelope with his name on it. No stamp. No address. He put it in his pocket. It could wait.

It was getting close to Christmas, and the railroad station was lively. Besides, the sun was shining, and the Kievans were taking advantage of the thaw to send packages by rail and to reserve tickets for holidays, north to Bryansk and Smolensk, to Borodino and Moscow, and on to St. Petersburg, or south to the towns along the Black Sea.

The train was late, which made for good business. Ragged boys with old faces minded horses for the coachmen who had gone inside to stand at the long counter sucking lumps of sugar and drinking hot tea. Peasant women in long coats and drab shawls hawking hot food faced each other over charcoal burners. Tall, loose-limbed Cossacks in gray karakul hats eyed the girls who, with unchanging smiles, were selling services. And there were well-dressed women standing with well-dressed men, buying trinkets and souvenirs and handing the packages to their liveried footmen, who stood like statues beside satin-lined carriages.

As the train slowed down, the Brusilovs stepped into the corridor and looked out on the station platform, a world in itself—donkey carts, droshkies on thin runners, grays hitched to sleighs, roan-colored mares to wagons.

Frowning a little, Katya said, "I don't see Boris."

Alexis looked about and saw a team of three black horses hitched to an elegant carriage emblazoned with the Pirov colors. "He's here. There's the carriage."

"But I wonder where he is."

"Here," said Boris, coming up beside her and swinging her off her feet.

He planted a brotherly kiss on her lips and set her down. He and Alexis exchanged a warm embrace.

"How's Ronya?" Katya asked.

"There's no one in the world like her," Boris said proudly, his spirits high.

Alexis smiled indulgently.

Eyes sparkling in anticipation, Katya said, "And David?"

Alexis observed that there was an instant's silence before Boris said: "Big."

On the way home, they talked about Rifka.

"What final disposition have you made?" Alexis asked.

"That is by no means decided," Boris answered. "We have waited for you."

That evening Ronya had almost to tear Katya away from David and force her to go down to the library, where everyone was gathered to discuss the problems presented by the theft. At length Katya made her appearance in a richly brocaded gown and her rubies. The greeting between her and Paul was especially warm, between her and Tamara perfunctory, though naturally she offered the proper condolences. Both Katya and Alexis were taken with Mischuk. As Mischuk told Paul later, "I would never have believed it possible to lose my heart to an enchanting lady and her two beautiful daughters all at the same time."

Boris had carried Ronya, wrapped in a wine-red velvet dressing gown and a silk quilt, down from her room and made her cozy amid a pile of silk cushions on the sofa near the fire.

Alexis asked every question he could think of. It was Tamara who supplied him with the answers. Alexis said it seemed the perfect crime.

"Yes," said Paul, "except for one particular. The stolen stones are false, though set in gold."

"As for that," said Katya, "could it be that theft was not the motive? Mother, you knew her longer and perhaps better than any of us. Do you suppose it possible that someone wanted her, not her jewels—someone who loved her—someone she once loved?"

"To me that seems unlikely," Ruth answered.

"Perhaps someone who hated her," Ronya said.

The two policemen, the professionals, turned to Ronya. "Now, that's a possibility, though remote," said Paul. He looked at Ruth intently. "Did Rifka ever have any significant encounter with a deranged person?"

Mischuk added, "Think hard, Madam von Glasman. Can you remember a name, an incident? Who hated her? And"—Mischuk looked back at Katya—"who loved her?"

Ruth could not think of Rifka without a sharp sense of loss. She could not say to Rifka's children, "Several men loved her, and had her, but she played at love, always capricious. As for hate—yes, there were those too, which was not surprising. She often coveted other women's husbands."

230

And so she said in reply: "Rifka was a woman of fastidious taste. She chose her friends with correctness, and those she chose considered themselves the most fortunate of men. I find it impossible even to speculate about a man dishonoring Rifka, or committing such a sacrilege against her memory."

The small silence was suddenly broken by Tamara, who bent forward in a quick movement toward Ruth. "Who was my father?" The question was spontaneous, but after a moment's deliberation, she added emphatically, "I have the right to know."

"Does anyone want another drink?" Boris asked.

No one answered him. He shrugged his shoulders, replenished his own glass, and lit a cigarette. Tamara reached out, and he gave her the cigarette. Ronya gave him a murderous look, which he did not see.

Ruth murmured, "Oh, dear, what bad luck. Rifka meant to take care of that. She left so much unfinished. Well," she said more to herself than the others, "I must take care of it for her. I simply cannot tell you his name, Tamara. I am sure your mother had no wish for you to know it."

Tamara inhaled once more and gave Boris back his cigarette. "I was hoping—"

Instinctively Ronya lowered her eyes to hide her rage. Paul touched her hand gently.

Ruth forced herself to go on. "All I can tell you is this: your half-brothers are Romanovs on their mother's side. The connection antedates our present Tzar by two generations."

Ruth had revealed too much. Paul and Alexis—both of whom were vitally interested—and Mischuk—who was not—knew where and how to ask about the man who sired Tamara.

Boris had his own notion who Tamara's father might be. He considered it a perilous subject, the sooner dropped the better. "It is extremely important," he said to Ruth, "that we learn what disposition Rifka made of her wealth. It could give us a clue—though I doubt it."

In reply, Ruth produced a small key from a pocket in her skirt. "Here," she said, giving it to Boris. "You know where to look. Please bring only the strongbox."

In a little while he was back with a strongbox, which he gave into Ruth's hands.

"Here are Rifka's jewels," she said, "the real ones. She gave them to me some time ago with a letter. When it is read, you'll know how Rifka divided her estate."

The letter contained no clue to the crime. Mischuk was fascinated to learn that Rifka had four sons, only one of whom, the gypsy Fedor, was mentioned by name, and stunned by the size of her fortune. Even Alexis was amazed at that.

Ruth held out the strongbox to Tamara.

"Thank you, no," said Tamara. She glanced at Ronya. "Keep them for me, will you?"

"No."

"Surely you're joking?"

"No," Ronya repeated angrily. "Important jewels belong in a bank vault. That's where mine are."

"Since when?"

"Since I am protected by a Tartar's name."

Tamara gave a shrug. Unable to recall any recent wrongdoing, Boris raised an eyebrow.

Paul came to the rescue. "Well," he said, "with all our talk, we've decided nothing."

"Permit me a question," said Mischuk. "Why must we do anything? Eventually the crime will be solved, or it won't be solved."

"It's really not that simple," Boris said.

"Unless Rifka is buried," Ronya told him, "her soul is doomed. Barred from the kingdom of the dead, it will kill the living."

A strange expression appeared on Mischuk's face, but he stayed politely silent.

Boris said quietly with a grin, "I can promise you that my wife doesn't believe one word of that rubbish."

"That's right," Ronya said immediately, without a glance at Boris, "I don't. However, the gypsies do, and unless Rifka is properly buried and mourned there'll be more than one occasion when her soul will be accused of murder."

Mischuk's eyes flicked over to Ruth.

"That's true," she agreed.

"The accursed soul will harass even future generations," Katya volunteered.

Tamara appealed to Ronya. "Have you a plan in mind?"

"Have you?" Ronya turned to Paul. "Do please light a cigarette for me."

Paul frowned at her but said, "Of course," put two cigarettes between his lips and lit them, giving her one.

Boris watched for a long minute. Then he walked over to Ronya, took the cigarette from her, and put his hand under her chin, forcing her to meet his eyes. "Something wrong?"

With all eyes on her, Ronya was forced to say no.

"If you're tired, I'll take you upstairs."

"No."

Boris flipped the cigarette into the fireplace and sat down beside Katya.

Amused, Alexis smiled at Boris over his wife's head. "Tell us what you have in mind, Ronya, my pet."

"I suggest we get another coffin, a replica of the one that vanished. We announce that Rifka has been found. With the obliging cooperation of the police, we produce the coffin and go through with the burial, doing everything exactly as it should be done, except for the burning. Tamara can invent some magic hocus-pocus to cover that."

"Do you agree?" Paul asked abruptly.

Tamara replied, "There's great danger in cheating."

"You're the queen," Paul said.

"On the other hand," Tamara reasoned, "if we don't— Either way—"

They waited, but Tamara did not complete her thought. She rose and went over to Ronya. "I thought of the same scheme. We'll do it." With a slow smile full of mischief, she added, "And I know of a way to outwit the devil. I'll wait for the full moon and kill a black hen."

In spite of herself, Ronya smiled. "And I'll cut a white sheet into seven equal strips and tie them together into a rope. When the devil comes to supper on your bloody black hen, I'll throw the magic rope around his neck. While I hold him, you cast your spell."

Ruth and Katya paid no attention. It was an old story for them. Still, they were plainly relieved when the door opened and Lydia came in wheeling a table laden with mouth-watering delicacies.

Boris ignored the food and the talk. His eyes lingered on Ronya, stretched out somewhat tense on the sofa, her red-brown hair shining in the light from the chandelier. It seemed to him that there was a kind of intimacy between her and Paul; this was bearable, because it included Katya, but not to be borne was the fact that for him Ronya had nothing at all—no smile, not even an occasional glance.

He got to his feet as soon as politeness allowed, pressing Mischuk to stay the night. Then he gathered up Ronya, silk quilt and all. His leave-taking, which included them all, was affable but brief, and he took the stairs two at a time.

When Ronya got into bed beside him, he hardly glanced at her, and when she looked at him from under high, quizzical eyebrows, he did not budge. Ronya inched nearer to him, not quite touching. He caught the faint smell of her special, delicate perfume, and a warm feeling began to steal over him. In his heart, he considered their difference done. He gave Ronya a big open grin. "I accept your apology."

Her dark eyes, big and unhappy, met his in a long look, and when he put his arms around her and asked, "What bothers you, dove? Why were you agitated all evening?" she answered, "I can't help it. I hate it when I'm forced to endure small familiarities between you and Tamara."

Boris held her more firmly. "Familiarities? What do you mean?"

"You let Tamara have your cigarette, and then you took it back. From your mouth to hers—from hers to yours."

"For Christ's sake—"

Ronya pressed her body against his. "I was so worried. Becoming queen has cleansed Tamara—at least for a time. I thought—perhaps—"

"You lovable little fool," said Boris, silencing her speculations with kisses.

Back in his own room, Boris saw the white envelope again. It must have fallen out of his pocket and been placed on his night table by a maid. Boris yawned and very nearly put off reading it for the second time, but did not. Gone was all hope of sleep that night.

> Boris Pirov. You are headed for a fall. You are not married to Ronya von Glasman. You have no legal claim to her. Even if Ronya von Glasman makes out that she is married to you, just for appearances' sake, she does not need your consent for a divorce or even an annulment. Nor will getting rid of you bring the slightest disgrace on her and her family, including the sons you fathered. Among the Jews, children belong to the mother, because they follow the religion of the mother.
>
> Rid of you, Ronya von Glasman will marry. Her second choice will be someone more like her father. She'll simply look among the great Jewish families of Europe and the Orient and add her luster and money to theirs. Remember, all the Jews are in league with each other. It's a world conspiracy.
>
> I feel sorry for you, but you can always go back to being what you were before.
>
> Don't waste a lot of effort and time, and maybe money, trying to puzzle out who I am. You might come to harm.

By morning his decision was made.

Ronya was asleep. Suddenly, out of nowhere, a thought came and jarred her awake. Ringing for Lydia, she dragged a quilt off the rumpled bed, threw it over her shoulders, and walked out onto her balcony. The stone floor was cold to her slippered feet, but the fresh air felt good and she took deep breaths, exhaling slowly.

In a few minutes, Lydia came rushing out to the balcony. "Dear Jesus—you'll catch your death. Come in here at once."

Ronya seemed not to have heard. "Where's everyone?"

"They've all left for the camp."

"Igor and the Blond One, too?"

234

"No. They're sledding near one of the barns. Boris, my master, put a couple of the older stable boys in charge."

"Then except for David and the servants, we're alone," Ronya said, sitting on the edge of the bed.

Lydia lifted Ronya's bare feet onto her lap and began warming them in her hands.

"That feels nice. Lydia, when did you last see Tanya?"

Lydia sighed, "Not for days and days." She frowned. "She wasn't at church Sunday."

Ronya said in an even tone, "With all that's happened this past week, it's no wonder you didn't think of Tanya. But now I want you to go to her grandfather's house and investigate immediately. It's my guess that Tanya's husband—and maybe his friend the General, too—came for her. And if, as I suspect, they've disappeared, take a look in the barn and see if they've snatched the horse and taken the wagon."

"Holy Mother!" Lydia gasped, making the sign of the cross. "Why didn't I think—"

"Why didn't I?" Ronya broke in. With a quick gesture, she took both Lydia's hands into hers. "I've spent hours and hours trying to solve the mystery of Rifka's disappearance. I seized on Tanya because I know her husband is a full-time thief and liar. But that's not proof, so let's not jump to any conclusion." She let go of Lydia's hands. "Hurry over and come right back—and don't talk to anyone, not even Father Tromokov if you should run into him."

Lydia nodded. Red-faced from the heat of her excitement, she mopped her forehead with the back of her hand. "Suppose, Ronya my mistress, they're there. What do I do then?"

"Talk to him for a few moments, and then ask Tanya to help out tomorrow. Tell her that, because of the *briss*, we expect a lot of callers."

In less than an hour Lydia was back. Without removing her coat, she slumped heavily into a chair.

Ronya had never seen her so upset. She let her sit awhile and then said, "Let me help you off with your coat. It's warm in here."

Ronya's voice seemed to startle Lydia, but she took off her coat. After a silence, she said, "They ransacked the house and took the horse, but if they stole Rifka I don't know what they did with her. I went looking and sniffing like a ghoul. There's no dead body in that house."

Ronya put her arms around Lydia and embraced her. "It can't be helped, so don't worry about it. Just be on your guard, because I don't want a soul to know until after David's *briss*. Then I'll confide in Boris. He'll figure out a safe plan of action."

Lydia glanced up at her with great curiosity. "You think she's there?"

As always, Ronya was kind to Lydia. "Not necessarily. The two disappearances may be totally unrelated."

For a second or two, Lydia believed her. Then, coming to her senses, she said in mock vexation, "Heavens! Get up off your knees. Back into bed with you."

"All right. And you take a hot bath and a rest. That's an order."

They were expecting Mischuk at any moment. Meanwhile they talked trifles. Katya began to notice that Paul had a faraway look. Her voice soft and thoughtful, she asked, "Does being here bring back memories?"

He looked up and said with careless charm, "As it happens, I was thinking about you, Katya."

Katya answered with a faint smile. "Go on."

For some moments Paul remained thoughtful. "I was trying to imagine what turn my life would have taken if you had been born David's son with a passion for power," he admitted honestly.

Katya laughed at that.

Paul and Katya sat in silence for a time. As with two people who like and admire each other, the silence was pleasantly companionable. Katya was remembering things about Paul from her childhood. In her heart, she recalled, she was sad when her father took him away.

"Why so somber, Katya? Are you nervous?"

"Yes."

"Don't be. The gypsies are willing to be hoodwinked so that no horrifying mystery will mar Tamara's coronation next July."

There was a rap on the door; imposing, in a white shirt tucked into a ruffled skirt sashed in red velvet, her thick black hair in a chignon at the nape of her long, graceful neck, Tamara led Mischuk and Krasmikov into Rifka's bedroom. She flung a bright patchwork quilt over the bronze casket and put a match to the tall candles standing ready in highly shined brass candlestands. Then she brought them back into the living room.

Paul had drinks ready.

When Mischuk asked, "Do you want me to wait?" Tamara nodded. "Please. A police officer, a bystander, will lend validity to my words."

My God, what a woman! Mischuk thought to himself. *Damn shame she's a strumpet.*

Krasmikov looked at Tamara with loving eyes. "When do we start?"

"Quite soon. They are digging the grave." Tamara turned to Katya with a question in her eyes, and she nodded and said, "Boris is bringing Mother. If Alexis can, he'll be here, too."

The sound of excited voices had been rising outside the house. Tamara, accompanied by Ruth and Katya, with Boris and Alexis following, finally answered the summons. Paul and the policemen joined them, leaving the lamps burning in the living room.

Tamara's eyes were fixed on Old Auntie, who was standing at the front of the crowd of gypsies. She said nothing and let the silence grow. Only when she sensed that Boris' patience was coming to an end did she begin.

"For days and days now," Tamara said, "I have called to Rifka my mother and made ready for her, putting out food and drink and keeping her bed fresh and soft. Before daybreak, she came to me. 'You see me?' she asked.

" 'Clearly,' I answered.

" 'Shall I speak?'

" 'Speak,' I implored.

" 'When I left here,' she said, 'I was still mated to life. Now I am once more in my coffin. Glad to be there, I am ready to be put into the earth.'

"I felt my mother wanted something special of me, and so I said, 'Whatever your pleasure, Rifka my queen, that I shall do.'

"She said, 'I have come back to tell you not to destroy by fire. This house belongs to Old Auntie. She was devoted to me beyond usual devotion.' "

This was totally unexpected. All eyes turned to the aged woman.

"*Arva, arva,*" she said, supporting Tamara. "Our late queen called upon me, too. With reverence, instructions were laid upon me. 'Let no one be wretched. Let there be no lament for the dead. Let no Gajo band play. Let no fire be kindled. Let no statue mark my grave. I want only a stick.' "

Old Auntie looked up at Tamara. There was pride in the wrinkled, old face.

Tamara went to her, took her hand, and kissed it.

In a dense fog, with two helpers to shovel the wet dirt, Kako and Yokka buried the rock-filled coffin on an incline overlooking the camp.

24

When Ronya and Boris were first married, the Jews of Kiev assumed he had embraced Judaism. However, as time went on and it became evident he was not a convert, many sided with Joseph Levinsky and refused to listen to the old rabbi's gentler advice.

Public opinion was strong, and Ronya was more or less isolated from the Jewish community. But with stubborn fidelity she clung to her Jewish identity and made a point of finding out how the Jews who lived in the Jewish quarter were getting on. Ronya was always the first to know who needed help. Sometimes it was money to celebrate a circumcision, sometimes money to send a wife and children to America, sometimes money to pay for a medical specialist. But money was not always needed, and she helped in other ways. Ronya once heard of an orphaned girl who was taken to live with relatives who had become rich. To enable her to hold up her head among the daughters of the house who wore fashionable clothes, Ronya gave the girl a beautiful wardrobe of clothes; and, instead of a poor cousin in rags, an elegant young lady arrived in a Pirov carriage.

The rich Jews looked upon Ronya more charitably; among the rich there was considerably less orthodoxy. They were no strangers to a son who was Russified or a daughter who lost her heart to a Gentile.

Some cloaked their pride in Ronya in this fashion: "God, wiser than the wisest of men, must have chosen her to serve His purposes. Why else bestow upon her more than He bestows upon the pious wives of pious men?"

There were those who, despite their belief that Ronya lived in sin with a man whose ancestors drove the Jews into hiding or into graves, still loved her. Not because she gave alms, but because God made her beautiful, because He made her unafraid.

And so it was that on the eighth day of his life, when Ronya's second son was to receive his name, there was a wide difference of opinion among the Jews.

When asked for advice, Rabbi Simon Levinsky said, "Yes, it is a time for jubilation. We are all invited. Let us go. I myself have made the preparations for Elijah, the Prophet, the Messenger of the Covenant. A chair has been placed for him, facing west. Lemon myrtle await him."

Rabbi Joseph Levinsky differed. He said, "Let the boy be bathed and laid in his cradle. Let the rite of circumcision be performed according to the Law. Let David von Glasman Pirov be consecrated to the faith of Jehovah. Let us send gifts. But let us not eat and drink and make merry with Boris Pirov until it is our duty to honor him because he has served us."

The congregation elected to follow the son.

When the Pirov horses arrived, Rabbi Simon Levinsky entered the carriage alone. "My last months in Kiev," he said dejectedly, "and no Jews accompany me. I stand alone to taste the wine."

Ten o'clock came, ten thirty, and Ronya, excluded as was customary from the rite, was frantic with worry. She was sure that something terrible must have happened. She wandered about the room touching, straightening, her tasks useless, her movements mechanical.

Shortly after she had forced herself down on the chaise, forced herself to pick up a book, Boris strode through the door, reassuring her hastily as he came toward her. "I fed him a full teaspoon of brandy. He liked it. The *mohel* was quick and sure. The rabbi blessed David. It's over. They wanted to come up here to congratulate you, but I said I'd carry you downstairs."

He knelt on the carpet and put his arms around her. "Why are you so pale, dove?"

"Can we talk a minute?"

Boris knew what she wanted to know. "Joseph did not come. No one came. Presents came by the wagonload. Joseph sent a gold mezuzah and two gold nails. I fastened it to the nursery door."

Ronya looked away.

"Don't turn your face from me, Ronya." He touched her chin with his fingers, and slowly and gently forced her to look at him. It was strange the way the sadness in her dark eyes always affected him.

He now startled himself by saying, almost before the idea crossed his mind, "Ronya, I came here not meaning to spoil a surprise, but I'm going to. Your precious Joseph will be here."

"Really? Are you sure? Who told you?"

Boris saw the happiness in her face and, lifting her from the chaise, he rose to his feet with her in his arms and said, "I'll get you settled and go fetch him."

The radiance of her smile was thanks enough for what he was about to do.

Ruth and Ronya were delighted when the *mohel* left. As Simon Levinsky remarked: "A clever fellow at his profession, but in other ways a *nudnick*."

They were astounded when Father Tromokov appeared. He was not expected until much later. "I'm here," he said, "to pay my respects to the rabbi."

The rabbi returned the compliment instantly. "A pleasure, Father, always a pleasure to see you."

It was curious. When Simon Levinsky was chief rabbi he mistrusted Father Tromokov, believing a priest was the instrument by which anti-Semitism was kept alive. Once he had resigned in favor of his son, his feelings changed. He began to think of the priest as a man of God, with the respect that one good professional has for another. He regretted the years of being polite strangers when they could have been friends and mused, "My Joseph fails his own intellect, as I failed mine." He gave the huge priest, slouching back in the velvet chair, a glance of affection and said, "Promise me something, Father."

"Anything," the priest said agreeably.

"Joseph, my son, is young; and Joseph, my son, is wise—but not as wise as he imagines. Fortunately, you are far closer to his age than to mine. Be generous, Father. Give him a helping hand. After all, there is not such an immense difference between us. The first Christians were Jews. We share some of the same virtues and many of the same faults."

The priest, despite his gusto, his propensity for vodka, his dislike for stuffy generalizations, had eloquence when he wished. He understood, far better than Ruth or Ronya or Katya, what the rabbi was saying. "Isn't it odd," he replied, "that man can understand the nature of his world but can't understand man? Perhaps if we, the priests, who are the leaders and scholars, truly esteemed the dignity and nobility of *all* mankind, we could touch the hearts of men and incite them to goodness."

If only all priests were as good as Ivan and all rabbis as compassionate as Simon, Ruth thought. She knew, however, as did they all, that some were hypocrites, some bigots, some driven by ungodly aims, and some actually the enemy of man because they put pride, ceremony, and victory before human life. Sad to say, this was more true in Russia than in other parts of the world.

One thing cheered the priest: his trust in a benevolent, tender, infinitely patient God. And then in the silence, the rabbi's voice came in a harsh whisper. "I have sinned against my Lena."

The priest looked at him and did not speak. Ruth and Ronya wondered if they had heard right. Their eyes met and locked, and neither made a sound. Katya looked down. The rabbi, the picture of distress, eyed the ceiling.

"Yes," he said, "for all my fine pretenses, I am a hollow article." Regarding his friends, he said softly, "Confession will not sweep away my remorse, and confession will profit my Lena nothing. Still my wish to speak is strong, even though I do not know exactly why." The rabbi saw that he had their complete attention. That was the best part of talking to real friends; they cared.

He began his story. The language he used was not Russian but the language of the people—Ukrainian.

"It is not enough that she has spent her life in a country where the people—hers, in particular—are oppressed. For my Lena, there has been a special and unique oppression. Who oppressed her? I! She was born into a family that no longer conformed strictly to Jewish tradition. She came to me a child bride thinking me only mildly orthodox —Westernized—a man who smiled upon liberal ideas.

240

"I said, 'Cut off your hair.'

"She cried. Oh, how she cried. 'I'll kill myself first,' she wailed.

"I quieted her. I said, 'When we are alone I'll thread pearls in your hair. I will decorate your head with flowers. I will cradle your hair on a cushion of silk. Don't cry and don't kill yourself. In public you will wear a *sheitel*, the customary wig. When we have children, God willing, even in front of them you will wear a *sheitel*. And nobody will know that under the *sheitel* is hair like that of the siren Lorelei.'

"What could she do? Object?

"The pattern was laid down. At night, before we went to sleep, we washed, we brushed, we combed her yellow treasure.

"It was a remarkable hardship for my Lena, for a woman's natural inclination is to seek praise and veneration for her beauty.

"Then came the great and wonderful day when, with the help of David von Glasman—may his soul rest in peace—I was made chief rabbi of Kiev. Vivid in my recollection of that day is the memory of my Lena saying, 'I shall throw away my *sheitel*. As *rebbetzen* to the great ladies of Kiev, I shall be as modern as they.'

"I rebuked her. 'What vanity!'

" 'You force such ugliness on me,' she said bitterly. 'When you go out, you will go alone.'

"I went. I mingled with the people. And she, who loved people and good times, stayed behind."

Father Tromokov was a professional listener. He understood that the value was in the telling and in the listening, and that there was a time for answering and a time for not answering.

Ronya had very definite ideas about a marriage in which the husband made all the rules and all the decisions, but she left it to her mother to deal with the rabbi's revelation.

"Why, Simon," Ruth said diplomatically, "how amazing! I never suspected that Lena ever wanted to move outside her pious circle."

Father Tromokov noticed the warm and intimate look the rabbi gave her and stood up. "Ronya," he said, "you'd better rest."

He helped her to her room, while Katya went to look in on David.

The effect of their departure on Simon Levinsky was astonishing. Immediately, he forgot the long story he had told against himself. He ignored the probability that if Ivan Tromokov had stayed, he would have been willing to talk on indefinitely. He turned to Ruth and said indignantly, "Ah, alone, at last!"

"It is you who forgot the time," Ruth answered, amused. "You always do when you are talking."

With a hint of a smile, the rabbi agreed. *"Taka."* Becoming serious, he asked, *"Nu,* it worked?"

"With spectacular success. Boris waits only for this day to be over. He is inviting a policeman, whose name is Mischuk, and the editor of the newspaper to be his witnesses. He says there'll be no more loose talk about the legality of his marriage."

"What about Ronya?"

"She thinks the whole business totally asinine. When Boris started to talk about a civil ceremony, she broke out in a blaze of fury and said it would be making a mockery of their love and their marriage. She was magnificent, but this time Boris is ignoring what she thinks."

His brow wrinkled in sober thought, the rabbi inquired, "They suspect nothing?"

"Heavens, no! Who would believe you, of all people, capable of such a letter?"

There was a pause, and then the rabbi said, "David, may he rest in peace, was such a brilliant man. He held a university degree in law. He was well informed. Why didn't he protect Ronya, why didn't he legalize her marriage with a civil ceremony? He knew Joseph, my son, would not take a lenient line with Boris. Worse, much worse, he knew that Ronya would have no chance in a legal battle with Boris. In Russian courts of law a Jewess is not a Tartar's equal."

Ruth nodded. "Certainly David knew. However he was hyper-careful. He did not want Ronya *too* married. He wanted the security of an easy annulment if that were to become necessary or desirable. And secondly, David had a sharp sense of power. He counted on great wealth and the Romanov assurance that the Von Glasmans would command the rights and privileges accorded the nobility."

"Well," Rabbi Levinsky said, "let us assume that Nicholas II will be an honorable monarch and that my Joseph will be a reasonable rabbi. Still, legality is a serious business. I shall go to Jerusalem much easier in mind knowing that there is no need to worry."

The door stood slightly ajar. Boris knocked and went in.

"Who is there? You, Joseph?" The voice belonged to Simon's wife.

"Please don't be uneasy, ma'am. I am Boris Pirov." The agreeable aroma of spices led Boris into the kitchen, where Lena stood over the stove, a wooden stirring spoon in her hand.

After several moments of intense and speechless confusion, Lena began to stammer. "This is so unexpected. I never dreamed—I am still unable to believe—" She paused and collected herself. "You must excuse me. My son, I hope, is better prepared for the unexpected than I."

Boris saw that she was not distressed, not frightened; she was equal to the situation; she wanted to be friendly. He liked her instantly. He was surprised that she was still quite young and, in spite of the hideous brown wig on her head, rather pretty. Smiling at her, he said, "I am here on a private matter. When your son gets home, I'll provide you with a proper explanation." He saw that she did not understand in the least and simply did not know what to do. Still smiling, he said, "Meanwhile, you had better offer me something to eat. I'm as hungry as a wolf."

"Please," Lena said, "come sit. The meal is ready."

Boris knew she meant to take him into the dining room. "I'd rather eat here. May I?"

Lena was holding her apron. "Oh, no!" she said, deeply shocked, and then, "Really?"

"It's nice here."

The *rebbetzen* smiled tentatively. "Shall I serve?"

Boris gave her a big grin. "By all means."

Boris ate everything. Gefillte fish, a dish of which he was not over-fond. Kreplach with chicken broth. Kosher meat, bloodless and over-cooked—he liked his meat rare. Mashed carrots, sugared and cooked with prunes. Boris considered a carrot in its natural state a fitting root for a horse. But Lena's noodle kugel was delicious. So was the fruit compote.

Deeply impressed with his appetite and highly pleased with his generous praise, Lena thought, *It is no wonder that Ronya von Glasman walks proud. She has caught a rare eagle.* The thought startled her.

When Joseph returned from the synagogue, he found his mother and Ronya's husband sitting opposite each other in the kitchen. They were drinking tea, boiling hot, from tall thin glasses and talking animatedly. It was easy to see, as they turned their faces toward him, that they were having a good time. Lena's pale blue eyes were shining.

At once, Boris rose, and Joseph was shocked. His mother, the *rebbetzen*—the most exemplary, the most estimable, the paragon of piety—giving a bare-headed man food! She had dined with him!

Boris eyed Joseph. Joseph eyed Boris. They each took a long appraising look.

Boris saw a neat-bearded, intelligent-eyed man of slight physique, a pontifical man who needed to speak truth as he saw it.

Joseph saw a prodigiously lusty male, a charmer, a mixture of hero and rogue. Already his emotional response to Boris was making it difficult for him to cling to his stiff prejudgments.

Joseph spoke first. "Obviously you have something special to ask of me. What is it?"

"Don't ask me why Ronya wants you, but she does. Will you come with me?" Boris replied, adding firmly, "No one suggested that I come here. Please remember that."

Joseph's face lost its bleak look. "Since you make your appeal to my heart, how can I refuse?"

"Thank you. I appreciate that."

Lena gave a great sigh of relief. She went quickly to the stove, filled a plate, and set it on the table. "Eat," she said to Joseph. "I'll get ready."

Joseph looked startled.

His mother left the kitchen and went to her room, there to array her plump figure in her sabbath best and to fashion her own hair into a multitude of fat curls. This took a full hour, which provided the men with an opportunity to get acquainted. First Joseph excused himself and came back in a few minutes, washed, with two neatly folded skull-caps.

In the quiet of the cozy kitchen—with immaculate white curtains and winter berries in pewter urns—the rabbi, all-powerful among the Jews, and the Tartar, prince to his fierce, proud, ruthless people, took their first creeping step into friendship, neither quite sure whether he wanted to or not.

It took Joseph approximately another quarter century to understand the enigma of Boris, to convince himself that he loved Ronya with every pounding beat of his heart, and to learn that lust, adultery, and Tamara were trivial things when compared to the fearful challenges Boris met and the choices he made.

Now, however, when Joseph heard his mother coming back, he was glad, and Boris was equally so. At the first slight rustle of silk, Boris was on his feet, and when Lena made her way through the open door, he eyed her with open admiration.

No man had ever given her such approval. She adored it. A couple of seconds later, her eyes crept to Joseph.

Boris gave Lena his arm. Together they walked out, leaving an agitated Joseph to follow.

They were very late in arriving at the house. Boris took into account the frightfully restricted life Lena had led and decided to make memorable the day she made her daring gesture of defiance and discarded her *sheitel*. Boris drove, stopped, drove, pointed, explaining his Kiev, the Paris of the Ukraine. And Lena, sitting between him and Joseph on the coachmen's seat, questioned and marveled and exclaimed in delight.

Boris took twisting dirt roads covered with slush and snow-filled streets that passed weathered old churches, the handsome Opera House, and the majestic Cathedral of Hagia Sophia. He climbed the Vladimir Hill, high above Kiev's rooftops, and they looked down on the Dnieper, glinting in the winter sun. He approached the big house in the most roundabout manner, by driving first to the rim of the forest and then swinging around to show Lena the peasant church surrounded by cottages clustered in a space that amounted to a small village, the thatched roofs of the guest cabins, the carefully tended gardens and orchards, the full-grown pine grove, the barns and carriage houses, and the painted gypsy wagons with their tongues resting on wooden blocks.

They reached the house, soft and golden in the receding sun, just as Simon Levinsky was preparing to leave. He saw Lena before she saw him. Even Katya, who was on the stair landing, heard his gasp.

"Lena, my *rebbetzen*, are you in your right senses? Think how more dazzling is paradise than your crown of yellow that shines so brilliantly on earth."

The rabbi's lofty phrasing left the *rebbetzen* unmoved. Taking measure of the barely perceptible twinkle that accompanied Ruth's warm welcome, she smiled and nodded and said, "Joseph, my son the rabbi, and I are happy to be here. *Mazel tov.*" Then she became completely absorbed in Ronya, who, in a burst of gratitude, stood on tiptoe and threw her arms around Boris' neck before turning away to Lena and Joseph, offering them her thanks for coming.

"A *mazel tov* to you, Ronya," Joseph answered gravely.

Lena found her tongue again. "On your feet! Such a *tsimmes* over Joseph. You should be in bed."

A great sadness rose in Ronya's eyes. "He recited Kaddish for David, my father," said she.

Boris picked her up into his arms and started for the stairs. Her long black lashes swept upward, and she said with a laugh, "Come along, Joseph. I want you to meet our sons."

When the time for the ceremony of Tamara's prophecy drew near, the Levinskys talked things over among themselves and announced their decision. No one pressed Joseph to stay. As he drove out in a Pirov carriage with a Pirov coachman in the box, the carriages of the gentry drove up in a steady stream, and the peasants and the gypsies, already tipsy, were gathering.

Tamara felt desperate. Three times she had cast the molten lead. Three times she saw the white wings of death. She went to the secret cards, shuffled, and laid them out; she read the awful truth: David was fated to die early. She tried other magic; this time she saw a shadow shrouded in black. The similarity between the white and the black was unmistakable.

Tamara knew Boris was resigned to the power of fate. Certain of his own, these words once fell from his lips: "There is no way out. And since I cannot change it, why complain of it?" Not Ronya. She set herself against the idea that one is helpless in the grip of fate, and she fought gallantly. Tamara knew she had to invent a false fortune for David.

Carrying David, Tamara came into the reception hall from the adjacent drawing room and took her place on a dais draped in white velvet. She was dressed in a daringly low-cut purple dress with splashes of pink and green. Her skirt puffed and flared over embroidered lace petticoats. She sent a searching glance around the room and found Boris, longing to look him in the face and command him to step forward, but because she thought he might not obey she did not dare. Dramatically she fixed her eyes upon David, making a long pause to underscore the importance of the occasion. Taking a line from a play, she exclaimed, "Hear me!" Then, her throaty voice melodious: "Sky and earth. Stones and water. Earth and stones. Matched serpents in disguise." She switched her gaze from David to the listening crowd, and her voice grew stronger. "Wings without dust. Clouds soaring aloft. Clover and amber." Slowly she turned, stepped down, and ascended the stairway.

Liveried waiters appeared, carrying heavy silver trays with goblets of champagne.

Alexis stepped forward. "To David. Long may he live."

Simon Levinsky bent over Lena as, bothered by the bubbles, she wrinkled her nose. "*Nu*—did you ever?" he whispered. "Such a *meshuggeneh megillah!*"

"Ssh." In a low tone, she confided, "Simon, I like it here."

Simon Levinsky took her by the elbow and hastily steered her over to Ruth. "Please," he said, "we must go."

Ruth realized that her friend was uneasy about the nonkosher food, and she, equally uneasy about the gay hours to follow, did not offer them an omelette served on glass as she had intended to do. Instead she summoned a servant and ordered a carriage.

Because the rabbi and the *rebbetzen* left before Tamara exhibited her dazzling dancing, they were able to say to the Jews of Kiev, "A family united in innocence and trust. No Russian hilarity, no abandonment. And Boris Pirov—more host than lusty eagle."

The ballroom, softly illuminated by sparkling chandeliers and heated by a roaring fire, was beautified with dwarf trees in fat brass pots and masses of hothouse roses and white and purple orchids. Through supper and until midnight, the professional musicians played fast dance tunes and lively waltzes; then the gypsies took over. Before Tamara's performance, Boris said a few words to a passing footman, and soon a sofa was carried in for Ronya. Boris placed a chair near her, and a number of guests crowded around them.

Tamara relished the hush that fell over the ballroom the moment she entered. She twirled across the room to Boris, stopped, and waited. He nodded courteously, correctly. Tamara made a curtsy, which half included Ronya.

The gypsy violins struck up her music. She waited, then, her legs spread apart, she shook her head. Her hair flew down and fell wantonly about her shoulders as she gave herself up to the music. Men leaped on chairs and whistled, dazed by drink and excited by Tamara's provocative dancing, but the swelling, fire-hot cheers came from the Cossack chiefs. When the applause subsided and the music started again, Tamara made a move toward Boris, who immediately drew himself to his feet and offered his arm to the woman nearest him. Tamara blushed and took his place next to Ronya. They stared at each other for a few seconds, and then Ronya raised her eyebrows a little and asked, "Why were you so worked up about David? Why all the hocus-pocus nonsense phrases?"

For a split second, Tamara's face went blank, but she recovered quickly. "Just before I read, I had an accident with the lead and, believe it or not, I was too superstitious to summon the fates after such carelessness. I'll cast the molten lead another time when there is no danger of offending."

Before Ronya had a chance to reply, Krasmikov came up to claim Tamara, and Paul joined her. As he looked at her, he said, narrowing his eyes, "You must be aching with tiredness. Can I persuade you to let Lydia put you to bed?"

Ronya's lips parted in a smile. "As soon as the presents are distributed, I'll go."

Excusing himself, Paul left her to find Boris, now in the company of a visitor from Bucharest, a tall good-looking blonde with an expanse of white bosom. The lady called upon all her charms to please, but Boris, strongly tempted to dedicate himself to her attractions for an hour or two, called up Ruth's seraphic face and the sublime magic of his fiery-tempered dove. He stayed resolute and sober.

25

"How long have you been standing here barefoot in the cold?" Boris glanced at the clock, yawning: eight forty—the party had not ended until three. He pulled Ronya into bed and felt a stab of apprehension. She was bracing herself—he could feel her tense under his fingers. "All right, Ronya," he said, "what have you done?"

Ronya curled her toes and pushed one foot hard into his abdomen. "Promise not to get angry."

Boris swore. "Come on, I haven't got all day."

"I think I've solved our mystery. I've had a lot of time to think and suddenly, I remembered: How unlike Tanya. She's never passed up a present before. Once she came into my mind, the rest was easy." Snuggling against him, she reconstructed the crime pretty much as it happened.

In cold, measured tones, Boris said, "You kept this all to yourself and let us go through with the burial farce."

"Yes, Boris."

"You had better come up with a good reason."

"First of all, the hole was dug, everyone was prepared, and Mischuk was already on his way with the substitute coffin."

"I said a *reason*, Ronya."

"I'm coming to that. I couldn't let Rifka spoil David's *briss*, because his naming was too important to my mother. That was one reason— the lesser one. The bigger reason is that I won't let a terrible bloodbath between the gypsies and the peasants destroy all that I was born to cherish and nurture and pass on to Igor."

"How can we hide a thing like this?"

Her heart in her eyes, Ronya said, "We must."

Boris was deeply touched. He took her in his arms and kissed her, a gentle kiss. "Dove, that's exactly what we'll do."

For the first time, Ronya was uncertain. "Suppose Rifka isn't there? Lydia looked everywhere and couldn't find her."

"She's there," Boris replied evenly. "Lydia didn't know where to look. Go back to your own room, Ronya. I'll meet you there in about —" he glanced at the clock, "I doubt that it'll be later than noon."

As soon as she saw his face, Ronya knew Rifka had been found.

Boris gave her precise instructions.

Ronya promptly agreed.

He asked her two questions.

"Can we trust Tamara?"

With no hesitation, she replied, "Totally."

"Paul?"

After a second's thought, she said, "If you find him still here this evening, the answer is yes."

Boris laid his hand on her shoulder. "Until later," he said.

Not least among Paul's reasons for being in Kiev was his need to confer with Ronya privately.

Waiting for her alone in the library, Paul allowed himself to think of David, her father, whose death marked the end of a significant part of his own life.

Not all his memories were pleasant.

Generally, Paul refused to dwell upon the past, and he had long since stopped tormenting himself about his illegitimacy, but seeing the Blond One and compassionately observing the child's ambiguous position in the Von Glasman-Pirov ménage brought back his own suffering. He had decided to adopt the boy. He did not think he would encounter any difficulty.

Ronya came in, looking lovely in a simple skirt and a snow-white lacy blouse. Paul's eyes sparkled with admiration as he bowed and kissed her hand. He followed her over to the sofa, hovering solicitously one step behind her, and sat down beside her.

"You mustn't tire yourself. Put your feet up."

Ronya laughed and obeyed. "You sound more like Boris all the time."

Paul looked at her sharply but made no answer, and in a few seconds his transitory displeasure passed and he began to talk about Igor.

"Paul, I could sit here for the rest of the day and talk about the children, but we don't have much time."

"We have more time than you think. Boris has a four o'clock appointment with His Honor Gregory Grekov."

"Oh—that ridiculous letter!" A puzzled wrinkle appeared. "How can Boris take it seriously?"

He remained silent.

Ronya looked at him steadily and said, "Paul, do you want to work for me?"

"Yes," Paul said quietly.

Her thoughts were busy with the many things she wanted from him, but first there were terms to be settled. It seemed strange to be mentioning money to Paul, but it had to be done. "Will you accept a yearly retainer?"

He stared at her, shocked. "I don't want money from you."

"I have no other way of expressing my gratitude, Paul."

Paul suddenly realized his hand was on her knee and quickly removed it. He got up from the sofa and went in silence for a whiskey and water, and when he sat down again it was in Boris' armchair. His equanimity restored, he said, "Allow me the same arrangement I had with David. When I wanted something very much, I asked for it."

"Ask now, Paul. Then I needn't worry about taking advantage."

"At this moment," he said with a half smile, "there isn't anything—No, that isn't quite true. There is something. I want my mother's St. Petersburg house. I've even thought of making Tamara an offer."

Ronya nodded. "The house is mine. Your mother had the right of occupancy in her lifetime but not the right to pass it on. The deed is among my father's papers. I'll have my lawyer draw up the transfer."

"I should have known," he said, somewhat taken aback. Then he went on directly to his second request. "Ronya, I want the Blond One. I'll provide him with a good home, and I'll be a good father to him."

Her eyes flashed. "You can't have him. I love him," she said, more softly. "I love him almost as much as I love Igor, and more than I love David."

"Good God, Ronya!"

"And I can't tell you why, because I don't know why."

After a long appraising glance, Paul said, "Little *krasavitza,* you're quite a woman." He took two cigarettes from a handsome gold cigarette case, lighted them and handed her one. "Well, Ronya," he said, "make me earn my exorbitant fee."

"You might start by pretending I am my father. What would you be telling him?"

"If you want me to talk as I did to David, you must learn to be specific. Your father always wanted to know about some particular thing or about some particular person. For instance, he'd say, 'Get me a copy of all the correspondence between Constantine Pobiedonostsev and the chief of the secret police.' Or, 'What knowledge do you have of a priest, Ivan Tromokov by name? He foolishly expresses revolutionary ideas. I'm wondering if—' "

He stopped in midsentence.

"Ivan Tromokov is a Russian," Ronya said calmly, "he loves to eat, drink, and talk."

Paul nodded with approval, but he was deadly serious. "Silence him, Ronya. On the surface things seem normal, but fear and mistrust grip the country. Our orders are to disband all political clubs, to arrest all the inflamed intellectuals, and to cooperate with the Cossack Cavalry Militia in beating the hell out of the disgraceful students."

"Is it that bad?"

Paul nodded.

Ronya sighed deeply. "You believe then that there'll be more repressive measures?"

"I know it."

"What's in store for the Jews, Paul?"

"A difficult time."

"Isn't there any hope that the Tzar will adopt at least some of his mother's humanitarian attitudes?"

"The Tzar will follow Pobiedonostsev. Expect humiliation, harassment, and brutality for the Jews."

A shiver passed over Ronya. "Pogroms?"

Paul nodded.

"Where?"

"In the Ukraine, Odessa, Kiev, the villages. Mostly Odessa."

"When?"

He shrugged his shoulders. "That is something I don't know. But don't worry, I'll get you the information you need. With luck we'll outsmart the Cossacks a few times. In any case, you yourself will have no trouble. Frankly, with Boris for a husband and Alexis for a brother-in-law, you're in a better position under Nicholas than David was under Marie."

"I know," Ronya said very sadly, "and that calls for atonement."

"You shouldn't think that, Ronya," he said in alarm.

"Why not? At times I feel so guilty. Here I live, rich and safe, while my people live in fear and misery."

Paul leaned forward. His impulse was to touch her, but he restrained himself. "Because of you, Ronya, many will be left in peace. There's no reason for you to feel guilty. None."

Ronya refused to be comforted. "That," she mocked, "is just what my Tartar husband says."

After supper, Boris built up the fire in the library and opened a bottle of fine old brandy. Lydia, privy to almost all family matters, was not admitted to the conference, but Paul was there, and of course Tamara, resplendent in beads, fringes, and dangling gold bracelets.

Ronya held them mesmerized as she described what she suspected had been done with Rifka's coffin. There were no comments, no exclamations. There was just one question in their faces, and Boris answered it.

"I found her. The casket is in a shallow hole in the cellar, barely covered. There's not the faintest suggestion of decay. There's a layer of ice an inch thick on the coffin."

Shivering, Tamara drew closer to the fire.

"Not one of us is blind to the dangers of a peasant-gypsy war," Boris said. "There's only one thing we can do."

"I agree," Paul came quickly to his support.

Tamara turned to Paul. "Where?" she demanded. "Some meadow is not good enough for Rifka, the queen."

"I expect you all remember the lots to the left and right of my David," Ruth said gravely. "I'm quite certain that Rifka would want us to move her quietly to her final resting place near David, so that the three of us will eventually lie side by side in death."

"No!" Katya said fiercely.

Betraying no feeling, Ronya asked, "Why not?"

The sisters looked into each other's eyes. With the intensity of an antagonist, Katya replied, "Because our father knew the Tartars will bring a white stallion for Boris and take him away. He saved that place for you."

"Did he, Mother?"

Ruth was conscious of the tension. She went over in her mind all that David had planned that was not to be. Sophia, his sister, had an iron will of her own. "My child, do you want your last rest to be beside David, your father?"

Ronya wanted to please her mother, Tamara, and Paul; yet, suspecting—rightly—that Boris and Alexis sided with Katya, she wanted to please them, too. "Where I'm buried makes little or no difference to me. I'm only concerned with how I live."

That was not exactly the answer anyone expected, but Ruth grasped at it as a solution. "In that case, dear—"

"Didn't Father want Ronya to his left?" interrupted Katya, persisting.

"No, he did not," Ruth said firmly.

No one suspected the degree to which Ronya felt comforted. "Katya," she said, "I think only Mother has the right to decide."

Katya had no appetite left for dissent. Reverting to her usual composure, she said, "I defer to that."

Boris and Paul went upstairs and came down again in rough clothes. Unexpectedly, they found Alexis, who had been silent most of the evening, ready to go with them.

They were an hour getting what they needed from the stables—cast-iron lanterns, pickaxes, heavy shovels, tarpaulins, and a big wagon.

"I'll drop you and Alexis at the house and hide the wagon in the weeds. There's no point in doing anything more until it's light."

As the front door shut behind Alexis and Paul, Boris turned the horse toward the river. The road ran through a grove of great pines. The horse set its feet down carefully. Where the road came out into the open it became a mass of slush—in some ways the recent thaw made the going rougher. Then they were in the woods. Behind an incline, at the edge of the woods, Boris secured the wagon. Not far away was that remote part of the estate where the Von Glasmans lay buried.

At dawn, they attacked the hard earth. With Boris' help, Paul buried his mother.

26

Every eye in the room was on Ronya. Serenely impervious, she sat with her hands folded, her eyes on the picture of the Tzar.

The white-haired judge, normally an impatient man, decided to make one last effort to persuade her to go through the usual wedding ceremony. He admired her steadfast refusal to deny, even implicitly, her marriage; but he would try again, because Boris' way was the safer way.

"Must I remind you, Ronya, that I have taken great care to assure myself that the thoroughly sincere and justifiable uneasiness Boris has expressed regarding the legality of your marriage cannot be dismissed. Since doubt indeed exists, I agree with Boris, who insists upon full civil ratification. That means that I, with the authority vested in me by my Sovereign, and as proxy for a priest, will perform the marriage ceremony."

Ronya went on looking at the Tzar. Boris glared at her savagely.

The judge rose from his heavy leather chair. Straight and stiff, he crossed the room to Boris. "We're beaten," he said, his voice gruff and a little amused. "We shall have to do it her way."

Katya, a fluttering in her stomach, stole a sidelong glance at Boris. Alexis chuckled to himself, more amused than ever.

Paul, staring intently at Ronya, was transplanted back in time when he had looked at David and asked incredulously, "Are you really going to let her marry the Tartar?" And David had shrugged: "We'll see."

Boris managed to hold in his temper, but still his voice had the sound of thunder. "Will it be legal?"

"Airtight, watertight, hermetically sealed!"

Somewhat mollified, Boris gave a nod. "Go ahead."

Swiftly Ronya went to Boris and held out her hand. He gripped it hard and held it tightly. Feeling her wince, he eased his hold and his face lost some of its hardness. Ronya looked gravely at the judge, who gathered the witnesses into position.

In the centuries-old, wood-paneled room, as the clock struck three, the judge contemplated the huge golden Tartar with the piercing look and the bewitching Jewess, her beautiful face luminously alive. He spoke solemnly.

"In considered judgment, I, as representative of his Imperial Highness Nicholas II, Emperor and Autocrat of all the Russias, do declare

253

that no concubinary relationship has ever existed between Boris Pirov and Ronya von Glasman Pirov. The purpose of this gathering is to certify with total legality the sureness of a marriage contracted, sanctified, and consummated some five years ago. We are, consequently, concerned not with a marriage but with the reaffirmation of that marriage. That makes the usual query and the concomitant 'I do' superfluous." The old man's voice softened. "I give you both my blessing, and may I add that it gives me pleasure to see two married people so much in love. It happens all too seldom."

Alexis was ready with a golden goblet filled with wine, but Boris still held Ronya's hand, and neither stirred. There was something else. "Sir," Boris said, "I wish to remind you—"

"Ah, yes!" The judge sounded very hearty. "The document."

Boris nodded gravely.

From his desk drawer the judge produced a paper. Boris and Ronya put their names to a notarized statement that acknowledged that each renounced irrevocably the right to divorce and even to legal separation.

27

It was June 26, six days before Tamara's coronation, when trouble with the gypsies flared up. Paul had just arrived, and Katya and Alexis were expected in a day or so.

Igor and the Blond One had been restless all day looking for Boris. He had promised to teach them how to build a smoke fire, but he was nowhere to be found. He never broke his promise. Ronya had to snatch an hour from planning for the coronation to soothe them and take them riding, leaving David with Ruth, who was spending more and more time with the children now that the time for her departure was near.

That night, Boris broke the news of his discovery to Ronya.

"As I said, I wasn't thinking when I promised Igor yesterday, so I got going an hour earlier this morning, thinking I'd give Rifka's plot a hurried glance and still get to the stables in time to lay out a full day's work for the men before taking the boys into the woods." Boris paused, noted Ronya's bewildered frown, and went on. "I was a fair ride away from the camp, when I noticed wheel tracks where they had no right to be. Then I found fresh signs indicating heavy traffic. While I was looking around, I caught the sound of horses moving furiously through brush. I got off to the far side of the road and hid in the high grass. Presently, Tamara came riding along at the head of twenty men. They had the look of men on a job—no talking, no horseplay.

"I let them get ahead and then started after them. It was about a five-mile ride, up to the extreme northwest corner of your land. I tethered Black Beauty and worked my way to where I could see them without being seen.

"In a clearing along the stream—oh, about an acre strip—there are a couple of wooden shanties hidden by a clump of trees and an open area with a roofed overhang. Tamara stood watch while the men set to work. It's an illegal still, Ronya."

Boris reached for his glass and glanced down at Ronya with keen interest. She looked like some warrior goddess, stony, still with anger and outrage. Half sorry for her, yet half pleased—it seemed to him that Tamara's betrayal released Ronya from all obligation toward her—he decided to go on and finish.

"At noon, they stopped and ate. I took off my boots, stripped off my shirt, and went to sleep. Around two, they started getting ready to leave. They covered the works with weathered tarpaulins and blanketed everything with cones and boughs—a hell of a good camouflage. They rode off and I rode in. In the sheds I found a stack of wood, kegs, casks, bottles, tubs, copper tubing, and a huge supply of barley, wheat, and rye.

"It's a clever operation, Ronya. They're distilling enough vodka to supply the whole province. Tamara must be coining a fortune. The hell of it is that she has involved you in an offense against the crown. It's your land. Anyone caught in the illegal manufacture and sale of vodka—" There was no need for Boris to conclude the sentence. Ronya was fully aware of the consequences.

Ready to burst with temper, Ronya cursed—not Tamara, but her hunger for gold and more gold. Then her mood changed. "How could she? On my land. What possible excuse?"

Boris frowned and let the glass drop softly to the carpeted floor. He put an arm around her and his grip tightened. "Some people, dove, are by nature outlaws. My mother is such a person. She embodies all that is savage. Crossed, she's more dangerous than a wolf or a bear. Tamara is the same breed. The difference is, a pogrom is excitement to my mother whereas Tamara gets her charge from—" As Boris sought the right word, Ronya said, "Risk and daring."

"Yes," he agreed. "And variety."

Ronya was reminded of herself and Tamara as children. Even then, Tamara was recklessly impervious to danger, even then, she gave way to every whim. And Rifka never thwarted her. For a fleeting second, Ronya's mind lingered on Tamara—an unwanted vision—a shimmering, wanton Tamara.

"Ronya," Boris asked, "how do you want this handled?"

"I just hope that when we get there in the morning some of them get reckless enough to start looking for trouble."

She sounded so ferocious, Boris threw his head back and laughed aloud.

"We'll take Ivan Tromokov and Paul with us. The gypsies might not see their latest loss of revenue from our point of view."

"Hmm." He grinned. "Your whip. My fists. Who needs help?"

Ronya smiled mischievously. "I'm serious. Besides, I think Paul ought to share the fun. Until Father put him in perfect attire and sent him to school, brawls were meat and potatoes to him."

"What prompts you to include Ivan?"

This time Ronya did not answer lightly. "We'll need him."

Boris shrugged. "Yes. I guess so." Then, "Dove, do you trust my judgment?"

"Always," she said softly.

"Get rid of Tamara."

Ronya's lashes fell. "How?"

"Make a deal with her, Ronya. Deed her the camp—no part of the forest, no river front—only the campsite and an easement, so that the wagons can move in and out. We don't go there, she doesn't come here and, henceforth, we tolerate no encroachment upon us from the gypsies."

"The Blond One. Here or there?"

Boris glared at her. "There!"

"Boris, please listen." Leaning forward, she placed her fingers on his face. "It won't work, my love. Tamara seethes. If I give her the land, I lose all control over her."

With swift judgment, Boris immediately accepted the truth of her statement. "Dove, let's get some sleep."

"Promise you'll wake me."

Taking her into his arms, he promised.

Feeling his clean, sweet breath in her face, Ronya awakened from a dream. She remembered only that somehow her beloved pine-scented trees were completely blackened and destroyed.

"We ought to get there by sunup," Boris was saying, brushing a tendril of her hair back from her face.

"Yes, darling. We must."

Boris took another glance to make sure she was prepared to get up and said, "I'll wake Paul and pick up Ivan."

256

Paul shook himself into wakefulness. His reaction to the situation swelled Boris' violent resentment toward Tamara.

"My God, I've been a week trying to hunt out an illicit still around Kiev. You can thank your lucky stars that you found it. This area is our next objective."

Boris looked at him speculatively.

Paul said, "We've got twenty-four hours."

A cold grin touched Boris' lips. He made no comment.

In fifteen minutes Paul was downstairs with Ronya, thoroughly savoring the sight of her, slim and beautiful in tight-fitting pants, a long-sleeved blouse, and an embroidered vest.

"How lovely you look," he said, taking her hand.

For a long moment their hands stayed fingered together. Then Ronya glanced at the clock, and Paul let go, cherishing the delusion that his feeling for Ronya was innocent. She was David's daughter, therefore part of his life.

In a short time, Boris returned with Father Tromokov. After a simple breakfast of bread and cheese and scrambled eggs, they set out in an open carriage hitched to two horses. Among them, only Ronya delighted in the superb sunrise. It wasn't often that she saw her land at this peaceful time of morning. The priest stormed about Tamara's forbidden venture. Boris, itching for a fight, felt elated. Paul passed the time gazing at the reddish glow in Ronya's hair.

They pulled up in front of Tamara's fine, new, seven-room house. There was no garden, but it had three great trees. The sun was climbing high, and the camp was filling with day noises. A donkey brayed, hens scratched, and dogs stretched and barked. Tied to a tree stump well to the rear of Tamara's house, a horse, reluctant host to big flies, snorted and kicked. Not twenty feet away, a deer stared at the horse with soft, solemn eyes.

Boris recognized the horse at once.

"Tamara is entertaining a friend."

Paul peered at Boris over Ronya's head. "How do you know that?"

"I sold that fine thoroughbred saddle horse to a loud-mouthed Cossack whose uncle, the chief, traded him and about twenty others to Grand Duke Vladimir for some government land. They'll be sworn in here at the Cavalry post in a few days and sent to St. Petersburg."

Ronya spoke. "The shutters are drawn."

Eyes hard, thinking of his own childhood, Paul asked, "What arrangements does she make for the Blond One?"

"Who knows?" Boris said coldly.

"When Tamara wants him out of the house for the night," Ronya told them, "she sends him to Old Auntie or she sends me a note and I keep him."

Leaning over Boris' shoulder, Ivan Tromokov said, "What now?"

Boris swung the wagon around. He jumped down and onto Tamara's porch. Frightening the birds out of the trees with a wild, fiendish, Tartar howl, he sounded the high-pitched emergency bell.

No one knew what was happening. Men stumbled out of houses and wagons, half dressed and armed with daggers. Others came, brandishing guns. Barely robed, hair flying loose to her waist, Tamara came out breathlessly, rifle in hand. The women came barefoot, clutching their children; the old people struggled along after them. Paul spotted Old Auntie. She was the last one out.

He whispered to Ronya, "Do you see him?"

"He spent last night with Igor. It was a special concession from Boris to the boys."

That gave Paul pause for a few seconds. Then he riveted his eyes on Boris.

Boris' speech was short and to the point, and every person there understood fully the ferocity concealed beneath its unperturbed delivery.

"You," he said, pointing to Tamara, "will order the gang I pick to destroy, under my direction, your moonlight vodka operation. You will never again start any project before obtaining permission from Ronya, your mistress. And—"

Tamara stiffened, but before she could reply, Boris silenced her.

"And," he continued, "you will pay, in gold, such reparations as we deem proper for the danger in which you have involved us."

Her people waited silent and expectant.

This time her answer was not long in coming. "Ronya, my mistress —indeed not. Ronya, my cousin. In my veins flows the Von Glasman blood enriched by that of royalty."

Tamara was beginning to enjoy herself. She was confident that Ronya would understand her bravado. Her people egged her on.

"And you're mistaken about the gold." She held up her hand to the crowd. "Quiet. I want my words to reach Ronya my cousin and the policeman by her side. I invite him who wants gold to turn me in for the reward. And that's not all—" Tamara was so absorbed that she did not hear the Cossack.

He was unshaved, his torso bare, his belt buckle unfastened, his breeches skin-tight over muscular thighs and tucked into black boots. "Boris! How about you, me, and the girls having a little party? I'll take Ronya. I'd give a lot for a little hell-raising with that Jew—"

Boris brought up his fist. The Cossack never knew what hit him.

With a whoop of pleasure, the priest slapped his thigh. The gypsies yelled.

Tamara ran into the house, came back with a pail of water, and flung it at the Cossack.

Boris dragged the man to his feet, and—as women clapped and children gaped—pounded him unmercifully. His fury spent, he let him fall.

Two men hurried over and carried the young Cossack into Old Auntie's house. Until he was able to mount a horse and ride out, he would be her special charge, and then if he set foot in the camp ever again he'd get a knife in his heart and it would be Old Auntie who wielded it. That was the law.

Boris walked down the porch steps and over to Ronya. "Lift me down, darling. I must talk to Tamara."

Boris caught her waist in his big hands. He kissed her reverently on the mouth before putting her gently on her feet.

Half an hour later, Boris rode out with Tamara's men and a dozen wagons. The priest gave thought to skipping mass but decided instead to catch up with them later.

Paul went with Ronya into the house, and Tamara followed. Hardly making a sound on the thick Oriental carpeting, they stepped into the high living room, clean and cool and filled with the scent of small red roses and honeysuckle tumbling from a big cut-glass bowl. Tamara opened the shutters. Bright sun filled the room.

Paul looked around and was not surprised. In a small way, Tamara had patterned the appointments on the big house. The fireplace itself was almost a replica. There was a small but priceless Belgian tapestry on one wall and two fine oils in gilded frames on another. The furniture was English, Queen Anne mixed with a few William and Mary pieces. Low tables were crowded with gold and crystal and boxes of inlaid enamel.

"Like it?" Tamara asked him.

"Very nice."

"Ronya thinks it's overmuch, overbusy, overcrowded." Tamara laughed aloud. "And it is."

Paul could not help smiling.

"Sit down," Tamara said pleasantly. "I'll get dressed."

When she reappeared a full hour later, Tamara saw at a glance that some important decision had been made in her absence. Taking a cup of coffee, she turned questioningly to Ronya.

Ronya smiled. "Paul and I have already decided it would be wise to appease the Cossack chief. Paul will take him gold and persuade him to see his nephew's misfortune as a bit of good-natured sport."

Tamara agreed at once. "That's the clever thing to do."

"Now, get the gold. Paul must be on his way if he's to get back tonight."

This was not the first time Tamara had seen that particular look of

Ronya's—no ifs, buts, or maybes. Tamara turned on Paul. "Some brother you are!"

"Some fool you are! Taking a chance on Siberia for some paltry money you don't need!"

Tamara laughed. "Who's going to send me there? You? Krasmikov?"

Paul reddened.

"Tamara," Ronya said. "Go dig up the gold. Plenty of it."

Tamara rushed out, slamming the door.

"She's not really upset," Ronya said, pouring more hot coffee.

Paul shook his head. "I'll never get accustomed to you two. But while she's gone for that gold, there's something you should know. I tracked down the unholy trio."

Ronya put the cup down. "Tanya? The two others? How?"

With a satisfied smile, he said, "I'm a good policeman."

Her look implored him to go on.

"They're in a Warsaw slum, holed up in a miserable cage of a room."

"All three of them?"

He nodded. "The men, drunk most of the time, pimp for Tanya."

"My God—how awful!"

"Save your pity. I let Tanya pick me up in a workman's café. I offered her the chance to escape. She turned it down." He laughed sharply. "But not before telling me what she thought of a greasy Polack like me."

Ronya could imagine his disguise and she laughed too, but not for long. "Paul, Warsaw is too close for comfort. If they've squandered that much gold in so short a time, they'll eventually be back for more."

He nodded. "I'll get rid of them."

"How?"

"Leave that to me."

"I won't allow you to hurt Lydia's niece," she said, her face grave. "See to it that all three get to America, and that once there Tanya is given the chance of a fresh start."

Paul had no use for sentimentality, but the important thing was to please Ronya—at least, not to disappoint her. He patted Ronya's arm. "Consider it done."

28

In later years, it was said that the coronation of the third Tamara, the gilded aristocrat of the gypsies, was an event of spectacular opulence. The myth grew and grew, and they said that the pageantry and the feasting lasted twenty-one days and that gypsies, led by kings and dukes, came from as far away as Scotland. There were stories of bejeweled ladies with parasols, fashionable gentlemen in top hats, provincial governors, and dashing officers in uniform coming to honor Tamara. They said that Boris—his golden hair ablaze in the brilliant sunlight, his face as if fixed in stone—led bands of galloping Tartars on parade and that Ronya, in pants and boots with diamonds in her hair, rode with the Tartars astride a black mare.

These fanciful stories of viewing platforms built along the edge of the forest, of the Tzar's generals and admirals decorated from shoulder to shoulder, of dances on Ronya's flowering terraces, of banquets created by French and Italian chefs, were told on cold winter nights around campfires. It was natural that the gypsies should believe in a bright time, and this was the picture they liked to paint of Tamara.

The truth was far less contrived and far more fascinating.

There was disagreement. . . .

Boris saw nothing marvelous in Tamara's band of sedentary gypsies. As far as he was concerned, over the generations they had fashioned an easy life for themselves, leaving the Von Glasmans with burdens and responsibility. To him the customs practiced by the gypsies on the occasion of a queen's crowning and a queen's death were especially foolish. Tamara herself did not help matters.

Still for a time, Boris, whose natural inclination was live and let live, did not pay much attention to the preparations. That is, not until he began to speculate on the consequences of several hundred strangers—many dirty, thieving, and quarrelsome—pasturing horses in Ronya's meadows, trampling her fields of marigolds and chrysanthemums, polluting her fresh, clean streams. He envisioned covered wagons spread out in wide circles, hordes of children dressed in rags, fat women with greasy hair squatting by fires preparing foul-smelling dishes, growling dogs, boisterous merrymaking, outbursts of drunken violence.

He took his thoughts to Ruth.

Ruth was by nature patient, she listened well. To Boris, whom she cherished, she was especially attentive. "We've had a dry summer," he said. "The danger of fire frightens the hell out of me."

"All you say is so. Tell Ronya. Tell her of the perils involved. In Katya's name and in mine, you may add that we find Tamara's constant encroachment upon us tiresome."

There was loyalty. . . .

"It helps very little," Ronya said, after hearing him out, "that you are right," and added as an afterthought, "Poor Tamara, she'll have a bad time when I tell her."

261

"You've no choice. Your first responsibility is to the welfare of the estate and to its future."

But Ronya was troubled. Without further word to Boris, she sat down at her writing table and wrote out a long list of names. It was eleven o'clock in the morning when she started her first invitation, addressed to the commanding officer of the Cavalry post, and well over two hours later before she put down her pen. By then, every officer and his lady, every landowner and his family, every person of consequence in Kiev, was cordially urged to witness Tamara's coronation and to stay for an evening of feasting and dancing.

There was bitterness. . . .

"My mother warned us that Boris and Katya would conspire to ruin my coronation."

"Evidently, Tamara, you haven't heard one word I said. We're all looking forward to the splendor and excitement. Only we must be practical. We can't be hosts to the entire Rom nation."

Tamara thrust her hands angrily into her pockets. "To give substance to my reign, I must have—"

"Your vanity," Ronya interrupted, "may endanger us all."

Tamara's voice rang with derision. "Boris must be naïve if he thinks I can stop the gypsies at this late date."

"You're talking to me—Ronya. You can, and you will, stop them. And remember—you may *never* consider this land your private domain."

"You know," Tamara said, with a glint in her eyes, "it was a mistake to teach you all our secrets. If I don't stop them coming, you will. You know how."

"How clever of you to remember. I must go. Good-bye, Tamara."

Tamara followed her through the door. "Have you heard from St. Petersburg?"

"Katya will be here tomorrow. Alexis, too, I hope."

"I was thinking about Paul."

"He says he can't come."

"Neither can Sergei. And neither can Alexander."

"I'm sorry," Ronya said, and meant it.

There was jubilation. . . .

Until her death, Tamara remembered every detail of this day. She awoke to music. As soon as she was dressed, she went out on the porch and stood there gazing dreamily at the sky, watching clouds drifting slowly on a gentle breeze. She heard the plaintive gypsy chords and turned toward the sound. In the heavy shade of an oak, dressed in gaudy sparkling costumes, stood a band of musicians from Hungary. They ceased playing and bowed, while from behind them came the

262

leaders of the free nomads: a duke from England, a duke from Spain, a duke from Romania, a prince from Germany, and another from Serbia. Representing close to a million gypsies, they had come to honor Tamara. They were all vital men, with strong sparkling white teeth and shining blue-black hair. Each wore a single ring.

The hours went by; the time had come. Tamara was now covered in gold from head to toe.

"Here they come," she said to her guests in a hushed voice. "Here they come, my Von Glasman cousins. With them is Count Alexis Brusilov. The children are Ronya's son Igor and my son the Blond One. The golden giant in the white uniform is Boris Pirov."

Tamara, still able to deceive herself, surrendered to a vision of delight: For her, to add color and joy to her coronation, Boris wore scarlet epaulets fringed in gold and had covered his chest with medals. She glowed with pride. Behind the family was every notable in Kiev. The peasants with their children, all dressed in their Sunday best, walked behind Father Tromokov, in his summer cassock. All were encumbered by the gifts they carried. As they neared the cooking fires, the peasants began to sing and the gypsies around the wagons joined in; their voices filled the sun-flooded camp.

Ronya, dressed completely in white, walked up to Tamara alone. She welcomed the visitors, then took Tamara's hand and led her to the center of the camp, where they climbed the seven steps of a newly erected wooden platform strewn and carpeted with rose petals.

The gypsies swarmed about, thunderously shouting and cheering. Some of the women wept. Ronya raised her hand and ordered quiet. Catching sight of the Blond One carrying the jeweled crown on a deep-blue velvet cushion, the crowd fell back.

Taking the crown in her hands, Ronya said very quietly, "Go, darling, stand next to your mother."

"I want to go back to Igor," he said, tugging at her skirt.

Tamara nodded and Ronya smiled and whispered, "Your mother says you may."

Ronya waited. Then as Tamara stood before her, beautiful in the blazing sunset, she lifted her arms, placed the wreath of sapphires and rubies on the sleek black head, and said solemnly, "I, Ronya, crown thee Queen Tamara the Third. Long may you reign."

Tamara's people strained forward, standing on tiptoe, craning their necks to see the new queen, yelling, whistling, cheering, and kissing all at once, their shouts louder than the deafening clang of bells.

After receiving these cries of loyalty and homage from her people, Tamara made her way with Ronya to Old Auntie, whose age entitled her to homage even from the queen and whose blessing, if bestowed, carried weight with the spirits. Later, as they went into the house to change into clothes more suitable to outdoor feasting and dancing, Ronya consoled Tamara: "Don't be upset. You know she's half blind, she mistook me for you."

Tamara answered lightly, "On the contrary. I feel that in blessing you, she blessed me." She held out her hand. "I hear violins."

Ronya smiled. In another moment, they were outside, and their reappearance was the signal for the party to go into full swing. Peasants, gypsies, gentry, the military, all equal on this occasion, downed vodka in prodigious amounts and consumed round after round of roasted beef and suckling pig.

Until midnight couples swayed to the gypsy beat, drenched in moonlight, and then it was time for Tamara to perform. But even at her coronation Tamara had thoughts only of Boris—who was nowhere to be seen. She sought out Ronya, who was surrounded by officers and gay young cadets, and shepherded her to a quiet torch-lit spot some distance away where guests were still eating and drinking.

"What's wrong?" asked Ronya.

"I can't find Boris. Where is he?"

Ronya suppressed her rising anger. "If you must know, the last time I saw him he was dancing with my mother."

"That was over an hour ago." Tamara's obsession caused her to lose all sense of caution. "Most likely he's in one of the wagons with the door bolted."

With cold revulsion, Ronya walked off to find Katya. She asked if she had seen Boris.

"Yes, he and Alexis are together," Katya said. "They said we are to go on as if they were with us. I'll tell you more about it when we get home."

At that moment Tamara slowly started to dance to the moaning gypsy violins, and Ronya had to remain.

The dance, which began in slow motion, soon became fast and sensuous, and the merriment of the crowd got boisterous. They shouted for more, and though Tamara was dominated by one desire—to find Boris—still, duty to her guests kept her dancing, and habit kept the dance at a feverish pitch.

The priest finished his vodka, blew his nose, turned his back on Tamara, and walked off toward the big house. It was time to say goodbye to Ruth.

Finally the music died down and waiters appeared with trays of drinks. Partly because of her training, partly because she wanted nothing with which to reproach herself later, Ronya stayed on, while avoiding Tamara.

264

Instead of being pleased, Tamara was overwrought that everyone was staying so late. She fidgeted with nervous strain. Where was Boris?

At last, toward dawn, the guests began taking their leave. Tamara scarcely knew to whom she gave her hand. The moment the last guest departed, she changed into boots and a broad skirt and rushed out to search after Boris.

The mystery of Boris' disappearance was solved by the two notes that lay on Ronya's pillow.

July 2, 1886

My dear and Precious Ronya,
    I find that I am unable to say good-bye. If I were to wait until the day after tomorrow, I'm afraid I'd be unable to tear myself away from you and the children. And yet I do not want to turn from the direction I have set for myself. Darling, time will pass in a flash, and I'll be home.
    It is good of my daughters to furnish me with such dashing and gallant escorts. Alexis goes with us as far as Odessa. Only my selfishness justifies my taking Boris as far as Antwerp.
    I love you, Ronya. I love Igor. I love David.

Until my return,
Your mother, Ruth

Ronya, my dove,
    It is better so.
    Miss me.

All my love,
Your Boris

Tamara looked everywhere and failed to find Boris. She returned to her house and found waiting in her bedroom a handsome, mahogany-colored Serbian. Quickly fevered, she answered the question in his eyes with a long kiss full on the mouth.

29

As the clock softly chimed nine on the evening of Boris' return home, the wind began shaking the trees and rattling the windows. The last thing Boris wanted to do was venture outside again, but he could not ignore the possibility of a real storm.

"Dove, I must go back to the stables," he said, putting down his drink and rising from his armchair. "I won't be long."

Boris remained only long enough to place some of his men on all-night watch and to put Sad Eyes in charge. Getting back to the house was a struggle—even Boris, for all his size and strength, was nearly knocked to the ground by the wind. Once inside, he bolted all the doors and shuttered all the windows.

In just four hours the wind reached gale ferocity. Ronya, frightened from sleep, cried out for Boris. "What's that awful screaming sound? The wind?"

"Yes, dove," Boris answered, taking her into his arms.

Ronya's first thought was the children. Boris lit the lamps and went in search of Igor and the Blond One, both of whom he found huddled under the blanket clinging to each other. He carried them to Ronya, who opened the covers and helped the boys crawl into bed. Boris started for the nursery, but Ronya told him Lydia had David in bed with her.

Boris stood undecided, until Ronya said, "Please, Boris, get into bed with us. I'm afraid."

Igor weighed the remark, then dismissed it. He understood that grown-ups say the strangest things at times. He knew nothing could frighten his mother.

At six o'clock the maids came in with an enormous breakfast. With his second cup of coffee, all at once Boris became alert and attentive.

"The fury of the wind is over, dove." From the balcony he could see felled trees, devastated thatch, overturned wagons, smashed poles. The church's onion-shaped dome was down. As for Ronya's golden wheat fields— His face revealed none of his gloomy forebodings as he returned inside and quickly got dressed.

Boris lost no time in getting to the fields.

In astonishment he stood in the saddle, his eyes sweeping the horizon. They were untouched. The thought came to him that some force mightier than the wind had protected Ronya's crop.

After he brought Ronya the good news, he rode out again, this time in the hope that their neighbors had been as lucky. But hope did not last long. As far as he could see there was almost total destruction. On the way back, the rain began to fall.

Rain fell all day and all night, and all the next day, and the next— an unending, torrential downpour. Roads were washed away; the river, made turbulent, rose. In places the ground gave way and animals were swept into whirlpools of dirt and water. And still the driving deluge poured down.

266

Boris and Ronya shared their concern.

"The hell with brooding over the damage caused by the storm," Boris said. "The wheat isn't going to be saved unless we save it."

"So far we've been lucky. Maybe we'll stay lucky."

"Not luck, Ronya. Topography. The land dips down to the river. We've been getting a fair measure of natural drainage, but once we overflow—" Boris dropped his half-smoked cigarette into the fireplace. "We've got to sacrifice a small part of the crop. If we dig trenches down the slope, the water will flow down them into the river."

"What will you do with the mud?"

"We'll haul it away."

"Between the digging and the hauling, you'll need an army."

"Yes," Boris said quietly, thinking of all the people who lived on the land, "and I've got an army."

Boris hoisted the red emergency flag high above the main barn, then took a hammer and struck the circular iron band suspended from a rafter. While he waited for the peasants to assemble, he organized his stable hands into crews for hauling the mud. "Scoop it up," he said, "and take it away in wheelbarrows, pushcarts, buckets, anything you can lay your hands on." Then he called Sad Eyes aside and ordered a couple of rounds of vodka for the men.

Every able-bodied man and all the older lads arrived, wearing all possible protection against the rain. They stood in the mud and heard the plan. Then, on Boris' order, they moved out.

At midday, Tamara arrived at the house in a canvas-covered wagon drawn by two black oxen. She invited her driver into the kitchen for a hot drink.

"You've brought a driver!" exclaimed Ronya. "That's just what I need. Keep him here and tell the maids to start boiling eggs, cutting chunks of cheese, cooking potatoes in their skins—I want them to gather as much food as possible. I'm going upstairs to change my clothes."

Even with oxen, the going was bad, and the wagon moved forward at a crawl. Once Ronya knelt behind the driver and peered over his shoulder at the flattened gardens. She kept saying to herself, "The gardens don't matter," but the havoc wreaked on flowers upset her deeply, though not for long. They turned off the water-filled road and stopped in a narrow clearing alongside the wheat fields, and Ronya saw the men's sober faces streaming with sweat, their bodies lashed with rain, their feet sunk in the mud.

The peasants stared at Ronya and Tamara; they expected only their own women to turn out in such weather, not their mistress and the gypsy queen. Boris threw down his shovel, dabbed his face with the back of his hand, and walked over.

"Hello, dove. The men are wet, hot, and tired. Food and drink will be a shot in the arm."

Tamara glanced around sharply. "You need help."

"Yes," Boris admitted matter-of-factly.

"Amin," Tamara called to her driver, "round up the men and tell the women to start collecting storm lamps."

"Listen," said Boris, "we need more shovels and a couple of oxcarts. And—"

"More food," Ronya broke in.

"And," Tamara said with a laugh, "I recommend my vodka. I made it myself."

Ronya caught Boris' eye, and she smiled a private little smile. He cupped his hands and called to the men.

They moved up to the wagon in groups of ten. Tamara brought out jugs of beer and vodka and sugared tea in iron kettles. Ronya, from her improvised kitchen under the canvas, handed out corn, potatoes, slices of meat, hunks of cheese, and hard-boiled eggs.

The men ate and talked in low voices, until the food ran out. The men stirred and went back to digging.

Boris told Ronya to go home, but she pleaded with him to let her stay.

None of them noticed the priest until he said, "No, Ronya. You've got to go back. We need you more than we need the wheat."

More rain fell that day without carrying away the wheat. It ran down the deep channels, and the Dnieper looked more like a wintry sea than a river.

It was dark and still raining when, from the platform of an over-turned wagon, Boris thanked his diggers and haulers. "Don't despair about personal losses and property damages due to the storm. We'll work out something."

The men stood mute, each absorbed in his own tiredness and his raw, blistered palms.

One old peasant, wrapped in a wet shawl, stepped forward. Holding his lantern high, he cleared his throat and spoke for all of them. "It's good," he said, "that our Ronya has a real man to lean on. God bless you for that."

"Thank you," Boris said, smiling, and stepped off the wagon and walked rapidly away. The night engulfed him.

Muddied, sweat-stained, and rain-soaked, Boris entered the house through a back door. He rinsed his mouth with cold tea in the old kitchen and glanced up at the clock. Two in the morning. Outside in the narrow corridor, he pulled off his boots and carelessly dropped his clothes. He went up the rear stairway and started down the long, wide hall, coming to a stop at Ronya's open door. Her lights were on. He saw her and the happiness in her face at the sight of him. She came slowly to him and lifted her face. When their lips met, her eyes closed.

Boris gazed down at her. "Ronya, my dove. We saved the wheat."

Ronya nodded gravely. "I never doubted that you would." Then she smiled up at him. "Your bath is ready."

Boris lit a cigarette and followed her into the bathroom. He finished smoking and bathing, and afterward, naked, he edged himself into bed. Ronya pulled the quilt up over the sheet. "You must sleep," she said to him. And because he could see her and touch her and feel the warmth of her, Boris slept in peace.

Part II

30

There were days like ordinary days; there were days of gentle sunshine or of shrieking winds; there were white days when Boris put a radiant Ronya, wrapped in sable, on a sled and pulled her along the icy roads; there were gray days when Boris slipped back into libertine indulgence with women taken in brutal indifference and quickly dropped in ennui; there were days when Boris held Ronya strongly and she was tranquil; and there were black days when the Tzar's troops disarmed Jews of their pitiful sticks but left unmolested the drunken mobs who invaded the synagogues and dishonored the women.

So four years passed. It was again late summer. The year was 1890, and Georgi, their third son, was five months old. Ronya sat holding her pen, about to write to her mother.

For a little while she sat thinking. What she found hard to understand, and what bewildered Boris, was that Ruth could spend years away from them. In the four years she had been away, Ruth had met with Katya and Alexis twice, once in Copenhagen and once on the French Riviera; now she was in America, staying in a place called Oyster Bay, Long Island, with a woman she called "my dear friend Sophia." Ronya wondered about this dear friend. Ruth had never in her life spoken of Sophia before she went to America, and Ronya could not imagine where her mother had met her and why she had never been mentioned.

Aug. 25, 1890

Ruth, my Mother,

The nursery door is open, and I can hear Katya humming. Since her return to Kiev, she has been with Georgi constantly. At first I worried over David, thinking he'd be jealous, but all he wants is horses. His joys are sleeping in one of the barns stretched out on straw and sharing a meal with the stable boys. If the Cavalry were willing to take him, he'd be ready to go now. Boris says: "At least, he'll have no difficulty choosing a career, he'll be the horseman I hoped to make out of Igor."

He and Igor quarrel. Fortunately, David needs no one to protect him. He'll soon be taller than Igor. He gets more handsome every day, but he does not have Igor's dashing dimple or the Blond One's effortless goodness. To Katya's despair, he swears like a drunken hussar.

Katya says that Georgi was born ready to love, and that's true. He's gay and trustful, he adores being fussed over, and he goes to strangers as happily as he goes to me or Katya. He is truly the golden one. Boris finds this frightening—he remembers the curse and the legend. The fear comes unbidden, usually in his sleep.

I can provide you with some news of interest, but on the whole it isn't good. Paul is of enormous worth to us. I can assure you that in a few instances we have averted trouble and prevented tragedy. However, my latest information is that large-scale repressive measures are being planned in the strictest secrecy. Blood accusations will be revived. Mother, I often wonder—why were the Jews chosen, for what? Ignore my pessimism. Possibly it is not quite as bad as Paul thinks.

Incidentally, I depend upon Tamara for information almost as much as upon Paul. You won't believe the organization she operates. When the police, even the local secret police, need help, they go to Tamara, and they pay her outrageous fees.

We miss you dreadfully and want you home. Why don't you bring Sophia with you? It might be nice for her to see Russia. Of course we should be pleased to see her, especially if it brings you home even one day sooner. We all join in sending you our love.

Your devoted daughter,
Ronya

One Wednesday morning, Ronya awakened at six o'clock to find she was in bed alone; Boris' side of the bed was rumpled and his pillow smelled faintly of his wonderful male smell. For a moment she lay quietly, listening unconcerned for his return, but all at once, for no apparent reason, she began to feel anxious. She told herself not to be a fool and tried to force herself back to sleep, but after a few minutes she sprang out of bed and flew downstairs.

Only the maid lighting the stove in the kitchen looked up to greet her. Now thoroughly worried, though still scolding herself for being so irrationally alarmed, Ronya struggled into riding clothes and high-topped boots and hurried to the stables. A number of the men were already there, working in the warmth of the summer morning with their shirt sleeves rolled up. Boris had ridden off ten minutes ago, they said. In a voice that cracked like a whip lash, Ronya demanded a horse and, after a single startled glance, a groom rushed to saddle Yelena, a well-behaved mare. Purely by happenstance, as Ronya said later, she took a horse path that led to the camp.

274

The morning was still and the air heavy with moisture. The grass on either side of the winding path was a deep dark green amid the poplars and weeping willows. As Ronya emerged into the sunlit clearing in front of Tamara's house, she reined in, stunned, and for seconds made no move. Right in front of her eyes, placidly twitching its ears free of flies, was Boris' horse, the reins thrown over its head. Her mind filled with pictures of Boris with Tamara—hot and triumphant, happy and satiated. Hardly aware of what she was doing or where she was going, she set off at breakneck speed. The white dusty road, the yellow fields, the fruit-laden trees flew by, but she saw nothing but the flickering scenes behind her eyes. Dogs ran out to bark at the mare's heels, and peasant women straightened from their labors to gaze after her openmouthed. The mare pulled up of her own accord, sweating and tired, in Kreshchatik, Kiev's busiest thoroughfare, her way blocked by a cartload of wood. Ronya straightened in the saddle, suddenly conscious of the load of stacked timber, the paved street, the brick houses on either side, the curious stares of the passers-by. She turned her horse's head and the mare brought her home, where completely given over to overpowering, anguished resentment, Ronya went straight to her room.

Boris was already there.

"Ronya, where in hell—"

Ronya raised her arm.

Instinctively, he recoiled from her, at the same time noting her eyes full of agony, the loose ends of her shining hair falling carelessly, the coiling of her slender, graceful body—

Boris heard the whip's harsh hum before he felt its sharp sting. It all happened very quickly, and until she heard Katya's scream, Ronya was not aware of blood or even of the whip in her hand. Later, she vividly remembered her sister standing rooted in the doorway dressed in a morning gown, her hair tied with a blue silk ribbon; Boris moving fast into the bathroom, already pressing a wet towel to his right eyebrow, unable to stop the bright red flow; Katya rushing after him.

Katya was perceptibly rattled, but Ronya, in spite of her anger, sent for the surgeon. Then she went downstairs and ate her breakfast.

Katya remained with Boris, making cold compresses in a vain effort to staunch the blood. "What in heaven's name got into Ronya?" she asked him incredulously.

"It's all right, Katya," he said smiling, as the blood welled out of the open wound.

Katya wrung out a towel, unable to understand how Ronya could be so brutal and how Boris could be so mild.

Finally the doctor came. In the bedroom Ronya watched as he stitched the wound with black silk thread.

"It's nothing," the doctor said. "It won't leave a scar—only a thin line that will soon fade. I've fixed you up as good as new."

"Too bad," Ronya said, glaring at Boris.

The doctor, an old friend of the family, smiled politely and bowed himself out.

Boris walked slowly over to Ronya. "You had better take a bath and cool off."

"You can go straight to—"

"Don't say it, Ronya." Turning away, Boris put his arm around Katya and went off for breakfast.

Ronya watched them go, mechanically twisting a bloody compress in her fingers. Why didn't Boris look guilty? He had slept with Tamara—seen Ronya's anger—felt her whip—why was he so cool and untroubled?

At breakfast Katya was eagerly listening to Boris' explanation.

"When I awakened, it was still too early to get up, so I decided to look in on Igor—I often do. It was a shock when I found the Blond One in his place. I thought Igor might be with David. The minute I entered the room, David opened his eyes. You know," Boris said, "David gets that trait from me. Igor sleeps like Ronya—dead to the world. I asked David if he knew why the Blond One was alone in Igor's bed. He said, 'Igor stayed with Tamara.' I didn't like it, but I was willing to leave him there for the present, until David said, 'Krasmikov came in and told us to get out of bed, but Igor wouldn't because Tamara promised him she'd sing.' You can imagine how fast I got over to Tamara's. Do you know, Katya"—Boris held out his cup to her—"they were all three properly night-shirted and peacefully asleep, Igor in the middle."

Katya filled his cup and pursed her lips without comment.

"Well, I picked Igor up without disturbing them, and just as I came out onto the porch I saw Ronya riding away. The way she galloped that mare, I think she was trying to outstrip the wind."

When Boris opened her door it was already late in the afternoon. Ronya looked at him searchingly. "How do you feel?"

"Fine."

"Katya told me." She took a breath and went on with some difficulty, "Boris, I want to explain. I honestly didn't know I held that damn whip in my hand."

Boris considered her with a slightly mocking grin.

"I mean it," she protested.

"Sit down, Ronya. I want to talk to you."

Ronya hurried over to the sofa. He looked suspiciously at the vodka, the fresh caviar, and the thin-sliced black bread, the tiny plum tomatoes, the cigarettes—even his favorite ashtray.

276

"Darling," Ronya murmured, "do you absolutely insist upon a quarrel?"

Boris almost laughed aloud.

"Tamara came to tell me there was nothing to reproach her with."

Astonished that Ronya was not seriously angry, he said, "I don't want Igor sleeping with Tamara."

"It doesn't happen often."

"It's not to happen *at all*. I'm relying upon you to remember that, Ronya."

"Very well," she agreed, "I promise it won't happen again . . . Boris . . . I suppose I owe you an apology. I did jump to quite the wrong conclusion."

"Forget it," he said harshly.

He walked over to the tall window and stood looking out at the reds and yellows of the dahlias, now at their peak and blooming luxuriantly in every bed in the garden.

Ronya came to him. He turned, for a moment looked at her, then without a word, took her into his arms.

Katya spent much of the day chastising Ronya.

At length she whirled on Katya in self-defense. "All right, he didn't lie with Tamara today, but he did once, and maybe he will again. Perhaps that's why he took that blow. He felt he deserved it."

The month between Katya's departure from Kiev and the arrival of Sophia's letter to Ronya with its tragic news might have been—should have been—a glorious month. The weather was perfect, gay sunshine and warm. Boris, still in a devoted mood, was tender and splendid to Ronya and, as she confided to her journal, "behaving himself like a legendary knight, shining pure." But the rivalry between him and David grew deeper every day.

People said of David, now almost five, "Incredible!"—in the face of his size, it was not surprising. David gloried in the attention he attracted. He was intelligent, strong, and agile—he could keep up with Igor and the Blond One when they took him into the woods. Riding he loved and was nearly as good at it as Igor. While the men in the stables bragged about this, Boris hated it; he did not want David, half Igor's age, pulling ahead.

But there was more: David was cruel. True, Igor had a temper and was a brawler, but he got into fights without intending to do so. David, when crossed, doggedly planned his revenge. He punished Boris by coming between him and Ronya and by loving Tamara. Instinctively, he knew this was the way to hurt his father.

Boris struggled with his hostile feelings, especially when Ronya said to him, "It must be dreadful for him, darling, knowing that you favor Igor and are beginning to adore Georgi. Perhaps if he had you to himself, he might begin to feel important to you and that might bring about a big change."

"Goddamn it, Ronya, I try."

Speaking softly, Ronya pleaded, "Boris, try a little harder. Please."

Boris realized that a good part of his dislike of the boy came from a feeling that he was being displaced by the boy. And he resented it. This especially plagued him, because he knew that he was being unfair.

In the first week of September, he sought David out and suggested a few days in the forest. "Just the two of us, son."

David's eyes grew colder.

It was Boris who felt uncomfortable. "Don't you want to?"

"Well, no," David said, "not with you alone."

"Forget it!" Boris said gruffly.

A few days later, Boris presented David with a six-inch silver-cased pocketknife.

David took it, not much impressed. He lost it the same day.

Drunk with vodka, drunk with desolation, drunk with exhaustion, Boris fell into merciful sleep. Ruth was dead. Gentle, loving, gracious Ruth, flung from a yacht into the ocean off Montauk Point in a terrible freak storm that hit the tip of Long Island. Amid wreckage and debris, the coast guards went out in the pelting rain, but they pulled no survivors from the sea.

Jews filled the synagogue. Ronya sat on a wooden bench in the upstairs section with Igor and David. Everyone was there to hear the rabbi conduct a special memorial service.

Rabbi Joseph Levinsky ascended the pulpit. Trembling, his eyes overflowing with tears, he prayed. The swaying men prayed with him, uttering loud cries. Some were personal prayers, words that did Ruth honor. In the balcony, the women asked themselves, "Why does Ronya not weep? Is she made of stone?"

Ronya, keeping a firm grip on David, felt suffocated by the smell of the many bodies in the airless building declared to be the House of God. She was beset by the pictures in her mind: Ruth tossed overboard—Ruth spinning in the surging sea. She was torn by thoughts of Boris—his savage sob, "No, Christ, no!"—his misery. There was madness in it. She prayed he stay blinded and senseless until she could stretch out on the bed beside him and comfort him. David squirming brought her out of her private grief.

278

The prayer done, the rabbi gave the eulogy and he revealed Ruth's lineage. Ronya did not relish the disclosure.

"Ruth's name was not Ruth. Her name was Vera Theresa Augusta. She was not Russian, she was Austrian. Vera Theresa Augusta left her father and mother and the land of her nativity, and she cast her lot among us. Ruth won favor in our sight, for she clung passionately to our traditions, she took pride in our past, she learned our language.

"Just as Ruth of old cleaved unto Naomi, so our Ruth cleaved unto David von Glasman. She said, 'Whither thou goest, I will go, and where thou lodgest, I will lodge, thy people shall be my people, and thy God, my God.' "

The congregation thought: *Surely the daughters of so noble a Jewess should not have been given in marriage to Gentiles.* They beat their breasts. The rabbi thought: *Perhaps what was good enough for his beloved mother-in-law will be good enough for Boris.* In silent prayer, he called to God to lead Boris into righteousness. "Everything is possible to God."

Ronya alighted from her carriage, turned David over to Lydia and warned Igor to behave himself, and went up to Boris' room. His door was locked. Ordering a ladder put to his window, she kilted up her skirts and climbed up. She pushed aside the curtains and entered the room. He lay in his clothes, unshaved, feet bare, stretched on his back, his arms spread out, sleeping soundly. Silently, she gathered bottles and ashtrays, unlocked the door, and tiptoed softly away. She left the house and set off for Tamara.

It was a melancholy day with the smell of autumn in the air. Tamara was waiting.

The Blond One heard his mother say, "That child is even more silent than usual," and heard Ronya's answer, "He loved her." The Blond One put his mouth organ to his lips, and the sound that reached the women was sad, sobbing. He was begging Ronya to understand.

Ronya was deeply torn. The children, her children, were to go to Moscow that very day, and she was letting them go because she knew Boris needed her and Katya needed them. Alexis' telegram had been brief: KATYA INCONSOLABLE. But this meant that the Blond One was being abandoned by Igor. It excluded him from the manor house, from Ronya, and from warmhearted Lydia, who welcomed him with heavenly treats—giant prunes stuffed with nuts, glazed apples, Vienna tarts filled with currants—and who shooed him out of sight in time. Boris was still hugging his self-deception: "Of Tamara's flesh is no blood of mine."

There was very little that escaped Tamara. She went down the hall to the Blond One, shut her eyes to the hard look he gave her, and sent him kindly to Ronya. She started to pack his clothes.

The Blond One gazed at Ronya with all the speechless sadness of seven years old. The sight of him decided her; she opened her arms.

When Ronya returned from the gypsy camp, the Blond One was with her. At three o'clock, accompanied by the wet nurse, two dependable nursemaids in starched white, a tutor, and Igor's golden retriever, Boris' four sons departed from Kiev. Only his bastard missed him.

Ronya turned from the train without a backward glance. Her driver, a young competition rider in training with Boris, tilted his hat to a rakish angle and waved his whip. The coach gave a jolt. Ronya called, "Faster." When the carriage stopped, the driver swung down, and as he opened the door, said, "I'm willing to wager that only the champion, and maybe the priest, could have made it faster." Ronya jumped down unaided. "You did well." She ran through the front door and up the splendid stairway. Lydia ran after her, puffing. Ronya gave kitchen orders, then vanished into the bathroom.

When she reappeared, she took Lydia's breath away. Gone the bereaved daughter, the devoted mother, the loyal sister, the responsible mistress, the businesswoman, the passionate Jewess bound to the tear-wet faces of her people. In a sheer dressing gown that revealed her nakedness, her hair bound with a scarlet ribbon, her feet sandaled in gold, Ronya smelled of a soft dreamy fragrance.

Boris opened his eyes. To his surprise, he felt well. He went out into the balcony, and looked at the familiar trees, and breathed the fresh open air. By the time Ronya came softly into the room, he had bathed, shaved, and gotten back into bed. He was pretending to be asleep. She put her tray down and nuzzled her face in his hair.

"Hello, dove."

"Hello, my eagle. How are you?"

"I'm hungry."

He ate in silence. Then he asked, "Did I give you a bad time? Did I hurt David?"

The sound of her laughter startled him. She kicked off her gold sandals and said, "What do you remember?"

"That I picked him up by the seat of his pants."

"He got less than he deserved."

Boris smiled wryly.

"You made a few dire threats and shook him pretty hard, and you put him down abruptly. Now he won't drink milk. He says he wants vodka to drink, because he wants to grow as strong as his father."

"Remember, Ronya," Boris said calmly, "I wanted to leave before I started to drink. Do you regret not letting me go?"

"No, darling," Ronya replied. "I needed you near me—desperately."

280

Boris nodded slowly and was silent.

"She never lectured me," he said at length, "she never tried to change me. She loved me." Sadly, almost to himself, he added, "She wasn't old. I thought we'd have a long time."

It took all Ronya's strength not to weep at the thought of life without her mother. Slowly she slipped out of her robe and under the quilt. Her lips nearing his, she whispered, "Hold me tight."

Boris' arms moved and closed around her. His mouth moved and lingered on hers, his hold tightened, his muscles hardened. Swiftly he took her and in possessing was possessed.

The next morning, after a long dreamless sleep, Boris went back to the stables. For the white stallion the whole world was golden light again.

Ronya stayed in seclusion for eight days, devoting herself only to Boris. She did not forget Ruth, her sorrow did not lessen, but she did give Boris back his vigor. When he was with Ronya, the dimly remembered horrors from his past sank back into the darkness.

In Moscow, Katya devoted herself mostly to the infant Georgi, while Alexis tried to cope with David. It was a struggle. The boy paid little heed to rules or regulations. If scolded, he raised his arched pale eyebrows and looked so dauntlessly self-assured that the restraining adult doubted himself. Even more disconcerting was his response to approval: not the slightest trace of concern.

"No wonder it took so long and it was so hard to liberate Russia from the Tartars," Alexis said to Katya. "My pet, our middle nephew is no ordinary youngster. We are dealing with a throwback to the golden horde."

Igor and the Blond One were left very much on their own; only lessons, conducted five mornings a week from eight thirty until noon, were required. The rest of the time they played with the dogs, harnessed ponies to carts, batted tennis balls, and raced Alexis' horses. Sometimes they were accompanied by David, who might be well behaved or a terror. Once, he defended himself in a fight so well that the Blond One had to rescue his opponent from a cruel beating. There were harsh words between David and Igor, because David called the, Blond One a meddling bastard.

The boys saw nothing of the dazzle of Moscow; Katya was in mourning. However, sometimes there were dinner guests, jeweled ladies with soft hands and dandified men of fashion. At such times the children dined alone or with Igor's tutor.

On Sundays, when Katya and Alexis went to one of the great onion-domed cathedrals, they left Boris' Jewish sons at home. The

281

Blond One, who was technically of the Orthodox faith, was offered the opportunity of going to church, but he disliked the lengthy mass, standing for hours holding a candle, and the smell of smoking incense. He did not like to kiss the hand of the priest either, even a priest in the robes of a bishop.

One Saturday morning when all the boys were raking up leaves, they heard a voice say, "Gracious, what industry!" The voice belonged to his Grace the Bishop of Moscow. Igor grinned, showing his dimple. The Blond One gazed up respectfully at the tall, portly, bearded figure. David smiled charmingly. He was ingratiating himself with his brothers; after lunch they were going down to the river, and he wanted to go with them.

The bishop, turning his dark Von Glasman eyes alternately upon Igor, the Blond One, and David, said, "Come along, let's get acquainted." Apart from Father Tromokov, whom they much admired and approached with easy familiarity, the boys knew no priests; yet they needed no one to tell them that this was a very special priest, and when he said, "Come," one went. Igor was the first to put down his rake and glanced over at David sternly. He saw it was unnecessary. David, all attention, was reaching for the bishop's outstretched hand.

The midday meal was something to remember. The chrysanthemums in a bright porcelain bowl were the only note of fall on the summery, sunlit table. Hurrying in and out of the kitchen with platters of delicious concoctions, the sturdy-legged serving maids peered under their lashes at his Grace, a welcome but infrequent guest. He seldom came to visit and then rarely lingered, but today he kept them long at the table, making the boys laugh, asking questions. "When I was just a little boy—not almost nine years old like Igor, or even like the Blond One, but more the age of my young friend David—my grandmother took me on a visit to her ancestral home. It was surrounded by thousands of acres of rich black soil—what we called black gold—and there was a cherry orchard. Even now I can remember those red cherries. Nothing since has ever tasted so good."

The bishop was thinking of more than cherries and wheat, however. He remembered a beautiful lady, lips painted red, fingers covered with rings, feet moving lightly to the sounds of a violin and guitar. The dance over, she sank to her knees and with a gentle motion took him in her arms and kissed him.

His Grace did not name the place or mention that his first remembered kiss was from the mouth of a gypsy queen, so he believed no one would guess what he was talking about. But he was wrong; the Blond One placed the black gold, and he knew the best-tasting cherries on earth were on Ronya's land.

282

An idea crept into the bishop's mind which he shrugged away—it seemed too farfetched. But it persisted, and he began to think: Why had he waited so long to pay his condolence call? Why had he called on that particular day? Fate? God's will? The boy was heaven-sent.

"I have been thinking," the bishop said to the Blond One. "I have no son. To whom do I leave my name? I believe you'd make a fine son. Stay the winter in Moscow. By next spring it should be clear if we are suited for each other."

Hearing this, the ordinary bastard might have thought life suddenly beautiful: son to a prince of the church, heir to his wealth. But not the Blond One. He felt his heart beat as though it would burst. He felt sick. He got up and ran from the table, and no one was foolish enough to believe he ran to hide tears of joy. Igor lagged behind for an instant to spit out in fury, "And I thought you were our friend!"

David promptly vanished too. Igor and the Blond One were not going down to the river.

When Katya raised her eyes they were moist, yet there was a radiance about her face. Alexis found that at this moment he loved the Blond One most of Boris' sons.

The bishop rose and took Katya's hand. "Tell your sister that I, the bishop of Moscow, kneel before her and bow my head."

"Your Grace," Katya smiled, "may I send for Georgi?"

"Of course."

The bishop was completely captivated. "I swear," he said as Georgi lay happily cushioned in his arms, his gaze a little elfish, a little bold, "this one spreads light like the sun. May God be his overseer."

In a remarkably short time they were prepared. They took out their stoutest boots and bundled themselves up in as many layers of clothes as they could wear. Igor took bread, cheese, lumps of sugar, apples, and all that was left of a veal roast. On the way out of the kitchen he saw some hard-boiled eggs and a package of raisins and added them to his sack. The Blond One got hold of a jug of cider, a cake of soap, a pack of playing cards, matches, a coffee pot, and fine powdered coffee. He and Igor were partial to a powerful brew. David envied them their short daggers in leather sheaths. "All right," Igor said, "I'll let you have my pocketknife, but be careful, it's sharp." But then David grumbled, "I haven't anything to carry," so the Blond One gave him a handful of gold coins. "Put them in your pockets," he said. His own were full.

They walked along the bank of the Moskva River at a leisurely pace, circled by Satan, the golden retriever. Away from the current of city life, they encountered peasant women with bright kerchiefs under their chins, carrying bundles of wood in their arms. An old man went by dragging a donkey; the donkey dragged a cart full of wood. They met chipmunks scurrying about gathering nuts.

Sucking a blade of grass, Igor tried to sound like Boris: "It'll be a cold winter."

The Blond One mimicked back: "Sure will."

"I guess it was stupid taking David along."

The Blond One grinned. "He'll do all right. He always manages to keep up with us."

David made himself heard. "Why are we running away? It was nice with Tante Katya and Uncle Alexis."

"That priest wants the Blond One," Igor answered.

David looked up at Igor. "Oh! Wait till Mother hears that."

The Blond One was touched. "Want a drink?"

"He'll drink when we drink," Igor said.

David did not want a drink; he wanted to urinate. He fell behind. The same urge overtook Satan. Sharing a tree with Satan, David spotted an old barn at the end of a dirt lane. It would protect them from the night.

Recently abandoned by a tenant farmer who had left the fields to work in a factory, the barn was reasonably clean and a scant hundred paces from a well. Igor sent David to gather dry sticks; soon he was back with a haul of potatoes. "Look what I brought you." Igor simply took the potatoes and nodded, but David laughed happily. "We're having fun."

The boys were famished. Igor and the Blond One ate with intensity and David devoured his food, but Satan, by contrast, ate with marked indifference. Afterward, the sack repacked, the Blond One played his harmonica. After a time, Igor said, "It's getting cold." The boys picked themselves up from the ground and threw handfuls of dirt on the remains of the fire. David had a bed made of hay; Igor and the Blond One stretched out on the board floor.

The floor was damp and cold. Huddled close together, Boris' sons shut their eyes to fear and slept until sunup.

After a breakfast of cheese and cider—Satan had veal, water, and one lump of sugar—they set out again, keeping their ears and eyes open for a gypsy caravan. They had no doubt they would meet one. At this time of year, the gypsies were heading southwest to Tula, Kursk, Kiev, or directly south to Rostov and Baku—and maybe on to Baghdad.

That second day on the road they were careful. The clatter of hoofs, a sudden cloud of dust, and they hid. The sounds they were waiting for were special gypsy sounds—wagon wheels on rutted roads, the yelping of boisterous dogs. The Moscow police had no experience with boys trained in Tartar tactics and gypsy cunning. They hunted out in the open, advancing noisily.

In Kiev, Ronya refused to get upset—not even by Katya's telegram. The children's disappearance had all the marks of a boyish adventure, and Tamara supported her story. They knew the gypsy caravans were leaving the sub-zero north and coming south, and Tamara sent out the word: "Find them and bring them home." All over Russia dirty, swarthy men driving painted wagons and gaudily dressed women tramping along in the dust were keeping a lookout for three little boys and a retriever.

Boris was far from complacent. He was already angry with Ronya for sending the Blond One to Katya and amazed at her lack of concern. For the moment he agreed to heed her heart and not act on his fear that the boys had been kidnapped, but still he had made sure that he in Kiev, Alexis in Moscow, and Paul, alerted in St. Petersburg, had large amounts of hard currency ready.

The more Katya thought, the more certain she felt that it was Igor who had got it into his head to run away and that the Blond One had been drawn into the venture by his attachment to Igor. Surprisingly, she felt no alarm over David. Remembering how years ago his mother had struggled free from a nursemaid and embarked with Tamara on a similar feat, she could imagine him unaware of danger, in love with the whole romantic undertaking. Immersed in Georgi, she wished the adventurers godspeed.

Sharp ears. A traveling caravan. The boys roused David from sleep and crept through the tall brown grass. Without hesitation, they ran toward the wagons waving. The high-wheeled wagons slowed to a stop. It was the third day of their flight.

"Good timing, my lads," said the driver, smiling with such amusement that his eyes almost disappeared between his heavy brows and high cheekbones. "About seven miles back we were stopped by the police and searched." He waved a piece of paper. "Our clearance." His wife, an understanding, comfortable woman, pressed on them hot red peppers, cold fried meat, stale bread smeared with melted fat, and milk. The boys ate and drank greedily, sharing everything with Satan.

Night fell early. The three boys and the dog slept together under a feather bed that smelled of urine.

For the next few days the caravan did not linger over campfires: With two tow-headed children along, the gypsies felt insecure. When they neared a town or village they skirted it, avoiding the local constabulary who were savagely hostile to gypsies, sure that they kidnapped blond children and used them obscenely. But gradually the mood of caution relaxed, and they traveled more leisurely, camping within village boundaries, where they could steal chickens and eggs, buy milk, beer, and razors, tell fortunes, mend harnesses, and sell charms.

To David this was life as it was meant to be lived. The gypsies, generally indulgent with the very young, spoiled him completely. They saw that he had strength and courage and were deeply impressed that he fought with the older boys, asking no quarter, and stayed aloof from the women, who were all taken with his pale blue eyes and light hair. It was obvious that the Blond One, too, had strength and courage. He could straddle a frisky stallion, handle a team of horses, raid a chicken coop (they never suspected he left gold coins for the eggs he took). They admired him—a strong, courageous, intelligent, capable boy, who looked them in the face, his eyes never wavering; but his cool dignity, his apartness, made them uncomfortable, and they never warmed to him.

But they were smitten with Igor—a *Gajo* boy who spoke Romani fluently, whose pedigreed pet answered to Rom commands. Igor could charm the birds out of the trees. He was the favorite of the toothless old crone who rocked all day on her haunches, and at the same time he was much respected by the men for the way he could leap over a fence and steal a chicken—and on a horse it was easy to see whose son he was.

Slowly the Blond One realized that something was happening, something of great importance. A rival had come into his life, a girl, small and dark, wise beyond her eleven years, with fire in her bold eyes and little gold rings in the lobes of her ears. Intrigued with Igor— his fair skin, his red-brown hair, his enchanting dimple—she schemed to be near him. Day after day she followed them everywhere, even into the woods; that Igor let her astonished him.

Igor liked the girl. She was pretty. However, because the Blond One brought it up, he told her to stop tagging him; the girl said, "I like you. Your eyes are the same color as mine." Igor shifted his feet and grinned.

The Blond One did not pursue the matter further, nor did he sulk. He tried to assure himself that Igor was entitled to friends, even friends who were girls, even a girl who glared at him and who took pleasure in coming between him and Igor. But he felt the grasp of shame as he watched her brush her coltish body against Igor and then move away, her eyes bright. It brought to mind those tainted times when, in the room next to Tamara's, he heard the big bed creak. The Blond One decided it was hard to like girls. They behaved in a bad way.

A mere six hours outside Kiev, the caravan spread out in a wide circle, lit the campfires, and brought out from the covered vans huge iron caldrons. The boys were given to understand that the ensuing feast was to honor them.

A cold wind was blowing. The married women, huddled in shawls, small children clinging to their skirts, took leave of their men and went inside the wagons. The men, warm with drink, ignored the cold and the dark clouds that drifted overhead. Faces flushed with excitement, they rubbed dust-filled, smoke-stung eyes and, singling out pretty girls, pulled them inside the circle of stamping feet and swinging arms.

The pounding of horses' hooves put an abrupt end to the merrymaking. In the last village through which they had passed, the peasants had reported seeing blond boys with the gypsies. The police, always on the lookout for bribes or for a bit of vicious sport, had taken to their mounts and galloped into the camp.

The men were silent. The women, pale and quivering, came out of the wagons. David pulled away from a restraining hand and ran to be with Igor and the Blond One. The older children crowded around, prodding them, "Hurry, tell them who you are." Igor's girlfriend pinched him. "Give them your brother's gold," she begged. "Make them go away."

The policeman jumped from their saddles. One of the men identified himself and greeted them politely, explaining, "This was a feast of parting. We are escorting them to their parents."

He was pushed aside. "Shut your ugly mouth, you swine," said a policeman. The Blond One felt ashamed when the gypsy replied, "Yes, sir. As you say, sir," ducking his head conciliatingly. Igor, too, was distressed at the gypsies' impotence. Until now he had admired the gypsy men for their many skills, but he knew that if this policeman had spoken so to his mother she'd have taken her whip to him. As for Tamara—lifting his chin proudly—an unconscious gesture that made him the image of Ronya—he took a step forward. So did the Blond One. So did David. "I am Igor von Glasman Pirov, sir," he said in a firm voice. "Our friends are good people, not swine."

A murmur of agreement ran around the circle. "Quiet," shouted the policeman. He turned on Igor menacingly, but the boys stood their ground, all three with something of their father's strong arrogant look.

Only that afternoon the policeman had heard something about the Pirovs, he could not remember exactly what. Confound those damn peasants!—he and his men riding all over the place—and three young pups making him look an ass.

"All right, gypsy scum," he barked, "get out of here."

The gypsies broke camp in haste and rode through the night as if pursued by wolves.

At daybreak—in rags, windburned, dirty, hair unkempt, faded kerchiefs knotted around their throats—the boys were home. The Blond One was passionately happy to be back.

31

Paul Zotov was a brilliant police officer, which provided him with a great deal of gratification. Paul had a tolerant wife, and until it occurred to him that she was colorless and dull, he was reasonably satisfied with her. His dissatisfaction was due, in large part, to Ronya. Until he shifted his professional loyalty to her, he was in the habit of thinking of her in impersonal terms; she was David's daughter: That was enough. He did not know when he first began to think of his arm around her waist, his lips on hers, her eyes bright with anticipation. When he did discover how much she was in his thoughts, he told himself to stop being stupid.

Initially, Paul had no plans to alter the relationship that existed between himself and Ronya. When they met (true, it was more often now that he found new excuses to justify his visits), he gave no sign of the pure pleasure he took just in being near her. Even when Boris caught her in his arms and put an end to conversation, he kept his eyes from betraying his raging jealousy. So no one had reason to worry. Ronya felt safe with Paul; he was like an older brother. And Boris, who had eyes in the back of his head where Ronya was concerned, saw no rival, no challenge, in Paul.

But if anyone had kept close watch, he would have noticed several things. Boris was a man of action; Paul provided Ronya with ideas. Boris paid no attention to Ronya's business affairs; Paul spent time— much time—in sharpening her business acumen. Boris lacked a penetrating interest in politics; Paul intensified his effort to educate Ronya politically. Boris ignored the Blond One; Paul treated him with special deference. Boris was rough on Igor. Igor was his favorite, and he wanted him to outdo much older boys in prowess and daring. By virtue of his years in England, Paul was exceptionally well educated and also exceptionally well acquainted with the West. He emphasized intellect and gave Igor books.

Time went on, yet nothing warned Ronya. When Paul visited Kiev
—his visits always brief—Father Tromokov and the banker Von
Kaufman would come to listen to Paul, just as they used to listen to
David von Glasman, for Paul knew what was going on beneath the
surface of events. He knew the professional terrorists, he knew the
leading revolutionary conspirators, when they quarreled, where they
hid. He knew the moving forces among the reactionaries and their
plans. He knew of Russia's expansionist tendencies. He knew where
the action was. Very useful information; very profitable, too.

Just about the time that Paul became conscious of his cold-blooded
desire for Boris' death, he decided to get rid of his wife. That, however,
presented difficulties. The sudden appearance of Ladislaus in St. Petersburg showed him the way. Intuitively aware that some complex
evil had taken hold of Paul, while remaining quite ignorant of the reason, Ladislaus directed Paul's thinking toward America, describing
the staggering opportunities in the New World. "And consider this,"
Ladislaus said, "in some ways it is a lax society. No one gives a damn
about a man's background. What counts is the man himself. The
motto seems to be 'Live and let live.' "

Paul started making plans. His intentions made Tamara's unashamed obsession with Boris seem wholesome. But fate intervened.

One evening, finding himself bored, Paul went to watch the gambling at his favorite casino, where long-limbed girl croupiers in revealing dresses were employed. He stood at one of the tables, his eyes on a
quite beautiful young woman with reddish hair whose face showed
that she was worried—so worried that she looked toward Paul with an
urgency that seemed to say, "Help me."

He drifted around the table and stopped casually at her chair.

"How much have you lost?"

"I've lost count."

"Can you afford it?"

"My husband will be angry," she answered in French. "He made
me promise not to come here."

"Do you often break your promises?"

She smiled. "Only to my husband."

"Where is your husband?"

"He has a grown son who lives in a monastery. He has gone there to
spend the night."

"I'll attend to your losses."

She went with him. When they climbed down from his carriage, he
knew her name was Anna and that her elderly aristocratic husband
was Grand Duke Gennady Dryayeva, the most vicious reactionary in
Russia, a man who had sworn to put a rope around the throat of all
who hungered for equality and freedom.

When Paul awoke, he had a mistress. At first, he told himself she scarcely counted. Until his plans took shape and arrangements for his future were made, it was enjoyable to bring her into the bed that was formerly his mother's. They met frequently, and Anna served to deaden the torment of his unfulfilled desire for Ronya. Still it was only a matter of weeks before he was beginning to consider their affair more of a nuisance than a convenience. Anna was a demanding mistress and a reckless gambler and, in spite of being a grand duchess with a splendid regal carriage, she was somewhat common. However, unlike his previous paramours, Anna was hard to send packing. Assessing the risks, Paul felt slightly alarmed.

Some days later, chance again directed Paul's life. On a particularly mild May afternoon, he left his office about two. He strolled down the left bank of the Neva, passing bare-armed buxom girls in embroidered dresses, splendid dusky-skinned Uzbekis from the Muslim East, spirited Georgian horsemen with daggers thrust into sheaths at their sides, Ukrainians in striking silk tunics. It was White Night Festival time. Coming into the Palace Square, he ran into Alexis.

"Ah," said Alexis, waving four tickets to the evening performance of the Imperial Ballet. "Just the man I'm looking for. Is your wife still in retreat?"

Paul's wife was a few miles away, entrenched in solid comfort in a pale pink rococo house with a formal garden and an ornamented gate.

"She'll be away a long time. Her true life is the church."

"Ronya arrives within the hour. It would be rather a shame for her to go to the ballet and to the ball unescorted."

Paul gave Alexis a lingering glance. "Ronya wrote that Boris accompanies her this visit. What happened?"

Alexis laughed. "A typical Boris excuse. A prize mare is about to foal."

"That's my good fortune."

"It's settled then."

Lost in anticipation, Paul nodded.

As it happened, Paul did not see the ballet.

"I'm sorry, I was delayed," he said, bowing over Ronya's hand outside the Mayinsky Theater after the ballet. "An unexpected bit of official business."

Anna's arrival early in the evening just as he was leaving for the Mayinsky had certainly been unexpected but, rather than risk tears and a scene, he had taken her to bed. Afterward, he had said, "I doubt very much I'll be free the next few days. Should anything change, I'll contact you." He carried no trace of her perfume to Ronya.

At the ball Katya, sumptuous in the glide of ice blue satin, ornamented with a dazzling jeweled belt, and Ronya, slim, radiant, and infinitely feminine in romantic sea mist green chiffon that sprang from her tiny waist to a full flowing skirt, were breathtakingly beautiful. Alexis behaved as he normally did—madly proud of the Von Glasman girls. Paul, ruggedly good-looking, freshly bathed, and expensively dressed, actually was in the grip of intense emotion, but he betrayed none of his feelings.

After the ball, Katya and Alexis retired to their baroque palace, but Paul and Ronya went for a ride. Her Oriental shawl draped lightly over her shoulders, Ronya came home in the early dawn; on the way they had passed peasant wagons loaded with vegetables, fruits, and flowers—tasseled donkeys weighted with kegs of hard cider. Every day was market day during the time of the festival.

It was two nights later, when Paul was leaving a restaurant with Katya, Alexis, and Ronya, that he next saw Anna, accompanied— most unusual for her—by her husband. They all met in the doorway; it was impossible to avoid the encounter. The effect on Anna was quite startling. Never one to hide her feelings, she fastened her nearsighted eyes on Ronya and said, "It's always interesting to see how and with whom one's friend spends his time."

Alexis immediately drew Ronya within the circle of his arm and said, smiling at Anna, "I am delighted, my dear, that you are jealous."

Only the grand duke was embarrassed.

Despite her confusion, Katya spoke easily, "You both remember my sister, Ronya Pirov."

Anna's blue eyes continued their myopic stare.

Ronya accepted the duke's bow with a nod and ignored Anna's rudeness.

"And now," Alexis said, "may I present Captain Paul Zotov—and then Katya and I must be on our way."

"Your wife and I know each other," Paul said, extending his hand. "We meet occasionally at the casino and spend a moment commiserating together about our losses." For a second, Paul was afraid that the grand duke would deny him his hand, but the duke extended a lean, impersonal hand and said in a tone full of meaning, "Captain, I am overcome by my wife's talent for acquiring comrades. Shall we go somewhere and get acquainted?"

Anna's eyes began to shine. "Let's take a boat to the Lighthouse Cabaret. They have the most exciting dance band there."

As they went down the three stone steps to the sidewalk, Paul touched Katya's elbow and led her aside. "Come with us," he urged.

"Not for the world," Katya whispered. "I despise those two."

They found other passengers inside the water taxi. Pressed tightly against the two women, Paul was torn between a desire to get away from Anna and a longing to stay close to Ronya, aware of her body and her scent. The grand duke was staring at the river; but his thoughts were not on the broken shimmer of reflected light and the little waves rippling away from the boat; he was visualizing Ronya's endless fields of yellow gold and seeing the dim outline of a possibility take shape. . . .

Patience and planning. The idea was there; the details could be arranged.

Half an hour later, they rounded a bend in the river and came to the Lighthouse Cabaret. It was still as light as day.

The decor was romantic, the music fast and melodious, and though the guests were varied indeed, their party met many friends and Anna was immediately seized by carousing dancing partners and drawn into the hilarious throng. The grand duke sipped his champagne at the table and proclaimed his disdain for the energetic one-step. However, when Paul and Anna waltzed, they had his fixed regard. In a rare instant of compassion, Paul pitied him his torment and tried to guide a protesting Anna back to the table. Luckily the musicians chose this particular moment for a brief pause and left the stage to a vocalist who sang folk ballads to the accompaniment of guitars. The singer was well received and would have continued indefinitely but for the musicians' return.

Paul, thinking it probable that Anna would again lay claim to him, turned to Ronya. "Shall we dance?"

"Let's make it the last one."

Anna opened her mouth to protest, but Paul was already on his feet. The grand duke took note of his wife's agitation.

The dance started in slow motion to slow music, and then all at once broke into the gay and sensuous rhythm of the *kazatzkale*.

Ronya was a natural dancer and not averse to showing to advantage in front of Anna; she whirled on her toes, hardly touching the floor at all.

Swinging her high, Paul laughed, "You're a marvel, Ronya. Truly a marvel."

The grand duke leaned back in his chair, his eyes moving from the dancers to his wife. Two spots of color high on her cheekbones glared from the dead white of her face. Without taking her gaze from Paul, she groped for her champagne glass and drained it at a draft. The grand duke picked up his own glass and raised it to her in a silent toast.

Paul and Ronya parted from the Drayayevas on the pier and walked the short distance home. Standing on the steps waiting for the porter to open the door, Paul fell silent, his arms aching to embrace her. It hurt him that she was not aware of his love; still, he dared not give her the slightest sign.

"Good-night, Paul."

Paul gazed straight into her face. "I may have some important information for you tomorrow. Will you come to the house for tea? Or would you rather—"

"I'm dying to see the house—I never have, you know."

For Paul the day's wait was a long one.

Ronya arrived a little after five, sumptuous in a dress of Chinese yellow, emerald earrings, a long emerald-green cape bordered in lynx, and a matching lynx hat. She looked around the hall and smiled. "I like it already."

Paul answered her smile. "Tour or tea? The samovar is bubbling."

"Tour."

When they had gone over the house and were settled in the study, Ronya glanced up, head tilted like a ballerina, and asked in a low voice, "What about your wife, Paul?" Noting his hesitation, she added, "Boris and I have discussed her. He says that I am not to intrude into your personal life."

By way of answer, Paul gave a noncommittal smile and got up to ring for the housekeeper and order tea and cakes.

Then he started to speak, picking his words carefully.

"Ronya, may I ask: Suppose—and this is hypothetical—" Paul placed a cigarette between his lips and took his time lighting it, "suppose Boris has a house where he acts . . . pretty much as he wishes. What would you do about it? Would you be very upset?"

That gave Ronya a jolt. "I know," she said, no longer friendly, "all about Boris' house, what use he makes of it, to whom he lends it. I know, too, that if I were to ask it of him, he'd lock the damn house and throw away the key."

Paul winced: His first tactical error. As his mind calculated the damage, he nodded and said with certainty, "I believe that." He paused, stared hard at her, and added, "What I don't know is why you allow it to go on? It makes me wonder if perhaps you have long-range plans that—" Deliberately, he paused again, "I hesitate to say more."

Ronya looked as if she wished she had her whip. Her voice now frankly raised in anger, she said, "I have no plans, long-range or otherwise, that do not include my husband."

Paul was clever enough to laugh. "Good for you! I admire a loyal wife."

Ronya frowned. Then her face crinkled into a smile. "I'm sorry, Paul, I guess I'm sensitive. That loathsome house is a painful subject."

293

He nodded understandingly, and Ronya persuaded herself that everything was right between them.

Paul smiled. "Don't worry, Ronya, I don't spy on Boris. He brought me there—a poker game that went on until morning."

"No other diversion?" she asked, a little too quickly.

"No. Unless you call supper a diversion. It was brought in from a restaurant around eleven."

"You won't tell Boris I know about the house, will you?"

Giving her a curious look, he said, "I won't tell."

Ronya drew a deep breath. She asked solemnly, "Do you have any information for me?"

"No, my informant didn't come today. I don't know why. Maybe tomorrow." Paul passed a hand over his face. As his fingers touched his lips, he said, "About my wife—"

She raised her eyes.

"My marriage is a legal fact, and that's all it is. I haven't touched her in years."

She felt her face burning.

Watching the blushes flood her cheeks, Paul went on doggedly, "I want you to hear this, Ronya. I committed myself, at a young age, for the wrong reason: I wanted someone the absolute opposite of my mother. And I wanted my own family—at least, I thought I did. For years I was neither happy nor unhappy. Now I have found the woman I want. I mean to marry her."

Ronya was terribly disappointed in him, but he was her good friend and her heart went out to him. "Forgive me, Paul," she said, "but I must say it. How long do you think you'll keep the duchess before she leaves you for some other man? Besides, think of the difficulties. You'll have to leave Russia."

Paul gaped at her in soundless astonishment. Anna!

Ronya's long eyes widened. "Not Anna?"

All the calculation in his nature told Paul he was making a mistake, but he could not stop himself. "Ronya—" he said, his voice hoarse, "Ronya, the woman I love is warm—her face is exquisite, endlessly expressive—she's used to being adored, used to being a beauty, she accepts it as naturally as a butterfly accepts its wings. But there's more to her than physical beauty—"

"Paul—" Ronya got up in dismay, her mind a jumble of appalled exclamations: *It can't be!—I'm a little sister to him!—always have been!*

Seeing the damage he had done, Paul got a grip on himself and forced his body to relax and his face to sketch a reassuringly unimpassioned smile. "I'm sorry, Ronya," he said in his usual cool voice, "I shouldn't burden you with all this."

294

Ronya looked down at him uncertainly. Calmed by his apparent ease, persuaded that her fleeting thought was very much in error, once more comfortable, she said, "Please, Paul, give yourself time to think."

"Yes. I'll bide my time. I must."

"And I must run."

"Will I see you tomorrow?"

"No—there's a morning train, and I'll be on it. Boris grumbled at this trip and tried to argue me out of it, but I promised Katya I'd bring Georgi, and I didn't want to disappoint her."

Paul hid his disappointment. "You'll hear from me in Kiev."

He went with her to the street to find a droshky, which was hard to find during busy hours. It seemed that they were going to be lucky. There was a droshky pulling up at Paul's door. Anna flew out. She stopped and gaped at Ronya. "You, again!"

At that moment, Ronya saw not the Grand Duchess Anna but the woman—the many kinds of women—who shared a bed with Boris, and Anna became the enemy.

"Yes, I." Deliberately she smiled up at Paul, stood on tiptoe and kissed him, pressing her lips firmly on his. "Good-bye, darling. I had a lovely afternoon." With a swish of her cape, she got into the droshky.

Anna forgotten, Paul stared after her; though the kiss was a lie, it warmed him like the sun. Moments later, he found his voice and it was chilled.

"Go home, Anna."

"Paul, don't let that Jewess come between us."

He started for the door.

Anna was beside him immediately. "Push me out of your life, Paul, and I'll tell my husband you corrupted me."

Paul walked through the open door without looking at her, without answering her. He went back into the study and locked the door.

Anna abandoned herself to screaming without restraint. Finally, the housekeeper persuaded her to leave.

It has been said that a man in Paul's profession must be a little in love with death. Paul flirted with death, but he was in love with life, and it was alertness and experience that kept him alive.

When Anna left her husband's ancestral palace the next day at noon, Paul was following her. Within fifteen minutes he knew for certain that two officers of the secret police were also trailing her. Since when—today, yesterday, last week?—that was the question. Paul's astute mind leaped to a conclusion. Ronya was the duke's target. Through her he'd gain his revenge. A cunning smile twisted Paul's face, he felt exhilarated. He had long been tired of his life in St. Petersburg, ready for a new life in the New World. This situation provided him with the impetus he needed to jump the hurdle.

Shortly after two o'clock Anna entered the house Ronya had given him, whereupon one policeman settled himself against a fence on the opposite side of the street, his eyes fixed on the front entrance, while the other watched the rear. Walking away unobtrusively, Paul wondered how long Anna would wait. He made sure he was not being followed and then went to his official residence. Though he had not set foot in the house for some time, his reappearance created no stir. His wife Helena greeted him in a mild, unsurprised way, just as though he had left for work that morning like any ordinary husband. Her maiden sister, a permanent guest, was cordial.

When he called Helena into the bedroom, his suitcase was packed and his pockets bulky with the money he had always kept ready for an emergency. "Listen," he told her, "I am going to Switzerland. The journey there is safe, my business there dangerous. If I'm not back in thirty days, know yourself to be a widow, free to remarry or do anything you please. I've made ample provision for you. You'll never go hungry."

For a second Helena wondered why Paul should want her to think him dead, but she never asked him for explanations, simply assuming that the bureau wanted word to get about that Paul was deceased.

She let his words slide from her mind. "Of course, you'll come back," she said, blinking her faded eyes.

Paul smiled sardonically. "Is that all you have to say?"

Helena realized that wifely solicitude was required. She groped for suitable words. "Take a muffler. It can be very chilly this time of year."

He turned away, his face expressionless. "I'll send for my suitcase."

Helena accompanied him as Paul got on his hat and coat, opened the door an inch or two, then closed it. For the first time he felt it would be wrong merely to walk out of the house as though he were a stranger.

I once cared about this woman, he reflected, his eyes traveling over the untidy mousy hair, the drooping shoulders, the dim dowdy clothes that had never looked fresh and bright even when new. With genuine curiosity he asked, "Have you found it lonely being married to me?"

"Not at all," she replied, undisturbed. "I've had an agreeable life. In some ways, you've been the perfect husband."

"Really? How?"

Helena allowed herself a moment to consider carefully. When she spoke, it was with total concentration. "You never pushed me into things. You've been generous—overgenerous to my family, especially to Papa. And"—Helena gave him a strangely engaging smile; Paul wondered why he had never seen that smile before—"when I felt compelled to visit the young holy man, the teacher, the new saint Rasputin, in his retreat and ask for guidance, you let me go, even though you found his fervor repulsive and his unwashed person disgusting. I'll always remember that, Paul, and be grateful."

Helena's face seemed to have become younger, softer, more alive. Her cheeks were faintly flushed. Perplexed, Paul wrinkled his brow and said, "Tell me, when you went to see Rasputin, was he in the Khlysty?"

Her eyes kindled and she nodded.

All at once it dawned on him. Staring at her disbelievingly, he cried, "God Almighty—with that slimy fraud!—with that dirty hypocrite!—you climaxed your devotion!"

Unashamed, Helena said, "I did it for God."

There was a moment of silence, then Paul wrenched at the door handle and ran from the house.

Neither of them had made any mention of their two daughters, the elder a novitiate in a closed order, the younger in school abroad.

Paul sat in a hired carriage thinking of Helena, frigid, prudish, unobtrusive, soft-sounding Helena, and the image in his mind's eye now was obscene and hateful—cuckolded by the likes of Rasputin— the swine—in the name of Jesus! He drew a deep, shuddering sigh.

"I'm well rid of her," he muttered.

By the time he had reached the railroad station and paid off the driver, he was again completely indifferent to Helena, his mind full upon himself. He bought a one-way ticket to Harbin, Manchuria—a common escape route—on the first available train, which left from Moscow on Thursday. This was Saturday. In a few hours half a dozen agents would start asking questions at the station, and they would scrutinize every passer-by until the train pulled out for Harbin. This was routine.

To kill an hour Paul walked aimlessly about the streets, then went into an ordinary restaurant, accepted a quiet corner table, and ordered a full meal starting with hot soup and ending with a baked apple. He ate like a man without pain or grievance. Finished, he lit a cigarette, then, shoulders squared, he left the restaurant. The eyes of the well-tipped waiter followed him out of the door. The waiter, a burdened man, envied the stride of a marvelously self-satisfied man.

Paul's next stop was beneath a big tree on a slight incline overlooking an unostentatious church constructed on piles. Alongside the church, also built on piles, stood two houses, which belonged to the church. To the rear of the second, almost completely surrounded by trees, was a third house. It was not easy to see, not easy to find. The front entrance was padlocked and the windows heavily curtained and barricaded with black iron grilles. The back entrance, down a short but steep flight of steps into an alley, was especially hard to find. The risk of being seen entering the house, particularly at night, was very slight; and indeed, not one of its patrons would ever dream of going there except at night. The talk in the street was that a rich eccentric inhabited the sinister-looking house, but since he bothered no one and took excellent care of the grounds, no one bothered him. Even the children avoided coming too near. In fact, the house was a luxurious homosexual bordello where the rich and noble caroused with soft-eyed young boys.

Paul considered the house a long time. It was a good hideout, but everyone knew of it, including the two men assigned to follow Anna. Still, this might not matter, since the house was protected by such influential persons that no policeman ever came here to apprehend a man. He had learned this a long time ago when assigned to work with the intelligence of a friendly foreign power. The double agent he was after stayed there for weeks and got away in the end because it was not expedient to expose the great men who gave him sanctuary.

Paul forced himself to abandon his station under the tree. It was getting late. He walked slowly to the house and, though he stopped at the door, turned, and then walked away in the direction of the Admiralty; his male pride would not let him pretend he belonged there. Later, he found a droshky driver he had known a long time and who, for a fat wage, had worked for him before. The driver was only too happy to believe that Paul was engaged in an official investigation and needed an inconspicuous carriage he could drive himself. The man took his money and turned over the reins to Paul. As always, it was understood that the fee included the price of silence.

Peering ahead into the fog, Paul crossed three islands connected by bridges and came to a waterfront slum, which like the rest of St. Petersburg was laced with canals. The crooked cobblestone alleys were populated by sailors, criminals, drug addicts, drunks, merchant seamen, fishermen, pimps, street vendors, beggars, prostitutes eager for business, the nefarious and the neglected of many nations—Russians, Germans, Danes, Swedes, Finns, Poles, Chinese. The whole district was an obscenity.

In a depressing dungeon-like café with upstairs accommodations, Paul ordered a bottle and waited. His patience was rewarded. The gypsy owner, who called herself Madam Titiana, had reason to be grateful to him—he had once saved her life.

"My esteemed cousin," said the big-rumped lump of a woman, "there are two reasons that bring you here. An arrest or a purchase. With the second, I prosper."

298

"I need a room."

They climbed the rickety stairs. At the far end of the narrow hall, she produced a key and unlocked a door. The room was ugly, dank, poorly furnished, but there was an unhoped-for blessing—it was clean. Paul sat down on the bed. Madam Titiana lowered herself onto the single chair.

"All right," she said, "get it off your chest. I owe you a debt."

"I'm on the run."

The woman moved her weight and the chair creaked. "Did you eat?"

Paul laughed aloud. Always with women—be it Ronya or this gross, sin-soaked seller of bad liquor and damaged baggage—the lavish outpouring of the maternal instinct: "Eat something, you'll feel better."

To please her, he said, "I could use a bite."

She came back with a tray bearing meat spread on black bread, sliced cucumbers sprinkled with parsley, and a bottle of good chilled champagne. Careful not to drop a single crumb, she ate with him. After finishing her share and all that Paul left and washing it down with champagne, she said, "Talk. The money drawer is unwatched."

"I need space on a merchant ship."

"Where to?"

"Anywhere."

"You're in luck."

"Good. Can you get a message to Kiev?"

"Sure, write it out."

Paul shook his head. "This one goes committed to memory. Whom can you trust?"

"No one."

"Then go yourself."

Madam Titiana concentrated so hard that her eyes seemed to disappear completely into folds of fat. Gradually they opened and she asked, "What's it worth?"

Paul grinned. "Half the asking price."

The fat woman mopped her face with her sleeve. "Cousin, you're holding my attention."

Paul briefed her on the situation.

Their eyes met: his intelligent and at the moment unguarded and completely honest; hers small, sharp, and greedy.

"Let me get this straight. You want me to go to Boris Pirov and tell him that his wife came to see you alone, and that when she left—"

"Yes, I want Boris to know everything there is to know beforehand. It's not compromising for me, it's not compromising for Ronya. This way there won't be any surprises, he'll know what he's up against when he has to deal with the grand duke."

Madam Titiana peered at Paul and frowned. "Cousin, how old are you?"

Paul hesitated a moment. "Thirty-eight."

"Too young to die."

"So you know Boris."

"Who doesn't? And I figure I ain't helping you any by telling him you kissed his wife." She paused deliberately, "No, it was the other way around. She kissed you."

Paul grinned. "I'll be out of the Gulf of Finland and in the Baltic Sea."

Again her eyes narrowed. She stuck a fingernail between two yellow teeth and picked at a fragment of meat. She was thinking about his house. She wanted it, but she knew that was foolish. It would connect her with Paul, and anyway it would probably be confiscated—that was the way the crown did business.

"Well?"

She sucked her finger once. "I'll do it. I've always wanted to see that gypsy camp. But there's an easier way out. A thousand rubles to a friend of mine puts the grand duke in the cemetery."

Paul smiled. "No. That's too good for his next-of-kin."

Madam Titiana gave his answer a moment's consideration. "Well, you're first fiddler, you call the tune." She heaved herself to her feet. "You'd better get some sleep. I'll call you in a few hours."

"A few more things." He gave her the name of a street and a number. "There's an unattended droshky outside. See that it gets to its owner tonight. And give this message to Ronya. Tell Tamara to give it to Ronya if you don't see Ronya, but tell it to no one else. Tell her I've had enough of bluff and pretense. Tell her that each step away from Europe is one step closer to fate, and afraid or not we will all have to face it."

Her little eyes stared unwinking as she memorized the words.

"You know, Paul, something has been ticking," she tapped her head, "up here. Now it comes to me. You and Boris Pirov are a lot alike."

"Really?"

"Yes. You don't approach him in fire, but you catch a woman's eyes. You're not as honest, but you can be trusted. Not his toughness, not his charm—but tough and charming enough. Smart? I figure you're smarter. Yes, I can imagine his woman liking you."

"Thanks."

His tone made her feel she had said the wrong thing. Her eyes lingered upon his face a moment more, then she was on her way.

Paul stretched out fully dressed. Accustomed to excitement all of his life, he went straight to sleep.

300

Aside from barges and yachts in the harbor, there were about twenty ships moored at the harbor piers—schooners, freighters, tankers, passenger liners.

One small Danish freighter of about five thousand tons was ready to sail—loaded with smoked fish in barrels, caviar, and vodka—Southampton her first port of call. Her captain, also her owner, wasted no time in hurrying to Madam Titiana, once he got her summons. He heard her through in silence. "It will cost more than you're offering."

"Fine," said Madam Titiana, "name your price. I can afford to be generous, it costs me nothing."

"Will he be needing papers? Clothes?"

"Yeah. And he's a smart dresser."

"That'll cost more."

"You needn't worry about that either."

"Good. Let's have a look at him." The captain waved her ahead and waited at the top of the stairs while she went to get Paul, who emerged from his room neat and spruce, as though ready for a day's work behind an office desk.

Titiana introduced them. Paul was immediately aware that the madam and the captain were colleagues in skulduggery and smiled inwardly.

When the greetings were over, the captain's intelligent glance rested on Paul, but not in a questioning manner. "Let's go, if we're to get a good start."

They walked at a steady pace.

"Here she is," said the captain, pointing up at the ship.

The captain conducted Paul to an outside cabin furnished with a clean bed, a lantern, a bowl and pitcher on a marble-topped washstand, a built-in closet, and two wooden chairs and invited him to breakfast in half an hour.

Left alone, Paul sat down on the bed and stared at the bare scrubbed floor. He had been planning this move for some time, ever since he had become obsessed with Ronya, sure that all the ugliness in Russia would one day turn inexorably into danger; that Ronya, whose love of life was stronger than the bonds that held her to Kiev, would run to where friends and safety beckoned, and Paul would be ready to receive her. In America he would bend all his energies and all his intelligence to becoming rich, so that when the time came, when her world crumbled, he would be able to give her the moon and the stars. He would have her in the end; it was inevitable.

In the bleak dawn, Paul Zotov disappeared from Russia without a backward glance. They were way out to sea before the fog lifted.

32

It was Madam Titiana's fault that Boris and Tamara, ignorant of his escape, went to so much trouble to save Paul. After he sailed, the madam eyed her establishment and sighed heavily. Who could take her place?

"I don't know, I don't know," she said to herself for nearly a week, but then she thought of Yevgenia, once one of her girls, now retired. It took her two days to find Yevgenia's address. Yevgenia was not sure she wanted to preside over Titiana's café—she kept house for a widower who was still full of bounce and liked it—but finally, for old time's sake, she agreed to take over the café while Titiana was away.

Meanwhile in Kiev, Mischuk and Krasmikov had both been dragged into the affair. Forty-eight hours after Paul's escape, Mischuk called on the Pirovs. He had sent word that he wanted to talk to them privately about a matter of some importance, and Boris, forewarned by this unusual message, had cautioned Ronya to let him deal with Mischuk.

When the policeman came into the library that night, they could see that beneath his official manner he was ill at ease.

"Dry?" Boris asked, waving Mischuk to a chair.

Mischuk nodded, and Boris gave him a drink before rejoining Ronya on the sofa.

Mischuk took a long drink and licked his lips. They still felt dry, his hands moist. He lifted his head and looked straight at Boris. "It's against all my principles as a policeman, and for me most unprecedented—but I've decided to share a state secret with you. It's about Paul. The charge will be a crime against the crown."

Ronya bit back an exclamation.

Boris' mouth went hard. "What crime?"

"Dealings with a foreign power, marketing state papers, disclosing military intelligence, stealing files, accepting bribes—it's not difficult to think one up. They all lead to the barren wasteland of eternal ice."

Boris eyed Mischuk with raised brows. "A frame?"

"Yes. I smell it."

"Since when does the secret police work through civil authority? And why a Kievan policeman?"

This was the moment Mischuk was dreading. Avoiding Ronya's eyes, he mumbled through stiff lips. "Ronya."

"Go on, I'm listening," Boris said.

"I'm involved because Ronya was seen entering a house in St. Petersburg that was being watched. A search revealed that the house, now Paul's, formerly belonged to Ronya." He stirred uncomfortably. "My orders are: 'Find out why the Jewess, known as Ronya von Glasman Pirov, has given a mansion to an intelligence officer in the Tzar's employ.'"

Ronya had become very still.

Slowly, Boris lit a cigarette. "Who says it was a present?"

"I suggested that, but they said, 'Where does a policeman get that kind of money?' I said maybe he's from a rich family, and I was told, 'Find out.' But the worst thing is what they said at the end. I'm sorry, Ronya"—Mischuk looked directly at her for the first time—"but it's better that I tell you. They said, 'What remains to be decided is the reason for Ronya von Glasman Pirov's visit to Captain Paul Zotov. Better that she be an adulteress than a traitor.'"

Boris shot a quick, silencing look at Ronya, instinctively sure that it was best not to reveal why Ronya met with Paul, not to tell of the secret information sent, the warnings made, the bribes offered, the pogroms averted. Not even Mischuk must know. Ronya must be free of the smallest political connection with Paul. As for the other charge, he would take care of that personally. At the very thought his eyes narrowed, his nostrils flared, and his lips tightened in a savage grin. Now Boris looked more as Mischuk expected him to look and, in a strange way, it comforted him, made things seem more natural.

Boris spoke again. "The sharing of one secret deserves another."

Mischuk held up his hand. "I may be obliged to pass on anything you divulge."

"Agreed." Boris swallowed the rest of his drink. "Paul is Tamara's brother. The house, ostensibly their mother's, was in fact my father-in-law's, but he meant it to be Rifka's and Ronya inherited the house by an oversight. That error she corrected by transferring the property to Paul, its rightful owner."

Well, well, thought Mischuk. *Her brother. Closer, much closer than I suspected. That makes him Ronya's cousin. So that's why Boris lets him hang around. Now I understand.* Aloud, he said, "If we must, let us leave the impression that a romantic alliance existed between the gypsy queen and David von Glasman—far better than revealing a kinship between Paul and Ronya."

The wisdom of Mischuk's advice was only too clear. Boris nodded.

Appalled, Ronya burst out, "No!"

"Look here, Ronya—" But Ronya held her ground.

Boris saw that a striking change had come over Ronya. "Well, all right, dove," he said at last. "The choice is yours."

Mischuk frowned thoughtfully.

Gradually the tension that had gripped the room since Mischuk had walked in drained away, and Ronya felt it in order for her to ask, "Who accuses Paul? And why?"

Mischuk had a good many knowledgeable friends in St. Petersburg. The tale he had pieced together from several sources was remarkably accurate.

"Think of Paul as Count Vronsky. He met an Anna. Paul's Anna is married to a much older man whom she does not love. For Paul she forgets discretion, perhaps deliberately lets her husband see that she is making a fool of him. But Anna's husband is not timid, helpless, or without pride. He has Anna watched. She leads him to Paul, whom he must destroy but not with a bullet. Paul must live in order to suffer, and the world must never know that he has been cuckolded by a policeman of dubious antecedents. I calculate we have a few days, possibly a week, before Paul is seized and branded an enemy of the crown, and when I tell you the husband's name, you'll understand why: the Grand Duke Gennady Drayayeva!"

"Drayayeva!" Boris exclaimed. "I don't like it. Paul has to be smuggled out of Russia. We must move fast."

"Ronya," Mischuk said, "what are you thinking?"

"Only that Paul, in or out of uniform, is no Count Vronsky."

Taken by surprise, both men stared at her for a minute and, as if answering another question, she said, "I'm afraid."

"I, too, am afraid," Mischuk said. "The grand duke has an eye for valuable land—everyone knows that, and everyone knows that he is not altogether scrupulous about how he obtains it."

But Boris was not afraid. "The duke can be dealt with. Now, there are two ways to get Paul out of St. Petersburg," he said. "One, the gypsies. Two, the Tartars. I'll wait for him in Odessa and take him the rest of the way."

Ronya drew Boris' hand into hers. "Send your Tartars, my darling. Paul has no taste for gypsies."

The clock was striking three when Mischuk left.

The clock was striking three when Krasmikov climbed into Tamara's bed. She was dreaming of her father, a man she had never seen, but still she knew the man in her dream was her father and that she loved him in a way she had never loved before. Tamara was struggling to hold on to the dream when Krasmikov's strong arms clutched her nakedness. With a deep sigh, her dream gone, Tamara rolled against him and opened her eyes. "What time is it?"

"Sh! It's late. Go back to sleep."

"You don't have to whisper. The Blond One isn't here."

For years now, Krasmikov had pleaded with Tamara to marry him.

He could no longer count the number of times she had refused him. Occasionally she would give him a reason, but usually she did not even bother to answer. In the beginning Krasmikov had been taken aback by Tamara's indifference to marriage, but now he accepted it, as he accepted her constant need for violent sensation and her confidence that one day Boris would come to her. The amazing thing about Krasmikov was that he felt no resentment toward Boris, he never brooded over Tamara's lovers. To him nothing she did seemed sordid, and his feeling for her remained steadfast. For this, and because he clung to her, Tamara gave him a key to her house. That her doors were never locked was irrelevant.

A faint glimmer of daylight showed through the curtains as Krasmikov approached Tamara. Her body, immediately magnetized by his maleness, did not deny him. As for her heart, he might as well have been a mechanical object.

The moment of suspended time over, Tamara fell swiftly into sleep. The man uttered a long, convulsed groan and rolled over on his side; but sleep did not come. For days now, Krasmikov had suffered from acute insomnia. A delicate piece of business had been put into his hands. If he yielded to ambition and avarice—a nice bit of hard money was involved—this was the last time he would take this large, delicious warmth from Tamara. Not only would she be lost to him, but he would spend the rest of his life far from Kiev looking over his shoulder.

Krasmikov decided there was nothing to be done but confide in Tamara. His decision made, he plummeted into a sleep of complete exhaustion.

When breakfast was almost ready, Tamara woke him reluctantly. Sharing the morning meal with her bedmate was always a tiresome ordeal. This morning, however, as Krasmikov told his story, very similar to Mischuk's, her attention was firmly held. However, who the elder man was, who the woman, he had no idea. All he knew was that they were rich and powerful. In the silence that followed, he realized that never before had Tamara been so completely his. He only wished he had more to say.

Tamara was genuinely shocked. What a hypocrite Paul had been! Not that it mattered with whom he slept, but by coming to Kiev so often he had led the secret police to Ronya.

"Be quiet," she said, rolling two cigarettes and giving him one, "while I think. Your report must draw attention away from Ronya."

"Tamara, the difficulty is I am instructed to provide damaging information, to produce something shameful, a complete fabrication if necessary. Truth has nothing to do with it. Still, if I should chance upon—"

305

"Shut up. Let me think."

Krasmikov laughed, not offended. "What I write isn't important as long as I hold it up long enough for Paul to get out. Once he has flown the coop—"

"Must you be so obvious? It's Ronya's association with Paul that needs defining."

Krasmikov looked at Tamara quizzically. "Why are you so concerned about Ronya? I thought Paul was Boris' friend."

"Because—" Suddenly the solution flashed through her mind. "Listen, Krasmikov"—it hurt him that she never addressed him with an endearment or even by his first name—"about that report. Tell them that Paul came to see me—that we're lovers. He stayed with the Pirovs because it seemed more correct—after all, he's a married man. Tell them that when he wanted the house in St. Petersburg it was I who produced the money. Tell them it cost me high, Ronya drives a hard bargain."

"Did you—" Krasmikov stopped and controlled his voice, "did you really go to bed with Paul?"

Tamara looked at him. Surely he knew— She checked the answer on her tongue and said mischievously, "When I was a little girl, I remember times when Ronya and I both crawled into his bed."

Tamara kept her face straight at the look on Krasmikov's face. "He came to see my mother."

"Funny," Krasmikov added reflectively, "I don't think I could ever mind Boris. The casuals—the devil take them. But I don't like sharing you with Paul."

Laughter came into Tamara's eyes. Far more affectionately than usual, she said, "Go now, I've work to do."

The instant he was gone, she rang a bell at the rear of the house, and within the hour the wagons were on their way. Pulled by horses bred for speed and endurance and driven by trustworthy men, they carried no loads; thrash wheels, chopped wood, tools, scythes would be dumped into them later. One wagon had a false bottom.

Despite the estrangement between Boris and his mother, neither regarded the other with any degree of animosity. Quite the reverse. Boris had provided her with three grandsons, two of whom were golden ones (his bastard didn't count), and Jewess or no Jewess, they were hers. Besides, the Tartar woman still felt that Boris would find some way of shaking Ronya out of her unreasonable stubbornness and save himself, not to mention the children.

From the beginning Boris had believed in his mother's curse, and if that was the price he had to pay for marrying Ronya he was willing to pay it. Yet there was an extraordinary sort of relationship between them, and areas of mutual interdependence.

306

As soon as the Tartar woman got Boris' urgent message, and not long after Tamara's wagons moved out, twenty men and sixty horses, dispersed in groups, were on their way to St. Petersburg by way of Kiev. Men and horses were well matched, and the Tartar woman smiled with the knowledge that they were worth more than a hundred Cossacks in a fight.

At a walking pace, Boris set out on the stallion to meet them.

As the sun sank in the sky, Boris saw the distinct forms of riders spread over a hilltop a mile and a half away. He slackened the rein, and the stallion immediately broke into a run. The Tartars thundered down on him, pulling up sharply when they recognized the cap of golden hair and the still, erect figure. Boris raised his hand. They saluted respectfully.

Boris dismounted and motioned to Pavel, the headman, a big, steady-eyed mustachioed Tartar who had been riding ahead and a little apart from the young men. Pavel slid down from his sleek black horse, which stood quiet with the reins flung over his head, very wild but well trained in the Tartar way.

Boris handed him a photograph. "This is Paul Zotov. He's the most competent policeman in Russia, so he must realize what's in the wind. Don't approach him directly. Once he becomes aware of you, he'll catch up with you. Get to my father, the general, as quick as you can, because there's where you'll find your orders from Zotov if he's already made for a hideout."

Pavel ran his fingers through his thick black hair. "Hunting a man is the same as hunting game. I should know his habits."

"He's a quick thinker, a good liar, almost as fast with a gun and a knife as I am, and he reacts a lot as I do, too."

The headman nodded. "We'll find him."

The Tartars mounted, and the dust rose as they galloped off, with Boris riding beside them. When the stars came out, Boris turned and headed for home.

It was a balmy afternoon, lazy and sweetly fragrant, when Madam Titiana made her appearance at Tamara's door four days later. Tamara fed her royally, listened to her story, and determined to keep this vulgar, garrulous old woman well away from Ronya and Boris. The kiss Ronya had given Paul she felt sure was something to conceal from Boris, no matter what Paul had said. Boris was not a man to dismiss a kiss, however innocent.

After she had gotten rid of Madam Titiana the following morning, fobbing off her avid desire to meet the Pirovs with a story of sickness among the children, Tamara sent off a messenger to recall her rescue party and walked over to give the news to Ronya, whom she found in bed eating breakfast.

Tamara helped herself to coffee and said abruptly, "News of Paul."

Ronya caught her breath, but seeing that Tamara appeared unworried, let it out slowly.

Tamara repeated Madam Titiana's story in all its detail.

"Well," Ronya said, "at least Alexis can deal with that evil old goat who wanted Paul counting birch trees in Siberia and me separated from my land."

"Alexis?" Tamara echoed disappointedly.

"I know," Ronya said. "You and I were taught to fight back in kind, and I was perfectly willing to let Boris tackle him, but Mischuk advised us to go cautiously and suggested that we should leave it to Alexis. In St. Petersburg they'll listen to the Count Brusilov, and Alexis can even use his friendship with the Tzar. Boris eventually let us persuade him—reluctantly."

"Ronya, there's something I left out. Paul told Madam Titiana to give you a message. He told her to tell you that he's had enough of bluff and pretense, that each step away from Europe is one step closer to fate, and that afraid or not, we will all have to face it."

Ronya gave no indication that she understood anything personal and private in Paul's message. She remained silent, seemingly content to let Tamara go on talking.

Tamara gave her a speculative look. "Paul is a lot like me—oh, not on the surface but inside. He covets just as I covet. Have you ever wondered what he feels about you?"

Color suffused Ronya's cheeks at the thought of Paul describing to her the woman he loved.

"You're blushing," Tamara remarked. "Listen, Ronya, why do you think Paul has gone to America? From what I've heard of her, the grand duchess isn't the sort of woman Paul could ever care for, and he slid out of Russia within a few hours, without a backward glance. He could have arranged things differently; Madam Titiana offered him a hired killer, which he refused—Paul isn't so squeamish."

"I don't know about that. Paul doesn't strike me as a scoundrel."

"No?" Tamara's eyes snapped fire. "Well, I've been thinking back and I should have realized long ago there was something about his attitude toward you—"

"Tamara, this conversation is ridiculous."

Now Tamara was even more certain. "No, it isn't. What Paul wants he'll try to get. He'll slip back into Russia as easily as he slipped out. He doesn't give a fig for Boris. He'll get rid of him if he can without our knowing it. You must warn Boris. Tell him to be on the watch."

"Are you out of your mind—Paul, an assassin?"

Tamara's eyes never left Ronya. "Yes. He's killed before."

"My God," said Ronya. Then, slowly, "I don't believe it. That Paul belongs to the past."

"I know Paul," Tamara said somberly, getting up. "He hasn't changed."

That night Boris came into her bed. He had spent most of the day in the stables. "Tomorrow I'll have to go after Pavel," he said wearily. "He'll be turning St. Petersburg upside down for Paul." He stroked her shoulder. "Where did you finally find David?"

Ronya smiled. "In the chicken coop, pretending to be a fox. He had pinned on a real foxtail and wouldn't unpin it. 'A fox isn't a fox without a foxtail,' he said."

Contemplating his son, Boris' brow knitted in a frown. "I don't understand that boy. Last week, when he was a rattler, writhing in the dirt, he hissed so realistically that my mare reared and David almost got himself killed."

"He's full of mischief."

"No, Ronya, Georgi is full of mischief. David is something else again. He's a terror." Boris' arms encircled her and, as he pulled her toward him, Ronya said tentatively, "Tamara thinks it's not the grand duchess Paul loves."

"She's right."

"How do you know that?"

"If Paul loved her he'd have made a widow of her before he turned her into an adulteress."

"Boris, suppose—just suppose—Paul didn't think of his love as a betrayal. Doesn't that sometimes happen? Two people meant for each other have the misfortune of giving themselves over in good faith to the wrong person first."

"It happens, Ronya; it could have happened to us."

"What would you have done in such a case?"

"What Paul didn't do—taken you with me."

"Then the only thing we can conclude is that one day Paul will come back for the woman he loves."

"I'd say that depends a lot upon who the woman is. Maybe she's already in the right arms."

Ronya felt her heart had stopped beating. "When did you first guess?"

"I didn't, dove," Boris answered truthfully. "Tamara told me when I went over late in the afternoon to thank her for keeping that vulgar old whore away from you."

She was so obviously relieved, Boris had to grin.

Very softly, Ronya said, "Until today, I didn't dream that Paul—"
Boris put his fingers to her lips. "Sh—I know. Don't ever talk of him again."

With spring came the first letter from America. It came midmorning, on a day when Boris was away from Kiev, and so Ronya loitered in her room by the window, staring out across the garden at David softly stroking Igor's old retriever. The dog had a special hold on David's affection.

Handing over the letter, Lydia said, sorely grieved, "Only someone as devilishly clever as Paul would wait until the master stopped inquiring about the mail. It's almost as if he'd left a disembodied eye here."

Ronya turned from the window. "Honestly, Lydia, you must spend your life at keyholes—" She sighed. "Oh, well."

Not content with a single protest, Lydia sighed too, a sigh that expressed all her indignation.

"For goodness sake, Lydia!"

"A good solution, Ronya my mistress, would be to destroy the letter unopened."

"I can't bring myself to do that," Ronya said, her feelings roused. "It wouldn't be right. Have you forgotten what a friend he was to my people?"

Lydia said no more, but it was in a stormy mood that she went back to her duties.

April 5, 1891

Dear, dear Ronya,

In seven months, I feel I know this land better than I know Russia. I arrived in New York toward the end of September and devoted the next seventeen weeks to travel. I traveled by rail—there are more railroads here than in all of Europe—by river boat, and by schooner. I saturated myself in the magnificent scenery. I made myself knowledgeable. The free way of living, Ronya, is a better way of living. The distribution of power with sovereignty vested in the people is a better kind of government. A land where the schools are free, where in business as in private life the rule is *laissez faire*, is a better land. Oh, Ronya, if only I were a lyrical essayist! It is a pity that I have to rely upon my unadorned reportage to make you see what I see.

Ronya, I am after prodigious profits, and I have an inkling that they are to be made in the oil fields. With financial backing from Sergey, I have become involved in an oil trust organized by a shrewd pirate named John D. Rockefeller. I am also investing in land, particularly in New York City. Here the increase in population is not to be believed, the city swelled daily by the influx of im-migrants. And I have an enthusiasm for railroading. I believe in America's great destiny. I believe in my destiny. No matter when, Ronya, or why, or how, a letter posted to P.O. Box 379, New York City, N.Y., will get to me.

Time and distance do not blur my image of you. My mind is churning with words I want to write, but I shall say only that I see you, and your hair captures the glints of the sun. I see you, and your eyes are mischievous. I see you with the four boys, with Katya and Alexis, and I long for you.

Yours always,
Paul

April 28, 1891

Dear Paul,

It was my intention to write, "You will never hear from me again, and you must never write to me again." Then I remembered that David my father condemned words like never and always. As you know, he was partial to the wait-and-see approach, in true Rus-sian style—possibly, perchance, maybe, if, and God willing.

It saddens me that, like Tamara, you are in the grip of an obses-sion. However I think your consuming infatuation is not with me but with my father still, and this, I think, accounts for your drive for money and power. But whatever the reasons, I wish you well. I hope you never regret your decision to leave Russia. I hope that part of you, the good part, remembers a wife and one daughter who has not separated herself from the world—*her* at least you should have with you. Don't be too consumed with your destiny, Paul, and do con-template the years of solitude you are imposing on yourself.

My great regret is that I have been distanced from a friend. Also, you've certainly put a damper on my ever again being allowed a re-lationship (aside from Ivan Tromokov and Joseph Levinsky) with a man who still perambulates without a cane.

Since I have already said more than I intended, I add: Knowing there is P.O. Box 379 gives me a feeling of security, it seems to me a possible solution for the Blond One if, one day, he becomes dis-satisfied here.

Enough—and, no more.

Good-bye,
Ronya

Ronya readied her letter for mailing; Paul's she locked away with her private papers. She spent the afternoon hours on business affairs, listening to her banker, hearing about the wheat market and land values. She gave Georgi his supper and put him to bed. She spent time with David and Igor. At eight o'clock, in a brocaded kimono coat edged and lined with pink satin and with the Von Glasman pearls around her neck, she came downstairs to dine with Father Tromokov.

An hour later the priest put down his wine glass, sighed, "A delicious dinner, Ronya," and lazily inched himself out of his chair. Smiling, Ronya preceded him into the library. For a time they said nothing. The priest sipped his brandy and, except for the crackling fire and the sound of rain and wind through the trees in bud, all was quiet.

"Ronya," said Father Tromokov, "a kopek for your thoughts."

"They're about the letter I received from Paul today."

"You don't say!" he exclaimed, his voice raised with pleasure. "A letter from Paul!"

"I was thinking, Father, that I'd like to tell you about a bizarre situation."

"Bizarre?"

"Yes, bizarre—meaning irrational, unusual, absurd."

"All three?"

"Yes. Paul thinks he is in love with me. He talks about destiny and fate."

Slowly the priest started to nod. Slowly he began to rub his chin. "S-o-o. David sent Paul to England. Only Ruth, your mother, ever laid eyes on the real Ladislaus. David felt the weight and foresaw the danger. He knew, he was a student of human nature. Man's secret wish is to possess his master's daughter."

Ronya thought of her father. She thought of Paul. Then, in great seriousness, she asked, "What is Paul's wife like?"

"Do you promise not to tell Tamara?"

"I promise."

Sipping his second brandy, Father Tromokov asked, "Have you ever heard the name Gregory Rasputin?"

"No."

"Have you ever heard of the Khlysty?"

"No."

"Have you ever heard of a sect of men and women who believe that holiness is reached through sin?"

Wide-eyed, Ronya merely shook her head.

Father Tromokov drank a little brandy. "Ronya," he said, "listen then, and listen well. Gregory Rasputin is a grimy, gross, rough Siberian muzhik, a fraudulent monk who should be torn limb from limb. The time will come when I shall rue the day I saved that bastard from drowning."

It was on the tip of Ronya's tongue to say, "Where?" but the priest allowed no time for interruption.

"Somewhere in his wanderings through Russia, Rasputin met Paul's wife, and he offered to guide her soul to God. Melancholy in nature, fanatically religious, she fell into his power, but she was not completely disloyal to her husband. She brought Rasputin to their summer house and introduced him to Paul. Paul loathed him immediately, but he let him stay on as house guest, and when Paul went back to St. Petersburg a few days later Rasputin took his new disciple to a monastery where the Khlysty held their meetings. There she was indoctrinated with the belief that God is reached through sexual encounter, and the more vile and frenzied the orgy, the closer the union with the Almighty. Helena surrendered to Rasputin totally and became a full-fledged member of the Khlysty. Some years later, she sent her elder daughter to Rasputin to be united with God, but the girl was terrified, rebuffed him, and fled to a nunnery, where she is today."

All Ronya could feel was shock and horror. "Did Paul ever find out?"

Father Tromokov shrugged. "I have no idea."

"Then how in heaven's name do you know all this?"

Ivan Tromokov debated a few minutes. "This must go no further. I was once the guest of a high prince of the church at his cousin's villa in the country outside Moscow. The cousin, an old maid by our standards, a quite ordinary person, was enormously rich. Her twenty-four-hour companion, much to everyone's embarrassment, was Rasputin. He took an enormous liking to me, because the vodka that made him drunk was just a warm-up for me and because I could bend as many horseshoes with my bare hands as he. He urged me to become a member of the Khlysty or at least to come to the monastery and stay awhile.

"Privately my host commanded me to go. 'Consider that you are on a mission for the church,' he said. 'I want to know what happens there. I fear that God is not their goal.'"

Ronya pushed back a fallen lock of hair from her brow. "Go on."

"There's not much more to tell. I met Helena Zotov there. Don't ask me what it was like. Even in recall, I blush with shame at what I saw."

In a way, Ronya was pleased with what she had heard. It confirmed all Paul said of his wife and absolved him from wrongdoing. Her sin of carnality transcended his of desertion. In the silence that followed Ivan Tromokov's disclosures, she reached into her pocket and handed over Paul's letter.

The priest read slowly, reflecting sadly that the only time Boris had opened his home to a resolute man of action, it had been a mistake. He noted the care with which Ronya folded the letter and replaced it in her pocket. Not liking what he saw at all, he asked, "When does Boris get back?"

"That depends upon the weather. Boris and his riders are bringing in a large herd. This sudden spring storm is bound to slow them down."

"Ronya," there was a hard note in the priest's voice, "don't fan Boris' jealousy."

"I don't intend to."

"Then," said the priest evenly, "burn the letter."

"I don't want to."

"Why not?"

"Oh, I don't know." After a moment's pensiveness she added, "It just doesn't seem right."

With a rare display of temper, the priest said, "Be honest, Ronya, speak the truth."

A mischievous smile spread over her lovely face. "You can't expect me to dislike a man like Paul for loving me."

The priest laughed unhappily. "Women!"

33

There was hardly any rain the whole month of May. In June, one meager drizzle. July saw two useless short-lived showers. The meadow grass was burnt, and Ronya's gardens were bleached and dry—no radiant colors, no gigantic blooms, no wonderful scents. In Russia, along the Volga, there was no rain at all. Everything—grass, grain, flowers, vegetables—withered and died. The terrible drought-stricken summer of 1891 was remembered by the people for many years—the land was bewitched. The blistering sun and choking dust snuffed out the peasants' vitality and, though most prayed for rain, many held aloof from the church and slumped sadly into black, brooding fatalism.

By mid-July, Ronya was frantic. Boris tried to comfort her, promising, "We'll be all right," but Ronya heard her father's voice saying, "Feed the peasants." With these words burning in her mind, she tossed and twisted in her sleep. Early one morning she woke with a start.

"I was dreaming," she told Boris. "A nightingale's tear on a single blade of grass. It was such a sad little tear."

"Reconcile yourself to the drought, dove," he said quietly.

"It's no use, darling, I can't. With no crops there'll be famine."

Boris longed to dissipate her dread, but what was there to say?

"The peasants need to be compelled to work. Will you advise me?"

Boris grinned in response and got to his feet. He opened the French doors that led to the balcony. The sky was clear. Another hot, dry day, and the water was sinking in the wells and the water holes.

They walked out of the house and across lawns scorched brown; the orchards and the meadows were the same drab color. Ronya stared down the road at the dogs panting in the shade of the poplars and at the peasants dragging indifferently through great clouds of dust. The only sound was the occasional tinkle of cowbells.

Boris let his eyes roam over dead leaves, withered grass, fallen branches. There was extreme danger here; there was much to do. Everywhere there were signs of peasant indolence.

He proposed a general housecleaning for the estate. "We'll cut, rake, and burn. But first the hay must be cut."

She nodded in agreement.

"This is not a job for the peasants alone, dove," he said seriously. "We can't make them do the toil and then expect them to share everything we salvage with the gypsies. I say all hands to work."

"Tamara won't mind that at all."

By midmorning, they were all in the fields. Already oppressively hot, the sun's glint dropped flame upon the wheat.

The morning decided Ronya.

"We've got to do something," she told Boris, "otherwise the people will starve and our friends will be ruined and there will be terrible trouble with the Cossacks. I've been trying to think of what to do, and I think I've hit on a plan that will feed our peasants, tide our neighbors over the drought, wipe out our losses, provide white flour for the Sabbath loaves, and pacify the local Cossacks. With a gift of wheat from us, they may leave our Jews alone."

Only half in jest, Boris said, "How about my Odessa Tartars? Do I get grain for them?"

"Of course, darling. We'll need them."

"Ronya, what are you talking about?"

"I want to tell Sergey of our circumstances and instruct him to purchase all the wheat, corn, barley, rice, groats—all the grain he can get—plus staples such as white flour and potatoes. I want boatloads of them."

Boris contained his excitement. "But to buy in the international marketplace, we'll have to deal in English pounds. The ruble is so weak no one accepts it."

Nevertheless, he was impressed with the size of the venture she proposed and the many risks it presented. Already his mind had begun to grapple with the tough problems of execution: manpower, transport, storage. The shipment had to be transferred from boats to wagons and hauled great distances, secreted from prying eyes. Rodentproof, waterproof storage bins, well concealed and easy to guard, had to be constructed. Harbor officials had to be bribed. Nothing could be left to chance.

"I was afraid," she confessed, "you'd consider my idea grandiose and dangerous, and reject it."

"Your idea is brilliant, my cerebral dove, but you're talking about millions and millions of rubles. Can you handle it?"

"Not alone—especially since I don't want to sell or mortgage anything."

"Are you thinking of a combine with the other wheat growers?"

"No, they'll see only an opportunity for big profits. They won't give a damn about our starving people."

"That's true."

"We don't need outsiders. Among us—you and I, Tamara, and Katya—we have the money."

"Me?" Boris' voice carried a strong note of surprise.

Ronya smiled at him. "Yes, darling. You're quite rich. I've taken very little of what Father left you. The rest is still entrusted to Sergey, and he has piled up nice profits for you. Also, I've indulged in some studied speculation and been lucky."

"What if we run into costly snags? How do we get out?"

"I'll borrow from Alexis."

"Alexis! Not Sergey?"

Ronya sensed his surprise. Her mind flew to Paul—what a difference it would make if he were in St. Petersburg to handle matters there. "Sergey," she said, "is committed elsewhere."

Boris' eyes narrowed. He had heard Sergey's name mentioned in connection with investments in the United States.

Ronya kept her face expressionless.

After the brief moment, Boris' face lost its ill-humor. "Well, it'll take the better part of a month to get things organized here. Then I must go see about enlisting my mother's help. In Odessa even the tide rolls in under her watchful eye. No one clears port without her nod."

Ronya's look was direct. So was her appeal. "Boris, when the time comes, send Ivan Tromokov to St. Petersburg to lead the wagons. You're too conspicuous."

"I'll see."

She saw he was completely unconcerned with the danger.

The old woman opened the door, and Ronya stepped into darkness. The hall reeked of decay and the smell of strange roots and herbs.

"I've brought you fruit candies," Ronya said, offering her a jar.

Old Auntie took possession both of the jar and of Ronya's hand. "Good," she said, "I like to suck," and escorted Ronya into a room that once was Rifka's. Here nothing was changed, yet nothing was the same. The room used to be full of light and color. Now the wooden shutters were tightly shut. Old Auntie had no interest in the morning sun. Her blindness, developing over the years, was now complete. Every morning the gypsies brought her warm food, and every night someone helped her with a warm bath. The rest she managed by herself.

Ronya said, "I had a dream. There was a slender blade of grass. The grass was almost all brown, except in one tiny spot. That was vivid green. The secret of the green was one tear, left there by a nightingale."

The old woman's sightless eyes stared at her. "The single island of green is a good sign. The drought will not put this land to death. A tear can be read in many ways. Sometimes it is punishment. Here that does not follow. The moisture of the tear gave the leaf back its speck of beauty. I believe you are the nightingale, Ronya, and the tear is the love you feel and the love you give. The brown is God's curse on the earth, for God knows that man and the devil are lovers."

When the old woman led Ronya back to the door, she said, "Come soon, Ronya. Bring *bronfin* and *chaleh*, and celebrate the morning I am one hundred and two."

Ronya took her old friend in her arms and kissed her. "I'll come."

It was Tamara's thirtieth birthday, and all day she waited for Ronya, but only Ronya's gift came. Toward evening, clad in her birthday finery, she went out with an officer, a Major Andrei Rakov.

On the way home, he made his blunt proposal.

"Some other time," Tamara said wearily.

The major took out a roll of bills. "Will this change your mind?"

Concealing her hurt, Tamara replied, "I'm in the habit of taking, not selling."

Because they told him at the post that Tamara was a born slut, he insisted.

There was a piece of old cracked whip on the seat between them. She picked it up and hit him with it.

"Gypsy bitch! Whore!" But he held the horses in control.

Tamara pulled a knife (later, the man wondered where on her person she kept it hidden). "Behave yourself," she said, "or, so help me, I'll kill you."

Because of Ronya, Tamara went to bed in rejected wretchedness.

Because of Boris, she lay under her summer blanket shivering—she was thirty years old and alone. Toward morning she fell into a ligh' sleep, but the luxury of rest did not last long. She heard her name ; . knew it was Boris calling. Her heart stood still. She pulled on a . ɟe and ran outside. He was there, the sun shining down on his hair.

"What's the matter, Boris?"

"Plenty. Can you see a single rabbit in the meadow?"

"It will rain," Tamara said softly.

Boris gazed from the seared earth to the cloudless sky. "Did you see rain in your crystal ball?" he scoffed.

Tonelessly Tamara answered, "I did not look."

Just then the Blond One appeared. Before he could turn and run, Boris said, "Come here." They looked at one another, and Boris said, "I want you and Igor in the stables each morning at seven. You'll eat your noon meal with the men and work until sunset."

"Yes, sir," the Blond One said.

Boris looked down at the boy from his great height. "I'll give you a lift to the stables."

The boy regarded him with such worship that Boris grew uncomfortable. "Go eat your breakfast," he said. "You have time."

"I've had bread and cheese."

Boris turned back to Tamara. "Get some clothes on. Come and tell your people they take their orders from me."

"Boris, I have to know—"

"Do as I say."

Tamara sent the Blond One to ring the bell.

While Tamara dressed, her people gathered. When she told them they would be taking their orders from Boris, the gypsies stirred in sudden interest. Boris spoke without emphasis, giving no details, but no one doubted his seriousness. Looking into their upturned faces, he stated the situation and concluded, "Work through the next few months and you'll eat." To Tamara he said, "I need women to rake in dry hay. I want your men assembled in front of the stables within the hour."

"Boris," she said directly, "what task do you have for me?"

"Unless you want to pitch hay, none."

Conscious that her people watched and judged, Tamara smiled. "If Ronya is willing to descend from her lofty perch to toil in the fields with the peasants, then I am willing to put aside my position as queen and do likewise."

Boris stalked off with the Blond One at his heels.

Tamara could not drive Andrei Rakov out of her mind. It wasn't only that he had offered her money "like a streetwalker," she kept repeating to herself; on the drive home he had sniffed at her as though she were a creature ready to take on any male animal. By the time Ronya arrived, she was in a foul mood. "And where," she snapped, "were you yesterday?"

"I came as soon as I could with a cake I baked, but you were gone. This may be the last cake for some while. We'll need the flour for bread."

Somewhat mollified, Tamara said, "I've started to lay in supplies."

Ronya sighed, "That's a drop in the bucket."

"Boris hinted that you've a plan for feeding us. Is that true?"

When Ronya had explained her scheme, instead of enthusiastic endorsement Tamara raised objections.

"Look, Ronya, I'll give you stout wagons and brawny men, but you know I'm bitterly against parting with gold."

"You're not parting with gold, you're using it. Besides, you'll get it all back, and more."

"How soon?"

Ronya shrugged. "I don't know. It depends."

On guard, Tamara said, "How much is 'more' in money?"

"Ten, maybe twelve percent on your investment."

"That's a trifle, a tiny return on a gigantic gamble."

"Well, profit isn't the primary motive."

Tamara's expression was comment enough.

Thoroughly disappointed, Ronya said, "If you don't like it—you don't. We'll manage without you."

"Oh, shut up, Ronya," Tamara said impulsively. "I'm trying to figure—" Then she groaned. "This is impossible. We can't make money. You're giving too much away. Even if we don't get caught—or ransacked—or looted—"

"Of course we can."

"All right. Show me how."

"One, we eliminate the middleman. Two, we sell for cost plus. In plus we take the normal markup. But in cost we include the full worth of everything we distribute for free."

Tamara smiled with delight. "I'm in for a third."

"One fourth."

"Katya, you, me—and who else?"

"Boris."

Tamara had no idea Boris was so rich but bit her tongue.

Once committed, Tamara leaped with her customary recklessness into schemes and arrangements. "We must have guns and ammunition."

"No! All security will be entrusted to Boris' Tartars."

319

"Why them," she demanded, "with hundreds of our own on the land, peasants and gypsies?"

"Do you want me to present Pobiedonostsev with a ready-made case against me? I can just imagine him: Ronya von Glasman Pirov, the accused, did knowingly and willfully incite the peasants to revolt."

Tamara's gaze fell.

Ronya rose. "I must go. I'm going to see Joseph Levinsky."

"Ronya," Joseph cried in surprise, "what brings you here?"

"I thought perhaps you'd give me tea."

Joseph knew at once she brought no reassuring news. "Come," he said, motioning her inside.

Ronya removed her big, soft-brimmed hat and her white lace gloves and surveyed the small, neat room, pausing to gaze at a painting of the old rabbi and *rebbetzen*, a gift from the congregation. "How long since you've heard from your parents?" she asked.

"About a month. You simply cannot conceive their contentment. They speak to each other in Hebrew. They venture out at night. There are no edicts limiting the Jews to restricted quarters. My father writes the very air they breathe is filled with the myths and legends of three thousand years."

"About once a year, Boris hears from your mother."

"She is very kindly disposed toward him," Joseph replied coolly. "Settle yourself, Ronya. I'll be right back."

He returned with two glasses on a tray.

"To your good health," Ronya said, and drank the bitter wine.

His quiet eyes rested gently on her face. "You look lovely, Ronya, lovelier than ever. It must be that what you chose satisfied your nature." Suddenly, he felt his face burn and looked away.

Ronya's black eyes danced with devilment.

"I understood from our last conversation," Joseph said, his composure regained, "that you felt your brother-in-law might have some influence on Pobiedonostsev. Did he agree to try?"

"Yes. He pleaded for our people, but Pobiedonostsev told him that the only solution is for the Jews to become Christians. The greatest rewards will go to those who accept conversion and assimilation. The others shall perish.

"Then Alexis was summoned to the palace. The Tzar told him that the house of Von Glasman will remain under imperial protection. This was supposed to reassure us."

"The Tzarina hates us," Joseph said reflectively.

"She hates everyone cordially—Jews, Roman Catholics, Muslims, and her in-laws. When she finishes hating, there won't be anyone left to love."

Joseph swallowed his disappointment. "You know, Ronya," he said, like a teacher explaining to a child, "there are documents that speak of Jewish settlements in European Russia at the time of Christ. Organized Jewish communities prospered on the shores of the Black Sea in the first centuries of the Christian era. Jewish explorers ventured far into the Caucasus and were parent to the mountain Jews. Of the Khazar Empire and its orthodoxy we all know. Upon the destruction of the Khazars, somewhere around 980, the Kievan Vladimir converted from paganism to Byzantium Christianity, which was quite intolerant to the Jews and the Muslims. Nevertheless, the Jewish community in Kiev grew enormously in numbers, in importance, and in opulence. Moses of Kiev was probably the leading scholar of the twelfth century. Even after the Tartar conquest, the Jews remained strong in the Crimea. So you see, Ronya my dear, the Jews were here before the Romanovs. We shall be here when the Romanovs are long gone."

"Joseph, that's irrelevant. It looks as though twenty thousand Jews are going to be expelled from Moscow. Scholars may be fascinated by events long past, but most of us derive small comfort from what was and what will be, particularly women. Women are not ascetics. We take no interest in dry bread, and abstract ideas, and theoretical discussion. We are committed to the living. We want a safe world."

There were things about Ronya of which Joseph disapproved. She did not observe form, she sometimes meted out justice with her whip, she had given herself to a Tartar. Yet she was his favorite human being, and always his heart went out to her. Now he felt that more than the Moscow Jews were in her mind.

"What has happened, Ronya? What troubles you? We have lived with anti-Semitism all our lives. Why, at this time when nothing is really definite, are you so full of anxiety?"

"Anxiety." Ronya considered the word. "It fits," she conceded, "God knows, it fits. The drought is definite. There'll be famine—that's definite. The starvation and the suffering hate, the need to blame someone, that's definite. Durnovo and Pleve, for their own protection, will give them the Jews. We shall be the elected, once more, the chosen."

"You have strength, Ronya. Where is your faith? Without faith there is no hope."

Her face averted, Ronya asked, "Has God forgotten us?"

He looked at her thoughtfully. "You are not the first to ask." He laid a hand reassuringly on hers. "Ronya, in each generation there are those who believe and those who think they can get along without belief. I am your rabbi. With a troubled heart, I speak. Have faith and you can have heaven. Have faith and you can live in paradise. Have faith and you can keep your soul."

"You sound exactly like Father Tromokov when he gives his Sunday sermon to the peasants. 'For what shall it profit man, if he shall gain the whole world and lose his own soul?' "

"Nothing is ours alone, not even wisdom."

Ronya felt censured. "I'm sorry, I've had a trying day."

"That's all right."

"Joseph."

He noted the change in her voice. "Yes?"

Ronya heeded her judgment and told him a little of her scheme.

For a time Joseph Levinsky remained silent, weighing the pros and cons.

"It's a big gamble," he said at last, "and the risks run high. What if you're caught importing without a permit?"

"Don't be alarmed. I've passed the entire project on to Boris. Believe me, he can take care of himself."

With a serious chuckle, Joseph said, "All right, Ronya, let Boris lead. It is his earthly joy. I shall concentrate on prayer. That is my responsibility."

Ronya reached out and touched his hand. "Why don't you sometimes come see us?"

"That's hardly a mystery."

"It's a mystery to me."

"Because it is impossible not to admire Boris once close—don't be deluded into the thought that I now approve of your—"

Ronya stopped him. "Please, Joseph—don't."

The rabbi nodded. "All right, Ronya. Perhaps this is not the time."

The lady smiled. Boris grinned and picked up his glass.

The steward bent deferentially toward Boris and murmured discreetly, "The lady has half occupancy of a compartment for two, sir. Shall I move your things?"

Boris' eyes went to the table opposite his and rested there. He had noticed her earlier, the amber flecks in her eyes, the rise of her rounded breasts against her dress. If only the fine line of her chin and the high cheekbones had not reminded him of Ronya—even her hair was very nearly the same burnished chestnut. Almost ready to let her vague resemblance draw him on, Boris had a sudden change of mind. The thought of afterward—the hours, confined in a small space, listening to the sound of her breathing—filled him with a quick aversion.

He shook his head. "Don't bother."

The lady stood up and left the dining car.

The next morning Boris stepped down from the train, dropped his suitcase to the ground, and lit a cigarette. He paused in the hot brilliance of the Odessa sunlight and breathed in the piny sea air. A hard-looking horse-soldier from the Odessa garrison leading a saddled Cavalry trooper approached him from the far end of the street. In well-trained silence, the soldier saluted, waited until Boris had mounted, picked up the suitcase, and turned away in the direction of the barracks.

Boris rode down to the sea and picked his way along the quay. Perfect. Who would trouble watching for Ronya's cargo in this harbor, port of call for the ships of a hundred countries?

Leaving the café-lined quayside, he headed for his mother's place.

High on a narrow, shady lane, the house stared down on the warm Black Sea. Over the door, heavily carved and ornamented with gold, hung a leather whip, a symbol of power. The three rooms comprising the interior (there was a kitchen, also, but it was mainly ornamental) were a museum, a treasure house. Everything in the house had been stolen by Tartars in the course of centuries: ancient Uzbekistan carpets, a fifteenth-century mural from the palace of a shah in the ancient city of Baku, a stone sculpture from the Dmitrievsky Cathedral in Vladimir, an icon from the mighty Kievan Rus, a jewel from a tomb in Samarkand, Chinese panels inlaid with ivory. It was all exactly as it used to be in Boris' childhood.

Boris found his mother cooking in the courtyard over an open fire. As the delicious aroma of shashlik rose in the air, the past came flooding back. He stood quietly watching her.

The Tartar woman motioned him to the rug on the ground and fetched vodka. They drank from the bottle, turn and turn about.

"You still married?"

"Yes," Boris answered firmly.

Handing him a skewer, his mother said, "Eat."

"I'm not hungry."

"Take it," she said sharply. "This one is ready."

Knowing that if he refused there would be no help from the Tartars, Boris took the skewer of shashlik. When his mother was certain he meant to eat, she turned back to the fire.

Boris couldn't help contrast this with the sumptuous elegance of Ronya's candlelit table. "Let's take coffee inside," he said when they were done.

"Why?"

"Because it's civilized."

"I don't like arguments." Then, with a shrug of her broad shoulders, "Well, all right."

Wonderfully inconsistent, she served him heavily sweetened Turkish coffee in old Meissen china and with the aplomb of a duchess said, "Tell me about the boys."

323

Boris talked mostly about David, because his violent antics were what she liked to hear.

"As long as he's good with horses," she said complacently. "The rest is damn nonsense."

This seemed the moment to tell her about Ronya's plan.

The Tartar woman heard Boris out and said, after a moment's consideration, "Smart, real smart. Pity she won't be my daughter."

Boris knew then that he had her support. There were still terms to be agreed upon, and he waited to hear what price she would demand.

"This is business, you know."

Boris nodded.

"I'll take ten wagonloads for me."

"Eight."

"Nine."

"Nine—I pick the wagons and I load. Eight—you load."

The Tartar woman looked at him and grinned. "I'll take eight."

Boris laughed.

The Tartar woman watched him silently for a moment. "Let me know when the ships drop anchor. So far as I'm concerned, there's nothing for you to do. I'll get the wagons to Kiev."

"Good. That leaves me free for St. Petersburg."

Boris stood up and, with sudden emotion, touched his mother's shoulder.

"You staying at the Jewess's dacha?" the Tartar woman asked hoarsely.

"No, the barracks."

It was mid-September when four cargo ships dropped anchor just outside the harbor. The Odessa Tartars were ready. A disturbing rumor was spread about the docks that the plague was sweeping the coast of Europe. The preceding months of heavy heat gave impetus to the stevedores' fears. They did not stop to argue; they believed the rumor; they walked off the docks. The harbor stewards had some doubts about the truth of the rumor, but not one official was willing to back up his doubts with an investigation. When a reasonable time elapsed and no ship's captain tied up to a pier, the port authorities marched off, leaving the area unpoliced. Word got around that the waterfront was a dangerous place, and a trek started to the safety of the hills.

The Tartar woman gave the signal, and ships and wagons moved. It was a neat job, and in due time the loaded wagons reached their destination unnoticed.

Boris delayed long enough to store the grain and put it under armed guard and then, handing over the command in Kiev to Ivan Tromokov, he rode north. An immense amount of preparation was necessary and, with bland self-assurance, he employed a few tricks worthy of David von Glasman. He tried to anticipate every possible danger, especially pillaging—there were dozens of roaming bands of Cossacks between St. Petersburg and Kiev—and turned his attention to the provision of an armed escort for his wagons. The solution to thises lem was easy. Boris estimated that both the Cavalry and his father owed him a favor—though he had no wish to make his request official.

Itil Pirov maintained a luxurious suite in St. Petersburg. With a regular stipend from Ronya in addition to his salary, he could well afford the elegant Europa Hotel.

Boris knew the key girl, so he picked up the key to his father's rooms at her desk at the end of the corridor and let himself in. He filled a glass with vodka, not bothering to fetch the ground pepper from the drawer at hand, and took his drink into the bedroom. Stretched out on the bed, he fell asleep only to be roused by his father's voice from the doorway: "Boris! I didn't know you were in town."

"I've made a point of avoiding my usual haunts," Boris said, getting to his feet.

"Anything wrong?"

His father was actually anxious about him. Itil Pirov being fatherly —it was almost too much. Boris' face creased with a grin. "Not a thing."

Over supper Boris explained his plans, and his father listened and nodded and agreed to everything without hesitation.

"Will there be feed for my horses?"

"Yes, all you need."

For a moment Boris thought his father was going to ask for supplies for his men, but his next remark was: "I suppose it doesn't matter to you if I keep my engagement for the evening."

"Will you be bringing her back here?"

His father laughed. "No. Stay the night."

As they were finishing their coffee, Boris said, "A final word. Breathe a word of this, and father or no father I'll have your heart."

Itil Pirov looked up quickly. "Don't worry."

Boris eyed his father at some length. Tall and trim, he was still a marvelously good-looking man.

The streets of the rowdy waterfront quarter were empty in the quiet dawn. Boris gazed at the aging merchant ships inching lazily into the becalmed harbor. As soon as they lay at anchor tied to wharves, he sent for his own men. By this time, the bribes had been paid, the har-

325

bor officials had issued Boris a blanket permit, and no attention was paid to either ships or men. Meanwhile, officers and merchant crew took turns patronizing the taverns and brothels in the twisting, squalid alleyways, and they got themselves into the usual harbor scrapes from which Boris coolly extracted them. He himself waited with patience, upholding his reputation for vodka and sport, but the job on hand remained uppermost in his mind, and the girls on the streets told each other, "The eagle's yearnings are stilled." Yet their eyes dwelled upon him longingly, and they hoped. So two weeks passed.

The brawl was staged one night in Madam Titiana's bar. Ivan Tromokov, looking more warlike than priestly in his rough clothes and high boots, advanced on Boris menacingly and wavered to an inebriated halt in front of him.

"I don't like your face."

Boris moved away from the group surrounding him. "Do something about it," he said, a lurking smile in his eyes.

The priest complied.

Boris wasn't at all surprised at the power in that raised right hand, nor was Ivan perturbed that Boris' punch nearly sent him sprawling. He grunted and straightened. The free-for-all started a little ahead of schedule. The Russian looked up at the big brute stupidly and toppled. Pulling a knife and taking a step toward Ivan Tromokov, the Swede said to Boris, "Let me get at him." With a fiendish Tartar yell, Boris kicked the knife from the Swede's hand and then came the crack of his fist. The Swede fell to his knees. Father Tromokov threw another admirable right, and another man fell.

Madam Titiana was viewing the scene with sadistic delight. A nod from Boris, and the fracas spread to the street. Finally the harbor police arrived; it was they for whom Boris had been waiting. The captain knew his instructions. The streets were cleared and the entire area proclaimed out of bounds. The police disappeared. Boris gave the signal. The wagons moved in.

Boris took over Madam Titiana's café and made it his headquarters; the saloon was the mess hall, the upstairs a barracks dormitory. He worked the men at fever pitch, and they gave him all he expected of them. Drenched in sweat, their wet bodies shivering in the cold, they set their teeth and slaved on, uncomplaining. Boris did the work of three men, and as soon as a wagon was loaded he hurried it off. Some were ferried across the river; most went over bridges. More often than not, the priest drove the lead wagon. The rendezvous was a shady park in the little town of Petrodvorets, where for two centuries the Tzars had summered. Now, deep into fall, the area was deserted.

Waiting under the trees in the gathering darkness, Boris and his

326

men had a drink together and in a few hours General Pirov arrived with their Cavalry escort.

The waterfront was crowded and wild again. Madam Titiana, her café returned now to its habitual condition, sold her cheap liquor dear, and the floor shook with the stamp of sailors and prostitutes dancing to a blaring band. She sat at her cash register thinking enviously about Ronya's shrewd scheme. That night she dreamed of money.

On the road to Kiev, under a moonless sky full of stars, Boris dreamed too. His dream was about Ronya.

34

The weather changed and an early frost set in, adding to the suffering of the people. Along the Volga, the starving wandered from village to village, looking for food. Many got lost in the snowdrifts and were not found until the thaw. Swollen-bellied children ate snow and sucked icicles and died. The women wrung their hands and wailed; men wept because they were helpless. And those with a little food were afraid.

In and around Kiev and in most of the Ukraine things were not so bad. Moscow was hard hit. In St. Petersburg the poor sobbed, but the rich ate well: They had plenty of sweet butter, fresh milk, and honey. They slept on silk sheets. Well wrapped in furs, they journeyed by sled over the icy roads, pursuing pleasure. The white winter was gay.

Leo Tolstoy said of them, "They are a depraved society." His voice jumped national frontiers, and France, England, and Germany answered his call. The United States sent seven boatloads of grain. Indignantly, the Tzar denounced the benefactors and issued an official statement: "There is no famine in Russia. A few localities reaped a poor harvest."

Decent people throughout Russia were appalled. The Tzar's remarks meant death by starvation for thousands of people.

More than the famine was making Ronya unhappy. She had a sixth sense about the house on the hill and knew instinctively when Boris was drawn there not by a card game but by a woman—or by a thirst.

Fretting over the famine had made her thin and now, as November

327

came in with freezing winds, fretting over the house on the hill made her thinner. She said nothing, but Boris had a sixth sense too where she was concerned, and one night, catching a glimpse of her lips trembling as she listlessly turned the page of a book, he determined to rid himself then and there of the current tenant. From Nina, as from her predecessors, he got a carnality that afterward filled him with repugnance.

Waiting until Ronya drifted into her deepest sleep, he got out of bed without making a sound, dressed, and opened a drawer and filled his pockets with money.

Outside it was bitter cold and pitch black, but the stallion knew his way up the steep, deserted incline that led to the house. Arriving at the top of the hill, Boris took off his long fur-lined coat, draped it gently over the stallion, and led him to shelter under a bare weeping willow. "Stand," he said. "I won't be long."

Boris used the knocker, not his key. "Open."

Nina came sooner than he expected. He stepped in and the door slammed. It was difficult to be sure, but Boris sensed the presence of a third person. He took note of her disarray: tousled blond hair, flushed face, a robe hastily dragged around her full body. She looked terrified.

"Pour drinks," he said.

Thankful for the excuse to turn away, Nina obeyed.

Boris took the drink from her hand. "Sit down."

She sat looking at him with a mixture of fear and perplexity, but when he said, "I want you out of here," sudden anger deprived her of fear.

"Just like that!" she said, snapping her fingers.

Boris knew she had been born into a wretched little house in Central Asia where life for a girl is far from easy. He relented. "You've got three weeks."

Nina looked sadly into her vodka. "What have I done?"

In Boris' mind there lurked the conviction that behind the bedroom door lay a second lodger, but it did not matter. "It isn't personal, Nina."

She began to regain her confidence—he couldn't possibly know there was a man in the bedroom—and got up the courage to say, "I'd have moved out weeks ago if I had somewhere to go. Being cooped up here isn't my idea of a good time."

Boris placed a fistful of money on the table. "Don't forget."

He was at the door when she called his name softly. "Would it be all right if I give myself a farewell party?" A party was the difference between an honorable departure and a dismissal—but only if he were there. "Boris, won't you come, please, and bring some friends? Please. On the twenty-sixth."

328

Once again he was moved to a degree of pity. "Don't count on it," he said, and left quickly.

She secured the door and made her way back to the bedroom, saying, "He's gone."

"Damn it, Ronya." Boris was angry. "You've done your fair share, and then some."

Ronya looked up from a sheet of figures. "Darling, I didn't think you'd mind. I haven't given a party in a long time."

"This isn't a party, it's a three-ring circus with wenches auctioning kisses and you ready to dance with any confounded intruder who hands you a ticket."

"It's for medicines and warm clothing, Boris."

"It's for sons of bitches who'd cut your throat if they weren't afraid of me," Boris said.

Ronya smiled ruefully. "Women all over Russia are opening their homes to raise money."

"Don't fool yourself, Ronya. Their philanthropy's an excuse for courting strangers."

Ronya's eyebrows went up. "The Grand Duchess Xenia, the Grand Duchess Elizabeth, Princess Ella—climbers?"

"They demolish lobster and pastry thick with cream every night. Raising money's an excuse for a party. The famine has nothing to do with it."

She took his hand and stroked it gently. "The party isn't responsible for your mood. What's wrong, darling?"

"It's one goddamned thing after another. I never have you all to myself."

Ronya stared into his eyes, thinking of the times she lay waiting in the darkness and he did not come.

He knew what she was thinking.

Never taking his eyes from her face, and with no mockery in his voice, Boris said softly, "But remember, Ronya, this is an ultimatum. You'll sell no dances, or there'll be no party."

Finishing her accounts, Ronya went down the hall to what used to be her mother's sitting room to give David a reading lesson. David was wonderfully bright but impatient. He wanted always to be doing. Sometimes she felt that Igor was almost as difficult a child; piqued with him because he pitted himself against the old Hebrew teacher, she was equally annoyed with Boris, because he sided with Igor and laughingly suggested to the old man that he bequeath Igor to the Gentiles and quit—which was exactly what he eventually did. Even Georgi—marvelous, lovable Georgi—was a handful. The only one who never vexed her was the Blond One, and the only reason Igor managed to learn some Hebrew, in spite of himself, was because the Blond One sat through all the Hebrew lessons and afterward drummed everything into his head by turning it into a word game. Any contest revived Igor's interest. As always, he had to win.

This morning of November 12, David was good as gold, because at lunch Ronya had promised she would start teaching him how to use a whip and show him a few tricks.

"Bribes," Boris had roared disapprovingly.

"A reward is *not* a bribe."

Boris glared at David. "No doubt you're being rewarded for acquiring one hell of a gruesome infection."

David gave him a withering look. "I told you, I didn't know I had it. It didn't hurt."

"Christ! It bled, didn't it?"

"Please, Boris," Ronya said.

"All right, Ronya. Pour honey, offer gifts—but don't save the egg and lose the hen."

David grinned at Igor and rolled his eyes—a performance ignored with difficulty by Boris.

As Ronya's mind circled around the antagonism between Boris and David, Tamara's voice floated upstairs. With alarming dexterity for a boy with a bandaged foot, David bounded down the hall, yelling out her name like a red Indian. Tamara laughed gaily and opened her arms.

Actually, as far as Ronya was concerned, the truce was ended. There had been no trouble—each wagonload of grain reached its destination safely and, all in all, the venture was a complete success with all goals attained: In the Ukraine the famine was no threat to the solvency of the landowners, and on a modest scale the peasants had wheat sufficient to meet their needs. The Cossack chiefs, well stocked, left the Jews to their Sabbath loaves in peace. In no time at all, it seemed, Ronya had paid Tamara off in gold, giving her an overall profit of eighteen percent. But at this moment there was nothing she could do but be civil; she felt she owed it to David. And, too, she was about to ask Tamara for her assistance. Fortunately, nothing pleased Tamara more than being called upon to lend her resourcefulness in planning a party.

They all three went to the playroom for a demonstration of using the whip to back a person into a corner. Then, with a rapid flick, Ronya made a handkerchief disappear from the top of David's head without touching a hair. She made melodious sounds with the whip, and to David it was music.

"Ronya, my mother, make it sound like hard rain in the wind."
Rain in the wind filled the room.

He reached up and kissed Ronya. She hugged him and handed over
the whip. "Practice your swings, darling. And if you feel your bandage
getting wet, that means you're bleeding. Go at once to Lydia."

David said, "All right," but it was perfectly obvious that he had no
intention of doing any such thing.

Ronya sighed.

Curled up on a sofa in the library drinking Lydia's marvelous
steaming hot coffee, Tamara said hesitantly, "It strikes me that you
heckle David."

"I have to," Ronya admitted. "He could break a leg and he
wouldn't complain of pain. Imagine! Walking around for days with a
piece of glass in his foot."

"How is it you didn't know?"

Ronya shrugged. "Boris won't let me bathe him, and he won't let
me dress him. 'I'm not a baby,' he says."

"Maybe it's his nature to stay unperturbed."

Ronya brought the mug to her lips. "No," she said reluctantly, putting down the mug, "it's nothing to do with his character. I used to
think it was perversity, but I did him an injustice. More likely he is
not aware of an injury—at least, not to the same degree as most children."

"You ought to take him to a doctor," Tamara said in a troubled
voice.

"I've spoken to a couple of local doctors. Stupid ignoramuses. One
said, 'Fear has big eyes, Madam Pirov. There's nothing the matter
with the boy.' The second agreed with the first and advised me to be
grateful that I don't have a sniveling crybaby on my hands. He collected his fee and bowed himself out. Then I suggested to Boris that I
should take David to a diagnostician in Vienna. What a blowup! He
accused me of wanting to see Erick Stiller again. Remember him?"

Tamara nodded. "You can't go against Boris. But Katya could take
David."

"Maybe—if I get more sure." Ronya refilled the mugs. "You look
suddenly gloomy."

"I have good reason. Krasmikov was over last night. After breakfast,
he took it into his head to drop over to the stables and say hello to
Boris. When he came back he—"

Ronya's highly arched brows rose higher.

Tamara misunderstood. "All right," she said savagely, "I have a
feeble character. I'm corrupt. I sin. To coin a proverb, 'What good is
virtue in an empty bed?' "

"I didn't say anything."

"You did," Tamara said accusingly. "You have the most judgmental brows on earth. You and that panther-footed Blond One. I'd rather face a wolf baring his teeth than—"

"Stop croaking like an angry hen. What did Krasmikov tell you?"

"Oh—" Tamara burst into tears. "Why don't you put an end to his whoring? You could, you know."

Seeing her so tormented over Boris made Ronya sick and angry. Her hands tightened into fists. "Tamara! You tell me what Krasmikov said."

Wiping her eyes with the back of her hand, Tamara said through the last of her tears, "Boris invited him to a party and told him not to bring me—the stupid ox, thinking he could tell me that much and no more! I snatched up his pants and threw them in his face." She gave Ronya another long glance. "Guess what she looks like."

"I don't have to guess. She's tall, a blonde or a redhead. Easygoing, and five to ten years away from fat. She's got good teeth. Boris is very particular about teeth. And she's free from venereal disease. He's particular about that, too."

Krasmikov's words had been: "Tall, fair, not really pretty but attractive—a real nice smile. Stripped naked, I bet she's got meat on her."

"How did you know?" Tamara said to Ronya.

"They're all the same. The same size, the same arrangement of parts."

Tamara pouted. "This one is young."

"No, the age doesn't vary. They seem younger, because we're getting older."

"Oh, Christ! Don't remind me."

"Don't look so tragic. We'll never be fair and fat, and we're far from forty."

Tamara wet her lips with the tip of her tongue. "What are you going to do?"

"When is this great social event going to be?"

"On the twenty-sixth."

"Do you know where?"

Tamara shook her head. "Krasmikov went dumb. He just wouldn't answer that. But I'll find out, don't you worry."

"Don't bother. Tell Krasmikov to decline Boris' invitation. You are both coming to my party. *All* of Boris' friends are coming to my party. It happens that it falls on the same night."

Tamara brightened. "What party?"

"A charity. A really showy party to raise money for the wretched victims of the famine."

332

"How marvelous!"

"I'll need all your pretty girls to act as hostesses and a full gypsy orchestra. We'll discuss the details another time."

Tamara leaned forward and clasped Ronya's hands in hers. "I'll dance. I'll be a sensation. I'll outdo all the whores in Kiev."

Ronya laughed. "In that case, I'll make the price of admission a shocker."

"We'll make a fortune," Tamara said, giving Ronya's hands a gentle squeeze. All at once, she realized: "But what about Boris? He's already made his plans—"

"He'll be here."

It was barely light on November 26 when Father Tromokov, just back from a peasant village on the landlocked Caspian, came bareheaded into Ronya's kitchen. He removed his heavy overcoat and flung it over a chair. A few minutes later he was stretched lazily in Boris' rocker uncorking a bottle. Tilting and dozing, he waited. The clock was striking six as he heard Lydia's footsteps.

"Away from here," he said, brandishing the bottle, now only half full, "they ring bells often but not for dinner. Pray to God, Lydia, but put the kettle to boil."

"Welcome home, Father," said Lydia cheerfully, and soon the priest was filling his lungs with the delicious aroma of chicken livers cooking in sweet butter.

Lydia could scarcely wait to tell about the party and soon launched into a flow of talk. "Most gratifying to my Ronya is the contribution from the Jews. Each family is pledging one week's wages, be they full or poor as mice."

The priest was impressed. "I'll be damned."

Lydia chuckled and then, giving him a conspiratorial look, said, "Somebody had better keep an eye on Tamara. She's up to something. That whoring she-devil is a blasphemy against decency."

"About the Jews, Lydia. Has the rabbi raised his ban? Will he let the Jews accept her?"

The answer came almost at once from Boris, who was standing in the doorway. "No, it still stands. Ronya remains isolated." He advanced, holding out his hand, and Ivan Tromokov gripped it warmly.

Rising, Lydia went to the stove. Presently she came back with Boris' scrambled eggs, and though she knew that Boris liked and trusted her, she removed herself from the kitchen.

Boris poured his own coffee. "How did it go?"

Ivan Tromokov was not one to mock God, but his first utterance was a blasphemy. He added bitterly, "Polluted, corrupted, stinking

333

Holy Mother Russia. And that, my friend, is an understatement." He tilted the vodka bottle, gulped a long drink, and grimaced. Vivid in his mind was the exhaustion and helplessness of the inarticulate and the unorganized. "I found a total collapse of the economy, deliberate and gross profiteering, and control by the bayonet. The list of horrors is endless."

There was a lengthy silence during which Ivan Tromokov mustered his courage. Then, with a rush, he plunged in. "Sooner or later, Boris, the Ukraine must free itself from the Romanovs. Let's seize power now. The famine provides a rare opportunity."

The look in Boris' eyes was savage. "If what you're really saying is the peasants should help themselves to privately owned land, I can only recommend that you don't try it here."

The priest sighed. "Would I hurt Ronya?"

"For your peasants." Boris stopped. "I don't know." He stood. "Swear allegiance to Ronya, or I crush you beneath my heel."

The priest answered mildly, "I assure you, my friend—" Then, his voice deepened. "Dammit, you know I'm talking plain good sense. Why shouldn't we regulate our own way of life on our own soil?"

Boris shook his head. His features relaxed. "Start a civil war? Don't be a fool."

The priest saw that with Boris, as with Ronya, persuasion was useless for now. He got to his feet. "Tell Ronya I'll be back to liven up the party."

Evening came, a splendid evening. The full moon glittered on the snow, and snow crystals glittered on bare, weather-beaten trees. There was nothing in Kiev to approach the magnificence of the Von Glasman house; on this gala evening the house outrivaled itself in splendor and hospitality.

One after another, troikas on runners and sleighs drawn by trotters drove up to the front entrance at a steady pace. Gentlemen in evening clothes or dress uniform handed down ladies wrapped in furs under which were gowns of the latest and most dazzling French fashions. The coachmen swung around and continued in a long line to the rear of the house, where waiting for them in the servants' hall was hot borsch, dough turnovers filled with meat, and plenty of vodka.

All four units of the Cavalry were well represented. Hussars dressed in red pants and jackets braided with five rows of cord; lancers, lean and handsome, sabers swaying; white-bloused Cossacks with swords, daggers, and cartridge belts; and dragoons, every boot, every button shining. The bachelor officers arrived in twos, come to enjoy a Russian's greatest pleasures—to eat and drink, talk and joke, and dance with merry, bare-armed girls.

The reception started in the central hall, extended into the drawing room, and spilled over into the morning room. Standing side by side under the graceful swing of the mahogany banister, Boris—seven rows of gold braid arrayed across his chest, his tunic belted and held fast with a gold buckle—and Ronya—young and as fresh as a spring flower among the glittering brocades and lush velvets in a delicate blouse and a skirt—welcomed their guests warmly. The babble of gaiety mounted, as six butlers supervised twenty waiters pouring champagne and a glossy array of gypsy girls passing hors d'oeuvres.

The spacious library had been turned into a treasure room, which the guests paid to enter. A murmur of envy and admiration hovered over the silk embroideries, the valuable books and manuscripts, the paintings and drawings, the lapis lazuli and jade, the beautiful cut glass, the crystal and gold, and the rare porcelain snuffboxes.

Presently, at a prearranged signal, the musicians of the Cavalry band began playing a waltz—not to invite the guests to dance but to tempt them into the ballroom. The hilarity and flirtations were a bit too lively for so early in the evening.

In the ballroom, twenty tables set with gleaming silver and crystal on pure white linen had been arranged in groups along three walls. On a stage by the fourth wall, two groups of musicians were waiting, the gypsies ready to strike up their music as soon as the sounds of the military orchestra ceased.

All through dinner, a prolonged feast, there was entertainment: a famed basso accompanying himself on the guitar, a soldiers' chorus, a Hungarian violinist. During the purposely protracted wait between the entrée and dessert, Boris made his way across to Ronya.

"Ready?" he asked.

"I am."

They walked to the stage to soft music played by both orchestras. Although nothing had been announced in advance, the guests shifted their chairs to obtain a good view.

Boris handed Ronya her whip, which had been placed in a corner of the stage that morning. The tilt of her head told him she was ready. He smiled at her reassuringly, signaled to the musicians, and lit a cigarette.

But for the music, all was quiet. Ronya raised her arm, swung the whip—and the cigarette dangling from his lips disappeared. He lit another and held it up. Another flick of the whip, and the cigarette was extinguished, the white tube still steady between his fingers. The applause was wild. Boris held up his hand for silence. Still the hurrahs went on, punctuated with the tinkling of glass. The crack-crack of Ronya's whip—each crack as sharp and sure as a pistol shot—silenced them. She performed to the music of a mazurka, her dancing a miracle of sustained grace, each crack of the whip in perfect rhythm. The music changed to a slow, romantic tune. Boris stood still as a statue. In the same slow rhythm, Ronya's whip missed Boris' eyes, nose, mouth, by a breath, her movements were so graceful, so beautiful that the performance took on the lightness and charm of a lyrical dance. Finally, Boris took the whip from Ronya's hand and raised the hand to his lips. Amid mounting applause, he proudly escorted her back to her table.

It was after dinner, when the noise and gaiety and drinking were at their height, that Tamara danced.

Weeks afterward, at a social gathering far from Kiev, a very strait-laced lady said, with genuine admiration, "One cannot describe the gypsy queen. A fire burns in her. When she danced, some of us averted our heads, but we soon conceded that she was a priestess born to entice men, even the unconquerable, and compel brief surrender."

That night the ladies of Kiev paid Tamara homage—handmaidens to Astarte.

Tamara whirled about the dance floor. One number was carefree, one amazingly funny, one as airy and light as a snowflake, one wild and unfettered. One was of love and longing, and men who had been drinking for hours made no attempt to hide the emotions she unleashed in their fevered imaginations.

Flushed with pleasure, Tamara rose from her bow and held out her arms to Boris.

"Dance with me," she said provocatively. Boris, who had been matching his guests glass for glass, cast her an appraising glance and caught her low on her hips.

His hair blazed like streaks of hardened sun, and he danced with the dash and daring with which he speeded an unsaddled stallion down a mountain gully.

Wild with excitement, the crowd joined in—first only the men, then men and women joined hands and, in beat with the music, circled Boris and Tamara.

Ronya watched. Mercifully, only the priest was paying attention to her. When the dance came to an end, she forced her stiff face into a smile and took a glass of vodka from a passing waiter. She did not drink but instead held the glass watchful. As soon as he could get away from the crowd that surrounded him and Tamara, Boris came to her. Mimicking his own style, she raised her glass and tossed down the vodka in one gulp. "I want another drink."

Boris raised a finger and beckoned a waiter.

This was unexpected.

Ronya drew a deep breath and said, "I've changed my mind. It's time to start the auction."

Boris was amused.

Ronya presented her back to him, but before she could take a step, he had an arm about her waist. She looked back at him over her shoulder.

"You know perfectly well Ivan Tromokov is the auctioneer."

Ronya turned and met his gaze. "I am only going to introduce him," she said innocently.

"All right, dove." Boris let her go, smiling but feeling guilty about the dance. "I'll wait for you right here."

Ronya hesitated. He whispered in her ear, "I love you."

"That's nice," Ronya said meekly.

Boris frowned.

On the stage, Ronya stood directly in front of the musicians and under the glow of the chandelier. The noise and babble slackened.

Boris began to walk toward Ronya along with the others. He felt an undercurrent of foreboding, there was something about Ronya, something that demanded attention. He looked up at her—her figure at once slim and sensuous, her hands shapely and strong. Nothing different there. Her face—hard to tell. Lips rosy and faintly moist. Hair the same luxuriant sweep that framed her face like a glorious copper halo.

Ronya turned her face to his. Searching her eyes, Boris found the answer. Her eyes had a strange fire in them.

Ronya began as if nothing extraordinary were about to take place. She thanked the guests for their generous and enthusiastic response, complimented the musicians, praised the staff and, although she made no great point of it, very graciously gave Tamara credit for the unusual table decorations.

For some reason, everyone seemed to guess something was in the air. The silence was complete.

"You've been told," Ronya went on with an enchanting smile, "that our beloved Father Tromokov will, in the name of charity and for a most worthy cause, take on the role of auctioneer. And, so he will.

"However, it is I, your hostess, who shall start the auction. Gentlemen: my lips in one lingering kiss. What am I bid?"

A prolonged roar rose from the men, almost smothering the first bid from a handsome, dark officer in the uniform of a hussar.

But Boris heard the bid; Ronya did, too.

Punctuating his bid, "One thousand rubles!" Boris shoved forward. Those around him fell back.

To everyone's surprise, Ronya laughed. "That, Boris Pirov, is an insult. I myself bid three thousand rubles and cheerfully present it to"—Ronya paused and looked around as if unable to decide. Her eyes found the hussar—"a gentleman of my choosing."

It was Ronya who had put him in this absurd position, yet it was the hussar whom Boris wanted to strangle with his bare hands.

Haughtily, Ronya counted: "Three thousand, once. Three thousand, twice. T-h-r-e-e—"

"Five thousand."

When the long-drawn-out clapping subsided, Ronya called out in a ringing voice, "Do I hear six thousand?"

Tamara's voice came from the center of the room. "Yes, I bid six thousand rubles."

Boris' eyes filled with disgust.

The crowd yelled and stamped and roared with glee.

Ronya felt both annoyed and silly. As Tamara pushed her way forward, she said, "You can't bid."

"Yes, I can."

Giving her a tigerish look, Ronya snapped, "Your bid is idiotic."

"You have no right to refuse the high bid," Tamara countered defiantly.

Ronya walked straight to the center of the stage. Her dark eyes sought Boris'. His lost some of their amusement and with one leap he was next to her. Taking her hand into his, he said, "Ladies and gentlemen, the bidding is closed at seven thousand rubles. And now—"

There were renewed cheers.

Ronya and Boris hardly noticed. Their kiss left them both breathless.

Father Tromokov, roaring with vodka and relief, took Ronya's place. Never were the Kievan landowners so united with the military. Never, with one accord, did they so generously give.

The rain of money ended with the guests crowding around the buffet tables for breakfast.

Routed out from the warm kitchen, the vodka, and the flushed kitchen maids, the coachmen drove their cheerful ladies and gentlemen into the first glimmerings of dawn.

35

Events seldom begin when they occur, and the suicide that created a scandal in Kiev started months before. There were some who blamed Ronya. They said, "It's her land. If she had not let Tamara have her own way, the tragedy would not have occurred."

Ronya let their conjectures stand.

The truth was that a curious combination of circumstances had brought the death about, and the tragic affair could have ended in no other way.

One hot day the previous July, Lydia opened the rear door to a fair-headed young man, slight and barely above medium height. Looking him up and down appraisingly, she noted the blond hair on his bare arms, and the blond hairs sprouting from his chin, and the tuft of blond hair on his chest. His faded blue shirt was unbuttoned. What particularly intrigued her were the knapsack on his back and the roll of canvases under his arm.

"Please," he said, "may I make bold to ask a favor? I must see Gospodin Pirov."

Schooled by Ronya, Lydia never turned a stranger away. "Please wait here," she said. "It happens the master is presently at home."

Boris was in the library dozing. At five that morning, he had delivered a hundred horses to small dealers at a horse fair.

"A stranger asks to see you, sir."

Such crypticness was out of character for Lydia. Boris looked at her. "Why the brevity?"

"You'd think I'd have the sense not to barge in," she said dolefully. "It's getting that I permit myself too much liberty."

"You're a damned fake. Tell me about the stranger."

Now that he was grinning, Lydia chuckled. "He's a painter. He looks proud and poorly fed. His bones stick out."

"Show him in."

Boris was fixing his tie into a neat bow when the man came into the room. He turned from the mirror and held out his hand. "I'm Boris Pirov."

The man's eyes slid away from the outstretched hand. He seemed to have to force himself to offer his own. It was cold and damp.

Boris could see that the poor fellow was in pretty bad shape.

"Why don't you make yourself comfortable? I'll fix us a drink. What'll you have?"

"My name is Leo Vassily. I am an artist."

"All right, Leo Vassily. What can I do for you?"

Tears welled up in Vassily's eyes. Clutching his work tightly, he said, "I am self-taught. I have a lot to learn. But I am an artist, not a painter. An artist!"

Boris simply nodded and served himself a vodka and his caller a sherry.

Scarcely aware of his knapsack falling to the floor, Vassily looked up at him, and for the second time his eyes filled with tears. "You don't know how hard it is. Nobody cares."

"Sit down," Boris said kindly and firmly. "If you want to sell me a picture, show them to me."

"No," Vassily said, with a quick shake of the head. "I have nothing to sell."

"Then why are you here?"

Vassily leaned forward. "I have a pencil sketch of your wife. It's the best thing I've ever done. I want you to have it. In return I ask leave to wander about and the chance to do odd jobs when I need supplies."

A fierce look came into Boris' eyes. "Give me the sketch," he said sharply.

The sketch was abstract and uniquely inventive, yet the slim form that curved so intriguingly, and the shape of the face, expressed in an arrangement of lines, were Ronya's alone.

"How do you know my wife?"

Vassily had not known that so great a change in a man's face was possible. "I don't," he answered, barely above a whisper. "I saw her once—only once. I did the sketch from memory."

Again Vassily was startled. The savage look had gone as suddenly as it had come. "Sir, I did not think you'd mind. There's no reason to mind. I even thought you'd be pleased."

"You say you saw my wife," he said, pleasantly now. "When? Where?"

"Some weeks ago when I was painting near here. I looked up and found myself being watched by a woman. She had a blond boy with her. She apologized for intruding, and then she said, 'You're extremely good.' Then she called to the boy, and they raced downhill through the grass, and I was left alone.

"I'm afraid I did not paint much after that. I decided to have a glass of tea in a café where there is a girl who sometimes talks to me. I told her about the lady and the boy, and that's how I found out the lady's name. The waitress said her name was Ronya, the wife of Boris Pirov."

Boris reached for the bell cord. "You're to go with Lydia, our housekeeper. While you eat, I'll look over the rest of these canvases."

"I have no appetite. I—"

"Fortunately, Lydia has a remedy for that."

Boris separated the canvases, and the more he looked, the more enthusiastic he grew. None was realistic. Some were harsh, even fierce. Boris was no expert on technical craftsmanship, but he knew that what he saw was first-rate. Boris was no physician, but he knew that Leo Vassily was a highly imaginative misfit ill-adapted to the average environment. Boris was no oracle, and he did not divine that Vassily was ill-omened, but he needed no clairvoyance to be sure that he did not want Vassily near Ronya and the boys.

340

He came into the kitchen carrying the knapsack and the oils. "Come, we've a call to make."

Leo Vassily gave Lydia a shy smile. "I've ruined your tablecloth."

It was with difficulty that Lydia lifted her eyes from the crayon drawing of her own face, her own silk-covered head, her own wide hips. She beamed with pleasure. "I've never had a picture of me before."

They went out, but an instant later Boris put his head around the door. "When your mistress returns, don't discuss our caller. I'll tell her myself. And it might make it easier to have that tablecloth out of here."

The look on Lydia's face made him smile.

In front of a table cluttered with dye stuffs, rouges of varying tints, blue and green for beautifying the eyes, creams, perfumes, Tamara sat peering into the mirror immersed in her own image. The tub was full, she was undressed, yet still she sat. She was trying to decide what to do about six gray hairs. "It's ridiculous to start pulling out hair," she told herself. "Far better— No," she sighed. "If once you start with artificial coloring—" As usual, self-pity suddenly seized her. "Why did this have to happen to me? Why not Katya? She's older." The thought of Katya graying comforted her. She threw back her head. "To hell with it. I'll comb my hair so they won't show." Her mind made up now, she walked over to the tub. She had just reached out to turn on more hot water, when she heard a man's voice under the window.

Annoyed—"Who needs *him* early?"—Tamara paused long enough to snatch up a bath towel and looked out of the window. "Good God, Boris!" There were at least a dozen wrappers and robes in a closet not five feet away. Tamara made a rapid appraisal of herself in the long mirror, let the towel fall a little lower, and ran to open the door. She stood stock-still, mortified. "I thought you were alone."

Tamara was at the peak of her beauty, and a man had to be made of wood to remain unmoved. Boris was made of flesh and blood. Slowly he pulled his gaze from the curve of the towel. Looking over his shoulder, he surveyed Vassily's embarrassment. Haunted eyes averted, the lad was politely trying to keep his face empty. Poor devil!

During dinner, Ronya and Boris had a quarrel. Boris' guest provided the reason, but it was David who brought it on.

When Boris came in, there was time only to strip off his clothes, shave, and bathe. He opened Ronya's door softly. It was nearly eight o'clock, but she was still in her robe, lying on the bed telling a story. His four sons were sprawled all over her. No one greeted him. She looked up with a smile, but her voice hardly paused. Boris tiptoed into the room, his only intention to sit quietly and listen.

David pursed his lips. "Sh-sh-sh!"

Boris gave him a look. David returned exactly the same look.

My God! Ronya thought. *That's pure Tartar. It's illogical to think that David just mimics him.* She stopped the story and in the silence that followed David fumed, "You interrupted *my* mother."

Boris smoldered. He took one step nearer, but the attack came from Igor. In a rage, he let fly. "Yours—since when?" David ducked, and Ronya took the blow. Suddenly there was nothing loving and laughing about Georgi. He was digging his hands into Igor's face ready to tear holes in it. "You hurt *my* mamma."

Boris groaned. "Christ, another one!" But he was touched. Georgi was putting up a good fight.

Ronya began to laugh.

That decided David. He lent Georgi a hand. In the bedlam that followed—the Blond One wisely did nothing—Boris roared, "Stop, before I cripple all three of you."

As if Ronya were one of the children, Boris turned on her. "If you're not downstairs by the time I finish one drink—one, Ronya—"

Ronya giggled. "I'll be there."

When supper was finished, Ronya listened without interruption while Boris told her of Leo Vassily, breaking in on his own story to show her the sketch. "See what he did of you."

It was awhile before Ronya put it down. Almost in one breath, she said, "He has a splendid talent. What arrangements have you made for him?"

"I took him to Tamara and left him in her charge. She'll see that he has everything he needs."

She stared at him with a look of outrage. "Why didn't you house him in a brothel?"

"Rubbish. Tamara wouldn't give that undersized mouse the time of day."

"If a lion may come to be beholden to a mouse, so can Tamara," she said furiously.

"I don't care a damn what they do."

Her voice rose high. "You could have given him one of the guest cabins, you could have found him a good home with a peasant family —but no. You planted him in the camp, because you want an excuse to go calling. And even if Tamara does seduce him, that won't interfere with you, will it? After all, Krasmikov doesn't, the Cossacks don't."

Boris said quietly, "You're overwrought, Ronya. Go to bed." He watched her pick up her wine glass and raise her arm. He shook his head. "Don't do that."

342

"I will if I want to," Ronya snapped back at him.

"Good-night, Ronya." He got to his feet. "Tomorrow is another early morning—a few green hired hands. I want to keep an eye on them."

The gypsies called him Tamara's painter and accepted him but thought him a little crazy—a man who would rather paint Old Auntie than a pretty girl, a tiny toad beneath a huge mushroom than a sunflower or the river under the summer sky.

Gradually, and mainly because Boris had taken a fancy to him, Tamara became interested in Vassily. She arrived at his wagon one morning with a basket of groceries and found him standing at his easel. She could not tell whose face was in the charcoal drawing; there were no details certifying this is a nose, these are eyes. But she knew the face was familiar.

"Do you like it?"

Unlike Boris and Ronya, Tamara did not recognize his amazing talent. "No-no, not especially. She hasn't much except bones and eyebrows, but—"

"Before I'm through, she'll have hair and loops in her ears."

"Won't she have color?"

"She will when I do her in oils."

She put the groceries on a shelf and the perishables in the cold box. "Let me know if there's anything I can do for you," she said before going out.

In a rush, before he lost his courage, Vassily blurted, "You can pose for me. That way, maybe you'll recognize yourself."

"Oh, I'd love to," she said, intrigued.

He blushed and stammered, when?

"Right now. I haven't anything else to do."

Leo Vassily could hardly believe it.

She smiled at his awe. "Shall I take my clothes off?"

He was stunned.

Tamara smiled again and unhooked her skirt.

For all of Tamara's expertise, it was a long morning. For one thing, it was all too sudden; for another, Vassily did not know what to do. When Tamara realized this, she began to feel for him a kind of tenderness. She silenced his incoherent stammerings with kisses and guided his trembling fingers, until, at last, he was no longer innocent. And then, out of compassion, Tamara made him a present. "You were marvelous."

With tremendous surprise, Leo Vassily said, "Really?"

To Vassily what had happened was a miracle. His whole world changed. He was bewitched.

343

From the beginning Tamara argued, "Why capture a mere like-ness? I spend hours posing for you. Make the most of it. Besides, look-ing at that portrait, who would take me for a beauty? It's too disquiet-ing."

Vassily's style became more precise. He toiled over the portrait trying again and again, harder and harder. Finally, he got a physical likeness so true that it satisfied Tamara.

But the portrait was empty. The integrity in Vassily—what was left of it—rebelled against the emptiness, the meaninglessness he saw on the canvas. But he deluded himself, buoyed up by Tamara's delight. "What is the use of painting pictures," he asked himself, "if no one likes them? In art, nothing is absolute."

It seemed to Boris that Vassily's talent had vanished. He lost all in-terest in him.

For some weeks Tamara's spirit had been revolted by Vassily's ap-proaches, timid one minute, frantic and panting the next, but not until her portrait was completed to her satisfaction did she say, "Vass-ily, we're finished, and nothing that went on between us can change my mind."

"No!" Vassily cried out. "You can't!"

Desperately shamed by his stricken face, Tamara grew furious. "Don't feel yourself ill used. I paid for my portrait, I made you happy at my expense. You should be grateful."

"You're ill," Vassily sobbed, cruelly shaken, "you don't know what you're saying."

"Vassily, my friend," she said, pitiless in her plain speaking, "I hunt lovers. I collect them. And when I'm in the mood, any well-powered male does nicely. If I were you, I'd—"

Vassily fell to his knees weeping.

Now Tamara hated him. He had reminded her of herself, kneeling and weeping before Boris.

Vassily stopped painting. He stopped eating. Sunk in melancholy, he played his flute. Affected in spite of herself, Tamara sent for Boris.

He scribbled on the back of her note:

> Thanks to you, a talent is destroyed. As for Vassily's problem, I can't solve it. I haven't the right equipment.
> Be sensible, Tamara. I wish you luck.
>
> B.

Tamara wrote a second note and, by dispatching it to Ronya, she made certain of a more sympathetic response.

Boris:

You brought Vassily here, so you are committed to him. You can't let a man die merely because you've stopped thinking well of him. I'm sure that if Ronya had been Vassily's model, you'd have had no objections to his seeing her harmoniously. Because it was I he painted, you wanted fragments—a breast, a limb, or an ugly caricature.

Is your stubbornness more precious to you than a human life?

Tamara

Ronya instructed Lydia to fill a couple of jars, one with soup, and one with stewed fruits, and hurried off to the stables, catching Boris whittling a wooden whistle for the Blond One.

Far from pleased and cursing Tamara, Boris swung up in the saddle and rode out with the food. He came to the wagon in a cloud of dust, dismounted, and went in. He got Vassily to take the soup.

"And now," he said when he put down the soup spoon, "I want you to get the hell out of here." Dragging the knapsack from under the bed, he said, "Pack."

Vassily began to tremble with agitation. "I revered her."

"You wanted a kitten, and got struck down by a she-wolf," Boris said. "Let it go at that, and stop feeling sorry for yourself."

Boris was being watched by eyes far too bright. He emptied his pockets. "Take it."

"In the beginning," Vassily said excitedly, ignoring the money, "she received me in a motherly fashion, affectionate and patient. Then, all at once, without turning a hair, she attacked, saying all she wants from a man is muscle."

Boris nodded. "There's a saddled horse outside. A day's easy ride, and you can make camp miles from here. Fix your eyes on the landscape and paint. You used to be good. Maybe you can be great." Without further comment, he left. Shortly afterward, the bay caught up with him.

Vassily gave no trouble after that. He made no attempt to see Tamara. In the evening he appeared at someone's table and ate a little supper. The rest of the time he painted, and very well. Soon, nobody worried about him. Gypsy children played around his wagon, and occasionally Boris, curious to see the new work, dropped in and stayed a few minutes.

With the onset of the early frost, Vassily shut himself in. He started to paint Tamara, using memory as his model. Then he began to incorporate his dreams into the canvases, and in his dreams he was a bull. He ate practically nothing and fainted from exhaustion.

Around midday on a Tuesday late in November, he called on

Ronya. It took her a good five minutes to get him into the library; he wanted to talk in the hall. Finally he followed her, moving cautiously. Ronya sank into a chair and watched him put a bulky roll of canvases on a table between them. Suddenly he sagged into a chair. "The top two are for you, Mistress Ronya. I want you to look at them, please."

Ronya took up one, then the other, and caught her breath.

"Do you like them?"

"They're magnificent."

"Yes—yes—of course—they're magnificent. That's not the point. Do you like them?"

Ronya nodded slowly. "Very much."

His watery eyes fixed on her now, Vassily said, "The one with the shimmering sky and the figure of the boy with yellow hair symbolizes the day fate sent me here. The all-white painting is sacred. It is for the unscorned."

Ronya met his look. "Tamara had no wish to hurt you. She had no wish to hurt me. Do you understand?"

He said nothing.

"Tamara never means to hurt anyone."

His knees trembled. He began to shiver.

"Rest here. I'll come back later with tea."

"Mistress Ronya, will you give the remainder of my oils to your husband? He'll know what to do with them."

"Are you leaving us?"

His voice was quiet. "I'm staying."

"I'm glad," Ronya said with a smile. "Stay and paint. That'll reduce Tamara to proper size."

Vassily was the first to rise. Uneasy, Ronya noted his skeletal thinness as he disappeared through the door.

A moment later, Igor put his head inquiringly into the room, the Blond One behind him. To her amazement, Ronya found that the boys had long ago made Leo Vassily their concern.

"David, too?"

"Sure." This from Igor.

"Sit down and tell me."

Igor hesitated, his glance on the Blond One. The Blond One answered with a nod, Igor with another, and they both turned to Ronya.

"The sheets," Igor said with a grin. "David is the one who steals them."

Ronya laughed aloud. "Of course, the sheets. Vassily needs them for paint rags."

The Blond One smiled. "Don't tell Lydia."

Ronya's eyes went from the Blond One's face to Igor's. "I won't."

346

Igor said, "Ronya, my mother—for a mother you're certainly splendid."

The next day, before the camp was stirring, the Blond One had his bread and cheese with milk and walked out carrying leftovers and hard-boiled eggs tied in a bundle. Vassily's wagon stood silent at the end of the empty lane between the barns and the main road. His progress toward the wagon was leisurely, but as he came nearer and saw the windows heavily curtained he sensed that something was wrong, knowing how Vassily valued even one slit of daylight. He walked faster now. The door was chain-locked from the inside. The Blond One could not imagine Vassily locking his door. His fine blue eyes watchful, he listened. Not a sound but his own breathing. After a few minutes he dropped the bundle, threw off his overcoat, turned swiftly, and started to run. At the big house he climbed the stairs silently and halted outside Ronya's bedroom. Kneeling down, he gave the thrush call—the secret communication between Tartar and Tartar—and stood back.

In minutes, Boris was standing beside the Blond One. He gave no indication of surprise, but his face had the look of a man alerted for some catastrophe. "Come," he said in a low voice, moving across the hall into his own room. The Blond One followed on tiptoe. He peered up at his father. "You'd better get to Vassily's wagon." No explanation.

Boris nodded. He trusted the boy's instinct wholly. As he untied his dressing gown, the Blond One put a match to the paper beneath the kindling and, sitting down quietly, watched his father dress by the flames licking up over the logs. He wanted to ask if he might wake Igor but decided he had better not.

Boris guessed that the Blond One would rush to Igor as soon as he stepped out into the cold, gray morning. He did not mind. Secretly he was proud of the love between his son and his bastard. Just before he reached the closed door, he paused and said in a level voice, "You're to stay here. Tell Igor to keep his mouth shut."

Even as he was kicking the door down, Boris thought that Leo Vassily—frail-balanced and caught up in the tangle of Tamara's sexuality —had committed the act of self-destruction. Boris was right; he had. But Boris had never thought to set eyes upon the like of the hideousness that awaited him in the semidarkness beyond the door—the amputated blood-purple protuberance pushed like the twist of a serpent onto a horrible distortion of Tamara's face. Stacks of canvases were piled high on the table, and with them three of Ronya's missing sheets, two tied together, the third made into a hangman's noose. On the floor, Leo Vassily lay half-naked, dead in a sea of blood.

Boris reeled out of the wagon.

By the time Boris barged into Tamara's bedroom, intending that she should see what she was responsible for, he was no longer stumbling.

Krasmikov sat up, dazed. Tamara pushed herself up against the pillows. She looked into Boris' face—hard and menacing—and recoiled.

"I've come to congratulate you, Tamara. Leo Vassily has made you a gift."

Tamara cringed.

"The supreme gift. He castrated himself."

Tamara groaned; her lips blanched; she slumped down. "I meant him no harm."

Leo Vassily had no family, and the police cared nothing about a vagrant painter. Mischuk arranged a private inquest. Only Boris gave evidence. The doctor added one sentence. "He bled profusely." The verdict: "Demented, Leo Vassily met death by his own hand."

Tamara wept bitter tears of remorse and provided the bronze casket. Old Auntie dressed him in corduroy. Ronya choked back tears and stood by Tamara.

Boris' anger grew: "Why?"

Ronya put her hands on his shoulders and kissed him gently on the mouth. "Because I must." Early on Friday morning Ronya said, "Come with me, Boris."

"No!" His mind was made up. He was not going to change it.

The gypsies buried Leo Vassily in style. Then they burned the wagon.

In the church, the bell tolled.

36

It was Ronya who suggested a hunting expedition. Since the funeral, Boris had been silent and grim, weighed down by the horror of what he had seen. One evening a few days later when Father Tromokov and Mischuk had come to dinner, she broached the idea in the form of a demand for a new bearskin rug. All three men brightened at the thought of a bear-hunt, and next day Mischuk was arranging for some leave, Father Tromokov was sending to the next village for a priest to take his place, and Boris was busy cleaning his guns and stockpiling food, vodka, tobacco, and brandy.

Igor and the Blond One followed Boris around all day. David tagged along, too. Finally, Igor could no longer restrain himself. "Aren't you taking us?"

"No, son."

David turned on him. "Why not?"

"You're not quite ready."

"We are. None of us needs a padded saddle. We all three can ride as many hours as you without a break and follow wherever you lead."

Boris was not displeased at his eagerness and tried to refuse gently. "We'll be riding immense distances day after day through treacherous terrain, resting only a few hours before pushing on. I'll take you on a real hunt next fall, before the wolves are hungry and when we can manage it at a walking pace."

David's face clouded, but before he could open his mouth Igor had gripped him by the shoulders. "Shut up! It's on account of you that we can't go."

Like lightning David's expression changed from disappointment to ferocity; he closed with Igor.

Boris let them slug it out until David was panting and Igor, afraid to drop his guard and wipe the sweat from his eyes, was breathing heavily. Then he stepped in and separated them.

The Blond One watched, quiet as ever, his respect for David's fighting skill mixed with love for Igor.

"Why did you stop us?" David grumbled. "I nearly had him."

"No," Boris said mildly, "but you put up a good fight, and you're good at taking punishment. Shake hands with your brother, Igor."

Igor offered his hand.

Boris cleaned the boys up in his own bathroom and brought them down to supper in fine spirits. They went to bed blissfully happy, full of their father's tales of horses and hunts.

Dressed in windbreaking hooded parkas and wolfskin breeches tucked into light, thoroughly oiled boots, the men were in the saddle early the next morning. Three good comrades, on excellent mounts, rifles firmly braced, with dogs trained to be alert day and night and keep still and silent on command.

Boris rode in front on his stallion, reins loose, his eyes searching, constantly on the lookout for wolves. The deer signs were plentiful. A few yards to his rear came the priest and Mischuk, leading the pack horses. Quivering with excitement, the dogs ran ahead. Before dusk they were in bivouac on a wooded hill, tents pitched and fires lit. Nightfall put an end to their companionable talk. The dogs whined in their sleep, waking with a fusillade of barks and howls when any suspicious scent or sound came to them through the dark forest.

It was just daybreak when Boris heard the elusive sounds of deer browsing. Dressing quickly, teeth clenched against the bitter frost, he scrambled out of his tent and stretched luxuriously. The sky was lightening, revealing a white, quiet world. He sucked the thin, cold air deep into his lungs. There were deer tracks crisscrossed in the snow, and he followed in the wake of what looked to be a fine buck. At the end of the trail he found him bedded down in the snow, instinctively aware that there was no need to fear this man. The buck jumped up. They stared at each other for a moment, and then the buck nonchalantly sauntered off, the soft snow deadening his footfalls. Boris shook his head and smiled. When he returned to the camp, the cooking fire was crackling and Ivan Tromokov was preparing a hearty breakfast.

"Good morning, Boris," said the priest. "It looks to me as though you were up with the sun."

"That's right. Where's Mischuk?"

"With the horses, most likely."

The horses were watering at the foot of the hill, with Mischuk looking on absentmindedly. As the smell of food reached him, he turned and waved. Boris ran down the hill to give him a hand, dodging trees and drifts with easy skill. Together they tramped back to camp with the horses and fell ravenously on the meat, porridge, and coffee the priest had ready on the fire.

They spent the day setting fox traps.

Toward evening, Boris trekked upstream along the river bank. He had been reconnoitering about an hour when he caught sight of the bear. The bear sniffed and shuffled off, apparently without taking any notice of him.

Boris abandoned his tent early again next day. Well armed, he set off alone but for three savage, shaggy-coated dogs of Tibetan breed. Almost at the same spot, he saw the same bear barely twenty yards away. Aggressive by day, the bear stood on his hind legs and growled. Sharply Boris ordered the dogs back.

Well balanced, the butt of the rifle nestled against his shoulder, ready to swing easily in any direction, Boris aimed and advanced a few yards, keeping his eyes fixed on his quarry. The bear shuffled purposefully toward him. He stood absolutely still and fired. The bear fell, wounded. Boris did not rush him. He waited to see if the animal was hard hit—he had seen men die under the great paws of a trapped bear. He used a second cartridge before he walked up to the beast and finished him off with his knife. The bear was huge and in his prime. Boris stood over him, feeling intensely alive. He blinked wind tears from his eyes. The weather was changing. The sky was gray above the dark forest, and the wind was gathering force. He left the dogs to stand guard.

In camp, the priest sat cross-legged by the fire, feeding it with small dry sticks. Mischuk was squatting with his back to the wind, skinning a rabbit.

Boris drew close to the fire. "I got Ronya her bear."

Mischuk sighed without realizing it. "I got a rabbit."

The priest chuckled. "Well, at least we'll never go hungry."

That night Boris lay drowsily staring into the dark and thinking of Ronya—of her body fitting snugly along his, of pleasure shining from her eyes. He became acutely aware of his own body throbbing with excitement. He would be glad to be home.

Along with Ronya's breakfast tray, Lydia carried a letter. Ronya leaned her back against the pillow as her eyes traveled across her name on the envelope. "It's from the rabbi," she said. "I recognize his handwriting."

> Ronya.
> I regard your silence very strange—very strange indeed.
> Unless informed otherwise, I shall expect you at three o'clock.
> Yours,
> Joseph

It was clear that Joseph was angry. Ronya could only assume that it was the suicide of Leo Vassily that had made him write this curt, chilly note. With a sigh of resignation, she instructed Lydia to order her carriage in time for her to reach the Jewish quarter by three o'clock.

For several agonizingly long minutes, Joseph remained silent, his stern eyes condemning the woman sitting opposite—so richly elegant, so unconcernedly lovely, waiting for him to open the conversation.

At last he cried, "Why? Why did it happen?"

"I don't know why, Joseph. His talent was remarkable and, in my opinion, Boris was right to provide him with the opportunity to paint free and unhampered. Who could predict that Tamara would pay attention to him, that he would worship her, that he would destroy himself?"

The rabbi was speechless with surprise.

"I owe you an apology," he said at length with great solemnity. "I see now I have no cause to reproach you. You do not know what has happened.

"Some days ago, twenty thousand working-class Jews were snatched from their slumber and expelled from Moscow. Now only the rich Jews remain there. The new synagogue has been closed down."

Ronya's face reflected her shock and sorrow. That censorship was so tight that no hint of the expulsion had appeared in the local press, that such news had to travel by word of mouth, was frightening beyond imagination. The fate of the Moscow Jews reawakened in her a vein of guilt, even of despair. Almost unconsciously, she wondered whether her conscience would ease somewhat if for once she were personally affected. She put the thought from her in disgust, suddenly overcome by a surge of bristling indignation.

"What are you thinking?" Joseph asked gently, noting the glint of anger in her eyes.

"Where is exile for the twenty thousand?"

"To tell the truth, no one knows for sure. Everything was prepared in advance and carried out in strict secrecy. The rumor is that they are in camps and that those Jews already possessing permits to travel will possibly be allowed to return to Moscow long enough to gather up their possessions."

As her anger abated, Ronya grew thoughtful. "Are you thinking in terms of mass migration?"

Joseph's inner conflict was brought out into the open. Joseph Levinsky loved Russia deeply; still, he dreamed of a better land for the Jews, a land without ghettos and shadows, and he expected Ronya to strain her resources to help Baron Maurice de Hirsch in his colossal undertaking of establishing Jewish colonies in North and South America and in Africa. Now, with a sigh, he lifted his hands and let them fall. "What else?" he said. "The pretense of liberalism is—at least, for the time being—dropped, but the government wants to get rid of the Moscow Jews, so it is fairly certain that the restrictions on emigration will be eased."

"I don't believe the government wants to rid Russia of its Moscow Jews," Ronya countered swiftly. "If the silk factories are shut down, thousands of Christians will lose their jobs." She laughed bitterly as she caught Joseph's expression. "I can't help thinking that I have a genius for exasperating you."

"You are partly right." But he could never remain angry with her for long. "Ronya," he said, "millions of rubles are needed." Joseph cupped his face in his hands and rocked himself a little. "The Diaspora—ah—the centuries we Jews have wandered over the earth's surface, strangers in alien worlds." His voice strained by emotion, he went on in a weary tone, "This is what I want from you, Ronya: half a million rubles."

The fact that she had just purchased a thousand acres from an absentee landowner and had undertaken vast improvements for his tenants—and that this had vastly cut down her resources—she kept to herself. "You have it, Joseph."

"I'm grateful." But his gratitude was brief. Joseph got up and stood with his back to the fire. "I want more than money from you, Ronya, much more. I want the kind of assistance that nobody but a Jewess who shares an ancestor with a bishop and is sister to a countess can obtain for us."

"What about my Tartar connections?"

"I was hoping you would not remind me again, but to help the Jews, I will—so to speak—sit at the same table with the Tartars."

"That's mighty good of you," said Ronya; but her tone was friendly.

"May I tell you what I want?"

"Of course."

"Go to Moscow, Ronya. Who, more than you, can help arouse the conscience of good Christians?"

The train ride was pleasantly uneventful. The conductor brought her hot tea, and except for a stroll up and down the corridor Ronya never left her compartment. She had with her a picnic basket, the *Brothers Karamazov,* and a letter from Harbin, Manchuria, which had been waiting for her yesterday afternoon when she returned home from Joseph's.

To my dearest, to Ronya:

I am here because Ladislaus has been seriously ill. He has recovered, though he still looks gaunt and there is more gray in his hair.

Ronya, my dear, according to Ladislaus, the situation for the Jews—particularly in Moscow—is bad, and it will go from bad to nightmarish worse. Over a million Jews will be forced from Russia within a few years. The remaining Jews, with the exception of those few with whom the government wishes to maintain friendly relations, will be left to the pogromists.

According to Sergey, the Paris Rothschilds are withdrawing from the half billion loan the Tzar wants, and according to my sources in the States the firm of Kuhn and Loeb and Company will no longer extend loans to Russia.

If you are thinking of enlisting Alexis' aid, don't—not now. He'll only get into trouble. Alexis could be a great statesman, but he is no politician, and Katya's eyes are glowing Jewish. Alexis will be useful later.

Ronya dear, I saw Katya and Alexis in Paris. We talked of you.

Ronya, you are not under lock and key. Write to me—please. A line—just one.

All my love,
Paul

The letter was destined to be tied in ribbon with Paul's first letter and locked in Ronya's secret drawer. But for Paul there was no answer.

About an hour before the train pulled into Moscow, the porter gave Ronya two large pitchers of very hot water, and she devoted much care to herself. She alighted from the train the epitome of elegance, as flawlessly patrician as if she had just come out of her own boudoir. To approving masculine gazes, she stepped into a sleigh. The driver tucked her own fur robe around her and saw to her many suitcases of varying sizes and shapes but all of excellent leather, matching in color and hand-sewn.

The bishop of Moscow was considered an aloof man, tall and stately, with a fancy for port after dinner—yet the kinship between him and Ronya was there to see: in the eyes. And they had much in common. Both were profoundly honest, both were somewhat socially minded, and both possessed the ingrained assurance of the aristocrat. Both lived in noticeable lavishness; the Von Glasman money allowed them this indulgence.

Upon her arrival, Ronya was installed in a suite that wealth and taste had made a masterpiece of perfection. Classically formal, the furniture was of French rosewood, the marble fireplaces were from Italy, the mantel Meissen from Germany. Ronya's rooms were free of icons and scenes from the lives of saints.

It had been her intention to talk to the bishop and leave the next day, as soon as things were settled between them. Still, knowing the ways of the haut monde, she came prepared, which was a lucky thing for the bishop had arranged a reception in her honor. At seven o'clock, bewitching in low-cut velvet with diamonds in her elaborately high-piled hair, Ronya descended the circular staircase, accompanied by the bishop. Together they welcomed the most celebrated men and women of Moscow. At dinner, the banquet table stretched fifty feet, and there was a footman behind each chair. Between courses the guests danced to an orchestra of balalaikas.

Ronya let her dark eyes linger appreciatively over beautiful frocks and paid delicate compliments graciously; she listened enchantingly, and many a gentleman felt caressed when she smiled. As the evening progressed, Ronya understood that her father's cousin, once removed, had surmised the purpose of her visit and very deliberately planned to present the Jewess in splendor. Then and there, Ronya decided to stay on and make capital of his cunning. Since she was staying, she decided to indulge herself—to ice-skate, to attend plays, to end her day in a closed carriage at three in the morning coming home from a ball.

Almost a week went by, and for those six days, Ronya felt free. No

354

Boris towering over her, watching every movement, glaring at a shoulder a bit too bare, making it boundlessly clear to everyone that every breath she drew belonged to him. Ronya was tired. She needed a vacation.

On the morning of the seventh day, Ronya received a message from her host. "I shall be back at three. I have reserved the rest of the day for you."

They met in his study, a superb room with a high ceiling, tall windows, and a stone fireplace. Waving her into a chair, the bishop said with approval, "You have done your cause a world of good. The women like you. That is the best way of getting the men to help."

"It is you I entreat. Are you willing to help?"

"Not blindly, Ronya. However, as soon as I know what you're after, we can get down to the business of getting it done—that is, if I think what you want is a good thing for Moscow, as well as for the Jews."

"There are several aspects to what I want."

"Is that so? First, let me tell you something of what I've been thinking." The bishop began to pace up and down the room.

"My father was a Muscovite and Minister of the Interior. In general, he felt that the Jews should develop industry and trade. He expected the Jews to be extraordinarily useful, and he expected that eventually they would be absorbed into the Russian church.

"My father felt no alarm over my frequent stays with the Von Glasmans and—" The bishop smiled to himself. "Until I was almost fifteen," he confessed, "I was madly in love with Tamara's grandmother.

"I concluded that I was meant for the church. I was ordained at a very early age—an enigma to my brother priests. I remain an enigma." Again the bishop smiled. "When one is an enigma, great wealth is useful."

Ronya returned his smile. "It's always useful."

The bishop patted her hand affectionately and went on. "What I'm getting at is this, Ronya. I cannot deny my deep attachment to the Jewish people, but I do not regret that my branch of the family found its way to the baptismal font and orthodoxy. Similarly, many Jewish converts—nearly eighty-five thousand—have joined the Orthodox faith in this century. I myself have converted over fifty Jews within this last week. These Russians are in Moscow with all the rights of full citizenship bestowed upon them.

"I'm not saying that I condone forced baptism, but for thousands and thousands of Jews there is an easy way out." He glanced at Ronya. "Belonging is a splendid thing, my child."

When he thought her silence had lasted long enough, he said,

"Speak, Ronya. I promise to listen as politely as you listened, but with a mind far more open and with greater trust."

Ronya stirred. "I see no reason to discuss the easily assimilated intelligentsia, the ambitious careerists, the opportunists, or the few who truly believe in the teachings of Christ. I am here on behalf of the Moscow Jews crowded into miserable camps outside the city, on behalf of the masses of Jews who are shoved into ghettos and are sinking deeper and deeper into poverty and despair. I am here on behalf of the young Jews, who are being forced into Socialism, and even more on behalf of those who are turning to Jewish nationalism, especially the baptized Jews who are trying to find a way to return to Judaism."

The bishop's Von Glasman eyebrows came together in a deep frown. He drew his lips in tightly. "Baptized Jews back to Judaism?"

Ronya merely nodded, but she took note of annoyance and a deep satisfaction stirred in her heart. She added fuel to the fire. "And I know something else. The Tzar has lost the Rothschilds' loan." Slowly, significantly, she added, "No half billion francs."

The bishop knew how badly his government needed that loan.

"That is reprehensible and illustrates the very thing for which the Jews are resented, the zeal with which they avenge their own."

"I don't think that is reprehensible. I think it is magnificent. It is repayment, tradition, survival. Without it, we would be extinct by now."

"Ronya, it's astonishing how stubbornly Jewish you are. Why? Is it because Boris is a Tartar?"

A sudden sadness came into Ronya's face. "Partly."

The bishop looked at her with undisguised admiration. "At least you're honest. Tell me, when did you learn about the Rothschilds, and from whom?"

"Very recently, from a friend who thinks a great deal about my future."

"He spoke to you?"

"He wrote. He has also, in the past, urged me to put my money in a country whose government I can trust, a government that is fully behind its currency. He says Russia is a country bent on self-demolition."

The bishop examined her face closely. "Listen, my child," he said, "if Boris ever checks your correspondence, your friend had better worry about his own future. He may not have one."

Ronya took a very long cigarette out of the cigarette box and waited for her host to strike a match. "I'm very curious. What makes you say that?"

The bishop busied himself lighting a Spanish cigar. After a puff or two, he said, "Ronya, I have a feeling about your friend. I keep thinking I know him. Who is he?"

356

"An expert in the habit of dealing in facts."

He permitted himself a slight grin. "You talk like David von Glasman."

Here in Moscow, surrounded by the atmosphere of his great talent, politics, Ronya saw her father before her eyes with vivid clarity. "My father was important to the Empress, he was important to Russia. Had he lived, he'd have made Alexis Prime Minister—and why not Alexis? After all, the Tzar isn't a little boy any more. He doesn't need a tutor, he needs an adviser in whom he can believe, who believes in freedom."

The bishop gave Ronya an admiring look. A fusion of racial strains —yet the eternal Jewess. Extraordinary. Challenging. Inspiring.

The bishop rose. "I think it's time to have a sherry. We'll talk again." He went to the wine table and poured generously from a crystal decanter.

"Long live life," said the bishop.

Ronya's eyes sparkled. "*L'chaim,* my cousin."

After dinner, the bishop resumed their discussion. Ronya was well prepared. In fact, she had been rehearsing in her mind the questions she wanted to ask and the pledges she hoped to secure.

She made her first attack. "Are the Muscovites envious of the Jewish entrepreneurs?"

"I don't think so. From what I gather, precisely the opposite is true. Big business resents the adverse economic effects of the exodus."

Ronya smiled wryly. "Big business? Wouldn't you say that big business in Moscow is largely Jewish?"

"The salt and tobacco monopolies are in Christian hands," the bishop countered. "All the liquor trades are, too, including the distilleries." He attempted a small witticism. "In fact, I doubt that there is a single Jewish saloonkeeper in all of Moscow."

"Rubbish! That's like saying there are no Jewish prostitutes, no Jewish drunkards, no Jewish simpletons."

"Despite the differences in age, Ronya, you remind me of my Von Glasman grandmother. I recall that she was undeviatingly unamused by erroneous notions."

Ronya laughed, but her gaiety was brief. "How much better for Russia," he heard her say in a low, calm voice, "were the Tzar to rid himself of the Jew-haters. A night raid, and Russia loses millions and millions of badly needed rubles. In the villages, where for years the Jews and peasants have lived in harmony, in come the Tzar's police, the military, the religious zealots and create tensions, which they then fan with lies. 'The Jews poison cows and goats. The Jews contaminate virgin land. Human blood is their sacramental wine.'

"Jewish factories are closed. What happens? The Christian labor

357

force pays. Unemployment rises, wages fall, working hours become murderously long."

The bishop was amazed. "Is this the Ronya who whirls a whip and dances a wild *kazatzkale?*"

"You are a Christian leader. Your God preached brotherhood. Call for a change. Address yourself to the Tzar. Urge that the Jews be given at least the freedom to emigrate—and not half naked and penniless."

The old cry, "Let my people go." The bishop emitted a big sigh. "I am ready to defend the Jews against false accusations and gross injustices, but there is nothing I can do about the deep hatred."

"On the contrary, there is much the church can do. The people listen to you. You are the symbol of truth. Don't teach your children that the Jews killed Christ. Tell the story of Jesus as it really was."

The bishop shook his head unhappily and said, "The hatred did not start of a winter night in the year 1892. The solution will not be rapid."

Just as Ronya opened her mouth to reply, there was a knock on the door and the butler appeared. "A telegram for madam."

The telegram was from Boris. It said, ARE YOU COMING HOME, RONYA, OR DO I COME FOR YOU?

Ronya handed it to the bishop, who asked with a smile, "Is there no end to the Tartar yoke?"

"Boris holds all Muscovites, with the exception of Alexis, in contempt."

She wrote out a reply, folded it in an envelope, and gave it to the butler. It read:

> DEAR MIGHTY BORIS,
> I AM ON MY WAY.
>
> YOUR TERRIFIED RONYA

The bishop was none too pleased with Boris' summons; he was growing very fond of Ronya's company.

"Nothing is final," he said soothingly, lighting another cigar. "Many Jews will make their way home. More will accept baptism. For some there will be special permits. I have spoken on behalf of my bootmaker, and he has already reopened his shop. Other Muscovites are working just as hard for other Jews."

Ronya said wearily, "That's nice. Each Muscovite's favorite Jew gets a second chance. What about those who remain victims?"

The bishop prodded gently. "Doubtless you have some ideas?"

"In the name of Rome, Herod the Idumaean barbarian usurped a kingdom and secured death for the Jews. Please do not be the tool of today's barbarians, who in the name of the Tzar and the church seek annihilation for a people."

The bishop frowned and pulled hard on his cigar. "Ronya, what do you want?" he asked patiently.

"I want *time*, time to dispose of houses and property at fair market prices."

The bishop nodded. "I'll see what can be done."

"Thank you. But I was about to ask for more."

"Go on."

"I want the end of rapid deportation. From now on, let the exodus be directed in an orderly, humane fashion."

"No!" He shook his head. "No, Ronya. I am against organized emigration. Russia needs its Jews. We must find a way to live together."

Ronya did not answer at once. She smiled. "My idea exactly," Ronya said pointedly. Pleased, very pleased, the bishop said, "Am I to understand that you do not support the Jewish nationalists?"

"Oh, I give money," Ronya said. "It's my duty to help those Jews who can no longer make a life for themselves in Russia."

The bishop said, "I see." As they went through the door together, he put an affectionate arm around her shoulder and said, "I shall mies you very much, Ronya."

Waiting with Boris in the heavy six-horse sleigh were Katya and Alexis—whom Ronya had telegraphed to come home before she left for Moscow—as well as Igor, David, and Georgi. Ronya was a little surprised that Boris brought them, for she expected he would be infuriated by her precipitate departure for Moscow and come to meet her alone. In a way she was looking forward to a display of temper, but Katya and Alexis, having learned the circumstances from Lydia, persuaded Boris to put aside his anger.

"No home in Russia is more proper than the home of our bishop," Alexis said. "I am proud of her."

Nevertheless Boris still intended to tell Ronya that he regarded her behavior as recklessly inappropriate, but as he ran toward her his anger was forgotten. All he wanted was to take her into his arms. Their fevered kiss startled more than one passer-by.

"Hello, little dove," Boris said, taking Ronya's face in his hands and kissing her eyes.

"Do I have a new bearskin rug?"

Boris gave her a big grin. "All spread out in the library."

Ronya brought all sorts of presents from Moscow—toys and games and clothes and, for the Blond One, who had remained at the house, what he wanted most: books and a new guitar. Not until everything had been rejoiced over, played with, and stored away, were Ronya and Katya freed from the boys. As they were leaving, Ronya caught the Blond One to her and kissed him, and said, "I missed you."

Ronya waited until they sat down to their meal, prepared by Lydia and served by her alone, before telling them all that happened.

"In your opinion," Alexis asked, "will the Jews close their factories and participate in a general boycott?"

"It appears so. Many of the wealthier families are determined to emigrate. The rebels, the poets, and all who seek justice, strongly advocate a citywide strike."

"But wouldn't that ruin the economy of Moscow, to say nothing of the rest of the nation?"

"What of the snow and hunger and the ghetto walls?" Ronya exclaimed with passion. "What of people driven hither and yon? What of life and love and humanity?"

Boris' heart went out to her.

Alexis gave a sympathetic nod, but the expatriation of the rich Jews was not at all to his liking. Turning to Katya, he said with regret, "I think I must go to Moscow. I'm sorry to cut our visit short."

"Yes, of course we must. If Ronya will lend me Georgi." She looked at her sister, "One week—that's all I ask."

"All right with you, Boris?"

He nodded.

The next day when Ronya awakened they were already gone.

37

A scowl on his face, Boris accosted her with: "Where in hell have you been?"

"That's a nice welcome!"

"Well?"

"I felt obliged to make my report to Joseph Levinsky *before* he sent for me."

That seemed to pacify Boris. Ronya accompanied him into the library, where he retired to a corner chair with the newspaper.

Ronya started on the stack of mail that had accumulated in her absence, among which was a reminder from Colonel Gregory Veliki, the new commandant of the Cavalry post, of the date of his party.

"Darling."

Boris looked up.

"Listen: 'Kiev is full of people but only Major and Madam Pirov can turn a party into a celebration. Please come on the eighteenth of January and make my welcome complete. Respectfully, Gregory Veliki.'"

"I'm glad we're going to a party. It'll be a nice respite. Besides, I can't wait to wear the gown Katya brought from Paris."

Boris flung the paper aside. "That get-together is not for you, Ronya. Hardened drinkers and women of all sorts—any sort."

"No wives?"

"Some. Not the kind that attend church on Sunday."

"What's Colonel Veliki like?"

Without understanding why, Boris felt vaguely alarmed and was annoyed with himself. "Now how could that possibly matter to you, Ronya?"

"Just curious," she said amiably.

Boris was fully aware he was being unreasonable. He summoned his good sense and answered, "Veliki is a hard-drinking, hard-riding Cossack from an island below the rapids of the Dnieper. He always carries a whip, and his saber never leaves his saddle."

"Hmm. Sounds fascinating."

"Ronya," said Boris, "you can be irritating."

She laughed. Straightening her skirt, she asked, "How will you justify our regrets?"

"Our regrets are not precisely what I have in mind. Only yours."

"That's not fair," Ronya protested. "You know I want to go. Besides, both of us are invited. It's rude of you to go alone."

"He's a man of the world. He'll understand." As far as Boris was concerned, the conversation was closed.

Ronya forced her eyes to the letters before her until she was able to control her desire to slam things about with abandon. Finally she looked up and asked, as if nothing had happened, "Do you want a vodka?"

Boris stood and put his hand on her shoulder. "I think I'll ride in and have a drink with the Cossacks."

Ronya threw back her shoulders. With a defiant toss of her head, she said, "If you're so anxious to be out of the house, what was your telegram all about?" Ronya had an irresistible desire to infuriate him.

His face darkened. "Ronya," he said, "that whole week out in that intense cold I was thinking of you and looking forward to having you

361

all to myself when I got home. Instead, I returned to an empty house."

Ronya had her retort ready. "Oh, damn you, Boris Pirov, you're a rotten father."

Boris made no comment and stalked from the room. He saw Lydia had been eavesdropping but treated it as one of her perquisites; Lydia, on her behalf, saw no reason to explain or apologize. She bounced after him as he mounted the staircase. "Boris, my master, she didn't mean it. I know my Ronya. She's already eating her words."

Boris glanced down on the chunky, rosy-cheeked meddler. "Listen, Lydia. Make sure she eats her dinner and gets some rest. She needs it."

"Yes, sir." Lydia was going to say more but thought better of it.

After her long bath, Ronya lay in bed thinking. Before she went to sleep, she decided what she would do on the night of the colonel's party. When Boris came in at about 3 A.M., her door was locked. He had a mind to put his shoulder to it but instead went to his own room and came back with an envelope which he slipped under her door. Ronya found it before she came down to breakfast. Along withies - dreds and hundreds of rubles was a scrap of paper saying: "I won this for the Moscow Jews, dove."

At about eleven thirty, Ronya appeared at the stables.

Boris looked up with a smile and went back to heating a horseshoe over a glowing fire. He was an expert shoer; it was a job he liked. Ronya watched for a while, then saddled a hunter (no one offered to help; the men seemed to know she wanted to do it herself) and rode him for miles across her property. Friendly peasants waved at her and she waved back.

That night, when Boris arrived at Ronya's door, it was open.

Boris started to get ready for the party. He took long appraisal of himself in the mirror and liked what he saw. He was dressed in full-dress uniform; and he adjusted the medals that decorated his chest.

To his surprise, Ronya came to see him off. Dressed in a wrapper with her hair falling all over her shoulders, she let herself be kissed.

Boris took her hands. "Next week, little dove, I'll take you to the theater, and then for supper and dancing. You'll wear your new dress and we'll celebrate until dawn, just the two of us."

"Fresh sturgeon and French champagne?"

"The best and the most." He kissed her hands and, at the sound of carriage wheels on the drive below, said, "Ronya, I'll make a real effort to come home tonight."

Ronya smiled enchantingly. "I know you will, my darling."

Boris left easily.

She closed his windows, deeply breathing the river's breeze, and ran across the hall to her own room, where Lydia and her hairdresser were waiting for her.

Colonel Veliki gaped. "A goddess! She must be the most beautiful woman on earth." He was staring at Ronya, ablaze in emeralds and gowned all in white, her waist romantically sashed, her exquisite shoulders bare.

Boris did not turn around. He said, "I half promised my wife I'd come home early. If I should change my mind how about a wager?—five hundred rubles say I take the goddess upstairs."

Veliki made a grimace. "That's a lot of rubles. At least look before you leap, Boris. She's already surrounded and may be more than you bargained for. She's a lady. I know quality when I see it."

"Have we got a bet?"

"Spot me one dance?"

"All right. But at dinner, she sits between us."

"You've got a deal."

A practiced seducer, Colonel Veliki did not rush at Ronya like an overeager schoolboy. Resting his eyes on her, he continued his conversation with Boris. "One question. How do you risk five hundred rubles blind?"

Boris chuckled. "I have a Russian soul. I don't have to look to see. The minute that woman made her appearance, the whole room vibrated with excitement. Look around, we're practically alone at the bar—except for Krasmikov, and that's because Tamara's with him."

The orchestra struck up the last waltz before dinner. The colonel went to Ronya, who was waiting for him, poised and radiant.

Veliki gave her a formal bow. "Goddess of love and beauty, where do you come from?"

"From the foam of the sea."

"That means you're Venus. I knew it."

Ronya's mischievous smile made Veliki glow.

With studied correctness he put his arm around her tiny waist—by dancing on tiptoe she reached almost to his chin (whereas when dancing with Boris, the top of her head barely touched his shoulder).

Abruptly, Tamara left Krasmikov and came over to Boris.

He gave her a derisive glance. "May I suggest you return to your escort?"

"May I call your attention to your stupidity? I heard that wager."

"I seem to be surrounded by eavesdroppers tonight," he said without explaining the remark.

"Who in Kiev but Ronya has the dignity to make that seasoned hunter treat her with respect?"

Boris spun around. He caught a glimpse of Ronya floating like a feather in the Cossack's arms. He reached them as the dance ended.

"Colonel, my wife, Ronya."

"No wonder," Veliki said gallantly, "you make excuses to keep her hidden. I'd do the same—at all costs."

Boris took her hand. "I'm sure, Colonel," he said coldly, "that some lady waits for you."

The colonel laughed. "I brought no one. Madame Pirov sits on my right between us at dinner."

Ronya sensed something in the air between them and knew the gleam in Boris' eye meant trouble brewing. Pressing his hand, she said, "I'm thirsty, darling. Is there time for one glass of champagne before dinner?"

But just then dinner was announced.

"We'll have champagne to begin with," said the colonel.

Ronya was between them as they went into the dining room, but Boris kept hold of her hand as if to say, "She is mine!"

Aside from his officers, the commandant was entertaining sixty Kievans and their ladies at dinner, among whom there were quite a few perfectly respectable, church-going wives from estates neighboring Ronya's. They wore expensive clothes, elaborate hair styles, and an overabundance of jewels. The princesses of the night were there, too.

Tamara projected an image all her own. She held herself tall in a long evening dress intricately decorated in a gay embroidered design, and she was covered in gold—her ears, her neck, her arms. On her jet-black hair she wore her famed gold tiara embossed in diamonds.

The dinner was in strict imitation of the great splendor of a St. Petersburg banquet. The chefs were French; the menu was Russian; the volume and the variety were unbelievable. The diners were engulfed in dish after dish, each accompanied by its own wine.

Not Boris. He went through the motions of eating, but he was in a fury, though he felt obliged to keep his temper bottled up. The Cossack was being a well-mannered, attentive host, but his extreme politeness only made Boris more jealous and angry. And Ronya—it was not easy to fathom Ronya. She was beyond criticism: impeccably proper, her manners exquisite. Yet very skillfully by her well-bred but flattering regard, she was encouraging the Cossack, making him feel clever and important. Boris knew she wanted a reaction from him. She got it. His Tartar eyes began to glitter.

When dinner ended and the ladies retired, Tamara came across the hall to Ronya. Thus did Ronya learn about the five-hundred-ruble wager; she felt as if she had been struck. When she returned, her face showed nothing of her rage and sadness, but as soon as the music started, she turned her face toward the Cossack and he stood up immediately.

They were the first couple on the dance floor. Everyone crowded after them. Then they saw Boris threading his way toward them through the whirling dancers. The Cossack waited for Boris to reach them, holding Ronya more firmly; but he released her the instant Boris cut in.

They danced, each lost in thought. Ronya put her head lightly on his shoulder and tried to remember that the cocksure Cossack, with the dress sword at his belt, outranked Boris.

The Cossack—"A pox on him"—did not trouble Boris very much. He could kill him happily. What he had to think about was Ronya. But he could think only of how much he loved her. But he also could not help realizing that a change was beginning to take place in Ronya; she was beginning to take out her resentments, to retaliate in new, unexpected ways—Boris found it difficult to complete his thought. He realized he was frightened.

When the music stopped, Ronya tried to ease herself out of his arms but he held her in a grip like steel.

"I want to talk to you," he said in a hard voice.

Ronya saw his mouth tighten, and her eyes grew larger. She walked with him to one of the card rooms. Boris locked the door and sat down at a card table. He lit a cigarette.

"So you knew that I was destined to sleep home tonight."

"I have my own carriage and my own coachman," she replied, smiling. "If you are eager to stay on after the ball, by all means do. There's a rather stunning girl in green satin. I saw her make several moves in your direction. Maybe the colonel, if he has nothing better to do, will give you a second chance at a wager."

Boris pointed his cigarette at her like a pistol. "You won't be dancing with that Cossack again," he said coldly.

"Why not?"

"Lower your voice, Ronya."

Ronya slowly faced him. "That damn Cossack is more fun to dance with than you are. He dances. You do a solo, to show everyone what a great dancer you are."

Boris was thinking he'd like to cut out Tamara's tongue. "You will never again allow that Cossack's arms around you."

Ronya felt pleased at his ferocious jealousy. To provoke him further she said sweetly, "You can always break it."

Boris suddenly swung to his feet and pulled her to him, but she struggled, holding her head back, twisting her mouth away from his.

"Please," he whispered in her ear.

She stopped resisting.

"Sh-h-h, dove. That wager was damn stupid. I'm sorry about it, genuinely sorry." He leaned over her, and his lips came down slowly on hers. "Do you want to dance with me?"

Ronya's smile lit up her whole face. "All the rest of my life, my love."

Boris could hardly contain his elation. There was nothing different about Ronya. His own fanciful fears had created the delusion that she was changing, that she needed him less.

They reappeared in the ballroom in time to complete a waltz. Colonel Veliki, a sage and cunning rogue, let Ronya alone. One look had shown him how pointless it was to continue his pursuit now and, besides, he wanted no unpleasantness with Boris Pirov. He turned his attention to Tamara, throwing aside the careful correctness he had employed with Ronya.

"I had you in mind from the start," he whispered into her hair.

Tamara laughed. "You're really afraid of Boris, aren't you?"

An angry light sprang into his eyes.

Tamara answered his stare with an amused glance. "Try that French whore in green satin."

The colonel's eyes traveled from Tamara to the girl. "Thanks, I shall. I'll get back to you another time," he promised.

However, he was at Ronya's shoulder when she and Boris prepared to leave. Boris refused an invitation, addressed to them both, to drink a last brandy in the colonel's private quarters and shepherded Ronya out to the waiting carriage. He took the salute from the sentries, stepped into the carriage, and gave his hand to Ronya. The colonel gallantly supported her elbow. Both Pirovs said good-night quickly, and Boris drew shut the carriage door. The colonel stood there in the cold to see if Ronya would glance back. She never did.

The following day, toward evening, Boris called on Colonel Veliki.

"Hello, Boris," the colonel said easily, "I had a curious premonition you'd come."

"Shall we waste time as I lose a few hands, or will you accept five hundred rubles?"

"Does it really matter?"

"To me, yes. I'm anxious to get home."

"I'd rather have your friendship than take your money—yours and Ronya's."

"Here at the barracks and around town we'll see each other. I don't want you in my home. And keep away from my wife."

"How can you doubt—"

366

"I don't choose to discuss my reasons with you," Boris cut in. With that, he put down the money and left the room.

About five days later, the key girl on General Itil Pirov's floor at the Europa gave him a letter from Ronya.

> My dear Father-in-law,
> I am writing to ask a favor. Just recently you sent us Colonel Gregory Veliki. Please transfer him elsewhere. He has antagonized Boris, and that ends his usefulness here.

The favor Ronya knew would be immediately and discreetly granted; the invitation with which she ended the letter she knew would be appreciatively but immediately declined:

> Please do come spend the holidays with us. Imagine—1893 just one week away.
>
> Devotedly and with love,
Ronya

38

Boris Pirov did not see God as an elderly, bearded Jew. He did not know or care whether he was a Jew. All Boris saw was the divine in life itself and, in a large measure, his attitude rubbed off on his sons.

In the winter of 1895, as Igor was approaching his thirteenth birthday, he was trapped between his desire to please Ronya, whom he idolized, and his antagonism to the pious old tutors who taught him Hebrew and the intricacies of the Talmud. In any case, he considered the Cavalry the only manly way of life.

One day, as they were coming back from the stables, he appealed to his father. "Do I really have to be bar-mitzvahed?"

"You're a Jew, Igor. Remember that."

"So what's so important about being a Jew?"

"I don't know, son, but clearly it's important because nobody is ever going to let you forget it."

Igor was a smart lad with good practical sense. It occurred to him that with a Tartar father and a half-gypsy half brother, he was not much of a Jew.

When Ronya came into the library bearing the afternoon tea tray, Boris took the tray from her and set it on a table. Then he drew up two armchairs to the fireplace.

"Ronya," he said, sipping his tea, "this is probably a futile appeal. Postpone Igor's bar mitzvah. Pushing him into a ceremony against his wishes makes little sense."

"Joseph Levinsky's sentiments exactly," Ronya said calmly.

"What? How come?"

"He wrote that Igor isn't ready. He must prepare for another six months, at least."

Boris put down his glass, a grin at the corners of his mouth. "I'll tell Igor he's got a reprieve."

So Boris regarded it as deliverance! Ronya began to feel angry. "Tell *your* son that, ready or not, he'll be in *shul* the morning of July twelfth, and that on the occasion of his bar mitzvah his Tartar father will give him a *tallis*. Tell him to guard it well. He may need it to serve as a canopy during his marriage ceremony."

Boris' grin widened. "Yes, dove. I'll tell him all that."

As the bar mitzvah date approached, Boris began looking around for an excuse to be away from Kiev. In the middle of June he had a talk with the commandant at the barracks. By evening, it was all over Kiev that Boris Pirov, who for years had stayed away from competition riding, had agreed to represent the Ukraine in an event whose stakes were, simply, survival.

It went like this:

From all parts of Russia, horsemen gathered in Moscow. They had strength, skill, and confidence in common; all were born and bred to the saddle. Aside from his horse and the clothes on his back, each man was allowed his whip and his gun, his sword, dagger, and hunting knife, one water canteen, matches, and tobacco. No food or money. Riding a single horse, the contestant had to make his way from inside the Kremlin to the central square in the oasis town of Samarkand in Central Asia—a distance of some two thousand miles. Anyone who came in with a damaged horse was disqualified. Otherwise everything went.

Though it was near sunup when Boris came back from the barracks, Ronya's reading light was still on. Her thick hair tumbled over her bare shoulders. He bent his tousled head, kissed her gently on the mouth, then stepped into the bathroom. When he emerged, he smelled of soap and the cool fresh morning, and there was no golden stubble on his handsome face. They made love rapturously. When Ronya opened her eyes, she heard the robins singing, and it seemed to her that the whole world was filled with bird songs.

But when he told her about the marathon—"Three hundred mounted men, Ronya—from the Kremlin to a bright, hot, Moslem outpost in Central Asia"—her eyes filled with tears. He misunderstood:

"Don't be afraid, dove. I'll run into Tartar clansmen at streams and water holes and they'll give me food and vodka. I'll win easily," he said, intensifying the reassurance. "I'll come riding in at a full gallop through the red dust to a welcome of rifle volleys and pealing bells. Before you realize it, I'll be home."

Sudden fury swept her; Ronya's eyes blazed. "Because I failed him and married a Tartar, my son must pay the price. He has no father to accompany him to the synagogue."

Boris set his jaw. "Let's get some sleep."

"Sleep!"

"Move over."

In spite of her wretchedness, Ronya slept, looking little-girl-young in her sleep.

At the stroke of eleven, he brought her a pot of black coffee. Along with it, he provided a warm washcloth for her hands and a cool one for her face. Gently he rested her against the pillows.

"Hear me out, Ronya," he said. "If this were solely a matter of horsemanship, I'd not be concerned about a couple of wasted days. I'm as good at forty as I ever was, and I don't think anyone better has come along. But this is an endurance contest, and I need to build my stamina. I can't concentrate on a goddamn thing when you're unhappy."

"Your stamina is stupendous," Ronya said mischievously.

Boris kissed her. "I'll bring Katya and Alexis home, and we'll have a family celebration."

All at once it no longer really mattered to her when, exactly, Igor was bar-mitzvahed as long as it took place in his thirteenth year. What did matter was that the boys should see three hundred gallant men setting out on such a stupendous undertaking and hear the Moscow crowds cheering their father. "Besides, I want to share in the excitement and I want to be there to wish you godspeed."

This was the best and greatest surprise. It had never entered his head that she would come to Moscow to cheer him on. He was smiling as he left the room to start training.

The rabbi's reply to Ronya's request came by return messenger.

Ronya:

First, you ask for an alternate date. Then you tie up three months to suit your pleasure. *Chutzpa!*

Perhaps you are right in taking Igor to Moscow. I am not certain I'd have permitted your firstborn to take part in the bar mitzvah service at the present time. He is lacking in Hebrew. He has no knowledge of the Haftarah. He has no love in his heart for Judaism.

Why should special concessions be made to Igor? Because it is in his mother's heart to love a Tartar?

No, Ronya, Igor is on trial.

Your Rabbi,
Joseph Levinsky

Ronya was startled by the depth of her own anger. Knowing it unwise to do so, she replied at once.

Dear Rabbi:

Thank you for your letter. You have opened my eyes.

I can imagine no one less forgiving than you.

Please leave it to God to punish. He is mightier than you.

Sincerely,
Ronya von Glasman Pirov

The rabbi's conciliatory note reached Ronya at Katya's soon after her arrival. It traveled on the same train.

Dear foolish, impossible Ronya,

Come back from Moscow counting on a November bar mitzvah. I myself shall prepare Igor. That Boris will not participate is—*this once*—no formidable obstacle. A minyan we shall have.

In advance, I send my *mazel tov.* No man alive can outride or outlast Boris. Greet Katya and her distinguished husband.

Your friend,
Joseph

The stallion gave out a terrifying, ringing neigh. Rearing and plunging, he would let no one approach him. David braced his legs and made a wild snatch at the stallion's halter, but Igor seized him and held him in an iron grip.

"You damn fool. Do you want to get yourself killed?"

Struggling to break Igor's hold, David bellowed, "I reckon he remembers me—don't you, Boy?"

The stallion's nostrils flared, and he threw back his head.

Sad Eyes cursed under his breath and went looking for Boris in the gun room. "Sir, the stallion's crazed with temper. He won't go into the horsebox."

370

Boris grinned. "He wants to go to Moscow on his own four legs." He tossed Sad Eyes the key. "Lock up."

The stallion raised his head and sniffed. It was Boris' scent. He jerked his head in his master's direction.

David pushed the hair out of his eyes and gave Igor a hard kick in the shin.

"Hold it, son." Boris took in the situation and said to Igor, "Let him go." He moved gently toward the stallion. "Hell-o-o, Boy."

The stallion picked up his ears.

"Until Moscow, you take it easy, my tough old friend. It's no picnic we're going on, and you're no three-year-old. There'll be no paths— just pine thickets and fallen trees and sucking sands. There'll be wolves and wild birds, and—"

The stallion buried his nose in Boris' chest.

With one eye on the horse, Boris clapped David on the shoulder. "All right, he'll go now. Take him in."

Warily, Sad Eyes closed in, ready to help the boy, but David needed no assistance.

"Come," he said softly, making his voice like his father's, "you'll laugh after you win."

Meek as a tame mare, the stallion let himself be jailed in a big pen on wheels fastened to a strong wagon. Eight sorrel horses were backed into the shafts.

It was midmorning, hot and sultry, when Boris gave the order, "Prepare to leave," and went off to find Ronya.

Hardly had he left, when Igor and the Blond One dragged up a canvas huge enough to hide three wild boars, which they stored carefully in the back of the wagon.

David came bearing down on them. "You'll take me, or I'll tell."

Igor and the Blond One exchanged a look.

"You've got to get your own food," Igor said.

"We'll share," said the Blond One.

David grinned. "Besides, Father has enough to feed a regiment."

All at once, and seemingly from nowhere, Georgi appeared. "What about me?"

"Where'd you come from?" Igor demanded.

"From in there. Way in."

The three boys turned as one and stared into the stallion's stall. Georgi's slanted hazel eyes followed theirs. "He lets me do anything. I smell like Father."

"For Christ's sake!" Igor exclaimed with disgust. The Blond One howled with laughter. David did not want Georgi to spoil their scheme. Reluctantly he yielded.

371

"Listen, Georgi, we can't take you, but you can ruin it for us." Igor smiled at him. "Be a good sport and go with Mother. We'll make it up to you in Moscow."

Georgi stared up at Igor. "I don't tell."

"Mother'll get it out of you," David said.

"I'll hide until it's too late for her to send horsemen after the train."

"Where will you hide, Georgi?" the Blond One asked.

Georgi grinned. "At your house. I'll tell Tamara she has to help us."

"Well," Igor warned, "don't depend on her unless you have to. If she's feeling friendly toward Mother she'll inform on us."

"She's mad at Mother."

Igor and the Blond One looked at David. "She's mad at us all except Georgi," he said. "It hurt because no one in the family told her about Father."

By the time Boris reappeared with Ronya, the peasants and many of the gypsies were assembled, prepared to follow Boris and the stallion to the railroad station. Boris flashed his glance to Igor, who said eagerly, "May we ride in the wagon?"

"Climb in back."

Igor lifted Georgi, and Boris lifted Ronya. As the three older boys scrambled aloft, Boris seated himself next to Ronya and took the reins. At the edge of the property, he reined in the horses. "Darling, I'll see you at Katya's tomorrow night," she said.

Boris kissed her lustily on the mouth and lifted her down. One of the grooms led up her mount and Ronya rode off, calling back to the boys, "We leave the first thing in the morning. Come directly home."

They had just cleared the town boundaries when Tamara, riding astride, her hair streaming down behind her, whirled her mare to a stop. Behind her galloped a band of her best riders, who pulled in with such force that the horses reared in the air before their hooves thundered down. The gypsies jumped to the ground and unhitched the sorrels. Together with Boris' stable hands, they pulled the wagon in slow parade through the shouting, elbowing crowd all the way to the horse-car at the end of the freight train. Along the route, women hung over fences throwing rose petals and men followed singing, their voices almost drowned by the pealing church bells of all the churches in Kiev. A good hundred Cossacks, full of vodka, rode wildly through the crowd. The thousands of spectators at the railroad tracks trying madly to reach Boris were kept in line by the police and foot soldiers.

Boris grinned and waved, and his golden hair fell in a forelock over his brow.

The stallion rode with his nose high in the air.

At five o'clock Ronya closed the last suitcase and got up from her knees. From the quietness of the house, she might have been the only mortal in Kiev. About six thirty Lydia came in, out of breath with excitement and happiness. "If only Ruth, your mother—may her blessed soul rest in peace—could have lived to see the glory of this day," she puffed. "You know how Father Tromokov feels—just like me. His pride in Boris, our master, pierced my heart."

"Father Tromokov? I thought he was still in St. Petersburg with another petition to the Tzar and not expected back for days."

"He practically flew to say good-bye. Besides, he thought you'd be needing him here to help look after the stables."

Ronya's eyes filled with gratitude. "I'll be needing him to help look after the estate. Please ask him to come and dine with me."

Ronya had just gotten into the tub, when Lydia came in with the news. "The rooms are empty. No one is here."

"No one?"

"The tutor is home, and some of the servants— About the time the train was pulling out of the station, I spotted Georgi standing all by himself. I started for him, but Tamara got there first. They rode off together."

Ronya picked up a bar of French soap. "Then they're all with Tamara. Send a runner, please. I want them at once."

"Yes, ma'am."

It seemed forever before Georgi appeared.

Like David and the Blond One, he was extraordinarily large for his age, bright, and amazingly good-looking: hair that shone like Boris', white skin, and clear, hazel eyes. Like both parents, he had high cheekbones, and his wide mouth showed strength.

Georgi loved the world, and the world loved him in return. He got on well with his brothers. The relationship between him and Boris was infinitely easier than that between Boris and Igor, whom Boris so strongly favored, or between Boris and the Blond One, whom Boris resented and respected, or between Boris and David, whom Boris rejected.

Georgi was infinitely secure with Ronya. He knew she loved him and never bothered about how much she loved the others. The one Georgi adored was Katya—no wonder.

It took a certain amount of questioning on Ronya's part and a certain amount of hedging on Georgi's—until he was quite sure it was too late for anyone to ride after the train—before Georgi confessed.

"Did the Blond One hide under the canvas, too?" Ronya asked.

Georgi nodded. "He went under first. Igor went last."

The Blond One interested Ronya most, for it meant Boris was an accomplice. *No one* stowed away in his wagon without his knowing it.

373

A few weeks later, a telegram arrived for Father Tromokov.

BORIS WON. MOSCOW PREPARING A CELEBRATION FOR RUSSIA'S CHAMPION. BOYS ECSTATIC.

LOVE FROM ALL,
RONYA

39

Summer came to an end quickly that year.

Igor did not bother his head much with Hebrew or with the Torah, but he remembered enough not to shame Rabbi Levinsky, and when the bar mitzvah ceremony ended, men who had never seen him before commented, "One has to admit, he possesses the Von Glasman looks and the Von Glasman charm."

Igor, muscular and already dashingly handsome, had Ronya's magnificent black eyes, but the expression in those eyes was Boris'. His dimple fascinated girls, a fact Igor fully realized. More than one Jewish mother dreamed of one day seeing her daughter standing under the marriage canopy with Ronya's heir, with Ronya's pearls around her neck.

Igor entertained a hearty contempt for his tutors and paid no attention to his studies. It was a sore grief to Ronya that her firstborn cared only for horses and, she sensed, girls. When she implored him to make the most of the great opportunities offered him, he replied, smiling, "I do." When she pleaded, "Don't waste your time," he laughed, "I don't."

Still, he took his examination for the gymnasium at the proper time and passed, getting the more satisfactory grades in his orals. He grinned, his black eyes twinkled mischievously when he faked his way through an answer, and points were stretching leniently in his favor. When weeks later his education was progressing exactly as before, to the continued despair of his tutors, Boris decided he wanted an explanation. He sent for his oldest son.

The library was cheerful and warm, the pungent smell of polished wood mingled with winter greenery.

Igor came in breezily, almost defiantly.

374

"Look here, Igor," Boris said, coming directly to the point, "don't you want to go to school with boys of your own age?"

"Sure, if I had a choice."

"If you had a choice?"

"I've spoken to Mother twice about gymnasium. It seems she wants me here with those idiot tutors."

"Why?"

Igor shrugged. "I wish I knew."

"Maybe you should have come to *me* and told *me* what you told your mother," Boris said evenly. "You have two parents."

"I had only a mother at my bar mitzvah."

Boris blinked. *So that's it,* he thought, *that's the reason for her infuriating coolness.* She knew he could never find it in his heart to go to the synagogue. That's why he had invented the urgent summons from his mother. The way she accepted it so calmly, so convinced, only confirmed the fact that she understood his mind. Yet all the while, she harbored resentment. Leaping to his feet, Igor forgotten, he tracked her down in her kitchen. Ronya was checking the shine on pots and pans: a bad sign.

"That summons to Odessa was pure invention, wasn't it?" she said, anticipating him. "You couldn't find it in your Tartar heart to enter the synagogue, so you devised—"

"Yes," Boris cut in honestly, "I thought it would make it easier for you if I got out of Kiev for a couple of days."

"And all those presents—they were meant to bedazzle me, weren't they? And Igor too?"

Boris gave her a pained look. "That wasn't exactly a commonplace watch I gave him, you know."

"But it had none of the sentimental attachment of the gift I gave him when we came home from the synagogue—my father's watch and gold chain."

David and Georgi came clattering down the passage and Boris snapped his mouth shut. Under other circumstances he might have stayed to argue, but at the moment he was unwilling to embark upon an encounter with David, whom he found hard to take even when the boy was behaving comparatively well. It seemed to him that the boy was never satisfied unless he was threatening Igor, bullying Georgi. More and more, David fought for the upper hand in everything and outdid himself in trying to force Ronya to make a choice between him and his father.

Whenever Boris complained to Ronya, she searched around for excuses. "He imitates you." Or, foolishly, "Confess—the only difference between you is age and size. It's a rare moment when you're not insisting upon being first—most—best. Why, at your age, do you still pour your strength into breaking horses?" And when she was angry enough or anxious enough, she would turn the argument from David to his father. "The country needs leaders," she would say, impassionedly. "There will be no progress, Boris, until men like you— Russia's heroes—take a stand. But most important, you should be living up to your potential." And lately, perhaps because of such urging, Boris had begun to see himself in that role.

It was not until evening that Boris was given a chance to bring up the subject of Igor's education.

"I think you had better cut the cord, Ronya," he told her. "You've got to let Igor grow up."

"What?"

"Why isn't Igor attending high school classes where he'll waste less time or where at least he'll waste it with boys of his own age? The new term starts in January. I'll give the tutors their notice tomorrow."

Ronya's retort carried the ring of silver against glass. "It is not fitting for the son of Boris Pirov to deprive a Jewish boy of his chance of an education."

"What in hell are you getting at?"

"The Jewish quota."

"That's idiotic."

"Do you want Igor to deny that he is a Jew?"

"Oh, Christ!" Boris struck the arm of his chair with his fist. "Through each of us our sons have hereditary rights and privileges. The quota has absolutely nothing to do with Igor."

"Hmph! Tell that to the new minister of education. Hereditary rights get short shrift in his decrees."

"Stop talking in riddles. What decrees?"

" 'With no exception,' " she recited, " 'for the sons of old and valorous families, all nonbaptized applicants come under the quota.' That is one decree."

Boris gave her a glance. "How long have you known this?"

Ronya looked suddenly appealing in her confusion and obvious embarrassment.

"Why," he inquired, striving to maintain a stern attitude, "was I kept in ignorance?"

Ronya shrugged her shoulders. All she could recall were the many times Boris said, "Dammit, Ronya, don't bother me with problems, I'm home to enjoy you." Even Paul's occasional letters, from Venezuela or Saudi Arabia, but routed to her via Sergey in Switzerland, gave her a support and understanding she could get nowhere else.

How can I make Boris see? she thought. *Hardly a month passes but I urge him to acquire political power and fulfill his responsibility to his sons.*

Earnestly, she said, "The Von Glasmans have fought all their lives against quotas and restrictions. That's why they educated their sons privately all through secondary school and then sent them to European universities. That's why I keep Igor home."

"Well, we're not waiting for the new semester. Come morning, Igor's going where he should have been from the start of the school year. *You* get rid of the tutors, Ronya. I don't want to see their constipated faces around here ever again."

Ronya cast him a bewildered glance.

"Don't fret, dove. I don't propose to let the bastards put a number on our Igor."

The sudden early morning appearance of Boris Pirov astride his white stallion on the Jewish street caused many a resident to rush to a window. They saw him dismount in front of the rabbi's house and talk to his stallion before ascending the few steps to the rabbi's door.

"This can't be a purely social visit," Joseph said after he had got over his initial surprise. "What brings you here?"

"What do you know about the director of education?"

"Konstantinovich?"

Boris nodded.

"He's nothing but grief to the Jews."

"In what way?"

"It's a complicated matter."

"Simplify it. I'm short on time."

"It's difficult to say in a few words, but I'll try. Konstantinovich, unlike his predecessors, can't be reached with money, and an official who can't be bribed and whose position is so at variance with ours makes things singularly difficult for us."

"What specifically do you know about him?"

"Under his administration, the primary and secondary schools are used to induce Jews to change their religion. He believes also that education is useless for those born into the lower classes, a superfluous luxury that profits the state nothing. The man was sent to us from Kostroma. I wish I knew why."

"Tell me about the quota system. How does it work?"

"It used to be ten percent within the Pale and five percent outside the Pale, except in Moscow and St. Petersburg, where it was less," Joseph said bitterly. "Subsequently, it was reduced to seven percent in and three percent out of the Pale, with two percent in Moscow and St. Petersburg.

"But what's the difference? Well over eighty percent of the students are the children of the nobility and of officials. Here in Kiev aside from officials, they are mainly the landed gentry and the military."

"Would you say," Boris asked, "that the quota is filled?"

Joseph's first impulse was to remind Boris that no Jew got anywhere without friends in high places, but Boris was not Ronya, and he confined himself to saying emphatically, "Not at all! And keep in mind the tens of thousands of Jews in the villages, where there are no government schools. They, too, are included in Kiev's quota."

Boris was beginning to appreciate why Ronya was sensitive about sending Igor to gymnasium. "Apart from money—that's no problem —how many qualified boys of Igor's age can you have ready by tomorrow?"

"Ready for school?"

"That's right."

Joseph Levinsky made some mental calculations. "At least forty boys would flock to the eighteen unfilled places."

"Tomorrow at seven, when you hear the sound of wagon wheels outside the synagogue, send out your eighteen boys. Igor and I will be waiting." Coming to his feet, Boris added, "And please, Joseph, no frightened faces. Pick fine samples, boys of at least average height and sturdy frame. Let's have a bit of Jewish brawn as well as brain."

The rabbi looked at him dumbfounded.

From his conference with Joseph, Boris went straight to Konstantinovich. "It's a pleasure to welcome you, Gospodin Pirov," said the director. Shaking hands, Boris saw a gray and balding middle-aged man who looked acutely uncomfortable, like a man forced into a situation not at all to his liking. There was no sign of the hard-headed tyrant described by Joseph Levinsky.

Boris dropped into a chair. "I have just run into a friend from Kostroma," he said without preliminary. "Very enlightening."

The man facing him turned dead white.

Boris carefully kept his face expressionless. His stab in the dark had succeeded beyond his hopes.

"Your friend?"

"My friend."

"Your friend," Konstantinovich asked slowly, "what does he do?"

"He's with the secret police."

There was a brief but grim silence. "What did he tell you?"

"Everything!" Boris snapped.

The man's eyes filled with fear. "I'm at your mercy," he said in a low voice, "therefore at your service."

Boris stared at him coldly. "Good. Let's begin. You probably know I have a son, Igor."

Konstantinovich nodded. "Certainly. I kept my eyes open for him at the start of the fall semester. I saved a place for him."

378

Boris laughed, a mean Tartar laugh. "You saved eighteen places, thereby making two mistakes. Very stupid of you."

This was exceedingly awkward for the director. Should he apologize? The boy clearly listed himself a Jew on his test papers.

"Those eighteen places are filled," Boris went on. "Extend every courtesy to the new boys—and no proselytizing, you hear?"

"I hear," Konstantinovich said meekly.

"About Igor. If the Tzar were to ride in parade in Odessa, he'd ride behind Igor's Tartar grandmother. When the Emperor and Autocrat of all the Russias parades in the Crimea, he finds himself to the rear of Igor's great-uncle."

Boris' speech was a comfort to Konstantinovich. Pirov was telling him that his son was no Jew boy!

"Igor's claim to rights and privileges," Boris continued, closing off this new hope, "is further strengthened through his mother. I'm sure you've heard what the Von Glasman name stands for in Russia."

Knowing it was useless to dispute with Boris, he said, "I know, but it's not the Jews we shun, it's their religion. Some of my friends were once Jews—or their parents were."

"No!" Boris said, in mock astonishment.

"It is we who are shunned by the Jews," Konstantinovich said righteously, "a nation within a nation, the rich with their imported German tutors and imported brides too. The Tzar greatly wishes Russian men to marry Russian-bred women."

"Christ!" Boris said. "The Tzar brought home Alix Victoria, Princess of Hesse-Darmstadt, born near the Rhine and raised in England."

"Her conversion to orthodoxy was immediate. The Empress Alexandra is utterly devout."

Boris grinned. "That makes me indescribably happy." He rose.

Konstantinovich was tempted to ask for some sort of reassurance, but he understood that if he kept his part of the bargain he had nothing to fear from Boris Pirov. "I am told," he said, attempting some gesture of propitiation, "that your Igor has a magnetic personality."

"My Igor," Boris replied, "is a rotten student and a brawler who fancies himself a devil with the girls."

"My God," said Krasmikov, "I can't let you read a file classified 'A.' I haven't read it myself."

"Too bad. We used to be good friends. So long."

"Come back," Krasmikov shouted.

Boris turned at once. "Gladly," he said, settling himself comfortably in Krasmikov's big chair.

The policeman looked at the clock. Five minutes to five. "I can't go to the vault until everyone's gone for the day."

"We wait." Boris opened the center drawer of Krasmikov's desk and took out a deck of cards. "Let's play."

"No," Krasmikov said. "I don't choose to give you my money, too."

Boris smiled. "I'll try to lose."

"Hell—that's not necessary," Krasmikov said affectionately. "I'm glad to do you a favor."

At six sharp, Krasmikov left his office, and it was not until a quarter of seven that he handed Boris a document and said, "I read it and the supplementary sheet, too."

Embezzlement of school funds. Statutory rape. The girl was barely fifteen. Boris looked up. "So the son of a bitch can't be reached with money."

"How's that?" Krasmikov said.

"Embezzlement and rape," Boris said thoughtfully. "They don't usually go together, do they?"

"They do if the rapist—really the victim—is being blackmailed."

"So," said Boris, "an extenuating circumstance? Why the whitewash?"

"His record," Krasmikov said, handing over the supplementary sheet. "Pobiedonostsev interceded in his behalf, and he is paying back every cent."

It seemed that Konstantinovich was doing the kind of work Pobiedonostsev really admired. He held the record for leading Jewish students into Russian orthodoxy. His zeal was indefatigable.

"Do you want him caught?" Krasmikov asked, gathering up the papers. "I'll put someone on to watch him. Once smitten, who knoies It's quite possible that he might fool around with a minor again. Fundamentally, people don't change."

Boris reflected. "No," he said, "leave him alone. I don't think he'll be any more trouble."

Three months after Boris saw him, Konstantinovich died. It had not gone unnoticed in St. Petersburg that there were no new converts in his district. The letter he got telling him, none too kindly, that such failure on his part was not to be tolerated also told him, in essence, that his time on earth was over. One evening he did not go home. He waited until quite late, and went up to the roof of the school and looked down. It was a long way to the white-covered cobblestones. As he jumped, he screamed hideously into the howling wind that carried the cold rains and heavy snows across Russia. Next morning he was found by a dog. The snow that whirled across the city had already blanketed him. His death caused no stir, it was just another death of many who were dying from the relentless cold.

When Pobiedonostsev was informed of Konstantinovich's suicide, he shrugged. The Tzar brushed away the whole incident, just as he declined to notice the rural suffering. He went skating; he liked skating. He went to the opera; he was especially fond of the opera. Mostly, he stayed home with his beloved Alix—shy, proud, pious Alix. Heat from gaily colored porcelain stoves kept them warm, and booted Cossacks in fur caps kept them safe.

"In a way," Ronya said to Boris, "it's our fault that a man like Konstantinovich is sent to Kiev. What have we done to prevent it? This time let's not wait for another Konstantinovich. I have good friends among the landowners and among the bankers and merchants. The local politicians are all admirers of yours. We have some contacts in the church. I think my cousin, the bishop, will intercede for us."

"We'll need no help from Moscow," said Boris, taking the lead. Under pressure from the Christian community, a dedicated educator with no ulterior motive was made director of education and put in charge of the Kiev primary and secondary schools.

40

Was it blind chance? Do the fates, as it is said, spin the thread of human destiny? Or was Ronya's carelessness unwittingly planned? Did she deliberately leave open the drawer where she kept Paul's letters? And if so—why? To drive Boris to the pinnacle of rage? To see him devoured by jealousy? Now that Boris seemed less interested in dalliance with other women, was life that golden summer too good to be true?

When Boris came into Ronya's room late one summer afternoon, hot and tired from the day's work, he hardly noticed the packet of letters tied with red ribbon. He had quite forgotten Paul, and it never entered his head to suspect Ronya of anything clandestine. It was while shaving that the red ribbon intruded itself into his consciousness, and the less he wanted to give it a thought the more the silly piece of ribbon gave him no peace. Impatient with himself, he strode back to the open drawer.

Ronya came in twenty minutes later. Still beside himself with rage, though the beast within him had been brought somewhat under control, Boris pushed her toward the fireplace with such fury that she dropped to her knees.

"Look!"

Boris forced her head around: Paul's letters were on fire; the tongues of flame had demolished all but one bit of red ribbon.

Boris gripped her wrists and pulled her to her feet. "Why have you deceived me?"

Her eyes almost as fierce as his, her jaw no less set, Ronya freed herself from his grip. "How dare you criticize me! Blame yourself, Boris Pirov. You accept everything as your due but, by your law, I—" Her lower lip began to quiver. "I won't cringe, and I won't excuse myself or Paul, and I won't beg your forgiveness. So wipe the slate clean, Boris. As you so conveniently say about your own conduct when it suits you, 'Done is done.'"

There was no torment Ronya could have invented greater than mentioning Paul's name.

"End it, Ronya, or so help me, I'll find him—no matter where— and kill him."

Ronya stared up into fire-filled eyes. "I am *Ronya*. I am not your personal property."

Boris picked her up and tossed her on the bed. "You make a grave mistake, Ronya, if you think that. You *are* mine."

She had only to look at him to know that he was on his way to buy a woman. "I hope you're unable—incapable—impotent."

Boris gave her a savage grin. And he was gone.

Ronya felt drained. But in a short time she had recovered sufficiently to write in the journal she still addressed to her father: "Whatever else, my swashbuckling eagle will never turn into the kind of old man who drinks warm milk as he ponders a lonely sleep." She locked the drawer. Next she wrote to Katya, telling her everything that had happened: "I entreat you to come if you can. This is bound to be one of his more monumental carousals, because it is aimed at teaching me a lesson. Boris has transferred so much of the worship he had for Mother to you, and you seem to have her calming effect upon him."

Katya's reply was immediate: TONIGHT, WE TAKE TRAIN.

Ronya was wrong about Boris: He did not want a strange woman; his passion was for her. He wanted to drink, and brood, and be alone. And sleep.

Colette provided the best hotel service in Kiev. The guest rooms were quiet, the liquor the best. Food was served from an immaculate kitchen: Her chef was acknowledged superb. More procuress than

382

madam, Colette represented highly attractive harlots with good manners and no morals, whom she introduced to gentlemen able to pay an immense price for services performed. She kept herself exclusively for three regulars, who never dropped in without an appointment, but sometimes she gave in to the young imp she once was and treated herself to a whirl with a well-proportioned youth.

Colette appeared delighted to see Boris. "Where in the world have you been hiding yourself? My ladies are distressed by your neglect." She looked at him and inquired, without further tiresome nonsense: "What is your pleasure, Boris?"

"Rent me a room. I feel a great thirst."

Colette sought his eyes, but he shook his head. "Just vodka. Keep it coming."

"You'll regret your decision, Boris. I've imported several new beauties—they're good, awfully good. And safe."

Boredom in his shrug, he said, "Maybe. We'll see."

With a notable celebrity like Boris Pirov, Colette did not send for a servant. She took the trouble to take him upstairs herself and leave him well provisioned.

During his five-day stay, Boris made Colette terribly unhappy. An unsatisfied client was more damaging to the good reputation of a house than a dissatisfied one.

The first woman who touched him, he resented. He resented her immediate, extravagant familiarity, the bright red on her lips, and the feverish patches of red high on her cheeks. Boris, who was never overly nice to a harlot, even when she appealed to him, made no attempt to hide his displeasure.

Next, Colette turned to a woman she thought no man could resist. She even coached her a little. "Be professional. In a good mood, he's quite easy to handle." After a time, the woman came down. "I could do nothing—neither could he."

Colette rather enjoyed hearing that.

The next came down in less than ten minutes. "Critical bastard," she muttered contemptuously.

The last one said, "It's no use."

Colette was desperate. She went to Boris herself. Too late: his door was bolted from the inside. She found comfort in the size of his bill, and it gave her pleasure that it was the stuck-up Jewess' money he was spending.

Boris was relieved to hear the footsteps fade. He picked up the newspaper and found that Ronya had used it to communicate to him. It was announced that the Count and Countess Alexis Brusilov were expected from Moscow tomorrow.

The wardrobe door was open. Sorely tempted to put on his clothes and leave, Boris set down his glass and got out of bed. He tried his legs: fine, he could manage them all right. He went into the bathroom and stood staring at himself in the mirror that hung over the washbasin. He had never before noticed that there was some silver streaked through the growth of gold on his face. He fetched what was left of the vodka, poured every last drop into the sink, and got into bed, determined to get a good night's sleep. It was no use.

Late in the night he fell into a light sleep and dreamed a slightly different version of his recurrent dream. No longer was the candle bent; now it was cracked. In his dream, Boris knew he had to get to Ronya, for only she could make the candle whole and strong again.

He opened his eyes and stared up at the frescoed ceiling of voluptuous nudes. Boris grunted and got to his feet.

With the paper and his morning tea the maid brought a message: "Madam Colette invites you to breakfast. She asks that you accept."

Boris nodded a dismissal.

Slightly annoyed, he went downstairs to an alcove off the ornamental drawing room, where Colette was seated at a round, lace-covered table, already drinking coffee and sucking on a lump of sugar.

She examined him appraisingly, disappointed to see how well he looked.

"Really, Boris," she began, "how could you? I've had hard-to-please customers in my day, but—" Suddenly realizing this was not the right approach, she became very gracious: "Any one of them was able and more than willing to meet any wish of yours."

"Colette, I don't give a damn about the proficiency of your whores. To me they're all alike. They look alike. They smell alike."

Colette was tempted to suggest that occasional impotence in a robust man was not uncommon, especially if the man sought oblivion in vodka, but one did not prosper in a competitive business by deflating a celebrity. Pouring more coffee, she treated herself to a moment's savory anticipation of what she had in store for him.

"Please, Boris, understand I speak out of friendship," she said, pretending an uneasiness she did not feel. "I've been wanting to tell you and not tell you. I've had repeated arguments with myself."

Did she think he was taken in by her performance? All he said was, "Go on."

"Your Igor was here last week. Thinking he required the right instruction, and knowing that his mother could well afford it, I took care of him personally. He paid the house fee in gold, and he was—to put it mildly—overgenerous to everyone."

The shot went home, but holding himself in control, Boris asked, "Who brought him here?"

"No one. He came with the other youngster—the tall, blond one."

Boris was boiling and knew that Colette was enjoying his discomfiture, but he spoke in the same mild tone: "I want all the facts, Colette."

"It'll take time."

"No hurry." Boris wondered why it hurt so much that his Igor was no longer a fledgling experimenting in the hayloft.

Colette went into the details as she had heard them from the boys.

The week before, on a Friday, the Blond One pulled the buggy to a stop on a corner opposite the school and waited for Igor. He frequently met Igor and gave him a lift home. Today he was troubled. He wanted no part of the fun Igor promised him, but he had brought the gold, an extravagant amount of gold. Just fifteen, he knew that tall, willowy girls with makeup on their faces whose business it was to remove their clothes and make rhythmic motions, preferably on a bed, were expensive.

The late afternoon sun was going down when the horses came to a stop in front of Colette's mansion. Igor jumped down, and the Blond One followed slowly, staring curiously at the man lounging outside the house whose eyes flickered briefly over the boys' faces.

"I take the horses, gentlemen."

Before the Blond One could say anything, Igor whipped out a five-ruble gold piece and thrust it into the attendant's hand.

The man's smile widened. "Thank you, sir. I hope you gentlemen have a good time."

The Blond One could feel the mockery and wanted to give the man one good punch in the nose, but Igor was already at the front door.

The maid who answered Igor's ring said, "Sorry, boys, but we don't buy at the front door."

Igor whipped out another gold coin. The maid stepped aside and Igor pushed past her.

At first, the receptionist was amused. When Igor gave his name, her smile became warmer. Igor put his hand in his pocket, and at the sight of gold she straightened her corset, took them both by the elbow, and steered them into the drawing room, talking all the while. She pushed Igor gently into a chair and said, "Don't go away."

Left alone, the boys inspected their surroundings. The Blond One thought the room with its purple and gold, its crystal and pink marble, a superb example of the awful, but to Igor it was just right—exactly what his boyish romanticism expected of a whorehouse.

Colette arrived on the scene a little uncertain of what to expect, though automatically flashing her practiced smile. Igor leaped to his feet. "Hello," he said, happily, "I'm Igor Pirov. This is my brother. We call him the Blond One."

Noting the extraordinary grace of Boris' bastard, and not failing to appreciate the beauty of Igor's sensuous mouth, Colette decided to handle the boys in style and do herself proud. "I think," she said, "we should sit down, have a drink, and get acquainted."

"I don't think so, ma'am," the Blond One said. "On one drink Igor gets sleepy. On two he gets drunk."

Igor agreed. "That's the truth. On three I pass out, and I don't want to do that. I want to go to bed with you."

"Why, bless your heart," said Colette. She turned her attention to the Blond One. "I really haven't got anyone for you, but I'll find someone."

"Please don't bother, ma'am."

"Oh, that's no bother. There's bound to be a cancellation or two." With a sudden surge of trust, she confided, "Wives are so damn cunning. You've no idea the lengths they go to. And just like that," she snapped her fingers, "someone's evening is completely wasted."

"I don't want anyone, ma'am."

"Why not?" she asked in surprise.

Igor and the Blond One exchanged a long, even glance, and Igor said, "He means it."

Not knowing what to make of it, Colette shrugged. Still the good hostess, she asked, "Would you like a bit of supper while you wait?"

Without hesitation the Blond One made his request: "Please ma'am, may I have Igor's books? They were left in the buggy."

Books! This was too much for Colette. She laughed aloud and pulled a velvet cord. "What will you be doing with Igor's books?"

Igor laughed. "I go to school, and he gets the education."

By the time the maid had fetched the books and escorted the Blond One to a third floor room where, sprawled on a divan, he started Chapter XII of *The Romantic Movement in France,* Colette and Igor were settled in bed.

Assuming that Igor, despite the wicked gleam in his eyes, would be doing what he came to do for the first time, Colette was astonished, then impressed, and soon dazzled by the exuberant vitality with which he made love. "Good God, Igor! You've got a talent."

"That was just the warm-up."

"Wonderful."

Igor raised his eyebrows in amusement, and his wayward hands started their journey all over again. Colette closed her eyes and pretended that she was young again.

Christ! Boris thought to himself. *A practiced veteran, an old hand at sixteen.*

After a silence, he got to his feet and said harshly, "So you took care of him personally."

Colette smiled up at him smoothly.

Narrowing his eyes, he said, "Wonderful." Flint-hard, he went on, "If anything bad happens to that boy, so help me, I'll—" He stopped himself. There was a better way of handling this.

"Boris, I have a favor to ask. Will you spare me another minute?" She rapidly continued, "I have a relative coming to live in Kiev. She's a stunner, and she moves only in the highest circles. Would you mind lending her your house until she makes some friends here?"

"What's wrong with here?"

"Vera is used to her own place, and her own carriage, and a generous allowance. That's why I thought of you."

"All right," Boris said wearily, "so long as she realizes I don't give a long lease." At the door, he paused. "One more thing: Tell her she may have one hell of a wait, but if I happen to call she'd better be there alone."

"I'll tell her," Colette said matter-of-factly.

From Colette's, Boris went to see Mischuk.

The policeman stopped writing and looked up. "Hello, stranger. What a coincidence. I'm just accepting Ronya's invitation."

"Are we entertaining?" Boris asked tiredly.

"Katya and Alexis are arriving today."

"I know." Boris' voice was remote.

It was obvious that this was no casual visit. Offering Boris a comfortable chair, Mischuk waited.

"Igor," Boris said wearily, "is whoring. The Blond One supplies him with gold and does his lessons while he fiddles. His performance is sensational, I'm told."

Mischuk understood the pain locked up in his friend. It fascinated him that where his son was concerned Boris was a prude. "I suppose you're sure."

Boris nodded slowly.

"Where?" he asked, extremely put out. As a policeman, Mischuk thought it shameful that Kiev was littered with whorehouses.

"Who knows?" Boris answered with a shrug. "Last week he turned up at Colette's."

"You're not serious!"

For a time the two men sat in silence. Mischuk's thoughts had nothing to do with lovemaking. Boris let his mind slip back to his own introduction to sex. He had done none of the things his mother thought he was doing, and not until he was a cadet had he had his first experience. The woman was gracious and tender; he hated her because she was married and cheated.

Boris came out of his reverie. "I intend to keep Igor busy, but I can't lock him up. He's bound to give me the slip. I want him watched. At whatever whorehouse he lights, I want the madam and the pimps warned. I'll tear limb from limb anyone who harms him."

"Do you want him stopped?"

"No. Just make sure he gets girls who are clean, and no tricksters."

"Very well. But while I'd like to put on a regular police officer, I can't."

"I know. My preference is for someone I can use around the stables. That way he can keep an eye on Igor's comings and goings."

"That's easy. You'll have him tomorrow at nine." Then: "Why do you think—?" Mischuk broke off in confusion.

"You're wondering about the Blond One."

"I suppose."

"I suspect he's scared. There's the possibility he doesn't like girls. Hell, I don't know."

"The Blond One is as strong as a bull and as smart as a whip. He likes girls all right, but he likes only nice ones. Remember, I'm the one who told you."

"Why the stress?"

"I don't know," Mischuk said. "Maybe because I see a little of me in him."

The grandfather clock was chiming five as Boris entered the house. The dining room table was set for seven, but none of the family was downstairs. He sought out Lydia, an astonishingly accurate indicator of Ronya's moods. She was sitting at the kitchen table having a quiet glass of tea by herself.

"Don't get up." Boris picked up an apple but did not bite into it. It stayed cradled in his hand. "Have Katya and Alexis arrived?"

"Yes, sir. Hours ago."

"Company for dinner?"

"Only the family," Lydia answered quickly.

Boris cocked an eyebrow. "Georgi, too?"

Lydia nodded. "For this, he stayed out of mischief nearly all week."

"See if Katya can persuade him to rest before dinner."

"Hopeless," Lydia responded happily, "but don't worry, Boris, my master, I'll serve them all a long tea."

There was no need to warn Lydia to delay dinner. Boris put the apple on the table.

Upstairs in her room, Ronya was at the open window staring out into the garden, where Katya and Georgi were sharing some wonderful joke. The sound of their laughter reached her, but she was lost in sadness. Now she was sure that the news in the paper had escaped

Boris' notice—or worse. **Perhaps** he had seen it and was beyond caring.

When Boris came up behind her and whispered, "Hello, dove," she jumped and then her arms were around his neck and her head burrowed into his chest. He held her quietly and stroked her silken hair.

"I love you, Ronya."

"I have to talk, darling. I want you to understand why—"

"No!"

"At least, let me explain—"

"Don't!"

The vehemence in his voice gave her panic.

"Ronya, please come to bed with me," he said, recovering his gentleness.

Ronya sat down on the bed and started to take the pins out of her hair.

She gave him back his full manhood. And when, after a long while, he asked, "Did you miss me, dove?" she answered, "Oh, my darling."

As a rule, the family gathered in the library, but this evening they were in the drawing room where Alexis, *apéritif* in hand, was having a serious talk with David about the Army.

"Even if it is the career second sons frequently choose, it's not for you. It's all rules, procedure, discipline. I must say I'd find that a wretched way to live. I'm hoping that you'll consider my Moscow estate. There's a real career for you there."

Before David could answer, his parents walked in holding hands. Boys learn a lot by the time they are twelve. It was hateful that Boris had the power to transfigure his mother, to make her radiant. Immediately he was on his feet and next to Ronya.

"Ah, my dear brother." Alexis put down his glass and gave Boris an embrace.

The exchange between Boris and David was cool, but then Katya and Georgi came in, and Boris lifted Katya off her feet and kissed her soundly on the mouth. Looking up at him, she found it hard to believe that he was not just back from a day's healthy exercise in the open air. Boris read her correctly and winked.

They had already begun dinner when Igor came bursting into the room full of breathless apologies. From his place at the head of the table, Boris gave his eldest son a level look. Igor's eyes sparkled with happy-go-lucky excitement; he was almost laughing.

"How's school?" Boris asked.

"It *was* all right."

"*Was?*" Boris said with raised brows.

"Yes, darling," Ronya said. "Summer recess started last Friday."

"I understand," said Boris with a sarcastic grin, "you gave yourself quite a treat in celebration."

Igor gave him a curious glance. "It was nothing special," he replied with mocking brevity.

Alexis wondered: *What now?*

Katya thought: *Some youthful prank.*

Ronya's heart said: *They duel.*

The silence was heavy. Boris picked up his wine glass and said to Alexis, "So you were saying. The Tzar's expenses are prodigal. . . ."

41

Summer faded into gold and rust, and again it was autumn. There was an invigorating coolness in the air, and the darkness came earlier. Around Kiev the landowners had reaped a rich harvest, and the celebration which started with a citywide festival was still on. So was the war of wills between Boris and David. Between Ronya and Tamara there was a curious, delicately balanced mixture of allegiance and intense rivalry.

Boris was deplorably shorthanded. The tremendous victory of Pirov horses and by Pirov riders had set in motion a series of wild celebrations from which the riders and trainers were not yet recovered—a fling that Boris overlooked in view of the prize money. Sad Eyes, upon whom he depended, was on his once-a-year spree. This time it already had lasted a couple of weeks, so this morning two men had ridden out to search for him. Even if some of the hands did stagger back, Boris could not rely on them. Accordingly, he labored from early morning well through late afternoon, shouting orders to the Blond One and David, and the three of them did the work of twenty hands. The Blond One carried easily the load of four good men, and David—big and brawny and no longer a child—worked and worked, for he alone among Boris' sons proudly embraced his Tartar roots and promised himself, "I'll be the tallest, the strongest, the toughest, the best. And the most powerful." He thought to succeed his grandmother, the Tartar woman, even dreaming of marching across Russia at the head of a Tartar army to retake Moscow and all of Central Asia. At twelve David greatly lamented the Romanov rule. As for the Jews, he was willing to leave them free—unless, of course, they bothered him. All this he shared with Tamara, who took him seriously and entered into his fantasy, offering her men for his army and discussing military strategy with enthusiasm.

At the red of sunset, David began to drag through the last of the chores. He was thinking of Tamara. She was his enchantress, and when she danced the most exciting imaginings ran through his mind. David was precocious in every way.

"You've done enough, David," the Blond One said. "I'll finish." The Blond One was always good to David. In contrast to David's eagerness to get to the camp, the Blond One had no wish to leave the stables. He had no affection for his mother; her sensuality had set the mark of disgrace upon him. When she danced, all he could see was a gypsy woman with disheveled hair and sweat on her forehead.

Boris could hear them. The last thing he wanted was for the Blond One to nursemaid David, and the boy's deep emotional involvement with Tamara made him uneasy. He went into the stable in an irritable mood. He noticed at once that David was again going about his tasks in bare feet, despite repeated warnings.

"How many times have I told you to wear boots in the barns?"

Without ever really knowing why, David loved to drive Boris into pure Tartar fury. It gave him physical pleasure to watch Boris' face change. "My feet aren't cold," he said at last.

Boris refused to be tricked into an explosion of temper. "It's not a matter of temperature, son," he said reasonably. "It *can* be a matter of life or death."

David's pale, cold eyes narrowed to slits. "Why don't you admit you'd like me dead and out of the way so that you could have *more* of *my* mother for yourself."

Boris lifted the flat of his hand and knocked him off his feet.

"That was senseless," the Blond One said with a sigh, helping David to his feet.

Looking after Boris' departing form, David said, "Do you think we are *ever* going to be as strong as he?"

"You, yes, and Georgi, too. Igor, I think, is more Von Glasman than Pirov. He'll never have the size. Very likely, he'll stay his present six feet one."

"What about you?"

"I don't want to be better than Igor," the Blond One answered.

"Why not?"

"It's complicated. Sometimes I'm not even sure I know why. I just know it's fitting."

Greatly mystified, David shook his head. How could anyone choose not to compete?

The Blond One laid his hand on David's shoulder. "You'd better get to the camp. Old Auntie will be storytelling soon."

As David shot out of the stall, tossing a farewell over his shoulder, his foot landed upon a nail which drove right up into the sole. The first quick, hot stab made him swear, but after that it did not hurt. He went into the tack room, got a pair of pliers, and dragged out the nail. Then, sticking his dirty feet into clean socks and soft leather boots, and whistling a tune, he went on his way. He arrived at the camp with a light heart and a big hunger and went straight to the laden tables. Nearby suckling pigs were roasting over open fires; there were dishes of salads, seafoods, cold cuts, and cheeses.

Everything was gay under the bright stars and around the fires of fir and pine—dark-faced men with full lips and bulging muscles dancing, gypsy girls flushed with excitement humming melodies in tune with balalaikas, and flat-faced peasants eating and drinking and clapping their hands in time to the music.

David picked up a stick and started down a path to where Old Auntie, aged and bent and shawled, was telling a story of witches and astrologers and spells.

In the glow of the fire, he drew a face on the ground with his stick. It was meant to be Boris' face, but it looked oddly like his own.

Three days went by; on the fourth David spent a long time squeezing the pus from his foot, washing it in hot water, after which he put on a bandage. Before he unlocked the door to the bathroom he splashed water on his hair, so that when Ronya asked what had taken him so long he could say he'd washed his hair.

"I'd like it better if you'd let me wash your hair."

David scowled. "He told me I'm too big for you to bathe. He told you, too. I heard him. Everyone did."

Ronya remembered well the way Boris had roared at the top of his lungs: "I know him, Ronya. He's a troublemaker and a cold-blooded liar to boot."

"He hates me."

"No, David, he doesn't hate you," Ronya hastened to say. "He feels hurt and angry because you're not even civil to him. All he's trying to do is prepare you for life."

"Well, I don't need him."

Now David's sore was completely healed. He examined the sole of his left foot carefully—not a mark. He was proud of his lie and the way everyone had believed him.

The first symptoms occurred six days after the accident. He was restless and irritable and had a violent headache. The next Friday morning, sore and stiff and sweating heavily, he forced himself out of bed, but ate no breakfast and had a terrible outburst of temper. A strange feeling of stiffness followed, which frightened even him. He confessed to a headache, and Lydia took him to Ronya's room. As he ran to his mother, he fell heavily on the floor, and when Ronya reached him he clung to her frantically, sobbing. "I hurt all over."

Ronya glanced up at Lydia, who shrugged her shoulders.

Presently the pain eased, and the boy stopped sobbing and was able to walk unaided, though stiffly, to Ronya's bed. She helped him climb in, then asked him a number of questions—among them whether he had been wandering about in his bare feet again.

"No."

"Think hard. This is the time for truth. Don't be afraid to tell me."

David gave her a resolute "No," wondering as he said it why he felt compelled to lie to his mother.

"Are you sure?"

He grew agitated. "No, no. How many times do I have to tell you: No!"

"Listen, David, do you think I like upsetting you?"

David thought this over. "No."

"Have you been careless in the stables? Are you sure you have no cuts anywhere?"

"No."

Ronya sponged him with a washcloth, her eyes alert for any marks or cuts, but she could find nothing.

"Now do you believe me?" David demanded.

He slept a little, but when the doctor came, he was unmanageable.

The doctor listened to Ronya attentively but thought she was making a mountain of a molehill—a female peculiarity. However, as Ronya sat by her sleeping son, she could not shake off a feeling of doom. One thing for certain: Whatever the doctor's opinion, she knew she was not going to the party being given by the new commandant of the Cavalry post tomorrow night. Boris would be disappointed; he had been looking forward to it.

As if to confirm the fact, Boris sent a message telling her that he would stay at the post overnight—the commandant had invited him to an all-night card game; and she deliberated whether to summon him home, but David was sleeping normally and she put the thought aside.

By evening David's temperature had soared, and spasms convulsed his left leg. He tore at Ronya's arms as she held him, droning "Mamma, mamma." Between seizures he slept uneasily, beset by nightmares. Toward morning he seemed better, less hot, and the spasms were fewer.

Faithful Lydia heaved herself out of Boris' chair and returned quickly with a soft-boiled egg and warm milk, but David refused to eat and complained he was cold. Lydia immediately built up a roaring fire. Ronya persuaded him to drink milk spiked generously with brandy.

The first thing Boris noticed when he walked into Ronya's room was the oppressive heat. He stood looking down at Ronya and David, side by side in the big bed.

"Darling," she said, deeply relieved that he was home, "awake he's in the most frightful pain, asleep he suffers the most frightening dreams."

David stirred and sat up. He looked much better.

Boris shot her a quick glance.

"Feel him, Boris. He's hot."

"How can he avoid being hot? This room is stifling. Open the windows." Boris turned to David. "Your mother says you're in pain. Is that true?"

"No."

"She says that you've been having nightmares. Is that true?"

"No."

"Are you saying your mother is a liar?"

"No."

Boris' eyes blazed. "Then what in the hell are you saying?"

Pain shot through David's head, but he said defiantly: "I've been drinking your brandy. Smell my breath."

Ronya could scarcely believe this was the same muttering, pain-racked child she had nursed all night.

"That's all right, son," Boris said, his face stone. "Have another with me." He strode over to the brandy bottle and poured a glass for David and a tumblerful for himself.

He waited until David had choked down the brandy, picked him up, and carried him to his own room, deaf to Ronya's protests.

He returned and took Ronya's arm. "Let's go. We'll sleep in my room."

"Listen to me, Boris."

"You're easily fooled, Ronya. My remedy for a malingerer is military school."

"Darling, I've been with him nearly twenty-four hours. I've watched him. Perhaps he picked up a nail or got himself a deep cut that healed, but now—" Ronya found she could not say the word lockjaw.

Boris cursed under his breath. "That can't be. I've told you once, I'm telling you again—don't mollycoddle the boys." But Ronya could tell he was alarmed. "You've got absolutely nothing to go on." He let go of her arm. "I'm going to sleep. I suggest you do the same. You look like hell."

She stood there, sorry she had said as much as she had.

"Did you call the doctor?"

She nodded.

"Did *he* say—?"

She shook her head.

Cursing mightily, Boris slammed the door.

For five hours Boris slept poorly, his nightmares full of David and Paul. He came awake to the sound of steady rain. He went into David's room to find the boy sleeping, his breathing even.

Later, her voice hoarse with weeping, Lydia told Father Tromokov, "I tell you, Father, when Boris walked in, the devil walked in too. Otherwise how do you explain it? David breathed and moved normally, a nice healthy color in his cheeks, no sign of pain."

Without a greeting or even a smile, Ronya asked from the doorway, "What do you want? I must go to David at once."

Since getting up, he had had plenty of time to brood over his resentment of her pampering the boy. "Don't smother the boys, Ronya!"

She was startled at his ferocity. Especially now. "Why do you so stubbornly refuse to believe me? He's terribly sick."

Her suffering twisted his heart, but Boris had an established rule: Once he took a stand, he would not budge. He threw her a handful of rubles from the bedside table.

"Hire nurses. Engage a resident physician. When this is gone, I'll win more for you. All I want is this: Rest. Get rid of the shadows under your eyes. Tonight you're going to look your best."

"Tonight?" she repeated, bewildered.

"Commandant Ignatov's reception."

She stared at him, dumbfounded. "I'm not going anywhere tonight, and neither are you."

He saw, to his fury, that David had driven their promised evening together quite out of her head. He took her by the shoulders. "Don't crack the whip, Ronya. Six o'clock. Be ready." He let his hands run over her, then he let her go.

Almost sick with disappointment, Ronya ran to David.

David was quite rational that afternoon when the doctor examined him. Afterward Ronya took the doctor down to the library. She had sent Igor to look for Boris. In the space of one day, he had matured. Ronya could see that. Exactly how was hard to say—maybe a new hardness to his sensuous mouth, a sadness to his eyes. Igor said, "We can't find him."

When the door closed behind Igor, the doctor said, "Well, my dear, I had hoped to spare you."

She swallowed. "I think I know."

The doctor realized it was better not to utter the awful word "tetanus." He nodded and said instead, "A disease as old as the centuries. Descriptions can be found in ancient writings—a baffling mystery."

Ronya remembered a little girl she knew when she was seven. When the girl fell ill and it was known that she would soon die, Tamara and Ronya went together to say good-bye. They were with her when she began to froth at the mouth.

"How long do we have, Doctor?"

The doctor was struck by the directness of her gaze. "Let us not give up all hope. With no history of an open wound, the chances of recovery are better."

"Better? Better than what?" Ronya asked piteously.

The physician was angry because he was helpless. He walked stiffly to the window and said, with his back turned to her, "Hundreds of years, Ronya—fruitless, unproductive—a good ninety-five percent is the mortality rate."

Ronya's mouth trembled.

Feeling hollow inside, she went to the doctor and stood beside him, wordless. He tried to soften the stark horror. "But we must hope. I have never seen a boy physically David's equal. He has a will of iron, and that, too, makes a difference. If he continues to take nourishment, maybe the outcome will be favorable."

"Thank you, Doctor."

They smiled at each other joylessly.

"Give him anything he finds comforting. Keep him quiet in a darkened room removed from noise. Warm baths twice a day. A whiff of chloroform as needed."

"I'll remember."

"Good-bye, Ronya. I'll look in tomorrow."

A little before six, Ronya left David sleeping lightly with Igor and the Blond One to watch over him and settled down to wait for Boris. In full-dress uniform, exuding strength and vigor, he walked into her room at the first stroke of six. He took one look at her and stopped short.

"The doctor has made his diagnosis," she began, and then stopped, as a sudden flood of grief overwhelmed her.

Boris' face was convulsed with rage. "Spare me the posturing of the anguished Jewish mother," he said brutally. "I told you to be ready."

"For heaven's sake, Boris, listen to me, please. David—"

A slave to his own need to bend her to his will, Boris was beyond hearing. "You listen to me! I'm leaving the big carriage behind for you, and when you get to the post I don't want to see big sorrowing eyes staring out of a pale face."

A dull cold pain closed around Ronya's heart. "You are a fool, Boris."

"If you don't join me, it won't be the end of the world," he said maliciously. "I've got a whore lined up who's the perfect antidote to a lying son and a hysterical wife."

Ronya's head jerked up.

"Don't bother to come back."

Clearly Boris did not believe her: She could no more do without him than he could without her.

David was racked with spasms all evening, teeth clenched, mouth drawn down, barely able to cry "Mamma, mamma—my back—the pain in my back."

Igor's eyes were filled with tears, and cold shivers ran through his body. He had never in his life felt despair. But when David needed lifting, his trembling ceased and he carried him gently into the bathroom to ease his torment in a tub of tepid water.

Ronya swore to herself that she would keep calm, but when David's brow started to wrinkle and his lips set in a terrible Satanic grin, her resolve almost left her. She mastered her panic and gulped down her tears, and the face David saw was serene, the voice he heard cheerful.

"David, darling," she said, bending over his pillow, "I want you to have milk and a sedative."

David's devil-look was hideous, and the effort to speak was beginning to take its toll, but he was still alert and his will remained ironstrong. "I—want—vodka," he whispered.

She filled a glass with vodka and added fifteen drops of laudanum. Holding him up, she put the glass to his lips, and David swallowed every drop.

David held on to her with all his strength. "Tamara—" he uttered.

"Tamara doesn't know you're sick, darling," Ronya said soothingly. "I'll send for her in the morning if you like."

David managed to say, "Now," before Igor put the chloroform-soaked cotton under his nose.

Somewhere between midnight and one in the morning, Tamara, still in the extravagance of flashy rings, fine embroidery, and red ruffles, brushed past Lydia, asleep in an easy chair in the hall, and entered the bedroom, to see David's form on the bed and Ronya dozing in the rocker. Filled with foreboding she halted at the head of the bed: She saw that the white angel was near. Ronya caught her in the middle of a scream that brought Lydia running.

In a few minutes, Tamara was recovered enough to follow Ronya out to the hall, but she had to drag herself through the door. "How bad is he, Ronya?"

"My poor David. Even though he's heavily drugged, just our voices trigger his spasms now."

Squatted at the foot of the bed, Lydia stared after them contemplatively. She was imagining them before Boris, before Tamara went wrong; but Lydia knew in her stout peasant heart that it was too late for either of them to go back.

"Did Boris send you?" Ronya asked abruptly, putting down her glass of tea on the kitchen table.

Tamara looked blank. Suddenly she cried: "My God—isn't he here?"

"No, he isn't."

"What! Damn it, Ronya, where is he?"

"Maybe you'd better tell me what made you come here."

"Well, when I saw Boris watching the entrance—he looked forbidding—I said to Semoshkov, 'I wonder what's keeping Ronya.' And he—"

"Did Boris dance?"

"A duty-dance with the colonel's wife. When we went in to supper, he was gone. Semoshkov told me that he had given the colonel your regrets and asked to be excused.

"When I danced with Ignatov, I said, 'What in the world happened to Boris?' and he said, 'Don't you know? His son David is mildly ill. Nothing to fret over, still he felt he must go to his wife.'

"For the rest of the evening, I could think only of David. Semoshkov was very decent. He offered to drive me back, and here I am." Tamara put down her glass and stared at Ronya. "Ronya, where *is* Boris?"

"I don't know."

"Well, I do," Tamara almost shrieked. "He's in that fancy French brothel behind a closed door."

"Maybe," said Ronya, starting to rise. "Go to David, while I take a bath. I won't be long."

Tamara was with David when he had his first serious convulsion. After that, he deteriorated fast. Lydia ran to wake Igor and the Blond One. Twenty minutes later, the Blond One rode from the stables into the rainy darkness for the doctor. Igor raced into town hoping to find Boris.

The doctor had the most unforgettable ride of his life. The Blond One drove as though he were Boris.

"Go right to Georgi, please," Ronya asked the Blond One when he returned. He touched her hair and he said quietly, "I think heaven is a pasture with angels guarding the horses. Heaven is a garden of apple blossoms and rosebuds of all colors. It's the sea. And the woods are there. David will like heaven."

Mostly out of pity for Ronya, the doctor kept everyone busy, but he told Tamara, "Before the disease kills him, death will come from acute exhaustion."

Tamara knew better. She understood David's savage strength. She knew he would die, but not from the inability to endure the unendurable. She was right. By three o'clock in the afternoon, his temperature had risen to 107 degrees. His arms and legs were completely bent, and his body was a single curve. He was foaming at the mouth.

Lydia came in and whispered in Ronya's ear, "Igor is back. The boy is a wreck." Together they stepped out of the room. Raging against his father, Igor cried, "The earth has opened and swallowed him."

Ronya reached up and brushed Igor's hair from his eyes. "You must get out of those wet clothes, dear."

"How's David?"

"Not good."

"I want to stay with him," Igor said huskily.

"Leave him in Tamara's care for a while, dear."

Igor stared. It seemed unfair to him that Tamara, who had made his mother suffer, should be with David now.

"You're forgetting, darling," Ronya said softly, "David loves her."

If ever Tamara proved her love for David, it was now. The convulsion that seized him nearly threw him from the bed. Tamara seized a wad of cotton, saturated it with chloroform, and held it over his face.

Ronya reentered the darkened room filled with the unmistakable odor of chloroform. One glance at Tamara, and she knew. She flung open the windows and let in the high wind and the teeming rain. She went to David, and straightened his arms and his legs, and put his face in an expression of repose. She leaned forward and brushed her lips across his mouth. Then she turned her magnificent eyes on Tamara and thanked her.

"He was born in a storm."

"Yes."

Tamara went into the bathroom and returned with a basin of water. She washed and dried David's face and combed his hair, and as Ronya covered him with a fresh sheet, she thought back to the time when she had read his fate.

"Oh Ronya," she cried, tears streaming down her face, "I loved him so much."

Ronya refused to give way. "You must do me one more service, Tamara. You must go for Boris and bring him home."

Wiping her eyes with the back of her fists, Tamara drew away. "For God's sake, Ronya. How do I do that?"

Ronya told her about the house on the hill. "It's a narrow structure, with a small barn to the side, completely hidden from the street by a high wall. A narrow path leads to the rear. Be careful. From there it's a straight drop to the river."

Tamara saw that all too obviously Ronya was willing to put up with the house and whatever Boris did there as long as its doors were closed to her.

Ronya stared at Tamara's departing back. Her face twisted and the tears started. She threw herself down on the floor. Great, terrible sobs racked her slender frame.

Outside, the rain had stopped. A pallid half moon streaked through the window.

42

Tamara was trying to smash the door of the house on the hill with her fists. Each blow gave her pleasure and fed the blaze of her jealous rage.

The door swung open, and Boris stood bewildered on the threshold; barefoot, dressed only in trousers and an unbuttoned shirt, a day's stubble on his face, he looked half crazed.

"David's dead," Tamara screeched.

She stepped back from the blaze of his eyes.

Boris jumped past her, swung onto her sorrel mare, and lashed the horse into a gallop.

Lydia had sent away the servants and bolted all but the front door. She waited for Boris in the hall.

"Where's Ronya?" he demanded as the door swung to behind him.

Lydia came closer. "Boris, my master, you've no shoes on your feet." And she led him up to his room.

"Lydia, was it—" his voice faltered, "tetanus?"

"Yes, that's what it was. It was terrible."

Boris felt his stomach contract in agony. "Tell me about Ronya, please."

"She cried until she had no tears left. Now she's empty and fearfully white."

Lydia turned away and left him.

When Boris had made himself presentable, he went first to his dead son. Screaming out an unspeakable obscenity against himself, his tears ran like rainwater. At last he made his way back to his own room, grateful that no one was in the hall. Calmed down, he opened Ronya's door, there to be confronted by a total stranger.

Ash on her forehead, without shoes, Ronya sat in a straight chair facing him, piteous, pathetic, vindictive. She let him come within two feet of her, and no more. "Stay where you are. I don't want you near me."

"Ronya, Ronya." Boris gave a great sigh, weary and helpless. "Can't I sit down?"

"Tired?" Her voice was caustic.

He admitted he was.

Ronya's smile made him want to beg for mercy, but he knew it was useless; she would not be placated.

Horrified as she uttered them by the smallness, the inappropriateness of her words, Ronya mocked him: "You're not looking well. Perhaps you put too much strength in servicing your whore. You weren't lying awake worrying over David. Perhaps you spent yourself with remorse for letting down Igor, who wanted you so desperately, or the Blond One and Georgi, whose god you were."

No mention of herself, Boris thought. His apprehensiveness deepened. "How long have you known?" The asking cost him a great effort.

"You mean the house?" All these years she had kept to herself her knowledge of his private rendezvous.

Dumbly he nodded.

"Who do you think made good your overdraft?"

He looked stunned. "Why, Ronya? Why?"

"That's what David, my father, asked. 'Why, Ronya, why?' "

"It's unbelievable. You must have had a reason. What was it, Ronya?"

She was about to deliver a stinging retort—"Isn't that the sort of thing an heiress does, anything to hang on to—" when she saw his eyes glazed with tears. She ached with pity for him, but there was a demon pushing her on. "How dare you concern yourself with such rubbish! Why don't you concern yourself with David?" Her passion rose. "Why doesn't the frost melt around your Tartar heart? He was ours. We lay in love and gave him life."

Boris fell on his knees. He buried his head on her lap. "Forgive me, my love."

"Take your hands off me."

He made another desperate attempt to reach her. "Help me, Ronya. And don't deny me the right to help you."

"Get up from your knees, please," she said in a restrained voice and waited until he had done so. "I do not want our estrangement to be known to all the world—at least, not until I have decided what I want to do. Therefore, I leave to you what is considered a father's right and duty. Please make the arrangements for the coffin and go to the rabbi. Tell Joseph I want no eulogy and no sentimental farewell."

"Ronya, I've been a coward—that's what it was, dove, plain cowardice. I've seen tetanus, and I dared not let myself think that such horror could cross our doorstep. I retreated to that dark corner you spoke of with a bottle, and while I hid, I pictured David strong and haughty and determined to outdo me. Sometimes I secretly hoped he would some day. Well—I was wrong on all counts. I'll regret it for the rest of my life, and I fully intend to make it up to you. But—done is done."

Ronya felt her resolve diminishing, but just then he slapped his chair with his huge hand. "I don't ever want to hear the word 'estrangement' again—not ever. And no matter what, you're *mine*. Make no mistake about that, Ronya."

She stood up. "I am so tired." She looked ready to drop.

"I love you, Ronya," Boris said.

When the door closed behind him, Ronya rubbed her eyes. "That's good," she told herself. "How else can I get Igor to the university? How else can I give the Blond One your name?"

When Lydia came into the library with coffee, Boris drank it. When she said, "Eat," he took a slice of bread and ate it. When she brought him his coat from the closet, he accepted it and looked at her as if he expected her to say something.

Lydia shook her head. "I'm sorry. They're still not here."

"Does Igor know I'm back?"

Lydia picked up the tray. "Yes, Boris, my master."

"Well," Boris said, in a matter-of-fact tone, "I'd better get going. There's a lot to do."

Boris lay on his back. Sleep did not come. He tried another position; no help. He decided to forget sleep and turned up the lamp, opened the draperies to let in the breeze, and settled down to read.

A rap on the door made his heart beat faster: Perhaps that was Igor at last.

"I've been walking," the priest said. "I can't sleep. So I've brought a bottle—yours. I've even brought glasses—also yours."

Boris smiled slightly. "I see."

The priest handed him a glass and sagged down on the bed. Boris could feel the piercing glance and looked over the rim of his glass.

"You're disappointed," said the priest.

Boris did not deny it.

"Overlook the slight, Boris. It was no dying sparrow, it was his brother. Besides, Igor is brooding over another worry. He's convinced that Ronya's sweet gaiety is gone forever."

Boris shook his head. "Igor is wrong. When the Blond One was born, I saw for the first time how Ronya handles grief. She has to lock her door and be by herself. I used to climb to her balcony and watch her by the hour. Sitting in her darkened corner, staring at nothing, she looked a doomed little spirit. It was the same after her father's death.

"Then, one day, Ronya feels an overpowering urge to live, and her mourning is over. The color comes back to her cheeks, her black eyes sparkle, and her proud mouth smiles."

The priest got up from the bed and sat down on a chair. "Listen," he said, wondering how he could make Boris understand, "it's different this time, my friend. Ronya is running. She has told me to take Georgi to Moscow right after the burial and break the sad news to Katya and Alexis. Ronya is going to Odessa. The servants there have already been warned she is coming."

Boris' eyes became slits as his temper rose. "Oh, no she isn't! Christ —no!"

The priest paid no attention. "Fill me up. I have an aversion to thirst."

Boris gave him the bottle.

The priest filled his glass and set the bottle down. He took a mouthful of vodka. "Are you ready to listen?"

"Hand me the bottle."

The priest smiled and tossed it over. Boris caught it and put it to his lips. The priest saw a softer look about the Tartar.

"I agree with you, Boris. I've no intention of taking Georgi to Moscow. I propose to bring Katya here."

"Katya!" Boris nodded, as if all had been settled to his satisfaction.

"Katya is only a beginning. She leads me to my main point, which is: Remember, you're dealing with Ronya von Glasman."

"What do you mean by that?"

When he saw no tearing rage in that penetrating stare, when Boris did not remind him of Ronya's married name, the priest then knew that Boris would be reasonable and respect Ronya's need to renew herself in her own way. "Remember," he said gently, "the girl who had to have you—only you. She's yours, Boris. Give her time."

Boris felt his eyes misting again.

They sipped vodka until three in the morning. Part of the time they talked and part of the time they stayed silent, each with his own thoughts. Boris' mind went back to Ruth swept overboard into a crashing sea, it went back to David, but mostly he thought about Ronya in her desolate loneliness. His arms ached to hold her. Finally, he said, "Go home, Ivan."

"Lydia has prepared a room for me here." He got to his feet. "If you would believe in God, Boris, ask for his support—"

"God!" Boris exploded. "Go down the hall and look at David."

Boris waited for morning and for Igor. Morning came; Igor did not. At seven o'clock, he rose and dressed and went to David to say good-bye. He stared at his son, and then went to the windows, opened them, and let the sun pour in.

The news of David's death spread quickly, but friends and acquaintances alike went out of their way not to intrude. The pious peasants and the tenant farmers went to the early mass and prayed: "Good Jesus, lead his soul to a sunny place." The church bells pealed. The peasants believed that David had departed for a better life.

Among the gypsies there was great tumult. The white-winged angel of death had severed the life of David, their queen's favorite, and so they sought the angel, in order that he, too, should perish. Attired in bizarre colors, they whirled ropes and brandished daggers and fired pistols into the air, and they cried in loud voices to the blare of guitars and violins: "Make yourself visible." Most of them were drunk.

Little by little the children joined in, throwing stones and, like their elders, challenging the angel: "Show yourself."

The old women ridiculed him, baring toothless gums in evil smiles, lifting their skirts to show him their wrinkled bottoms.

He did not make himself visible.

The gypsies were consoled. The white-winged angel of death feared them.

Tamara came to the cemetery immediately from the camp, decked out in a flamboyant fuchsia vest over a blazing yellow blouse, a mulberry-colored skirt, a chain of gold bangles glittering about her waist —a costume designed to irritate the evil spirits.

Simultaneously, the Blond One arrived, all in white.

"Who gave you a white yarmulkah?" Tamara asked petulantly.

"Ronya did, when I was thirteen."

"Why weren't you at the camp?"

Straightening as he saw Ronya approaching, he said, "I went to church."

Ronya was supported by Igor. Georgi followed between Boris and the rabbi. Lydia, her bonnet askew, walked alone. The males all wore yarmulkahs.

At the open grave, Ronya uttered a moan. In a moment Boris was by her side.

The rabbi moved to the grave, opening his prayer book. Slowly, rocking to and fro, he chanted the prayer. Ronya stared with eyes fixed straight ahead.

Then came the horrifying instant when the first shovelful of dirt fell over the coffin. Igor put his arm protectively around his mother. They turned and made their way back to the house. The others followed—all but the Blond One. He cut David's name into a tree in the pine grove, then went down to the river and sat on a boulder waiting for Igor and Georgi.

Hands in lap, Ronya sat contemplating the Persian rug. Her hair shone in the sunlight that streamed through the open window, and she looked young, hardly more than a girl. It was almost as if sorrow intensified her loveliness. Even so, her face was changing—the high cheekbones were slightly sharper, the firm chin a little more precise, the beautiful mouth parted a little less eagerly.

Tamara slid from her chair. "My men are ready to leave for Odessa whenever you are," she said.

Damn her, Boris muttered to himself. Aloud, he said savagely, "Thanks, Tamara, that's a favor I won't soon forget."

Carefully avoiding the rabbi's eyes, Tamara said, "Good-bye, Joseph," and slipped quietly from the room.

If Ronya was relieved to see Tamara go, Joseph was even more so. The years had mellowed Joseph Levinsky, but his insight into a woman's nature—especially a nature as complex as Ronya's—was still woefully inadequate. He believed, for example, that Ronya's departure was an aimless indulgence because she was sorry for herself. He missed a whole range of reasons: Igor was one, the Jews were another. He could not realize that Ronya had grown up and longed for a man who had grown up too.

As for resuming the conjugal relationship, the very idea of making love now was repugnant to her.

He made an even bigger mistake. He was taken in completely by Boris' gentleness with Ronya, his patience and endless excuses for her behavior.

After all, even a non-Jewish father is still a father.

Joseph reminded her of the ritual of *shivah:* seven solemn days mourning on a low stool, dressed in cloth and shod with slippers. That would help her come to her senses.

"Ronya," he concluded, "have faith in God. He raises up the fallen."

There was no softening her. She wet her lips. "You praise the Lord, Joseph. I must change my clothes. I'll be back to bid you good-bye."

"Are you packed?" Boris said with surprise.

"I'm not taking much, mainly walking and riding outfits."

"Then that means—?"

"I don't know what it means."

Ronya had barely returned downstairs, when Tamara burst into the room.

"Hurry, Ronya, Old Auntie sent me to fetch you. She is dying and said you must hear her vision. She insists she saw it in the sky the morning the sun came out."

For a moment no one knew what to do—the summons was too bizarre and too soon after David's death. But tragedies have a way of coming in pairs. The rabbi broke the silence. "Go, Ronya—it's a *mitzvah*."

"Don't linger, dove," Boris agreed.

Boris touched her face with his hands. He kissed her eyelids.

At the front door, Ronya embraced Lydia tenderly. "Look out for him," she said softly. "I love him with all my heart." Then she picked up her shawl and followed Tamara into the waiting buggy.

There was no record of Old Auntie's age. Tamara thought she was somewhere between one hundred and two and one hundred and five, but in reality she was older. Old Auntie was born on Von Glasman land the year Catherine the Great suppressed the Pugachev uprising, in the year 1783. Now, at the culmination of her life, her sightless eyes sought and found Ronya's, and she told this tale:

"Rifka sent out her soul ornamented with false jewels. She was punished for this because the fates have a lien upon the jewels of a queen. They sent the wind and the snow. Her body disappeared, and her soul had no place to go. The soul cried bitterly.

"In that very storm, Ronya, you gave birth to a boy. The babe came early because it was needed. He was blond and royal, and he was David von Glasman's grandson. Rifka's soul found sanctuary and ceased its weeping.

"For twelve long years the soul and the boy lived in peace and contentment. And then the fates ordered the soul to paradise. But the soul loved the boy and refused to abandon him; and the boy had no soul of his own. The fates ordered the white angel to take David, too, and guide him to heaven."

Her tale was completed. Ronya said nothing, but Tamara asked, "When you looked up into the sky, what did you see? What is the prophecy?"

406

A wrinkled hand, cold and clammy, touched Ronya's lips. "Thou shalt behold the grace of it," Old Auntie said to her, "blond for golden. Be comforted." Her hand fell away, and Ronya knew it was the end.

Tamara bent over Old Auntie and kissed her. They left her to the ministrations of the women.

"Do you remember," Ronya said as they went out together, "when we were children she told us she was the reincarnation of a rare bird that lived long ago in unexplored Africa? And afterward she commanded me to bring an eagle to this place?"

Tamara remembered. Ronya had done so.

Igor and the Blond One were waiting for Ronya with their present —an ivory-handled whip. They kissed her upturned face. Tamara gave her a cigarette case. "I rolled the cigarettes myself."

Then Igor lifted her into the closed carriage. His strong hands were so much like Boris' that Ronya trembled, making a determined effort to maintain her composure until the doors were shut and no one could see her misery as the carriage set off along the muddy slippery roads toward Odessa.

Thirty-six hours after Ronya's departure, Katya arrived in Kiev. Ivan Tromokov carried her bags to the Pirov carriage and opened the door. Katya found herself in Boris' arms.

She half lay across the seat leaning against him, her eyes swollen from crying, her head aching with misery.

Boris removed her hat and gently stroked her hair. "Katya, Katya, you're even paler than Ronya."

He waited until she quieted, wiped the tears from her eyes and cheeks, and laid a bouquet of bronze and yellow chrysanthemums in her lap.

"From Georgi."

He put his arm around her shoulder and told her what had passed —a lot less than there was to tell but more than she wanted to hear. When he spoke of the house on the hill, he felt her recoil, even though he made little of the woman and emphasized the vodka.

"Not very attractive, is it, Katya?"

She shook her head.

"But it's what you'd expect of me, isn't it?" He didn't wait for her answer. "I had to tell you, because I don't want you hearing it first from Tamara. Igor has hardly spoken to me since David's death. Now he won't even look at me."

As soon as Katya entered the house, Georgi pounced on her. She took him in her arms, and he leaned his head against her bosom. "Oh, Georgi darling," she cried, "I've missed you so."

Not far from the house, on a quiet bank by the Dnieper, there was a little world of marble—tombstones and benches set about with fragrant flowers and lawns and guarded by silver birches and lindens, where flocks of birds chirped and frolicked and filled the air with their song. It was here that generations of Von Glasmans slept eternal sleep.

Boris went there more often than Ronya knew. He had an attachment to the place, liked sitting tranquilly, watching the river sparkle in the sun. Now, forty-eight hours after Ronya had left, and after having put a watch around the estate and set up a warning system, he was there, but not for his usual reasons.

Sitting near a sheltered spot by David's grave, he reached for the vodka bottle and took a swallow. He was listening for the quiet jingle of harness, for the cautious rustle of leaves that would warn of the approach of the men who had come to do the Tartar woman's bidding.

He heard sounds coming loudly toward him. Soon his eyes made out the two figures—Igor and the Blond One, pistol belts girding their waists, rifles in their hands.

"For Christ's sake," Boris swore. "I told them to stay out of it."

He remained motionless until the boys were standing in front of him.

"You came in wide open. I could have—"

"We meant you to hear us," Igor said. "No one can sneak up on you."

"I can," said Georgi, coming out of a hiding place, his pony well hidden behind a clump of bushes.

Boris laughed aloud as he saw the amazement on Igor's face. "Take one," he said, offering him his cigarette case. "You need it."

Igor turned on Georgi. "You got here first—before father."

Georgi's eyes sparkled roguishly. He could hardly conceal his high spirits—he had outsmarted Igor. "How else?" He saw this banter was having a good effect: He had not seen his father laugh, or even smile, since David's death. Emboldened, he stepped forward, his hunting gun gripped firmly in his hand. "We've a right to be here. David was our brother."

Igor seized on this. "That's right. Absolutely right. Let's make it clear to the Tartars—legend or no legend, if they want to come for the body of our brother we're none of us afraid of them." Igor stole a cautious glance at the Blond One. "If we don't stop them now, what's to prevent the Tartars from taking you from us one day? Then, Georgi, they'll want him, too. Let's show them now. The Pirov men stay here —legend be damned."

The eyes that Boris turned on Igor had changed from hazel to steel-gray. "All right. I'll take the dusk to dawn watch. In case they come when I'm not here, don't waste your breath talking and don't attack. Nothing is going to happen in a hurry. All you need do is fire three pistol shots, two fast, the third after a pause. That's the signal. Georgi, take your orders from Igor, but remember, you're expected home for meals on time."

Boris turned to the Blond One. He said nothing, but gave him a quiet nod. Almost at once he was gone.

The swirl of manes and the clatter of hooves came in a dense murky dawn: six black Tartars, brutal men on savage horses, riding in single file a pace apart. The last man led a white horse. Boris was relieved to see them; the wait had been long—seven days and seven nights. The Tartar woman surprised him as she had surprised herself by granting the Jewess her week of tears and ashes undisturbed.

Reining in, the leader halted the column and dismounted. Heavily armed, wrapped in a thick, high-collared coat of sheepskin, Pavel was sore from rough riding; but he was more than sore. He was curiously troubled. Sworn to serve the Tartar woman, body and soul, he also loved Boris. Slowly he walked up to Boris, leading the white horse, and delivered the Tartar command: "The Tartar woman says he is flaxen-haired. Therefore the legend says he is ours."

Boris covered him with his rifle. It was not a threat or an act of self-defense. It was his answer.

Unable to understand why Boris should choose to defy his mother and violate tribal law, Pavel said in a hard voice, "All I know is: The golden ones have ascendancy over all of us. In death the remains are carried home regally and laid to rest in Tartar soil. There's no escape."

Eying him from head to silver spurs, Boris said, "You may not have Ronya's son."

Pavel glanced around. Boris' uncompromising tone had had its effect. The men shifted, ready for Pavel's commands. His eyes went back to Boris. "Boris, don't make us take him by force."

Boris lowered his gun. "Did my mother grant you the right to kill me?"

"We are not assassins," the black Tartar said with dignity.

Boris smiled with his mouth only.

Pavel was a fierce fighter but no thinker. For several minutes he concentrated, all the while rotating a fleshy thumb over his short nose. Behind him, the men were fidgety. In their hearts they knew that they did not want to fight Boris. Pavel cleared his throat, blew out air with a puff, and said, "Hmm. This means we shall meet here again, perhaps as enemies."

"When?"

Pavel calculated aloud. "A good twenty-four, and twenty-four, and if there's no delay—"

Boris remembered Pavel's slowness with figures. Flashing him a fond grin, he said, "Better give it three full days."

Pavel nodded slowly. "Agreed."

Now that Pavel had ceased to be an adversary, Boris said to the Tartars, "Await my mother's decision in comfort. The stables are yours. Whatever you need from the house is yours."

After a moment's hesitation, Pavel shook his head. "Better not—we're on orders. We'll make camp in the forest."

43

Odessa had barren hills and thin soil. It had lumber. It had pretty stone churches with tent-shaped wooden roofs, but it had no cathedral like the Hagia Sophia of Kiev. It had its art, though for the most part this was unknown to the outside world. It had its saints. It had wealth, and it had poverty. It had priests and monks, Jews, nomadic Turks, and Persians. It had an imperious people, whose origins did not fade—the Odessa Tartars.

Odessa was an important city. It had the Black Sea.

As did all cities, Odessa had conflict which, as could be expected, produced anguish for its Jews. The centuries of anti-Semitism were not the will of God nor part of the divine plan; but this gave no solace to the Odessa Jews, for the Tzar's government put the seal of approval on persecution, restriction, and impoverishment. Not that all Odessa's Jews were impoverished; the rich lived in solid comfort and respectability as doctors, druggists, dentists, merchants. But the poor led dismal disfranchised lives in the lowest of dwellings in a harsh ghetto.

Above all, the Jews survived, enduring the purges, the persecutions, the pogroms, and they remained in Odessa in hope, always in hope—"*L'chaim*—To Life. Tomorrow will be better." They cared for their own.

The Black Sea had a corner on the hearts of all Ukrainians, and those who could afford it came to Odessa during the summer months to breathe the salt-laden air. The very fortunate owned their own dachas in the endless, sea-lashed hills. The Von Glasman house was more imposing and more lavish than most, built to withstand gales and squalls, sun and salt. Each generation preserved its splendor. Inside its weathered exterior, the house glowed with bold colors, with elegant paneling, with shiny brass and Chinese pewter. The family living room was a wonderful place, cool in summer when it offered a spectacular view of the Naval base and warmed in winter by two fireplaces. The principal bedroom was a full twenty feet square, with long windows opening out onto stone terraces and an incomparable four-poster bed, designed to accommodate Tzar Peter the Great.

The news of Ronya's arrival created a stir in the caretaker's cottage. Mikhail said to his wife, Galina, and his widowed daughter, Joanna, "We have three days to bring in provisions, and shower the house with attention."

"Yes," said Galina, "back to work. Our lazy days are behind us."

"Won't she be lonely?" Joanna asked.

"Ronya was never one to be lonely," her mother answered. "Even when she was a little girl, she was perfectly content to be by herself. She'd climb and swim, walk with the cranes, and talk to the sea gulls."

"Stop your talk, woman," Mikhail said. "There are windows to unshutter, curtains to hang, brass to polish. I have my share of work in the stable. She is coming by carriage."

"I wish the master were coming with her," Joanna said.

At the crest of the hill the carriage came to a halt. Ronya had reached the end of her journey. Unaided, she stepped to the ground and began to walk up to the house, stopping to gaze at the terraces which in summer were filled with sunlight, great flowering trees and shrubs of brilliant blue and purple, bushes of yellow and white. Now all color was gone—only sea spray and thin, bare branches.

Travel-weary, she went on. The servants, who had been on the watch for her, were at the door to make her welcome. Once inside the house, glowingly clean and comfortably warm, Ronya told them about David. She told the news quickly, without embellishment; even so, the telling was an ordeal.

Mikhail groped for words and found none. Abruptly he said, "I'll go look after the gypsies." Joanna, wiping her eyes, went into the kitchen. Galina and Ronya were left staring at each other. The old housekeeper opened her arms wide, and Ronya took a step forward and let her head drop on Galina's shoulder. She clung to her for a moment.

"No more talking," Galina said. "Take your bath, have your supper, rest. The last week has been too much for you."

Ronya did not sleep much. In the quiet of the night, thoughts came crowding in. The next morning she dressed early and went to walk the deserted beach.

The next day the wind blew hard, the sea was dark and choppy. Ronya walked to the harbor, climbed a high cliff, and watched the fishing fleet put out to sea. So passed two more solitary days. She could not rest. During daylight she rode over the vast stretches of dunes and walked on the bleak hills. She spoke very little, but she began to sleep at night and felt her first stirrings of hunger.

Early in the morning of the fourth day she awakened to a persistent banging and a voice urgently raised. She looked at the clock on the mantel: five thirty-five. Snatching up a cape, she ran down the stairs. At the front door she hesitated and looked out of a window. "Good God!" she said to herself, and unlocked the door to Boris' mother.

Ramrod straight, her handsomely boned face stern, the Tartar woman regarded Ronya with clear blue-gray eyes. "I can see you're a heavy sleeper," she said. "That's a curse. I've seen men die because they were drugged with sleep and didn't move quickly."

"Please come in."

"Of course. Why else should I come?" She gave a boot to the door, and it closed with a slam.

Automatically falling into the role of hostess, Ronya said, "My servants sleep in their own quarters. May I offer you coffee, or do you prefer tea?"

"Coffee—tea. Both no good.'and

"Milk? Hot chocolate?"

The Tartar woman said, "I'll drink what you drink," and followed Ronya into the kitchen.

Ronya waited until the tea was boiling before excusing herself for a moment. Her bare feet were freezing on the stone floor, and she wanted to run up to her room for slippers.

The Tartar woman picked up the tray. "Let's go." When they were in Ronya's room, she put the tray on the bedside table and said, "Get in bed." She took off her sheepskin jacket, dragged up a chair, and planted herself in it unceremoniously.

The Tartar woman poured the tea; then her eyes moved from object to object. "Real nice," she said. She examined the four-poster and its occupant. "No doubt about it. You're real pretty. How is it you're not fat? Aren't Jewesses supposed to get fat?"

More amused than irked, Ronya replied, "I don't think there are set rules about that."

The Tartar woman narrowed her eyes, but she did not look away.

In all her recollection, the Tartar woman had no remembrance of having to ask a favor. She ruled in a man's world of horses, and to her people her faintest word was a command. Angered, she gloried in savagery and left strong men quivering. Sexually, she was an animal; in heat she seized a worthy male creature. But she was inexorably bound to Boris' father. She respected herself and her stallions. She hated Jews with a passion.

The decision to speak to Ronya had come to her slowly, only after she had sought and failed to find another way. Her mind made up, she had put a bottle of vodka to her mouth, adjusted her holster, thrown on a jacket, and five minutes later was on her way. She knew exactly where Ronya was; she made it her business to know Ronya's whereabouts at all times.

The Tartar woman found it pleasant to sit in the cushioned armchair drinking tea and gazing closely at the Jewess. She liked the way Ronya sat in the majestic bed. She liked the absence of fear in Ronya's eyes. She liked the long, heavy braids, like a little girl's, falling down Ronya's back. For a moment she even envisioned the Jewess embracing the Tartar way and kissing the cross. It was all most perplexing.

At length, she went to the windows, pulled the draperies apart, opened the shutters, and let the early morning light fill the room. Back in her chair, she broke the silence. "I got my rights. I'm human—and make no mistake about that."

Then came the maniacal laugh.

Involuntarily, Ronya hugged herself and shivered.

The Tartar woman glared. "Make Boris a present of his life."

Assailed by fear but clinging to control, Ronya said, "What do you mean by that?"

"Persuade him to give up the boy to us. I don't want to kill him. I gave him life. I made him the world's greatest horseman. But he's an imbecile if he thinks I'll let him stand in my way. I won't be defeated at the second try. The legend says the golden ones are royal."

Ronya understood what she was facing. According to the legend, going back through the centuries, David, because of his coloring, was no ordinary mortal. The Tartars revered a golden one. Fabled to be royal—in instances divine—he is assigned a unique destiny. As his life draws near its end, the Tartars somehow know and Tartar warriors then go for him. On a young stallion, pure white, they bring the golden one home, where he is laid to rest on a forbidding, sea-pummeled hill, alongside a Tartar woman. Ronya understood that reason, appeals, would merely work up the Tartar woman to crazed ferocity. More important, she understood that legend can be fought only with legend. To thwart Boris' mother and triumph over the Tartars, she had to invoke a stronger magic. "David," she began carefully, "was not golden, only blond."

The Tartar woman cared little for such distinctions. "Same thing."

Composing a silent tribute to Old Auntie, and with the virtuosity of a born storyteller, Ronya shared with Boris' mother the story of Rifka's soul:

"The ways of the gypsies are strange. To fully understand about David, you must accept truths foreign to you. Just as I accept much that is amazing and fantastic in the long chapters of Tartar lore. This is what happened:

"The gypsy queen Rifka fell from grace and favor. When she died she was punished—the fates refused her soul. But when they beheld Rifka's sorrow, even the angel of death felt pity for her. The angel went to God and spoke of Rifka's soul, and the words filled God with such sorrow He bestowed a reprieve upon the soul. In the presence of all the fates, He laid his hand upon the infant David and sent him forth in a fierce storm, his own soul denied him. The lost soul of the gypsy queen then found David and entered his living flesh. No sooner had this happened than the storm that brought him abated and the soul cried out: 'The boy David and I are one.' To which the fates replied: 'This second chance is your last, Rifka, queen of the gypsies.'

"One day the angel again revealed himself. 'Come,' he said, 'you may now ascend into heaven.' Thereupon, the soul addressed the fates. 'You put me into the body of this blond boy. During the twelve years I inhabited this body I learned to love it. I shall not leave David.'

"But the angel reminded Rifka this was her last chance. 'We are concerned only with you. The boy has no soul. He was sent only to serve you.'

"And so," concluded Ronya, "we lost our David, creature of Boris' flesh and mine. Tamara bent over and kissed him and he departed with her mother."

The Tartar woman felt her head spinning. She got up, paced, muttered black curses, sat down again, and began to question Ronya.

She began with the storm. "Was there lightning and great rolls of thunder? Did it seem as though the wind blew in the boy and gave him life?"

"Yes. Lightning, thunder, wind, and rain."

"How did Boris view the boy? Did he find him lacking in any way?"

Sadly, Ronya recalled the enmity between Boris and David.

"Was he strange?" the Tartar woman asked shortly.

"He was rebellious, he could be cruel, but he loved the gypsies and they loved him."

That enraged the Tartar woman even more. She looked about the room for a drink.

"There's brandy in the cabinet," said Ronya, following her eyes.

Four long pulls from the bottle and the Tartar woman went back to questioning Ronya. "Were you ever afraid of him?"

414

"Never! But," Ronya added truthfully, "I was often afraid for him."

The Tartar woman pondered, chin in hand. Ronya weighed her strategy, hoping it was adequate.

"Describe his eyes."

"They bore no resemblance to Boris' eyes or mine."

The Tartar woman seemed impressed. From the expression on her face, it was clear to Ronya that she had won, David was hers. She knew she must show no triumph; if anything she had better confuse the Tartar woman still further. So she embellished her tale. "I never told Boris," she said, "I didn't have the heart. Perhaps that's why he did not deliver David to your emissaries. Perhaps he felt David not fit to lie beside the Tartars."

The Tartar woman cursed. "I never heard of a thing like that. It sure is a pity."

"Yes, it is, I resent it, too." She sank deeply, luxuriously into the pillows. "But I have reason for thanks, too. My caretaker tells me that your patrol comes regularly, and that he and his family find your protection very comforting."

"You pay for it, ma'am." The Tartar woman was standing now.

As Ronya recalled it later, there were no good-byes. All at once she was alone in her room.

Back in her own home, the Tartar woman sent this message to Pavel: "I call back the white stallion. Trouble Boris no more."

It was the third day after Ronya's departure. Except for the servants, Katya was quite alone in the house, worried and unhappy. But for one brief note there had been no word from Ronya; and she had Tamara to cope with. With Ronya gone there was no getting rid of her. Every day Katya was forced to repeat, "Go home. He does not want you here." And she had Boris and the Tartars to disturb her thoughts. She sat down at the piano; playing soothed her nerves.

She swung around when Boris came in.

"Have you found Georgi?"

"No, but I found a special reception in the stables—a hundred men or more carrying weapons. It was almost impossible to get rid of them."

"I wonder what has happened to Georgi?"

"I see no reason to worry. He often goes off exploring."

In her mind's eye Katya saw Georgi challenging the huge black-haired Tartar in the forest. She saw Igor defending his brother's coffin. She saw Boris, bold as a lion but outnumbered by six mounted savages.

Feeling a tightness in her chest, Katya laid her hand upon his arm. "You've got to take me with you. I can't wait here alone."

"Shall I take you to Ivan?" Boris asked, gazing sympathetically into her warm brown eyes. "Do you want to pray?"

Katya smiled ruefully. "Oh, Boris, you are a dear, but no."

For a moment Boris thought he was looking into Ruth's face, and then Katya again was urging him not to oppose the Tartars.

"Let them have David. What possible difference can it make to him, or to us?"

Boris gave her some sherry, which she took with a shaking hand.

"I can only tell you I have a feeling that if my mother has a decision forced upon her, she'll find some excuse to disclaim David."

"What if she doesn't?"

Boris shrugged. "We'll win. Those men waiting in the forest are far from enthusiastic; they're hoping as desperately as we for an order to return to Odessa. Whereas I have a motive: I want to hear 'Well done' from Ronya."

"I can understand that, but I only hope you'll remember that Ronya wants you to stay alive."

"I'll remember," Boris promised.

If it was hard to protect Boris from danger, it was twenty times harder with the boys. Igor came in, determined to be with his father when the Tartars' messenger returned. It took all Boris' effort to persuade the boy the meeting with Tartars was nothing: the fight would come later. He sent Igor happily off to devise a plan of campaign.

On the way to the stables, Boris met the Blond One. With inward pleasure, Boris took note of his majestic size and shining good looks. Though they did not speak, there was understanding between them.

Alone in the workshop, Boris tested the edges of the two knives and fitted them into sheaths. He whetted an ax at the grindstone until it was razor-sharp. He re-coiled his rope and checked his rifle and revolver. His weapons ready, he changed his clothes in the tack room. Boris had made sure he would be richly dressed: a silk-sashed shirt under a fur parka, a silk bandana tied loosely around his neck, skin-tight pants neatly tucked into highly polished boots, a fur hat for his head.

When he went to fetch the stallion, he was stunned to find Georgi perched on the horse's back, treating him to an animated monologue. Boris caught the last remarks. "They'll have daggers and rifles and they outnumber us, but we have weapons too and the forest belongs to us. We know it. They don't."

"True," said Boris.

In the best of spirits, Georgi said, "You'll have to take me with you. I'm golden. The Tartars won't be able to fight until they hear what grandmother says about killing me."

416

The golden eagle rode out a Tartar prince, the stallion his royal throne, a glint of fiery Tartar savagery in his eyes.

The campsite was encircled by fires to stave off wolves, but the men were sitting around a cook-fire making a meal of sausage and roast potatoes and washing it down with beer.

Boris rode up openly and eased himself out of the saddle, throwing the reins to one of the men. "Take care of him while I talk to Pavel."

Pavel, who was sitting by himself at the far end of the fire, peered up at Boris speculatively. "What brings you here?"

"The sausage. It smells good."

Pavel let Boris eat his supper in peace, and it pleased him that the men brought out vodka and pestered Boris with hospitality, but he could see at a glance that Boris was playing at drinking. Frequently he raised his glass and made the toast, "To Long Life," but took only small sips. Pavel's men themselves got drunk.

Beckoning to Boris, Pavel strolled across to his tent.

Boris noted the wide mattress on the floor. "You're getting soft," he said with a grin.

"That I am," Pavel responded without banter. "Let's sit down."

As they settled themselves on the mattress, Pavel remarked, "It's not hard to see that you're your mother's son."

"Don't fret. They'll wake sober."

After a silence, the big man looked up at Boris. "What do you think?"

"How many riders in the relay?"

"Twenty, each posted about twelve miles apart."

"Is Yuri the last rider?"

Pavel nodded.

"He's hours late," Boris said.

Pavel sat with lowered gaze. This could only mean that she was having second thoughts about seizing the white coffin by force. Good news, really, but Pavel did not wish to think about it. It was safer not to think. Better to have a talk with Boris. If someone had asked him how he came to think of his idea and how he came to speak freely, he would not have been able to explain.

Now, as he was floundering about searching for an opening remark, Boris helped him out. "So you've reached a decision."

"Evidently it shows when I think."

Boris smiled.

Pavel rested his eyes on Boris only a moment, then fixed them on the lantern slung from the center pole of the tent. "If only you could get your wife to come over to us and take root in our ways, everything would be perfect," he said. "Your mother would gladly revoke the curse, and I would take it upon myself to promise that never again in Ronya's lifetime would any one of us take part in a pogrom." Now he turned to Boris. "That's a fine offer. What good Jewess would dare refuse it?"

A trace of a smile still lit Boris' face, and since he offered no immediate resistance to the idea Pavel dared to hope it might be accepted. In an effort to further his cause, he revived a bit of history.

"You are not the first in the family to marry a Jew. The mighty Prince Tamen was a blue-eyed Jew. He came to Odessa from Genoa and fell in love with a Tartar princess. That was way back in time, before we even had an alphabet of our own, so the Court wrote in Hebrew letters when it engaged in official correspondence. But in everything else we kept to our Tartar ways and he came over to us."

Boris lit a cigarette and surveyed the smoke as it curled between them. "I haven't forgotten the Prince Tamen, but—" He stopped abruptly and went back to watching the smoke curl.

"But what! What's your answer? Will you try, at least?"

"No, Pavel. I will not try."

Pavel's eyes fell.

Boris capitulated to a point; he tried to explain. "Pavel, were the Jews the many and we the few, were they the powerful and we the weak, were they the high in power and we the low, were they the judges and we the misunderstood, was theirs the right to be brutal and were we without rights, Ronya's remaining a Jewess would be meaningless. But as things are—"

Pavel sighed. "You're a good man, Boris. A good man," he repeated. He turned down the lantern. "Get some sleep." He leaned over and pulled off Boris' boots and went out of the tent. He kept watch outside while gusts of wind tore through the trees and lashed the fires. Finally, the last lurking star left the sky, and day came.

The smell of coffee brought Boris awake. He made his way to water the stallion. From the stream he saw Yuri sweep into camp at a gallop.

All but Pavel were at breakfast when Boris returned, and the expression on their faces was one of immense relief. Without a word he walked into the tent.

Pavel nodded slowly. "You get to keep the boy. Your mother and your wife had tea."

"Tea!"

"Tea." Wondering how it had happened, he offered, "Your mother poured the tea from a silver pot."

Boris turned on him and seized him by the arm. His eyes flashed. "Goddamn it, Pavel. If anything—"

"It was all right," Pavel said with a smile. "Go get something to eat."

A wave of relief swept over Boris. "Christ!" he said. "I need a drink."

Pavel extracted a bottle from his gear, chuckling, and burst out laughing as he handed it to Boris.

Boris broke into a grin. He drank, lifted the bottle in salute, and put it down. His mother and Ronya tête-à-tête: Inconceivable! Just thinking about it gave him pleasure. Yet on his way home, Boris was not smiling. What strange events were set in motion by David's death! His mind encumbered with puzzles, Boris sought only two answers. Why did his mother go calling? This was not her way, especially while her men sat encamped in Ronya's forest. And what had happened? Somehow, Ronya had beaten her. He was sure of it.

The hoofbeats of many horses being driven hard put an end to his reflections. Boris shook the rein lightly, and the stallion started to travel faster. Where the gypsy camp ended and the forest began he met Tamara.

"We began to get worried about you. Father Tromokov is there," Tamara said, pointing in the direction of the cemetery, "with Katya and Georgi and the peasants."

Boris scanned the armed mounted gypsies spread out behind her and shook his head. "Where's Igor?"

"That hellion," Tamara smiled.

Boris followed her glance. Igor and the Blond One were perched in trees guarding the entrance to the estate from the forest side.

Boris smiled wearily. "Did you arm the peasants?"

"They armed themselves," Tamara laughed, "with pitchforks."

Boris looked up at Igor and the Blond One in turn. "Come down," he called to them. "The Tartars are on their way back to Odessa."

44

The League of Russian People, known also as the Union of Russian People (later to become known by a more fitting name—the Black Hundreds), were a number of organizations made up of unidentified rightists and the most extreme reactionaries dedicated to preserving the status quo. Supplied with funds by the Tzar's secret police, they concentrated their attention principally upon the Jews, because they were easy targets and because pogroms and massacres against the Jews went unpunished and unreported. Pogroms were extremely useful. They shifted interest away from strikes, lockouts, taxes, the agrarian problem, the influx of peasants into the cities, widespread unemployment, peasant unrest (the mass of peasants were still loyal to the Tzar), Nicolas' wanton extravagance, the lack of bread.

Though the villainous Cossacks, a reliable force of professional mercenaries, directed the slaughter of the Jews, the alliance was not exclusively between the league and the Cossacks. It included the brutish, stupid element of the peasantry. This triple alliance was not formal, it was an understanding that provided for dividing the spoils. To the reactionary league went control of schools, press, and local police. Destruction, physical cruelty, and murder were in the hands of the crude, illiterate, angry rabble. Rape and looting were left to the local Cossacks.

The League of Russian People was planning something—that much the Tartar woman knew. Instinct warned her that they made ready to strike at the Jews. She made inquiries and learned of a plot to let loose a pogrom, with the Department of Police ready to accuse the Jews of the false charge of ritual murder. She brooded upon it and disliked it, not because it was immoral but because the scheme had been hatched in St. Petersburg. An onslaught from outside, death and destruction upon the city she regarded as her own, was unquestionably wrong. In addition, she feared the ascendancy of the Cossacks over the Tartars. The Tartar woman sighed deeply and concluded that it was in her interest to make a deal with her rival Ilya Dolinyuk, a Cossack chief. The Tartar woman usually took the broad outlook.

Ilya Dolinyuk, a stocky figure with a big blond head and a thick neck set on massive shoulders, was a snub-nosed, mean-mouthed middle-aged man revered by the local Cossacks by virtue of his combination of audacity, cruelty, and shrewdness. It was rumored that his father's sudden death fit his wishes well, since it made him head man and freed him to take his young stepmother to bed.

Ilya Dolinyuk ruled over three hundred families on a collective farm well away from Odessa, away from the sea, and spread over so many streets and squares that it was as big as a village. It had no pretty farmhouses, no modern barns; it had only an ancient church half buried on a hill that once, long ago, was a fortified stronghold.

Life was no burden to the men. Besides the washtub and the cooking stove, besides baking the bread and churning the butter, the women worked the land, harvested the wheat, raised the pigs, milked the cows, tended the chickens, and grazed the sheep in distant pastures.

But a Cossack remains a Cossack no matter where he lives. He has no culture apart from his songs. He loves only his horse, and his sport is killing.

Pushing her horse, the Tartar woman reached Ilya Dolinyuk's house in record time. He was more than glad to see her; he needed colts.

As he accompanied her into the stone house, he paused to call his woman, and as soon as they had sat down at the wooden table she brought in vodka, herring, coarse black bread, pickled cucumbers, and soured green tomatoes.

Ilya Dolinyuk and Boris' mother slowly assessed each other.

Dolinyuk was wondering just what the Tartar woman wanted. "Strange that you should come here. I want young horses—to train for fighting and hunting."

The Tartar woman did not bother to answer him or waste time. "Look here," she said, pointing a finger at him, "you're planning to attack the Jews. Be careful not to cheat me of my fair share of the loot."

Dolinyuk stared. Then it dawned on him: She had come to drive a bargain. "Ha-ha! You give me the horses, and I split the Jews' riches with you. Right?"

"Wrong."

His anger flamed, but he dared not risk her enmity. Not only were the Tartars unquestionably stronger and richer than the Cossacks, but Boris Pirov was her son and every Cossack in Russia was awed by his might.

"So help me," said he, slapping a thigh, "if there's a woman your equal I've yet to hear of her. You're priceless."

"I want half."

"No!" he protested. "I have to pay the stinking peasants, turn over a percentage to the police, and—"

"Don't haggle—I spit on what you have to do. Listen well: Swindle me, and you'd better dig a deep hole to lie in. I'll lower you into it myself."

Fear overrode greed, and he capitulated. "All right," he said. "Now about the horses, is it possible to work out an exchange?"

But the Tartar woman was still thinking about the pogrom and the Jewess, who presented yet another problem. "That's the hell of it," she said aloud, "I'm bedeviled by her."

"What?" Dolinyuk said in surprise.

"None of your damn business," the Tartar woman replied, angry that she had spoken her thoughts.

He tightened his lips.

Suddenly the Tartar woman was on her feet. "When?"

"Friday."

"How many days?"

"Four. We'll meet late Saturday."

"I'll send Pavel. Stay away from my part of town," she warned.

Aware of her Jewish daughter-in-law, Dolinyuk merely grunted. "Don't we always?"

Pavel saw her urging her horse through a clump of trees and went to meet her. The Tartar woman dismounted and together they walked back to the house. Her horse followed. There was no need to lead him, or to tie him, or to throw the reins over his head. He would stand, and when the Tartar woman called he would go to her and to no one else.

She came swiftly to the point. "I want no harm to come to her."

Pavel missed nothing. Boris' mother was thinking of the sons Boris had by this Ronya, thinking that Boris' strength rested in her small hands. "Perhaps I'd better place a watch around the dacha and a constant guard on her. I hear she rides alone a lot."

"You echo my thought."

"Say, twenty men?"

"Yes."

At a later date Ronya knew why, but not when, she was made captive. All she knew was that a giant of a man called Pavel, accompanied by twenty Tartars all almost as tall and broad as he, showed up one day. They carried with them tents, guns, and supplies—even food for the horses. They set up a long table built on sawhorses, and when they ate they covered the table with a bright checkered tablecloth of red and white. Like the gypsies, they sprinkled all the food liberally with pepper.

"Why are you putting guards around the house?" she asked Pavel.

"We don't want strangers wandering about."

"I haven't noticed anyone."

"That's lucky."

But Ronya was not so easily put off, so Pavel invented a few convincing details—a nasty situation on the waterfront. "The shipowners have brought in strikebreakers, real ruffians. The thing to do is to stay comfortably close to home."

On impulse, Ronya invited him to eat with her, and soon Pavel was telling her stories about Boris when he was a boy.

The household accepted the Tartars, feeling safer with them than without them. It made no difference to Ronya that on rides and hikes high in the hills a two-man escort holding rifles closed around her. Joanna liked the campers. It was pleasant to run to the window in the morning, clutching a sheet, and see men about. She was only thirty. Only Galina was not exactly overjoyed.

422

The bad time for the Odessa Jews began one Friday evening in October. It was a little after sundown when the synagogues were stormed. Drunken mobs of ruffians and peasants, recruited from the outlying districts, stormed the holy places and defiled the sacred scrolls. The Cossacks, comrades in infamy, roared the orders: "Burn!" From the hills, the citizenry watched the ghastly flames.

After the first moments of paralyzing fear, the Jews threw themselves upon the attackers and fought furiously. Little by little the mob gave way—there was no sense in burning to death with the wretched Jews.

That night the Jews did not sleep.

From the synagogues, the hired rabble, full of exhilaration, were led into the districts populated by the poor Jews. The destruction was total; the slaughter shocked the entire civilized world.

The profitable plunder began on Saturday. This pogrom was well planned, the shops singled out for pillage well reconnoitered. The police mingled with the looters and protected them from determined resistance. It was the Jews the authorities labeled "bloodthirsty attackers."

On Saturday night, hundreds of Jewish women of all ages, many with children, hid from the drunken mobs in Christian cemeteries. Surrounded by crosses, they huddled together in groups, whispering among themselves, "Here we are safe." The bitter irony did not matter; their first duty was to live.

On Sunday, amid the tolling of church bells, the Christian conscience was aroused. Priests in white vestments, ringed by candles and a haze of incense, scathingly denounced the brutality. Consequently— seeing that authority spoke—Jews, tired, cold, hungry, numb with the weight of their losses, were welcomed into Christian homes and saved.

Monday had been set aside for rape and drunken orgies. Houses were invaded by Cossacks, with room-to-room searches for Jewish daughters and comely matrons.

Word of the bloody massacre in Odessa was brought to Tamara by a gypsy scout riding two days in advance of a caravan. His purpose went beyond spreading the news. The caravan was in need of food, blankets, and warm clothes. The horses needed rest. In time of a pogrom, no gypsy tribes remained in the stricken area, for when the muzhiks and Cossacks went after the Jews, the gypsies were the next target.

It was David von Glasman who once said to Tamara: "The Jews and the gypsies have this in common: Each is resolved to live life in his own way. Each lives amid—but apart."

Tamara promptly left the gypsy and dispatched a messenger on horseback to the stables. "Tell them," she ordered, "that Boris needs his stallion with plenty of feed tied to its saddle." She herself burst into the house just as Boris and Katya were finishing breakfast.

"There's a pogrom in Odessa."

Katya felt herself grow cold as stone.

Boris said, "You're sure?"

"The Jewish streets are littered with their dead. The children with their eyes gouged out can be heard screaming for miles." Tamara hesitated, uncertain if she should go on, and decided the choice lay with Boris. If he asked, she had the answers—women dragged naked into the streets, what was done to them then by many.

"Oh my God," Katya cried. "Ronya!"

Boris took Katya into his arms and said, "I'll grudge my horse its water, but no matter how hard I press on, the pogrom will be over when I get there. Even so, you're not to be apprehensive. The wife of Boris Pirov is far removed from the uproar in Odessa."

Katya was shaking, speechless, and Boris could imagine what flashed through her mind—no Jewess, not even a countess, was spared the frenzy of a drunken mob. "It's true, Katya. In Odessa only Ronya's connection with the Tartars is significant."

Katya barely managed a whisper. "Truly?"

"You *must* believe it."

Katya raised her hands to his shoulders. "Fly to Ronya. God give you speed."

Every nerve in Boris' body bade him: "Ride!" but he turned on Tamara mercilessly. "Tell Igor what you told us, and so help me, I'll have your tongue. I don't want him a target silhouetted against the Odessa sky."

Tamara took his words meekly. Her thoughts now were only of Boris, of his safety. "Please, Boris, don't be fool enough to fight against overwhelming odds."

Boris scarcely heard. He was looking at Katya. "Send for Alexis." A moment later, he was gone.

Her body weighted with lead, Katya reached Tamara's side. She put her hand on Tamara's arm. "Let's go upstairs."

"Your fingers are cold."

"Of course, the gypsy scout may have exaggerated."

"No, he told the truth."

"Boris said we have nothing to fear."

"I'll tell you this," said Tamara, "with a whip in her hand, she's stronger than the strongest man."

"Far away and high above the city, she's safe."

"There's the boat."

"Did you say something?"

"Yes. I said she swims like a fish."

"And she rides like a man. But it's hard to imagine anyone as small as Ronya capable of defending herself."

"Ronya is not in danger," Tamara said, thinking back to the molten metal. "Remember: Two lives in two lands—that's her fate."

Boris paused only to water the stallion and then grudgingly, telling him to make haste, he ate in the saddle. He dozed in the saddle with his rifle across his thighs, one hand guarding the leather bags stuffed with ammunition, counting on his stallion to hold direction and speed. As he pushed on toward the sea at a murderous pace, avoiding towns and villages, he grieved for his stallion. He knew he was killing him.

Boris had intended to go directly to Ronya, but something came between him and his intention. He told himself, "It's Monday. It's over. The fires are out, the smashing is over, the spoils are divided, and the dead are buried. The living are walking down their own streets. The killers, the drifters, have disappeared." His thoughts turned to clean, white-skinned bellies and soft naked breasts. "Damn the Cossacks— the sons of bitches—they're back with their own women, keeping out of things until the stink of their brutality blows away." Boris told himself, "I'm mad. I'm a fool." Nevertheless, that something wore him down. With a last look in the direction of the dachas, he turned the horse away from the hills and dashed down into the Jewish sector, galloping into the heart of it with a clatter and Tartar roar, knowing well that if the streets were still awash with muzhiks and Cossacks, wild on drink and bestiality, they would rush forward to embrace their hero.

The Cossacks were not in the street. Drenched in drink, the despoilers were in a beer hall fighting among themselves, because now it seemed likely the pogrom would end before its time. It was incredible: While the Cossacks waited for Monday, their day set aside for rape and defilement, the Jews had vanished. Thousands of women of all ages—and not a soul left. Not one!

Ilya Dolinyuk stood ripping at the beer house walls with a hunting knife and lashing out at his men. "Where are the women?"

The police were on their way to the Jewish streets, and they were hours ahead of schedule. A drab stream of humanity followed them, and behind them were friendly Christian families from around the quarter, and tagging after them were more Jews.

All this came about in this way:

Pavel had taken a tremendous liking to Ronya. Food was a bond between them—Pavel prized a woman with a big appetite and a slim figure—and the way she sat a horse was beautiful. But what attracted

425

him to Ronya most was her whip. A swinging whip in her hand, and she was transformed into a goddess. He was puzzled by her, too. How could she read half the night and sleep late every morning? Still, on the whole, his admiration for her was boundless.

At noon on Sunday, as they finished their eggs and coffee, Ronya said, "Pavel, is it really true that the trouble in town is between the stevedores and the strikebreakers?"

Pavel nodded, preferring to lie to Ronya without words. He found it difficult to look into her eyes now that he was so fond of her.

"Today is Sunday. Almost everyone will be in church. I'd like to go down to the waterfront and see for myself."

"Fine with me. I'll talk to Boris' mother," was Pavel's reply.

In an astonishingly short time the guard around Ronya was doubled, but she gave it no thought at first, although she abandoned her desire to see the waterfront. In the evening she talked to Pavel again, more curious this time. He was no match for her determined questioning, and she got the truth out of him—or part of the truth. He could not bear to tell her how bad the pogrom was.

Nothing happened around Odessa without the Tartar woman's knowledge. Consequently, Boris' approach was reported, and by seven o'clock on Monday morning Tartars with rifles were on lookout duty on the rooftops of the Jewish quarter.

By eight o'clock the chief of police and the Tartar woman were breakfasting on caviar and red wine, and as they ate and drank, the crafty official agreed to all her demands.

"Let Boris catch a fish or two," said she. "It'll please the Jewess. Then I want the pogrom over."

"Ahead of time?"

"Right."

"Understand, Catherine, if the Cossacks are not appeased, they will go on the rampage independently."

"Warn Dolinyuk. His Cossacks behave, or I myself will plunge a Tartar dagger into his heart."

"What about the other chiefs?"

"Others? Why? They weren't hired for this job."

The chief of police agreed quickly. "True." While he waited to light her cigarette, his hard, slate-gray eyes watched her sculptured face. "Catherine, may I ask a personal question?"

The Tartar woman had an aversion to direct questions of any kind, but she liked the chief and, besides, she needed him. "Ask," came her answer. "I let you call me Catherine, don't I?"

"Damn it, Catherine, why are you doing this for the Jewess? You put the curse on Boris."

426

The Tartar woman nodded. Her answer was slow in coming. "I owe her a debt. Recently she did me a great service. Then there's the matter of succession. Georgi is golden, he's next in line. He still needs a mother." Then she said, "Besides, she'll turn."

The police chief was no fool, though he was amazed to see the Tartar woman show such a weakness. He placed a hand over hers. "I'm sorry, Catherine, but Ronya von Glasman belongs to the Jews."

"So—that's to your way of thinking," the Tartar woman roared. "Answer me this: Did you ever hear of a Jewess who eats pork? Walks lonely roads in the rain? Wears a pistol in a holster at her belt? Sleeps with a whip in her hand? That's a brave girl—that black-eyed Ronya from Kiev."

The police chief chuckled. "All right. I'll send a hundred men."

"Fifty. My men are crawling all over the place. Send out messages. Tell the goddamned Jews to go home."

Though he could see no Cossacks, the muzhiks were in the streets and, as Boris had guessed, flocked around him, eager to pay homage. Meanwhile, his eyes took in the smashed furniture, the broken glass strewn here and there, the buildings gutted by fire, the ruined stalls, the marketplace in a shambles. Then he saw a single crutch lying beneath a charred tree. A surge of rage beat up to his head. He fired one well-aimed shot from his revolver, and a venal drunken muzhik went down. Sodden, the muzhiks scarcely had time to comprehend what had happened before Boris leaped to his feet on the stallion's back, firing more shots into the air. The muzhiks fell back, dumbfounded, and many fled down side alleys. Meanwhile, the inquiring police came on the run. The Cossacks rushed out, led by Dolinyuk, who made straight for Boris. "What happened?" he panted, staring up at the towering figure on the white horse. "We heard shots."

"Nothing. I shot a mad dog."

Stooping down, Dolinyuk saw this was no Jew a Tartar bullet had killed. Now everything was clear—Pirov had made common cause with the Jews. Eyes blazing with anger at this insolence, knife-hand outstretched, he shouted, "Kill Pirov."

But as his own men fumbled with the bolts of their rifles, the Tartars fired a warning down from the rooftops.

Dolinyuk grudged the Tartars their easy victory. He called a greeting to the police, sure they were on his side, and feeling himself strong, challenged Boris. "Well, Pirov, that leaves me and you."

Sitting calmly on his stallion, Boris played with the Cossack. He threw down his rifle, unloosened his holster belt and let it drop, tossed away his whip, freed his dagger from its sheath and let it fall.

Enraged, and still somewhat addled by drink, and conscious of the curious and excited crowd pressing around him and the mounted Tartar, Dolinyuk threw back his head contemptuously. "Your fist is a useless weapon against my knife. Take advantage of my generous nature. Ride on. Have no fear."

Boris' grin mocked him. Still grinning, he jumped.

In many ways, Boris was stronger than ever before. The years had simply added a few pounds to his hard, powerful frame, making him even more brawny. Never was he more sure of himself. A right to the jaw and a boot to the groin, and Dolinyuk was helpless.

Boris called out loud enough for Ronya's people to hear, "I'm on my way to my wife, the Jewess, but I'll spare a minute for any Cossack with a fighting instinct."

A fight with Boris Pirov was not what the Cossacks had expected when the day started, and with Dolinyuk down they had no confidence left in the police or in themselves. No one was moved to accept the offer.

The chief of police came up to Boris and put an arm around him. "Your wife is waiting."

Boris turned on him furiously. "What effort did you make to put an end to this pogrom?"

With a leap, Boris was on the stallion and riding away, fast.

45

The stallion made his way along the path and came up to the house. Boris had no idea that his mother was waiting until she suddenly appeared. She stormed, by way of greeting, "What delayed you? You had the Cossacks at your mercy."

Memories came flooding back, and Boris was reminded of the times he had nearly killed himself trying to please her. He saw that now, as always, she was unable to show her softer feelings.

His lips parted in a grin. "Hello, Mother."

The Tartar woman gave a little nod. She laughed and made one of her random remarks: "She's a late sleeper. Probably dead to the world right now."

"Let's have a cigarette, Mother. I want a few answers."

"If you are thinking that I had something to do with the pogrom, well, I didn't."

428

There was no point in challenging her. Boris said nothing as he took in the same handsomeness, the same narrowness of hips, the same masses of gleaming yellow braids. It came to him that he felt, mixed together, wonder and the stirrings of a remembered love.

The Tartar woman saw the same beauty in him as she saw in her white stallions, the purest white horses in existence. It was she who took the conversational reins. "We gave your Jewess a trumped-up story. It worked until late last night, but then Pavel couldn't keep it secret any longer—not that Pavel told her everything. He said there was a bit of rioting, a few fights in the streets, some sacking."

Without taking his eyes from her, Boris asked, "How did she take it? Pretty badly?"

"Pavel said she just looked at him and went up to her room. He placed men outside her door and under her windows because he didn't trust her to stay put."

"Mother, I'm much obliged."

"Christ Almighty, you talk a lot."

The stallion waited patiently, his sides heaving heroically, for his master's return. Boris buried his head in his stallion's mighty neck and turned away. The Tartar woman took the reins and led him off.

Ronya was not asleep. She had lain sleepless most of the night, sorrowing for the Odessa Jews and trying to master her chaotic emotions. Though Pavel had said only that Boris was on his way, somehow she knew, lying in the dark, that he was near and that by morning her isolation would be over. Her thoughts were complex and full of contradictions. One minute she wanted Boris with an almost savage passion; the next, thinking of David and the pogrom, she was ashamed of herself. Then she would think of Kiev, and the boys, and of all the people who depended upon her. And she realized she could best serve them by coming back to life. A person is born to live. By morning she was calm.

On a gown Boris liked she fastened her heart-shaped diamond pin, knowing it would please him and knowing that it was the quickest way of announcing, "I've pulled myself together, Boris, my husband." She wanted to add, "Not that I'll ever forget where you were the night we needed you." She went over to the mirror and combed her hair, pulling it into a hard bun on top of her head. Boris would know how to interpret this, too.

Boris stepped through the front door to find Ronya waiting for him. He thought, *I hope she wants me as much as I want her.* Aloud, he said, "Hello, dove." Suddenly she was in his arms, and he was whispering, "Ronya, Ronya."

Trembling, she lifted her face.

"I'm covered with dust."

"It doesn't matter," Ronya answered quickly, and yielded her lips. For an eternity nothing existed except the kiss. When thought returned, she said, "Come, I'll fill your tub, and for once you'll have your breakfast in bed."

Ronya helped with his boots. She bent over him in the tub and washed his hair. She would not let him talk until he had eaten eggs and toast and warm milk. When he asked her to let down her hair, she did and lay beside him in bed as she listened to his account of the pogrom.

He told her about the stallion, exhausted by the killing ride.

He admitted to the killing.

Dazed by the pogrom, incredulous that a muzhik lay dead in a Jewish street, Ronya asked, "Why him? Why that particular one?"

"So far as I was concerned, Ronya," he said, his eyes unflinching, "I was willing to shoot them all."

He gathered her into his powerful arms, holding her body close to his, tired to the marrow of his bones.

Ronya saw his utter exhaustion, and all else ceased to matter. "Shut your eyes," she whispered softly. She curled close to him and lay perfectly still until he rolled over and hid his face in the crook of his arm. She eased herself noiselessly out of the bed and drew the curtains so that no light came into the room. She dressed attractively in creamy white and brown and gold and went out of the bedroom carrying his dirty clothes. At the foot of the stairs she was met by the Tartar woman, who gave a snort. "Jewess, there's something damn puzzling about you. Are you a witch?"

"Why do you ask?"

The Tartar woman strode into the sitting room, saying, "I sent them away. They disturb me."

"Sent them away?"

The Tartar woman looked at her sharply. "Not my men—your servants." She scooped Boris' clothes out of her arms. "Did you know I need his clothes to fool a stallion into thinking I'm Boris?" The Tartar woman swung herself into a chair. "Sit down and listen to me."

Ronya sat on the edge of a chair.

"Are we friends?"

A shadow of a smile appeared on Ronya's face. "Yes, I think we are."

"What I am asking is: Do you want to be my daughter?"

"Nothing would please me more."

"Belong to me," said the Tartar woman, reaching out to touch Ronya's hair. "Be a Tartar woman, pretty one."

430

"I can't," was Ronya's soft-spoken answer.

The Tartar woman frowned and took away her hand, her eyes narrowing in displeasure.

"Anything else Boris asked of me, I would do."

"Jewess, I tried."

"Yes, you did," Ronya said.

"You Jews are strange people," the Tartar woman said, preparing to leave.

Ronya felt sorry for her. She knew that in her heart, Boris' mother still hoped she would embrace the cross. Her thoughts drifted to the pogrom. This once the Tartar woman had done something good for the Jews; Ronya wanted to do something for her. Quietly she rose and pushed the door shut again. "Wait, please."

The Tartar woman's eyes glittered. "Why?"

"You've got a grandson who is not a Jew. He's fine, he's bright, he's blond. You two could care for each other. He needs a name, and you need someone close to love, someone who won't leave you."

The Tartar woman exploded with fury. "He's a bastard—born in sin to a gypsy whore. He's no kin of mine." Abruptly she turned but, as the angry flush went out of her face, she brought her eyes back to Ronya and said, "Tell Boris they are the same, no different. The same. He'll know what I mean."

Many hours later, Boris awakened. Dressed only in a silk robe, he went downstairs to find Ronya seated at the candlelit dining table. His heart beating fast, Boris reached to embrace her. Ronya felt herself lifted. Her arms went around his neck and their lips met.

The bedroom was lighted, the crisp bed turned down for the night, and a friendly fire burned in the grate. Boris sat her down in the middle of the bed and pulled the pins from her hair. He unbuttoned her shoes. He drew off her clothes. Her ravishing whiteness was a glorious sight. Boris gave her a quick hard glance and buried his face between her breasts. Ronya clung to him shivering.

They made love hungrily, violently, and the thud of his heart was louder to Ronya than her own.

Afterward, Boris raised himself on one elbow. His eyes roamed over her, lingering lovingly on her face.

Ronya looked back at him without stirring.

"Tell me something," he said.

"I love you, my darling."

"Say it again."

"Kiss me."

Once during the night, Boris thought he heard the neigh of a wild stallion. He squinted through the blurred windowpanes and even went

431

downstairs and peered out into the misty blackness from the open door, but he could see nothing. He climbed back up the stairs and got into the warm bed.

Ronya had given him his mother's message: "The same, no different. The same."

He put a cigarette between his lips and struck a match. His eyes fixed on the ceiling, he could see him: a pure-bred, milk-white stallion born to a royal line—haughty, swift, spirited, stout in fighting, strong in mating—a majestic companion.

By six fifteen, having gulped down some hot coffee, Boris was on his way to prove the reality of the neigh he had heard. It was at six thirty that the Tartar woman, sweaty and dirty in Boris' clothes, decided to materialize into the mist from behind a clump of bushes. She started downhill to the stable, thereby adding to his certainty: She had selected the successor to his stallion. He walked beside her with no mind for talk.

"Can't you make a Tartar wife out of that Jewess of yours?" she said abruptly.

If there was anything Boris did not want it was a Tartar wife, but his grave eyes told her nothing. Haunted by the curse she herself had put on him, obsessed with Ronya, she said with a flush of hope, "Her sister turned. For a Muscovite. Incredible!"

Even as Boris marveled at the compelling instinct of mother-love, he grinned inwardly. Never would his mother accept a Muscovite as her social equal. He tried to explain Ronya's feelings. "How can she betray her father and abandon her people?"

The Tartar woman tramped on in glum silence. "I think," Boris said thoughtfully, "my love for Ronya has something to do with her Jewishness."

The Tartar woman stopped dead in her tracks, her eyes glinting, her whole face hard. "Almighty Christ! What in hell do you mean by that?"

From the remote depths of his mind, Boris called up the lonely boy, denied a childhood, wholly dependent upon the Tartar woman. He thought of how it was now between Ronya, the Jewess, and his sons. He felt cheated, but he knew he could never explain this to his mother, so he said, "You wouldn't understand. I'm not sure I do."

"Damn Jews!" the Tartar woman growled, out of her depth. "Let them load guns and fight."

"That's easy for you to say."

"You'll fulfill the curse," she said heavily, "make no mistake about it."

"I accept that," said Boris. "Meanwhile I want to forget it."

432

They walked on, while she told him about the stallion. "He's slightly bigger and a better swimmer than your old stallion. I've given him his first instructions. He knows he belongs to you." At the barn door she handed Boris his parka. "I'll keep the boots."

Boris viewed his mother with the eyes of a son. He took hold of her rich blond braids and smiled into her face. "If I kissed you, would I get a kiss in return?"

"Ride your stallion," the Tartar woman said in a flat voice. "His name is Boy. Same as the other."

The new stallion's eyes, a mixture of eagerness, curiosity, and acceptance, were fixed on Boris, who was drifting slowly toward him, murmuring endearments.

With every step he took, he appreciated even more the stallion's vigorous splendor. Soon Boris' fingers were caressing his nose. The stallion tossed his great head in delight. "Boy," Boris laughed, "you're so beautiful." He jumped on the horse's back. "Out there," he said, "is the sea. We'll watch the sea gulls dive for fish." They went down to the shore, but everything, even the sea, was hidden by mist. "Never mind, Boy." Boris' voice grew tender. "I'll introduce you to Ronya later. Her black eyes sparkle like diamonds and there's a raspberry sweetness to her lips, and you're to love her because she's mine."

They shared the next two hours in perfect communication. With no reins, not even a rope, to guide him—only Boris' knees and soothing murmurs of praise—the stallion gave all that was demanded of him. The mist lifted, and the sea was revealed a rich blue-green. They rode home in sunshine, but not along roads or trails—along the sea beach, from which they made the steep climb to the stable through clumps of low-branched fir and pine, over boulders and ditches, along sheer cliffs barren of brush and grass where a fall was a drop straight into the sea.

Boris was hard at work when Ronya came into the stable. He flashed her a happy grin. "I'm almost done. Come over and meet Boy."

She came forward, stirred by the stallion's breathtaking perfection.

Boris rose from his knees and ran his fingers through the stallion's mane. "Within a month Boy will be the greatest horse on earth. I wouldn't trade him for all the—"

Her mind darted to the old stallion and how much David had loved him. She could not bear the eagerness in Boris' voice, the ardent look in his eyes. She ran out of the barn.

Boris frowned, wiping his forehead with the back of his hand. "Don't worry about it, Boy. She'll come around."

When he came into Ronya's room, she was reading.

"What are you reading, dove?"

"A book."

He sank down beside her on the bed. "What is it, Ronya?"

Ronya hurled the book clear across the room. "I wonder, if I were to die, how long it would be before you married again."

"I'd wait a bit."

"I don't believe you'd wait a day! You don't know the meaning of constancy."

"Dove," Boris said quietly, "you don't mean that."

Disarmed by his patience and by the touch of his hand, she laid her head on his shoulder. "I can't understand how you've been able to put him out of your heart so quickly."

Engulfed in the memory of David, Boris clenched his fist so tight that the knuckles showed white.

Effortlessly she moved closer, one finger tracing an invisible line down his cheek. "It just can't be true that you love this stallion as much as the other."

Damning his hellish guilt, Boris unclenched his hand; his head sank back against the headboard, and he let out his breath in a great slow sigh of relief. "Dove," said he, "you gave me the most awful scare." The fingertip stopped. "That's right, a guilty conscience hears unclearly."

Her dark eyes filled with tears and she said softly, "The guilt belongs to me, also. I did not love him as much as the others."

"You never failed him, dove. I did. That's a cold, bitter load I'll carry to the grave."

Her arms encircled his neck, her eyes closed, and he bent his face to hers. Breathing in the delicate perfume she wore, his arms tightened about her. For a moment she stayed very still, taken aback by the sudden fierce assault of her hot primitive need. . . .

Boris had gone, and Ronya lay alone, once more prey to her thoughts. The tears rose until her sobs filled the room.

"Poor, poor David. All goes on without you."

46

Though born in Odessa, Boris thought of Kiev as home. He was, on the whole, indifferent to Ronya's wealth. He liked hard work, he liked taking care of horses, he liked the company of men and, much as he liked Ronya all to himself, he was quickly bored with leisure. He thought it time to depart; but Ronya had said nothing about going home. Thinking that she wished only to prolong their time together, he hesitated to speak.

Exactly a week after the pogrom, Ronya was suggesting that they ask Pavel to dinner some evening.

Boris looked at her curiously. "Why?"

She was leaning against a window breathing in the fragrance of the sea mist. "Because I like him."

"I have a better suggestion, Ronya. Pack."

"What for?" she asked without turning.

"For the trouble we're causing Katya and Alexis."

Ronya turned away from the window. "Let's send for them. I miss the boys."

"No!"

She shrugged and turned back to the window.

Three letters came that day.

The first letter was brief.

> "Adam had a son and he died. Adam allowed himself to be comforted. God gives and God takes away.
> Come home, Ronya."

The letter was signed Joseph and Ivan. Ronya folded it and put it away.

The second letter was from Alexis. This letter Ronya kept to show to Boris.

> Dearest Ronya,
> I must return to St. Petersburg, and much as Katya will miss Georgi she will not send me back alone. I must persuade the Tzar that Russia needs Sergius Witte. Not everyone likes Witte, but everyone concedes his genius. We shall need his help, and when he is Minister of the Interior we shall have it. He will make Russia prosperous, and with prosperity will come the end of anti-Semitism.
> Come home, Ronya. The boys need you.
>
> Alexis

The third letter was from Paul. Ronya read it in frenzied haste. There was a postscript:

On bad days, Ronya, I ache with longing. On good days I incline to Boris' way of thinking. "Why struggle with fate? What will be will be."

Yours,
Paul

Ronya looked at the envelope, a plain envelope with no return address. It had been mailed within Russia and forwarded unopened from Kiev. This letter was quickly destroyed in the fireplace.

Ronya flew down to the kitchen.

"Elizabeth, we've about two free hours to get me ready, and remember—hide my suitcases."

"Where?"

"I don't particularly care, as long as he doesn't see them."

"Anything else, Ronya, my mistress?"

"Yes. See that my sister gets a telegram. Tell her she'd better expect us on Sunday."

Ronya undressed. The robe she chose was of brocaded velvet tinted in blues and greens and golds. She arranged her hair and caught it with a jewel. Her wind-tanned face she left fastidiously clean of powder.

The evening wore on, and Boris came in.

Ronya lifted her head from her book.

He gave her a smile of admiration and made ready for the night, before coming to sit by the bed with a glass of brandy and a cigarette.

Gently rubbing her foot, he said, "Tomorrow we leave. I've reserved a compartment for you. I'll be in the boxcar with the horses."

Ronya's eyes met his with defiance. "You've made arrangements without consulting me?"

"Ronya, what's wrong?"

"My God!" she sighed. "Do you really think I came here to look at the sea or walk in the hills? Every day I waited for you to come for me, simply for this reason: I go back to Kiev only on my terms."

"Really?" Boris said mildly.

"What about the muzhik? There'll be an inquiry. Can you ignore the law?"

Boris' eyes sparkled. "I've arranged all that."

She looked at him in dismay. "I tell myself the muzhik's death was well justified, I tell myself: 'Thank God Boris took a stand,' but I've been worried to death, so don't sit there keeping me in the dark. Whom have you talked to?"

"The mayor, the magistrate, and the chief of police. They're giving me a medal."

Ronya tucked her feet under her robe. "Boris, you had better give me an intelligent explanation."

"All right. I hadn't expected so much as a lifted brow when today I am told that I rode into an armed mob, and single-handed saved scores of policemen from being injured. Because I quelled the riot, the city of Odessa wishes to decorate me for valor."

Ronya did not laugh heartily as he had expected. She said, "Russia is an immoral country."

"You're tired, dove."

"No, I'm not. I'm concerned over Igor. I'm in despair over the Blond One."

"Now listen, Ronya, there's something I never want to hear again, so if that's what you've in mind, forget it. He's nearly seventeen, and six foot three, and too attached to you."

Ronya opened her eyes wide.

"That's right. I'd be a fool to let him hover around."

Ronya was shattered. "You ought to be ashamed of yourself!" She snatched her hand away, but then she thought: *I must be wrong—he couldn't have meant* that! Slowly she took his hand again. "Boris, I said to him, 'One day your father will call you son. I promise.' Please, my darling, give him your name."

"Never!"

Ronya felt herself trembling; she let go his hand. The minutes passed, and Boris said, "What about Igor?"

"He's got to be educated at a university, and I want him to learn a profession." She was trying to stay calm, but her voice shook a little. "The only security one has in this world is what one carries inside one's head—and heart."

"I'm not opposed to that view in principle."

"But your actions are opposed to it. All you do is drill him in horsemanship, so study seems irrelevant to Igor—it won't win him the championship."

With a sudden spurt of words she rushed on, proving a saying in the Talmud: "Much talk, much foolishness," for Ronya's loose tongue reaped a strange harvest: "Our way of life is over—only a blind man or a fool fails to realize that the horse is on its way out. We're approaching a new century. It'll be a mechanized one. That, my dear husband, is progress." Had Ronya given Boris even a fleeting glance, she would not have uttered another word, but she swept on: "In the United States the manufacture of auto cars is staggering. It will change every aspect of life."

"Where do you get your information about the United States?" Boris thundered.

437

Ronya was ready to bite her tongue out. "I—I—read a lot."

"You expect me to believe that? Look at me!"

Ronya lifted her eyes and looked at him.

Boris waited, but she said not a word.

All his patience and forbearance exploded in a paroxysm of jealousy. He put his big hands on her shoulders and shook her with all his strength. "Did you hear me? From whom do you get your information about the United States?"

Suddenly inflamed, Ronya's temper triumphed over wisdom. She sprang to her feet. "Eighteen years of unfaithfulness, and you *dare* question me! Are you bored with Odessa? Are you eager to be off to your current fancy woman in Kiev? Are you tired of our tame bed? Well, maybe I'm tired of it too, and I freely admit to one of Paul's rare letters—"

Boris could hardly believe his ears—"tame bed"—"Paul"— Goaded beyond endurance, he picked her up, tossed her onto the bed, grasped her robe, and ripped it open with one great tear. As he stooped over her, she whispered, "Don't, please." He neither heard nor cared. Consumed with hatred for Paul, he vented his fury on Ronya. She fought him, amazing him with the strength of her resistance, but he took her with deadly coldness. When it was over, overwhelmed by what he had done, drained and exhausted, he rolled away.

Ronya moved at last. Bending over him, she whispered, "I burned the letter."

Boris lifted his head and looked into the beloved face. "If ever he sets foot in Russia, I'll kill him. That I promise you." He left her, then, to fill a tub to the brim with steaming water.

He bathed her, rubbing gently.

"Can you stand the water any hotter, dove?"

"No, I don't think so."

"Do you hurt?"

"No."

He brought her a tumblerful of brandy. "Drink it, dove."

He bent over and kissed her tenderly on the mouth, tasting the brandy. "I love you, Ronya."

He kept her in the tub for twenty minutes, adding hot water all the while. When she was bright pink all over, he lifted her out of the tub and dried her briskly with an immense towel. Pulling from a drawer the first nightdress he laid his hands on, he slipped it over her head and carried her back to bed. He got in beside her.

"Boris."

"Sh-sh. Sleep, dove."

438

"I'm packed and ready."

"Then why were you complaining?" Boris asked without anger.

She extended her arms to him. "I feel like a bride. Hold me tight."

Boris held Ronya as a man holds the woman he loves. Above them the rising wind blew through the treetops.